THE OXFORD
MODE
WOMEN'S STORIES

Patricia Craig was born and educated in Belfast before moving to London where she now lives. She is a freelance critic and reviewer and has edited several anthologies including the Penguin Books of *British Comic Stories* and *British Comic Writing* and Oxford Books of *English Detective Stories* and *Schooldays*.

Also available from Oxford Paperbacks

The Oxford Book of Modern Fairy Tales
Edited by Alison Lurie

The Oxford Book of Children's Stories
Edited by Jan Mark

The Oxford Book of Fantasy Stories
Edited by Tom Shippey

THE OXFORD BOOK OF
Modern Women's Stories

Edited by

PATRICIA CRAIG

Oxford   New York

OXFORD UNIVERSITY PRESS

1995

Oxford University Press, Walton Street, Oxford OX2 6DP

Oxford New York
Athens Auckland Bangkok Bombay
Calcutta Cape Town Dar es Salaam Delhi
Florence Hong Kong Istanbul Karachi
Kuala Lumpur Madras Madrid Melbourne
Mexico City Nairobi Paris Singapore
Taipei Tokyo Toronto
and associated companies in
Berlin Ibadan

Oxford is a trade mark of Oxford University Press

First published 1994
First issued as an Oxford University Press paperback 1995

British Library Cataloguing in Publication Data
Data available

Library of Congress Cataloging in Publication Data
The Oxford book of modern women's stories / edited by Patricia Craig.
p. cm.
1. Short stories, English—Women authors.
2. Short stories, Commonwealth (English)—Women authors.
3. Short stories. American—Women authors. 4. American fiction—20th century.
5. English fiction—20th century. 6. Women—Fiction.
I. Craig, Patricia.
PR1309.W709 1994 823'.0108091—dc20 94-657
ISBN 0-19-283204-2

1 3 5 7 9 10 8 6 4 2

Printed in Great Britain
Biddles Ltd.,
Guildford & King's Lynn

CONTENTS

Contents

INTRODUCTION

Commentators on the short story are generally in agreement about one or two things: it's a modern art form, a 'child of this century', as Elizabeth Bowen put it; it depends for its impact on an individual angle of vision; it's more concerned with the essence of a situation than with its development. What it needs to guard against, above all, is vagueness—vagueness of intention, or of effect. Qualities essential to it are 'punch and poetry', as Sean O'Faolain has it in his spirited study of this branch of literature, *The Short Story* (1948). Punch and poetry—but these may be arrived at in surprising, or even devious, ways. When you come down to it, there are no rules—or none that can't be overturned by the right practitioner. What matters is the force of the writer's inspiration and his or her command of technique.

The story, in other words, can be realistic or fantastic; it can describe an incident, harp on a single theme, evoke a mood or an atmosphere, miraculously (and succinctly) connect various strands of plot, or set up certain resonances in the mind of the reader. It can approach its subject directly or obliquely; it may contain an anecdotal core, but it must have something over and above this to cause reverberations. 'Personal voltage': this is another of Sean O'Faolain's terms to describe the mysterious extra element in short-story writing that makes all the difference between unadorned competence, and the power to captivate. It's not that the author's personality should be plastered all over the prose—this, indeed, would repel most readers—but that it should subtly and irresistibly suffuse the narration.

And here we come to the crux of the matter for an *Oxford Book of Modern Women's Stories*. The author's personality, and its inimitable manifestations: this, indeed, has nothing to do with gender, one way or the other. Take a really superlative story, any story: if it's written by a man, it is misleading to assert that no *woman* could have written it, when the truth is that no other person could have achieved that particular blend of inspiration and expertise. To merit its derogatory connotation, the 'woman's story' (or the 'man's story', for that matter) would need to be based on the most facile assumptions about the nature of men and women— to be, in other words, the kind of story with which no worthwhile anthology need concern itself. I don't believe, for example, that it's possible to isolate an intrinsically 'feminine' way of looking at things: what exists is just sexually undifferentiated perceptiveness, or imperceptiveness, on the part of one author or another. 'Every artist is either a man or a woman,'

Mary Ellman wrote in her illuminating study of 1968, *Thinking About Women*, 'and the struggle is pretty much the same for both.' Quite so. However, I don't wish to minimize the part played by extra-literary criteria in determining the conditions in which women wrote, or the way in which their work was sometimes received. Mary Ellman quotes Warren Coffey on Flannery O'Connor: 'a man would give his right arm to have written Flannery O'Connor's "Good Country People".' This is the highest praise he can offer the story: that it wouldn't seem amiss for a man to have written it. As a standard of judgement (in 1965), it tells us something about persisting fears of undue 'femininity' in women's writing.

The most accomplished women writers, all along, have assimilated the social factors operating at the time, or risen above them, or studied them with subversive intent, or simply, and with great economy, converted them into the subject-matter of one sharp fable after another (as Fay Weldon does: see in particular her amusing and polemical story 'In the Great War'—the war, the truces, and all the shifts of allegiance between men and women, or women and women). They write *as* women (which is inescapable), not *like* women (which carries—still—imposed characteristics of weakness and inferiority). Angela Carter makes this distinction in her essay on Christina Stead,[1] in which she praises Stead for writing out of a profound consciousness of what it is to be a woman, without displaying any of that 'collusive charm which is supposedly a mark of the feminine genius'. (There is a branch of feminist story-telling and criticism that would like to flaunt the faults traditionally ascribed to women's writing—excessive emotionalism, sensibility, soul-searching, sisterly solidarity, or whatever—in the interests of fostering some intangible feminine principle. My own view is that this is counter-productive; I am drawn all the time to work that attracts, in Mary Ellman's phrase, 'asexual approval'.)

A story is a story is a story—to adapt the most celebrated pronouncement of an author not included here, Gertrude Stein—and isn't it somehow contradicting this premiss to hive off a body of work from what may be called the mainstream of twentieth-century fiction? At a first glance, it may look as if nothing unifies the stories in this collection but the gender of their authors, and that this is an artificial unity. (So it is, in a sense, but hardly more than that pertaining to twentieth-century stories *tout court*, or midwestern stories, or stories about the sea.) Two lines of defence come to mind immediately. First, the effectiveness or otherwise of an anthology depends to an extent on the arrangement of the pieces selected for inclusion, with each, ideally, gaining something from 'the presence of neighbours'

---

[1] *London Review of Books*, 1982; reprinted in *Expletives Deleted* (1992).

(as Hortense Calisher remarks in the preface to her own *Collected Stories*), and nothing to strike a jarring note, unbalance the collection, or cause a sudden swoop in quality. I don't mean that one should aim for uniformity of tone, even if such a thing were possible, just that the stories should be, in some indefinable way, and for all the variety of their distinctive voices, complementary. This is the only kind of unity available to an anthology.

When it comes to the matter of separating women from men—as far as I am concerned there is only one justification for doing this, and that is to redress the balance. Faced with the whole range of short-story writing, by men and women, most anthologists have opted first of all for the acknowledged giants of the form—Poe, Kipling, Joyce, Lawrence, Faulkner, O'Faolain, O'Connor, William Trevor, and so on—and then either found themselves with insufficient space to squeeze in many women contributors, or in the grip of preconceptions with regard to the latter ('how many others I've missed, and all the women, all the lady writers, bless them': this is Norman Mailer—the well-named Norman Mailer— in 1966, in *Cannibals and Christians*, after listing 36 of his fellow-authors who've had a piece of the 'Great Bitch', as he sees fit to term the novel at this point).[1] *The Greatest American Short Stories*, published by McGraw Hill in 1953, includes one woman, Willa Cather. *The Penguin Book of English Short Stories* (1967) scores two out of sixteen. V. S. Pritchett's *Oxford Book of Short Stories* (1981)? Not much better—seven out of forty-one. *The Penguin Book of Modern British Short Stories*, edited by Malcolm Bradbury, has ten women out of a total of thirty-four contributors: perhaps things are beginning, just beginning, to look up. But then, Walter Allen's otherwise bracing and valuable study, *The Short Story in English* (1981), gives serious consideration to less than twenty female writers, and more than seventy male. And so on, and so on. The need to make up for this has been apparent for some time, and works by women authors are now being assembled in various forms. Feminist anthologies, of which a fair number have appeared over the last ten years, have tended to be grouped around a single theme, such as mothers and daughters, or something along the lines of Angela Carter's *Wayward Girls and Wicked Women*. This is fine, but a bit constricting. Good general anthologies, such as Hermione Lee's two volumes, *The Secret Self 1* and *2* (1985 and 1987) do exist, but my aim is to indicate in a single volume the extent of women's contribution to the short-story form.

The above are all admirable attempts to bring about an adjustment of emphasis in literary matters, if you accept (as I do) that the inadequate

---

[1] Twenty years later, you still find Mailer asserting that 'there are countries in the world where there are no good women writers'.

acknowledgement of women short-story writers in standard anthologies
is a cause for wonder or affront. How else, indeed, can you view it, given
the riches overlooked? Twentieth-century riches, perhaps one should
specify: confronted by a choice between (for example) Jewett and Joyce,
one wouldn't hesitate long before coming to a decision, whereas things
are much more problematic in the case of O'Connor—do you go for
Flannery, or for Frank? Perhaps it took the *fin de siècle* drive towards
emancipation to spark off repercussions in the field of literature, to
engender the dedication and deliberate charmlessness of a Dorothy
Richardson (say), the androgynous innovations of a Woolf, or the journal-
istic high spirits of a Rebecca West. Around this time, it seems that
women were quick to take up the challenge to prove themselves: no
literary mode remained closed to them. They showed that they weren't,
for reasons of innate incapacity (as contemporary misogynists would have
liked to believe), cut off from any degree of authority or enlightenment.
George Eliot got it right. 'We have only', she wrote, 'to pour in the right
elements—genuine observation, humour and passion'[1] to confute the charge
of silliness—and all other charges—levelled against writing women.

Like other anthologists, I have had it firmly in mind to avoid the too-
familiar tale; and also like them, I've had to give in, in one or two
instances. *The Oxford Book of Modern Women's Stories* opens with 'Paul's
Case' by Willa Cather, which treats the tactical expedients of a young
man ill at ease in the world, and is justly admired for its doughty and
matter-of-fact telling. (It's not so much written from a standpoint of
psychological enquiry—though clearly it influenced the 'psychological
realism' of an English novelist like May Sinclair—as geared to express
some heightened version of the clinical condition of its central character.)
It is not an unexpected choice, and neither is Edith Wharton's 'Afterward'
though this, indeed, is likely to be confined to those anthologies that
bring together exercises in the supernatural. However, just as no one
would think of excluding Poe from a short-story collection on the grounds
that he produced only 'sensation' or embryo detective fiction, the fact
that 'Afterward' is a ghost story shouldn't debar it from inclusion here. It
is simply among the best short pieces that Edith Wharton wrote. It is free
of the lushness, the *beau monde* gloss, that sometimes deforms *fin de siècle*
writing (not excluding Edith Wharton's own); and it relies for its effect
on the power of suggestion, making something pungent and disquieting
out of what might easily have been presented as a commonplace episode
of business malpractice. It leads us, along with its heroine, up a mellow

---

[1] 'Silly Novels by Lady Novelists' (1856).

garden path, with its 'charmed winter days', its 'long house front with its twisted chimney stacks and blue roof angles . . . drenched in the pale gold moisture of the air', before backtracking to engender to the fullest degree the *frisson* which is a requirement of this particular genre.

'Miss de Mannering of Asham', by F. M. Mayor, is another ghost story, an English one this time (though to be sure, the Wharton one is set in England), written in sedate and formal English prose, and with a strong tragic incident at its centre. The ghost, Edith Wharton noted, is peculiar to English and Germanic fiction, having its origins in those 'lands of long twilights and wailing winds; and it certainly did not pass through French or even Russian hands to reach us'. (French and Russian influences filtered through in other areas, however: one has only to cite, for example, Katherine Mansfield's well-known debt to Chekhov.) I wanted to expand the scope of this anthology slightly by choosing some stories not absolutely attached to the mainstream of twentieth-century fiction (though it's hard to be dogmatic about exactly what this consists in); and as well as the two mentioned above, the reader will find a semi-horror story by Patricia Highsmith, a gloriously refurbished fairy tale and a few examples of historical fiction (two of these, at least, are among the most masterly pieces in the book). There's also an unclassifiable story by Stevie Smith from which one gathers that being dead has all the surrealism and absurdity of a dream.

The Highsmith story offers an interesting combination of social realism and atavistic unease, while Angela Carter's festive 'Puss-in-Boots' is full to the brim of erotic exuberance and high jinks. 'First Love', by Eudora Welty, set in Natchez, Mississippi, in the winter of 1807, 'the bitterest winter of them all', with a deaf 12-year-old as its protagonist, and numbering an ex-Vice President of the United States[1] among its characters, is a work of great strangeness and power. Just as highly-charged, and constructed with as perfect artistry, is Alice Munro's 'Meneseteung'—also set in the past, mostly in 1879, but with a contemporary vantage-point, and imagining the life of a minor Canadian poet named Almeda Roth; a story about seclusion, provincial life, psychic withdrawal, and reclamation.

'Lives of Girls and Women', the title of Alice Munro's best-known work, continues to provide writers with their subject-matter (though not exclusively so). 'As woman's predicament has shifted and changed, as she has gained advantages and lost them, the serious woman novelist [or short-story writer] has made it her business to depict the state of play

---

[1] Aaron Burr, who was acquitted on a charge of treason. See Walter Allen, *The Short Story in English* (1981).

in her time, noting, guiding, warning, exhorting.' So wrote Anthea Zeman in her buoyant study of serious women's fiction, *Presumptuous Girls* (1977), and you have only to turn to the stories by, for example, Margaret Atwood, Jean Rhys, Elizabeth Taylor, Grace Paley, Sylvia Townsend Warner, or Edna O'Brien, to see the truth of this observation. All these, to a greater or lesser extent, go in for ruefulness, cogency, animation, and a light touch; and all arrive unerringly at what it's proper to present as significant (even something as seemingly inconsequent as Jean Rhys's engaging 'Overture and Beginners Please'). Grace Paley recasts charm as toughness—toughness of outlook, which is necessary for survival in the underprivileged, racy, heterogeneous New York world she writes about. It's a far cry from the mannered, intellectual filigree of 'The Butterfly and the Traffic Light' by Cynthia Ozick, another Jewish writer, just as strongly, and ironically, alive to the implications of all that intoxicating ancestry—just as that is light years away from the forceful, brick-wall prose of Christina Stead (surely among the most uncompromising of twentieth-century writers).

Stead's 'UNO 1945' was originally published as a story in 1962, before being incorporated into what became her last (posthumous) novel, *I'm Dying Laughing* (1987). The story, which stands quite well on its own, takes a hard look at an ebullient marriage, against a background of United States politics in the 1940s (before the Left fell out of favour). Another fragment first presented as a single piece is Mary McCarthy's vengeful 'Yonder Peasant, Who Is He?', the closest the story comes, in this collection, to unadulterated autobiography. These two eventually became part of longer works—while, to reverse the process, Jean Stafford's marvellous 'Tea Time of Stouthearted Ladies' reads like a novel, a highly compressed novel, so much is going on in it. (It comes as no surprise to learn from her biographer that this is how it was conceived, before she abandoned the project. We should be grateful that the story remains.) With Jean Stafford, I found myself torn between this story and the one called 'Bad Characters'. This, of all her stories, is the one that smacks most strongly of another author (Mark Twain), and it is wonderfully sharp and funny. However, I wanted to keep stories about children to a minimum, along with those about housewives, or girlfriends, or sewing-parties, or any other topic graciously allotted to women short-story writers, since it posed no challenge to masculine hegemony in the genre. (I haven't kept them out altogether: turn, for example, to Ellen Gilchrist's diverting 'Victory Over Japan'. 'When I was in the third grade I knew a boy who had to have fourteen shots in the stomach as the result of a squirrel bite,' it opens, with button-holing verve. Impossible not to read on.)

Other authors, besides Jean Stafford, posed a problem of selection, since their entire output seems of such an astonishing quality (I am thinking of Alice Munro, for example, or Flannery O'Connor, or Eudora Welty, or Nadine Gordimer). With some, though, the choice was easily made. No one can be unaware that Virginia Woolf's short fiction is mediocre in comparison with her novels; 'A Legacy', however, has something that most of the other short pieces don't—dramatic interest. And, just as Olivia Manning's other novels are inferior to her *Balkan* and *Levant* trilogies, so her story, 'In a Winter Landscape', is head and shoulders above her other stories—and for the same reason. This material—train journeys under difficult conditions, foreign landscapes, displaced people, aggrieved Poles, all the exigencies of wartime—clearly suggested itself to her with a force that wasn't to be resisted. Another wartime adventure, in the summer of 1944, with V-I bombs raining down on London, is recounted in Muriel Spark's 'The House of the Famous Poet'; this one, though, to intriguing effect, superimposes a playful metaphysical conceit over the toned-down realism of its setting.

Many of the stories in this collection deal with realities of the day, social, sexual, and political; and sometimes a combination of these. As Nadine Gordimer has said in an interview, 'in South Africa, society *is* the political situation', a view that's borne out in her superb stories concerning complex relations between blacks and whites, all chock-full of irony and authority. 'Which New Era Would That Be?' (quite an early story) is an outstanding example. Doris Lessing has also written well about Africa, but I've chosen her London story, 'The Day Stalin Died', for its wryness and strong period flavour. (Perhaps I should mention an oddity here: this collection, quite by chance, turns out to contain three stories with titles alluding to some notable death. Notable in two cases at least: to complement Stalin and E. M. Forster—in the story by A. S. Byatt—we have Sylvia Plath's amiable 'The Day Mr Prescott Died', a more obscure and funnier demise.) Turning to America—Hortense Calisher in 'The Rehabilitation of Ginevra Leake' makes a comedy out of the Communist party and its sometimes inappropriate recruits; and Flannery O'Connor in her extraordinary story, 'Good Country People' gets to grips with a farouche, clever girl and a Bible salesman who isn't exactly what he seems. This one is marked by black humour and astringency.

For some short-story writers, plot, or at least the adumbration of a story-line, is all-important; while in the case of others, it's evocation that's essential. Some provide both, an electrifying atmosphere *and* a striking story. In Elizabeth Bowen's 'Look at All Those Roses', the story-within-a-story, the implied sensational core, is all the more striking for being withheld from the reader. Nadine Gordimer, again, has remarked that 'in a certain sense, a writer is "selected" by his [or her] subject—his subject being the *consciousness* of his own era', a view that's enacted in A. S. Byatt's 'On the Day that E. M. Forster Died'. In this, the narrator plans to write a novel composed out of 'the knowledge that she had lived through and noticed a certain amount of history'. This clever, literary, self-reflexive story is about writing, about plot-making—with the idea of plotting giving a focus to the plot. Of those writers who, on the other hand, go in for extremes of evocation, one should perhaps single out Joyce Carol Oates, whose fiercely impressionistic 'Scenes of Passion and Despair' plunges us right into the middle of an episode of adultery; it is all feverishness and fluctuation. Joyce Carol Oates likes to arrange her stories according to theme, and this one comes from the volume entitled *Marriages and Infidelities*. It is ironic and felicitous, if not exactly typical— in so far as *anything* can be said to be typical of this most versatile and prolific of authors, whose underlying aim is perhaps to give expression, in as many ways as possible, to the plenitude of American life.

American life—or life in England—is one thing, and the lives of immigrants another (as a writer like Grace Paley has been merrily demonstrating for the last forty-odd years). American writing, in recent times, has been enriched by an influx of foreign voices, all of them extracting something new and clear-toned out of the cacophony of racial conglomeration. Bharati Mukherjee, for example—born in Calcutta, now living in California—is among the most enterprising and audacious of modern short-story writers; Anjana Appachana is just as energetic and stylish; and Amy Tan's writing is marked by a West-Coast openness and briskness, while reaching out simultaneously towards some kind of Oriental resolution. (The Tan story included here, 'A Pair of Tickets' from the volume of linked stories *The Joy Luck Club*, recounts a trip to Shanghai but is centred, memorably, on an image of twin baby girls abandoned in wartime on the road to Chungking.) These three (and others) seem to me to be perfectly attuned to the spirit of the time (the late 1980s and after) while staying within a tradition of more-or-less naturalism and moderation in short-story writing in English.

The literary tastes of any anthologist are bound to proclaim themselves all over the collection, and it should be plain that mine run in the line of traditionalism (however this is modified by the individual approach). I am drawn to idiosyncrasy, indeed, but not to extremism; I believe, with Elizabeth Bowen, that the short story should give pleasure to the reader, 'of however disturbing, painful or complex a kind'. I don't propose to draw attention to exclusions, whether these are deliberate or have come about as a result of ignorance, except to say that a few things I wanted proved to be too long, such as Julia O'Faolain's 'Man in the Cellar', or unavailable, as in the case of Elizabeth Bishop. The inclusions, of course, should speak for themselves. They are all here because they seem to me to be among the very best examples of their kind—Katherine Anne Porter's 'That Tree', Caroline Gordon's sturdy 'Hear the Nightingale Sing', Ruth Prawer Jhabvala's urbane 'A Star and Two Girls', Jane Gardam's delightful study of English eccentricity thrown into even higher relief abroad—all these, no less than the others, would earn their place in *any* collection of short stories. They all, or nearly all, achieve a classic expression of the subject, or the mood, or the emotion they have set out to encompass. Indeed, every story in this anthology calls to mind, in one way or another, the observation of Muriel Spark's heroine Fleur Talbot (also a writer) in her novel of 1981, *Loitering with Intent*: 'the thought came to me in a most articulate way: "How wonderful it feels to be an artist and a woman in the twentieth century".'

I should like to thank, first and foremost, Jeffrey Morgan and Gerry Keenan; and thanks are also due to the following for help of various kinds: Nora T. Craig, Nigel and Naomi May, Judith Luna, Araminta Whitley, and Bernard Hills.

P.C.

WILLA CATHER

Paul's Case

A Study in Temperament

❧

It was Paul's afternoon to appear before the faculty of the Pittsburgh
High School to account for his various misdemeanours. He had been
suspended a week ago, and his father had called at the Principal's office
and confessed his perplexity about his son. Paul entered the faculty room
suave and smiling. His clothes were a trifle out-grown and the tan velvet
on the collar of his open overcoat was frayed and worn; but for all that
there was something of the dandy about him, and he wore an opal pin
in his neatly knotted black four-in-hand, and a red carnation in his
button-hole. This latter adornment the faculty somehow felt was not
properly significant of the contrite spirit befitting a boy under the ban of
suspension.

Paul was tall for his age and very thin, with high, cramped shoulders
and a narrow chest. His eyes were remarkable for a certain hysterical
brilliancy, and he continually used them in a conscious, theatrical sort
of way, peculiarly offensive in a boy. The pupils were abnormally large,
as though he were addicted to belladonna, but there was a glassy glitter
about them which that drug does not produce.

When questioned by the Principal as to why he was there, Paul stated,
politely enough, that he wanted to come back to school. This was a lie,
but Paul was quite accustomed to lying; found it, indeed, indispensable
for overcoming friction. His teachers were asked to state their respective
charges against him, which they did with such a rancour and aggrievedness
as evinced that this was not a usual case. Disorder and impertinence were
among the offences named, yet each of his instructors felt that it was
scarcely possible to put into words the real cause of the trouble, which lay
in a sort of hysterically defiant manner of the boy's; in the contempt
which they all knew he felt for them, and which he seemingly made not
the least effort to conceal. Once, when he had been making a synopsis of
a paragraph at the blackboard, his English teacher had stepped to his side
and attempted to guide his hand. Paul had started back with a shudder
and thrust his hands violently behind him. The astonished woman could

scarcely have been more hurt and embarrassed had he struck at her. The insult was so involuntary and definitely personal as to be unforgettable. In one way and another, he had made all his teachers, men and women alike, conscious of the same feeling of physical aversion. In one class he habitually sat with his hand shading his eyes; in another he always looked out of the window during the recitation; in another he made a running commentary on the lecture, with humorous intention.

His teachers felt this afternoon that his whole attitude was symbolized by his shrug and his flippantly red carnation flower, and they fell upon him without mercy, his English teacher leading the pack. He stood through it smiling, his pale lips parted over his white teeth. (His lips were continually twitching, and he had a habit of raising his eyebrows that was contemptuous and irritating to the last degree.) Older boys than Paul had broken down and shed tears under that baptism of fire, but his set smile did not once desert him, and his only sign of discomfort was the nervous trembling of the fingers that toyed with the buttons of his overcoat, and an occasional jerking of the other hand that held his hat. Paul was always smiling, always glancing about him, seeming to feel that people might be watching him and trying to detect something. This conscious expression, since it was as far as possible from boyish mirthfulness, was usually attributed to insolence or 'smartness'.

As the inquisition proceeded, one of his instructors repeated an impertinent remark of the boy's, and the Principal asked him whether he thought that a courteous speech to have made a woman. Paul shrugged his shoulders slightly and his eyebrows twitched.

'I don't know,' he replied. 'I didn't mean to be polite or impolite, either. I guess it's a sort of way I have of saying things regardless.'

The Principal, who was a sympathetic man, asked him whether he didn't think that a way it would be well to get rid of. Paul grinned and said he guessed so. When he was told that he could go, he bowed gracefully and went out. His bow was but a repetition of the scandalous red carnation.

His teachers were in despair, and his drawing master voiced the feeling of them all when he declared there was something about the boy which none of them understood. He added: 'I don't really believe that smile of his comes altogether from insolence; there's something sort of haunted about it. The boy is not strong, for one thing. I happen to know that he was born in Colorado, only a few months before his mother died out there of a long illness. There is something wrong about the fellow.'

The drawing master had come to realize that, in looking at Paul, one saw only his white teeth and the forced animation of his eyes. One warm afternoon the boy had gone to sleep at his drawing-board, and his master had noted with amazement what a white, blue-veined face it was; drawn and wrinkled like an old man's about the eyes, the lips twitching even in his sleep, and stiff with a nervous tension that drew them back from his teeth.

His teachers left the building dissatisfied and unhappy; humiliated to have felt so vindictive toward a mere boy, to have uttered this feeling in cutting terms, and to have set each other on, as it were, in the gruesome game of intemperate reproach. Some of them remembered having seen a miserable street cat set at bay by a ring of tormentors.

As for Paul, he ran down the hill whistling the Soldiers' Chorus from *Faust* looking wildly behind him now and then to see whether some of his teachers were not there to writhe under his light-heartedness. As it was now late in the afternoon and Paul was on duty that evening as usher at Carnegie Hall, he decided that he would not go home to supper. When he reached the concert hall the doors were not yet open and, as it was chilly outside, he decided to go up into the picture gallery—always deserted at this hour—where there were some of Raffaelli's gay studies of Paris streets and an airy blue Venetian scene or two that always exhilarated him. He was delighted to find no one in the gallery but the old guard, who sat in one corner, a newspaper on his knee, a black patch over one eye and the other closed. Paul possessed himself of the place and walked confidently up and down, whistling under his breath. After a while he sat down before a blue Rico and lost himself. When he bethought him to look at his watch, it was after seven o'clock, and he rose with a start and ran downstairs, making a face at Augustus, peering out from the cast-room, and an evil gesture at the Venus of Milo as he passed her on the stairway.

When Paul reached the ushers' dressing-room half-a-dozen boys were there already, and he began excitedly to tumble into his uniform. It was one of the few that at all approached fitting, and Paul thought it very becoming—though he knew that the tight, straight coat accentuated his narrow chest, about which he was exceedingly sensitive. He was always considerably excited while he dressed, twanging all over to the tuning of the strings and the preliminary flourishes of the horns in the music-room; but to-night he seemed quite beside himself, and he teased and plagued the boys until, telling him that he was crazy, they put him down on the floor and sat on him.

Somewhat calmed by his suppression, Paul dashed out to the front of the house to seat the early comers. He was a model usher; gracious and smiling he ran up and down the aisles; nothing was too much trouble for him; he carried messages and brought programmes as though it were his greatest pleasure in life, and all the people in his section thought him a charming boy, feeling that he remembered and admired them. As the house filled, he grew more and more vivacious and animated, and the

colour came to his cheeks and lips. It was very much as though this were
a great reception and Paul were the host. Just as the musicians came out
to take their places, his English teacher arrived with checks for the seats
which a prominent manufacturer had taken for the season. She betrayed
some embarrassment when she handed Paul the tickets, and a *hauteur*
which subsequently made her feel very foolish. Paul was startled for a
moment, and had the feeling of wanting to put her out; what business had
she here among all these fine people and gay colours? He looked her over
and decided that she was not appropriately dressed and must be a fool to
sit downstairs in such togs. The tickets had probably been sent her out of
kindness, he reflected as he put down a seat for her, and she had about as
much right to sit there as he had.

When the symphony began Paul sank into one of the rear seats with a
long sigh of relief, and lost himself as he had done before the Rico. It was
not that symphonies, as such, meant anything in particular to Paul, but
the first sign of the instruments seemed to free some hilarious and potent
spirit within him; something that struggled there like the Genius in the
bottle found by the Arab fisherman. He felt a sudden zest of life; the
lights danced before his eyes and the concert hall blazed into unimaginable splendour. When the soprano soloist came on, Paul forgot even the
nastiness of his teacher's being there and gave himself up to the peculiar
stimulus such personages always had for him. The soloist chanced to be
a German woman, by no means in her first youth, and the mother of
many children; but she wore an elaborate gown and a tiara, and above all
she had that indefinable air of achievement, that world-shine upon her,
which, in Paul's eyes, made her a veritable queen of Romance.

After a concert was over Paul was always irritable and wretched until
he got to sleep, and to-night he was even more than usually restless. He
had the feeling of not being able to let down, of its being impossible to
give up this delicious excitement which was the only thing that could be
called living at all. During the last number he withdrew and, after hastily
changing his clothes in the dressing-room, slipped out to the side door
where the soprano's carriage stood. Here he began pacing rapidly up and
down the walk, waiting to see her come out.

Over yonder the Schenley, in its vacant stretch, loomed big and square
through the fine rain, the windows of its twelve stories glowing like those
of a lighted card-board house under a Christmas tree. All the actors and
singers of the better class stayed there when they were in the city, and a
number of the big manufacturers of the place lived there in the winter.
Paul had often hung about the hotel, watching the people go in and out,
longing to enter and leave school-masters and dull care behind him forever.

At last the singer came out, accompanied by the conductor, who helped her into her carriage and closed the door with a cordial *auf wiedersehen*, which set Paul to wondering whether she were not an old sweetheart of his. Paul followed the carriage over to the hotel, walking so rapidly as not to be far from the entrance when the singer alighted and disappeared behind the swinging glass doors that were opened by a negro in a tall hat and a long coat. In the moment that the door was ajar, it seemed to Paul that he, too, entered. He seemed to feel himself go after her up the steps, into the warm, lighted building, into an exotic, a tropical world of shiny, glistening surfaces and basking ease. He reflected upon the mysterious dishes that were brought into the dining-room, the green bottles in buckets of ice, as he had seen them in the supper party pictures of the *Sunday World* supplement. A quick gust of wind brought the rain down with sudden vehemence, and Paul was startled to find that he was still outside in the slush of the gravel driveway; that his boots were letting in the water and his scanty overcoat was clinging wet about him; that the lights in front of the concert hall were out, and that the rain was driving in sheets between him and the orange glow of the windows above him. There it was, what he wanted—tangibly before him, like the fairy world of a Christmas pantomime, but mocking spirits stood guard at the doors, and, as the rain beat in his face, Paul wondered whether he were destined always to shiver in the black night outside, looking up at it.

He turned and walked reluctantly toward the car tracks. The end had to come sometime; his father in his night-clothes at the top of the stairs, explanations that did not explain, hastily improvised fictions that were forever tripping him up, his upstairs room and its horrible yellow wall-paper, the creaking bureau with the greasy plush collar-box, and over his painted wooden bed the pictures of George Washington and John Calvin, and the framed motto, 'Feed my Lambs', which had been worked in red worsted by his mother.

Half an hour later, Paul alighted from his car and went slowly down one of the side streets off the main thoroughfare. It was a highly respectable street, where all the houses were exactly alike, and where business men of moderate means begot and reared large families of children, all of whom went to Sabbath-school and learned the shorter catechism, and were interested in arithmetic; all of whom were as exactly alike as their homes, and of a piece with the monotony in which they lived. Paul never went up Cordelia Street without a shudder of loathing. His home was next the house of the Cumberland minister. He approached it to-night with the nerveless sense of defeat, the hopeless feeling of sinking back forever into ugliness and commonness that he had always had when he came home. The moment he turned into Cordelia Street he felt the waters close above his head. After each of these orgies of living, he experienced all the physical depression which follows a debauch; the loathing of respectable beds, of common food, of a house permeated by kitchen odours; a shuddering repulsion for the flavourless, colourless mass of every-day existence; a morbid desire for cool things and soft lights and fresh flowers.

The nearer he approached the house, the more absolutely unequal Paul felt to the sight of it all; his ugly sleeping chamber; the cold bathroom with the grimy zinc tub, the cracked mirror, the dripping spigots; his father, at the top of the stairs, his hairy legs sticking out from his night-shirt, his feet thrust into carpet slippers. He was so much later than usual that there would certainly be inquiries and reproaches. Paul stopped short before the door. He felt that he could not be accosted by his father to-night; that he could not toss again on that miserable bed. He would not go in. He would tell his father that he had no car fare, and it was raining so hard he had gone home with one of the boys and stayed all night.

Meanwhile, he was wet and cold. He went around to the back of the house and tried one of the basement windows, found it open, raised it cautiously, and scrambled down the cellar wall to the floor. There he stood, holding his breath, terrified by the noise he had made, but the floor above him was silent, and there was no creak on the stairs. He found a soap-box, and carried it over to the soft ring of light that streamed from the furnace door, and sat down. He was horribly afraid of rats, so he did not try to sleep, but sat looking distrustfully at the dark, still terrified lest he might have awakened his father. In such reactions, after one of the experiences which made days and nights out of the dreary blanks of the calendar, when his senses were deadened, Paul's head was always singularly clear. Suppose his father had heard him getting in at the window and had come down and shot him for a burglar? Then, again, suppose his father had come down, pistol in hand, and he had cried out in time to save himself, and his father had been horrified to think how nearly he had killed him? Then, again, suppose a day should come when his father would remember that night, and wish there had been no warning cry to stay his hand? With this last supposition Paul entertained himself until daybreak.

The following Sunday was fine; the sodden November chill was broken by the last flash of autumnal summer. In the morning Paul had to go to church and Sabbath-school, as always. On seasonable Sunday after-noons the burghers of Cordelia Street always sat out on their front 'stoops', and talked to their neighbours on the next stoop, or called to those across the street in neighbourly fashion. The men usually sat on gay cushions placed upon the steps that led down to the sidewalk, while the women, in their Sunday 'waists', sat in rockers on the cramped porches, pretending to be greatly at their ease. The children played in the streets; there were so many of them that the place resembled the recreation grounds of a kindergarten. The men on the steps—all in their shirt sleeves, their vests unbuttoned—sat with their legs well apart, their stomachs comfortably protruding, and talked of the prices of things, or told anecdotes of the sagacity of their various chiefs and overlords. They occasionally looked over the multitude of squabbling children, listened affectionately to their high-pitched, nasal voices, smiling to see their own proclivities reproduced in their offspring, and interspersed their legends of the iron kings with remarks about their sons' progress at school, their grades in arithmetic, and the amounts they had saved in their toy banks.

On this last Sunday of November, Paul sat all the afternoon on the lowest step of his 'stoop', staring into the street, while his sisters, in their rockers, were talking to the minister's daughters next door about how many shirt-waists they had made in the last week, and how many waffles some one had eaten at the last church supper. When the weather was warm, and his father was in a particularly jovial frame of mind, the girls made lemonade, which was always brought out in a red-glass pitcher, ornamented with forget-me-nots in blue enamel. This the girls thought very fine, and the neighbours always joked about the suspicious colour of the pitcher.

To-day Paul's father sat on the top step, talking to a young man who shifted a restless baby from knee to knee. He happened to be the young man who was daily held up to Paul as a model, and after whom it was his father's dearest hope that he would pattern. This young man was of a ruddy complexion, with a compressed, red mouth, and faded, near-sighted eyes, over which he wore thick spectacles, with gold bows that curved about his ears. He was clerk to one of the magnates of a great steel corporation, and was looked upon in Cordelia Street as a young man with a future. There was a story that, some five years ago—he was now barely twenty-six—he had been a trifle dissipated, but in order to curb his appetites and save the loss of time and strength that a sowing of wild oats might have entailed, he had taken his chief's advice, oft reiterated to his employees, and at twenty-one had married the first woman whom he could persuade to share his fortunes. She happened to be an angular school-mistress, much older than he, who also wore thick glasses, and who had now borne him four children, all near-sighted, like herself.

The young man was relating how his chief, now cruising in the Mediterranean, kept in touch with all the details of the business, arranging his office hours on his yacht just as though he were at home, and 'knocking off work enough to keep two stenographers busy'. His father told, in turn, the plan his corporation was considering, of putting in an electric railway plant at Cairo. Paul snapped his teeth; he had an awful apprehension that they might spoil it all before he got there. Yet he rather liked to hear these legends of the iron kings, that were told and retold on Sundays and holidays; these stories of palaces in Venice, yachts on the Mediterranean, and high play at Monte Carlo appealed to his fancy, and he was interested in the triumphs of these cash boys who had become famous, though he had no mind for the cash-boy stage.

After supper was over, and he had helped to dry the dishes, Paul nervously asked his father whether he could go to George's to get some help in his geometry, and still more nervously asked for car fare. This latter request he had to repeat, as his father, on principle, did not like to hear requests for money, whether much or little. He asked Paul whether he could not go to some boy who lived nearer, and told him that he ought not to leave his school work until Sunday; but he gave him the dime. He was not a poor man, but he had a worthy ambition to come up in the world. His only reason for allowing Paul to usher was, that he thought a boy ought to be earning a little.

Paul bounded upstairs, scrubbed the greasy odour of the dish-water from his hands with the ill-smelling soap he hated, and then shook over his fingers a few drops of violet water from the bottle he kept hidden in his drawer. He left the house with his geometry conspicuously under his arm, and the moment he got out of Cordelia Street and boarded a down-town car, he shook off the lethargy of two deadening days, and began to live again.

The leading juvenile of the permanent stock company which played at one of the downtown theatres was an acquaintance of Paul's, and the boy had been invited to drop in at the Sunday-night rehearsals whenever he could. For more than a year Paul had spent every available moment loitering about Charley Edwards's dressing-room. He had won a place among Edwards's following not only because the young actor, who could not afford to employ a dresser, often found him useful, but because he recognized in Paul something akin to what churchmen term 'vocation'.

It was at the theatre and at Carnegie Hall that Paul really lived; the rest was but a sleep and a forgetting. This was Paul's fairy tale, and it had for him all the allurement of a secret love. The moment he inhaled the gassy, painty, dusty odour behind the scenes, he breathed like a prisoner set free, and felt within him the possibility of doing or saying splendid, brilliant, poetic things. The moment the cracked orchestra beat out the overture from *Martha*, or jerked at the serenade from *Rigoletto*, all stupid and ugly things slid from him, and his senses were deliciously, yet deli-cately fired.

Perhaps it was because, in Paul's world, the natural nearly always wore the guise of ugliness, that a certain element of artificiality seemed to him necessary in beauty. Perhaps it was because his experience of life else-where was so full of Sabbath-school picnics, petty economies, wholesome advice as to how to succeed in life, and the unescapable odours of cooking, that he found this existence so alluring, these smartly-clad men and women so attractive, that he was so moved by these starry apple orchards that bloomed perennially under the limelight.

It would be difficult to put it strongly enough how convincingly the stage entrance of that theatre was for Paul the actual portal of Romance. Certainly none of the company ever suspected it, least of all Charley Edwards. It was very like the old stories that used to float about London of fabulously rich Jews, who had subterranean halls there, with palms, and fountains, and soft lamps and richly apparelled women who never saw the disenchanting light of London day. So, in the midst of that smoke-palled city, enamoured of figures and grimy toil, Paul had his secret temple, his wishing carpet, his bit of blue-and-white Mediterranean shore bathed in perpetual sunshine.

Several of Paul's teachers had a theory that his imagination had been perverted by garish fiction, but the truth was that he scarcely ever read at all. The books at home were not such as would either tempt or corrupt a youthful mind, and as for reading the novels that some of his friends urged upon him—well, he got what he wanted much more quickly from music; any sort of music, from an orchestra to a barrel organ. He needed only the spark, the indescribable thrill that made his imagination master of his senses, and he could make plots and pictures enough of his own. It was equally true that he was not stage-struck—not, at any rate, in the usual acceptation of that expression. He had no desire to become an actor, any more than he had to become a musician. He felt no necessity to do any of these things; what he wanted was to see, to be in the atmosphere, float on the wave of it, to be carried out, blue league after blue league, away from everything.

After a night behind the scenes, Paul found the school-room more than ever repulsive; the bare floors and naked walls; the prosy men who never wore frock coats, or violets in their button-holes; the women with their dull gowns, shrill voices, and pitiful seriousness about prepositions that govern the dative. He could not bear to have the other pupils think, for a moment, that he took these people seriously; he must convey to them that he considered it all trivial, and was there only by way of a jest, anyway. He had autograph pictures of all the members of the stock company which he showed his classmates, telling them the most incredible stories of his familiarity with these people, of his acquaintance with the soloists who came to Carnegie Hall, his suppers with them and the flowers he sent them. When these stories lost their effect, and his audience grew listless, he became desperate and would bid all the boys goodbye, announcing that he was going to travel for awhile; going to Naples, to Venice, to Egypt. Then, next Monday, he would slip back, conscious and nervously smiling; his sister was ill, and he should have to defer his voyage until spring.

Matters went steadily worse with Paul at school. In the itch to let his instructors know how heartily he despised them and their homilies, and how thoroughly he was appreciated elsewhere, he mentioned once or twice that he had no time to fool with theorems; adding—with a twitch of the eyebrows and a touch of that nervous bravado which so perplexed them—that he was helping the people down at the stock company; they were old friends of his.

The upshot of the matter was, that the Principal went to Paul's father, and Paul was taken out of school and put to work. The manager at Carnegie Hall was told to get another usher in his stead; the doorkeeper at the theatre was warned not to admit him to the house; and Charley Edwards remorsefully promised the boy's father not to see him again.

The members of the stock company were vastly amused when some of Paul's stories reached them—especially the women. They were hard-working women, most of them supporting indigent husbands or brothers, and they laughed rather bitterly at having stirred the boy to such fervid and florid inventions. They agreed with the faculty and with his father that Paul's was a bad case.

The east-bound train was ploughing through a January snow-storm; the dull dawn was beginning to show grey when the engine whistled a mile out of Newark. Paul started up from the seat where he had lain curled in uneasy slumber, rubbed the breath-misted window glass with his hand, and peered out. The snow was whirling in curling eddies above the white bottom lands, and the drifts lay already deep in the fields and along the fences, while here and there the long dead grass and dried weed stalks protruded black above it. Lights shone from the scattered houses, and a gang of labourers who stood beside the track waved their lanterns.

Paul had slept very little, and he felt grimy and uncomfortable. He had made the all-night journey in a day coach, partly because he was ashamed, dressed as he was, to go into a Pullman, and partly because he was afraid of being seen there by some Pittsburgh business man, who might have noticed him in Denny & Carson's office. When the whistle awoke him, he clutched quickly at his breast pocket, glancing about him with an uncertain smile. But the little, clay-bespattered Italians were still sleeping, the slatternly women across the aisle were in open-mouthed oblivion, and even the crumby, crying babies were for the nonce stilled. Paul settled back to struggle with his impatience as best he could.

When he arrived at the Jersey City station, he hurried through his breakfast, manifestly ill at ease and keeping a sharp eye about him. After he reached the Twenty-third Street station, he consulted a cabman, and had himself driven to a men's furnishing establishment that was just opening for the day. He spent upward of two hours there, buying with endless reconsidering and great care. His new street suit he put on in the fitting-room; the frock coat and dress clothes he had bundled into the cab with his linen. Then he drove to a hatter's and a shoe house. His next errand was at Tiffany's, where he selected his silver and a new scarf-pin. He would not wait to have his silver marked, he said. Lastly, he stopped at a trunk shop on Broadway, and had his purchases packed into various traveling bags.

It was a little after one o'clock when he drove up to the Waldorf, and after settling with the cabman, went into the office. He registered from Washington; said his mother and father had been abroad, and that he had come down to await the arrival of their steamer. He told his story plausibly and had no trouble, since he volunteered to pay for them in advance, in engaging his rooms; a sleeping-room, sitting-room and bath.

Not once, but a hundred times Paul had planned this entry into New York. He had gone over every detail of it with Charley Edwards, and in his scrap book at home there were pages of description about New York hotels, cut from the Sunday papers. When he was shown to his sitting-room on the eighth floor, he saw at a glance that everything was as it should be; there was but one detail in his mental picture that the place did not realize, so he rang for the bell boy and sent him down for flowers. He moved about nervously until the boy returned, putting away his new linen and fingering it delightedly as he did so. When the flowers came, he put them hastily into water, and then tumbled into a hot bath. Presently he came out of his white bathroom, resplendent in his new silk underwear, and playing with the tassels of his red robe. The snow was whirling so fiercely outside his windows that he could scarcely see across the street, but within the air was deliciously soft and fragrant. He put the violets and jonquils on the taboret beside the couch, and threw himself down, with a long sigh, covering himself with a Roman blanket. He was thoroughly tired; he had been in such haste, he had stood up to such a strain, covered so much ground in the last twenty-four hours, that he wanted to think how it had all come about. Lulled by the sound of the wind, the warm air, and the cool fragrance of the flowers, he sank into deep, drowsy retrospection.

It had been wonderfully simple; when they had shut him out of the theatre and concert hall, when they had taken away his bone, the whole thing was virtually determined. The rest was a mere matter of opportunity. The only thing that at all surprised him was his own courage—for he realized well enough that he had always been tormented by fear, a sort of apprehensive dread that, of late years, as the meshes of the lies he had told closed about him, had been pulling the muscles of his body tighter and tighter. Until now, he could not remember the time when he had not been dreading something. Even when he was a little boy, it was always there—behind him, or before, or on either side. There had always been the shadowed corner, the dark place into which he dared not look, but from which something seemed always to be watching him—and Paul had done things that were not pretty to watch, he knew.

But now he had a curious sense of relief, as though he had at last thrown down the gauntlet to the thing in the corner.

Yet it was but a day since he had been sulking in the traces; but yesterday afternoon that he had been sent to the bank with Denny & Carson's deposit, as usual—but this time he was instructed to leave the book to be balanced. There was above two thousand dollars in checks, and nearly a thousand in the bank notes which he had taken from the book and quietly transferred to his pocket. At the bank he had made out a new deposit slip. His nerves had been steady enough to permit of his returning to the office, where he had finished his work and asked for a full day's holiday to-morrow, Saturday, giving a perfectly reasonable pretext. The bank book, he knew, would not be returned before Monday or Tuesday, and his father would be out of town for the next week. From the time he slipped the bank notes into his pocket until he boarded the night train for New York, he had not known a moment's hesitation. It was not the first time Paul had steered through treacherous waters.

How astonishingly easy it had all been; here he was, the thing done; and this time there would be no awakening, no figure at the top of the stairs. He watched the snow flakes whirling by his window until he fell asleep.

When he awoke, it was three o'clock in the afternoon. He bounded up with a start; half of one of his precious days gone already! He spent more than an hour in dressing, watching every stage of his toilet carefully in the mirror. Everything was quite perfect; he was exactly the kind of boy he had always wanted to be.

When he went downstairs, Paul took a carriage and drove up Fifth Avenue toward the Park. The snow had somewhat abated; carriages and tradesmen's wagons were hurrying soundlessly to and fro in the winter twilight; boys in woolen mufflers were shovelling off the doorsteps; the avenue stages made fine spots of colour against the white street. Here and there on the corners were stands, with whole flower gardens blooming under glass cases, against the sides of which the snow flakes stuck and melted; violets, roses, carnations, lilies of the valley—somehow vastly more lovely and alluring that they blossomed thus unnaturally in the snow. The Park itself was a wonderful stage winter-piece.

When he returned, the pause of the twilight had ceased, and the tune of the streets had changed. The snow was falling faster, lights streamed from the hotels that reared their dozen stories fearlessly up into the storm, defying the raging Atlantic winds. A long, black stream of carriages poured down the avenue, intersected here and there by other streams, tending horizontally. There were a score of cabs about the entrance of his hotel, and his driver had to wait. Boys in livery were running in and out of the awning stretched across the sidewalk, up and down the red velvet carpet laid from the door to the street. Above, about, within it all was the rumble and roar, the hurry and toss of thousands of human beings as hot for pleasure as himself, and on every side of him towered the glaring affirmation of the omnipotence of wealth.

The boy set his teeth and drew his shoulders together in a spasm of realization; the plot of all dramas, the text of all romances, the nerve-stuff of all sensations was whirling about him like the snow flakes. He burnt like a faggot in a tempest.

When Paul went down to dinner, the music of the orchestra came floating up the elevator shaft to greet him. His head whirled as he stepped into the thronged corridor, and he sank back into one of the chairs against the wall to get his breath. The lights, the chatter, the perfumes, the bewildering medley of colour—he had, for a moment, the feeling of not being able to stand it. But only for a moment; these were his own people, he told himself. He went slowly about the corridors, through the writing-rooms, smoking-rooms, reception-rooms, as though he were exploring the chambers of an enchanted palace, built and peopled for him alone.

When he reached the dining-room he sat down at a table near a window. The flowers, the white linen, the many-coloured wine glasses, the gay toilettes of the women, the low popping of corks, the undulating repetitions of the *Blue Danube* from the orchestra, all flooded Paul's dream with bewildering radiance. When the roseate tinge of his champagne was added—that cold, precious bubbling stuff that creamed and foamed in his glass—Paul wondered that there were honest men in the world at all. This was what all the world was fighting for, he reflected; this was what all the struggle was about. He doubted the reality of his past. Had he ever known a place called Cordelia Street, a place where fagged-looking business men got on the early car; mere rivets in a machine they seemed to Paul,—sickening men, with combings of children's hair always hanging to their coats, and the smell of cooking in their clothes. Cordelia Street—Ah! that belonged to another time and country; had he not always been thus, had he not sat here night after night, from as far back as he could remember, looking pensively over just such shimmering textures, and slowly twirling the stem of a glass like this one between his thumb and middle finger? He rather thought he had.

He was not in the least abashed or lonely. He had no especial desire to meet or to know any of these people; all he demanded was the right to look on and conjecture, to watch the pageant. The mere stage properties were all he contended for. Nor was he lonely later in the evening, in his loge at the Metropolitan. He was now entirely rid of his nervous misgivings, of his forced aggressiveness, of the imperative desire to show himself different from his surroundings. He felt now that his surroundings explained him. Nobody questioned the purple; he had only to wear it passively. He had only to glance down at his attire to reassure himself that here it would be impossible for any one to humiliate him.

He found it hard to leave his beautiful sitting-room to go to bed that night, and sat long watching the raging storm from his turret window. When he went to sleep, it was with the lights turned on in his bedroom; partly because of his old timidity, and partly so that, if he should wake in the night, there would be no wretched moment of doubt, no horrible suspicion of yellow wall-paper, or of Washington and Calvin above his bed.

Sunday morning the city was practically snow-bound. Paul breakfasted late, and in the afternoon he fell in with a wild San Francisco boy, a freshman at Yale, who said he had run down for a 'little flyer' over Sunday. The young man offered to show Paul the night side of the town, and the two boys went out together after dinner, not returning to the hotel until seven o'clock the next morning. They had started out in the confiding warmth of a champagne friendship, but their parting in the elevator was singularly cool. The freshman pulled himself together to make his train, and Paul went to bed. He awoke at two o'clock in the afternoon, very thirsty and dizzy, and rang for ice-water, coffee, and the Pittsburgh papers.

On the part of the hotel management, Paul excited no suspicion. There was this to be said for him, that he wore his spoils with dignity and in no way made himself conspicuous. Even under the glow of his wine he was never boisterous, though he found the stuff like a magician's wand for wonder-building. His chief greediness lay in his ears and eyes, and his excesses were not offensive ones. His dearest pleasures were the grey winter twilights in his sitting-room; his quiet enjoyment of his flowers, his clothes, his wide divan, his cigarette and his sense of power. He could not remember a time when he had felt so at peace with himself. The mere release from the necessity of petty lying, lying every day and every day, restored his self-respect. He had never lied for pleasure, even at school; but to be noticed and admired, to assert his difference from other Cordelia Street boys; and he felt a good deal more manly, more honest, even, now that he had no need for boastful pretensions, now that he could, as his actor friends used to say, 'dress the part'. It was characteristic that remorse did not occur to him. His golden days went by without a shadow, and he made each as perfect as he could.

On the eighth day after his arrival in New York, he found the whole affair exploited in the Pittsburgh papers, exploited with a wealth of detail which indicated that local news of a sensational nature was at a low ebb. The firm of Denny & Carson announced that the boy's father had refunded the full amount of the theft, and that they had no intention of prosecuting. The Cumberland minister had been interviewed, and expressed his hope of yet reclaiming the motherless lad, and his Sabbath-school teacher declared that she would spare no effort to that end. The rumour had reached Pittsburgh that the boy had been seen in a New York hotel, and his father had gone East to find him and bring him home.

Paul had just come in to dress for dinner; he sank into a chair, weak to the knees, and clasped his head in his hands. It was to be worse than jail, even; the tepid waters of Cordelia Street were to close over him finally and forever. The grey monotony stretched before him in hopeless, unrelieved years; Sabbath-school, Young People's Meeting, the yellow-papered room, the damp dish-towels; it all rushed back upon him with a sickening vividness. He had the old feeling that the orchestra had suddenly stopped, the sinking sensation that the play was over. The sweat broke out on his face, and he sprang to his feet, looked about him with his white, conscious smile, and winked at himself in the mirror. With something of the old childish belief in miracles with which he had so often gone to class, all his lessons unlearned, Paul dressed and dashed whistling down the corridor to the elevator.

He had no sooner entered the dining-room and caught the measure of the music than his remembrance was lightened by his old elastic power of claiming the moment, mounting with it, and finding it all sufficient. The glare and glitter about him, the mere scenic accessories had again, and for the last time, their old potency. He would show himself that he was game, he would finish the thing splendidly. He doubted, more than ever, the existence of Cordelia Street, and for the first time he drank his wine recklessly. Was he not, after all, one of those fortunate beings born to the purple, was he not still himself and in his own place? He drummed a nervous accompaniment to the Pagliacci music and looked about him, telling himself over and over that it had paid.

He reflected drowsily, to the swell of the music and the chill sweetness of his wine, that he might have done it more wisely. He might have caught an outbound steamer and been well out of their clutches before now. But the other side of the world had seemed too far away and too uncertain then; he could not have waited for it; his need had been too sharp. If he had to choose over again, he would do the same thing to-morrow. He looked affectionately about the dining-room, now gilded with a soft mist. Ah, it had paid indeed!

Paul was awakened next morning by a painful throbbing in his head and feet. He had thrown himself across the bed without undressing, and had slept with his shoes on. His limbs and hands were lead heavy, and his tongue and throat were parched and burnt. There came upon him one of those fateful attacks of clear-headedness that never occurred except when he was physically exhausted and his nerves hung loose. He lay still and closed his eyes and let the tide of things wash over him.

His father was in New York; 'stopping at some joint or other', he told himself. The memory of successive summers on the front stoop fell upon him like a weight of black water. He had not a hundred dollars left; and he knew now, more than ever, that money was everything, the wall that stood between all he loathed and all he wanted. The thing was winding itself up; he had thought of that on his first glorious day in New York, and had even provided a way to snap the thread. It lay on his dressing-table now; he had got it out last night when he came blindly up from dinner, but the shiny metal hurt his eyes, and he disliked the looks of it.

He rose and moved about with a painful effort, succumbing now and again to attacks of nausea. It was the old depression exaggerated; all the world had become Cordelia Street. Yet somehow he was not afraid of anything, was absolutely calm; perhaps because he had looked into the dark corner at last and knew. It was bad enough, what he saw there, but somehow not so bad as his long fear of it had been. He saw everything clearly now. He had a feeling that he had made the best of it, that he had lived the sort of life he was meant to live, and for half an hour he sat staring at the revolver. But he told himself that was not the way, so he went downstairs and took a cab to the ferry.

When Paul arrived at Newark, he got off the train and took another cab, directing the driver to follow the Pennsylvania tracks out of the town. The snow lay heavy on the roadways and had drifted deep in the open fields. Only here and there the dead grass or dried weed stalks projected, singularly black, above it. Once well into the country, Paul dismissed the carriage and walked, floundering along the tracks, his mind a medley of irrelevant things. He seemed to hold in his brain an actual picture of everything he had seen that morning. He remembered every feature of both his drivers, of the toothless old woman from whom he had bought the red flowers in his coat, the agent from whom he had got his ticket, and all of his fellow-passengers on the ferry. His mind, unable to cope with vital matters near at hand, worked feverishly and deftly at sorting and grouping these images. They made for him a part of the ugliness of the world, of the ache in his head, and the bitter burning on his tongue. He stooped and put a handful of snow into his mouth as he walked, but that, too, seemed hot. When he reached a little hillside, where the tracks ran through a cut some twenty feet below him, he stopped and sat down.

The carnations in his coat were drooping with the cold, he noticed; their red glory all over. It occurred to him that all the flowers he had seen in the glass cases that first night must have gone the same way, long before this. It was only one splendid breath they had, in spite of their brave mockery at the winter outside the glass; and it was a losing game in the end, it seemed, this revolt against the homilies by which the world is run. Paul took one of the blossoms carefully from his coat and scooped a little hole in the snow, where he covered it up. Then he dozed a while, from his weak condition, seeming insensible to the cold.

The sound of an approaching train awoke him, and he started to his feet, remembering only his resolution, and afraid lest he should be too late. He stood watching the approaching locomotive, his teeth chattering, his lips drawn away from them in a frightened smile; once or twice he glanced nervously sidewise, as though he were being watched. When the right moment came, he jumped. As he fell, the folly of his haste occurred to him with merciless clearness, the vastness of what he had left undone. There flashed through his brain, clearer than ever before, the blue of Adriatic water, the yellow of Algerian sands.

He felt something strike his chest, and that his body was being thrown swiftly through the air, on and on, immeasurably far and fast, while his limbs were gently relaxed. Then, because the picture making mechanism was crushed, the disturbing visions flashed into black, and Paul dropped back into the immense design of things.

EDITH WHARTON

Afterward

❦

I

'Oh, there *is* one, of course, but you'll never know it.'

The assertion, laughingly flung out six months earlier in a bright June garden, came back to Mary Boyne with a new perception of its significance as she stood, in the December dusk, waiting for the lamps to be brought into the library.

The words had been spoken by their friend Alida Stair, as they sat at tea on her lawn at Pangbourne, in reference to the very house of which the library in question was the central, the pivotal 'feature'. Mary Boyne and her husband, in quest of a country place in one of the southern or southwestern counties, had, on their arrival in England, carried their problem straight to Alida Stair, who had successfully solved it in her own case; but it was not until they had rejected, almost capriciously, several practical and judicious suggestions that she threw out: 'Well, there's Lyng, in Dorsetshire. It belongs to Hugo's cousins, and you can get it for a song.'

The reason she gave for its being obtainable on these terms—its remoteness from a station, its lack of electric light, hot water pipes, and other vulgar necessities—were exactly those pleading in its favor with two romantic Americans perversely in search of the economic drawbacks which were associated, in their tradition, with unusual architectural felicities.

'I should never believe I was living in an old house unless I was thoroughly uncomfortable,' Ned Boyne, the more extravagant of the two, had jocosely insisted; 'the least hint of convenience would make me think it had been bought out of an exhibition, with the pieces numbered, and set up again.' And they had proceeded to enumerate, with humorous precision, their various doubts and demands, refusing to believe that the house their cousin recommended was *really* Tudor till they learned it had no heating system, or that the village church was literally in the grounds till she assured them of the deplorable uncertainty of the water supply.

'It's too uncomfortable to be true!' Edward Boyne had continued to exult as the avowal of each disadvantage was successively wrung from her; but he had cut short his rhapsody to ask, with a relapse to distrust: 'And the ghost? You've been concealing from us the fact that there is no ghost!'

Mary, at the moment, had laughed with him, yet almost with her laugh, being possessed of several sets of independent perceptions, had been struck by a note of flatness in Alida's answering hilarity.

'Oh, Dorsetshire's full of ghosts, you know.'

'Yes, yes; but that won't do. I don't want to have to drive ten miles to see somebody else's ghost. I want one of my own on the premises. *Is* there a ghost at Lyng?'

His rejoinder had made Alida laugh again, and it was then that she had flung back tantalizingly: 'Oh, there *is* one, of course, but you'll never know it.'

'Never know it?' Boyne pulled her up. 'But what in the world constitutes a ghost except the fact of its being known for one?'

'I can't say. But that's the story.'

'That there's a ghost, but that nobody knows it's a ghost?'

'Well—not till afterward, at any rate.'

'Till afterward?'

'Not till long long afterward.'

'But if it's once been identified as an unearthly visitant, why hasn't it *signalement* been handed down in the family? How has it managed to preserve its incognito?'

Alida could only shake her head. 'Don't ask me. But it has.'

'And then suddenly'—Mary spoke up as if from cavernous depths of divination—'suddenly, long afterward, one says to one's self "*That was it?*"'

She was startled at the sepulchral sound with which her question fell on the banter of the other two, and she saw the shadow of the same surprise flit across Alida's pupils. 'I suppose so. One just has to wait.'

'Oh, hang waiting!' Ned broke in. 'Life's too short for a ghost who can only be enjoyed in retrospect. Can't we do better than that, Mary?'

But it turned out that in the event they were not destined to, for within three months of their conversation with Mrs Stair they were settled at Lyng, and the life they had yearned for, to the point of planning it in advance in all its daily details, had actually begun for them.

It was to sit, in the thick December dusk, by just such a wide-hooded fireplace, under just such black oak rafters, with the sense that beyond the mullioned panes the downs were darkened to a deeper solitude: it was for the ultimate indulgence of such sensations that Mary Boyne, abruptly exiled from New York by her husband's business, had endured for nearly fourteen years the soul-deadening ugliness of a Middle Western town, and that Boyne had ground on doggedly at his engineering till, with a suddenness that still made her blink, the prodigious windfall of the Blue Star Mine had put them at a stroke in possession of life and the leisure to taste it. They had never for a moment meant their new state to be one of idleness; but they meant to give themselves only to harmonious activities. She had her vision of painting and gardening (against a background of grey walls), he dreamed of the production of his long-planned book on the 'Economic Basis of Culture'; and with such absorbing work ahead no existence could be too sequestered: they could not get far enough from the world, or plunge deep enough into the past.

Dorsetshire had attracted them from the first by an air of remoteness out of all proportion to its geographical position. But to the Boynes it was one of the ever-recurring wonders of the whole incredibly compressed island—a nest of counties, as they put it—that for the production of its effects so little of a given quality went so far: that so few miles made a distance, and so short a distance a difference.

'It's that,' Ned had once enthusiastically explained, 'that gives such depth to their effects, such relief to their contrasts. They've been able to lay the butter so thick on every delicious mouthful.'

The butter had certainly been laid on thick at Lyng: the old house hidden under a shoulder of the downs had almost all the finer marks of commerce with a protracted past. The mere fact that it was neither large nor exceptional made it, to the Boynes, abound the more completely in its special charm—the charm of having been for centuries a deep dim reservoir of life. The life had probably not been of the most vivid order: for long periods, no doubt, it had fallen as noiselessly into the past as the quiet drizzle of autumn fell, hour after hour, into the fish pond between the yews; but these backwaters of existence sometimes breed, in their sluggish depths, strange acuities of emotion, and Mary Boyne had felt from the first the mysterious stir of intenser memories.

The feeling had never been stronger than on this particular afternoon when, waiting in the library for the lamps to come, she rose from her seat and stood among the shadows of the hearth. Her husband had gone off, after luncheon, for one of his long tramps on the downs. She had noticed of late that he preferred to go alone; and, in the tried security of their personal relations, had been driven to conclude that his book was bothering him, and that he needed the afternoons to turn over in solitude the problems left from the morning's work. Certainly the book was not going as smoothly as she had thought it would, and there were lines of perplexity between his eyes such as had never been there in his engineering days. He had often, then, looked fagged to the verge of illness, but the native demon of worry had never branded his brow. Yet the few pages he had so far read to her—the introduction, and a summary of the opening chapter—showed a firm hold on his subject, and an increasing confidence in his powers.

The fact threw her into deeper perplexity, since, now that he had done with business and its disturbing contingencies, the one other possible source of anxiety was eliminated. Unless it were his health, then? But physically he had gained since they had come to Dorsetshire, grown robuster, ruddier and fresher eyed. It was only within the last week that she had felt in him the undefinable change which made her restless in his absence, and as tongue-tied in his presence as though it were *she* who had a secret to keep from him!

The thought that there *was* a secret somewhere between them struck her with a sudden rap of wonder, and she looked about her down the long room.

'Can it be the house?' she mused.

The room itself might have been full of secrets. They seemed to be piling themselves up, as evening fell, like the layers and layers of velvet shadow dropping from the low ceiling, the rows of books, the smoke-blurred sculpture of the hearth.

'Why, of course—the house is haunted!' she reflected.

The ghost—Alida's imperceptible ghost—after figuring largely in the banter of their first month or two at Lyng, had been gradually left aside as too ineffectual for imaginative use. Mary had, indeed, as became the tenant of a haunted house, made the customary inquiries among her rural neighbors, but, beyond a vague 'They dü say so, Ma'am,' the villagers had nothing to impart. The elusive specter had apparently never had sufficient identity for a legend to crystallize about it, and after a time the Boynes had set the matter down to their profit-and-loss account, agreeing that Lyng was one of the few houses good enough in itself to dispense with supernatural enhancements.

'And I suppose, poor ineffectual demon, that's why it beats its beautiful wings in vain in the void,' Mary had laughingly concluded.

'Or, rather,' Ned answered in the same strain, 'why, amid so much that's ghostly, it can never affirm its separate existence as *the* ghost.' And thereupon their invisible housemate had finally dropped out of their references, which were numerous enough to make them soon unaware of the loss.

Now, as she stood on the hearth, the subject of their earlier curiosity revived in her with a new sense of its meaning—a sense gradually acquired through daily contact with the scene of the lurking mystery. It was the house itself, of course, that possessed the ghost-seeing faculty, that communed visually but secretly with its own past; if one could only get into close enough communion with the house, one might surprise its secret, and acquire the ghost sight on one's own account. Perhaps, in his long hours in this very room, where she never trespassed till the afternoon, her husband *had* acquired it already, and was silently carrying about the weight of whatever it had revealed to him. Mary was too well versed in the code of the spectral world not to know that one could not talk about the ghosts one saw: to do so was almost as great a breach of taste as to name a lady in a club. But this explanation did not really satisfy her. 'What, after all, except for the fun of the shudder,' she reflected, 'would he really care for any of their old ghosts?' And thence she was thrown back once more on the fundamental dilemma: the fact that one's greater or less susceptibility to spectral influences had no particular bearing on the case, since, when one *did* see a ghost at Lyng, one did not know it.

'Not till long afterward,' Alida Stair had said. Well, supposing Ned *had* seen one when they first came, and had known only within the last week what had happened to him? More and more under the spell of the hour, she threw back her thoughts to the early days of their tenancy, but at first only to recall a lively confusion of unpacking, settling, arranging of books, and calling to each other from remote corners of the house as, treasure after treasure, it revealed itself to them. It was in this particular connection that she presently recalled a certain soft afternoon of the previous October, when, passing from the first rapturous flurry of exploration to a detailed inspection of the old house, she had pressed (like a novel heroine) a panel that opened on a flight of corkscrew stairs leading to a flat ledge of the roof—the roof which, from below, seemed to slope away on all sides too abruptly for any but practiced feet to scale.

The view from this hidden coign was enchanting, and she had flown down to snatch Ned from his papers and give him the freedom of her discovery. She remembered still how, standing at her side, he had passed his arm about her while their gaze flew to the long tossed horizon line of the downs, and then dropped contentedly back to trace the arabesque of yew hedges about the fish pond, and the shadow of the cedar on the lawn.

'And now the other way,' he had said, turning her about within his arm; and closely pressed to him, she had absorbed, like some long satisfying draught, the picture of the grey-walled court, the squat lions on the gates, and the lime avenue reaching up to the highroad under the downs.

It was just then, while they gazed and held each other, that she had felt his arm relax, and heard a sharp 'Hullo!' that made her turn to glance at him.

Distinctly, yes, she now recalled that she had seen, as she glanced, a shadow of anxiety, of perplexity, rather, fall across his face; and, following his eyes, had beheld the figure of a man—a man in loose greyish clothes, as it appeared to her—who was sauntering down the lime avenue to the court with the doubtful gait of a stranger who seeks his way. Her shortsighted eyes had given her but a blurred impression of slightness and greyishness, with something foreign, or at least unlocal, in the cut of the figure or its dress; but her husband had apparently seen more—seen enough to make him push past her with a hasty 'Wait!' and dash down the stairs without pausing to give her a hand.

A slight tendency to dizziness obliged her, after a provisional clutch at the chimney against which they had been leaning, to follow him first more cautiously; and when she had reached the landing she paused again, for a less definite reason, leaning over the banister to strain her eyes through the silence of the brown sun-flecked depths. She lingered there till, somewhere in those depths, she heard the closing of a door; then, mechanically impelled, she went down the shallow flights of steps till she reached the lower hall.

The front door stood open on the sunlight of the court, and hall and court were empty. The library door was open, too, and after listening in vain for any sound of voices within, she crossed the threshold, and found her husband alone, vaguely fingering the papers on his desk.

He looked up, as if surprised at her entrance, but the shadow of anxiety had passed from his face, leaving it even, as she fancied, a little brighter and clearer than usual.

'What was it? Who was it?' she asked.

'Who?' he repeated, with the surprise still all on his side.

'The man we saw coming toward the house.'

He seemed to reflect. 'The man? Why, I thought I saw Peters; I dashed after him to say a word about the stable drains, but he had disappeared before I could get down.'

'Disappeared? But he seemed to be walking so slowly when we saw him.'

Boyne shrugged his shoulders. 'So I thought; but he must have got up steam in the interval. What do you say to our trying a scramble up Meldon Steep before sunset?'

That was all. At the time the occurrence had been less than nothing, had, indeed, been immediately obliterated by the magic of their first vision from Meldon Steep, a height which they had dreamed of climbing ever since they had first seen its bare spine rising above the roof of Lyng. Doubtless it was the mere fact of the other incident's having occurred on the very day of their ascent to Meldon that had kept it stored away in the fold of memory from which it now emerged; for in itself it had no mark of the portentous. At the moment there could have been nothing more natural than that Ned should dash himself from the roof in the pursuit of dilatory tradesmen. It was the period when they were always on the watch for one or the other of the specialists employed about the place; always lying in wait for them, and rushing out at them with questions, reproaches or reminders. And certainly in the distance the grey figure had looked like Peters.

Yet now, as she reviewed the scene, she felt her husband's explanation of it to have been invalidated by the look of anxiety on his face. Why had the familiar appearance of Peters made him anxious? Why, above all, if it was of such prime necessity to confer with him on the subject of the stable drains, had the failure to find him produced such a look of relief? Mary could not say that any one of these questions had occurred to her at the time, yet, from the promptness with which they now marshalled themselves at her summons, she had a sense that they must all along have been there, waiting their hour.

II

Weary with her thoughts, she moved to the window. The library was now quite dark, and she was surprised to see how much faint light the outer world still held.

As she peered out into it across the court, a figure shaped itself far down the perspective of bare limes: it looked a mere blot of deeper grey in the greyness, and for an instant, as it moved toward her, her heart thumped to the thought 'It's the ghost!'

She had time, in that long instant, to feel suddenly that the man of whom, two months earlier, she had had a distant vision from the roof, was now, at his predestined hour, about to reveal himself as *not* having been Peters; and her spirit sank under the impending fear of the disclosure. But almost with the next tick of the clock the figure, gaining substance and character, showed itself even to her weak sight as her husband's; and she turned to meet him, as he entered, with the confession of her folly.

'It's really too absurd,' she laughed out, 'but I never *can* remember!'

'Remember what?' Boyne questioned as they drew together.

'That when one sees the Lyng ghost one never knows it.'

Her hand was on his sleeve, and he kept it there, but with no response in his gesture or in the lines of his preoccupied face.

'Did you think you'd seen it?' he asked, after an appreciable interval.

'Why, I actually took *you* for it, my dear, in my mad determination to spot it!'

'Me—just now?' His arm dropped away, and he turned from her with a faint echo of her laugh. 'Really, dearest, you'd better give it up, if that's the best you can do.'

'Oh, yes, I give it up. Have *you?*' she asked, turning round on him abruptly.

The parlormaid had entered with letters and a lamp, and the light struck up into Boyne's face as he bent above the tray she presented.

'Have *you?*' Mary perversely insisted, when the servant had disappeared on her errand of illumination.

'Have I what?' he rejoined absently, the light bringing out the sharp stamp of worry between his brows as he turned over the letters.

'Given up trying to see the ghost.' Her heart beat a little at the experiment she was making.

Her husband, laying his letters aside, moved away into the shadow of the hearth.

'I never tried,' he said, tearing open the wrapper of a newspaper.

'Well, of course,' Mary persisted. 'The exasperating thing is that there's no use trying, since one can't be sure till so long afterward.'

He was unfolding the paper as if he had hardly heard her; but after a pause, during which the sheets rustled spasmodically between his hands, he looked up to ask, 'Have you any idea *how long?*'

Mary had sunk into a low chair beside the fireplace. From her seat she glanced over, startled, at her husband's profile, which was projected against the circle of lamplight.

'No; none. Have *you?*' she retorted, repeating her former phrase with an added stress of intention.

Boyne crumpled the paper into a bunch, and then, inconsequently, turned back with it toward the lamp.

'Lord, no! I only meant,' he exclaimed, with a faint tinge of impatience, 'is there any legend, any tradition, as to that?'

'Not that I know of,' she answered; but the impulse to add 'What makes you ask?' was checked by the reappearance of the parlormaid, with tea and a second lamp.

With the dispersal of shadows, and the repetition of the daily domestic office, Mary Boyne felt herself less oppressed by that sense of something mutely imminent which had darkened her afternoon. For a few moments she gave herself to the details of her task, and when she looked up from it she was struck to the point of bewilderment by the change in her husband's face. He had seated himself near the farther lamp, and was absorbed in the perusal of his letters; but was it something he had found in them, or merely the shifting of her own point of view, that had restored his features to their normal aspect? The longer she looked the more definitely the change affirmed itself. The lines of tension had vanished, and such traces of fatigue as lingered were of the kind easily attributable to steady mental effort. He glanced up, as if drawn by her gaze, and met her eyes with a smile.

'I'm dying for my tea, you know; and here's a letter for you,' he said.

She took the letter he held out in exchange for the cup she proffered him, and, returning to her seat, broke the seal with the languid gesture of the reader whose interests are all enclosed in the circle of one cherished presence.

Her next conscious motion was that of starting to her feet, the letter falling to them as she rose, while she held out to her husband a newspaper clipping.

'Ned! What's this? What does it mean?'

He had risen at the same instant, almost as if hearing her cry before she uttered it; and for a perceptible space of time he and she studied each other, like adversaries watching for an advantage, across the space between her chair and his desk.

'What's what? You fairly made me jump!' Boyne said at length, moving toward her with a sudden half-exasperated laugh. The shadow of apprehension was on his face again, not now a look of fixed foreboding, but a shifting vigilance of lips and eyes that gave her the sense of his feeling himself invisibly surrounded.

Her hand shook so that she could hardly give him the clipping.

'This article—from the *Waukesha Sentinel*—that a man named Elwell has brought suit against you—that there was something wrong about the Blue Star Mine. I can't understand more than half.'

They continued to face each other as she spoke, and to her astonishment she saw that her words had the almost immediate effect of dissipating the strained watchfulness of his look.

'Oh, *that*!' He glanced down the printed slip, and then folded it with the gesture of one who handles something harmless and familiar. 'What's the matter with you this afternoon, Mary? I thought you'd got bad news.'

She stood before him with her undefinable terror subsiding slowly under the reassurance of his tone.

'You knew about this, then—it's all right?'

'Certainly I knew about it; and it's all right.'

'But what *is* it? I don't understand. What does this man accuse you of?'

'Pretty nearly every crime in the calendar.' Boyne had tossed the clipping down, and thrown himself into an armchair near the fire. 'Do you want to hear the story? It's not particularly interesting—just a squabble over interests in the Blue Star.'

'But who is this Elwell? I don't know the name.'

'Oh, he's a fellow I put into it—gave him a hand up. I told you all about him at the time.'

'I dare say. I must have forgotten.' Vainly she strained back among her memories. 'But if you helped him, why does he make this return?'

'Probably some shyster lawyer got hold of him and talked him over. It's all rather technical and complicated. I thought that kind of thing bored you.'

His wife felt a sting of compunction. Theoretically, she deprecated the American wife's detachment from her husband's professional interests, but in practice she had always found it difficult to fix her attention on Boyne's report of the transactions in which his varied interests involved him. Besides, she had felt during their years of exile, that, in a community where the amenities of living could be obtained only at the cost of efforts as arduous as her husband's professional labors, such brief leisure as he and she could command should be used as an escape from immediate preoccupations, a flight to the life they always dreamed of living. Once or twice, now that this new life had actually drawn its magic circle about them, she had asked herself if she had done right; but hitherto such conjectures had been no more than the retrospective excursions of an active fancy. Now, for the first time, it startled her a little to find how little she knew of the material foundation on which her happiness was built.

She glanced at her husband, and was again reassured by the composure of his face; yet she felt the need of more definite grounds for her reassurance.

'But doesn't this suit worry you? Why have you never spoken to me about it?'

He answered both questions at once. 'I didn't speak of it at first because it *did* worry me—annoyed me, rather. But it's all ancient history now. Your correspondent must have got hold of a back number of the *Sentinel*.'

She felt a quick thrill of relief. 'You mean it's over? He's lost his case?'

There was a just perceptible delay in Boyne's reply. 'This suit's been withdrawn—that's all.'

But she persisted, as if to exonerate herself from the inward charge of being too easily put off. 'Withdrawn it because he saw he had no chance?'

'Oh, he had no chance,' Boyne answered.

She was still struggling with a dimly felt perplexity at the back of her thoughts.

'How long ago was it withdrawn?'

He paused, as if with a slight return to his former uncertainty. 'I've just had the news now; but I've been expecting it.'

'Just now—in one of your letters?'

'Yes; in one of my letters.'

She made no answer, and was aware only, after a short interval of waiting, that he had risen, and, strolling across the room, had placed himself on the sofa at her side. She felt him, as he did so, pass an arm about her, she felt his hand seek hers and clasp it, and turning slowly, drawn by the warmth of his cheek, she met his smiling eyes.

'It's all right—it's all right?' she questioned, through the flood of her dissolving doubts; and 'I give you my word it was never righter!' he laughed back at her, holding her close.

III

One of the strangest things she was afterward to recall out of all the next day's strangeness was the sudden and complete recovery of her sense of security.

It was in the air when she woke in her low-ceiled, dusky room; it went with her downstairs to the breakfast table, flashed out at her from the fire, and reduplicated itself from the flanks of the urn and the sturdy flutings of the Georgian teapot. It was as if in some roundabout way, all her diffused fears of the previous day, with their moment of sharp concentration about the newspaper article—as if this dim questioning of the future, and startled return upon the past, had between them liquidated the arrears of some haunting moral obligation. If she had indeed been careless of her husband's affairs, it was, her new state seemed to prove, because her faith in him instinctively justified such carelessness; and his right to her faith had now affirmed itself in the very face of menace and suspicion. She had never seen him more untroubled, more naturally and unconsciously himself, than after the cross-examination to which she had subjected him: it was almost as if he had been aware of her doubts, and had wanted the air cleared as much as she did.

It was as clear, thank heaven, as the bright outer light that surprised her almost with a touch of summer when she issued from the house for her daily round of the gardens. She had left Boyne at his desk, indulging herself, as she passed the library door, by a last peep at his quiet face, where he bent, pipe in mouth, above his papers; and now she had her own morning's task to perform. The task involved, on such charmed winter days, almost as much happy loitering about the different quarters of her domain as if spring were already at work there. There were such endless possibilities still before her, such opportunities to bring out the latent graces of the old place, without a single irreverent touch of alteration, that the winter was all too short to plan what spring and autumn executed. And her recovered sense of safety gave, on this particular morning, a peculiar zest to her progress through the sweet still place. She went first to the kitchen garden, where the espaliered pear trees drew complicated patterns on the walls, and pigeons were fluttering and preening about the silvery-slated roof of their cot. There was something wrong about the piping of the hothouse, and she was expecting an authority from Dorchester, who was to drive out between trains and make a diagnosis of the boiler. But when she dipped into the damp heat of the greenhouses, among the spiced scents and waxy pinks and reds of old-fashioned exotics—even the flora of Lyng was in the note!—she learned that the great man had not arrived, and, the day being too rare to waste in an artificial atmosphere, she came out again and paced along the springy turf of the bowling green to the gardens behind the house. At their farther end rose a grass terrace, looking across the fish pond and yew hedges to the long house front with its twisted chimney stacks and blue roof angles all drenched in the pale gold moisture of the air.

Seen thus, across the level tracery of the gardens, it sent her, from open windows and hospitably smoking chimneys, the look of some warm human presence, of a mind slowly ripened on a sunny wall of experience. She had never before had such a sense of her intimacy with it, such a conviction that its secrets were all beneficent, kept, as they said to children, 'for one's good', such a trust in its power to gather up her life and Ned's into the harmonious pattern of the long long story it sat there weaving in the sun.

She heard steps behind her, and turned, expecting to see the gardener accompanied by the engineer, from Dorchester. But only one figure was in sight, that of a youngish slightly built man, who, for reasons she could not on the spot have given, did not remotely resemble her notion of an authority on hothouse boilers. The newcomer, on seeing her, lifted his hat, and paused with the air of a gentleman—perhaps a traveler—who wishes to make it known that his intrusion is involuntary. Lyng occasionally attracted the more cultivated traveler, and Mary half expected to see the stranger dissemble a camera, or justify his presence by producing it. But he made no gesture of any sort, and after a moment she asked, in a tone responding to the courteous hesitation of his attitude: 'Is there anyone you wish to see?'

'I came to see Mr Boyne,' he answered. His intonation, rather than his accent, was faintly American, and Mary, at the note, looked at him more closely. The brim of his soft felt hat cast a shade on his face, which, thus obscured, wore to her shortsighted gaze a look of seriousness, as of a person arriving on business, and civilly but firmly aware of his rights.

Past experience had made her equally sensible to such claims; but she was jealous of her husband's morning hours, and doubtful of his having given anyone the right to intrude on them.

'Have you an appointment with my husband?' she asked.

The visitor hesitated, as if unprepared for the question.

'I think he expects me,' he replied.

It was Mary's turn to hesitate. 'You see this is his time for work: he never sees anyone in the morning.'

He looked at her a moment without answering; then, as if accepting her decision, he began to move away. As he turned, Mary saw him pause and glance up at the peaceful house front. Something in his air suggested weariness and disappointment, the dejection of the traveler who has come from far off and whose hours are limited by the timetable. It occurred to her that if this were the case her refusal might have made his errand vain, and a sense of compunction caused her to hasten after him.

'May I ask if you have come a long way?'

He gave her the same grave look. 'Yes—I have come a long way.'

'Then, if you'll go to the house, no doubt my husband will see you now. You'll find him in the library.'

She did not know why she had added the last phrase, except from a vague impulse to atone for her previous inhospitality. The visitor seemed about to express his thanks, but her attention was distracted by the approach of the gardener with a companion who bore all the marks of being the expert from Dorchester.

'This way,' she said, waving the stranger to the house; and an instant later she had forgotten him in the absorption of her meeting with the boiler maker.

The encounter led to such far-reaching results that the engineer ended by finding it expedient to ignore his train, and Mary was beguiled into spending the remainder of the morning in absorbed confabulation among the flower pots. When the colloquy ended, she was surprised to find that it was nearly luncheon time, and she half expected, as she hurried back to the house, to see her husband coming out to meet her. But she found no one in the court but an undergardener raking the gravel, and the hall, when she entered it, was so silent that she guessed Boyne to be still at work.

Not wishing to disturb him, she turned into the drawing room, and there, at her writing table, lost herself in renewed calculations of the outlay to which the morning's conference had pledged her. The fact that she could permit herself such follies had not yet lost its novelty; and somehow, in contrast to the vague fears of the previous days, it now seemed an element of her recovered security, of the sense that, as Ned had said, things in general had never been 'righter'.

She was still luxuriating in a lavish play of figures when the parlormaid, from the threshold, roused her with an inquiry as to the expediency of serving luncheon. It was one of their jokes that Trimmle announced luncheon as if she were divulging a state secret, and Mary, intent upon her papers, merely murmured an absent-minded assent.

She felt Trimmle wavering doubtfully on the threshold, as if in rebuke of such unconsidered assent; then her retreating steps sounded down the passage, and Mary, pushing away her papers, crossed the hall and went to the library door. It was still closed, and she wavered in her turn, disliking to disturb her husband, yet anxious that he should not exceed his usual measure of work. As she stood there, balancing her impulses, Trimmle returned with the announcement of luncheon, and Mary, thus impelled, opened the library door.

Boyne was not at his desk, and she peered about her, expecting to discover him before the bookshelves, somewhere down the length of the room; but her call brought no response, and gradually it became clear to her that he was not there.

She turned back to the parlormaid.

'Mr Boyne must be upstairs. Please tell him that luncheon is ready.'

Trimmle appeared to hesitate between the obvious duty of obedience and an equally obvious conviction of the foolishness of the injunction laid on her. The struggle resulted in her saying: 'If you please, Madam, Mr Boyne's not upstairs.'

'Not in his room? Are you sure?'

'I'm sure, Madam.'

Mary consulted the clock. 'Where is he, then?'

'He's gone out,' Trimmle announced, with the superior air of one who has respectfully waited for the question that a well-ordered mind would have put first.

Mary's conjecture had been right, then. Boyne must have gone to the gardens to meet her, and since she had missed him, it was clear that he had taken the shorter way by the south door, instead of going round to the court. She crossed the hall to the French window opening directly on the yew garden, but the parlormaid, after another moment of inner conflict, decided to bring out: 'Please, Madam, Mr Boyne didn't go that way.'

Mary turned back. 'Where *did* he go? And when?'

'He went out of the front door, up the drive, Madam.' It was a matter of principle with Trimmle never to answer more than one question at a time.

'Up the drive? At this hour?' Mary went to the door herself, and glanced across the court through the tunnel of bare limes. But its per-spective was as empty as when she had scanned it on entering.

'Did Mr Boyne leave no meassage?'

Trimmle seemed to surrender herself to a last struggle with the forces of chaos.

'No, Madam. He just went out with the gentleman.'

'The gentleman? What gentleman?' Mary wheeled about, as if to front this new factor.

'The gentleman who called, Madam,' said Trimmle resignedly.

'When did a gentleman call? Do explain yourself, Trimmle!'

Only the fact that Mary was very hungry, and that she wanted to consult her husband about the greenhouses, would have caused her to lay so unusual an injunction on her attendant; and even now she was detached enough to note in Trimmle's eye the dawning defiance of the respectful subordinate who has been pressed too hard.

'I couldn't exactly say the hour, Madam, because I didn't let the gentleman in,' she replied, with an air of discreetly ignoring the irregularity of her mistress's course.

'You didn't let him in?'

'No, Madam. When the bell rang I was dressing, and Agnes—'

'Go and ask Agnes, then,' said Mary.

Trimmle still wore her look of patient magnanimity. 'Agnes would not know, Madam, for she had unfortunately burnt her hand in trimming the wick of the new lamp from town'—Trimmle, as Mary was aware, had always been opposed to the new lamp—'and so Mrs Dockett sent the kitchenmaid instead.'

Mary looked again at the clock. 'It's after two! Go and ask the kitchenmaid if Mr Boyne left any word.'

She went into luncheon without waiting, and Trimmle presently brought her there the kitchenmaid's statement that the gentleman had called about eleven o'clock, and that Mr Boyne had gone out with him without leaving any message. The kitchenmaid did not even know the caller's name, for he had written it on a slip of paper, which he had folded and handed to her, with the injunction to deliver it at once to Mr Boyne.

Mary finished her luncheon, still wondering, and when it was over, and Trimmle had brought the coffee to the drawing room, her wonder had deepened to a first faint tinge of disquietude. It was unlike Boyne to absent himself without explanation at so unwonted an hour, and the difficulty of identifying the visitor whose summons he had apparently obeyed made his disappearance the more unaccountable. Mary Boyne's experience as the wife of a busy engineer, subject to sudden calls and compelled to keep irregular hours, had trained her to the philosophic acceptance of surprises; but since Boyne's withdrawal from business he had adopted a Benedictine regularity of life. As if to make up for the dispersed and agitated years, with their 'stand-up' lunches, and dinners rattled down to the joltings of the dining cars, he cultivated the last refinements of punctuality and monotony, discouraging his wife's fancy for the unexpected, and declaring that to a delicate taste there were infinite gradations of pleasure in the recurrences of habit.

Still, since no life can completely defend itself from the unforeseen, it was evident that all Boyne's precautions would sooner or later prove unavailable, and Mary concluded that he had cut short a tiresome visit by walking with his caller to the station, or at least accompanying him for part of the way.

This conclusion relieved her from further preoccupation, and she went out herself to take up her conference with the gardener. Thence she walked to the village post office, a mile or so away; and when she turned toward home the early twilight was setting in.

She had taken a footpath across the downs, and as Boyne, meanwhile, had probably returned from the station by the highroad, there was little likelihood of their meeting. She felt sure, however, of his having reached the house before her; so sure that, when she entered it herself, without even pausing to inquire of Trimmle, she made directly for the library. But the library was still empty, and with an unwonted exactness of visual memory she observed that the papers on her husband's desk lay precisely as they had lain when she had gone in to call him to luncheon.

Then of a sudden she was seized by a vague dread of the unknown. She had closed the door behind her on entering, and as she stood alone in the long silent room, her dread seemed to take shape and sound, to be there breathing, and lurking among the shadows. Her shortsighted eyes strained through them, half-discerning an actual presence, something aloof, that watched and knew; and in the recoil from that intangible presence she threw herself on the bell rope and gave it a sharp pull.

The sharp summons brought Trimmle in precipitately with a lamp, and Mary breathed again at this sobering reappearance of the usual.

'You may bring tea if Mr Boyne is in,' she said, to justify her ring.

'Very well, Madam. But Mr Boyne is not in,' said Trimmle, putting down the lamp.

'Not in? You mean he's come back and gone out again?'

'No, Madam. He's never been back.'

The dread stirred again, and Mary knew that now it had her fast.

'Not since he went out with—the gentleman?'

'Not since he went out with the gentleman.'

'But who *was* the gentleman?' Mary insisted, with the shrill note of someone trying to be heard through a confusion of noises.

'That I couldn't say, Madam.' Trimmle, standing there by the lamp, seemed suddenly to grow less round and rosy, as though eclipsed by the same creeping shade of apprehension.

'But the kitchenmaid knows—wasn't it the kitchenmaid who let him in?'

'She doesn't know either, Madam, for he wrote his name on a folded paper.'

Mary, through her agitation, was aware that they were both designating the unknown visitor by a vague pronoun, instead of the conventional formula which, till then, had kept their allusions within the bounds of conformity. And at the same moment her mind caught at the suggestion of the folded paper.

'But he must have a name! Where's the paper?'

She moved to the desk, and began to turn over the documents that littered it. The first that caught her eye was an unfinished letter in her husband's hand, with his pen lying across it, as though dropped there at a sudden summons.

'My dear Parvis'—who was Parvis?—'I have just received your letter announcing Elwell's death, and while I suppose there is now no further risk of trouble, it might be safer—'

She tossed the sheet aside, and continued her search; but no folded paper was discoverable among the letters and pages of manuscript which had been swept together in a heap, as if by a hurried or a startled gesture.

'But the kitchenmaid *saw* him. Send her here,' she commanded, wondering at her dullness in not thinking sooner of so simple a solution.

Trimmle vanished in a flash, as if thankful to be out of the room, and when she reappeared, conducting the agitated underling, Mary had regained her self-possession, and had her questions ready.

The gentleman was a stranger, yes—that she understood. But what had he said? And, above all, what had he looked like? The first question was easily enough answered, for the disconcerting reason that he had said so little—had merely asked for Mr Boyne, and, scribbling something on a bit of paper, had requested that it should at once be carried in to him.

'Then you don't know what he wrote? You're not sure it *was* his name?'

The kitchenmaid was not sure, but supposed it was, since he had written it in answer to her inquiry as to whom she should announce.

'And when you carried the paper in to Mr Boyne, what did he say?'

'The kitchenmaid did not think that Mr Boyne had said anything, but she could not be sure, for just as she had handed him the paper and he was opening it, she had become aware that the visitor had followed her into the library, and she had slipped out, leaving the two gentlemen together.

'But then, if you left them in the library, how do you know that they went out of the house?'

This question plunged the witness into a momentary inarticulateness, from which she was rescued by Trimmle, who, by means of ingenious circumlocutions, elicited the statement that before she could cross the hall to the back passage she had heard the two gentlemen behind her, and had seen them go out of the front door together.

'Then, if you saw the strange gentleman twice, you must be able to tell me what he looked like.'

But with this final challenge to her powers of expression it became clear that the limit of the kitchenmaid's endurance had been reached. The obligation of going to the front door to 'show in' a visitor was in itself so subversive of the fundamental order of things that it had thrown her faculties into hopeless disarray, and she could only stammer out, after various panting efforts: 'His hat, mum, was different-like, as you might say—'

'Different? How different?' Mary flashed out, her own mind, in the same instant, leaping back to an image left on it that morning, and then lost under layers of subsequent impressions.

'His hat had a wide brim, you mean, and his face was pale—a youngish face?' Mary pressed her, with a white-lipped intensity of interrogation. But if the kitchenmaid found any adequate answer to this challenge, it was swept away for her listener down the rushing current of her own convictions. The stranger—the stranger in the garden! Why had Mary not thought of him before? She needed no one now to tell her that it was he who had called for her husband and gone away with him. But who was he, and why had Boyne obeyed him?

IV

It leaped out at her suddenly, like a grin out of the dark, that they had often called England so little—'such a confoundedly hard place to get lost in'.

A confoundedly hard place to get lost in! That had been her husband's phrase. And now, with the whole machinery of official investigation sweeping its flashlights from shore to shore, and across the dividing straits; now, with Boyne's name blazing from the walls of every town and village, his portrait (how that wrung her!) hawked up and down the country like the image of a hunted criminal; now the little compact populous island, so policed, surveyed and administered, revealed itself as a Sphinxlike guardian of abysmal mysteries, staring back into his wife's anguished eyes as if with the wicked joy of knowing something they would never know!

In the fortnight since Boyne's disappearance there had been no word of him, no trace of his movements. Even the usual misleading reports that raise expectancy in tortured bosoms had been few and fleeting. No one but the kitchenmaid had seen Boyne leave the house, and no one else had seen 'the gentleman' who accompanied him. All inquiries in the neighborhood failed to elicit the memory of a stranger's presence that day in the neighborhood of Lyng. And no one had met Edward Boyne, either alone or in company, in any of the neighboring villages, or on the road across the downs, or at either of the local railway stations. The sunny English noon had swallowed him as completely as if he had gone out into Cimmerian night.

Mary, while every official means of investigation was working at its highest pressure, had ransacked her husband's papers for any trace of antecedent complications, of entanglements or obligations unknown to her, that might throw a ray into the darkness. But if any such had existed in the background of Boyne's life, they had vanished like the slip of paper on which the visitor had written his name. There remained no possible thread of guidance except—if it were indeed an exception—the letter which Boyne had apparently been in the act of writing when he received his mysterious summons. That letter, read and reread by his wife, and submitted by her to the police, yielded little enough to feed conjecture.

'I have just heard of Elwell's death, and while I suppose there is now no further risk of trouble, it might be safer—' That was all. The 'risk of trouble' was easily explained by the newspaper clipping which had apprised Mary of the suit brought against her husband by one of his associates in the Blue Star enterprise. The only new information conveyed by the letter was the fact of its showing Boyne, when he wrote it, to be still apprehensive of the results of the suit, though he had told his wife that it had been withdrawn, and though the letter itself proved that the plaintiff was dead. It took several days of cabling to fix the identity of the 'Parvis' to whom the fragment was addressed, but even after these inquiries had shown him to be a Waukesha lawyer, no new facts concerning the Elwell suit were elicited. He appeared to have had no direct concern in it, but to have been conversant with the facts merely as an acquaintance, and possible intermediary; and he declared himself unable to guess with what object Boyne intended to seek his assistance.

This negative information, sole fruit of the first fortnight's search, was not increased by a jot during the slow weeks that followed. Mary knew that the investigations were still being carried on, but she had a vague sense of their gradually slackening, as the actual march of time seemed to slacken. It was as though the days, flying horror-struck from the shrouded image of the one inscrutable day, gained assurance as the distance lengthened, till at last they fell back into their normal gait. And so with the human imaginations at work on the dark event. No doubt it occupied them still, but week by week and hour by hour it grew less absorbing, took up less space, was slowly but inevitably crowded out of the foreground of consciousness by the new problems perpetually bubbling up from the cloudy caldron of human experience.

Even Mary Boyne's consciousness gradually felt the same lowering of velocity. It still swayed with the incessant oscillations of conjecture; but they were slower, more rhythmical in their beat. There were even moments of weariness when, like the victim of some poison which leaves the brain clear, but holds the body motionless, she saw herself domesticated with the Horror, accepting its perpetual presence as one of the fixed conditions of life.

These moments lengthened into hours and days, till she passed into a phase of stolid acquiescence. She watched the routine of daily life with the incurious eye of a savage on whom the meaningless processes of civilization make but the faintest impression. She had come to regard herself as part of the routine, a spoke of the wheel, revolving with its motion; she felt almost like the furniture of the room in which she sat, an insensate object to be dusted and pushed about with the chairs and tables. And this deepening apathy held her fast at Lyng, in spite of the entreaties of friends and the usual medical recommendation of 'change'. Her friends supposed that her refusal to move was inspired by the belief that her husband would one day return to the spot from which he had vanished, and a beautiful legend grew up about this imaginary state of waiting. But in reality she had no such belief: the depths of anguish enclosing her were no longer lighted by flashes of hope. She was sure that Boyne would never come back, that he had gone out of her sight as completely as if Death itself had waited that day on the threshold. She had even renounced, one by one, the various theories as to his disappearance which had been advanced by the press, the police, and her own agonized imagination. In sheer lassitude her mind turned from these alternatives of horror, and sank back into the blank fact that he was gone.

No, she would never know what had become of him—no one would ever know. But the house *knew*; the library in which she spent her long lonely evenings knew. For it was here that the last scene had been enacted, here that the stranger had come, and spoken the word which had caused Boyne to rise and follow him. The floor she trod had felt his tread; the books on the shelves had seen his face; and there were moments when the intense consciousness of the old dusky walls seemed about to break out into some audible revelation of their secret. But the revelation never came, and she knew it would never come. Lyng was not one of the garrulous old houses that betray the secrets entrusted to them. Its very legend proved that it had always been the mute accomplice, the incorruptible custodian, of the mysteries it had surprised. And Mary Boyne,

sitting face to face with its silence, felt the futility of seeking to break it
by any human means.

V

'I don't say it *wasn't* straight, and yet I don't say it *was* straight. It was
business.'

Mary, at the words, lifted her head with a start, and looked intently at
the speaker.

When, half an hour before, a card with 'Mr Parvis' on it had been
brought up to her, she had been immediately aware that the name had
been a part of her consciousness ever since she had read it and at the head
of Boyne's unfinished letter. In the library she had found awaiting her
a small sallow man with a bald head and gold eyeglasses, and it sent a
tremor through her to know that this was the person to whom her husband's last known thought had been directed.

Parvis, civilly, but without vain preamble—in the manner of a man
who has his watch in his hand—had set forth the object of his visit. He
had 'run over' to England on business, and finding himself in the
neighborhood of Dorchester, had not wished to leave it without paying
his respects to Mrs Boyne; and without asking her, if the occasion offered,
what she meant to do about Bob Elwell's family.

The words touched the spring of some obscure dread in Mary's bosom.
Did her visitor, after all, know what Boyne had meant by his unfinished
phrase? She asked for an elucidation of his question, and noticed at once
that he seemed surprised at her continued ignorance of the subject. Was
it possible that she really knew as little as she said?

'I know nothing—you must tell me,' she faltered out; and her visitor
thereupon proceeded to unfold his story. It threw, even to her confused
perceptions, and imperfectly initiated vision, a lurid glare on the whole
hazy episode of the Blue Star Mine. Her husband had made his money in
that brilliant speculation at the cost of 'getting ahead' of someone less
alert to seize the chance; and the victim of his ingenuity was young
Robert Elwell, who had 'put him on' to the Blue Star scheme.

Parvis, at Mary's first cry, had thrown her a sobering glance through
his impartial glasses.

'Bob Elwell wasn't smart enough, that's all; if he had been, he might
have turned round and served Boyne the same way. It's the kind of thing
that happens everyday in business. I guess it's what the scientists call the
survival of the fittest—see?' said Mr Parvis, evidently pleased with the
aptness of his analogy.

Mary felt a physical shrinking from the next question she tried to frame: it was as though the words on her lips had a taste that nauseated her.

'But then—you accuse my husband of doing something dishonorable?'

Mr Parvis surveyed the question dispassionately. 'Oh, no, I don't. I don't even say it wasn't straight.' He glanced up and down the long lines of books, as if one of them might have supplied him with the definition he sought. 'I don't say it *wasn't* straight, and yet I don't say it *was* straight. It was business.' After all, no definition in his category could be more comprehensive than that.

Mary sat staring at him with a look of terror. He seemed to her like the indifferent emissary of some evil power.

'But Mr Elwell's lawyers apparently did not take your view, since I suppose the suit was withdrawn by their advice.'

'Oh, yes; they knew he hadn't a leg to stand on, technically. It was when they advised him to withdraw the suit that he got desperate. You see, he'd borrowed most of the money he lost in the Blue Star, and he was up a tree. That's why he shot himself when they told him he had no show.'

The horror was sweeping over Mary in great deafening waves.

'He shot himself? He killed himself because of *that*?'

'Well, he didn't kill himself, exactly. He dragged on two months before he died.' Parvis emitted the statement as unemotionally as a gramophone grinding out its record.

'You mean that he tried to kill himself, and failed? And tried again?'

'Oh, he didn't have to *try* again,' said Parvis grimly.

They sat opposite each other in silence, he swinging his eyeglasses thoughtfully about his finger, she, motionless, her arms stretched along her knees in an attitude of rigid tension.

'But if you knew all this,' she began at length, hardly able to force her voice above a whisper, 'how is it that when I wrote you at the time of my husband's disappearance you said you didn't understand his letter?'

Parvis received this without perceptible embarrassment: 'Why, I didn't understand it—strictly speaking. And it wasn't the time to talk about it, if I had. The Elwell business was settled when the suit was withdrawn. Nothing I could have told you would have helped you to find your husband.'

Mary continued to scrutinize him. 'Then why are you telling me now?'

Still Parvis did not hesitate. 'Well, to begin with, I supposed you knew more than you appear to—I mean about the circumstances of Elwell's death. And then people are talking of it now; the whole matter's been raked up again. And I thought if you didn't know you ought to.'

She remained silent, and he continued: 'You see, it's only come out lately what a bad state Elwell's affairs were in. His wife's a proud woman, and she fought on as long as she could, going out to work, and taking sewing at home when she got too sick—something with the heart, I believe. But she had his mother to look after, and the children, and she broke down under it, and finally had to ask for help. That called attention to the case, and the papers took it up, and a subscription was started. Everybody out there liked Bob Elwell, and most of the prominent names in the place are down on the list, and people began to wonder why—'

Parvis broke off to fumble in an inner pocket. 'Here,' he continued, 'here's an account of the whole thing from the *Sentinel*—a little sensational, of course. But I guess you'd better look it over.'

He held out a newspaper to Mary, who unfolded it slowly, remembering, as she did so, the evening when, in that same room, the perusal of a clipping from the *Sentinel* had first shaken the depths of her security.

As she opened the paper, her eyes, shrinking from the glaring headlines, 'Widow of Boyne's Victim Forced to Appeal for Aid,' ran down the column of text to two portraits inserted in it. The first was her husband's, taken from a photograph made the year they had come to England. It was the picture of him that she liked best, the one that stood on the writing table upstairs in her bedroom. As the eyes in the photograph met hers, she felt it would be impossible to read what was said of him, and closed her lids with the sharpness of the pain.

'I thought if you felt disposed to put your name down—' she heard Parvis continue.

She opened her eyes with an effort, and they fell on the other portrait. It was that of a youngish man, slightly built, with features somewhat blurred by the shadow of a projecting hat brim. Where had she seen that outline before? She stared at it confusedly, her heart hammering in her ears. Then she gave a cry.

'This is the man—the man who came for my husband!'

She heard Parvis start to his feet, and was dimly aware that she had slipped backward into the corner of the sofa, and that he was bending above her in alarm. She straightened herself, and reached out for the paper, which she had dropped.

'It's the man! I should know him anywhere!' she persisted in a voice that sounded to her own ears like a scream.

Parvis's answer seemed to come to her from far off, down endless fog-muffled windings.

'Mrs Boyne, you're not very well. Shall I call somebody? Shall I get a glass of water?'

'No, no, no!' She threw herself toward him, her hand frantically clutching the newspaper. 'I tell you, it's the man! I *know* him! He spoke to me in the garden!'

Parvis took the journal from her, directing his glasses to the portrait. 'It can't be, Mrs Boyne. It's Robert Elwell.'

'Robert Elwell?' Her white stare seemed to travel into space. 'Then it was Robert Elwell who came for him.'

'Came for Boyne? The day he went away from here?' Parvis's voice dropped as hers rose. He bent over, laying a fraternal hand on her, as if to coax her gently back into her seat. 'Why, Elwell was dead! Don't you remember?'

Mary sat with her eyes fixed on the picture, unconscious of what he was saying.

'Don't you remember Boyne's unfinished letter to me—the one you found on his desk that day? It was written just after he'd heard of Elwell's death.' She noticed an odd shake in Parvis's unemotional voice. 'Surely you remember!' he urged her.

Yes, she remembered: that was the profoundest horror of it. Elwell had died the day before her husband's disappearance; and this was Elwell's portrait; and it was the portrait of the man who had spoken to her in the garden. She lifted her head and looked slowly about the library. The library could have borne witness that it was also the portrait of the man who had come in that day to call Boyne from his unfinished letter. Through the misty surgings of her brain she heard the faint boom of half-forgotten words—words spoken by Alida Stair on the lawn at Pangbourne before Boyne and his wife had ever seen the house at Lyng, or had imagined that they might one day live there.

'This was the man who spoke to me,' she repeated.

She looked again at Parvis. He was trying to conceal his disturbance under what he probably imagined to be an expression of indulgent commiseration; but the edges of his lips were blue. 'He thinks me mad; but I'm not mad,' she reflected; and suddenly there flashed upon her a way of justifying her strange affirmation.

She sat quiet, controlling the quiver of her lips, and waiting till she could trust her voice; then she said, looking straight at Parvis: 'Will you answer me one question, please? When was it that Robert Elwell tried to kill himself?'

'When—when?' Parvis stammered.

'Yes; the date. Please try to remember.'

She saw that he was growing still more afraid of her. 'I have a reason,' she insisted.

'Yes, yes. Only I can't remember. About two months before, I should say.'

'I want the date,' she repeated.

Parvis picked up the newspaper. 'We might see here,' he said, still humoring her. He ran his eyes down the page. 'Here it is. Last October—the—'

She caught the words from him. 'The 20th, wasn't it?' With a sharp look at her, he verified. 'Yes, the 20th. Then you *did* know?'

'I know now.' Her gaze continued to travel past him. 'Sunday, the 20th—that was the day he came first.'

Parvis's voice was almost inaudible. 'Came *here* first?'

'Yes.'

'You saw him twice, then?'

'Yes, twice.' She just breathed it at him. 'He came first on the 20th of October. I remember the date because it was the day we went up Meldon Steep for the first time." She felt a faint gasp of inward laughter at the thought that but for that she might have forgotten.

Parvis continued to scrutinize her, as if trying to intercept her gaze.

'We saw him from the roof,' she went on. 'He came down the lime avenue toward the house. He was dressed just as he is in that picture. My husband saw him first. He was frightened, and ran down ahead of me; but there was no one there. He had vanished.'

'Elwell had vanished?' Parvis faltered.

'Yes.' Their two whispers seemed to grope for each other. 'I couldn't think what had happened. I see now. He *tried* to come then; but he wasn't dead enough—he couldn't reach us. He had to wait for two months to die; and then he came back again—and Ned went with him.'

She nodded at Parvis with the look of triumph of a child who has worked out a difficult puzzle. But suddenly she lifted her hands with a desperate gesture, pressing them to her temples.

'Oh, my God! I sent him to Ned—I told him where to go! I sent him to this room!' she screamed.

She felt the walls of books rush toward her, like inward falling ruins; and she heard Parvis, a long way off, through the ruins, crying to her, and struggling to get at her. But she was numb to his touch, she did not know what he was saying. Through the tumult she heard but one clear note, the voice of Alida Stair, speaking on the lawn at Pangbourne.

'You won't know till afterward,' it said. 'You won't know till long, long afterward.'

CAROLINE GORDON

Hear the Nightingale Sing

❧

It was so dark in the ravine that at first she could not see the horses. Then her eyes grew accustomed to the gloom. She caught a gleam of white through the branches. She worked her way through the thicket and came upon Bess and Old Gray tethered to the ring that had been fixed in the trunk of a big pine. But the mule was not there.

She looked at the broken tether. 'Where's Lightning?' she asked.

The horses pressed up to her, nudging at the sack that was slung over her shoulders. She took hold of their halters and led them down the hill to the branch and up the stream to a place where the hazel bushes grew higher than her head. She let them drink their fill, then left them tethered to a little cottonwood, while she went on up the hill to look for the mule.

The woods were thin between here and the pike. She moved slowly, keeping a tree always between her and the road. At the top of the hill she climbed up on a stump to look down on the pike. There was a cloud of dust off in the direction of Gordonsville but she could not see any soldiers moving along the road. She could remember times—in the first year of the war, just after all the boys had gone away—when she used to walk in the late afternoons up to the top of this hill in the hope that somebody might be passing. There had hardly ever been anybody then. Now there was almost always something moving along the road—great, lumbering army wagons, regiments of infantry marching, squads of cavalry sweeping by in clouds of dust.

There was a rustling in the bushes along the fence. There the mule stood, looking at her. He ducked his head when he saw that she was looking at him, and moved off quickly. She got down off the stump, clumsily, in her homemade shoes, and went toward him, holding out an ear of corn. 'Cu-up! Cu-up!' she called in a whisper. He wheeled; his little hooves clattered against the rails. She turned and walked the other way, holding the nubbin of corn behind her back. When she felt him take hold of it she whirled and grasped his foretop. The nubbin had fallen to the ground. She stooped and retrieved it and held it before him on her open palm. 'Lightning!' she said, '*Lightning!*' and slipped her arms

down about his neck and closed her eyes and laid her cheek against
his side.

A long time ago—winter before last—she used to go down to the
stable lot early after breakfast on cold mornings and, finding him standing
in his corner, his breath steaming in the frosty air, she would cry out to
Uncle Joe that her little mule was freezing and put her arms about him
and bury her face in his shaggy hair. Uncle Joe would laugh, saying that
that mule had enough hair to keep both of them warm. 'Ain't no 'count,
nohow.'

Once Tom Ladd had come up behind them without their hearing him.
'I don't believe I'd have given you that mule if I'd known how you were
going to raise him,' he said. 'You can't get him back now,' she had told
him. 'I'm raising him to be the no 'countest mule in the country.'

He laughed. They walked in silence over the lightly frozen ground
up to the house. He had what her father called 'the gift of silence'. But
sometimes, sitting in company, you would look up and find him watching
you and it would seem that he had just said something or was about to say
something. But what it was she never knew. And it might be that he
never had any particularity for her. It might be that he noticed her more
than the other girls only because she had the mule for a pet. He liked all
animals.

She, too, had always been overfond of animals. When she was a little
girl and Uncle Joe would bring a team in to plow the garden in the
spring, she would look at the mules standing with their heads hung, their
great, dark eyes fixing nothing, and she would think how, like Negroes,
they were born into the world for nothing but labor, and her heart would
seem to break in her bosom and she would run barefoot down the rows
and when Uncle Joe cracked his whip she would clutch his elbow, shrieking,
'You, Uncle Joe. Don't you hit that mule!' until the old man would leave
his team standing and, going to the window where her mother sat,
sewing, would ask her to please make Miss Barbara come in the house.

When she became a young lady it had tickled her fancy to have a mule
for a pet. Lightning, nosing unreproved at the kitchen door or walking
across the flower beds, seemed, somehow, to make up for the pangs she
had suffered as a child. But even then, in those far-off days, when her
father was still alive and the servants were all still on the place and you
had only to call from the upper gallery to have somebody come and lead
him back to the pasture when he trespassed—even then in those days
that were so hard to remember now, he had been a trouble and a care.

He was old Lightfoot's colt. Lightfoot had gone blind in her last days.
Tom Ladd had turned her over to Jake Robinson to take care of. Jake had
taken good care of her but he could not resist the temptation to get one

more colt out of her. Tom had some business with her father and had been spending the night at their house. A Negro boy brought word from Jake that Lightfoot had foaled in the night. They were at breakfast. Her mother had just asked her to go to the kitchen to get some hot bread. Tom Ladd said, 'Miss Barbara, how'd you like to have one of Lightfoot's colts?' She was so taken aback that she did not answer. She came back with the biscuits and sat down and would have let what he had said pass unnoticed. But he looked at her as she came in and he spoke again. 'It'll be her last colt.'

Tom Ladd came to their house two or three times a week. A bed was kept ready for him in the office whenever he cared to spend the night. But he had never danced with her or with her sister and if he sat on the porch with them in the evenings it was to talk with her father about the crops or the stock. Tom Ladd loved horses better than people, her mother said, and he loved liquor better than he loved horses. Her father said that was because he was a bachelor, living alone in that big house, but her mother said it was in the blood: all the Ladds drank themselves to death.

She had felt her color rising, knowing that her mother's eyes were upon her. But it was no crime to love horses, and as for liquor, she had seen her father sprawling on the cellar steps, a jug in his hand.

She said, 'I'll have to see the colt first, Mr Ladd.'

Everybody laughed and the moment passed. After breakfast they drove over to Robinson's to see the new colt. Jake was sitting on the front steps, mending some harness. He did not quit his work, saying only, 'I'll be out there in a minute, Mister Tom.'

They walked out into the pasture. The mare stood at the far end, beside a willow sink. They could see, under her belly, the long, thin legs and little, wobbly feet. 'Sorrel,' Tom Ladd said, 'Lightfoot always breeds true,' and walked around the mare's hindquarters and stopped and swore out loud.

Her father laughed until he had to put a hand on her shoulder to steady himself. 'You never told him not to breed her,' he said, wiping his eyes.

'I never thought he'd breed her to a jackass with ears as long as his,' Tom Ladd said.

The colt stoppped sucking and flung his head up and stared at them. His ears were so long that they looked as if they might tip him over. He had eyes as large and dark and mournful as a Negro baby's. The fawn color about his muzzle gave him the look of a little clown. She put her arms about his furry rump and he kicked feebly, nuzzling against his mother's side.

'Hush,' she said, 'you'll hurt his feelings.'

It was a year later that Tom Ladd had given him to her, after Jake Robinson had had to give up trying to break him.

She led the mule down the hill. The horses heard them coming and whinnied. She led him up to them, so close that they could touch noses. Then she made a halter out of the broken rope and led the three of them back to the thicket. The old mare and the horse went quietly to their places beside the big pine but Lightning kept sidestepping and shaking his head. She led him off a little way and tied him to another tree and opened the sack and gave Bess and Gray four nubbins apiece and the clover that she had gathered in the orchard. When they had finished eating she tethered them again and mounted Lightning and rode him down the ravine.

The sun had set. Here in the thick woods it was dark. But she could see the light from the house, shining through the trees. They did not use the path at all now. No use in keeping your horses hid off in the woods if there was a path leading to them. But it was hard, riding through the underbrush. She had to lie flat on the mule's back to keep from being scraped off.

At the edge of the wood she dismounted and was about to open the gate when a sound down the road made her stop, chain in hand. Somebody was walking along the road, whistling softly. She let the chain fall with a little click against the post and led Lightning back a little way into the bushes. The sound grew. The man, or whoever it was, walked steadily, whistling as he came.

She pressed close against the mule, her arm over his withers. He stood quietly but the sound of his breathing seemed to fill all the thicket. Light from the house fell in a great fan across the road. A man's visored cap and the knapsack that bulged at his shoulder showed black against it for a second and then he passed on. But the sound of his whistling was all around her still. An old tune that she had always known:

> 'One morning, one morning, one morning in May
> I met a fair lady a-wending her way . . .'

She stood there until the sound had quite died away, then, lifting the chain with infinite care, she opened the gate and led the mule across the road and into the yard.

The front door opened. Her sister stood on the porch. 'Barbara!' she called.

Barbara did not answer. After a little Sophy went inside and shut the door. Barbara drew Lightning swiftly through the yard and toward the stable. Halfway there she stopped. The stable wouldn't do. That was the first place they went. Nor the hen house, though it was big enough. None of the outbuildings would do. They always searched outbuildings, to make sure they didn't miss anything. They would search an outbuilding when they wouldn't search the house itself. She turned back into the yard and ran down the cellar steps, the mule lumbering behind her.

He came down the last two steps so fast that he ran over her.

She felt the impact of his chest between her shoulders and knew that his forefoot had grazed her ankle before she went sprawling down in the dark. She lay there a moment, wondering how badly she was hurt, then got to her feet and felt her way to where he stood. She stroked his neck and talked to him gently. 'Poor little Lightning. Him have a hard time. Mammy *know* him have a hard time.'

A ray of light struck on the wall. Sophy stood at the head of the steps, a lighted lamp in her hand. She peered down into the cellar, then came a little way down the steps, holding the lamp high over her head.

'Have you gone distracted?' she asked.

'Why don't you see after the stock?' Barbara asked coldly. 'He's not hurting your old cellar.'

She poured what corn was left in the sack out upon the earthen floor, fastened the cellar doors, and followed Sophy up the steps.

Her twelve-year-old brother sat beside the stove, whittling. He looked up eagerly as she came in. 'You going to keep that mule in the cellar, sister? You going to keep him in there all the time?'

Barbara sat down in the big chair by the window. She lifted her skirt to examine her leg. Blood was caked on her shin and the flesh of the ankle was bruised and discolored. She felt her lip trembling. She spoke brusquely:

'I saw a soldier going past the house just as I was getting ready to cross the road.'

Sophy did not seem to have heard her. 'Why didn't you leave that mule out in the hollow?' she asked.

'He slipped his halter,' Barbara said. 'I had to walk all over the woods to find him.'

'It would have been a good thing if you couldn't find him,' Sophy said.

Barbara looked at her steadily. 'I'm going to keep him,' she said. 'I don't care what you say. I'm going to keep him.'

Sophy, compressing her lips, did not answer. Cummy had gone over and sat down at the kitchen table, where they always ate nowadays. 'Aren't we going to have any supper?' he asked.

Sophy went out on the back porch and returned with two covered dishes. 'There's some black-eyed peas,' she said. 'And Mrs Thomas sent us a pat of butter. I thought we might as well have it while it was fresh.'

She bent over the table, arranging knives and forks and plates. A frail woman of twenty-seven, who looked, Barbara thought suddenly, at least thirty-five. That was because she was just recovering from one of her asthmatic attacks. No, it was because she was so thin. She had never noticed until tonight how sunken her sister's temples were. And under her cheekbones, where even as a young girl she had had hollows, were deep wells of shadow.

'She can't stand it,' she thought. 'She's not strong like me. She can't stand it. . . . I ought not to keep him. Those nubbins I gave him today. I could have taken them to the mill and had them ground into meal.'

'There's two jars of preserves left,' she said, 'a jar of quince and a jar of peach.'

Cummy was up from the table and halfway down the cellar steps before she had stopped speaking. He brought up the two jars.

Sophy nodded. 'Might as well have them now. Preserves aren't any good without buttered bread, and no telling when we'll have butter again.'

Barbara did not answer. She was looking through the open door into the hall. 'Isn't that somebody on the porch?' she asked.

Cummy half rose from his chair. 'You sit still,' Barbara said sharply.

She got up and went through the hall toward the front door. When she was halfway there she stopped. 'Who is it?' she called.

The door swung slowly open. A man stepped into the hall. A tall, red-faced man in a dark cloak and cavalryman's boots. He looked at Barbara a moment before he took off his visored cap.

'Good evening, miss,' he said. 'This the way to Gordonsville?'

'Yes,' Barbara said, and stepped out onto the porch. 'You keep on down this lane till you hit the pike. It isn't more than a quarter of a mile.'

The soldier was looking back through the hall into the lighted kitchen. 'How about a bite of supper?' he asked, smiling a little.

Barbara moved past him to the door. She put her hand on the knob. 'I'm sorry but we haven't got a thing.'

He thrust his foot swiftly forward just before the door closed. He was laughing. 'That's too bad,' he said, and pushed past her into the kitchen.

Sophy got up slowly from her chair. Her face had gone dead white. Her mouth was open and then it shut, quivering like a rabbit's. She was always like that. In a minute she would be crying and telling him it was all right, the way she did last spring when the soldiers took all the meat out of the smokehouse.

Barbara thought of that time and her right hand clenched in the folds of her skirt. She put the other hand on Sophy's shoulder and pointed to the door. 'Go on,' she said, 'you go on and take Cummy with you.'

The soldier had sat down at the table and, pulling the dish of peas toward him, looked up at her, shaking his head a little. 'I'm mighty sorry,' he said, 'but I'm so hungry I could eat a horse.' He laughed. 'Horse gave out on me way back up the road. I must have walked three miles.'

Barbara leaned forward until her face was on a level with his. A vein in her forehead stood out, swollen and tinged faintly with purple. She spoke through clenched teeth.

'Aren't you ashamed to take the bread out of the mouths of women and children?'

The soldier stared. He seemed about to rise from his chair, but he sank back, shaking his head again, laughing. After a moment he spoke, his mouth full of peas. 'Lady, you got any pie?'

'We haven't got anything,' Barbara said. 'There isn't anything left on this place worth the taking. It doesn't make any difference which side they're on. They come and take everything.'

The soldier nodded. A mischievous light came in his eyes. 'Those damn Rebs,' he said. 'You turn 'em loose on a place and they'll strip it.'

'Don't you say "damn Reb" to me!' Barbara cried.

He put his knife and fork down and sat looking at her. His eyes sparkled. 'Damn Reb,' he said. 'Damn Reb. Damn Reb. . . . If you aren't the feistiest Reb I ever saw!'

Barbara left the room. Sophy and Cummy were on the front porch. She walked up and down a few minutes, then went into the deserted parlor and stood before one of the darkened windows. 'I wish I could kill him,' she said aloud. 'God! I wish I could kill him.'

'Hush!' came a fierce whisper. 'Here he comes.'

The soldier stood in the doorway. 'That was a fine dinner,' he said. He made a little bow. 'I'm much obliged to you.'

No one spoke. He lingered, fastened his cloak. He was humming that same tune.

> 'One morning, one morning, one morning in May
> I met a fair lady a-wending her way . . .'

'Very *much* obliged,' he said. His eyes sought Barbara's. She did not answer, staring at Sophy, who had moved over and was lighting one of the lamps that stood on the mantel, as if, Barbara thought, they had come in here to entertain a welcome guest. Sophy finished lighting the lamp and sat down on the old love seat, her hands folded in her lap. Cummy had slipped into the room and sat down beside her. On the mantel the lamp burned steadily, revealing objects unfamiliar from long disuse: the walnut chairs, upholstered in faded red, the mute piano, the damask curtains. Their mother had been proud of her parlor when all those things were new. The soldier was looking about him as calmly as if he had been invited to spend the evening in their company. A little smile played about the corners of his mouth. He walked over to a whatnot in the corner. Dresden figurines were on the top shelf and on the shelf below a hand-painted Japanese fan lay among a pile of Indian arrowheads that Cummy had picked up on the old chipping ground. He took one in his hand. The bits of mica embedded in the flint gleamed as he turned it over slowly. 'We get 'em like that on our home place,' he said, and looked into her eyes and smiled. 'Up in Indiana.' He laid the arrowhead down and picked up a larger flint. 'That's not for an arrow,' he said. 'That's a sword. A ceremonial sword. My grandfather knew an old Indian once told him what all the different kinds were.'

He spoke in a low, casual tone, as if to somebody who stood beside him, somebody who was listening and in a minute would say something back. But there was not anybody here who would listen to anything that he might ever say. And the room itself was not used to the sound of human voices. There had not been anybody in it for a long time, not since that night, two years ago, the night of Marie's wedding. They had pushed the chairs back and danced till dawn broke at the windows. Gil Lathrop played the fiddle. Sometimes he sang as he played:

> 'And the voice that I heard made the valleys all ring;
> It was fairer than the music when the nightingale sings.'

The soldier was humming again. That song, the song they all sang that night, seemed to go on inside him, and now he had to have something to listen to and words rang out in the still room:

> 'And if ever I return it will be in the spring
> For to see the waters flowing, hear the nightingale sing.'

He had a clear tenor voice. At home, among his own people, he would be the one to sing at the gatherings. He picked up the little, bright-colored fan. Over its rim his eyes sought hers again. 'Now which one of you ladies does this belong to?'

> 'For to see the waters flowing, hear the nightingale sing . . .'

But that night you could not tell who was singing: the song was on every lip. 'Look!' Ruth Emory said. 'There's Tom Ladd. I never saw him at a dance before.' He would have asked me to marry him, but for all their talk. 'It will be in the spring.' No, I will never see him again. There are some men do not come home from a war. If the music could only have gone on that night . . .

The man's eyes were blue, really, not gray. Blue, overlaid with white, like frozen water. There was no song in the room now. Black pinpoints grew in his eyes, glinted as he slowly turned his head. 'Now what was that?' he asked.

Barbara whirled and stood with her back to the window, her hands locked tight in front of her. She thought at first that she had not heard anything, that it was only the blood pounding in her ears. Then it came again, the slow beat-beat of the mule's hoof against the brick wall of the cellar.

She left the window and walked across the room. As she passed the fireplace she pushed the shovel with her foot. It fell to the floor with a clatter, taking the tongs with it. The Yankee picked them up and stood them on the hearth. He looked at her, his eyes grave and speculative.

'What was that?' he asked again.

She took a step toward him. 'It's my brother,' she said. 'He's armed.' She took another step. 'He'll shoot you.'

The Yankee laughed, cocking his head on one side. 'Now what good would it do you to get me shot?'

He walked in his heavy boots out into the hall and back into the kitchen. They followed him. He lifted the lighted lantern that sat on the table and beckoned to Cummy. 'Come here, son. I've got an errand for you.'

Cummy's face took on its stubborn look. 'I don't want to go down there,' he said.

Sophy was crying. 'Poor little motherless boy. Don't make him go.'

The Yankee put his arm about Cummy's shoulders. 'You come along with me, son. Nothing's going to hurt you.'

He opened the door into the cellar and, holding the lantern, leaned over Cummy's shoulder, to look down the stairs. He straightened up, laughing. 'That's a mighty peculiar brother you've got down there,' he said.

He handed the lantern to Cummy. 'You hold on to that, son, and don't get in the way of my right arm. I wouldn't be surprised if you had another brother down there.'

They started down the steps. The Yankee walked slowly, a step behind Cummy, his arm still about Cummy's shoulder. Barbara watched them until they were halfway down, then she ran out through the back door and around the side of the house.

The double cellar doors were still closed when she got there, but she could hear the Yankee fumbling with the bolt. He had pulled it out. The doors slammed back. Lightning came slowly up the steps. She waited until his head and shoulders were level with the ground before she reached up and caught the halter.

'This is my mule,' she said.

Lightning snorted and tossed his head. The whites of his eyes showed. His ears were laid back. She tugged at the halter again. 'You let him go,' she sobbed. 'You better let him go!'

The Yankee raised his arm and pushed her, so hard that she spun away from him to fall on the grass. He brought Lightning up the last two steps, then came and stood over her while she was getting to her feet. His hand was on her arm. The fingers pressed it for a moment, the firm, friendly, admonitory pressure a man might give your arm—at a dance, if there was some secret understanding between you that he wanted to remind you of. 'I didn't mean to hurt you,' he said, 'but you oughtn't to have come interfering. Between us we might have broken that mule's legs on those steps.'

She did not answer, staring past him at the mule where he stood in the wash of light from the window, gazing before him out of great, dark eyes. His coat and his little bristling mane shone red in the light. His nostrils were ringed with palest fawn color. If she went over now and cupped his nose in her hands, the nostrils, snuffing gently in and out, would beat against her palm like butterflies' wings.

She looked up into gray eyes that sparkled in the light. The soldier had a broad mouth that slanted a little to one side. The blunt lips seemed always just about to stretch into a smile. She looked away, thinking how you could set your thumbs at the corners of those lips and rend the mouth from side to side and then, grasping in your hands the head—the head that you had severed from the body—you would beat it up and down on the boards of the well sweep until you cast it, a battered bloody pulp, into those grasses that sprang up there beside the well.

She walked over and sat down on the wooden platform. The planks were cool and wet. She gripped them hard with both hands. The man was still there, making a throat latch out of a piece of twine. He was turning around. 'You haven't got a bridle to spare, Bud?'

Cummy spoke up shrilly. 'You better not take that mule. I'm telling you now. You better not take him. Can't anybody do anything with him but Tom Ladd and he's joined the army.'

The Yankee had thrown a leg over Lightning's back and was sitting there looking down at them. 'I'm swapping you a good mare for this mule,' he said. 'She gave out on me . . . About three miles up the road . . .'

Lightning had stood quiet while the man mounted but he reared suddenly and plunged forward, his small, wicked head tucked down, his ears flat on his neck. And now he plunged on, turned the corner into the lane, and broke into a mad gallop. The soldier's voice drifted back above the pounding of hooves. 'I'd be glad for you to have her . . . Lying down under a big oak . . . About three miles up the road.'

Cummy caught hold of Barbara's arm. 'Come on, sister. Let's go see if we can find that mare.'

Barbara did not move. Cummy waited a moment, and sat down beside her. 'One thing,' he said, 'he won't ever get Lightning through those woods. Lightning'll rub him off on the branches.'

Barbara had been sitting with her head lifted, staring off into the lane. When he began to speak again she raised her hand. 'Hush!' she said sharply and then: 'What's that?'

Cummy jumped to his feet. 'It's that Yankee,' he said. 'He's in trouble.'

He bounded across the yard and through the open gate. Barbara followed him. It was black dark in the lane. They could not see their hands before them. There was no sound except the thudding of their own feet and then it came again, the cry which rose and swelled and broke finally into hideous shrieks. Barbara caught up with Cummy and pulled him to the left. 'It's this way,' she panted, 'over in the woods.'

They crashed through the underbrush and came out in a little glade. They could not see anything at first, then they made out the white trunk of a sycamore and beside it, Lightning, stock-still under a low-hanging bough, his head sharply lifted, his forefeet planted wide apart. The dark mass between his spread legs was too dense for shadow.

Cummy was holding on to Barbara's hand. 'Somebody's coming,' he whispered.

Barbara did not look around. 'It's Sis Sophy,' she said. 'She's bringing the lantern.'

She stood motionless. The long rays of the lantern flickered across the tree trunk and fell on the soldier's face, on the place where his eyes had been, on the blood that oozed from the torn mouth onto the dead leaves.

Sophy was whimpering softly. The lantern shook in her hand. 'We'll have to bury him . . . We'll have to get somebody to help us bury him.'

Barbara's eyes came away from the dead man to rest on Sophy's face. 'I'm not going to help bury him,' she said.

She walked past Sophy to where the mule stood. She put her hand up and cupped it over his quivering nostrils. He gave a long sigh and stepped clear of the body. She slid her arm down to rest on his withers.

'Come on,' she said, 'let's go home.'

Je ne parle pas français

❧

I do not know why I have such a fancy for this little café. It's dirty and sad, sad. It's not as if it had anything to distinguish it from a hundred others—it hasn't; or as if the same strange types came here every day, whom one could watch from one's corner and recognise and more or less (with a strong accent on the less) get the hang of.

But pray don't imagine that those brackets are a confession of my humility before the mystery of the human soul. Not at all; I don't believe in the human soul. I never have. I believe that people are like portmanteaux—packed with certain things, started going, thrown about, tossed away, dumped down, lost and found, half emptied suddenly, or squeezed fatter than ever, until finally the Ultimate Porter swings them on to the Ultimate Train and away they rattle. . . .

Not but what these portmanteaux can be very fascinating. Oh, but very! I see myself standing in front of them, don't you know, like a Customs official.

'Have you anything to declare? Any wines, spirits, cigars, perfumes, silks?'

And the moment of hesitation as to whether I am going to be fooled just before I chalk that squiggle, and then the other moment of hesitation just after, as to whether I have been, are perhaps the two most thrilling instants in life. Yes, they are, to me.

But before I started that long and rather far-fetched and not frightfully original digression, what I meant to say quite simply was that there are no portmanteaux to be examined here because the clientèle of this café, ladies and gentlemen, does not sit down. No, it stands at the counter, and it consists of a handful of workmen who come up from the river, all powdered over with white flour, lime or something, and a few soldiers, bringing with them thin, dark girls with silver rings in their ears and market baskets on their arms.

Madame is thin and dark, too, with white cheeks and white hands. In certain lights she looks quite transparent, shining out of her black shawl with an extraordinary effect. When she is not serving she sits on a stool with her face turned, always, to the window. Her dark-ringed eyes search among and follow after the people passing, but not as if she was looking for somebody. Perhaps, fifteen years ago, she was; but now the pose has become a habit. You can tell from her air of fatigue and hopelessness that she must have given them up for the last ten years, at least. . . .

And then there is the waiter. Not pathetic—decidedly not comic. Never making one of those perfectly insignificant remarks which amaze you so coming from a waiter (as though the poor wretch were a sort of cross between a coffee-pot and a wine-bottle and not expected to hold so much as a drop of anything else). He is grey, flat-footed and withered, with long, brittle nails that set your nerves on edge while he scrapes up your two sous. When he is not smearing over the table or flicking at a dead fly or two, he stands with one hand on the back of a chair, in his far too long apron, and over his other arm the three-cornered dip of dirty napkin, waiting to be photographed in connection with some wretched murder. 'Interior of Café where Body was Found.' You've seen him hundreds of times.

Do you believe that every place has its hour of the day when it really does come alive? That's not exactly what I mean. It's more like this. There does seem to be a moment when you realise that, quite by accident, you happen to have come on to the stage at exactly the moment you were expected. Everything is arranged for you—waiting for you. Ah, master of the situation! You fill with important breath. And at the same time you smile, secretly, slyly, because Life seems to be opposed to granting you these entrances, seems indeed to be engaged in snatching them from you and making them impossible, keeping you in the wings until it is too late, in fact. . . . Just for once you've beaten the old hag.

I enjoyed one of these moments the first time I ever came in here. That's why I keep coming back, I suppose. Revisiting the scene of my triumph, or the scene of the crime where I had the old bitch by the throat for once and did what I pleased with her.

Query: Why am I so bitter against Life? And why do I see her as a rag-picker on the American cinema, shuffling along wrapped in a filthy shawl with her old claws crooked over a stick?

Answer: The direct result of the American cinema acting upon a weak mind.

Anyhow, the 'short winter afternoon was drawing to a close,' as they say, and I was drifting along, either going home or not going home, when I found myself in here, walking over to this seat in the corner.

I hung up my English overcoat and grey felt hat on that same peg behind me, and after I had allowed the waiter time for at least twenty photographers to snap their fill of him, I ordered a coffee.

He poured me out a glass of the familiar, purplish stuff with a green wandering light playing over it, and shuffled off, and I sat pressing my hands against the glass because it was bitterly cold outside.

Suddenly I realised that quite apart from myself, I was smiling. Slowly I raised my head and saw myself in the mirror opposite. Yes, there I sat, leaning on the table, smiling my deep, sly smile, the glass of coffee with its vague plume of steam before me and beside it the ring of white saucer with two pieces of sugar.

I opened my eyes very wide. There I had been for all eternity, as it were, and now at last I was coming to life. . . .

It was very quiet in the café. Outside, one could just see through the dusk that it had begun to snow. One could just see the shapes of horses and carts and people, soft and white, moving through the feathery air. The waiter disappeared and reappeared with an armful of straw. He strewed it over the floor from the door to the counter and round about the stove with humble, almost adoring gestures. One would not have been surprised if the door had opened and the Virgin Mary had come in, riding upon an ass, her meek hands folded over her big belly. . . .

That's rather nice, don't you think, that bit about the Virgin? It comes from the pen so gently; it has such a 'dying fall'. I thought so at the time and decided to make a note of it. One never knows when a little tag like that may come in useful to round off a paragraph. So, taking care to move as little as possible because the 'spell' was still unbroken (you know that?), I reached over to the next table for a writing-pad.

No paper or envelopes, of course. Only a morsel of pink blotting-paper, incredibly soft and limp and almost moist, like the tongue of a little dead kitten, which I've never felt.

I sat—but always underneath, in this state of expectation, rolling the little dead kitten's tongue round my finger and rolling the soft phrase round my mind while my eyes took in the girls' names and dirty jokes and drawings of bottles and cups that would not sit in the saucers, scattered over the writing-pad.

They are always the same, you know. The girls always have the same names, the cups never sit in the saucers; all the hearts are stuck and tied up with ribbons.

But then, quite suddenly, at the bottom of the page, written in green ink, I fell on to that stupid, stale little phrase: *Je ne parle pas français.*

There! it had come—the moment—the *geste*! And although I was so ready, it caught me, it tumbled me over; I was simply overwhelmed. And the physical feeling was so curious, so particular. It was as if all of me, except my head and arms, all of me that was under the table, had simply dissolved, melted, turned into water. Just my head remained and two sticks of arms pressing on to the table. But, ah! the agony of that moment! How can I describe it? I didn't think of anything. I didn't even cry out to myself. Just for one moment I was not. I was Agony, Agony, Agony.

Then it passed, and the very second after I was thinking: 'Good God! Am I capable of feeling as strongly as that? But I was absolutely unconscious! I hadn't a phrase to meet it with! I was overcome! I was swept off my feet! I didn't even try, in the dimmest way, to put it down!'

And up I puffed and puffed, blowing off finally with: 'After all I must be first-rate. No second-rate mind could have experienced such an intensity of feeling so . . . purely.'

The waiter has touched a spill at the red stove and lighted a bubble of gas under a spreading shade. It is no use looking out of the window, Madame; it is quite dark now. Your white hands hover over your dark shawl. They are like two birds that have come home to roost. They are restless, restless. . . . You tuck them, finally, under your warm little armpits.

Now the waiter has taken a long pole and clashed the curtains together. 'All gone,' as children say.

And besides, I've no patience with people who can't let go of things, who will follow after and cry out. When a thing's gone, it's gone. It's over and done with. Let it go, then! Ignore it, and comfort yourself, if you do want comforting, with the thought that you never do recover the same thing that you lose. It's always a new thing. The moment it leaves you it's changed. Why, that's even true of a hat you chase after; and I don't mean superficially—I mean profoundly speaking. . . . I have made it a rule of my life never to regret and never to look back. Regret is an appalling waste of energy, and no one who intends to be a writer can afford to indulge in it. You can't get it into shape; you can't build on it; it's only good for wallowing in. Looking back, of course, is equally fatal to Art. It's keeping yourself poor. Art can't and won't stand poverty.

Je ne parle pas français. Je ne parle pas français. All the while I wrote that last page my other self has been chasing up and down out in the dark there. It left me just when I began to analyse my grand moment, dashed off distracted, like a lost dog who thinks at last, at last, he hears the familiar step again.

'Mouse! Mouse! Where are you? Are you near? Is that you leaning from the high window and stretching out your arms for the wings of the shutters? Are you this soft bundle moving towards me through the feathery snow? Are you this little girl pressing through the swing-doors of the restaurant? Is that your dark shadow bending forward in the cab? Where are you? Where are you? Which way must I turn? Which way shall I run?

And every moment I stand here hesitating you are further away again. Mouse! Mouse!'

Now the poor dog has come back into the café, his tail between his legs, quite exhausted.

'It was a . . . false . . . alarm. She's nowhere . . . to . . . be seen.'

'Lie down, then! Lie down! Lie down!'

My name is Raoul Duquette. I am twenty-six years old and a Parisian, a true Parisian. About my family—it really doesn't matter. I have no family; I don't want any. I never think about my childhood. I've forgotten it.

In fact, there's only one memory that stands out at all. That is rather interesting because it seems to me now so very significant as regards myself from the literary point of view. It is this.

When I was about ten our laundress was an African woman, very big, very dark, with a check handkerchief over her frizzy hair. When she came to our house she always took particular notice of me, and after the clothes had been taken out of the basket she would lift me up into it and give me a rock while I held tight to the handles and screamed for joy and fright. I was tiny for my age, and pale, with a lovely little half-open mouth—I feel sure of that.

One day when I was standing at the door, watching her go, she turned round and beckoned to me, nodding and smiling in a strange secret way. I never thought of not following. She took me into a little outhouse at the end of the passage, caught me up in her arms and began kissing me. Ah, those kisses! Especially those kisses inside my ears that nearly deafened me.

When she set me down she took from her pocket a little round fried cake covered with sugar, and I reeled along the passage back to our door.

As this performance was repeated once a week it is no wonder that I remember it so vividly. Besides, from that very first afternoon, my childhood was, to put it prettily, 'kissed away'. I became very languid, very caressing, and greedy beyond measure. And so quickened, so sharpened, I seemed to understand everybody and be able to do what I liked with everybody.

I suppose I was in a state of more or less physical excitement, and that was what appealed to them. For all Parisians are more than half—oh, well, enough of that. And enough of my childhood, too. Bury it under a laundry basket instead of a shower of roses and *passons outre*.

I date myself from the moment that I became the tenant of a small bachelor flat on the fifth floor of a tall, not too shabby house, in a street that might or might not be discreet. Very useful, that. . . . There I emerged, came out into the light and put out my two horns with a study and a bedroom and a kitchen on my back. And real furniture planted in the rooms. In the bedroom a wardrobe with a long glass, a big bed covered with a yellow puffed-up quilt, a bed-table with a marbled top and a toilet set sprinkled with tiny apples. In my study—English writing-table with drawers, writing-chair with leather cushions, books, arm-chair, side table with paper-knife and lamp on it and some nude studies on the walls. I didn't use the kitchen except to throw old papers into.

Ah, I can see myself that first evening, after the furniture men had gone and I'd managed to get rid of my atrocious old concierge—walking about on tiptoe, arranging and standing in front of the glass with my hands in my pockets and saying to that radiant vision: 'I am a young man who has his own flat. I write for two newspapers. I am going in for serious literature. I am starting a career. The book that I shall bring out will simply stagger the critics. I am going to write about things that have never been touched before. I am going to make a name for myself as a writer about the submerged world. But not as others have done before me. Oh, no! Very naïvely, with a sort of tender humour and from the inside, as though it were all quite simple, quite natural. I see my way quite perfectly. Nobody has ever done it as I shall do it because none of the others have lived my experiences. I'm rich—I'm rich.'

All the same I had no more money than I have now. It's extraordinary how one can live without money. . . . I have quantities of good clothes, silk underwear, two evening suits, four pairs of patent leather boots with light uppers, all sorts of little things, like gloves and powder boxes and a manicure set, perfumes, very good soap, and nothing is paid for. If I find myself in need of right-down cash—well, there's always an African laundress and an outhouse, and I am very frank and *bon enfant* about plenty of sugar on the little fried cake afterwards. . . .

And here I should like to put something on record. Not from any strutting conceit, but rather with a mild sense of wonder. I've never yet made the first advances to any woman. It isn't as though I've known only one class of woman—not by any means. But from little prostitutes and kept women and elderly widows and shop girls and wives of respectable men, and even advanced modern literary ladies at the most select dinners and soirées (I've been there), I've met invariably with not only the same readiness, but with the same positive invitation. It surprised me at first. I used to look across the table and think 'Is that very distinguished young lady, discussing *le Kipling* with the gentleman with the brown beard, really pressing my foot?' And I was never really certain until I had pressed hers.

Curious, isn't it? I don't look at all like a maiden's dream. . . .

I am little and light with an olive skin, black eyes with long lashes, black silky hair cut short, tiny square teeth that show when I smile. My hands are supple and small. A woman in a bread shop once said to me: 'You have the hands for making fine little pastries.' I confess, without my clothes I am rather charming. Plump, almost like a girl, with smooth shoulders, and I wear a thin gold bracelet above my left elbow.

But, wait! Isn't it strange I should have written all that about my body and so on? It's the result of my bad life, my submerged life. I am like a little woman in a café who has to introduce herself with a handful of photographs. 'Me in my chemise, coming out of an eggshell. . . . Me upside down in a swing, with a frilly behind like a cauliflower. . . .' You know the things.

If you think what I've written is merely superficial and impudent and cheap, you're wrong. I'll admit it does sound so, but then it is not all. If it were, how could I have experienced what I did when I read that stale little phrase written in green ink, in the writing-pad? That proves there's more in me and that I really am important, doesn't it? Anything a fraction less than that moment of anguish I might have put on. But no! That was real.

'Waiter, a whisky.'

I hate whisky. Every time I take it into my mouth my stomach rises against it, and the stuff they keep here is sure to be particularly vile. I only ordered it because I am going to write about an Englishman. We French are incredibly old-fashioned and out of date still in some ways. I wonder I didn't ask him at the same time for a pair of tweed knickerbockers, a pipe, some long teeth and a set of ginger whiskers.

'Thanks, *mon vieux*. You haven't got perhaps a set of ginger whiskers?'

'No, monsieur,' he answers sadly. 'We don't sell American drinks.'

And having smeared a corner of the table he goes back to have another couple of dozen taken by artificial light.

Ugh! The smell of it! And the sickly sensation when one's throat contracts.

'It's bad stuff to get drunk on,' says Dick Harmon, turning his little glass in his fingers and smiling his slow, dreaming smile. So he gets drunk on it slowly and dreamily and at a certain moment begins to sing very low, very low, about a man who walks up and down trying to find a place where he can get some dinner.

Ah! how I loved that song, and how I loved the way he sang it, slowly, slowly, in a dark, soft voice:

> 'There was a man
> Walked up and down
> To get a dinner in the town . . .'

It seemed to hold, in its gravity and muffled measure, all those tall grey buildings, those fogs, those endless streets, those sharp shadows of policemen that mean England.

And then—the subject! The lean, starved creature walking up and down with every house barred against him because he had no 'home'. How extraordinarily English that is. . . . I remember that it ended where he did at last 'find a place' and ordered a little cake of fish, but when he asked for bread the waiter cried contemptuously, in a loud voice: 'We don't serve bread with one fish ball.'

What more do you want? How profound those songs are! There is the whole psychology of a people; and how un-French—how un-French!

'Once more, Deeck, once more!' I would plead, clasping my hands and making a pretty mouth at him. He was perfectly content to sing it for ever.

There again. Even with Dick. It was he who made the first advances.

I met him at an evening party given by the editor of a new review. It was a very select, very fashionable affair. One or two of the older men were there and the ladies were extremely *comme il faut*. They sat on cubist sofas in full evening dress and allowed us to hand them thimbles of cherry brandy and to talk to them about their poetry. For, as far as I can remember, they were all poetesses.

It was impossible not to notice Dick. He was the only Englishman present, and instead of circulating gracefully round the room as we all did, he stayed in one place leaning against the wall, his hands in his pockets, that dreamy half-smile on his lips, and replying in excellent French in his low, soft voice to anybody who spoke to him.

'Who is he?'

'An Englishman. From London. A writer. And he is making a special study of modern French literature.'

That was enough for me. My little book, *False Coins*, had just been published. I was a young, serious writer who was making a special study of modern English literature.

But I really had not time to fling my line before he said, giving himself a soft shake, coming right out of the water after the bait, as it were: 'Won't you come and see me at my hotel? Come about five o'clock and we can have a talk before going out to dinner.'

'Enchanted!'

I was so deeply, deeply flattered that I had to leave him then and there to preen and preen myself before the cubist sofas. What a catch! An Englishman, reserved, serious, making a special study of French literature. . . .

That same night a copy of *False Coins* with a carefully cordial inscription was posted off, and a day or two later we did dine together and spent the evening talking.

Talking—but not only of literature. I discovered to my relief that it wasn't necessary to keep to the tendency of the modern novel, the need of a new form, or the reason why our young men appeared to be just missing it. Now and again, as if by accident, I threw in a card that seemed to have nothing to do with the game, just to see how he'd take it. But each time he gathered it into his hands with his dreamy look and smile unchanged. Perhaps he murmured: 'That's very curious.' But not as if it were curious at all.

That calm acceptance went to my head at last. It fascinated me. It led me on and on till I threw every card that I possessed at him and sat back and watched him arrange them in his hand.

'Very curious and interesting. . . .'

By that time we were both fairly drunk, and he began to sing his song very soft, very low, about the man who walked up and down seeking his dinner.

But I was quite breathless at the thought of what I had done. I had shown somebody both sides of my life. Told him everything as sincerely and truthfully as I could. Taken immense pains to explain things about my submerged life that really were disgusting and never could possibly see the light of literary day. On the whole I had made myself out far worse than I was—more boastful, more cynical, more calculating.

And there sat the man I had confided in, singing to himself and smiling. . . . It moved me so that real tears came into my eyes. I saw them glittering on my long silky lashes—so charming.

After that I took Dick about with me everywhere, and he came to my flat, and sat in the arm-chair, very indolent, playing with the paper-knife. I cannot think why his indolence and dreaminess always gave me the impression he had been to sea. And all his leisurely slow ways seemed to be allowing for the movement of the ship. This impression was so strong that often when we were together and he got up and left a little woman just when she did not expect him to get up and leave her, but quite the contrary, I would explain: 'He can't help it, Baby. He has to go back to his ship.' And I believed it far more than she did.

All the while we were together Dick never went with a woman. I sometimes wondered whether he wasn't completely innocent. Why didn't I ask him? Because I never did ask him anything about himself. But late one night he took out his pocket-book and a photograph dropped out of it. I picked it up and glanced at it before I gave it to him. It was of a woman. Not quite young. Dark, handsome, wild-looking, but so full in every line of a kind of haggard pride that even if Dick had not stretched out so quickly I wouldn't have looked longer.

'Out of my sight, you little perfumed fox-terrier of a Frenchman,' said she.

(In my very worst moments my nose reminds me of a fox-terrier's.)

'That is my Mother,' said Dick, putting up the pocket-book.

But if he had not been Dick I should have been tempted to cross myself, just for fun.

This is how we parted. As we stood outside his hotel one night waiting for the concierge to release the catch of the outer door, he said, looking up at the sky: 'I hope it will be fine to-morrow. I am leaving for England in the morning.'

'You're not serious.'

'Perfectly. I have to get back. I've some work to do that I can't manage here.'

'But—but have you made all your preparations?'

'Preparations?' He almost grinned. 'I've none to make.'

'But—*enfin*, Dick, England is not the other side of the boulevard.'

'It isn't much farther off,' said he. 'Only a few hours, you know.' The door cracked open.

'Ah, I wish I'd known at the beginning of the evening!'

I felt hurt. I felt as a woman must feel when a man takes out his watch and remembers an appointment that cannot possibly concern her, except that its claim is the stronger.

'Why didn't you tell me?'

He put out his hand and stood, lightly swaying upon the step as though the whole hotel were his ship, and the anchor weighed.

'I forgot. Truly I did. But you'll write, won't you? Good night, old chap. I'll be over again one of these days.'

And then I stood on the shore alone, more like a little fox-terrier than ever. . . .

'But after all it was you who whistled to me, you who asked me to come! What a spectacle I've cut wagging my tail and leaping round you, only to be left like this while the boat sails off in its slow, dreamy way. . . . Curse these English! No, this is too insolent altogether. Who do you imagine I am? A little paid guide to the night pleasures of Paris? . . . No, Monsieur. I am a young writer, very serious, and extremely interested in modern English literature. And I have been insulted—insulted.'

Two days after came a long, charming letter from him, written in French that was a shade too French, but saying how he missed me and counted on our friendship, on keeping in touch.

I read it standing in front of the (unpaid for) wardrobe mirror. It was early morning. I wore a blue kimono embroidered with white birds and my hair was still wet; it lay on my forehead, wet and gleaming.

'Portrait of Madame Butterfly,' said I, 'on hearing of the arrival of *ce cher Pinkerton.*'

According to the books I should have felt immensely relieved and delighted. '. . . Going over to the window he drew apart the curtains and looked out at the Paris trees, just breaking into buds and green. . . . Dick! Dick! My English friend!'

I didn't. I merely felt a little sick. Having been up for my first ride in an aeroplane I didn't want to go up again, just now.

That passed, and months after, in the winter, Dick wrote that he was coming back to Paris to stay indefinitely. Would I take rooms for him? He was bringing a woman friend with him.

Of course I would. Away the little fox-terrier flew. It happened most usefully, too; for I owed much money at the hotel where I took my meals, and two English people requiring rooms for an indefinite time was an excellent sum on account.

Perhaps I did rather wonder, as I stood in the larger of the two rooms with Madame, saying 'Admirable', what the woman friend would be like, but only vaguely. Either she would be very severe, flat back and front, or she would be tall, fair, dressed in mignonette green, name—Daisy, and smelling of rather sweetish lavender water.

You see, by this time, according to my rule of not looking back, I had almost forgotten Dick. I even got the tune of his song about the unfortunate man a little bit wrong when I tried to hum it. . . .

I very nearly did not turn up at the station after all. I had arranged to, and had, in fact, dressed with particular care for the occasion. For I intended to take a new line with Dick this time. No more confidences and tears on eyelashes. No, thank you!

'Since you left Paris,' said I, knotting my black silver-spotted tie in the (also unpaid for) mirror over the mantelpiece, 'I have been very successful, you know. I have two more books in preparation, and then I have written a serial story, *Wrong Doors*, which is just on the point of publication and will bring me in a lot of money. And then my little book of poems,' I cried, seizing the clothes-brush and brushing the velvet collar of my new indigo-blue overcoat, 'my little book—*Left Umbrellas*—really did create', and I laughed and waved the brush, 'an immense sensation!'

It was impossible not to believe this of the person who surveyed himself finally, from top to toe, drawing on his soft grey gloves. He was looking the part; he was the part.

That gave me an idea. I took out my notebook, and still in full view, jotted down a note or two. . . . How can one look the part and not be the part? Or be the part and not look it? Isn't looking—being? Or being— looking? At any rate who is to say that it is not? . . .

This seemed to me extraordinarily profound at the time, and quite new. But I confess that something did whisper as, smiling, I put up the notebook: 'You—literary? you look as though you've taken down a bet on a racecourse!' But I didn't listen. I went out, shutting the door of the flat with a soft, quick pull so as not to warn the concierge of my departure, and ran down the stairs quick as a rabbit for the same reason.

But ah! the old spider. She was too quick for me. She let me run down the last little ladder of the web and then she pounced. 'One moment. One little moment, Monsieur,' she whispered, odiously confidential. 'Come in. Come in.' And she beckoned with a dripping soup–ladle. I went to the door, but that was not good enough. Right inside and the door shut before she would speak.

There are two ways of managing your concierge if you haven't any money. One is—to take the high hand, make her your enemy, bluster, refuse to discuss anything; the other is—to keep in with her, butter her up to the two knots of the black rag tying up her jaws, pretend to confide in her, and rely on her to arrange with the gas-man and to put off the landlord.

I had tried the second. But both are equally detestable and unsuccessful. At any rate, whichever you're trying is the worse, the impossible one.

It was the landlord this time. . . . Imitation of the landlord by the concierge threatening to toss me out. . . . Imitation of the concierge by the concierge taming the wild bull. . . . Imitation of the landlord rampant again, breathing in the concierge's face. I was the concierge. No, it was too nauseous. And all the while the black pot on the gas ring bubbling away, stewing out the hearts and livers of every tenant in the place.

'Ah!' I cried, staring at the clock on the mantelpiece, and then, realising that it didn't go, striking my forehead as though the idea had nothing to do with it. 'Madame, I have a very important appointment with the director of my newspaper at nine-thirty. Perhaps to-morrow I shall be able to give you . . .'

Out, out. And down the métro and squeezed into a full carriage. The more the better. Everybody was one bolster the more between me and the concierge. I was radiant.

'Ah! pardon, Monsieur!' said the tall charming creature in black with a big full bosom and a great bunch of violets dropping from it. As the train swayed it thrust the bouquet right into my eyes. 'Ah! pardon, Monsieur!'

But I looked up at her, smiling mischievously.

'There is nothing I love more, Madame, than flowers on a balcony.'

At the very moment of speaking I caught sight of the huge man in a fur coat against whom my charmer was leaning. He poked his head over her shoulder and he went white to the nose; in fact his nose stood out a sort of cheese green.

'What was that you said to my wife?'

Gare Saint Lazare saved me. But you'll own that even as the author of *False Coins, Wrong Doors, Left Umbrellas*, and two in preparation, it was not too easy to go on my triumphant way.

At length, after countless trains had steamed into my mind, and countless Dick Harmons had come rolling towards me, the real train came. The little knot of us waiting at the barrier moved up close, craned forward, and broke into cries as though we were some kind of many-headed monster, and Paris behind us nothing but a great trap we had set to catch these sleepy innocents.

Into the trap they walked and were snatched and taken off to be devoured. Where was my prey?

'Good God!' My smile and my lifted hand fell together. For one terrible moment I thought this was the woman of the photograph, Dick's mother, walking towards me in Dick's coat and hat. In the effort—and you saw what an effort it was—to smile, his lips curled in just the same way and he made for me, haggard and wild and proud.

What had happened? What could have changed him like this? Should I mention it?

I waited for him and was even conscious of venturing a fox-terrier wag or two to see if he could possibly respond, in the way I said: 'Good evening, Dick! How are you, old chap? All right?'

'All right. All right.' He almost gasped. 'You've got the rooms?'

Twenty times, good God! I saw it all. Light broke on the dark waters and my sailor hadn't been drowned. I almost turned a somersault with amusement.

It was nervousness, of course. It was embarrassment. It was the famous English seriousness. What fun I was going to have! I could have hugged him.

'Yes, I've got the rooms,' I nearly shouted. 'But where is Madame?'

'She's been looking after the luggage,' he panted. 'Here she comes, now.'

Not this baby walking beside the old porter as though he were her nurse and had just lifted her out of her ugly perambulator while he trundled the boxes on it.

'And she's not Madame,' said Dick, drawling suddenly.

At that moment she caught sight of him and hailed him with her minute muff. She broke away from her nurse and ran up and said something, very quick, in English; but he replied in French: 'Oh, very well. I'll manage.'

But before he turned to the porter he indicated me with a vague wave and muttered something. We were introduced. She held out her hand in that strange boyish way Englishwomen do, and standing very straight in front of me with her chin raised and making—she too—the effort of her life to control her preposterous excitement, she said, wringing my hand (I'm sure she didn't know it was mine), *Je ne parle pas français*.

'But I'm sure you do,' I answered, so tender, so reassuring, I might have been a dentist about to draw her first little milk tooth.

'Of course she does,' Dick swerved back to us. 'Here, can't we get a cab or taxi or something? We don't want to stay in this cursed station all night. Do we?'

This was so rude that it took me a moment to recover; and he must have noticed, for he flung his arm round my shoulder in the old way, saying: 'Ah, forgive me, old chap. But we've had such a loathsome, hideous journey. We've taken years to come. Haven't we?' To her. But she did not answer. She bent her head and began stroking her grey muff; she walked beside us stroking her grey muff all the way.

'Have I been wrong?' thought I. 'Is this simply a case of frenzied impatience on their part? Are they merely "in need of a bed," as we say? Have they been suffering agonies on the journey? Sitting, perhaps, very close and warm under the same travelling rug?' and so on and so on while the driver strapped on the boxes. That done—

'Look here, Dick. I go home by métro. Here is the address of your hotel. Everything is arranged. Come and see me as soon as you can.'

Upon my life I thought he was going to faint. He went white to the lips.

'But you're coming back with us,' he cried. 'I thought it was all settled. Of course you're coming back. You're not going to leave us.' No, I gave it up. It was too difficult, too English for me.

'Certainly, certainly. Delighted. I only thought, perhaps . . .'

'You must come!' said Dick to the little fox-terrier. And again he made that big awkward turn towards her.

'Get in, Mouse.'

And Mouse got in the black hole and sat stroking Mouse II and not saying a word.

Away we jolted and rattled like three little dice that life had decided to have a fling with.

I had insisted on taking the flap seat facing them because I would not have missed for anything those occasional flashing glimpses I had as we broke through the white circles of lamplight.

They revealed Dick, sitting far back in his corner, his coat collar turned up, his hands thrust in his pockets, and his broad dark hat shading him as if it were a part of him—a sort of wing he hid under. They showed her, sitting up very straight, her lovely little face more like a drawing than a real face—every line was so full of meaning and so sharp-cut against the swimming dark.

For Mouse was beautiful. She was exquisite, but so fragile and fine that each time I looked at her it was as if for the first time. She came upon you with the same kind of shock that you feel when you have been drinking tea out of a thin innocent cup and suddenly, at the bottom, you see a tiny creature, half butterfly, half woman, bowing to you with her hands in her sleeves.

As far as I could make out she had dark hair and blue or black eyes. Her long lashes and the two little feathers traced above were most important.

She wore a long dark cloak such as one sees in old-fashioned pictures of Englishwomen abroad. Where her arms came out of it there was grey fur—fur round her neck, too, and her close-fitting cap was furry.

'Carrying out the mouse idea,' I decided.

Ah, but how intriguing it was—how intriguing! Their excitement came nearer and nearer to me, while I ran out to meet it, bathed in it, flung myself far out of my depth, until at last I was as hard put to it to keep control as they.

But what I wanted to do was to behave in the most extraordinary fashion—like a clown. To start singing, with large extravagant gestures, to point out of the window and cry: 'We are now passing, ladies and gentlemen, one of the sights for which *notre Paris* is justly famous,' to jump out of the taxi while it was going, climb over the roof and dive in by another door; to hang out of the window and look for the hotel through the wrong end of a broken telescope, which was also a peculiarly ear-splitting trumpet.

I watched myself do all this, you understand, and even managed to applaud in a private way by putting my gloved hands gently together, while I said to Mouse: 'And is this your first visit to Paris?'

'Yes, I've not been here before.'

'Ah, then you have a great deal to see.'

And I was just going to touch lightly upon the objects of interest and the museums when we wrenched to a stop.

Do you know—it's very absurd—but as I pushed open the door for them and followed up the stairs to the bureau on the landing I felt somehow that this hotel was mine.

There was a vase of flowers on the window sill of the bureau, and I even went so far as to rearrange a bud or two and to stand off and note the effect while the manageress welcomed them. And when she turned to me and handed me the keys (the *garçon* was hauling up the boxes) and said: 'Monsieur Duquette will show you your rooms'—I had a longing to tap Dick on the arm with a key and say, very confidentially: 'Look here, old chap. As a friend of mine I'll be only too willing to make a slight reduction . . .'

Up and up we climbed. Round and round. Past an occasional pair of boots (why is it one never sees an attractive pair of boots outside a door?). Higher and higher.

'I'm afraid they're rather high up,' I murmured idiotically. 'But I chose them because . . .'

They so obviously did not care why I chose them that I went no further. They accepted everything. They did not expect anything to be different. This was just part of what they were going through—that was how I analysed it.

'Arrived at last.' I ran from one side of the passage to the other, turning on the lights, explaining.

'This one I thought for you, Dick. The other is larger and it has a little dressing-room in the alcove.'

My 'proprietary' eye noted the clean towels and covers, and the bed linen embroidered in red cotton. I thought them rather charming rooms, sloping, full of angles, just the sort of rooms one would expect to find if one had not been to Paris before.

Dick dashed his hat down on the bed.

'Oughtn't I to help that chap with the boxes?' he asked—nobody.

'Yes, you ought,' replied Mouse, 'they're dreadfully heavy.'

And she turned to me with the first glimmer of a smile: 'Books, you know.' Oh, he darted such a strange look at her before he rushed out. And he not only helped, he must have torn the box off the *garçon's* back, for he staggered back, carrying one, dumped it down and then fetched in the other.

'That's yours, Dick,' said she.

'Well, you don't mind it standing here for the present, do you?' he asked, breathless, breathing hard (the box must have been tremendously heavy). He pulled out a handful of money. 'I suppose I ought to pay this chap.'

The *garçon*, standing by, seemed to think so too.

'And will you require anything further, Monsieur?'

'No! No!' said Dick impatiently.

But at that Mouse stepped forward. She said, too deliberately, not looking at Dick, with her quaint clipped English accent: 'Yes, I'd like some tea. Tea for three.'

And suddenly she raised her muff as though her hands were clasped inside it, and she was telling the pale, sweaty *garçon* by that action that she was at the end of her resources, that she cried out to him to save her with 'Tea. Immediately!'

This seemed to me so amazingly in the picture, so exactly the gesture and cry that one would expect (though I couldn't have imagined it) to be wrung out of an Englishwoman faced with a great crisis, that I was almost tempted to hold up my hand and protest.

'No! No! Enough. Enough. Let us leave off there. At the word—tea. For really, really, you've filled your greediest subscriber so full that he will burst if he has to swallow another word.'

It even pulled Dick up. Like someone who has been unconscious for a long time he turned slowly to Mouse and slowly looked at her with his tired, haggard eyes, and murmured with the echo of his dreamy voice: 'Yes. That's a good idea.' And then: 'You must be tired, Mouse. Sit down.'

She sat down in a chair with lace tabs on the arms; he leaned against the bed, and I established myself on a straight-backed chair, crossed my legs and brushed some imaginary dust off the knees of my trousers. (The Parisian at his ease.)

There came a tiny pause. Then he said: 'Won't you take off your coat, Mouse?'

'No, thanks. Not just now.'

Were they going to ask me? Or should I hold up my hand and call out in a baby voice: 'It's my turn to be asked.'

No, I shouldn't. They didn't ask me.

The pause became a silence. A real silence.

'. . . Come, my Parisian fox-terrier! Amuse these sad English! It's no wonder they are such a nation for dogs.'

But, after all—why should I? It was not my 'job', as they would say. Nevertheless, I made a vivacious little bound at Mouse.

'What a pity it is that you did not arrive by daylight. There is such a charming view from these two windows. You know, the hotel is on a corner and each window looks down an immensely long, straight street.'

'Yes,' said she.

'Not that that sounds very charming,' I laughed. 'But there is so much

animation—so many absurd little boys on bicycles and people hanging
out of windows and—oh, well, you'll see for yourself in the morning.
. . . Very amusing. Very animated.'

'Oh yes,' said she.

If the pale, sweaty *garçon* had not come in at that moment, carrying
the tea-tray high on one hand as if the cups were cannon-balls and he a
heavy-weight lifter on the cinema . . .

He managed to lower it on to a round table.

'Bring the table over here,' said Mouse. The waiter seemed to be the
only person she cared to speak to. She took her hands out of her muff,
drew off her gloves and flung back the old-fashioned cape.

'Do you take milk and sugar?'

'No milk, thank you, and no sugar.'

I went over for mine like a little gentleman. She poured out another
cup.

'That's for Dick.'

And the faithful fox-terrier carried it across to him and laid it at his
feet, as it were.

'Oh, thanks,' said Dick.

And then I went back to my chair and she sank back in hers.

But Dick was off again. He stared wildly at the cup of tea for a
moment, glanced round him, put it down on the bed-table, caught up his
hat and stammered at full gallop: 'Oh, by the way, do you mind posting
a letter for me? I want to get it off by to-night's post. I must. It's very
urgent. . . .' Feeling her eyes on him, he flung: 'It's to my mother.' To
me: 'I won't be long. I've got everything I want. But it must go off to-
night. You don't mind? It . . . it won't take any time.'

'Of course I'll post it. Delighted.'

'Won't you drink your tea first?' suggested Mouse softly.

. . . Tea? Tea? Yes, of course. Tea. . . . A cup of tea on the bed-
table. . . . In his racing dream he flashed the brightest, most charming
smile at his little hostess.

'No, thanks. Not just now.'

And still hoping it would not be any trouble to me he went out of the
room and closed the door, and we heard him cross the passage.

I scalded myself with mine in my hurry to take the cup back to the table
and to say as I stood there: 'You must forgive me if I am impertinent . . . if
I am too frank. But Dick hasn't tried to disguise it—has he? There is
something the matter. Can I help?'

(Soft music. Mouse gets up, walks the stage for a moment or so before
she returns to her chair and pours him out, oh, such a brimming, such

a burning cup that the tears come into the friend's eyes while he sips—while he drains it to the bitter dregs. . . .)

I had time to do all this before she replied. First she looked in the teapot, filled it with hot water, and stirred it with a spoon.

'Yes, there is something the matter. No, I'm afraid you can't help, thank you.' Again I got that glimmer of a smile. 'I'm awfully sorry. It must be horrid for you.'

Horrid, indeed! Ah, why couldn't I tell her that it was months and months since I had been so entertained?

'But you are suffering,' I ventured softly, as though that was what I could not bear to see.

She didn't deny it. She nodded and bit her under-lip and I thought I saw her chin tremble.

'And there is really nothing I can do?' More softly still.

She shook her head, pushed back the table and jumped up.

'Oh, it will be all right soon,' she breathed, walking over to the dressing-table and standing with her back towards me. 'It will be all right. It can't go on like this.'

'But of course it can't.' I agreed, wondering whether it would look heartless if I lit a cigarette; I had a sudden longing to smoke.

In some way she saw my hand move to my breast pocket, half draw out my cigarette case and put it back again, for the next thing she said was: 'Matches . . . in . . . candlestick. I noticed them.'

And I heard from her voice that she was crying.

'Ah! thank you. Yes. Yes. I've found them.' I lighted my cigarette and walked up and down, smoking.

It was so quiet it might have been two o'clock in the morning. It was so quiet you heard the boards creak and pop as one does in a house in the country. I smoked the whole cigarette and stabbed the end into my saucer before Mouse turned round and came back to the table.

'Isn't Dick being rather a long time?'

'You are very tired. I expect you want to go to bed,' I said kindly. (And pray don't mind me if you do, said my mind.)

'But isn't he being a very long time?' she insisted.

I shrugged. 'He is, rather.'

Then I saw she looked at me strangely. She was listening.

'He's been gone ages,' she said, and she went with little light steps to the door, opened it, and crossed the passage into his room.

I waited. I listened too, now. I couldn't have borne to miss a word. She had left the door open. I stole across the room and looked after her. Dick's door was open, too. But—there wasn't a word to miss.

You know I had the mad idea that they were kissing in that quiet room—a long, comfortable kiss. One of those kisses that not only puts one's grief to bed, but nurses it and warms it and tucks it up and keeps it fast enfolded until it is sleeping sound. Ah! how good that is.

It was over at last. I heard someone move and tiptoed away.

It was Mouse. She came back. She felt her way into the room carrying the letter for me. But it wasn't in an envelope; it was just a sheet of paper and she held it by the corner as though it was still wet.

Her head was bent so low—so tucked in her furry collar that I hadn't a notion—until she let the paper fall and almost fell herself on to the floor by the side of the bed, leaned her cheek against it, flung out her hands as though the last of her poor little weapons was gone and now she let herself be carried away, washed out into the deep water.

Flash! went my mind. Dick has shot himself, and then a succession of flashes while I rushed in, saw the body, head unharmed, small blue hole over temple, roused hotel, arranged funeral, attended funeral, closed cab, new morning coat. . . .

I stooped down and picked up the paper, and would you believe it— so ingrained is my Parisian sense of *comme il faut*—I murmured 'pardon' before I read it.

MOUSE, MY LITTLE MOUSE,

It's no good. It's impossible. I can't see it through. Oh, I do love you. I do love you, Mouse, but I can't hurt her. People have been hurting her all her life. I simply dare not give her this final blow. You see, though she's stronger than both of us, she's so frail and proud. It would kill her—kill her, Mouse. And, oh God, I can't kill my mother! Not even for you. Not even for us. You do see that—don't you.

It all seemed so possible when we talked and planned, but the very moment the train started it was all over. I felt her drag me back to her—calling. I can hear her now as I write. And she's alone and she doesn't know. A man would have to be a devil to tell her and I'm not a devil, Mouse. She mustn't know. Oh, Mouse, somewhere, somewhere in you don't you agree? It's all so unspeakably awful that I don't know if I want to go or not. Do I? Or is Mother just dragging me? I don't know. My head is too tired. Mouse, Mouse—what will you do? But I can't think of that, either. I dare not. I'd break down. And I must not break down. All I've got to do is—just to tell you this and go. I couldn't have gone off without telling you. You'd have been frightened. And you must not be frightened. You won't— will you? I can't bear—but no more of that. And don't write. I should not have the courage to answer your letters and the sight of your spidery handwriting— Forgive me. Don't love me any more. Yes. Love me. Love me.—DICK.

What do you think of that? Wasn't that a rare find? My relief at his not having shot himself was mixed with a wonderful sense of elation. I was even—more than even with my 'that's very curious and interesting' Eng-lishman. . . .

She wept so strangely. With her eyes shut, with her face quite calm except for the quivering eyelids. The tears pearled down her cheeks and she let them fall.

But feeling my glance upon her she opened her eyes and saw me holding the letter.

'You've read it?'

Her voice was quite calm, but it was not her voice any more. It was like the voice you might imagine coming out of a tiny, cold sea-shell swept high and dry at last by the salt tide. . . .

I nodded, quite overcome, you understand, and laid the letter down.

'It's incredible! incredible!' I whispered.

At that she got up from the floor, walked over to the wash-stand, dipped her handkerchief into the jug and sponged her eyes, saying: 'Oh, no. It's not incredible at all.' And still pressing the wet ball to her eyes she came back to me, to her chair with the lace tabs, and sank into it.

'I knew all along, of course,' said the cold, salty little voice. 'From the very moment that we started. I felt it all through me, but I still went on hoping—' and here she took the handkerchief down and gave me a final glimmer—'as one so stupidly does, you know.'

'As one does.'

Silence.

'But what will you do? You'll go back? You'll see him?'

That made her sit right up and stare across at me.

'What an extraordinary idea!' she said, more coldly than ever. 'Of course I shall not dream of seeing him. As for going back—that is quite out of the question. I can't go back.'

'But . . .'

'It's impossible. For one thing all my friends think I am married.'

I put out my hand—'Ah, my poor little friend.'

But she shrank away. (False move.)

Of course, there was one question that had been at the back of my mind all this time. I hated it.

'Have you any money?'

'Yes, I have twenty pounds—here,' and she put her hand on her breast. I bowed. It was a great deal more than I had expected.

'And what are your plans?'

Yes, I know. My question was the most clumsy, the most idiotic one I could have put. She had been so tame, so confiding, letting me, at any rate spiritually speaking, hold her tiny, quivering body in one hand and stroke her furry head—and now, I'd thrown her away. Oh, I could have kicked myself.

She stood up. 'I have no plans. But—it's very late. You must go now, please.'

How could I get her back? I wanted her back. I swear I was not acting then.

'Do feel that I am your friend,' I cried. 'You will let me come to-morrow, early? You will let me look after you a little—take care of you a little? You'll use me just as you think fit?'

I succeeded. She came out of her hole . . . timid . . . but she came out.

'Yes, you're very kind. Yes. Do come to-morrow. I shall be glad. It makes things rather difficult because—' and again I clasped her boyish hand—'*je ne parle pas français.*'

Not until I was half-way down the boulevard did it come over me—the full force of it.

Why, they were suffering . . . those two . . . really suffering. I have seen two people suffer as I don't suppose I ever shall again. . . .

Of course you know what to expect. You anticipate, fully, what I am going to write. It wouldn't be me, otherwise.

I never went near the place again.

Yes, I still owe that considerable amount for lunches and dinners, but that's beside the mark. It's vulgar to mention it in the same breath with the fact that I never saw Mouse again.

Naturally, I intended to. Started out—got to the door—wrote and tore up letters—did all those things. But I simply could not make the final effort.

Even now I don't fully understand why. Of course I knew that I couldn't have kept it up. That had a great deal to do with it. But you would have thought, putting it as its lowest, curiosity couldn't have kept my fox-terrier nose away. . . .

Je ne parle pas français. That was her swan song for me.

But how she makes me break my rule. Oh, you've seen for yourself, but I could give you countless examples.

. . . Evenings, when I sit in some gloomy café, and an automatic piano starts playing a 'mouse' tune (there are dozens of tunes that evoke just her) I begin to dream things like . . .

A little house on the edge of the sea, somewhere far, far away. A girl outside in a frock rather like Red Indian women wear, hailing a light, barefoot boy who runs up from the beach.

'What have you got?'

'A fish.' I smile and give it to her.

. . . The same girl, the same boy, different costumes—sitting at an open window, eating fruit and leaning out and laughing.

'All the wild strawberries are for you, Mouse. I won't touch one.'

. . . A wet night. They are going home together under an umbrella. They stop on the door to press their wet cheeks together.

And so on and so on until some dirty old gallant comes up to my table and sits opposite and begins to grimace and yap. Until I hear myself saying: 'But I've got the little girl for you, *mon vieux*. So little . . . so tiny.' I kiss the tips of my fingers and lay them upon my heart. 'I give you my word of honour as a gentleman, a writer, serious, young, and extremely interested in modern English literature.'

I must go. I must go. I reach down my coat and hat. Madame knows me. 'You haven't dined yet?' she smiles.

'No, not yet, Madame.'

F. M. MAYOR

Miss de Mannering of Asham

❧

My dear Evelyn,

As you say you really are interested in this experience of mine, I am doing what you asked, and writing you an account of it. You can accept it as a token of friendship for, to tell you the truth, I had been trying to forget it, whatever it was. I hope in the end to bring myself to the belief that I never had it, but at present my remembrance is more vivid than I care for.

> Yours affectionately
> MARGARET LATIMER

You remember my friend, Kate Ware? She had been ill, and she asked me to stay in lodgings with her at an East Coast resort. 'It is simply Brixton-by-the-Sea, with a dash of Kensington,' Kate wrote, 'but I ought to go, because my aunt lives there, and likes to see me. So come, if you can bear it.'

'I think we might take a day off,' said Kate one morning, after we had been there a week. 'Too much front makes me think there really is no England but this. Let's have some sandwiches, and bicycle out as far away as we can.'

We came to a wayside inn, so quiet, so undisturbed, so cheerful in its quietness, that we felt at last we had found the soothing and rest we were in need of. Yes, I suppose our nerves were a little unstrung; at any rate, being high school mistresses, we knew what nerves were. But hitherto I have felt capable of controlling mine, only, as Hamlet says, I have bad dreams. And Kate is rather strange by nature; I do not think her nerves make her any stranger.

'Now,' said Kate, when we had finished our meal—she always settles everything—'I propose we borrow the pony here, and have a drive. I don't like desecrating these solitary lanes, which have existed for generations and generations before bicycles, with anything more modern than Tommy.'

Kate generally wants to have a map, and know exactly where she is going, but to-day we agreed to take the first turn to the left, and see where it led to. It was a sleepy afternoon, and Tommy trotted so gently that we were all three dozing, before we had gone a mile or two. Then we came to what had been magnificent wrought iron gates with stone pillars on either side. The pillars were now ruined, and the wall beyond was falling down. Kate said, 'Let's go in.' I said it was private, but we did go in.

We came into an avenue of laurels, resembling the sepulchral shrub-beries with which our fathers and our fathers' fathers loved to surround their residences, only those were generally more serpentine. It must have been there many years, and had had time to grow so high as to block out almost all the sky. It was very narrow, and the dankness, the closeness, the black ground that never gets dry, which have always oppressed me in such places, seemed almost intolerable here. I thought we should never get out to the small piece of white light we saw at the end of it. At the same time I dreaded what I expected to find there; one of those great, lugubrious, black mausoleums of a mansion, which so often are the complement of the shrubbery. But this avenue seemed to have been planted at haphazard, for it led only to another gate, and that opened on a neglected park. We saw before us an expanse of unfertile-looking grass, and then the horizon was completely hidden by ridges of very heavy greenish-black trees. There were other trees scattered about; they looked very old, and some had been struck by lightning. I felt sorry for their wounds; it seemed as if no one cared whether they lived or died.

There was a small church standing at the left-hand corner of the park, so small that it must have been a chapel for the private worship of the owners of the park; but we thought they could not have valued their church, for there was actually no path to it, nothing but grass, long, rank and damp.

I do not know when it was that I became so certain that I abhorred parks, but I remember it came over me very strongly all of a sudden. I was extremely anxious that Kate should not know what I felt. However, I said to her that grandeur was oppressive, and that after all I preferred small gardens.

'Yes,' said Kate, 'one might feel too much enclosed, if one lived in a park, as if one could never get out, and as if other things. . . .'

Here Kate stopped. I asked her to go on, and she said that was all she had to say. I don't know if you want to hear these minute details, but nearly everything I have to tell you is merely a succession of minute details. I remember looking up at the sky, because I wanted to keep my eyes away from the distant trees. I did not like to see them—it seems a very poor reason for a woman of thirty-eight—because they were so black. When I was six years old, I was afraid of black, and also, though I loved the country, I used to feel a sense of fear and isolation, if the sun was not shining, and I was alone in a large field; but then a child's mind is open to every terror, or rather it creates a terror out of everything. I thought I had as much forgotten that condition as if I had never known it. I should have supposed the weight of my many grown-up years would have defended me, but I assure you that I felt all at once that I was—what after all we are—as much at the mercy of the universe as an insect.

I remember when I looked up at the sky I observed that it had changed. As we were coming it had had the ordinary pale no-colour aspect, which it bears for quite half the days in the year. Some people grumble at it, but it is very English, and if you do not like it, or more than like it, relish it, you cannot really relish England. The sky had now that strange appearance to which days in the north are liable; I do not think they know anything about it in Italy or the south of France. It is a fancy of mine that the sudden strangeness and wildness one finds in our literature is due to these days; it is something to compensate us for them.

If I said the day was dying, you would think of beautiful sunsets, and certainly the day could not be dying, for it was only three o'clock in the afternoon, but it looked ill; and the grey of the atmosphere was not that silvery grey, which I think the sweetest of all the skies in the year, but an unwholesome grey, which made the trees look blacker still. I should have felt it a relief if only it had begun to rain, then there would have been a noise; it was so utterly silent.

Just as I was wondering where I should turn my eyes next, Tommy came to a sudden stop, and nearly jerked us out of the cart. 'Clever,' said Kate, 'you're letting Tommy stumble.'

But it was simply that Tommy would not go on. He was such a mild little pony too, anxious, as Kate said, to do everything one asked, before one asked him.

'Tommy's frightened,' said Kate. 'He's all trembling and sweating.'

Kate got out, and tried to soothe him, but for some time it was very little good.

'It's another snub for the men of science,' said Kate. 'Tommy sees an angel in the way. Animals are very odd you know. Haven't you noticed dogs scurrying past ghosts in the twilight? I am so glad we haven't got their faculties.'

Then Tommy all at once surprised us by going on as quietly as before.

We drove a little further, and we came to the hall. It was built 150 years before the mausoleum period, but it could not well have been drearier, though it must formerly have been a noble Jacobean mansion. It was not that it looked out of repair; a house can be very cheerful, in fact rather more cheerful, if it is shabby. And here there was a terrace with greenhouse plants in stucco vases placed at intervals, and also a clean-shaven lawn, so that man must have been there recently; nevertheless it seemed as if it had been abandoned for years.

I cannot tell you how relieved I was when a respectable young man in shirt sleeves made his appearance. It is Kate generally who talks to strangers, but the moment he was in sight I felt I must cling to him, as a protection. I felt Tommy and Kate no protection.

I apologized for trespassing in private grounds.

'No trespassing at all, miss, I'm sure.' He went on to say he wished it happened oftener, Colonel Winterton, the owner, being hardly ever there, only liking to keep the place up with servants, and 'if there wasn't a number of us to make it lively, one room being shut up and all,' he really did not know—

It did not seem right to encourage him on the subject of a shut-up room; we changed the conversation, and asked him about the church.

He said it was a very ancient church, and there was tombs and that, people came a wonderful way to see. Not that he cared much about them himself.

Kate, who is fond of sight-seeing, declared she would visit the church.

I would not go, though I should like to have seen the tombs. I said I must hold the pony. The young man said he was a groom, and would hold the pony for us. Then I said I was tired: Kate said she would go alone. She started.

'Don't go down there, miss,' said the groom, 'the grass is so wet. Round by the right it's better.'

His way looked the same as hers to me, but Kate followed his advice.

I talked to the groom while Kate was away, and I was glad to hear that he liked the pictures in reason, and that his father was a saddler, living in the High Street of some small town. This was cheerful and distracting to my thoughts, and I had managed to become so much interested that it was the young man who said, 'There's the lady coming back.'

'Well,' I said, 'what was the church like?'

'It was locked,' Kate answered, 'however, it was nice outside.'

'But Kate,' I said, 'how pale you are!'

'Of course I am,' said Kate. 'I always am.'

The young man hastened to ask if he should get Kate a glass of water.

'Oh dear no, thank you,' said Kate. 'But I think we might be going now. Is there any other road out? I don't want to drive exactly the same way back.'

There was, and we set off. As soon as we had said good-bye to the young man, Kate began: 'About Grace Martin; what do you think of her chances for the Certificate?' and we talked about the Certificate until we got back to the inn. As to that oppressed feeling, I could hardly imagine now what it was. It had passed, and the world seemed its usual dear, safe self, irritating and comfortable. It was clearing up, and the trees and hedges looked as they generally look at the end of August. They were dusty and a little shabby, showing here and there a red leaf, occasional bits of toadflax, and all those little yellow flowers whose names one forgets, but to which one turns tenderly in recollection, when seeing the beauty of foreign lands. My thoughts broke away from our conversation now and then to wonder what I could possibly have been afraid of.

They gave us tea at Tommy's home, and the innkeeper's wife was glad to have some conversation.

'Yes, the poor old Hall, it seems a pity the Colonel coming down so seldom. He only bought it seven years ago, and he seems tired of it already, and then only bringing gentlemen. Gentlemen spend more, but I always think there's more life with ladies. It's changed hands so often. Yes, there's a shut-up room. They say it was something about a housemaid many years ago and a baby, if you'll excuse my mentioning it, but I'm sure I couldn't say. If you listen to all the tales in a village like this, in a little place you know, one says one thing and one another. I come from Norwich myself.'

'The church looks rather dismal,' said Kate. 'The churchyard is so overgrown.'

'Yes, poor Mr Fuller, he's a nice gentleman, though he is so high. First when he come there was great goings on, services and antics. He says to me, "Tell me, Mrs Gage, is that why the people don't come?" "Oh," I says, "well, of course, I've been about, and seen life, so whether it's high or low, I just take no notice." I said that to put him off, poor gentleman, because it wasn't that. They won't come at all hardly after dark, particularly November; December it's better again; and for his communion service, what he sets his heart on so, we have such a small party, sometimes hardly more than two or three, and then he gets so downhearted. He seems to have lost all his spirit now.'

'But why is it better in December?'

'I'm sure I couldn't tell you, miss, but they always say those things is worse in November. I always heard my grandfather say that.'

I had rather expected that what I had forgotten in the day would come back at night, and about two, when I was reading *Framley Parsonage* with all possible resolution, I heard a knock at the door, and Kate came in.

'I saw your light,' said she. 'I can't sleep either. I think you felt uncomfortable in the park too, didn't you? Your face betrays you rather easily, you know. Going to the church, at least not going first of all, but as I got near the church, and the churchyard—ugh! However, I am *not* going to be conquered by a thought, and I mean to go there to-morrow. Still, I think, if you don't very much mind, I should like to sleep in here.'

I asked her to get into my bed.

'Thank you, I will,' said she. 'It's very good of you, Margaret, for I'm sure you loathe sharing somebody's bed as much as I do, but things being as they are—'

The next morning Kate was studying the guidebook at breakfast.

'Here we are,' said she. '"Asham Hall is a fine Jacobean mansion. The church, which is situated in the park, was originally the private chapel of the de Mannerings. Many members of the family are buried there, and their tombs are well worth a visit. The inscriptions in Norman French are of particular interest. The keys can be obtained from the sexton." Nothing about the shut-up room; I suppose we could hardly hope for it. We must see the tombs, don't you think so?'

Kate was one who very rarely showed her feelings, and I knew better than to refer to last night.

We bicycled to the Hall. It was a very sweet, bright windy morning, such a morning as would have pleased Wordsworth, I think, and may have brought forth many a poem from him.

'Now,' said Kate, 'when we get into the park, we'll walk our bicycles over the grass to the church.'

I began: then exactly the same feeling came over me as before, only this time there could be nothing in calm, beautiful nature to have produced it. The trees, though dark, did not look at all sinister, but stately and benignant, as they often do in late August, and early September. Whatever it was, it was within me. I felt I could not go to the church.

'You go on alone,' I said.

'You'd better come,' said Kate. 'I know just what you feel, but it will be worse here by yourself.'

'I think perhaps I won't,' I said.

'Very well,' said Kate. 'Bicycle on and meet me at the other gate.'

I said I was a coward, and Kate said she did not think it mattered being a coward. I meant to start at once, but I found something wrong with the bicycle. It took quite half an hour to repair, but as I was repairing it all my oppression passed, and I felt light and at ease. By the time I was ready, Kate had visited the tombs, and was coming out of the church door. I looked at her going down the path, and saw there was another woman in the churchyard. She was walking rather slowly. She came up behind Kate, then passed quite close to Kate on her left side. I was too far off to see her face. I felt thankful Kate had someone with her. I mounted; when I looked again the woman was gone.

I met Kate outside the church. She always had odd eyes; now they had a glittering look, half scared and half excited, which made me very uncomfortable. I asked her if she had spoken to the woman about the church.

'What woman? Where?' said Kate.

'The one in the churchyard just now.'

'I didn't see anyone.'

'You must have. She passed quite close to you.'

'Did she?' said Kate. 'She passed on my left side then?'

'Yes, she did. How did you know?'

'Oh, I don't know. We give the keys in here, and let's bicycle home fast, it's turned so cold.'

I always think Kate rather manlike, and she was manlike in her extreme moodiness. If anything of any sort went wrong, she clothed herself in a mood, and became impenetrable. Such a mood came on her now.

'I don't know why I never will tell things at the time,' said Kate next day. It was raining, and we were sitting over a nice little fire after tea. 'It's a sign of great feebleness of mind, I think. However, if you like to hear about Asham Church, you shall. I saw the tombs, and they are all that they should be. I hope the de Mannerings were worthy of them. But the church; perhaps being a clergyman's daughter made me take it so much to heart, but there was a filthy old carpet rolled up on the altar, all the draperies are full of holes, the paint is coming off, part of the chancel rail is broken, and it seems an abode of insects. I did not know there were such forsaken churches in England. That rather spoilt the tombs for me, also an uncomfortable idea that I did not want to look behind me; I don't know what I thought I was going to see. However, I gave every tomb its due. Then, when I was in the churchyard, I had the same feeling as last time; I could not get it out of my head that something I did not like was going to happen the next minute. Then I had that sensation, which books call the blood running chill; that really means, I think, a catch in one's heart as if one cannot breathe; and at the same time I had such an acute consciousness of someone standing at my left side that I almost felt I was being pushed, no one being there at all, you understand. That lasted a second, I should think, but after that I felt as if I were an intruder in the churchyard, and had better go.'

One afternoon a week later, the great-aunt of the smart townlike landlady at our lodgings came to clear away tea. First of all she was deferential and overwhelmed, but I have never known anyone have such a way with old ladies and gentlemen of the agricultural classes as Kate. In a few moments Mrs Croucher was sitting on the sofa with Kate beside her.

'Asham Hall,' said she. 'Why, my dear mother was sewing maid there, when she was a girl. Oh dear me, yes, the times she's told me about it all. Oh, it's a beautiful place, and them lovely laurels in the avenue, where Miss de Mannering was so fond of walking. It was the old gentleman, Mr de Mannering, he planted them; they was to have gone right up to the Hall, so they say. There was to be wonderful improvements, he was to have pulled down the old Hall and built something better, and then he hadn't the money. Yes, even then it was going down, for Mr William, that was the only son, that lived abroad, he was so wild. Yes, my mother was there in the family's time, not with them things which hev a-took it since.'

'You don't think much of Colonel Winterton, then?'

'Oh, I daresay he's a kind sort of gentleman, they say he's very free at Christmas with coals and that, but them new people they comes and goes, it stands to reason they can't be like the family. In the village we calls them jumped-up bit-of-a-things, but I'm sure I've nothing to say against Colonel Winterton.'

'Are there any of the family still here?'

'Oh no, mum. They've all gone. Some says there's a Mr de Mannering still in America, but he's never been near the place.'

'It's very sad when the old families go,' said Kate sympathetically.

'Oh, it is, mum. Poor old Mr de Mannering; but the place wasn't sold till after his death. My mother, she did feel it.'

'Was there a room shut up in your mother's time, Mrs Croucher?'

'Not when she first went there, mum.'

'It was a housemaid, wasn't it?'

'Not a housemaid,' with a look of important mystery. 'That's what they say, and it's better it *should* be said; I shouldn't tell it to everybody, but I don't mind telling a lady like you; it wasn't a housemaid at all.'

'Not a housemaid?'

'No; my mother's often told me. Miss de Mannering, she was a very high lady, well, she was a lady that *was* a lady, if you catch my meaning, and she must have been six or seven and forty, when she was took with her last illness. And the night before she died, my mother she was sitting sewing in Mrs Packe's room (she was the lady's maid, my mother was sewing maid, you know) and she heard Doctor Mason say, "Don't take any notice of what Miss de Mannering says, Mrs Packe. People get very odd fancies, when they're ill," he says. And she says, "No, sir, I won't," and she comes straight to my mother, and she says, "If you could hear the way she's a-going on. 'Oh, my baby,' she says, 'if I could have seen him smile. Oh, if he had lived just one day, one hour, even one moment.' I says to her, says Mrs Packe to my mother, 'Your baby, ma'am, whatever are you talking about?' It was such a peculiar thing for her to say," says

Mrs Packe. "Don't you think so, Bessie?" Bessie was my mother. "I'm sure I don't know," says my mother; she never liked Mrs Packe. "Miss de Mannering didn't take no notice," Mrs Packe went on, "then she says, 'If only I'd buried him in the churchyard.' So I says to her, 'But where did you bury him then, ma'am?' and fancy! she turns round, and looks at me, and she says, 'I burnt him'." Well, that's the truth, that's what my mother told me, and she always said, my mother did, Mrs Packe had no call to repeat such a thing.'

'I think your mother was quite right,' said Kate. 'Burnt! Poor Miss de Mannering must have been delirious. It is such a frightful. . . .'

'No, my mother didn't like carrying tales about the family,' said Mrs Croucher, engaged on quite a different line of thought. And whether it was that she had heard the story so often, or whether it was that they are still more inured to horrors in the country—I have observed far stranger things happen in the country than in the town—Mrs Croucher did not seem to have any idea that she was relating what was terrible. On the contrary, I think she found it homely, recalling a happy part of her childhood.

'Then,' went on Mrs Croucher, 'Mrs Packe, she says to my mother, "You come and hear her," she says, and my mother says, "I don't like to, whatever would she say?" "Oh," says Mrs Packe, "she don't take any notice of anything, you come and peep in at the door." "So I went," my mother says, "and I just peeped in, but I couldn't see anything, only just Miss de Mannering lying in bed, for there was no candle, only the firelight. Only I heard Miss de Mannering give a terrible sigh, and say very faint, but you could hear her quite plain, 'Oh, if only I'd buried him in the churchyard.' I wouldn't stay any longer," says my mother, "and Miss de Mannering died at seven in the evening next day." Whenever my mother spoke of it to me, she always said, "I only regretted going into her room once, and that was all my life. It was taking a liberty, which never should have been took."'

'But,' said Kate, framing the question with difficulty, 'did anybody —? Had anybody had a suspicion that Miss de Mannering—?'

'No, mum. Miss de Mannering was always very reserved, she was not a lady that was at all free in her ways like some ladies; not like you are, if you'll excuse me, mum. Not that I mean she would have said anything to anyone of course, and she had no relations, no sisters, and they never had no company at the Hall, and the old gentleman, he'd married very late in life, so he was what you might call aged, and the servants was terrible afraid of him, his temper was so bad; even Miss de Mannering had a wonderful dread of him, they said.

'There was a deal of talk among the servants after what Mrs Packe said, and there was a housemaid, she'd been in the family a long time, and she remembered one winter years before, I daresay eighteen or twenty years before, Miss de Mannering was ailing, and she sent away her maid, and then she didn't sleep in her own room, but in a room in another part of the house not near anyone, that's the room they shut up, mum. And they remembered once she was ill for months and months, and her nurse that lived at Selby, when she was very old, she got a-talking as sometimes old people will, she died years after Miss de Mannering, and she let out what she would have done better to keep to herself.

'It wasn't long after Miss de Mannering's death they began to say you could see her come out of that there room, walk down the stairs, out at the front door, down through the park, along the avenue, and back again to the house, and then across the park to the churchyard. And of course they say she's trying to find a place for her baby. Then there's some as says Mr Northfield, what lived at Asham before Colonel Winterton came, he saw her. They say that's why he sold it. Mr Fuller they say he's spoke to her; they say that's why he's turned so quiet.

'Then there's some say, Miss Jarvis—she kept The Blue Boar in the village, when I was a girl—she used to say, that Miss Emily Robinson, the daughter of Sir Thomas Robinson, who bought the place from Mr Seaton, who bought it after Mr de Mannering's death—he wasn't much of a "Sir" to my mind, just kept a draper's shop in London, the saying was—she was took very sudden with the heart disease, and was found dead, flat on her face in the avenue. Of course the tale was, she met Miss de Mannering and she laid a hand on her. The footman that was attending Miss Robinson—she was regular pomped up with pride *she* was, and always would have a footman after her—he says he *see* a woman quite plain come up behind her, and then she fell. He told Mr Jarvis. Poor Mrs Dicey—they was at the Hall before the Northfields—she went off sudden too at the end, but she was always sickly, and I don't hold with all those tales myself.

'But people will believe anything. Why, not long ago, well, perhaps twenty years ago, in Northfield's time, there was a footman got one of the housemaids into trouble, and of course there's new people about in the village since the family went, and they say the room was shut up along of *her*. It's really ridickerlous.'

'Did you ever see her, Mrs Croucher?'

'Not to say see her, mum, but more than once as I've been walking in the park, I've *heard* her quite plain behind me. That was in November. November is the month, as you very well know, mum,'—I could see Kate was gratified that it was supposed she should know—'and you could hear the leaves a-rustling as she walked. There's no need to be frightened, if you don't take no notice, and just walk straight on. They won't never harm you; they only gives you a chill.'

'Did your mother ever see her?'

'If she did, she never would say so. My mother wouldn't have any tales against Miss de Mannering. She said she never had any complaints to make. There was a young man treated my mother badly, and one day she was crying, and Miss de Mannering heard her, and she comes into the sewing-room, and she says, "What is it?" and my mother told her, and Miss de Mannering spoke very feeling, and said, "It's very sad, Bessie, but life is very sad." In general Miss de Mannering never spoke to anybody.

'My mother bought a picture of Miss de Mannering, if you young ladies would like to see it. Everything was in great confusion when Mr de Mannering died. Nothing had been touched for years, and there were all Miss de Mannering's dresses and her private things. No one had looked through them since her death. So what my mother could afford to buy she did, and she left them to me, and charged me to see they should never fall into hands that would not take care of them. There's a lot of writing I know, but I'm not much of a scholar myself, though my dear mother was, and I can't tell you what it's all about, not that my mother had read Miss de Mannering's papers, for she said that would never have been her place.'

Mrs Croucher went to her bedroom and brought us the papers and the portrait. It was a water-colour drawing dated Bath, 1805. The artist had done his best for Miss de Mannering with the blue sash to match the bit of blue sky, and the coral necklace to match her coral lips. The likeness presented to us was that of a young woman, dark, pale, thin, elegant, lady-like, long-nosed and plain. One gathers from pictures that such a type was not uncommon at that period. I should have been afraid of Miss de Mannering from her mouth and the turn of the head, they were so proud and aristocratic, but I loved her sad, timid eyes, which seemed appealing for kindness and protection.

Mrs Croucher was anxious to give Kate the portrait, 'for none of 'em don't care for my old things.' Kate refused. 'But after you are gone,' she said, for she knows that all such as Mrs Croucher are ready to discuss their deaths openly, 'if your niece will send her to me, I should like to have Miss de Mannering; I shall prize her very much.'

Then Mrs Croucher withdrew, 'for I shall be tiring you two young ladies with my talk.' It is rather touching how poor people, however old and feeble, think that everything will tire 'a lady,' however young and robust.

We turned to Miss de Mannering's papers. It was strange to look at something, written over a century ago, so long put by and never read. I had a terrible sensation of intruding, but Kate said she thought, if we were going to be as fastidious as all that, life would never get on at all. So I have copied out the narrative for you. I am sure, if Mrs Croucher knew you, she would feel you worthy to share the signal honour she conferred on us.

MISS DE MANNERING'S NARRATIVE

It is now twenty-two years since, yet the events of the year 1805 are engraved upon my memory with greater accuracy than those of any other in my life. It is to escape their pressing so heavily upon my brain that I commit them to paper, confiding to the pages of a book what may never be related to a human friend.

Had my lot been one more in accordance with that of other young women of my position, I might have been preserved from the calamity which befell me. But we are in the hands of a merciful Creator, who appoints to each his course. I sinned of my own free will, nor do I seek to mitigate my sin. My mother, Lady Jane de Mannering, daughter of the Earl of Poveril, died when I was five years old. She entrusted me to the care of a faithful governess and nurse, and owing to their affectionate solicitude in childhood and girlhood I hardly missed a mother's care. Of my father I saw but little. He was violent and moody. My brother, fourteen years older than I, was already causing him the greatest anxiety by his dissipation. Some words of my father's, and a chance remark, lightly spoken in my hearing, made an ineffaceable impression on me. In the unusual solitude of my existence I had ample, too ample, leisure to brood over recollections which had best be forgotten. Cheerful thoughts, natural to my age, should have left them no room in my heart. When I was thirteen years old, my father said to me one day, 'I don't want you skulking here, you're too much of a Poveril. Everyone knows that a Poveril once, for all their pride, stooped to marry a French waiting-maid. That's why every man Jack of them is black and sallow, as you are.' I fled from the room in terror.

Another day Miss Fanshawe was talking with the governess of a young lady who had come to spend the afternoon with me. They were walking behind us, and I heard their conversation.

'Is not Miss Maynard beautiful?' said Miss Adams. 'I believe that golden hair and brilliant eye will make a sensation even in London. What a pity Miss de Mannering is so black! Fair beauties are all the rage they say, and her eyes are too small.'

'Beauty is a very desirable possession for a young woman,' said Miss

Fanshawe, 'but one which is perhaps too highly valued. Anyone may have beauty; a milkmaid may have beauty; but there is an air of rank and breeding which outlasts beauty, and is, I believe, more prized by a man of fastidious taste. Such an air is possessed by Miss de Mannering in a remarkable degree.'

My kind, beloved Fan! but at fifteen how much rather would I have shared the gift possessed by milkmaids! From henceforth I was certain I should not please.

Miss Fanshawe, who never failed to give me the encouragement and confidence I lacked, died when I was seventeen and had reached the age which, above all others in a woman's life, requires the comfort and protection of a female friend. My father, more and more engrossed with money difficulties, made no arrangement for my introduction to the world. He had no relations, but my mother's sisters had several times invited me to visit them. My father however, who was on bad terms with the family, would not permit me to go. The most rigid economy was necessary. He would allow no guests to be invited, and therefore no invitations to be accepted. The Hall was situated in a very solitary part of the country, and it was rare indeed for any visitor to find his way thither. My brother was forbidden the house. Months, nay years passed, and I saw no one.

Suddenly my father said to me one day, 'You are twenty-five, so that cursed lawyer of the Poverils tells me; twenty-five, and not yet married. I have no money to leave you after my death. Write and tell your aunt at Bath that you will visit her, and she must find you a husband.'

Secluded from society as I had been, the prospect of leaving the Hall and being plunged into the world of fashion filled me with the utmost apprehension. 'I entreat you, sir, to excuse me,' I cried. 'Let me stay here. I ask nothing from you, but I cannot go to Bath.'

I fell on my knees before him, but he would take no denial, and a few weeks after I found myself at Bath.

My aunt, Lady Theresa Lindsay, a widow, was one of the gayest in that gay city, and especially this season, for she was introducing her daughter Miss Leonora.

My father had given me ten pounds to buy myself clothes for my visit, but, entirely inexperienced as I was, I acquitted myself ill.

'My dear creature,' said my cousin in a coaxing manner that could not wound. 'Poor Nancy in the scullery would blush to see herself like you. You must hide yourself completely from the world for the next few days like the monks of La Trappe, and put yourself in Mamma's hands and mine. After that time I doubt not Miss Sophia de Mannering will rival the fashionable toast Lady Charlotte Harper.'

My dear Leonora did all in her power to set me off to the best advantage, to praise and encourage me, and my formidable aunt was kind for my mother's sake. But my terror at the crowd of gentlemen, that filled my aunt's drawing-room, was not easily allayed.

'I tremble at their approach,' I said to Leonora.

'Tremble at their approach?' said Leonora. 'But it is their part to tremble at ours, my little cousin, to tremble with hopes that we shall be kind, or with fears that we shall not. I say my little cousin, because I am a giantess,' she was very tall and exquisitely beautiful, 'and also I am very old and experienced, and you are to look up to me in everything.'

I wished to have remained retired at the assemblies, but Leonora always sought me out, and presented her partners to me. But my awkwardness and embarrassment soon wearied them, and after such attentions as courtesy required they left me for more congenial company. Certainly I could not blame them; it was what I had anticipated. Yet the mortification wounded me and I said to my cousin, 'It is of no use, Leonora. I can never, never hope to please.'

'Those who fish diligently,' she replied, 'shall not go unrewarded. A gentleman said to me this evening, "Your cousin attracts me; she has so much countenance." Captain Phillimore is accounted a connoisseur in our sex. That is a large fish, and I congratulate you with all my heart.'

Captain Phillimore came constantly to my aunt's house. Once he entered into conversation with me. Afterwards he sought me out; at first I could not believe it possible, but again he sought me out, and yet again.

'Captain Phillimore is a connexion not to be despised by the ancient house of de Mannering,' said my aunt. 'There are tales of his extravagance it is true, and other matters; but the family is wealthy, and of what man of fashion are not such tales related? Marriage will steady him.'

Weeks passed by. It was now April. My aunt was to leave Bath in a few days, and I was to return home; the season was drawing to its close. My aunt was giving a farewell reception to her friends. Captain Phillimore drew me into an anteroom adjoining one of the drawing-rooms. He told me that he loved me, that he had loved me from the moment he first saw me. He kissed me. Never, never can I forget the bliss of that moment. 'There are,' he said, 'important reasons why our engagement must at present be known only to ourselves. As soon as it is possible I will apprise my father, and hasten to Asham to obtain Mr de Mannering's consent. Till then not a word to your aunt. It will be safest not even to correspond.' He told me that he had been summoned suddenly to join his regiment in Ireland and must leave Bath the following day. 'I must therefore see you once more before I go. The night is as warm as summer. Have you the resolution to meet me in an hour's time in the garden? We must enjoy a few minutes' solitude away from the teasing crowd.'

I, who was usually timid, had now no fears. I easily escaped unnoticed. The whole household was occupied with the reception. At the end of a long terrace there was an arbour. Here we met. He urged me to give myself entirely to him, using the wicked sophistries which had been circulated by the infidel philosophers of France; that marriage is a superstitious form with no value for the more enlightened of mankind. But alas, there was no need of sophistries. Whatever he had proposed, had he bidden me throw myself over a precipice, I should have obeyed. I loved him as no weak mortal should be loved. When his bright blue eye gazed into mine, and his hand caressed me, I sank before him as a worshipper before a shrine. With my eyes fully open I yielded to him.

I returned to the house. My absence had not been observed. My cousin came to my room, and said with her arch smile, 'I ask no question, I am too proud to beg for confidences. But I know what I know. Kiss me, and receive my blessing.'

I retired to rest, and could not sleep all night for feverish exaltation. It was not till the next day that I recognized my guilt. I hardly dared look my aunt and cousin in the face, but my demeanour passed unnoticed; for during the morning a Russian nobleman attached to the Imperial court, who had been paying Leonora great attentions, solicited her hand and was accepted. In the ensuing agitation I was forgotten, and my proposal that I should return to Asham a day or two earlier was welcomed. My aunt was anxious to go to London without delay to begin preparations for the wedding.

She made me a cordial farewell, engaging me to accompany her to Bath next year. 'But, Mamma,' said Leonora, 'I think Captain Phillimore will have something to say to that. All I stipulate is that Captain and Mrs Phillimore shall be my first visitors at St Petersburgh.'

Their kindness went through me like a knife, and I returned to Asham with a heavy heart.

'Where is your husband?' was my father's greeting.

'I have none, sir,' said I.

'The more fool you,' he answered, and asked no further particulars of my visit.

Time passed on. Every day I hoped for the appearance of Captain Phillimore. In vain; he came not. Certainty was succeeded by hope, hope by doubt, doubt by dread. I would not, I could not despair. Ere long it was evident that I was to become a mother. The horror of this discovery, with my total ignorance of Captain Phillimore's whereabouts, caused me the most miserable perturbation. I walked continually with the fever of madness along the laurel avenue and in the Park. I went to the Church, hoping that there I might find consolation, but the memorials of former de Mannerings reminded me too painfully that I alone of all the women of the family had brought dishonour on our name.

I longed to pour out my misery to some human ear, even though I exposed my disgrace. There was but one in my solitude whom I could trust; my old nurse, who lived at Selby three miles off. I walked thither one summer evening, and with many tears I told her all. She mingled her tears with mine. I was her nursling, she did not shrink from me. All in her power she would do for me. She knew a discreet woman in Ipswich, whither she might arrange for me to go as my time approached, who would later take charge of the infant. She suggested all that could be done to allay suspicion in the household and village.

At first my aunt and cousin wrote constantly, and even after Leonora's marriage I continued to hear from Russia. My letters were short and cold. When I knew that I was to be a mother, I could not bear to have further communication with them. My aunt wrote to me kindly and reproach-fully. I did not answer, and gradually all correspondence ceased. Yet their affectionate letters were all I had to cheer the misery of those ensuing months. I shall never forget them. Although it was now summer, the weather was almost continuously gloomy and tempestuous. There were many thunder storms, which wrought havoc among our elm trees in the Park. The rushing of the wind at night through the heavy branches and the falling of the rain against my window gave me an indescribable feeling of apprehension, so that I hid my head under the bedclothes that I might hear nothing. Yet more terrible to me were the long days of August, when the leaden sky oppressed my spirit, and it seemed as if I and the world alike were dead. I struggled against the domination of such fancies, fan-cies perhaps not uncommon in my condition, and in general soothed by the tenderness of an indulgent husband. I could imagine such tenderness. Night and day Captain Phillimore was in my thoughts. No female pride came to my aid; I loved him more passionately than ever.

On the 20th November some ladies visited us at the Hall. We had a common bond in two cousins of theirs I had met frequently in Bath. They talked of our mutual acquaintance. At length Captain Phillimore's name was mentioned. Shall I ever forget those words? 'Have you heard the tale of Captain Phillimore, the all-conquering Captain Phillimore? Major Richardson, who was an intimate of his at Bath, told my brother that he said to him at the beginning of the season, "What do you bet me that in one season I shall successfully assault the virtue of the three most innocent and immaculate maids, old or young, in Bath? Easy virtue has no charms for me, I prefer the difficult, but my passion is for the impregnable," and Major Richardson assures my brother that Captain Phillimore won his bet. Mr de Mannering, we are telling very shocking scandals; three ladies of strict virtue fallen in one season at Bath. What is the world coming to?'

My father had appeared to pay little heed to their chatter, but he now burst forth, 'If any woman lets her virtue be assaulted by a rake, she's a rake herself. Should such a fate befall a daughter of mine, I should first horsewhip her, and then turn her from my doors.'

During this conversation I felt a stab at the heart, so that I could neither speak nor breathe. How it was my companions noticed nothing I cannot say. I dared not move, I dared not leave my seat to get a glass of water to relieve me. Yet I believe I remained outwardly at ease, and as soon as speech returned, I forced myself to say with tolerable composure, 'Major Richardson was paying great attention to Miss Burdett. Does your brother say anything of that affair?'

Shortly afterwards the ladies took their leave.

I retired to my room. I had moved to one in the most solitary part of the house, far from either my father or the servants. I tried in vain to calm myself, but each moment my fever became more uncontrollable. I dispatched a messenger to my nurse, begging her to come to me without delay. I longed to sob my sorrows out to her with her kind arms round me. The destruction of all my hopes was as nothing to the shattering of my idol. My love was dead, but though I might despise him, I could not, could not hate him.

Later in the day I was taken ill, and in the night my baby was born. My room was so isolated that I need have little fear of discovery. An unnatural strength seemed to be given me, so that I was able to do what was necessary for my little one. He opened his eyes; the look on his innocent face exactly recalled my mother. My joy who shall describe? I was comforted with the fancy that in my hour of trial my mother was with me. I lay with my sweet babe in my arms, and kissed him a hundred times. The little tender cries were the most melodious music to my ears. But short-lived was my joy; my precious treasure was granted me but three brief hours. It was long ere I could bring myself to believe he had ceased to breathe. What could I do with the lovely waxen body? The horror that my privacy would be invaded, that some intruder should find my baby, and desecrate the sweet lifeless frame by questions and reproaches, was unendurable. I would have carried him to the churchyard, and dug the little grave with my own hands. But the first snow of the winter had been falling for some hours; it would be useless to venture forth.

The fire was still burning; I piled wood and coal upon it. I wrapped him in a cashmere handkerchief of my mother's; I repeated what I could remember of the funeral service, comforting and tranquillizing myself with its promises. I could not watch the flames destroy him. I fled to the other end of the room, and hid my face on the floor. Afterwards I remember a confused feeling that I myself was burning and must escape the flames. I knew no more, till I opened my eyes and found myself lying on my bed, with my nurse near me, and our attached old Brooks, the village apothecary, sitting by my side.

'How do you feel yourself, Miss de Mannering?' said he.

'Have I been ill?'

'Very ill for many weeks,' said he, 'but I think we shall do very well now.'

My nurse told me that, as soon as my message had reached her, she had set out to walk to Asham, but the snow had impeded her progress, and she was forced to stop the night at an inn not far from Selby. She was up before dawn, and reached the Hall, as the servants were unbarring the shutters. She hastened to my room, and found me lying on the floor, overcome by a dangerous attack of fever. She tended me all the many weeks of my illness, and would allow none to come near me but the doctor, for throughout my delirium I spoke constantly of my child.

The doctor visited me daily. At first I was so weak that I hardly noticed him, but my strength increased, and with strength came remembrance. He said to me one morning, 'You have been brought from the brink of the grave, Miss de Mannering. I did not think it possible that we should have saved you.'

In the anguish of my spirit I could not refrain from crying out, 'Would God that I had died.'

'Nay,' said he, 'since your life has been spared, should you reject the gift from the hands of the Almighty?'

'Ah,' I said in bitterness. 'You do not know—'

'Yes, madam,' said he, looking earnestly upon me, 'I know all.'

I turned from him trembling.

'Do not fear,' he said. 'The knowledge will never be revealed.'

I remained with my face against the wall.

'My dear Madam,' he said with the utmost kindness. 'Do not turn from an old man, who has attended you since babyhood and your mother also. My father and my father before me doctored the de Mannerings, and I wish to do all in my power to serve you. A physician may sometimes give his humble aid to the soul as well as to the body. Let me recall to your suffering soul that all of us sinners are promised mercy through our Redeemer. I entreat you not to lose heart. Now for my proper domain, the body. You must not spend your period of convalescence in this inclement native county of ours. You must seek sun and warmth, and change of scene to cheer your mind.'

His benevolence touched me, and my tears fell fast. Amid tears I answered him, 'Alas, I am without friends; I have nowhere to go.'

'Do not let that discourage us,' he said with a smile, 'we shall devise a plan. Let me sit by my own fireside with my own glass of whisky, and I shall certainly devise a plan.'

By his generous exertions I went on a visit to his sister at Worthing. She watched over me with a mother's care, and I returned to Asham with my health restored. Peace came to my soul; I learnt to forgive him. The years passed in outward tranquillity, but in each succeeding November, or whenever the winds were high or the sky leaden, I would suffer, as I had suffered in the months preceding the birth of my child. My mind was filled with baseless fears, above all that I should not meet my baby in Heaven, because his body did not lie in consecrated ground. Nor were the assurances of my Reason and my Faith able to conjure the delusion: yet I had—

Here the writing stopped.

'Wait, though,' said Kate, 'there's a letter.' She read the following:

> 3 Hen and Chicken Court,
> Clerkenwell.
> March 7, 1810.

Madam,

I have been told that my days are numbered. Standing as I do on the confines of eternity, I venture to address you. Long have I desired to implore your forgiveness, but have not presumed so far. I entreat you not to spurn my letter. God knows you have cause to hate the name of him who betrayed you. Yes, Madam, my vows were false, but even at the time I faltered, as I encountered your trusting and affectionate gaze, and often during my subsequent career of debauchery has that vision appeared before me. Had I embraced the opportunity offered me by Destiny to link my happiness with one as innocent and confiding as yourself, I might have been spared the wretchedness which has been my portion.

> I am Madam, your obedient servant,
> FREDERIC PHILLIMORE.

I could not speak for a minute; I was so engrossed with thinking what Miss de Mannering must have felt when she got that letter.

Kate said, 'I wonder what she wrote back to him. How often it has been folded and refolded, read and re-read, and do you see where words have got all smudged? I believe those are her tears, tears for that skunk!'

But I felt I could imagine better than Kate all that letter, with its stilted old-fashioned style, which makes it hard for us to believe the writer was in earnest, would have meant to Miss de Mannering.

'To-morrow is our last afternoon,' said Kate. 'What do you think,' coaxingly, 'of making a farewell visit to Asham?'

But though Miss de Mannering is a gentle ghost, I do not like ghosts; besides, now I know her secret, I *could* not intrude upon her. So we did not go to Asham again. Now we are back at school, and that is the end of my story.

That Tree

He had really wanted to be a cheerful bum lying under a tree in a good climate writing poetry. He wrote bushel basketfuls of poetry and it was all no good and he knew it, even while he was writing it. Knowing his poetry was no good did not take away much from his pleasure in it. He would have enjoyed just that kind of life: no respectability, no responsibility, no money to speak of, wearing worn-out sandals and a becoming, if probably ragged, blue shirt, lying under a tree writing poetry. That was why he had come to Mexico in the first place. He had felt in his bones that it was the country for him. Long after he had become quite an important journalist, an authority on Latin-American revolutions and a best-seller, he confessed to any friends and acquaintances who would listen to him— he enjoyed this confession, it gave him a chance to talk about the thing he believed he loved best, the idle, free, romantic life of a poet—that the day Miriam kicked him out was the luckiest day of his life. She had left him, really, packing up suddenly in a cold, quiet fury, stabbing him with her elbows when he tried to get his arms around her, now and again cutting him to the bone with a short sentence expelled through her clenched teeth; but he felt that he had been, as he always explained, kicked out. She had kicked him out and it had served him right.

The shock had brought him to himself as if he had been surprised out of a long sleep. He had sat quite benumbed in the bare clean room, among the straw mats and the painted Indian chairs Miriam hated, in the sudden cold silence, his head in his hands, nearly all night. It hadn't even occurred to him to lie down. It must have been almost daylight when he got up stiff in every joint from sitting still so long, and though he could not say he had been thinking, yet he had formed a new resolution. He had started out, you might almost say that very day, to make a career for himself in journalism. He couldn't say why he had hit on that, except that the word would impress his wife, the work was just intellectual enough to save his self-respect, such as it was, and even to him it seemed a suitable occupation for a man such as he had suddenly become, bent on getting on in the world of affairs. Nothing ever happens suddenly to anyone, he observed, as if the thought had just occurred to him; it had been coming on probably for a long time, sneaking up on him when he wasn't looking. His wife had called him 'Parasite!' She had said, 'Ne'er-do-well!' and as she repeated these things for what proved to be the last time, it struck him she had said them often before, when he had not listened to her with the ear of his mind. He translated these relatively harmless epithets instantly into their proper synonyms of loafer! and bum! Miriam had been a school teacher, and no matter what her disappointments and provocations may have been, you could not expect her easily to forget such discipline. She had got into a professional habit of primness; besides, she was a properly brought-up girl, not a prissy bore, not at all, but a— well, there you are, a nicely brought-up Middle-Western girl, who took life seriously. And what can you do about that? She was sweet and gay and full of little crazy notions, but she never gave way to them honestly, or at least never at the moment when they might have meant something. She was never able to see the amusing side of a threatening situation which, taken solemnly, would ruin everything. No, her sense of humour never worked for salvation. It was just an extra frill on what would have been a good time anyhow.

He wondered if anybody had ever thought—oh, well, of course everybody else had, he was always making marvellous discoveries that other people had known all along—how impossible it is to explain or to make other eyes see the special qualities in the person you love. There was such a special kind of beauty in Miriam. In certain lights and moods he simply got a clutch in the pit of his stomach when he looked at her. It was something that could happen at any hour of the day, in the midst of the most ordinary occupations. He thought there was something to be said for living with one person day and night the year round. It brings out the worst, but it brings out the best, too, and Miriam's best was pretty damn swell. He couldn't describe it. It was easy to talk about her faults. He remembered all of them, he could add them up against her like rows of figures in a vast unpaid debt. He had lived with her for four years, and even now sometimes he woke out of a sound sleep in a sweating rage with himself, asking himself again why he had ever wasted a minute on her. She wasn't beautiful in his style. He confessed to a weakness for the kind that knocks your eye out. Her notion of daytime dress was a tailored suit with a round-collared blouse and a little felt hat like a bent shovel pulled down over her eyes. In the evening she put on a black dinner dress, positively disappeared into it. But she did her hair well and had the most becoming nightgowns he ever saw. You could have put her mind in a peanut shell. She hadn't temperament of the kind he had got used to in the Mexican girls. She did not approve of his use of the word temperament, either. She thought it was a kind of occupational disease among artists, or a trick they practised to make themselves interesting. In any case, she distrusted artists and she distrusted temperament. But there was something about her. In cold blood he could size her up to himself, but it made him furious if anyone even hinted a criticism against her. His second wife had made a point of being catty about Miriam. In the end he could almost be willing to say this had led to his second divorce. He could not bear hearing Miriam called a mousy little nitwit—at least not by *that* woman . . .

They both jumped nervously at an explosion in the street, the backfire of an automobile.

'Another revolution,' said the fat scarlet young man in the tight purplish suit, at the next table. He looked like a par-boiled sausage ready to burst from its skin. It was the oldest joke since the Mexican Independence, but he was trying to look as if he had invented it. The journalist glanced back at him over a sloping shoulder. 'Another of those smart-cracking newspaper guys,' he said in a tough voice, too loudly on purpose, 'sitting around the Hotel Regis lobby wearing out the spittoons.'

The smart-cracker swelled visibly and turned a darker red. 'Who do you think you're talking about, you banjo-eyed, chinless wonder, you?' he asked explicitly, spreading his chest across the table.

'Somebody way up, no doubt,' said the journalist, in his natural voice, 'somebody in with the government, I'll bet.'

'Dyuhwana fight?' asked the newspaper man, trying to unwedge himself from between the table and his chair, which sat against the wall.

'Oh, I don't mind,' said the journalist, 'if you don't.'

The newspaper man's friends laid soothing paws all over him and held him down. 'Don't start anything with that shrimp,' said one of them, his wet, pink eyes trying to look sober and responsible. 'For crisesake, Joe, can't you see he's about half your size and a feeb to boot? You wouldn't hit a feeb, now, Joe, would you?'

'I'll feeb him,' said the newspaper man, wiggling faintly under restraint.

'*Señores'n, señores'n,*' urged the little Mexican waiter, 'there are respectable ladies and gentlemen present. Please, a little silence and correct behaviour, please.'

'Who the hell are *you*, anyhow?' the newspaper man asked the journalist, from under his shelter of hands, around the thin form of the waiter.

'Nobody you'd wanta know, Joe,' said another of his pawing friends. 'Pipe down now before these greasers turn in a general alarm. You know how liable they are to go off when you least expect it. Pipe down, now, Joe, now you just remember what happened the last time, Joe. Whaddayah *care*, anyhow?'

'*Señores'n*,' said the little waiter, working his thin, outspread, mahogany-coloured hands up and down alternately as if they were on sticks, 'it is necessary it must cease or the *señores'n* must remove themselves.'

It did cease. It seemed to evaporate. The four newspaper men at the next table subsided, cluttered in a circle with their heads together, muttering into their highballs. The journalist turned back, ordered another round of drinks, and went on talking, in a low voice.

He had never liked this café, never had any luck in it. Something always happened here to spoil his evening. If there was one brand of bum on earth he despised, it was a newspaper bum. Or anyhow the drunken illiterates that certain press agencies seemed to think were good enough for Mexico and South America. They were always getting mixed up in affairs that were none of their business, and they spent their time trying to work up trouble somewhere so that they could get a story out of it. They were always having to be thrown out on their ears by the government. He just happened to know that the bum at the next table was about due to be deported. It had been pretty safe to make that crack about how he was no doubt way up in Mexican official esteem . . . He thought that would remind him of something, all right.

One evening he had come here with Miriam for dinner and dancing, and at the very next table sat four fat generals from the North, with oxhorn moustaches and big bellies and big belts full of cartridges and pistols. It was in the old days just after Obregón had taken the city, and the town was crawling with generals. They infested the steam baths, where they took off their soiled campaign harness and sweated away the fumes of tequila and fornication, and they infested the cafés to get drunk again on champagne, and pick up the French whores who had been imported for the festivities of the presidential inauguration. These four were having an argument very quietly, their mean little eyes boring into each other's faces. He and his wife were dancing within arm's length of the table when one of the generals got up suddenly, tugging at his pistol, which stuck, and the other three jumped and grabbed him, all without a word; everybody in the place saw it at once. So far there was nothing unusual. The point was, every right-minded Mexican girl just seized her man firmly by the waist and spun him around until his back was to the generals, holding him before her like a shield, and there the whole roomful had stood frozen for a second, the music dead. His wife Miriam had broken from him and hidden under a table. He had to drag her out by the arm before everybody. 'Let's have another drink,' he said, and paused, looking around him as if he saw again the place as it had been on that night nearly ten years before. He blinked, and went on. It had been the most utterly humiliating moment of his whole blighted life. He had thought he couldn't survive to pick up their things and get her out of there. The generals had all sat down again and everybody went on dancing as though nothing had happened . . . Indeed, nothing had happened to anyone except himself.

He tried, for hours that night and on and on for nearly a year, to explain to her how he felt about it. She could not understand at all. Sometimes she said it was all perfect nonsense. Or she remarked complacently that it had never occurred to her to save her life at his expense. She thought such tricks were all very well for the Mexican girls who had only one idea in their heads, and any excuse would do to hold a man closer than they should, but she could not, could *not*, see why he should expect her to imitate them. Besides, she had felt safer under the table. It was her first and only thought. He told her a bullet might very well have gone through the wood; a plank was no protection at all, a human torso was as good as a feather pillow to stop a bullet. She kept saying it simply had not occurred to her to do anything else, and that it really had nothing at all to do with him. He could never make her see his point of view for one moment. It should have had something to do with him. All those Mexican girls were born knowing what they should do and they did it instantly, and Miriam had merely proved once for all that her instincts were out of tune. When she tightened her mouth to bite her lip and say 'Instincts!' she could make it sound like the most obscene word in any language. It was a shocking word. And she did not stop there. At last she said, she hadn't the faintest interest in what Mexican girls were born for, but she had no intention of wasting her life flattering male vanity. 'Why should I trust you in anything?' she asked. 'What reason have you given me to trust you?'

He was surprised at the change in her since he had first met her in Minneapolis. He chose to believe this change had been caused by her teaching school. He told her he thought it the most deadly occupation there was and a law should be passed prohibiting pretty women under thirty-five years of age from taking it up. She reminded him they were living on the money she had earned at it. They had been engaged for three years, a chaste, long-distance engagement which he considered morbid and unnatural. Of course he had to do something to wear away the time, so while she was in Minneapolis saving her money and filling a huge trunk with household linen, he had been living in Mexico City with an Indian girl who posed for a set of painters he knew. He had a job teaching English in one of the technical schools—damned odd, he had been a school teacher, too, but he never thought of it just that way until this minute—and he lived very comfortably with the Indian girl on his wages, for, naturally, the painters did not pay her for posing. The Indian girl divided her time cheerfully between the painters, the cooking-pot, and his bed, and she managed to have a baby without interrupting any of these occupations for more than a few days. Later on she was taken up by one of the more famous and successful painters, and grew very sophisticated and a 'character', but at that time she was still simple and nice. She took, later on, to wearing native art jewellery and doing native dances in costume, and learned to paint almost as well as a seven-year-old child. 'You know,' he said, 'the primitive style.' Well, by that time, he was having troubles of his own. When the time came for Miriam to come out and marry him—the whole delay, he realized afterward, was caused by Miriam's expansive notions of what a bride's outfit should be—the Indian girl had gone away very cheerfully, too cheerfully, in fact, with a new man. She had come back in three days to say she was at last going to get married honestly, and she felt he should give her the furniture for a dowry. He had helped her pile the stuff on the backs of two Indian carriers, and the girl had walked away with the baby's head dangling out of her shawl. For just a moment when he saw the baby's face he had an odd feeling. 'That's mine,' he said to himself, and added at once, 'perhaps.' There was no way of knowing, and it certainly looked like any other little shock-haired Indian baby. Of course the girl had not got married; she had never even thought of it.

When Miriam arrived, the place was almost empty, because he had not been able to save a peso. He had a bed and stove, and the walls were decorated with drawings and paintings by his Mexican friends, and there was a litter of painted gourds and carved wood and pottery in beautiful colours. It didn't seem so bad to him, but Miriam's face, when she stepped into the first room, was, he had to admit, pretty much of a study. She said very little, but she began to be unhappy about a number of things. She cried intermittently for the first few weeks, for the most mysterious and far-fetched causes. He would wake in the night and find her crying hopelessly. When she sat down to coffee in the morning she would lean her head on her hands and cry. 'It's nothing, nothing really,' she would tell him. 'I don't know what is the matter. I just want to cry.' He knew now what was the matter. She had come all that way to marry after three years' planning, and she couldn't see herself going back and facing the music at home. This mood had not lasted, but it made a fairly dreary failure of their honeymoon. She knew nothing about the Indian girl, and believed, or professed to believe, that he was virgin as she was at their marriage. She hadn't much curiosity and her moral standards were severe, so it was impossible for him ever to take her into his confidence about his past. She simply took it for granted in the most irritating way that he hadn't any past worth mentioning except the three years they were engaged, and that, of course, they shared already. He had believed that all virgins, however austere their behaviour, were palpitating to learn about life, were, you might say, hanging on by an eyelash until they arrived safely at initiation within the secure yet libertine advantages of marriage. Miriam upset this theory as in time she upset most of his theories. His intention to play the role of a man of the world educating an innocent but interestingly teachable bride was nipped in the bud. She was not at all teachable and she took no trouble to make herself interesting. In their most intimate hours her mind seemed elsewhere, gone into some darkness of its own, as if a prior and greater shock of knowledge had forestalled her attention. She was not to be won, for reasons of her own which she would not or could not give. He could not even play the role of a poet. She was not interested in his poetry. She preferred Milton, and she let him know it. She let him know also that she believed their mutual sacrifice of virginity was the most important act of their marriage, and this sacred rite once achieved, the whole affair had descended to a pretty low plane. She had a terrible phrase about 'walking the chalk line' which she applied to all sorts of situations. One walked, as never before, the chalk line in marriage; there seemed to be a chalk line drawn between them as they lay together . . .

The thing that finally got him down was Miriam's devilish inconsistency. She spent three mortal years writing him how dull and dreadful and commonplace her life was, how sick and tired she was of petty little conventions and amusements, how narrow-minded everybody around her was, how she longed to live in a beautiful dangerous place among interesting people who painted and wrote poetry, and how his letters came into her stuffy little world like a breath of free mountain air, and all that. 'For God's sake,' he said to his guest, 'let's have another drink.' Well, he had something of a notion he was freeing a sweet bird from a cage. Once freed, she would perch gratefully on his hand. He wrote a poem about a caged bird set free, dedicated it to her and sent her a copy. She forgot to mention it in her next letter. Then she came out with a two-hundred-pound trunk of linen and enough silk underwear to last her a lifetime, you might have supposed, expecting to settle down in a modern steam-heated flat and have nice artistic young couples from the American colony in for dinner Wednesday evenings. No wonder her face had changed at the first glimpse of her new home. His Mexican friends had scattered flowers all over the place, tied bunches of carnations on the door knobs, almost carpeted the floor with red roses, pinned posies of small bright blooms on the sagging cotton curtains, spread a coverlet of gardenias on the lumpy bed, and had disappeared discreetly, leaving gay, reassuring messages scribbled here and there, even on the white plastered walls . . . She had walked through with a vague look of terror in her eyes, pushing back the wilting flowers with her advancing feet. She swept the gardenias aside to sit on the edge of the bed, and she had said not a word. Hail, Hymen! What next?

He had lost his teaching job almost immediately. The Minister of Education, who was a patron of the school superintendent, was put out of office suddenly, and naturally every soul in his party down to the school janitors went out with him, and there you were. After a while you learn to take such things calmly. You wait until your man gets back in the saddle or you work up an alliance with the new one . . . Whichever . . . Meanwhile the change and movement made such a good show you almost forgot the effect it had on your food supply. Miriam was not interested in politics or the movement of local history. She could see nothing but that he had lost his job. They lived on Miriam's savings, eked out with birthday cheques and Christmas cheques from her father, who threatened constantly to come for a visit, in spite of Miriam's desperate letters warning him that the country was appalling, and the climate would most certainly ruin his health. Miriam went on holding her nose when she went to the markets, trying to cook wholesome civilized American food over a charcoal brazier, and doing the washing in the patio over a stone tub with a cold-water tap; and everything that had seemed so jolly and natural and inexpensive with the Indian girl was too damnifying and costly for words with Miriam. Her money melted away and they got nothing for it.

She would not have an Indian servant near her: they were dirty and, besides, how could she afford it? He could not see why she despised and resented housework so, especially since he offered to help. He had thought it rather a picnic to wash a lot of gaily coloured Indian crockery out-of-doors in the sunshine, with the bougainvillaea climbing up the wall and the heaven tree in full bloom. Not Miriam. She despised him for thinking it a picnic. He remembered for the first time his mother doing the housework when he was a child. There were half a dozen assorted children, her work was hard and endless, but she went about it with a quiet certainty, a happy, absorbed look on her face, as if her hands were working automatically while her imagination was away playing somewhere. 'Ah, your mother,' said his wife, without any particular emphasis. He felt horribly injured, as if she were insulting his mother and calling down a curse on her head for bringing such a son into the world. No doubt about it, Miriam had force. She could make her personality, which no one need really respect, felt in a bitter, sinister way. She had a background, and solid earth under her feet, and a point of view and a strong spine: even when she danced with him he could feel her tense controlled hips and her locked knees, which gave her dancing a most attractive strength and lightness without any yielding at all. She had her points, all right, like a good horse, but she had missed being beautiful. It wasn't in her. He began to cringe when she reminded him that if he were an invalid she would cheerfully work for him and take care of him, but he appeared to be in the best of health, he was not even looking for a job, and he was still writing that poetry, which was the last straw. She called him a failure. She called him worthless and shiftless and trifling and faithless. She showed him her ruined hands and asked him what she had to look forward to, and told him again, and again, that she was not used to associating with the simply indescribably savage and awful persons who kept streaming through the place. Moreover, she had no intention of getting used to it. He tried to tell her that these persons were the best painters and poets and what-alls in Mexico, that she should try to appreciate them; these were the artists he had told her about in his letters. She wanted to know why Carlos never changed his shirt. 'I told her,' said the journalist, 'it was because probably he hadn't got any other shirt.' And why was Jaime such a glutton, leaning over his plate and wolfing his food? Because he was famished, no doubt. It was precisely that she could not understand. Why didn't they go to work and make a living? It was no good trying to explain to her his Franciscan notions of holy Poverty as being the natural companion for the artist. She said, 'So you think they're being poor on purpose? Nobody but you would be such a fool.' Really, the things that girl said. And his general impression of her was that she was as silent as a cat. He went on in his pawky way trying to make clear to her his mystical faith in these men who went ragged and hungry because they had chosen once for all between what he called in all seriousness their souls, and this world. Miriam knew better. She knew they were looking for the main chance. 'She was abominably, obscenely right. How I hate that woman; I hate her as I hate no one else. She assured me they were not so stupid as I thought; and I lived to see Jaime take up with a rich old woman, and Ricardo decide to turn film actor, and Carlos sitting easy with a government job, painting revolutionary frescoes to order, and I asked myself, "Why shouldn't a man survive in any way he can?"' But some fixed point of feeling in him refused to be convinced, he had a sackful of romantic notions about artists and their destiny and he was left holding it. Miriam had seen through them with half an eye, and how he wished he might have thought of a trick to play on her that would have finished her for life. But he had not. They all in turn ran out on him, and in the end he had run out too. 'So you see, I don't feel any better about doing what I did finally do, but I can say I am not unusual. That I can say. The trouble was that Miriam was right, damn her. I am not a poet, my poetry is filthy, and I had notions about artists that I must have got out of books . . . You know, a race apart, dedicated men much superior to common human needs and ambitions . . . I mean I thought art was a religion . . . I mean that when Miriam kept saying . . .'

What he meant was that all this conflict began to damage him seriously. Miriam had become an avenging fury, yet he could not condemn her. Hate her, yes, that was almost too simple. His old-fashioned respectable middle-class hard-working American ancestry and training rose up in him and fought on Miriam's side. He felt he had broken about every bone in him to get away from them and live them down, and here he had been overtaken at last and beaten into resignation that had nothing to do with his mind or heart. It was as if his blood stream had betrayed him. The prospect of taking a job and being a decent little clerk with shiny pants and elbows—for he couldn't think of a job in any other terms—seemed like a kind of premature death which would not even compensate him with loss of memory. He didn't do anything about it at all. He did odd jobs and picked up a little money, but never enough. He could see her side of it, at least he tried hard to see it. When it came to a showdown, he hadn't a single argument in favour of his way of life that would hold water. He had been trying to live and think in a way that he hoped would end by making a poet of him, but it hadn't worked. That was the long and short of it. So he might have just gone on to some unimaginably sordid end if Miriam, after four years—four years? yes, good God, four years and one month and eleven days—had not written home for money, packed up what was left of her belongings, called him a few farewell names, and left. She had been shabby and thin and wild-looking for so long he could not remember ever having seen her any other way, yet all at once her profile in the doorway was unrecognizable to him.

So she went, and she did him a great favour without knowing it. He had fallen into the cowardly habit of thinking their marriage was permanent, no matter how evil it might be, that they loved each other, and so it did not matter what cruelties they committed against each other, and he had developed a real deafness to her words. He was unable, towards the end, either to see her or hear her. He realized this afterward, when remembered phrases and expressions of her eyes and mouth began to eat into his marrow. He was grateful to her. If she had not gone he might have loitered on, wasting his time trying to write poetry, hanging around dirty picturesque little cafés with a fresh set of clever, talkative, poverty-stricken young Mexicans who were painting or writing or talking about getting ready to paint or write. His faith had renewed itself; these fellows were pure artists—they would never sell out. They were not bums, either. They worked all the time at something to do with Art. 'Sacred Art,' he said, 'our glasses are empty again.'

But try telling anything of the kind to Miriam. Somehow he had never got to that tree he meant to lie down under. If he had, somebody would certainly have come around and collected rent for it, anyhow. He had spent a good deal of time lying under tables at Dinty Moore's or the Black Cat with a gang of Americans like himself who were living a free life and studying the native customs. He was rehearsing, he explained to Miriam, hoping for once she would take a joke, for lying under a tree later on. It didn't go over. She would have died with her boots on before she would have cracked a smile at that. So then . . . He had gone in for a career in the hugest sort of way. It had been easy. He hardly could say now just what his first steps were, but it had been easy. Except for Miriam, he would have been a lousy failure, like those bums at Dinty Moore's, still rolling under the tables, studying the native customs. He had gone in for a career in journalism and he had made a good thing of it. He was a recognized authority on revolutions in twenty-odd Latin-American countries, and his sympathies happened to fall in exactly right with the high-priced magazines of a liberal humanitarian slant which paid him well for telling the world about the oppressed peoples. He could really write, too; if he did say so, he had a prose style of his own. He had made the kind of success you can clip out of newspapers and paste in a book, you can count it and put it in the bank, you can eat and drink and wear it, and you can see it in other people's eyes at tea- and dinner-parties. Fine, and now what? On the strength of all this he had got married again. Twice, in fact, and divorced twice. That made three times, didn't it? That was plenty. He had spent a good deal of time and energy doing all sorts of things he didn't care for in the least to prove to his first wife, who had been a twenty-three-year-old school teacher in Minneapolis, Minnesota, that he was not just merely a bum, fit for nothing but lying under a tree—if he had ever been able to locate that ideal tree he had in his mind's eye—writing poetry and enjoying his life.

Now he had done it. He smoothed out the letter he had been turning in his hands and stroked it as if it were a cat. He said, 'I've been working up to the climax all this time. You know, good old surprise technique. Now then, get ready.'

Miriam had written to him, after these five years, asking him to take her back. And would you believe it, he was going to break down and do that very thing. Her father was dead, she was terribly lonely, she had had time to think everything over, she believed herself to blame for a great many things, she loved him truly and she always had, truly; she regretted, oh, everything, and hoped it was not too late for them to make a happy life together once more . . . She had read everything she could find of his in print, and she loved all of it. He had that very morning sent by cable the money for her to travel on, and he was going to take her back. She was going to live again in a Mexican house without any conveniences and she was not going to have a modern flat. She was going to take whatever he chose to hand her, and like it. And he wasn't going to marry her again, either. Not he. If she wanted to live with him on these terms, well and good. If not, she could just go back once more to that school of hers in Minneapolis. If she stayed, she would walk a chalk line, all right, one she hadn't drawn for herself. He picked up a cheese knife and drew a long, sharp line in the checked tablecloth. She would, believe him, walk *that*.

The hands of the clock pointed to half past two. The journalist swallowed the last of his drink and went on drawing more cross-hatches on the tablecloth with a relaxed hand. His guest wished to say, 'Don't forget to invite me to your wedding,' but thought better of it. The journalist raised his twitching lids and swung his half-focused eyes upon the shadow opposite and said, 'I suppose you think I don't know—'

His guest moved to the chair edge and watched the orchestra folding up for the night. The café was almost empty. The journalist paused, not for an answer, but to give weight to the important statement he was about to make.

'I don't know what's happening, this time,' he said, 'don't deceive yourself. This time, I know.' He seemed to be admonishing himself before a mirror.

1964

ELIZABETH BOWEN

Look at All Those Roses

❧

Lou exclaimed at that glimpse of a house in a sheath of startling flowers. She twisted round, to look back, in the open car, till the next corner had cut it out of sight. To reach the corner, it struck her, Edward accelerated, as though he were jealous of the rosy house—a house with gables, flat-fronted, whose dark windows stared with no expession through the flowers. The garden, with its silent, burning gaiety, stayed in both their minds like an apparition.

One of those conflicts between two silent moods had set up, with Lou and Edward, during that endless drive. Also, there is a point when an afternoon oppresses one with fatigue and a feeling of unreality. Relent-less, pointless, unwinding summer country made nerves ache at the back of both of their eyes. This was a late June Monday; they were doubling back to London through Suffolk by-roads, on the return from a week-end. Edward, who detested the main roads, had traced out their curious route before starting, and Lou now sat beside him with the map on her knees. They had to be back by eight, for Edward, who was a writer, to finish and post an article: apart from this, time was no object with them. They looked forward with no particular pleasure to London and unlocking the stuffy flat, taking in the milk, finding bills in the letter-box. In fact, they looked forward to nothing with particular pleasure. They were going home for the purely negative reason that there was nowhere else they could as cheaply go. The week-end had not been amusing, but at least it had been 'away'. Now they could foresee life for weeks ahead—until someone else invited them—the typewriter, the cocktail-shaker, the tele-phone, runs in the car out of London to nowhere special. Love when Edward got a cheque in the post, quarrels about people on the way home from parties—and Lou's anxiety always eating them. This future weighed on them like a dull burden . . . So they had been glad to extend today.

But under a vacant sky, not sunny but full of diffused glare, the drive had begun to last too long: they felt bound up in the tired impotence of a dream. The stretches of horizon were stupefying. The road bent round wedges of cornfield, blocky elms dark with summer: for these last ten miles the countryside looked abandoned; they passed dropping gates, rusty cattle-troughs and the thistly, tussocky, stale grass of neglected farms. There was nobody on the roads; perhaps there was nobody anywhere . . . In the heart of all this, the roses looked all the odder.

'They were extraordinary,' she said (when the first corner was turned) in her tired, little, dogmatic voice.

'All the more,' he agreed, 'when all the rest of the country looks something lived in by poor whites.'

'I wish we lived *there*,' she said. 'It really looked like somewhere.'

'It wouldn't if we did.'

Edward spoke with some tartness. He had found he had reason to dread week-ends away: they unsettled Lou and started up these fantasies. Himself, he had no illusions about life in the country: life without people was absolutely impossible. What would he and she do with nobody to talk to but each other? Already, they had not spoken for two hours. Lou saw life in terms of ideal moments. She found few ideal moments in their flat.

He went on: 'You know you can't stand ear-wigs. And we should spend our lives on the telephone.'

'About the earwigs?'

'No. About ourselves.'

Lou's smart little monkey face became dolorous. She never risked displeasing Edward too far, but she was just opening her mouth to risk one further remark when Edward jumped and frowned. A ghastly knocking had started. It seemed to come from everywhere, and at the same time to be a special attack on them. Then it had to be traced to the car's vitals: it jarred up Lou through the soles of her feet. Edward slowed to a crawl and stopped. He and she confronted each other with that completely dramatic lack of expression they kept for occasions when the car went wrong. They tried crawling on again, a few tentative yards: the knocking took up again with still greater fury.

'Sounds to me like a big end gone.'

'Oh my goodness,' she said.

All the same, she was truly glad to get out of the car. She stretched and stood waiting on the grass roadside while Edward made faces into the bonnet. Soon he flung round to ask what she would suggest doing: to his surprise (and annoyance) she had a plan ready. She would walk back to that house and ask if they had a telephone. If they had not, she would ask for a bicycle and bicycle to the place where the nearest garage was.

Edward snatched the map, but could not find where they were. Where they were seemed to be highly improbable. 'I expect you,' Lou said, 'would rather stay with the car.' 'No, I wouldn't,' said Edward, 'anybody can have it . . . You like to be sure where I am, don't you?' he added. He locked their few odd things up in the boot of the car with the suitcases, and they set off in silence. It was about a mile.

There stood the house, waiting. Why should a house wait? Most pretty scenes have something passive about them, but this looked like a trap baited with beauty, set ready to spring. It stood back from the road. Lou put her hand on the gate and, with a touch of bravado, the two filed up the paved path to the door. Each side of the path, hundreds of standard roses bloomed, over-charged with colour, as though this were their one hour. Crimson, coral, blue-pink, lemon and cold white, they disturbed with fragrance the dead air. In this spell-bound afternoon, with no shadows, the roses glared at the strangers, frighteningly bright. The face of the house was plastered with tea-roses: waxy cream when they opened but with vermilion buds.

The blistered door was propped open with a bizarre object, a lump of quartz. Indoors was the dark, cold-looking hall. When they had come to the door they found no bell or knocker: they could not think what to do. 'We had better cough,' Lou said. So they stood there coughing, till a door at the end of the hall opened and a lady or woman looked out—they were not sure which.'Oh?' she said, with no expression at all.

'We couldn't find your bell.'

'There they are,' she said, pointing to two Swiss cow-bells that hung on loops of string by the door she had just come out of. Having put this right, she continued to look at them, and out through the door past them, wiping her powerful-looking hands vaguely against the sides of her blue overall. They could hardly see themselves as intruders when their intrusion made so little effect. The occupying inner life of this person was not for an instant suspended by their presence. She was a shabby amazon of a woman, with a sculptural clearness about the face. She must have lost contact with the outer world completely: there was now nothing to 'place' her by. It is outside attachments—hopes, claims, curiosities, desires, little touches of greed—that put a label on one to help strangers. As it was, they could not tell if she were rich or poor, stupid or clever, a spinster or a wife. She seemed prepared, not anxious, for them to speak. Lou, standing close beside Edward, gave him a dig in a rib. So Edward explained to the lady how they found themselves, and asked if she had a telephone or a bicycle.

She said she was sorry to say she had neither. Her maid had a bicycle, but had ridden home on it. 'Would you like some tea?' she said. 'I am just boiling the kettle. Then perhaps you can think of something to do.' This lack of grip of the crisis made Edward decide the woman must be a moron: annoyance contused his face. But Lou, who wanted tea and was attracted by calmness, was entirely won. She looked at Edward placatingly.

'Thank you,' he said. 'But I must do something at once. We haven't got all night; I've got to be back in London. Can you tell me where I can telephone from? I must get through to a garage—a good garage.'

Unmoved, the lady said: 'You'll have to walk to the village. It's about three miles away.' She gave unexpectedly clear directions, then looked at Lou again. 'Leave your wife here,' she said. 'Then she can have tea.'

Edward shrugged; Lou gave a brief, undecided sigh. How much she wanted to stop. But she never liked to be left. This partly arose from the fact that she was not Edward's wife: he was married to someone else and his wife would not divorce him. He might some day go back to her, if this ever became the way of least resistance. Or he might, if it were the way of even less resistance, move on to someone else. Lou was determined neither should ever happen. She did love Edward, but she also stuck to him largely out of contentiousness. She quite often asked herself why she did. It seemed important—she could not say why. She was determined to be a necessity. Therefore she seldom let him out of her sight—her idea of love was adhesiveness . . . Knowing this well, Edward gave her a slightly malign smile, said she had far better stay, turned, and walked down the path without her. Lou, like a lost cat, went half-way to the door. 'Your roses are wonderful . . .' she said, staring out with unhappy eyes.

'Yes, they grow well for us, Josephine likes to see them.' Her hostess added: 'My kettle will be boiling. Won't you wait in there?'

Lou went deeper into the house. She found herself in a long, low and narrow parlour, with a window at each end. Before she could turn round, she felt herself being looked at. A girl of about thirteen lay, flat as a board, in a wicker invalid carriage. The carriage was pulled out across the room, so that the girl could command the view from either window, the flat horizons that bounded either sky. Lying there with no pillow she had a stretched look. Lou stood some distance from the foot of the carriage: the dark eyes looked at her down thin cheekbones, intently. The girl had an unresigned, living face; one hand crept on the rug over her breast. Lou felt, here was the nerve and core of the house . . . The only movement was made by a canary, springing to and fro in its cage.

'Hullo,' Lou said, with that deferential smile with which one approaches an invalid. When the child did not answer, she went on: 'You must wonder who I am?'

'I don't now; I did when you drove past.'

'Then our car broke down.'

'I know, I wondered whether it might.'

Lou laughed and said: 'Then you put the evil eye on it.'

The child ignored this. She said: 'This is not the way to London.'

'All the same, that's where we're going.'

'You mean, where you were going . . . Is that your husband who has just gone away?'

'That's Edward: yes. To telephone. He'll be back.' Lou, who was wearing a summer suit, smart, now rather crumpled, of honey-yellow linen, felt Josephine look her up and down. 'Have you been to a party?' she said, 'or are you going to one?'

'We've just been staying away,' Lou walked nervously down the room to the front window. From here she saw the same roses Josephine saw: she thought they looked like forced roses, magnetized into being. Magnetized, buds uncurled and petals dropped. Lou began to wake from the dream of the afternoon: her will stirred; she wanted to go; she felt apprehensive, threatened. 'I expect you like to lie out of doors, with all those roses?' she said.

'No, not often: I don't care for the sky.'

'You just watch through the window?'

'Yes,' said the child, impatiently. She added: 'What are the parts of London with most traffic?'

'Piccadilly Circus. Trafalgar Square.'

'Oh, I would like to see those.'

The child's mother's step sounded on the hall flags: she came in with the tea-tray. 'Can I help you?' said Lou, glad of the interim.

'Oh, thank you. Perhaps you'd unfold that table. Put it over here beside Josephine. She's lying down because she hurt her back.'

'My back was hurt six years ago,' said Josephine. 'It was my father's doing.'

Her mother was busy lodging the edge of the tray on the edge of the tea-table.

'Awful for him,' Lou murmured, helping unstack the cups.

'No, it's not,' said Josephine. 'He has gone away.'

Lou saw why. A man in the wrong cannot live where there is no humanity. There are enormities you can only keep piling up. He had bolted off down that path, as Edward had just done. Men cannot live with sorrow, with women who embrace it. Men will suffer a certain look in animals' eyes, but not in women's eyes. And men dread obstinacy, of love, of grief. You could stay with burning Josephine, not with her mother's patient, exalted face . . . When her mother had gone again, to fetch the teapot and kettle, Josephine once more fastened her eyes on Lou. 'Perhaps your husband will be some time,' she said. 'You're the first new person I have seen for a year. Perhaps he will lose his way.'

'Oh, but then I should have to look for him!'

Josephine gave a fanatical smile. 'But when people go away they sometimes quite go,' she said. 'If they always come back, then what is the good of moving?'

'I don't see the good of moving.'

'Then stay here.'

'People don't just go where they want; they go where they must.'

'Must you go back to London?'

'Oh, I have to, you know.'

'Why?'

Lou frowned and smiled in a portentous, grown-up way that meant nothing at all to either herself or Josephine. She felt for her cigarette case and, glumly, found it empty—Edward had walked away with the packet of cigarettes that he and she had been sharing that afternoon. He also carried any money she had.

'You don't know where he's gone to,' Josephine pointed out. 'If you had to stay, you would soon get used to it. We don't wonder where my father is.'

'What's your mother's name?'

'Mrs Mather. She'd like you to stay. Nobody comes to see us; they used to, they don't now. So we only see each other. They may be frightened of something—'

Mrs Mather came back, and Josephine looked out of the other window. This immediate silence marked a conspiracy, in which Lou had no willing part. While Mrs Mather was putting down the teapot, Lou looked round the room, to make sure it was ordinary. This window-ended parlour was lined with objects that looked honest and worn without having antique grace. A faded room should look homely. But extinct paper and phantom cretonnes gave this a gutted air. Rooms can be whitened and gutted by too-intensive living, as they are by a fire. It was the garden, out there, that focused the senses. Lou indulged for a minute the astounding fancy that Mr Mather lay at the roses' roots . . . Josephine said sharply: 'I don't want any tea,' which made Lou realize that she would have to be fed and did not want to be fed in front of the stranger Lou still was. Mrs Mather made no comment: she drew two chairs to the table and invited Lou to sit down. 'It's rather sultry,' she said. 'I'm afraid your husband may not enjoy his walk.'

'How far did you say it was?'

'Three miles.'

Lou, keeping her wrist under the table, glanced down covertly at her watch.

'We are very much out of the way,' said Mrs Mather.

'But perhaps you like that?'

'We are accustomed to quiet,' said Mrs Mather, pouring out tea. 'This was a farm, you know. But it was an unlucky farm, so since my husband left I have let the land. Servants seem to find that the place is lonely— country girls are so different now. My present servant is not very clear in her mind, but she works well and does not seem to feel lonely. When she is not working she rides home.'

'Far?' said Lou, tensely.

'A good way,' said Mrs Mather, looking out of the window at the horizon.

'Then aren't you rather . . . alone?—I mean, if anything happened.'

'Nothing more can happen,' said Mrs Mather. 'And there are two of us. When I am working upstairs or am out with the chickens, I wear one of those bells you see in the hall, so Josephine can always hear where I am. And I leave the other bell on Josephine's carriage. When I work in the garden she can see me, of course.' She slit the wax-paper top off a jar of jam. 'This is my last pot of last year's damson,' she said. 'Please try some; I shall be making more soon. We have two fine trees.'

'You should see mother climb them,' said Josephine.

'Aren't you afraid of falling?'

'Why?' said Mrs Mather, advancing a plate of rather rich bread and butter. 'I never eat tea, thank you,' Lou said, sitting rigid, sipping round her cup of tea like a bird.

'She thinks if she eats she may have to stay here for ever,' Josephine said. Her mother, taking no notice, spread jam on her bread and butter and started to eat in a calmly voracious way. Lou kept clinking her spoon against the teacup: every time she did this the canary stared and fluttered. Though she knew Edward could not possibly come yet, Lou kept glancing down the garden at the gate. Mrs Mather, reaching out for more bread and butter, saw, and thought Lou was looking at the roses. 'Would you like to take some back to London?' she said.

Josephine's carriage had been wheeled out on the lawn between the rosebeds. She lay with eyes shut and forehead contracted, for overhead hung the dreaded space of the sky. But she had to be near Lou while Lou cut the roses. In a day or two, Lou thought, I should be wearing a bell. What shall I do with these if I never do go? she thought, as she cut through the strong stems between the thorns and piled the roses on the foot of the carriage. I shall certainly never want to look at roses again. By her wrist watch it was six o'clock—two hours since Edward had started. All round, the country under the white, stretched sky was completely silent. She went once to the gate.

'Is there any way from that village?' she said at last. 'Any 'bus to anywhere else? Any taxi one could hire?'

'I don't know,' said Josephine.

'When does your servant come back?'

'Tomorrow morning. Sometimes our servants never come back at all.'

Lou shut the knife and said: 'Well, those are enough roses.' She supposed she could hear if whoever Edward sent for the car came to tow it away. The car, surely, Edward would not abandon? She went to the gate again. From behind her Josephine said: 'Then please wheel me indoors.'

'If you like. But I shall stay here.'

'Then I will. But please put something over my eyes.'

Lou got out her red silk handkerchief and laid this across Josephine's eyes. This made the mouth more revealing: she looked down at the small resolute smile. 'If you want to keep on listening,' the child said, 'you needn't talk to me. Lie down and let's pretend we're both asleep.'

Lou lay down on the dry, cropped grass alongside the wheels of the carriage: she crossed her hands under her head, shut her eyes and lay stretched, as rigid as Josephine. At first she was so nervous, she thought the lawn vibrated under her spine. Then slowly she relaxed. There is a moment when silence, no longer resisted, rushes into the mind. She let go, inch by inch, of life, that since she was a child she had been clutching so desperately—her obsessions about this and that, her obsession about keeping Edward. How anxiously she had run from place to place, wanting to keep everything inside her own power. I should have stayed still: I shall stay still now, she thought. What I want must come to me: I shall not go after it. People who stay still generate power. Josephine stores herself up, and so what she wants happens, because she knows what she wants. I only think I want things; I only think I want Edward. (He's not coming and I don't care, I don't care.) I feel life myself now. No wonder I've been tired, only half getting what I don't really want. Now I want nothing; I just want a white circle.

The white circle distended inside her eyelids and she looked into it in an ecstasy of indifference. She knew she was looking at nothing—then knew nothing . . .

Josephine's voice, from up in the carriage, woke her. 'You were quite asleep.'

'Was I?'

'Take the handkerchief off: a motor's coming.'

Lou heard the vibration. She got up and uncovered Josephine's eyes. Then she went to the foot of the carriage and got her roses together. She was busy with this, standing with her back to the gate, when she heard the taxi pull up, then Edward's step on the path. The taxi driver sat staring at the roses. 'It's all right,' Edward shouted, 'they're sending out from the garage. They should be here any moment. But what people— God!—Look here, have you been all right?'

'Perfectly, I've been with Josephine.'

'Oh, hullo, Josephine,' Edward said, with a hasty exercise of his charm. 'Well, I've come for this woman. Thank you for keeping her.'

'It's quite all right, thank you . . . Shall you be going now?'

'We must get our stuff out of the car: it will have to be towed to the garage. Then when I've had another talk to the garage people we'll take this taxi on and pick up a train . . . Come on, Lou, come on! We don't want to miss those people! And we've got to get that stuff out of that car!'

'Is there such a hurry?' she said, putting down the roses.

'Of course, there's a hurry . . .' He added, to Josephine: 'We'll look in on our way to the station, when I've fixed up all this, to say goodbye to your mother.' He put his hand on Lou's shoulder and punted her ahead of him down the path. 'I'm glad you're all right,' he said, as they got into the taxi. 'You're well out of that, my girl. From what I heard in the village—'

'What, have you been anxious?' said Lou, curiously.

'It's a nervy day,' said Edward, with an uneasy laugh. 'And I had to put in an hour in the village emporium, first waiting for my call, then waiting for this taxi. (And this is going to cost us a pretty penny.) I got talking, naturally, one way and another. You've no idea what they said when they heard where I had parked you. Not a soul round there will go near the place. I must say—discounting gossip—there's a story there,' said Edward. 'They can't fix anything, but . . . Well, you see, it appears that this Mather woman . . .' Lowering his voice, so as not to be heard by the driver, Edward began to tell Lou what he had heard in the village about the abrupt disappearance of Mr Mather.

OLIVIA MANNING

In a Winter Landscape

(To Prince Antoine Bibesco)

❧

Everyone who went there to ski for the first time took a photograph of the train. It had a little black engine with a tall funnel that bulged like an onion at the top. We thought it must date back to the '60s or the '70s, but on the side was written 'Munich, 1910'. It looked like a little muscular pony. Behind was an open truck for the wood. Behind that was the carriage, yellow-varnished, a platform back and front, big windows and long seats, like an old-fashioned tram-car. In this the hotel guests travelled. Last of all came a closed-in truck for the skis, luggage and any peasant who wanted to go from one halt to another in the valley. The truck had a coat of blue paint, weathered now so it looked like verdigris.

In the carriage the windows were sealed against the cold. The backsides of the respectable guests were packed like fruits in transit. The women wore hats copied from copies of the French, decorated coats, gloves, high-heeled shoes; the men wore their best city clothes. When they arrived they would dress correctly for 'the sport'—but until arrival no unconventionality could be tolerated. There were some children—little fur coats, muffs on strings, velvet bonnets, white bootees—who whimpered and gazed at the foreigners with round, unfriendly eyes. The hotel was a family hotel. Everyone was going there for Christmas.

As the journey was to last from early morning until supper-time, each family had brought a bag packed with rolls and salami and Thermos flasks. Immediately the engine gave its first jerk forward the rolls were split in half, filled with salami and handed out to the children. The children peeled off the salami-rind and dropped it on the floor. We were standing up, so they were able to wipe their fingers on our ski-trousers.

When we opened the door for air, someone slammed it indignantly shut: but that did not keep out the cold. It merely kept in the smell of garlic and sweat. At the first halt we left the carriage and went into the truck with the skis. On the return journey, we went all the way with the skis.

At the beginning of the long, slow climb up to the hotel, the valley lay about us coloured by sparse damp, winter grass. As we rose, we came into the snow region, but the snow was old. It was glassy and sinister in the grey light. We passed a little waterfall frozen into a glass waterfall. We felt, if we could get out and look, we would find dust on it.

It was dark when we reached the hotel. The snow was no better here and experienced skiers began grumbling at once, but next day there was a heavy fall. After that it snowed almost every day for a week. The new snow fell in grains like fluffy seeds. It settled in grains on the old snow and drifted about there with swansdown gentleness. The old snow had been white enough, but the new was whiter. It was like white light. We could not make it into balls. If we scooped it up and squeezed it, it just fell into powder again as soon as we opened our hands. When it froze hard it squeaked under our feet as we walked and had the dry, tight feel of boracic powder.

The mornings were beautiful. The snow flanked the paths in long, unbroken curves. We could put our hands into it and sift it about like sand and then shake every grain off our fingers. Up in the pine forests the trees were like sugar trees. After a while all this whiteness hurt the eyes and it became scarcely possible to see anything. Between the grizzled pines flashed the splinters of the low sun and above was the pure enamel blue of the sky.

Near the hotel was a little lake with a tea-house built out into the water for summer visitors. The tea-house was a shabby red, but now, outlined and glittering with frost, it had a Japanese look. The snow had been swept from the ice and a loudspeaker broadcast dance music; a few skaters pressed forward and turned and lifted feet to the rhythm of the music. People stood and watched them. Most kept cautiously to going forward; but one or two were good and conscious of their audience. These had all the attention they could want. Two young men in wind-jackets excelled everyone. They joined hands and swept forward to the music, their bodies leaning out like figureheads, their feet a little behind but following beautifully, knowing exactly what must be done and doing it exactly: now the right foot forward, now the left, now the right leg lifted and a swing round, arm in arm, a beautifully clean turn on one foot and away again in another direction to lift feet and change arms and cross and recross one another, all in time to the music and so smoothly. Their coarse faces expressed the nothingness of complete satisfaction.

Jake said: 'They're too conceited even to look pleased with themselves.'

Watching them for some reason made us feel sad and we thought that here we were in the centre of Europe with the enemy between us and our own country. We thought when we were refugees, perhaps we would look back on these as the happiest days of our lives.

The afternoons clouded over. It was dark by four o'clock. People began to leave the skiing slopes early, for wolves sometimes approached the hotel. If anyone lingered, they would see the figures of the others wavering and dwindling into the frightening twilight. Sometimes, while it was still light, a mist would come down through the pines and cut off everything. There was nothing to do but return to the hotel with its matchboarded walls and home-made electric light. The outdoor cold after sunset hurt one's whole body. The stream, too swift to freeze, steamed against the air. We hurried for relief to the heavy, oil-smelling, headache-heat of the hotel radiators.

The sun had not risen when we left. The air was grey. It was almost as cold as night. We knew what to do. There was an iron stove in one corner of the truck. We took two or three armfuls of logs from the tender-truck into the luggage-truck and made a fire in the stove. The passengers in the carriage watched out at us with amazement.

The damp logs, green fungus on the bark, smoked and perfumed the air. It was soon warm enough in the truck for comfort. There were two small windows without glass. We could kneel on the luggage and look out at the valley and feel the frozen air stream past our faces. As we descended, the snow lay thinner and we could see bushes and the hair-fine branches of the trees. A pewter and glass landscape repeated itself against a pewter sky. In places young trees covered the hills. The snow had blown from them, but lay thickly on the ground so the sloping hillsides were outlined through the smoke-fine fringing of trees. The hills rose and fell, rose and fell, drawn in white against the dark sky, detailed over with amazing delicacy by trees, houses and frozen rivers.

The houses were one-roomed, their windows boarded against the cold or hung with cloth. Each was topped by a straw roof like a peaked cap four times as high as itself. There was no telling barns and byres from dwelling-houses. They were all built the same and boarded up and extinguished by their tall, straw roofs. A few peasants followed the paths between the fields. They walked in single file—the men first in tight trousers and short coats of whitish frieze and sheepskin caps shaped like the roofs; the women followed in embroidered sheepskin jackets and red skirts. They turned their serious faces as we went past, but barely looked at us.

The river followed the train line. The ice, melting in parts, varied from white to a pale, icy green. Sometimes it was smashed to uncover the green-black waters below.

We stopped for five minutes at a half-way halt. There was a steady whine in the air. We got out to look. We had stopped beside a sawmill. There was an open fronted shed with a circular saw spinning round in the middle and enough logs stacked around to last a lifetime. The saw was cutting more logs. It could have cut four times as many a minute if the peasants had moved more quickly, but they saw no need to hurry. One of them held the wood to the saw, in an instant the steel slid through the wood, then he slowly pushed the pieces aside. The other peasant as slowly picked them up and stacked them—and all the time the saw whirred away with furious energy.

There were two stoves to heat the shed. We stood beside them and watched. One peasant looked at us with serious, disinterested, winter-bitten face, then went on slowly and disinterestedly feeding the saw. The other one kept his back to us.

Another man in a heavy overcoat, fur cap and jack-boots, was watching the saw. We knew he had not come from the carriage, which had remained sealed, its windows blurred, the faces showing through like tuberous plants in a conservatory. We supposed him to be a rich peasant, the owner of the sawmill, perhaps, or even of a small estate. He took no notice of us.

It was nearly noon. The day as light as it was likely to be, and still too cold to permit one to stand for more than a few minutes. Jake and David filled their arms with logs again and we went back to our truck. We stoked up the stove and sat round it on the suitcases. The brittle, white-pewter light struck upwards from the snow to the roof of the truck. The singing of the saw went on like a noise in nature. The stove burnt up a log in a few minutes. Its iron glowed rose-red, yet only thawed a few feet of the air about it.

The train gave a grunt. As it moved off someone jumped on to the platform of the truck and pushed open the door. In came the man in jack-boots. It was evident he had expected to have the truck to himself. He frowned at seeing us sitting round the stove and half-turned away. He would have sat by himself in some corner if he could, but there was nowhere to sit. David made room for him at once. He stood for a while then sat down in a withdrawn, resentful way.

We knew he could not be a Rumanian. It was only the first year of the war. A crowd of Rumanians, each drawing confidence from the others, might show resentment of our freedom, but one alone would be nervous, ingratiating, eager to assure us that the English had every right to think themselves a great people. If he were a Hungarian—and here we were almost on the frontier—he would surely be a more charming person!

This man had a sullen self-possession. Even David had nothing to say to him. Although he sat so close to us that he was pressing against Jake's arm, we three felt we sat together and apart from him and waited like an audience for him to speak.

He was a tall man, thin and bony, with a pallid, hard-boned face. He had a thin, down-drooping mouth like Dante's, but only his fixed expression of morose self-satisfaction—the expression of one who hopes his presence is causing discomfort—distinguished his face. His shineless leather boots sprawled surprisingly long and narrow in front of him.

He said suddenly in French: 'You're American, aren't you?'

'English,' David introduced himself: 'David Bailey: and this is my wife and this is Jake Jackson. We come from Bucharest.'

'I'm going there,' said the man without looking at us. He was beginning to feel the heat from the stove. He edged an inch or two from it and at last had to undo his overcoat. It fell open and we saw beneath it a greyish uniform with grey metal buttons. We knew at once he was a Polish soldier. We had seen hundreds like him coming in lorries to Bucharest. The lorries, riddled with shrapnel-holes and coated with mud, had swayed from side to side of the road, their drivers half-asleep at the wheel. The officers and civilians had come in cars. They parked anywhere. They just came to a stop. One could see them with the windscreens blotted out with mud, mattresses tied to the roofs, the people inside sprawling open-mouthed, asleep, their exhaustion overcoming for a while cold and hunger. The civilians who had money—and the wealthier ones brought bags of sovereigns, napoleons and golden dollars privately minted in Austria—took the Simplon at once for Paris. English money, and Englishmen to administer it, arrived in Bucharest to care for the rest. The soldiers were interned.

As soon as these refugees ceased to seem pitiable, stories began to circulate about their ingratitude and vanity and foolish, self-centred pride. Those who had lent them rooms or houses found their guests had settled in for good. In a few weeks everyone was bored with them and even ready to blame them for starting the war.

'What are you doing in Rumania?' asked the Pole.

'We work here,' said Jake.

'When our country was invaded,' said the Pole, 'every man who was abroad hurried back to defend her.'

'We were ordered to stay here,' said Jake. The Pole stared sullenly at the stove.

'They have more men in England than they can train,' David explained. 'We wanted to return, but we were told to stay here.'

'You should have been trained in readiness,' said the Pole. 'You should have been prepared to defend Poland.'

'We couldn't do more than we did,' said Jake sharply. 'And what about Poland being trained in readiness. Isn't it true you tried to fight the German tanks on horseback?'

'We have our traditions,' said the Pole. 'Poland suffered alone. She fought unaided. Now we will see how long the others fight.'

'They're all fighting for Poland,' said David.

'Nonsense,' said the Pole sourly, 'they're fighting for themselves.'

After that there was a long silence. At last I asked him what he was doing in this part of the country. He did not look at me, but answered: 'A few of us got down to Transylvania and were interned. We heard they were letting them escape from the bigger camps, but there were too few of us for anyone to bother. Nobody thought we would try to escape because we were too well off where we were. We had nothing to do. We'd lie on our bunks all day and think of Poland. Suddenly, last night, I knew I had had enough of it—and I knew I could get away. Why should these Rumanians care? They confiscated all the gold we brought from the banks and now they have to feed us—better for them if we go. I put a towel round me and crawled across the snow and under the wire. I spent the night walking east and this morning I came on this railway. I knew it must lead to the main line.'

'Have you had anything to eat?' asked David.

'I got bread and *ţuica* from a cottage.'

'You have some money?'

'No. Everything we had was taken from us at the camp.'

'Then how will you get to Bucharest?' asked Jake.

'I'll walk. I'll follow the line.'

'It will take you a month.'

'I have plenty of time.'

We settled down again into silence. The Pole interrupted. 'The war hasn't started for you yet,' he said. 'You do not think perhaps you will be refugees one day.' We did not answer and he said nothing more.

We came at last to the main-line halt. The carriage emptied itself in a squealing struggle to obtain one of the half-dozen peasants who acted as porters. While we were carrying our skis and bags across the line to the platform, we forgot the Pole. When we looked round, we saw he had followed us. He caught David's eye and, jumping down on to the line, he started walking determinedly eastwards. David shouted to him. He looked round.

'Don't go yet,' said David.

Without question or surprise, the Pole climbed back to the platform and waited.

David said in English to Jake. 'We'll have to get this fellow a ticket. He can't walk to Bucharest.'

'I don't see why not. He's got nothing else to do.'

'He'd freeze at night, or be eaten by wolves.'

'He doesn't seem the sort to freeze.'

'Don't be a fool, Jake; you know we'll have to get him a ticket.'

'And he knows it, too.'

'That makes no difference.'

'Oh, damn the Poles! They're everywhere.'

I followed David and Jake over to the waiting-room. It was crowded. Everyone had huddled there away from the wind. At the end was the ticket-office with its wooden shutter down and people rapping on the shutter, and shouting and making irritable Balkan gestures. Placed against the walls and on ledges and darkening the small, grimy windows, were plants in pots, all very dim and dry and dusty and shrunken with cold. The ticket-office shutter shot up suddenly and a red face above a dark uniform began shouting back at the travellers. David kept sending me outside to make sure the Pole had not run off. He remained where we had left him. Some twenty minutes later we got our tickets. David was afraid now that the Pole would not accept his, but he took it without comment.

I became angry then, but David said: 'What does it matter? We didn't do it for gratitude.'

The train, when it arrived, was crowded. Every train now was crowded. The whole country was under arms awaiting attack. The soldiers, who had to pay their own fares, travelled about the country in passenger trains. There were not many trains. All, even the 'expresses', stopped at every station and the peasants got on and off continually. Every journey was a long journey in time, if not in space.

Seven officers lay fast asleep in one carriage with their faces pressed against the bald, grimy plush and dirty curtains. David persuaded them to move so there was room for me, but he and Jake had to stand. The Pole disappeared.

The damp in the air had covered the carriage windows with long ferns of frost. One could scrape off the frost and see through the glass the white landscape going past. This was wheat-growing country, treeless, the fields repeating themselves in hills and hollows that looked barren, as though made of salt.

The peasants were packed in the corridors. Some lay on the floor. Some were prepared to stand for the full twenty hours of the journey to Bucharest. A girl in a wide red skirt sat on the handle of a basket. When she moved I could see beneath an embroidered linen covering, two geese in the basket. They were very big, very white, silent, dignified, but sick of being trodden on.

As we made our way along to the restaurant-car we looked for the Pole, but could not see him anywhere. When we reached the car, there he was lunching with a little dark man, who looked uncomfortable and annoyed.

He gave us a gloomy stare and turned his face away, as though we had ill-treated him. This amused Jake, who watched the two of them until the little man paid the bill and they passed us and went out. Neither of them had spoken during their meal. The Pole ignored us. We had decided to spend the night at Sighişoara, so we hoped to see no more of him.

But, when, at Sighişoara, we had got our luggage through the carriage window and fought our way out to join it, we found the Pole standing on the platform beside us.

He accused us: 'You are getting out here?'

'Yes, we're spending the night here.'

'And when does this train get to Bucharest?'

'Tomorrow morning.'

'I'll stay here too,' he said.

'Not with us,' said Jake, but he spoke in English. He hoisted his rucksack on to his shoulder and walked off.

David, following, sighed. He was always hoping circumstances would let him evade responsibility, but they never did.

With an air of obstinate peevishness, the Pole followed us. The waiting-room behind the platform was crowded with peasants eating from their bundles.

It was twilight. The air outside was a bright, frigid blue. The snow on the roofs was blue. The silhouette of the town with its towers and churches mounting the hillside, stood out in a plum-bloom blue against the frost-bitten blue of the sky.

We wanted a taxi because of the cold, but there were only sleighs. These were painted blue to match the town. They were small and close to the ground, with dirty straw on the floor, but their horses, unlike the wretched Bucharest horses, were plump under their woolly winter hair.

We got into a sleigh—David and I on one seat; Jake on the other. Jake put his rucksack on the fourth seat and smirked at the Pole, who was watching us. David lifted it down and said: 'Come on. There's room for you.'

Off we went with a jingle of bells through the blue streets with the air singing past our ears. Our faces became frozen so we could not feel them at all, but our ears hurt all the time.

We crossed a river. Blue snow lay on the ice. We could see the frosted branches of the weeping willows overhanging the invisible waters. The houses were dark but occasionally a little shop threw a glimmer of light on to the lumpy, dirty snow caked on the pavements. The hotel was surprisingly big. It looked like a barracks. When the sleigh stopped before it the driver, his frieze trousers fitting his legs like breeches, his jacket short and trimmed with fur, tumbled off the seat. 'Drunk,' said Jake, clicking his tongue. The driver picked himself up gaily and swayed with our bags into the hotel.

Inside was bare and new. David took three rooms—one was for the Pole, who accepted his key as he had his ticket—and we went upstairs to wash. The bedroom with its fumed oak and its golden satin eiderdown surprised us. Someone told us later that a lot of families from Bucharest spent the heat of the summer up here in the hills.

The Pole was waiting for us when we went downstairs and followed us out for supper. The hotel was in the main street. The shops were closed now. The whole place looked as though it were shuttered in against the cold. We felt the frozen snow like glass through our shoes. Snow was heaped in the gutters. The road was covered with snow that had been hardened flat by sleighs and looked like felt. We saw one or two private cars, probably belonging to factory owners, but everything else moved on sleighs.

Jake had been here before and knew where the restaurant was. It looked like a small shop and seemed as shuttered and dark as the rest of the street, but the door opened when we pushed it and inside we saw a counter for the sale of sausages, cheese, olives, pickles and *ţuica*. At one end of the counter, done in miniature but in the best traditions of old Rumanian restaurants, there was a display of the food on the menu: steak, garlic sausages, chicken and frankfurters. We were hungry.

The inner room was the restaurant. There were half a dozen tables covered with white paper and a couple of gipsies who started to play a modern dance tune as soon as we entered. At one table was a crowd of boys, friends of the waiter, who stopped talking and stared as soon as they saw us. We were not only visitors, we were foreigners—that must have been more than anyone hoped for in the middle of winter in Sighişoara.

We took the table farthest from the music before we realized it was also farthest from the stove. We sat with our coats on and ate grilled steak and drank *ţuica* that had been heated with sugar and pepper. The *ţuica* was very good. We ordered another half-litre and then another.

As we drank, the Pole, slowly and with the cumbersome movement of a tortoise wakening from age-long sleep, unbuttoned his coat and began to come to life. We had forgotten him. Jake and David had lapsed into English and were talking about the war. The Pole made a few slight hiccuping noises, then he joined in the conversation, which he did not understand, by giving an occasional '*Oui, oui*', and '*Non, non*'. When they were reminded of him, Jake and David started speaking again in French that he might not be excluded. As soon as he could understand what they were saying, he settled back again into gloomy silence. Then, suddenly, he shouted aloud: 'Poland has not perished yet.'

The town lads, who had lost interest in us by now, sat up and listened. The musicians paused in order to miss nothing. The Pole, with a look that showed he was aware of the expectancy, shut his mouth. When it was evident that nothing more was to be got out of him, everyone returned to his occupation, and the Pole gazed round, grieved, and after a pause, started mumbling: 'I remember when I worked in Lwow . . .' When no one took any notice, he repeated it more and more loudly until David and Jake broke off and looked at him. Then he drank a cup of *ţuica* slowly, swallowed slowly, and said impressively: 'I remember when I worked in Lwow . . .'

'Yes?' encouraged David.

'Ah!' said the Pole and stared gloomily into his empty cup.

None of us was very sober by now. The Pole had begun to seem a joke.

'Come on, cheer up!' shouted Jake, slapping him on the back. At first he did not seem to mind, then, as though he realized he ought to mind, he sat upright, his nostrils distended, his eyes starting, and said fiercely: 'How dare you! How dare you touch me! You, who did not fight for Poland!'

'Oh, shut up!' said Jake.

'Have some more *ţuica* and forget about Poland,' David said.

'I don't want any more *ţuica*,' said the Pole, but he let David fill his cup, 'and I shall never forget about Poland. Never.' He sipped meditatively: 'I remember when I was in Lwow . . .'

We did not interrupt. There was a long pause and at last he went on grudgingly, as though it were impossible now not to go on: 'I was in love with a girl. In the evenings we used to walk round the streets together and talk. Nothing else—but we had plenty to talk about. I told her every-thing. I thought she told me everything.'

He emptied his cup and refilled it. Another pause. He continued, not so grudgingly now, overlooking the injury for a time: 'I can remember we often went down a road by the canal. I can remember hearing some dogs barking, answering one another, somewhere behind the houses. It was dark. The roads were only half-lighted . . . and it all meant something. Yes, it meant something, but I don't know what. It seemed to me that I'd discovered something. Everything was important to me in those days.' He paused for so long now that David and Jake started talking again. At once the Pole interrupted them sternly: 'But nothing here is important. This place means nothing. You mean nothing. Your faces mean nothing.'

'Never mind,' said Jake.

David asked: 'Did you marry her?'

The Pole stared down darkly. 'No,' he replied, at last, 'I saved every penny to marry her, then one day she told me she was engaged to someone else. I'd kept her waiting too long. I didn't even know she knew another man. They got married and went to live in Warsaw. I used to get sent there sometimes and I always visited them. When the war started she was going to have a baby. Her husband was killed. She's probably still in Warsaw.'

'And you're trying to get back to her?' I asked.

'No,' the Pole looked surprised, 'I'm trying to get to France. I can fight for Poland there.'

'Poland is important?' asked Jake.

The Pole stared at him in silence. Jake, flushing slightly, gave a laugh, then called loudly for the bill.

When we got back to the hotel, the Pole walked straight upstairs to his room. He had not spoken again. We hoped he would catch the first train in the morning and when we awoke, we dressed slowly to give him time to get away. But we got down to the hotel café to find him sitting there reading a German newspaper mounted on a cane holder. His first words were: 'Everyone here speaks German.'

David explained: 'This is a Saxon town—the people are practically German. You know the Pied Piper legend? Well, these people are supposed to be descended from the children who disappeared.'

The Pole broke in as though he had been waiting for a chance to make a complaint: 'You shouldn't have brought me here.'

'No, I suppose we shouldn't,' said Jake. The Pole gave an irritated gesture and returned to his paper. We got Rumanian papers from the rack and ordered coffee and rolls for four.

Both the outer and inner windows were heavily frosted, but we could tell by the colour of the light that the sun was shining. As more people came into the café and the room warmed, the glass cleared in patches and we could look out at tiny pictures of the distant Gothic buildings climbing up the hillside. Against the delicate blue sky, with its stippling of green overhead, the snow-silvered glimpses of churches and towers were like pictures painted on china. We wanted to go out at once. The next train was not until one o'clock. We left the Pole to do what he pleased about it and, of course, he followed.

The light in the street was very bright. It was a New Year holiday and the shops were shut. The town seemed deserted. An occasional sleigh whipped past in a jingle of bells, but we passed no one on the pavements. We came to the main square. Here a solitary small boy was tobogganing down a slope and scattering as he went a multitude of pigeons. We took a path up between the roofs to the hilltop. When we got up a little way we looked back and saw the roofs below us like folded slips of white velvet. Each chimney held up its collar of snow. A smoke gauze lay over the frigid glitter of the snow. As the path grew steeper it turned into steps beside which the sedate houses rose one above the other, painted terracotta, pink, lime-green, grey-blue, orange or cocoa-brown. Everywhere the snow, unbroken and brilliant on roofs and ledges, heightened the colours.

The lower steps had been cleared, but as we rose higher we had to feel for foot-hold. The way was diverted at times under Gothic arches, corbelled, painted and gilded, that framed the bright corners of houses and the blinding glitter of light on snow. Suddenly we came to the top of the steps and saw the church—a dull piece of modern Gothic, but with ancient, very tall, black tombstones rising from snow behind an intricately-wrought railing. Whenever we paused, the Pole paused, too, but when we looked at him he stared blankly over our heads.

'Don't you think it's rather a pleasant town?' David asked him.

He shrugged his shoulders.

'We're just wasting his time,' said Jake.

We started up a new set of steps to the hilltop. As we rose from the protecting buildings, the air got colder and colder. It was almost impossible to breathe for cold. It tricked out everything with diamond-edged acuteness. The colours were bitten in with cold. It made us almost weep for our hands and nose and feet, but it also took away every haze of reflection that might dull the brain.

We were now walking up through public gardens. A large building stood at the top.

'What is it?' asked Jake. 'It's a school. The Rumanians would have put the Prefectura up there.'

'The French would have put the church,' said David.

'And we would have put a public monument—but we would have cleared the steps for appearances' sake.'

The school was closed for the holidays. Fall after fall of snow had blotted out the gardens, so one could not tell where there were paths and where grass or steps. Once or twice we sank down to our knees, or stepped on something unexpectedly hard and lost balance. The Pole tripped on a rail and came to his knees with a thud. He shouted out angrily in Polish. We laughed at him as he brushed himself down, but he did not laugh.

The summit, just behind the school, was a small, square garden with paths indenting the snow. Here, between the frost-tipped branches of the trees, we could survey the whole town running down the sides of the hill and crowded in a hollow round the central square. We could see the rapid horse-sleighs passing smoothly over the roads and the big, slow sleighs, loaded with wood, and drawn by heavy, fawn-coloured oxen. While we watched, the pigeons rose like a handful of seed flung into the air. They took three turns, flashing from iron-grey to white, then poured down like seed through a funnel to settle in a bunch on the road.

We could look out to the surrounding hills and see through the snow the division of fields, the ridges for vines or hops, the poles, the black rows of fruit trees and the isolated farms.

In the valley running between the hills were factory chimneys from which a red smoke rolled out to colour the sky so it looked like the sky in childhood pictures of biblical destruction.

From the other side of the garden, over a wall ribbed with wind-driven snow, we could see into a modern cemetery. Gravestones overhung gravestones, hundreds of them dropping acutely down and down out of sight.

'All so ugly,' I said. 'There were only a few of the old stones—but now there are too many people and one feels affronted by the sight of so much death,' and I returned to where the valley ran white into the distance. On either side the steep flanks of the hills were cultivated in terraces that hung there like the gardens of Babylon.

The Pole broke in on our conversation: 'We're late for the train.'

David looked at his watch. 'We haven't much time,' he agreed, 'but we haven't got to catch it. We're not due back until Monday.'

'Let us stay one more night,' I said.

The Pole interrupted irritably: 'There is no time to waste in talking.'

David said: 'We have decided to stay another day.'

'But I do not wish to stay.'

Jake said: 'If you hurry back, you'll catch the train. You can go straight to the station.'

'Don't worry about the hotel bill,' said David.

The Pole stared at us as though some inexcusable trick had been played on him, but we stood our ground remorselessly. After a moment he glanced down to the town, then swung round and away across the snow.

Suddenly David ran after him. Jake and I followed without enthusiasm. David overtook him and when we came up, was asking him: 'What are you going to do in Bucharest? I mean, for money?'

The Pole looked contemptuously from one to the other of us: 'I shall manage very well,' he said. 'All the buttons on my uniform are made of gold.'

We stared unbelievingly at the grey metal buttons.

'They're leaded over,' he said, 'I had them made two yeras ago.' His mouth dropped down further in a bitter smirk. 'You see, we were not unprepared.'

We had nothing to say. We watched him stride off.

'Damn him!' said Jake when the Pole was out of sight, 'how did he manage to put us in the wrong!'

'After all we did for him!' I said.

'What did we do for him?' asked David, giving me a push. 'We spent some money we could well afford.'

'What did he want?' asked Jake angrily. 'What did he expect from us?'

I said: 'He expected something. He followed us; he told us about the girl. He thought we had something to give.'

We all stood looking down where the Pole had gone. 'Well, it's too late now,' said Jake at last, 'and we're only worrying because it's too late. So let's be thankful we can go and eat in peace.'

We never saw the Pole again.

VIRGINIA WOOLF

The Legacy

❦

'For Sissy Miller.' Gilbert Clandon, taking up the pearl brooch that lay among a litter of rings and brooches on a little table in his wife's drawing-room, read the inscription: 'For Sissy Miller, with my love.'

It was like Angela to have remembered even Sissy Miller, her secretary. Yet how strange it was, Gilbert Clandon thought once more, that she had left everything in such order—a little gift of some sort for every one of her friends. It was as if she had foreseen her death. Yet she had been in perfect health when she left the house that morning, six weeks ago; when she stepped off the kerb in Piccadilly and the car had killed her.

He was waiting for Sissy Miller. He had asked her to come; he owed her, he felt, after all the years she had been with them, this token of consideration. Yes, he went on, as he sat there waiting, it was strange that Angela had left everything in such order. Every friend had been left some little token of her affection. Every ring, every necklace, every little Chinese box—she had a passion for little boxes—had a name on it. And each had some memory for him. This he had given her; this—the enamel dolphin with the ruby eyes—she had pounced upon one day in a back street in Venice. He could remember her little cry of delight. To him of course, she had left nothing in particular, unless it were her diary. Fifteen little volumes, bound in green leather, stood behind him on her writing table. Ever since they were married, she had kept a diary. Some of their very few—he could not call them quarrels, say tiffs—had been about that diary. When he came in and found her writing, she always shut it or put her hand over it. 'No, no, no,' he could hear her say, 'After I'm dead—perhaps.' So she had left it him, as her legacy. It was the only thing they had not shared when she was alive. But he had always taken it for granted that she would outlive him. If only she had stopped one moment, and had thought what she was doing, she would be alive now. But she had stepped straight off the kerb, the driver of the car had said at the inquest. She had given him no chance to pull up . . . Here the sound of voices in the hall interrupted him.

'Miss Miller, Sir,' said the maid.

She came in. He had never seen her alone in his life, nor, of course, in tears. She was terribly distressed, and no wonder. Angela had been much more to her than an employer. She had been a friend. To himself, he thought, as he pushed a chair for her and asked her to sit down, she was scarcely distinguishable from any other woman of her kind. There were thousands of Sissy Millers—drab little women in black carrying attaché cases. But Angela, with her genius for sympathy, had discovered all sorts of qualities in Sissy Miller. She was the soul of discretion; so silent; so trustworthy, one could tell her anything, and so on.

Miss Miller could not speak at first. She sat there dabbing her eyes with her pocket handkerchief. Then she made an effort.

'Pardon me, Mr Clandon,' she said.

He murmured. Of course he understood. It was only natural. He could guess what his wife had meant to her.

'I've been so happy here,' she said, looking round. Her eyes rested on the writing table behind him. It was here they had worked—she and Angela. For Angela had her share of the duties that fall to the lot of a prominent politician's wife. She had been the greatest help to him in his career. He had often seen her and Sissy sitting at that table—Sissy at the typewriter, taking down letters from her dictation. No doubt Miss Miller was thinking of that, too. Now all he had to do was to give her the brooch his wife had left her. A rather incongruous gift it seemed. It might have been better to have left her a sum of money, or even the typewriter. But there it was—'For Sissy Miller, with my love.' And, taking the brooch, he gave it her with the little speech that he had prepared. He knew, he said, that she would value it. His wife had often worn it . . . And she replied, as she took it almost as if she too had prepared a speech, that it would always be a treasured possession . . . She had, he supposed, other clothes upon which a pearl brooch would not look quite so incongruous. She was wearing the little black coat and skirt that seemed the uniform of her profession. Then he remembered—she was in mourning, of course. She, too, had had her tragedy—a brother, to whom she was devoted, had died only a week or two before Angela. In some accident was it? He could not remember—only Angela telling him. Angela, with her genius for sympathy, had been terribly upset. Meanwhile Sissy Miller had risen. She was putting on her gloves. Evidently she felt that she ought not to intrude. But he could not let her go without saying something about her future. What were her plans? Was there any way in which he could help her?

She was gazing at the table, where she had sat at her typewriter, where the diary lay. And, lost in her memories of Angela, she did not at once answer his suggestion that he should help her. She seemed for a moment not to understand. So he repeated:

'What are your plans, Miss Miller?'

'My plans? Oh, that's all right, Mr Clandon,' she exclaimed. 'Please don't bother yourself about me.'

He took her to mean that she was in no need of financial assistance. It would be better, he realized, to make any suggestion of that kind in a letter. All he could do now was to say as he pressed her hand, 'Remember, Miss Miller, if there's any way in which I can help you, it will be a pleasure . . .' Then he opened the door. For a moment, on the threshold, as if a sudden thought had struck her, she stopped.

'Mr Clandon,' she said, looking straight at him for the first time, and for the first time he was struck by the expression, sympathetic yet searching, in her eyes. 'If at any time,' she continued, 'there's anything I can do to help you, remember, I shall feel it, for your wife's sake, a pleasure . . .'

With that she was gone. Her words and the look that went with them were unexpected. It was almost as if she believed, or hoped, that he would need her. A curious, perhaps a fantastic idea occurred to him as he returned to his chair. Could it be, that during all those years when he had scarcely noticed her, she, as the novelists say, had entertained a passion for him? He caught his own reflection in the glass as he passed. He was over fifty; but he could not help admitting that he was still, as the looking-glass showed him, a very distinguished-looking man.

'Poor Sissy Miller!' he said, half laughing. How he would have liked to share that joke with his wife! He turned instinctively to her diary. 'Gilbert,' he read, opening it at random, 'looked so wonderful . . .' It was as if she had answered his question. Of course, she seemed to say, you're very attractive to women. Of course Sissy Miller felt that too. He read on. 'How proud I am to be his wife!' And he had always been very proud to be her husband. How often, when they dined out somewhere, he had looked at her across the table and said to himself, She is the loveliest woman here! He read on. That first year he had been standing for Parliament. They had toured his constituency. 'When Gilbert sat down the applause was terrific. The whole audience rose and sang: "For he's a jolly good fellow." I was quite overcome.' He remembered that, too. She had been sitting on the platform beside him. He could still see the glance she cast at him, and how she had tears in her eyes. And then? He turned the pages. They had gone to Venice. He recalled that happy holiday after the election. 'We had ices at Florians.' He smiled—she was still such a child; she loved ices. 'Gilbert gave me a most interesting account of the history of Venice. He told me that the Doges . . .' she had written it all out in her schoolgirl hand. One of the delights of travelling with Angela had been that she was so eager to learn. She was so terribly ignorant, she used to say, as if that were not one of her charms. And then—he opened the next volume—they had come back to London. 'I was so anxious to make a good impression. I wore my wedding dress.' He could see her now sitting next old Sir Edward; and making a conquest of that formidable old man, his chief. He read on rapidly, filling in scene after scene from her scrappy fragments. 'Dined at the House of Commons . . . To an evening party at the Lovegroves. Did I realize my responsibility, Lady L. asked me, as Gilbert's wife?' Then, as the years passed—he took another volume from the writing table—he had become more and more absorbed in his work. And she, of course, was more often alone . . . It had been a great grief to her, apparently, that they had had no children. 'How I wish,' one entry read, 'that Gilbert had a son!' Oddly enough he had never much regretted that himself. Life had been so full, so rich as it was. That year he had been given a minor post in the government. A minor post only, but her comment was: 'I am quite certain now that he will be Prime Minister!' Well, if things had gone differently, it might have been so. He paused here to speculate upon what might have been. Politics was a gamble, he reflected; but the game wasn't over yet. Not at fifty. He cast his eyes rapidly over more pages, full of the little trifles, the insignificant, happy daily trifles that had made up her life.

He took up another volume and opened it at random. 'What a coward I am! I let the chance slip again. But it seemed selfish to bother him with my own affairs, when he has so much to think about. And we so seldom have an evening alone.' What was the meaning of that? Oh, here was the explanation—it referred to her work in the East End. 'I plucked up courage and talked to Gilbert at last. He was so kind, so good. He made no objection.' He remembered that conversation. She had told him that she felt so idle, so useless. She wished to have some work of her own. She wanted to do something—she had blushed so prettily, he remembered, as she said it, sitting in that very chair—to help others. He had bantered her a little. Hadn't she enough to do looking after him, after her home? Still, if it amused her, of course he had no objection. What was it? Some district? Some committee? Only she must promise not to make herself ill. So it seemed that every Wednesday she went to Whitechapel. He remembered how he hated the clothes she wore on those occasions. But she had taken it very seriously, it seemed. The diary was full of references like this: 'Saw Mrs Jones . . . She has ten children . . . Husband lost his arm in an accident . . . Did my best to find a job for Lily.' He skipped on. His own name occurred less frequently. His interest slackened. Some of the entries conveyed nothing to him. For example: 'Had a heated argument about socialism with B. M.' Who was B. M.? he could not fill in the initials; some woman, he supposed, that she had met on one of her committees. 'B. M. made a violent attack upon the upper classes . . . I walked back after the meeting with B. M. and tried to convince him. But he is so narrow minded.' So B. M. was a man—no doubt one of those 'intellectuals', as they call themselves, who are so violent, as Angela said, and so narrow-minded. She had invited him to come and see her apparently. 'B. M. came to dinner. He shook hands with Minnie!' That note of exclamation gave another twist to his mental picture. B. M., it seemed, wasn't used to parlourmaids; he had shaken hands with Minnie. Presumably he was one of those tame working men who air their views in ladies' drawing-rooms. Gilbert knew the type, and had no liking for this particular specimen, whoever B. M. might be. Here he was again. 'Went with B. M. to the Tower of London . . . He said revolution is bound to come . . . He said we live in a Fool's Paradise.' That was just the kind of thing B. M. would say—Gilbert could hear him. He could also see him quite distinctly—a stubby little man, with a rough beard, red tie, dressed as they always did in tweeds, who had never done an honest day's work in his life. Surely Angela had the sense to see through him? He read on. 'B. M. said some very disagreeable things about—.' The name was carefully scratched out. 'I told him I would not listen to any more abuse of—' Again the name was obliterated. Could it have been his own name? Was that why Angela covered the page so quickly when he came in? The thought added to his growing dislike of B. M. He had had the impertinence to discuss him in this very room. Why had Angela never told him? It was very unlike her to conceal anything; she had been the soul of candour. He turned the pages, picking out every reference to B. M. 'B. M. told me the story of his childhood. His mother went out charring . . . When I think of it, I can hardly bear to go on living in such luxury . . . Three guineas for one hat!' If only she had discussed the matter with him, instead of puzzling her poor little head about questions that were much too difficult for her to understand! He had lent her books. *Karl Marx*, *The Coming Revolution*. The initials B. M., B. M., B. M., recurred repeatedly. But why never the full name? There was an informality, an intimacy in the use of initials that was very unlike Angela. Had she called him B. M. to his face? He read on. 'B. M. came unexpectedly after dinner. Luckily, I was alone.' That was only a year ago. 'Luckily'— why luckily?—'I was alone.' Where had he been that night? He checked the date in his engagement book. It had been the night of the Mansion House dinner. And B. M. and Angela had spent the evening alone! He tried to recall that evening. Was she waiting up for him when he came back? Had the room looked just as usual? Were there glasses on the table? Were the chairs drawn close together? He could remember nothing—nothing whatever, nothing except his own speech at the Mansion House dinner. It became more and more inexplicable to him—the whole situation; his wife receiving an unknown man alone. Perhaps the next volume would explain. Hastily he reached for the last of the diaries—the one she had left unfinished when she died. There, on the very first page, was that cursed fellow again. 'Dined alone with B. M. . . . He became very agitated. He said it was time we understood each other . . . I tried to make him listen. But he would not. He threatened that if I did not . . .' the rest of the page was scored over. She had written 'Egypt. Egypt. Egypt,' over the whole page. He could not make out a single word; but there could be only one interpretation: the scoundrel had asked her to become his mistress. Alone in his room! The blood rushed to Gilbert Clandon's face. He turned the pages rapidly. What had been her answer? Initials had ceased. It was simply 'he' now. 'He came again. I told him I could not come to any decision . . . I implored him to leave.' He had forced himself upon her in this very house. But why hadn't she told him? How could she have hesitated for an instant? Then: 'I wrote him a letter.' Then pages were left blank. Then there was this: 'No answer to my letter.' Then more blank pages; and then this: 'He has done what he threatened.' After that—what came after that? He turned page after page. All were blank. But there, on the very day before her death, was this entry: 'Have I the courage to do it too?' That was the end.

Gilbert Clandon let the book slide to the floor. He could see her in front of him. She was standing on the kerb in Piccadilly. Her eyes stared; her fists were clenched. Here came the car . . .

He could not bear it. He must know the truth. He strode to the telephone.

'Miss Miller!' There was silence. Then he heard someone moving in the room.

'Sissy Miller speaking'—her voice at last answered him.

'Who,' he thundered, 'is B. M.?'

He could hear the cheap clock ticking on her mantel-piece; then a long drawn sigh. Then at last she said:

'He was my brother.'

He *was* her brother; her brother who had killed himself. 'Is there,' he heard Sissy Miller asking, 'anything that I can explain?'

'Nothing!' he cried. 'Nothing!'

He had received his legacy. She had told him the truth. She had stepped off the kerb to rejoin her lover. She had stepped off the kerb to escape from him.

EUDORA WELTY

First Love

❧

Whatever happened, it happened in extraordinary times, in a season of dreams, and in Natchez it was the bitterest winter of them all. The north wind struck one January night in 1807 with an insistent penetration, as if it followed the settlers down by their own course, screaming down the river bends to drive them farther still. Afterwards there was the strange drugged fall of snow. When the sun rose the air broke into a thousand prisms as close as the flash-and-turn of gulls' wings. For a long time afterwards it was so clear that in the evening the little companion-star to Sirius could be seen plainly in the heavens by travellers who took their way by night, and Venus shone in the daytime in all its course through the new transparency of the sky.

The Mississippi shuddered and lifted from its bed, reaching like a somnambulist driven to go in new places; the ice stretched far out over the waves. Flatboats and rafts continued to float downstream, but with unsignalling passengers submissive and huddled, mere bundles of sticks; bets were laid on shore as to whether they were alive or dead, but it was impossible to prove it either way.

The coated moss hung in blue and shining garlands over the trees along the changed streets in the morning. The town of little galleries was all laden roofs and silence. In the fastness of Natchez it began to seem then that the whole world, like itself, must be in transfiguration. The only clamour came from the animals that suffered in their stalls, or from the wildcats that howled in closer rings each night from the frozen cane. The Indians could be heard from greater distances and in greater numbers than had been guessed, sending up placating but proud messages to the sun in continual ceremonies of dancing. The red percussion of their fires could be seen night and day by those waiting in the dark trance of the frozen town. Men were caught by the cold, they dropped in its snare-like silence. Bands of travellers moved closer together, with intenser caution, through the glassy tunnels of the Trace, for all proportion went away, and they followed one another like insects going at dawn through the heavy grass. Natchez people turned silently to look when a solitary man that no one had ever seen before was found and carried in through the streets, frozen the way he had crouched in a hollow tree, grey and huddled like a squirrel, with a little bundle of goods clasped to him.

Joel Mayes, a deaf boy twelve years old, saw the man brought in and knew it was a dead man, but his eyes were for something else, something wonderful. He saw the breaths coming out of people's mouths, and his dark face, losing just now a little of its softness, showed its secret desire. It was marvellous to him when the infinite designs of speech became visible in formations on the air, and he watched with awe that changed to tenderness whenever people met and passed in the road with an exchange of words. He walked alone, slowly through the silence, with the sturdy and yet dreamlike walk of the orphan, and let his own breath out through his lips, pushed it into the air, and whatever word it was it took the shape of a tower. He was as pleased as if he had a little conversation with someone. At the end of the street, where he turned into the Inn, he always bent his head and walked faster, as if all frivolity were done, for he was boot-boy there.

He had come to Natchez some time in the summer. That was through great worlds of leaves, and the whole journey from Virginia had been to him a kind of childhood wandering in oblivion. He had remained to himself: always to himself at first, and afterwards too—with the company of Old Man McCaleb who took him along when his parents vanished in the forest, were cut off from him, and in spite of his last backward look, dropped behind. Arms bent on destination dragged him forward through the sharp bushes, and leaves came toward his face which he finally put his hands out to stop. Now that he was a boot-boy, he had thought little, frugally, almost stonily, of that long time . . . until lately Old Man McCaleb had reappeared at the Inn, bound for no telling where, his tangled beard like the beards of old men in dreams; and in the act of cleaning his boots, which were uncommonly heavy and burdensome with mud, Joel came upon a little part of the old adventure, for there it was, dark and crusted . . . came back to it, and went over it again. . . .

He rubbed, and remembered the day after his parents had left him, the day when it was necessary to hide from the Indians. Old Man McCaleb, his stern face lighting in the most unexpected way, had herded them, the whole party alike, into the dense cane brake, deep down off the Trace— the densest part, where it grew as thick and locked as some kind of wild teeth. There they crouched, and each one of them, man, woman, and child, had looked at all the others from a hiding place that seemed the least safe of all, watching in an eager wild instinct for any movement or betrayal. Crouched by his bush, Joel had cried; all his understanding would desert him suddenly and because he could not hear he could not see or touch or find a familiar thing in the world. He wept, and Old Man McCaleb first felled the excited dog with the blunt end of his axe, and then he turned a fierce face toward him and lifted the blade in the air, in a kind of ecstasy of protecting the silence they were keeping. Joel had made a sound. . . . He gasped and put his mouth quicker than thought against the earth. He took the leaves in his mouth. . . . In that long time of lying motionless with the men and women in the cane brake he had learned what silence meant to other people. Through the danger he had felt acutely, even with horror, the nearness of his companions, a speechless embrace of which he had had no warning, a powerful, crushing unity. The Indians had then gone by, followed by an old woman—in solemn, single file, careless of the inflaming arrows they carried in their quivers, dangling in their hands a few strings of catfish. They passed in the length of the old woman's yawn. Then one by one McCaleb's charges had to rise up and come out of the hiding place. There was little talking together, but a kind of shame and shuffling. As soon as the party reached Natchez, their little cluster dissolved completely. The old man had given each of them one long, rather forlorn look for a farewell, and had gone away, no less pre-occupied than he had ever been. To the man who had saved his life Joel lifted the gentle, almost indifferent face of the child who has asked for nothing. Now he remembered the white gulls flying across the sky behind the old man's head.

Joel had been deposited at the Inn, and there was nowhere else for him to go, for it stood there and marked the foot of the long Trace, with the river back of it. So he remained. It was a noncommittal arrangement: he never paid them anything for his keep, and they never paid him anything for his work. Yet time passed, and he became a little part of the place where it passed over him. A small private room became his own; it was on the ground floor behind the saloon, a dark little room paved with stones with its ceiling rafters curved not higher than a man's head. There was a fireplace and one window, which opened on the courtyard filled always with the tremor of horses. He curled up every night on a highbacked bench, when the weather turned cold he was given a collection of old coats to sleep under, and the room was almost excessively his own, as it would have been a stray kitten's that came to the same spot every night. He began to keep his candlestick carefully polished, he set it in the centre of the puncheon table, and at night when it was lighted all the messages of love carved into it with a knife in Spanish words, with a deep Spanish gouging, came out in black relief, for anyone to read who came knowing the language.

Late at night, nearer morning, after the travellers had all certainly pulled off their boots to fall into bed, he waked by habit and passed with the candle shielded up the stairs and through the halls and rooms, and gathered up the boots. When he had brought them all down to his table he would sit and take his own time cleaning them, while the firelight would come gently across the paving stones. It seemed then that his whole life was safely alighted, in the sleep of everyone else, like a bird on a bough, and he was alone in the way he liked to be. He did not despise boots at all—he had learned boots; under his hand they stood up and took a good shape. This was not a slave's work, or a child's either. It had dignity: it was dangerous to walk about among sleeping men. More than once he had been seized and the life half shaken out of him by a man waking up in a sweat of suspicion or nightmare, but he dealt nimbly as an animal with the violence and quick frenzy of dreamers. It might seem to him that the whole world was sleeping in the lightest of trances, which the least movement would surely wake; but he only walked softly, stepping around and over, and got back to his room. Once a rattlesnake had shoved its head from a boot as he stretched out his hand; but that was not likely to happen again in a thousand years.

It was in his own room, on the night of the first snowfall, that a new adventure began for him. Very late in the night, toward morning, Joel sat bolt upright in bed and opened his eyes to see the whole room shining brightly, like a brimming lake in the sun. Boots went completely out of his head, and he was left motionless. The candle was lighted in its stick, the fire was high in the grate, and from the window a wild tossing illumination came, which he did not even identify at first as the falling of snow. Joel was left in the shadow of the room, and there before him, in the centre of the strange multiplied light, were two men in black capes sitting at his table. They sat in profile to him, tall under the little arch of the rafters, facing each other across the good table he used for everything, and talking together. They were not of Natchez, and their names were not in the book. Each of them had a white glitter upon his boots—it was the snow; their capes were drawn together in front, and in the blackness of the folds, snowflakes were just beginning to melt.

Joel had never been able to hear the knocking at a door, and still he knew what that would be; and he surmised that these men had never knocked even lightly to enter his room. When he found that at some moment outside his knowledge or consent two men had seemingly fallen from the clouds on to the two stools at his table and had taken everything over for themselves, he did not keep the calm heart with which he had stood and regarded all men up to Old Man McCaleb, who snored upstairs.

He did not at once betray the violation that he felt. Instead, he simply sat, still bolt upright, and looked with the feasting the eyes do in secret—at their faces, the one eye of each that he could see, the cheeks, the half-hidden mouths—the faces each firelit, and strange with a common reminiscence or speculation. . . . Perhaps he was saved from giving a cry by knowing it could be heard. Then the gesture one of the men made in the air transfixed him where he waited.

One of the two men lifted his right arm—a tense, yet gentle and easy motion—and made the dark wet cloak fall back. To Joel it was like the first movement he had ever seen, as if the world had been up to that night inanimate. It was like the signal to open some heavy gate or paddock, and it did open to his complete astonishment upon a panorama in his own head, about which he knew first of all that he would never be able to speak—it was nothing but brightness, as full as the brightness on which he had opened his eyes. Inside his room was still another interior, this meeting upon which all the light was turned, and within that was one more mystery, all that was being said. The men's heads were inclined together against the blaze, their hair seemed light and floating. Their elbows rested on the boards, stirring the crumbs where Joel had eaten his biscuit. He had no idea of how long they had stayed when they got up and stretched their arms and walked out through the door, after blowing the candle out.

When Joel woke up again at daylight, his first thought was of Indians, his next of ghosts, and then the vision of what had happened came back into his head. He took a light beating for forgetting to clean the boots, but then he forgot the beating. He wondered for how long a time the men had been meeting in his room while he was asleep, and whether they had ever seen him, and what they might be going to do to him, whether they would take him each by the arm and drag him on farther, through the leaves. He tried to remember everything of the night before, and he could, and then of the day before, and he rubbed belatedly at a boot in a long and deepening dream. His memory could work like the slinging of a noose to catch a wild pony. It reached back and hung trembling over the very moment of terror in which he had become separated from his parents, and then it turned and started in the opposite direction, and it would have discerned some shape, but he would not let it, of the future. In the meanwhile, all day long, everything in the passing moment and each little deed assumed the gravest importance. He divined every change in the house, in the angle of the doors, in the height of the fires, and whether the logs had been stirred by a boot or had only fallen in an empty room. He was seized and possessed by mystery. He waited for night. In his own room the candlestick now stood on the table covered with the wonder of having been touched by unknown hands in his absence and seen in his sleep.

It was while he was cleaning boots again that the identity of the men came to him all at once. Like part of his meditations, the names came into his mind. He ran out into the street with this knowledge rocking in his head, remembering then the tremor of a great arrival which had shaken Natchez, caught fast in the grip of the cold, and shaken it through the lethargy of the snow, and it was clear now why the floors swayed with running feet and unsteady hands shoved him aside at the bar. There was no one to inform him that the men were Aaron Burr and Harman Blennerhassett, but he knew. No one had pointed out to him any way that he might know which was which, but he knew that: it was Burr who had made the gesture.

They came to his room every night, and indeed Joel had not expected that the one visit would be the end. It never occurred to him that the first meeting did not mark a beginning. It took a little time always for the snow to melt from their capes—for it continued all this time to snow. Joel sat up with his eyes wide open in the shadows and looked out like the lone watcher of a conflagration. The room grew warm, burning with the heat from the little grate, but there was something of fire in all that happened. It was from Aaron Burr that the flame was springing, and it seemed to pass across the table with certain words and through the sudden noble-ness of the gesture, and touch Blennerhassett. Yet the breath of their speech was no simple thing like the candle's gleam between them. Joel saw them still only in profile, but he could see that the secret was end-lessly complex, for in two nights it was apparent that it could never be all told. All that they said never finished their conversation. They would always have to meet again. The ring Burr wore caught the firelight repeatedly and started it up again in the intricate whirlpool of a signet. Quicker and fuller still was his eye, darting its look about, but never at Joel. Their eyes had never really seen his room . . . the fine polish he had given the candlestick, the clean boards from which he had scraped the crumbs, the wooden bench where he was himself, from which he put outward—just a little, carelessly—his hand. . . . Everything in the room was conquest, all was a dream of delights and powers beyond its walls. . . . The light-filled hair fell over Burr's sharp forehead, his cheek grew taut, his smile was sudden, his lips drove the breath through. The other man's face, with its quiet mouth, for he was the listener, changed from ardour to gloom and back to ardour. . . . Joel sat still and looked from one man to the other.

At first he believed that he had not been discovered. Then he knew that they had learned somehow of his presence, and that it had not stopped them. Somehow that appalled him. . . . They were aware that if it were only before him, they could talk forever in his room. Then he put it that they accepted him. One night, in his first realization of this, his defect seemed to him a kind of hospitality. A joy came over him, he was moved to gaiety, he felt wit stirring in his mind, and he came out of his hiding place and took a few steps toward them. Finally, it was too much: he broke in upon the circle of their talk, and set food and drink from the kitchen on the table between them. His hands were shaking, and they looked at him as if from great distances, but they were not surprised, and he could smell the familiar black wetness of travellers' clothes steaming up from them in the firelight. Afterwards he sat on the floor perfectly still, with Burr's cloak hanging just beside his own shoulder. At such moments he felt a dizziness as if the cape swung him about in a great arc of wonder, but Aaron Burr turned his full face and looked down at him only with gravity, the high margin of his brows lifted above tireless eyes.

There was a kind of dominion promised in his gentlest glance. When he first would come and throw himself down to talk and the fire would flame up and the reflections of the snowy world grew bright, even the clumsy table seemed to change its substance and to become part of a ceremony. He might have talked in another language, in which there was nothing but evocation. When he was seen so plainly, all his movements and his looks seemed part of a devotion that was curiously patient and had the illusion of wisdom all about it. Lights shone in his eyes like travellers' fires seen far out on the river. Always he talked, his talking was his appearance, as if there were no eyes, nose, or mouth to remember; in his face there was every subtlety and eloquence, and no features, no kindness, for there was no awareness whatever of the present. Looking up from the floor at his speaking face, Joel knew all at once some secret of temptation and an anguish that would reach out after it like a closing hand. He would allow Burr to take him with him wherever it was that he meant to go.

Sometimes in the nights Joel would feel himself surely under their eyes, and think they must have come; but that would be a dream, and when he sat up on his bench he often saw nothing more than the dormant firelight stretched on the empty floor, and he would have a strange feeling of having been deserted and lost, not quite like anything he had ever felt in his life. It was likely to be early dawn before they came.

When they were there, he sat restored, though they paid no more attention to him than they paid the presence of the firelight. He brought all the food he could manage to give them; he saved a little out of his own suppers, and one night he stole a turkey pie. He might have been their safety, for the way he sat up so still and looked at them at moments like a father at his playing children. He never for an instant wished for them to leave, though he would so long for sleep that he would stare at them finally in bewilderment and without a single flicker of the eyelid. Often they would talk all night. Blennerhassett's wide vague face would grow out of devotion into exhaustion. But Burr's hand would always reach across and take him by the shoulder as if to rouse him from a dull sleep, and the radiance of his own face would heighten always with the passing of time. Joel sat quietly, waiting for the full revelation of the meetings. All his love went out to the talkers. He would not have known how to hold it back.

In the idle mornings, in some morning need to go looking at the world, he wandered down to the Esplanade and stood under the trees which bent heavily over his head. He frowned out across the ice-covered race-track and out upon the river. There was one hour when the river was the colour of smoke, as if it were more a thing of the woods than an element and a power in itself. It seemed to belong to the woods, to be gentle and watched over, a tethered and grazing pet of the forest, and then when the light spread higher and colour stained the world, the river would leap suddenly out of the shining ice around, into its full-grown torrent of life, and its strength and its churning passage held Joel watching over it like the spell unfolding by night in his room. If he could not speak to the river, and he could not, still he would try to read in the river's blue and violet skeins a working of the momentous event. It was hard to understand. Was any scheme a man had, however secret and intact, always broken upon by the very current of its working? One day, in anguish, he saw a raft torn apart in midstream and the men scattered from it. Then all that he felt move in his heart at the sight of the inscrutable river went out in hope for the two men and their genius that he sheltered.

It was when he returned to the Inn that he was given a notice to paste on the saloon mirror saying that the trial of Aaron Burr for treason would be held at the end of the month at Washington, capitol of Mississippi Territory, on the campus of Jefferson College, where the crowds might be amply accommodated. In the meanwhile, the arrival of the full, armed flotilla was being awaited, and the price of whisky would not be advanced in this tavern, but there would be a slight increase in the tariff on a bed upstairs, depending on how many slept in it.

The month wore on, and now it was full moonlight. Late at night the whole sky was lunar, like the surface of the moon brought as close as a cheek. The luminous ranges of all the clouds stretched one beyond the other in heavenly order. They seemed to be the streets where Joel was walking through the town. People now lighted their houses in entertainments as if they copied after the sky, with Burr in the centre of them always, dancing with the women, talking with the men. They followed and formed cotillion figures about the one who threatened or lured them, and their minuets skimmed across the nights like a pebble expertly skipped across water. Joel would watch them take sides, and watch the arguments, all the frilled motions and the toasts, and he thought they were to decide whether Burr was good or evil. But all the time, Joel believed, when he saw Burr go dancing by, that did not touch him at all. Joel knew his eyes saw nothing there and went always beyond the room, although usually the most beautiful woman there was somehow in his arms when the set was over. Sometimes they drove him in their carriages down to the Esplanade and pointed out the moon to him, to end the evening. There they sat showing everything to Aaron Burr, nodding with a magnificence that approached fatigue toward the reaches of the ice that stretched over the river like an impossible bridge, some extension to the West of the Natchez Trace; and a radiance as soft and near as rain fell on their hands and faces, and on the plumes of the breaths from the horses' nostrils, and they were as gracious and as grand as Burr.

Each day that drew the trial closer, men talked more hotly on the corners and the saloon at the Inn shook with debate; every night Burr was invited to a finer and later ball; and Joel waited. He knew that Burr was being allotted, by an almost specific consent, this free and unmolested time till dawn, to meet in conspiracy, for the sake of continuing and perfecting the secret. This knowledge Joel gathered to himself by being, himself, everywhere; it decreed his own suffering and made it secret and filled with private omens.

One day he was driven to know everything. It was the morning he was given a little fur cap, and he set it on his head and started out. He walked through the dark trodden snow all the way up the Trace to the Bayou Pierre. The great trees began to break that day. That pounding of their explosions filled the subdued air; to Joel it was as if a great foot had stamped on the ground. And at first he thought he saw the fulfilment of all the rumour and promise—the flotilla coming around the bend, and he did not know whether he felt terror or pride. But then he saw that what covered the river over was a chain of great perfect trees floating down, lying on their sides in postures like slain giants and heroes of battle, black cedars and stone-white sycamores, magnolias with their leavy leaves shining as if they were in bloom, a long procession. Then it was terror that he felt.

He went on. He was not the only one who had made the pilgrimage to see what the original flotilla was like, that had been taken from Burr. There were many others: there was Old Man McCaleb, at a little distance. . . . In care not to show any excitement of expectation, Joel made his way through successive little groups that seemed to meditate there above the encampment of militia on the snowy bluff, and looked down at the water.

There was no galley there. There were nine small flatboats tied to the shore. They seemed so small and delicate that he was shocked and distressed, and looked around at the faces of the others, who looked coolly back at him. There was no sign of weapon about the boats or anywhere, except in the hands of the men on guard. There were barrels of molasses and whisky, rolling and knocking each other like drowned men, and stowed to one side of one of the boats, in a dark place, a strange little collection of blankets, a silver bridle with bells, a book swollen with water, and a little flute with a narrow ridge of snow along it. Where Joel stood looking down upon them, the boats floated in clusters of three, as small as water-lilies on a still bayou. A canoe filled with crazily wrapped-up Indians passed at a little distance, and with severe open mouths the Indians all laughed.

But the soldiers were sullen with cold, and very grave or angry, and Old Man McCaleb was there with his beard flying and his finger pointing prophetically in the direction of upstream. Some of the soldiers and all the women nodded their heads, as though they were the easiest believers, and one woman drew her child tightly to her. Joel shivered. Two of the young men hanging over the edge of the bluff flung their arms in sudden exhilaration about each other's shoulders, and a look of wildness came over their faces.

Back in the streets of Natchez, Joel met part of the militia marching and stood with his heart racing, back out of the way of the line coming with bright guns tilted up in the sharp air. Behind them, two of the soldiers dragged along a young dandy whose eyes glared at everything. There where they held him he was trying over and over again to make Aaron Burr's gesture, and he never convinced anybody.

Joel went in all three times to the militia's encampment on the Bayou Pierre, the last time on the day before the trial was to begin. Then out beyond a willow point a rowboat with one soldier in it kept laconic watch upon the north.

Joel returned on the frozen path to the Inn, and stumbled into his room and waited for Burr and Blennerhassett to come and talk together. His head ached. . . . All his walking about was no use. Where did people learn things? Where did they go to find them? How far?

Burr and Blennerhassett talked across the table, and it was growing late on the last night. Then there in the doorway with a fiddle in her hand

stood Blennerhassett's wife, wearing breeches, come to fetch him home.
The fiddle she had simply picked up in the Inn parlour as she came
through, and Joel did not think she bothered now to speak at all. But
she waited there before the fire, still a child and so clearly related to her
husband that their sudden movements at the encounter were alike and
made at the same time. They stood looking at each other there in the
firelight like creatures balancing together on a raft, and then she lifted the
bow and began to play.

Joel gazed at the girl, not much older than himself. She leaned her
cheek against the fiddle. He had never examined a fiddle at all, and when
she began to play it she frightened and dismayed him by her almost
insect-like motions, the pensive antennæ of her arms, her mask of a
countenance. When she played she never blinked her eye. Her legs,
fantastic in breeches, were separated slightly, and from her bent knees she
swayed back and forth as if she were weaving the tunes with her body.
The sharp odour of whisky moved with her. The slits of her eyes were
milky. The songs she played seemed to him to have no beginnings and no
endings, but to be about many hills and valleys, and chains of lakes. She,
like the men, knew of a place. . . . All of them spoke of a country.

And quite clearly, and altogether to his surprise, Joel saw a sight that
he had nearly forgotten. Instead of the fire on the hearth, there was a
mimosa tree in flower. It was in the little back field at his home in
Virginia and his mother was leading him by the hand. Fragile, delicate,
cloudlike it rose on its pale trunk and spread its long level arms. His
mother pointed to it. Among the trembling leaves the feathery puffs of
sweet bloom filled the tree like thousands of paradisical birds all alighted
at an instant. He had known then the story of the Princess Labam, for his
mother had told it to him, how she was so radiant that she sat on the
roof-top at night and lighted the city. It seemed to be the mimosa tree
that lighted the garden, for its brightness and fragrance overlaid all
the rest. Out of its graciousness this tree suffered their presence and shed
its splendour upon him and his mother. His mother pointed again, and
its scent swayed like the Asiatic princess moving up and down the pink
steps of its branches. Then the vision was gone. Aaron Burr sat in front
of the fire, Blennerhassett faced him, and Blennerhassett's wife played on
the violin.

There was no compassion in what this woman was doing, he knew
that—there was only a frightening thing, a stern allurement. Try as he
might, he could not comprehend it, though it was so calculated. He had
instead a sensation of pain, the ends of his fingers were stinging. At first
he did not realize that he had heard the sounds of her song, the only thing
he had ever heard. Then all at once as she held the lifted bow still for a

moment he gasped for breath at the interruption, and he did not care to learn her purpose or to wonder any longer, but bent his head and listened for the note that she would fling down upon them. And it was so gentle then, it touched him with surprise; it made him think of animals sleeping on their cushioned paws.

For a moment his love went like sound into a myriad life and was divided among all the people in his room. While they listened, Burr's radiance was somehow quenched, or theirs was raised to equal it, and they were all alike. There was one thing that shone in all their faces, and that was how far they were from home, how far from everywhere that they knew. Joel put his hand to his own face, and hid his pity from them while they listened to the endless tunes.

But she ended then. Sleep all at once seemed to overcome her whole body. She put down the fiddle and took Blennerhassett by both hands. He seemed tired too, more tired than talking could ever make him. He went out when she led him. They went wrapped under one cloak, his arm about her.

Burr did not go away immediately. First he walked up and down before the fire. He turned each time with diminishing violence, and light and shadow seemed to stream more softly with his turning cloak. Then he stood still. The firelight threw its changes over his face. He had no one to talk to. His boots smelled of the fire's closeness. Of course he had forgotten Joel, he seemed quite alone. At last with a strange naturalness, almost with a limp, he went to the table and stretched himself full length upon it.

He lay on his back. Joel was astonished. That was the way they laid out the men killed in duels in the Inn yard; and that was the table they laid them on.

Burr fell asleep instantly, so quickly that Joel felt he should never be left alone. He looked at the sleeping face of Burr, and the time and the place left him, and all that Burr had said that he had tried to guess left him too—he knew nothing in the world except the sleeping face. It was quiet. The eyes were almost closed, only dark slits lay beneath the lids. There was a small scar on the cheek. The lips were parted. Joel thought, I could speak if I would, or I could hear. Once I did each thing. . . . Still he listened . . . and it seemed that all that would speak, in this world, was listening. Burr was silent; he demanded nothing, nothing. . . . A boy or a man could be so alone in his heart that he could not even ask a question. In such silence as falls over a lonely man there is childlike supplication, and all arms might wish to open to him, but there is no speech. This was Burr's last night: Joel knew that. This was the moment before he would ride away. Why would the heart break so at absence? Joel knew that it was because nothing had been told. The heart is secret even when the moment it dreamed of has come, a moment when there might have been a revelation. . . . Joel stood motionless; he lifted his gaze from Burr's face and stared at nothing. . . . If love does a secret thing always, it is to reach backward, to a time that could not be known—for it makes a history of the sorrow and the dream it has contemplated in some instant of recognition. What Joel saw before him he had a terrible wish to speak out loud, but he would have had to find names for the places of the heart and the times for its shadowy and tragic events, and they seemed of great magnitude, heroic and terrible and splendid, like the legends of the mind. But for lack of a way to tell how much was known, the boundaries would lie between him and the others, all the others, until he died.

Presently Burr began to toss his head and to cry out. He talked, his face drew into a dreadful set of grimaces, which it followed over and over. He could never stop talking. Joel was afraid of these words, and afraid that eavesdroppers might listen to them. Whatever words they were, they were being taken by some force out of his dream. In horror, Joel put out his hand. He could never in his life have laid it across the mouth of Aaron Burr, but he thrust it into Burr's spread-out fingers. The fingers closed and did not yield; the clasp grew so fierce that it hurt his hand, but he saw that the words had stopped.

As if a silent love had shown him whatever new thing he would ever be able to learn, Joel had some wisdom in his fingers now which only this long month could have brought. He knew with what gentleness to hold the burning hand. With the gravity of his very soul he received the furious pressure of this man's dream. At last Burr drew his arm back beside his quiet head, and his hand hung like a child's in sleep, released in oblivion.

The next morning, Joel was given a notice to paste on the saloon mirror that conveyances might be rented at the Inn daily for the excursion to Washington for the trial of Mr Burr, payment to be made in advance. Joel went out and stood on a corner, and joined with a group of young boys walking behind the militia.

It was warm—a 'false spring' day. The little procession from Natchez, decorated and smiling in all they owned or whatever they borrowed or chartered or rented, moved grandly through the streets and on up the Trace. To Joel, somewhere in the line, the blue air that seemed to lie between the high banks held it all in a mist, softly coloured, the fringe waving from a carriage top, a few flags waving, a sword shining when some gentleman made a flourish. High up on their horses a number of the men were wearing their Revolutionary War uniforms, as if to reiterate that Aaron Burr fought once at their sides as a hero.

Under the spreading live-oaks at Washington, the trial opened like a festival. There was a theatre of benches, and a promenade; stalls were set out under the trees and glasses of whisky, and coloured ribbons, were sold. Joel sat somewhere among the crowds. Breezes touched the yellow and violet of dresses and stirred them, horses pawed the ground, and the people pressed upon him and seemed more real than those in dreams, and yet their pantomime was like those choruses and companies whose movements are like the waves running together. A hammer was then pounded, there was sudden attention from all the spectators, and Joel felt the great solidifying of their silence.

He had dreaded the sight of Burr. He had thought there might be some mark or disfigurement that would come from his panic. But all his grace was back upon him, and he was smiling to greet the studious faces which regarded him. Before their bright façade others rose first, declaiming men in turn, and then Burr.

In a moment he was walking up and down with his shadow on the grass and the patches of snow. He was talking again, talking now in great courtesy to everybody. There was a flickering light of sun and shadow on his face.

Then Joel understood. Burr was explaining away, smoothing over all that he had held great enough to have dreaded once. He walked back and forth elegantly in the sun, turning his wrist ever so airily in its frill, making light of his dream that had terrified him. And it was the deed they had all come to see. All around Joel they gasped, smiled, pressed one another's arms, nodded their heads; there were tender smiles on the women's faces. They were at Aaron Burr's feet at last, learning their superiority. They loved him now, in their condescension. They leaned forward in delight at the parading spectacle he was making. And when it was over for the day, they shook each other's hands, and Old Man McCaleb could be seen spitting on the ground, in the anticipation of another day as good as this one.

Blennerhassett did not come that night.

Burr came very late. He walked in the door, looked down at Joel where he sat among his boots, and suddenly stopped and took the dirty cloth out of his hand. He put his face quickly into it and pressed and rubbed it against his skin. Joel saw that all his clothes were dirty and ragged. The last thing he did was to set a little cap of turkey feathers on his head. Then he went out.

Joel followed him along behind the dark houses and through a ravine. Burr turned toward the Halfway Hill. Joel turned too, and he saw Burr walk slowly up and open the great heavy gate.

He saw him stop beside a tall camellia bush as solid as a tower and pick up one of the frozen buds which were shed all around it on the ground.

For a moment he held it in the palm of his hand, and then he went on.
Joel, following behind, did the same. He held the bud, and studied the
burned edges of its folds by the pale half-light of the East. The bud
came apart in his hand, its layers like small velvet shells, still iridescent,
the shrivelled flower inside. He held it tenderly and yet timidly, in a kind
of shame, as though all disaster lay pitifully disclosed now to the eyes.

He knew the girl Burr had often danced with under the rings of tapers
when she came out in a cloak across the shadowy hill. Burr stood, quiet
and graceful as he had always been as her partner at the balls. Joel felt a
pain like a sting while she first merged with the dark figure and then drew
back. The moon, late-risen and waning, came out of the clouds. Aaron
Burr made the gesture there in the distance, toward the West, where the
clouds hung still and red, and when Joel looked at him in the light he saw
as she must have seen the absurdity he was dressed in, the feathers on his
head. With a curious feeling of revenge upon her, he watched her turn,
draw smaller within her own cape, and go away.

Burr came walking down the hill, and passed close to the camellia bush
where Joel was standing. He walked stiffly in his mock Indian dress with
the boot polish on his face. The youngest child in Natchez would have
known that this was a remarkable and wonderful figure that had humiliated
itself by disguise.

Pausing in an open space, Burr lifted his hand once more and a slave
led out from the shadows a majestic horse with silver trappings shining
in the light of the moon. Burr mounted from the slave's hand in all the
clarity of his true elegance, and sat for a moment motionless in the saddle.
Then he cut his whip through the air, and rode away.

Joel followed him on foot toward the Liberty Road. As he walked
through the streets of Natchez he felt a strange mourning to know that
Burr would never come again by that way. If he had left in disguise, the
thirst that was in his face was the same as it had ever been. He had eluded
judgment, that was all he had done, and Joel was glad while he still
trembled. Joel would never know now the true course, or the true outcome
of any dream: this was all he felt. But he walked on, in the frozen path
into the wilderness, on and on. He did not see how he could ever go back
and still be the boot-boy at the Inn.

He did not know how far he had gone on the Liberty Road when the
posse came riding up behind and passed him. He walked on. He saw that
the bodies of the frozen birds had fallen out of the trees, and he fell down
and wept for his father and mother, to whom he had not said good-bye.

STEVIE SMITH

Is There a Life beyond the Gravy?

It was a wonderfully sunny day; the willowherb waved in the ruins and the white fluff fell like snow. But alas—Celia glanced at the blue-faced clock in the Ministry tower—it was eleven o'clock.

She shook herself free of the rubble and stood up. The white earth fell from her hair and clothes.

'Are you all right?' said her cousin Casivalaunus, who was standing looking at her.

'Oh yes, thank you so much. Oh, hallo, Cas.'

'Hallo, Celia. Well, I'll be off. See you at Uncle Heber's.'

Celia took hold of her cousin's arm and hung on like grim death.

'You're sure you're all right?' said Cas, flicking at the white fluff with his service gloves. 'I say, would you mind letting go of my arm?'

'So long, Cas.'

'So long, Celia. You'll soon get accustomed to it.'

He saluted, and walking quickly with elegant long strides made off down an avenue lined with broken pillars.

Celia leaped over the waterpipes that lay in the gutter and tore across the garden in the middle of the square. This was a short cut to the Ministry. She was already an hour late, but she thought it was a good thing to take the short cut, and very important to run.

'How do you do, Browser?' she called out, as she ran past the porter and up the stairs.

'Same as usual, miss,' said the porter with a wink.

Well, it *was* much the same really; for one thing Celia had never in her life been early.

'You've never in your lifetime been early.' Browser's parting shot (what a very carrying voice he had to be sure) followed her up the stairs and across the threshold of her room.

Tiny was standing over by the window squashing flies on the curtain.

'Hallo, Tiny.'

'Hallo, Celia.'

Celia flung her gloves into the wastepaper basket and put her hat on the statue of the Young Octavius. What a really fine room it was, she thought, so high and square, with such a beautiful moulded ceiling. But rather untidy. Celia sighed. She began to count up the number of things that would have to be put away one day, but not just now. Perhaps Tiny would put them away.

There was a leather revolver holster on the radiator, a set of tennis-balls on the table by the window, a tin, marked Harrogate Toffee, with some cartridges in it, a large feather duster and a jigsaw puzzle. On the floor lay a copy of Sir Sefton Choate's monograph *Across the Sinai Desert with the Children of Israel*, and sticking out of the tall bronze urn by the fireplace were a large landing-net and a couple of golf-clubs with broken sticks. A long thin climbing plant had managed to take root in the filing tray and was already half way up the wall.

Celia sighed again and closed her eyes. 'Anything in today, Tiny, darling?'

'Just a telegram,' said Tiny, and read it out:

'*To Criticisms Mainly Emanating Examerica He Anxiousest More Responsible Ministers Be Associated Cumhim But Sharpliest Protested Antisuggestion Camille Chautemps*'—wang wang, Tiny struck a note and intoned the rest of it—'*Quote Eye Appreciate Joke Buttwas He Who Signed Capitulation Abandoned Allies Sentenced Leaders Deathwards Unquote General DeGaulle Postremarking He Unthought Hed See Andre Maurois Again.*'

'It is from our cousin,' said Tiny. '"Eye appreciate joke", I do not. Look,' he pointed to the signature, *Casivalaunus*.

Tiny and Celia began to laugh their aggravating high-pitched laugh. This noise was very aggravating for Lord Loop—Augustus Loop—Tiny's brother, who occupied the adjoining room. He began to pound on the wall. Tiny turned quite pale. 'Oh, lord, there goes Augustus,' he said. He flicked at the papers on his desk and put a busy expression on his face.

'This cablegram,' he said, 'is dated 1942.'

'I tell you what,' said Celia, 'I'll do the washing-up.'

Celia had a large red Bristol glass tumbler, out of which she drank her morning milk. She was delighted with the appearance of this tumbler in the wash-basin and swam it round for some time, admiring the reflection. 'But of course,' she said, for she had acquired the habit of talking to herself, 'it is to be seen at its best only with the white milk in it.' There was also Tiny's old Spode cup and saucer to be washed—he had pinched this from Augustus—and a rather humdrum yellow jug that belonged to Sir Sefton. Celia suddenly remembered Sir Sefton and wondered if he was in yet. She was Sir Sefton's Personal Assistant. How grand that sounded! Personal Assistant to Sir Sefton Choate, Bt, MP, MIME—yes, he was a famous mining engineer, or had been, before 'like the rest of us' he had been caught by the Ministry. Had he not written in his famous monograph on the Children of Israel, 'It is probable, in this rich oil-bearing district, that Lot's wife was turned into a pillar of asphalt, not salt'?

From somewhere in the distance came the sound of a harp—the thin beautiful sound. That must be Jacky Sparrow in Publications. He was a graceful harpist. Celia remembered that she was lunching with Jacky today. She must hurry up and get on with the morning. The morning was like a beautiful coloured ball to be bounced and played with till the next thing came along to be done, and that was lunch-time.

Tiny came and banged on the door. 'Hurry up, Celia! Crumbs, what ages you take. Sefton wants you.'

' 'Morning, Miss Phoze.'

' 'Morning, Sir Sefton.'

'I had a rotten night last night,' said the baronet. 'I don't know. This way and that. Couldn't get a wink. Then I got up and sat on the side of the bath with my feet in hot water. No good. So I took a tablet. Thought it was Slumber-o, but must have got the wrong bottle. Turned it up next morning. D'you know what it was? Camomile. I was up all night.'

Sir Sefton was sitting at his desk doing the *Morning Post* crossword puzzle.

'What's a difficult poem by Browning?'

'Paracelsus,' said Celia, who was trying to write an article for the *Tribune*—where was that envelope with the figures on it? Was it two-thirds or two-fifths?

'*Eight* letters,' said the baronet.

'Sordello.'

'Hrrump, hrrump! Yes, that's it. Thank you very much, Miss Phoze . . . I don't think there's anything very much here.' He began to rummage under his blotter, holding it up with one hand and paddling underneath with the other. 'Oh, here's a note from the LCC. Let's see, March 1942? Well, it's answered itself by now.' He went back to his puzzle.

'Where did the Kings of Israel reign?'

'Jerusalem,' said Celia.

'Now now, it's not as easy as that.'

'The Kings of Israel,' said Celia, and began to stare round the room rather desperately. 'I say, the charlady has left a packet of sandwiches in the curtain loop.'

'Good heavens!' said Sir Sefton absentmindedly. 'The Kings of Israel, the Kings of Israel?'

'Stead,' said Sir Sefton. 'I asked Jacky Sparrow about it, as a matter of fact; he's a dab at these things.' He grinned delightedly. '"And Jeroboam reigned in his stead." Smart, isn't it?' he said. 'Well, well, Miss Phoze, I think I'll buzz off now. I'm going to this lecture on Oil Surrogates at the Institute. Thought I'd take Bozey with me—cheer him up you know—he's never been the same since his wife died. I said to him: "Bozey, your good lady's gone, hasn't she? Very well, then, she's gone. No good moping, is there, we all have to go some time."'

'Don't forget the hare,' said Celia, as Sefton padded towards the door.

This was a large, dead animal, half wrapped in brown paper, that lay across the floor. Augustus had brought it up for Sefton from his farm (the beastly Augustus, thought Celia, for neither she nor Tiny could stand him). All the same, it was a fine animal, the hare, and stretched right across the room.

Sefton picked it up and went out rather burdened, with the creature trailing over one arm, and his umbrella on the other.

'God bless you,' he said, with a happy smile. 'God bless us all and the Pope of Rome.'

There was a message from Jacky Sparrow on Celia's desk, to say that he would not be able to lunch as he had to rush off to the dentist's.

Celia and Tiny decided to have lunch in their room, and Celia went to get it from the canteen, because Mrs Bones always gave her more ice-cream than Tiny. Halfway through their picnic lunch, Augustus came into the room with a made-up boisterous expression on his face.

'Hallo, you two, pack up there; we're off to the countryside for an excursion.'

Hand in hand Tiny and Celia went and stood in the garden of the square while Augustus went to get the car out. The garden now stretched for miles and was more full of flowers than it had been in the morning; indeed there was a rather alarming air of quickly growing vegetation.

'Perhaps we had better make a move,' said Celia.

They walked together down a narrow pathway, between the giant blue flowers which grew and flowered high above their heads. Suddenly, coming round a hairy oriental poppy plant, they ran full tilt into Sir Sefton.

'Good heavens,' he said, 'I must hurry, or I shall be late for the meeting. I shall see you next week at the Ministry, Miss Phoze? Ah, howdedo, Loop? So long, all.'

He went off in a fuss in the opposite direction.

'Next week?' said Tiny. 'What can he be thinking of?—the poor old gentleman.'

'Why, *this* week is the holidays, of course,' said Celia. 'We are going to stay with Uncle Heber.'

'Oh yes,' said Tiny, 'I'd forgotten. How quickly the time comes round.'

'Well, we'd better be getting on,' said Celia, disengaging her foot from a young oak tree that was shooting up from a split acorn.

'But Augustus told us to wait for him.'

'I don't care about Augustus,' said Celia recklessly, and tossed back her fine dark hair. 'After all, he can soon catch us up in his motor-car.'

'Perhaps we had better keep to the pathway,' said Tiny slyly.

The pretty grey grass was soft under their feet, but there was hardly room for the two of them to walk abreast.

'Yes, perhaps we had,' said Celia, laughing. 'It will save a lot of bother.'

'Why, look,' said Tiny, 'here comes Jacky Sparrow.'

Jacky came running along the narrow path towards them, jumping gracefully over the young shoots as he ran. He was carrying his harp in his outstretched arms.

'Hallo, hallo, hallo,' he said, 'can't stop, can't stop, can't stop. Sorry about the lunch, Celia; got to get me harp-string mended, got to catch the old chap before he lies down for the afternoon.'

'Phew!' said Tiny, as Jacky disappeared from sight. 'Everybody seems to be going in the opposite direction.'

The vista now opened before them upon a slight decline. There was a fine white marble viaduct down below them to the right, and upon the viaduct was an old-fashioned train, with steam coming out of the coal-black engine and the fire stoked to flame upon the fender.

'Hurry, hurry, hurry,' cried Tiny, catching Celia by the hand. 'We have just time to take the train!'

The train was beginning to move as they tore up the steps and into the last carriage.

'Jolly good show,' said Tiny; and then he said, 'I hope Uncle Heber will be pleased to see us.'

They both lay down on the carriage seat, and ate the sandwiches which Celia had brought with her from Sir Sefton's room.

The train was now running between high embankments. On the top of the embankment and down the side was the soft grass waving like beautiful hair; also on the top, against a Cambridge-blue sky, there were some poppies.

'Beautiful,' said Tiny; 'might be Norfolk.'

'One always comes back to the British School,' said Celia dreamily.

'What a dreamy girl you are,' said Tiny.

The train, gathering speed at the bend, shot through an old-fashioned station. There were rounded Victorian window-panes in the waiting-room and a general air of coal, sea, soot and steamer oil.

'What station was that?' asked Celia.

'Looked like Dover,' said Tiny.

'Can't be Dover,' said Celia. 'Dover isn't on the way to Uncle Heber's.'

After another mile or so the train pulled up with a jerk and they sat up quickly to look out of the window. It was an enormous, long, busy station. People were hurrying down the platform towards the refreshment-room; soldiers, sailors and airmen stood about in groups drinking cups of tea from the trolleys.

'Just time to get dinner if you hurry,' sang out a familiar voice, and there was Sir Sefton carrying a couple of bottles of hair-oil as well as the hare and the umbrella. 'So long,' he said, raising his hat to Celia and dropping one of the bottles, which smashed against the platform and released a beautiful odour. 'So long, all, see you later.'

'Must be Perth,' said Tiny. He pulled the blind down with a snap, and pushed Celia on to the bunk.

Celia looked round the carriage, at the wash-basin, the lights just where you wanted them, the luggage-table, the many different sorts of racks, the air-conditioning control, the neat fawn blankets and clean pillow-cases.

'What a good thing we managed to get a sleeper,' she said.

'I fancy we have to thank Sir Sefton for that.'

'I think Sefton is simply ripping,' said Celia.

'One of the best; jolly good show, sir,' said Tiny.

'Can't be Perth,' said Celia. 'Perth isn't on the way to Uncle Heber's.'

'We shall be in the mountains soon,' said Tiny; 'the mountain air is always so delicious. I trust that we shall catch a great many trout. It is a pity that we left the landing-net at home.'

'Uncle Heber's country,' said Celia, 'is as flat as a pancake.'

Tiny said, 'We must continue steadfastly to look on the bright side of things,' and promptly fell asleep.

There now came a great pounding at the door. It was Jacky Sparrow with his harp in his hand, and an inspector's cap on his head.

'All change, all change, all change,' he cried out. Then he said, 'So long, I simply must fly.'

Celia and Tiny got the suitcases shut at last and tumbled out on to a grass-grown platform. There were a couple of donkeys grazing on the siding, but no people at all. The train gave a shiver and a back-ward slide, then it pulled itself together and rushed off, leaving a patch of black smoke hanging in mid-air. The smoke bellied out and hung, first black, then grey, then white, against a pale-blue sky.

'Thornton-le-Soke,' read out Tiny from the station nameplate.

'You see,' said Celia, 'no mountains at all.'

The station was set in a beautiful sunbaked plain under a wide skyline.

The sea could be seen in the far distance, and a soft fresh wind blew inland over the samphire beds.

Tiny looked very happy. 'We have arrived,' he said. 'It is curious, do you know I have not thought of Augustus for several moments?'

'I fancy,' said Celia, 'that Augustus has taken the wrong turning.'

'Indeed?' said Tiny.

'Augustus was looking rather weird,' said Celia in her dreamy way. 'There he was, sitting high above the road in his old-fashioned motor-car, with his dust coat and his goggles, and the dust flying up behind the car and the chickens running away in front of it.'

'Oh, did you see him?'

'Did *you?*'

'Yes, as a matter of fact I did see Augustus in his motor-car. I said nothing about it,' said Tiny kindly, 'because I did not wish to disturb you.'

'Oh, not at all,' said Celia; 'thanks awfully all the same.'

They now sat down on their suitcases like a couple of school-children waiting to be fetched.

'Do you know who will fetch us, I think?' said Celia.

'It will be Uncle Heber for one.'

'Uncle is an old and established person, he may not come, but if he comes there will also be another one, and that other one will be our cousin, Casivalaunus.'

'Good heavens!' said Tiny. 'He was seconded to Intelligence, was he not? I fancied he was in the mountains.'

'You seem to have got the mountains on the brain.'

Celia began to count the wooden palings opposite, counting aloud in German, '*Ein, zwei, drei, vier, fünf.*'

'Mark my words,' said Tiny, 'that car of Augustus's will *konk out* on the hills.' He coughed. 'If you will excuse the expression.'

At this moment a long, thin person came in an elegant stroll along the platform towards them; he was wearing the uniform of a high-ranking British officer.

'There you are. What did I tell you?' said Celia. 'It is Cas.'

'I can't stand these clothes,' said Cas. 'You'll have to wait a minute while I change. Uncle's down below in the pony-trap. We drove it under the bridge, as Polly likes the shade. I'll just pop into the waiting-room, I won't be a tick.'

'I do think our cousin has a vulgar parlance,' said Tiny.

Celia tore down the station steps and climbed into the pony-trap beside Uncle Heber, and put her arms round him. Heber was wearing his shabby old clergyman's clothes, a clerical grey ankle-length mackintosh and a shovel hat. He was crying quietly.

'We must get home quickly,' he said. 'I have set the supper table because it is Tuffie's night out, but there is much to do; we must hurry.'

He pulled gently on the reins and Polly moved off at an amble, with the grass still sticking out of her mouth. Cas, in a light-green ski-jacket and flannel trousers, came running with Tiny. They caught hold of the trap and jumped in.

'All aboard,' said Heber in a hollow voice.

As they drove the quiet country miles to the rectory, Celia began to sing, 'Softly, softly, softly, softly, The white snow fell.'

'Now, Celia,' said Cas, 'we can do without that.'

They were bowling along the sands by this time, bowling along the white sea sand down below the high-tide level where the sands were damp and firm. The sea crept out to the far horizon, where some dirty weather was blowing up; one could see the line of stormy white waves beyond the seawhorl worms, and the white bones and white seashells that lay in the hollow.

'There's some dirty weather coming,' said Tiny.

'True, Tiny, true,' said Cas.

'I hope we shan't be *kept in*,' said Celia.

'I am sure we shall be able to *get out of the wind under the breakwater*, and that we shall be able to go for a *stretch*, a *blow*, a *turn*, a *tramp* and a *breather*,' said Cas, giving Tiny a sly pinch.

When they got to the rectory they had some sardines, some cheese, some bread, some margarine and some cocoa.

'There are some spring onions in the sideboard cupboard, if any person cares for such things,' said Heber.

The dark fell suddenly upon them as they sat at supper, and the rainstorm slashed across the window-pane.

'Off to bed with you all,' said Heber. 'There are your candles, take them with you. You are sleeping in the three rooms on the first floor at the back of the house overlooking the beechwoods. The rooms are called Minnie, Yarrow and Florence. You, Celia, are in Minnie. The boys can take their choice.'

'Oh, thank you sir, thank you so much,' said the boys.

'I must buzz off now,' said Heber, 'I have some business to attend to.'

He took his white muffler from the chest in the hall where the surplices were kept and a horn lantern from the porch. 'So long, all,' he said.

Tiny looked rather frightened.

'He is certainly going to the church,' said Celia.

They spoke in whispers together, and together went up the shallow treads of the staircase to bed.

Tiny pushed past Cas and went into the Florence room.

'Just what one might expect,' muttered Cas furiously. 'You know perfectly well, Tiny,' he called through the door, 'that I detest Yarrow.' He turned to Celia. 'I shall not be able to sleep a wink.'

Tiny sat on the window-seat crying. He leant far out into the night and his tears fell with a splash into the water-butt that was under the Florence window.

Then he got up and went into Celia's room. 'I keep thinking of Augustus,' he sobbed.

'Now, Tiny, now, Tiny,' said Celia, 'why do you do such a foolish thing?' But she was crying too.

'Then why are you crying, Celia?'

'Since I thought of Uncle going alone to the old, dark, cold church,' said Celia, 'I have had a feeling of disturbance.'

'One must continue to look on the bright side of things,' said Tiny.

As he spoke they heard the church bell tolling.

'It is tolling for the dead,' said Celia.

She went and stood in the middle of the room with her fingers in her ears. Her white cotton nightdress flapped round her legs in the wind that blew in from the open window.

'Be sure Augustus will not come,' she said. She stood quite still in a dull and violent stare. 'Do you not remember,' she said, 'what Augustus did to Brendan Harper the poet?'

'No.' said Tiny, cheering up a bit. 'What was that?'

'If you do not remember, then I shall not tell you. All *that*,' said Celia, 'belongs to the dead past.'

'To the *living* past,' said Tiny, rather to himself.

'Augustus is an abject character,' cried Celia, her voice rising to a high-pitched scream that quite drowned the wireless coming from Yarrow, where Cas sat sulking. 'Do you suppose for a moment that our uncle would have such a person to darken the threshold?'

'Well, it is already rather dark,' said Tiny. 'I say, Cas has got the radio on, I do think he's the limit.'

He began to pound on the wall.

'Starp that pounding!' yelled Cas.

'How vulgar he is,' Tiny sniffed in a superior manner. 'Well, so long, Celia, I'll be off.'

The next morning, after a broken night, they assembled early for breakfast. Tuffie, who had spent her evening at the pictures, brought in a large jorum of porridge and set it in front of Heber, who was looking rather severe in a shiny black suit and a pair of black wool mittens. The three visitors lolled in their chairs waiting for the porridge to be served.

Heber looked severely at Celia. 'Instead of lolling forever with your cousins in a negative mood, you should strive to improve. Do you all want to be sent back to school?' he inquired.

'Oh no, Uncle—oh no; oh, *rather* not!'

'Oh, Uncle,' said Celia, 'I will *try*.'

Heber gave them an equivocal look and rapped the table with a small silver crucifix. 'You will please stand,' he said. And then he said, 'For what we are about to receive.'

Cas intoned 'Et cetera' on a bell-like note, and they all sat down.

'What did you see last night, Tuffie?' inquired Celia politely.

'It was a lovely piece, duck,' said Tuffie; 'it was called Kingdom Kong.'

'Thy kingdom kong,' said Tiny with a giggle.

Cas kicked him under the table and turned to Heber.

'Who was it that arrived so late last night, sir, and was bedded down not without disturbance?'

Heber, who at Tiny's words had turned quite pale, spoke in a reedlike whisper.

'Sir Sefton Choate,' he said, 'has honoured us by an unexpected visit.'

'My word!' said Tiny. 'Not old Sefton? Well, I never!'

'Shut *up*, Tiny!' said Cas.

'You are so frivolous, Tiny,' Celia sighed. 'It is something one does not care to think about.'

'Will he be making a long stay, sir, and where have you put him?'

'To the first part of the question, I do not know,' said Heber in his ghostly voice. 'To the second part, in Doom.'

'Good heavens!' said Tiny, his mouth full of porridge. 'Not in Doom?'

'And why not in Doom, pray?' said Heber. 'Is not Doom our best bedroom, and does it not look out upon the cemetery?'

'It may be the best bedroom,' said Tiny, with a wink at Celia, 'and it may look out upon the cemetery, but the bed is pretty well untakable, sir, since Celia broke the springs last hols.'

'Shut up, Tiny!' said Cas, but they all began to giggle furiously, stuffing their handkerchiefs into their mouths.

'Poor old chap,' said Tiny, who was purple in the face by this time. 'He won't get a wink.'

'Not a wink, not a wink, not a tiddly-widdly wink,' sang Celia, beating time with her porridge spoon.

They all joined in.

Celia said, 'Mark my words, *he'll be up all night*.'

Heber rose to his feet like a lion in anger.

'It is Sunday today,' he said, 'you must all go to church.'

'I make it Thursday,' said Tiny. 'What do you make it, Celia?'

Celia answered in German, with a strong North German accent, finishing up with her aggravating laugh: '*Bei mir ist's Montag um halb sechs.*'

'No, no,' said Tiny, 'it is Thursday.' He smiled in an infatuated manner upon Celia and pointed to the lake that could just be seen from the kitchen window where they had set the table, '*C'est le lac de jeudi,*' he said, 'for, you see, it is Thursday today.'

Cas, who was getting rather restless, said, 'Heads Sunday, tails Thursday.' The coin came down heads.

'So long, Uncle,' they said.

When they got to the church the service was already over, so they turned back along the grass path bordered with poplar trees. The weather had cleared again and it was hot and fine.

'I am afraid we shall not be able to get our church stamps for attendance,' said Celia.

'I'm sorry about that,' said Tiny.

'I thought our uncle's sermon was extremely to the point,' said Cas.

'Quite affecting,' said Celia.

'I always think that is one of his best sermons,' said Tiny with a generous smile.

'I enjoyed the hymns so much,' said Celia.

'I thought Mr Sparrow's voluntary on the harp was in excellent taste,' said Cas. 'Was I right in detecting a slight flaw in one of the strings?'

The white butterflies flew round their heads in the hot sunshine and the tall flowers, red, white and blue, waved against their shoulders as they walked along.

'Marguerites, cornflowers, poppies,' drawled Celia, pressing the stalks in her hands.

'Don't pick the flowers, Celia,' said Cas. 'Do you wish to raise the devil?'

'How tall they grow,' said Celia.

'Very fine,' said Cas, with his eye still upon her.

'They would make a nice bouquet for the lunch-table,' said Celia.

'Don't pick the flowers,' said Cas and Tiny together, edging nearer to their cousin.

Celia now looked down at her clothes and found that she was dressed in a pink-and-white-striped sailor suit, white socks and black strapped pumps. She took off her hat to look at it and to ease the discomfort where the elastic was biting into her chin. It was a large floppy leghorn hat trimmed with cornflowers and daisies and a white satin bow.

'Do you realize, boys, that you are both wearing Eton suits?' she said, and took them by the hand.

'Why, look,' said Tiny, as they came up the drive to the rectory, 'there is old Sir Sefton standing in the doorway with our uncle.'

'Howdedo, little girl?' said Sefton, pressing a bar of Fry's chocolate cream into Celia's hand. 'We've put the hare in the fridg,' he added in a confidential aside.

Celia shook hands with Sir Sefton, and gave a little nick of a curtsy.

'Celia has recently returned from her school in Potsdam,' explained Cas, who was rather embarrassed by the curtsy.

'She had become quite Prussian,' said Tiny.

Cas trod on his toe. 'Shut up, Tiny,' he said.

'Well, well, well, very nice, I'm sure,' said Sir Sefton, who had not quite taken it in. He gave a large coloured ball to Tiny.

'I bought a model motor-car for you, my lad,' he said, turning to Cas, 'but it has not come yet.'

'Oh, hurrah,' said Cas. 'Oh, thank you so much, sir.'

'Are they going back to shcool after the holidays?' Sir Sefton inquired of Heber.

'Well,' said Heber, '*that depends*.'

Cas and Tiny and Celia sat in the long, cool nursery.

'That depends . . .' said Tiny, with a rather fearful look at Celia. 'Oh, Celia, I do hope we do not have to go back to school.'

'Not likely,' said Cas; 'nothing more to learn.'

'Cas is awfully smug,' said Celia, putting her arms round Tiny, who was beginning to cry. 'Cheer up, Tiny, you won't have Augustus, anyway.'

'I was flogged twice through Homer at Eton,' said Cas, with an ineffable smug smile.

Celia began to print a sentence in coloured chalks in her copy-book, there was a different chalk for each letter. Cas looked over her shoulder and read out what she had written: 'Is there a life beyond the gravy?'

'It's an "e",' he said, 'not a "y".'

At this moment there was a black shadow across the open window and a large, dark, fat boy fell into the room. He picked himself up and swaggered over to where Tiny was crouching beside Celia.

'I couldn't make anyone hear,' he said.

Then he looked round the room with a sneering expression. 'Crumbs,' he said, 'what a place, and what smudgy beasts you look! Why, Celia, the ink is all over your dress. There's no life here,' he said; 'you people simply don't know you're alive.'

It was Augustus.

Cas came over to him and stood threatening him with the heavy ruler he had snatched from Celia's desk.

'*You* don't know you're dead,' he said.

'It's better to know you're dead,' said Tiny.

'Oh, much better,' said Cas.

'There's no room here for anyone who doesn't know he's dead,' said Celia.

They took hands and closed round Augustus, driving him back towards the window. He climbed on to the window-sill.

'We're all dead,' cried the three children in a loud, shrill chorus that rose like the wail of a siren. 'We're all dead, we've been dead *for ages*.'

Tiny rushed forward, breaking hands with the others, and gave Augustus a great shove that sent him backwards out of the dark shadowed window.

'We rather like it,' he said, as Augustus disappeared from view.

Yonder Peasant, Who Is He?

Whenever we children came to stay at my grandmother's house, we were put to sleep in the sewing room, a bleak, shabby, utilitarian rectangle, more office than bedroom, more attic than office, that played to the hierarchy of chambers the role of a poor relation. It was a room seldom entered by the other members of the family, seldom swept by the maid, a room without pride; the old sewing machine, some cast-off chairs, a shadeless lamp, rolls of wrapping paper, piles of cardboard boxes that might someday come in handy, papers of pins, and remnants of material united with the iron folding cots put out for our use and the bare floor boards to give an impression of intense and ruthless temporality. Thin white spreads, of the kind used in hospitals and charity institutions, and naked blinds at the windows reminded us of our orphaned condition and of the ephemeral character of our visit; there was nothing here to encourage us to consider this our home.

Poor Roy's children, as commiseration damply styled the four of us, could not afford illusions, in the family opinion. Our father had put us beyond the pale by dying suddenly of influenza and taking our young mother with him, a defection that was remarked on with horror and grief commingled, as though our mother had been a pretty secretary with whom he had wantonly absconded into the irresponsible paradise of the hereafter. Our reputation was clouded by this misfortune. There was a prevailing sense, not only in the family but in storekeepers, servants, streetcar conductors, and other satellites of our circle, that my grandfather, a rich man, had behaved with extraordinary munificence in allotting a sum of money for our support and installing us with some disagreeable middle-aged relations in a dingy house two blocks distant from his own. What alternative he had was not mentioned; presumably he could have sent us to an orphan asylum and no one would have thought the worse of him. At any rate, it was felt, even by those who sympathized with us, that we led a privileged existence, privileged because we had no rights, and the very fact that at the yearly Halloween or Christmas party given at the home of an uncle we appeared so dismal, ill clad, and unhealthy, in contrast to our rosy, exquisite cousins, confirmed the judgment that had been made on us—clearly, it was a generous impulse that kept us in the family at all. Thus, the meaner our circumstances, the greater seemed our grandfather's condescension, a view in which we ourselves shared, looking softly and shyly on this old man—with his rheumatism, his pink face and white hair, set off by the rosebuds in his Pierce-Arrow and in his buttonhole—as the font of goodness and philanthropy, and the nickel he occasionally gave us to drop into the collection plate on Sunday (two cents was our ordinary contribution) filled us not with envy but with simple admiration for his potency; this indeed was princely, *this* was the way to give. It did not occur to us to judge him for the disparity of our styles of living. Whatever bitterness we felt was kept for our actual guardians, who, we believed, must be embezzling the money set aside for us, since the standard of comfort achieved in our grandparents' house— the electric heaters, the gas logs, the lap robes, the shawls wrapped tenderly about the old knees, the white meat of chicken and red meat of beef, the silver, the white tablecloths, the maids, and the solicitous chauffeur—persuaded us that prunes and rice pudding, peeling paint and patched clothes were *hors concours* with these persons and therefore could not have been willed by them. Wealth, in our minds, was equivalent to bounty, and poverty but a sign of penuriousness of spirit.

Yet even if we had been convinced of the honesty of our guardians, we would still have clung to that beneficent image of our grandfather that the family myth proposed to us. We were too poor, spiritually speaking, to question his generosity, to ask why he allowed us to live in oppressed chill and deprivation at a long arm's length from himself and hooded his genial blue eye with a bluff, millionairish gray eyebrow whenever the evidence of our suffering presented itself at his knee. The official answer we knew: our benefactors were too old to put up with four wild young children; our grandfather was preoccupied with business matters and with his rheumatism, to which he devoted himself as though to a pious duty, taking it with him on pilgrimages to Ste Anne de Beaupré and Miami, offering it with impartial reverence to the miracle of the Northern Mother and the Southern sun. This rheumatism hallowed my grandfather with the mark of a special vocation; he lived with it in the manner of an artist or a grizzled Galahad; it set him apart from all of us and even from my grandmother, who, lacking such an affliction, led a relatively unjustified existence and showed, in relation to us children, a sharper and more bellicose spirit. She felt, in spite of everything, that she was open to criticism, and, transposing this feeling with a practiced old hand, kept peering into our characters for symptoms of ingratitude.

We, as a matter of fact, were grateful to the point of servility. We made no demands, we had no hopes. We were content if we were permitted to enjoy the refracted rays of that solar prosperity and come sometimes in the summer afternoons to sit on the shady porch or idle through a winter morning on the wicker furniture of the sun parlor, to stare at the player piano in the music room and smell the odor of whiskey in the mahogany cabinet in the library, or to climb about the dark living room examining the glassed-in paintings in their huge gilt frames, the fruits of European travel: dusky Italian devotional groupings, heavy and lustrous as grapes, Neapolitan women carrying baskets to market, views of Venetian canals, and Tuscan harvest scenes—secular themes that, to the Irish-American mind, had become tinged with Catholic feeling by a regional infusion from the Pope. We asked no more from this house than the pride of being connected with it, and this was fortunate for us, since my grandmother, a great adherent of the give-them-an-inch-and-they'll-take-a-yard theory of hospitality, never, so far as I can remember, offered any caller the slightest refreshment, regarding her own conversation as sufficiently wholesome and sustaining. An ugly, severe old woman with a monstrous balcony of a bosom, she officiated over certain set topics in a colorless singsong, like a priest intoning a Mass, topics to which repetition had lent a senseless solemnity: her audience with the Holy Father; how my own father had broken with family tradition and voted the Democratic ticket; a visit to Lourdes; the Sacred Stairs in Rome, bloodstained since the first Good Friday, which she had climbed on her knees; my crooked little fingers and how they meant I was a liar; a miracle-working bone; the importance of regular bowel movements; the wickedness of Protestants; the conversion of my mother to Catholicism; and the assertion that my Protestant grandmother must certainly dye her hair. The most trivial reminiscences (my aunt's having hysterics in a haystack) received from her delivery and from the piety of the conext a strongly monitory flavor; they inspired fear and guilt, and one searched uncomfortably for the moral in them, as in a dark and riddling fable.

Luckily, I am writing a memoir and not a work of fiction, and therefore I do not have to account for my grandmother's unpleasing character and look for the Oedipal fixation or the traumatic experience which would give her that clinical authenticity that is nowadays so desirable in portraiture. I do not know how my grandmother got the way she was; I assume, from family photographs and from the inflexibility of her habits, that she was always the same, and it seems as idle to inquire into her childhood as to ask what was ailing Iago or look for the thumb-sucking prohibition that was responsible for Lady Macbeth. My grandmother's sexual history, bristling with infant mortality in the usual style of her period, was robust and decisive: three tall, handsome sons grew up, and one attentive daughter. Her husband treated her kindly. She had money, many grandchildren, and religion to sustain her. White hair, glasses, soft skin, wrinkles, needlework—all the paraphernalia of motherliness were hers; yet it was a cold, grudging, disputatious old woman who sat all day in her sunroom making tapestries from a pattern, scanning religious periodicals, and setting her iron jaw against any infraction of her ways.

Combativeness was, I suppose, the dominant trait in my grandmother's nature. An aggressive churchgoer, she was quite without Christian feeling; the mercy of the Lord Jesus had never entered her heart. Her piety was an act of war against the Protestant ascendancy. The religious magazines on her table furnished her not with food for meditation but with fresh pretexts for anger; articles attacking birth control, divorce, mixed marriages, Darwin, and secular education were her favorite reading. The teachings of the Church did not interest her, except as they were a rebuke to others; 'Honor thy father and thy mother,' a commandment she was no longer called upon to practice, was the one most frequently on her lips. The extermination of Protestantism, rather than spiritual perfection, was the boon she prayed for. Her mind was preoccupied with conversion, the capture of a soul for God much diverted her fancy—it made one less Protestant in the world. Foreign missions, with their overtones of good will and social service, appealed to her less strongly; it was not a *harvest* of souls that my grandmother had in mind.

This pugnacity of my grandmother's did not confine itself to sectarian enthusiasm. There was the defense of her furniture and her house against the imagined encroachments of visitors. With her, this was not the gentle and tremulous protectiveness endemic in old ladies, who fear for the safety of their possessions with a truly touching anxiety, inferring the fragility of all things from the brittleness of their old bones and hearing the crash of mortality in the perilous tinkling of a teacup. My grandmother's sentiment was more autocratic: she hated having her chairs sat in or her lawns stepped on or the water turned on in her basins, for no reason at all except pure officiousness; she even grudged the mailman his daily promenade up her sidewalk. Her home was a center of power, and she would not allow it to be derogated by easy or democratic usage. Under her jealous eye, its social properties had atrophied, and it functioned in the family structure simply as a political headquarters. Family conferences were held there, consultations with the doctor and the clergy; refractory children were brought there for a lecture or an interval of thought-taking; wills were read and loans negotiated and emissaries from the Protestant faction on state occasions received. The family had no friends, and entertaining was held to be a foolish and unnecessary courtesy as between blood relations.

Yet on one terrible occasion my grandmother had kept open house. She had accommodated us all during those fatal weeks of the influenza epidemic, when no hospital beds were to be had and people went about with masks or stayed shut up in their houses, and the awful fear of contagion paralyzed all services and made each man an enemy to his neighbor. One by one, we had been carried off the train—four children and two adults, coming from distant Puget Sound to make a new home in Minneapolis. Waving good-bye in the Seattle depot, we had not known that we had brought the flu with us into our drawing rooms, along with the presents and the flowers, but, one after another, we had been struck down as the train proceeded eastward. We children did not understand whether the chattering of our teeth and Mama's lying torpid in the berth were not somehow a part of the trip (until then serious illness, in our minds, had been associated with innovations—it had always brought home a new baby), and we began to suspect that it was all an adventure when we saw our father draw a revolver on the conductor who, in a burst of sanitary precaution, was trying to put us off the train at a small wooden station in the middle of the North Dakota prairie. On the platform at Minneapolis, there were stretchers, a wheelchair, redcaps, distraught officials, and, beyond them, in the crowd, my grandfather's rosy face, cigar, and cane, my grandmother's feathered hat, imparting an air of festivity to this strange and confused picture, making us children certain that our illness was the beginning of a delightful holiday.

We awoke to reality in the sewing room several weeks later, to an atmosphere of castor oil, rectal thermometers, cross nurses, and efficiency, and though we were shut out from the knowledge of what had happened so close to us, just out of our hearing—a scandal of the gravest character, a coming and going of priests and undertakers and coffins (Mama and Daddy, they assured us, had gone to get well in the hospital)—we became aware, even as we woke from our fevers, that everything, including ourselves, was different. We had shrunk, as it were, and faded, like the flannel pajamas we wore, which during these few weeks had grown, doubtless from the disinfectant they were washed in, wretchedly thin and shabby. The behavior of the people around us, abrupt, careless, and preoccupied, apprised us without any ceremony of our diminished importance. Our value had paled, and a new image of ourselves—the image, if we had guessed it, of the orphan—was already forming in our minds. We had not known we were spoiled, but now this word, entering our vocabulary for the first time, served to define the change for us and to herald the new order. Before we got sick, we were spoiled; that was what was the matter now, and everything we could not understand, everything unfamiliar and displeasing, took on a certain plausibility when related to this fresh concept. We had not known what it was to have trays dumped summarily on our beds and no sugar and cream for our cereal, to take medicine in a gulp because someone could not be bothered to wait for us, to have our arms jerked into our sleeves and a comb ripped through our hair, to be bathed impatiently, to be told to sit up or lie down quick and no nonsense about it, to find our questions unanswered and our requests unheeded, to lie for hours alone and wait for the doctor's visit, but this, so it seemed, was an oversight in our training, and my grandmother and her household applied themselves with a will to remedying the deficiency.

Their motives were, no doubt, good; it was time indeed that we learned that the world was no longer our oyster. The happy life we had had—the May baskets and the valentines, the picnics in the yard, and the elaborate snowmen—was a poor preparation, in truth, for the future that now opened up to us. Our new instructors could hardly be blamed for a certain impatience with our parents, who had been so lacking in foresight. It was to everyone's interest, decidedly, that we should forget the past— the quicker, the better—and a steady disparagement of our habits ('Tea and chocolate, can you imagine, and all those frosted cakes—no wonder poor Tess was always after the doctor'), praise that was rigorously comparative ('You have absolutely no idea of the improvement in these children') flattered the feelings of the speakers and prepared us to accept a loss that was, in any case, irreparable. Like all children, we wished to conform, and the notion that our former ways had been somehow ridiculous and unsuitable made the memory of them falter a little, like a child's recitation to strangers. We no longer demanded our due, and the wish to see our parents insensibly weakened. Soon we ceased to speak of it, and thus, without tears or tantrums, we came to know they were dead.

Why no one, least of all our grandmother, to whose repertory the subject seems so congenial, took the trouble to tell us, it is impossible now to know. It is easy to imagine her 'breaking' the news to those of us who were old enough to listen in one of those official interviews in which her nature periodically tumefied, becoming heavy and turgid, like her portentous bosom, like peonies, her favorite flower, or like the dressmaker's dummy, that bombastic image of herself that lent a museumlike solemnity to the humble sewing room and made us tremble in our beds. The mind's ear frames her sentences, but in reality she did not speak, whether from a clumsy sense of delicacy or from a mistaken kindness, it is difficult to guess. Perhaps she feared our tears, which might rain on her like reproaches, since the family policy at the time was predicated on the axiom of our virtual insentience, an assumption that allowed them to proceed with us as if with pieces of furniture. Without explanations or coddling, as soon as they could safely get up, my three brothers were dispatched to the other house; they were much too young to 'feel' it, I heard the grownups murmur, and would never know the difference 'if Myers and Margaret were careful'. In my case, however, a doubt must have been experienced. I was six—old enough to 'remember'—and this entitled me, in the family's eyes, to greater consideration, as if this memory of mine were a lawyer who represented me in court. In deference, therefore, to my age and my supposed powers of criticism and comparison, I was kept on for a time, to roam palely about my grandmother's living rooms, a dangling, transitional creature, a frog becoming a tadpole, while my brothers, poor little polyps, were already well embedded in the structure of the new life. I did not wonder what had become of them. I believe I thought they were dead, but their fate did not greatly concern me; my heart had grown numb. I considered myself clever to have guessed the truth about my parents, like a child who proudly discovers that there is no Santa Claus, but I would not speak of that knowledge or even react to it privately, for I wished to have nothing to do with it; I would not cooperate in this loss. Those weeks in my grandmother's house come back to me very obscurely, surrounded by blackness, like a mourning card: the dark well of the staircase, where I seem to have been endlessly loitering, waiting to see Mama when she would come home from the hospital, and then simply loitering with no purpose whatever; the winter-dim first-grade classroom of the strange academy I was sent to; the drab treatment room of the doctor's office, where every Saturday I screamed and begged on a table while electric shocks were sent through me, for what purpose I cannot conjecture. But this preferential treatment could not be accorded me forever; it was time that I found my niche. 'There is someone here to see you'—the maid met me one afternoon with this announcement and a smile of superior knowledge. My heart bounded; I felt almost sick (who else, after all, could it be?), and she had to push me forward. But the man and woman surveying me in the sun parlor with my grandmother were strangers, two unprepossessing middle-aged people— a great-aunt and her husband, so it seemed—to whom I was now commanded to give a hand and a smile, for, as my grandmother remarked, Myers and Margaret had come to take me home that very afternoon to live with them, and I must not make a bad impression.

Once the new household was running, our parents' death was officially conceded and sentiment given its due. Concrete references to the lost ones, to their beauty, gaiety, and good manners, were naturally not welcomed by our guardians, who possessed none of these qualities themselves, but the veneration of our parents' *memory* was considered an admirable exercise. Our evening prayers were lengthened to include one for our parents' souls, and we were thought to make a pretty picture, all four of us in our pajamas with feet in them, kneeling in a neat line, our hands clasped before us, reciting the prayer for the dead. 'Eternal rest grant unto them, O Lord, and let the perpetual light shine upon them,' our thin little voices cried, but this remembrancing, so pleasurable to our guardians, was only a chore to us. We connected it with lights out, washing, all the bedtime coercions, and particularly with the adhesive tape that, to prevent mouth-breathing, was clapped upon our lips the moment the prayer was finished, sealing us up for the night, and that was removed, very painfully, with the help of ether, in the morning. It embarrassed us to be reminded of our parents by these persons who had superseded them and who seemed to evoke their wraiths in an almost proprietary manner, as though death, the great leveller, had brought them within their province. In the same spirit, we were taken to the cemetery to view our parents' graves; this, in fact, being free of charge, was a regular Sunday pastime with us, which we grew to hate as we did all recreation enforced by our guardians—department-store demonstrations, band concerts, parades, trips to the Old Soldiers' Home, to the Botanical Gardens, to Minnehaha Park, where we watched other children ride on the ponies, to the Zoo, to the water tower—diversions that cost nothing, involved long streetcar trips or endless walking or waiting, and that had the peculiarly fatigued, dusty, proletarianized character of American municipal entertainment. The two mounds that now were our parents associated themselves in our minds with Civil War cannon balls and monuments to the doughboy dead; we contemplated them stolidly, waiting for a sensation, but these twin grass beds, with their junior-executive headstones, elicited nothing whatever; tired of this interminable staring, we would beg to be allowed to go play in some collateral mausoleum, where the dead at least were buried in drawers and offered some stimulus to fancy.

For my grandmother, the recollection of the dead became a mode of civility that she thought proper to exercise toward us whenever, for any reason, one of us came to stay at her house. The reason was almost always the same. We (that is, my brother Kevin or I) had run away from home. Independently of each other, this oldest of my brothers and I had evolved an identical project. The purpose dearest to our hearts was to get ourselves placed in an orphan asylum, for we interpreted the word 'asylum' in the old Greek sense and looked upon a certain red brick building, seen once from a streetcar near the Mississippi River, as a sanctuary for the helpless and a refuge from persecution. So, from time to time, when our lives became too painful, one of us would set forth, determined to find the red brick building and to press what we imagined was our legal claim to its shelter and protection. But sometimes we lost our way, and sometimes our courage, and after spending a day hanging about the streets peering into strange yards, trying to assess the kindheartedness of the owner (for we also thought of adoption), or after a cold night spent hiding in a church confessional box or behind some statuary in the Art Institute, we would be brought by the police, by some well-meaning householder, or simply by fear and hunger, to my grandmother's door. There we would be silently received, and a family conclave would be summoned. We would be put to sleep in the sewing room for a night, or sometimes more, until our feelings had subsided and we could be sent back, grateful, at any rate, for the promise that no reprisals would be taken and that the life we had run away from would go on 'as if nothing had happened'.

Since we were usually running away to escape some anticipated punishment, these flights at least gained us something, but in spite of the taunts of our guardians, who congratulated us bitterly on our 'cleverness', we ourselves could not feel that we came home in triumph so long as we came home at all. Our failure to run away successfully put us, so we thought, at the absolute mercy of our guardians; our last weapon was gone, for it was plain to be seen that they could always bring us back, however far we travelled, or that we would bring ourselves back, too soft to stand cold and hunger, too cowardly to steal or run away from a policeman; we never understood why they did not take advantage of this situation to thrash us, as they used to put it, within an inch of our lives. What intervened to save us, we could not guess—a miracle, perhaps; we were not acquainted with any *human* motive that would prompt Omnipotence to desist. We did not suspect that these escapades brought consternation to the family circle, which had acted, so it conceived, only in our best interests, and now saw itself in danger of unmerited obloquy. What would be the Protestant reaction if something still more dreadful were to happen? Child suicides were not unknown, and quiet, asthmatic little Kevin had been caught with matches under the house. The family would not acknowledge error, but it conceded a certain mismanagement on Myers' and Margaret's part. Clearly, we might become altogether intractable if our homecoming on these occasions were not mitigated with leniency. Consequently, my grandmother kept us in a kind of neutral detention. She declined to be aware of our grievance and offered no words of comfort, but the comforts of her household acted upon us soothingly, like an automatic mother's hand. We ate and drank contentedly; with all her harsh views, my grandmother was a practical woman and would not have thought it worth while to unsettle her whole schedule, teach her cook to make a lumpy mush and watery boiled potatoes, and market for turnips and parsnips and all the other vegetables we hated, in order to approximate the conditions she considered suitable for our characters. Humble pie could be costly, especially when cooked to order.

Doubtless she did not guess how delightful these visits seemed to us once the fear of punishment had abated. Her knowledge of our own way of living was luxuriously remote. She did not visit our ménage or inquire into its practices, and though hypersensitive to a squint or a dental irregularity (for she was liberal indeed with glasses and braces for the teeth, disfiguring appliances that remained the sole token of our bourgeois origin and set us off from our parochial-school mates like the caste marks of some primitive tribe), she appeared not to notice the darns and patches of our clothing, our raw hands and scarecrow arms, our silence and our elderly faces. She imagined us as surrounded by certain playthings she had once bestowed on us—a sandbox, a wooden swing, a wagon, and a toy fire engine. In my grandmother's consciousness, these objects remained always in pristine condition; years after the sand had spilled out of it and the roof had rotted away, she continued to ask tenderly after our lovely sand pile and to manifest displeasure if we declined to join in its praises. Like many egoistic people (I have noticed this trait in myself), she was capable of making a handsome outlay, but the act affected her so powerfully that her generosity was still lively in her memory when its practical effects had long vanished. In the case of a brown beaver hat, which she watched me wear for four years, she was clearly blinded to its matted nap, its shapeless brim, and ragged ribbon by the vision of the price tag it had worn when new. Yet, however her mind embroidered the bare tapestry of our lives, she could not fail to perceive that we felt, during these short stays with her, *some* difference between the two establishments, and to take our wonder and pleasure as a compliment to herself.

She smiled on us quite kindly when we exclaimed over the food and the nice, warm bathrooms, with their rugs and electric heaters. What funny little creatures, to be so impressed by things that were, after all, only the ordinary amenities of life! Seeing us content in her house, her emulative spirit warmed slowly to our admiration; she compared herself to our guardians, and though for expedient reasons she could not afford to depreciate them ('You children have been very ungrateful for all Myers and Margaret have done for you'), a sense of her own finer magnanimity disposed her subtly in our favor. In the flush of these emotions, a tenderness sprang up between us. She seemed half reluctant to part with whichever of us she had in her custody, almost as if she were experiencing a genuine pang of conscience. 'Try and be good,' she would advise us when the moment for leave-taking came, 'and don't provoke your aunt and uncle. We might have made different arrangements if there had been only one of you to consider.' These manifestations of concern, these tacit admissions of our true situation, did not make us, as one might have thought, bitter against our grandparents, for whom ignorance of the facts might have served as a justification, but, on the contrary, filled us with love for them and even a kind of sympathy—our sufferings were less terrible if someone acknowledged their existence, if someone were suffering for us, for whom we, in our turn, could suffer, and thereby absolve of guilt.

During these respites, the recollection of our parents formed a bond between us and our grandmother that deepened our mutual regard. Unlike our guardians or the whispering ladies who sometimes came to call on us, inspired, it seemed, by a pornographic curiosity as to the exact details of our feelings ('Do you suppose they remember their parents?' 'Do they ever say anything?'), our grandmother was quite uninterested in arousing an emotion of grief in us. 'She doesn't feel it at all,' I used to hear her confide to visitors, but contentedly, without censure, as if I had been a spayed cat that, in her superior foresight, she had had 'attended to'. For my grandmother, the death of my parents had become, in retrospect, an eventful occasion upon which she looked back with pleasure and a certain self-satisfaction. Whenever we stayed with her, we were allowed, as a special treat, to look into the rooms they had died in, for the fact that, as she phrased it, 'they died in separate rooms' had for her a significance both romantic and somehow self-gratulatory, as though the separation in death of two who had loved each other in life were beautiful in itself and also reflected credit on the chatelaine of the house, who had been able to furnish two master bedrooms for the greater facility of decease. The housekeeping details of the tragedy, in fact, were to her of paramount interest. 'I turned my house into a hospital,' she used to say, particularly when visitors were present. 'Nurses were as scarce as hen's teeth, and *high*—you can hardly imagine what those girls were charging an hour.' The trays and the special cooking, the laundry and the disinfectants recalled themselves fondly to her thoughts, like items on the menu of some long-ago buffet supper, the memory of which recurred to her with a strong, possessive nostalgia.

My parents had, it seemed, by dying on her premises, become in a lively sense her property, and she dispensed them to us now, little by little, with a genuine sense of bounty, just as, later on, when I returned to her a grown-up young lady, she conceded me a diamond lavaliere of my mother's as if this trinket were an inheritance to which she had the prior claim. But her generosity with her memories appeared to us, as children, an act of the graeatest indulgence. We begged her for more of these mortuary reminiscences as we might have begged for candy, and since ordinarily we not only had no candy but were permitted no friendships, no movies, and little reading beyond what our teachers prescribed for us, and were kept in quarantine, like carriers of social contagion, among the rhubarb plants of our neglected yard, these memories doled out by our grandmother became our secret treasures; we never spoke of them to each other but hoarded them, each against the rest, in the miserly fastnesses of our hearts. We returned, therefore, from our grandparents' house replenished in all our faculties; these crumbs from the rich man's table were a banquet indeed to us. We did not even mind going back to our guardians, for we now felt superior to them, and besides, as we well knew, we had no choice. It was only by accepting our situation as a just and unalterable arrangement that we could be allowed to transcend it and feel ourselves united to our grandparents in a love that was the more miraculous for breeding no practical results.

In this manner, our household was kept together, and my grandparents were spared the necessity of arriving at a fresh decision about it. Naturally, from time to time a new scandal would break out (for our guardians did not grow kinder in response to being run away from), yet we had come, at bottom, to despair of making any real change in our circumstances, and ran away hopelessly, merely to postpone punishment. And when, after five years, our Protestant grandfather, informed at last of the facts, intervened to save us, his indignation at the family surprised us nearly as much as his action. We thought it only natural that grandparents should know and do nothing, for did not God in the mansions of Heaven look down upon human suffering and allow it to take its course?

NADINE GORDIMER

Which New Era Would That Be?

Jake Alexander, a big, fat coloured man, half Scottish, half African, was
shaking a large pan of frying bacon on the gas stove in the back room of
his Johannesburg printing shop when he became aware that someone was
knocking on the door at the front of the shop. The sizzling fat and the
voices of the five men in the back room with him almost blocked sounds
from without, and the knocking was of the steady kind that might have
been going on for quite a few minutes. He lifted the pan off the flame
with one hand and with the other made an impatient silencing gesture,
directed at the bacon as well as the voices. Interpreting the movement as
one of caution, the men hurriedly picked up the tumblers and cups in
which they had been taking their end-of-the-day brandy at their ease, and
tossed the last of it down. Little yellow Klaas, whose hair was like ginger-
coloured wire wool, stacked the cups and glasses swiftly and hid them
behind the dirty curtain that covered a row of shelves.

'Who's that?' yelled Jake, wiping his greasy hands down his pants.

There was a sharp and playful tattoo, followed by an English voice:
'Me—Alister. For heaven's sake, Jake!'

The fat man put the pan back on the flame and tramped through the
dark shop, past the idle presses, to the door, and flung it open. 'Mr
Halford!' he said. 'Well, good to see you. Come in, man. In the back
there, you can't hear a thing.' A young Englishman with gentle eyes, a
stern mouth and flat, colourless hair which grew in an untidy, confused
spiral from a double crown, stepped back to allow a young woman to
enter ahead of him. Before he could introduce her, she held out her hand
to Jake, smiling, and shook his firmly. 'Good evening. Jennifer Tetzel,'
she said.

'Jennifer, this is Jake Alexander,' the young man managed to get in,
over her shoulder.

The two had entered the building from the street through an archway
lettered NEW ERA BUILDING. 'Which new era would that be?' the young
woman had wondered aloud, brightly, while they were waiting in the dim
hallway for the door to be opened, and Alister Halford had not known

whether the reference was to the discovery of deep-level gold mining that had saved Johannesburg from the ephemeral fate of a mining camp in the nineties, or to the optimism after the settlement of labour troubles in the twenties, or to the recovery after the world went off the gold standard in the thirties—really, one had no idea of the age of these buildings in this run-down end of the town. Now, coming in out of the deserted hallway gloom, which smelled of dust and rotting wood—the smell of waiting— they were met by the live, cold tang of ink and the homely, lazy odour of bacon fat—the smell of acceptance. There was not much light in the deserted workshop. The host blundered to the wall and switched on a bright naked bulb, up in the ceiling. The three stood blinking at one another for a moment: a coloured man with the fat of the man-of-the- world upon him, grossly dressed—not out of poverty but obviously be- cause he liked it that way—in a rayon sports shirt that gaped and showed two hairy stomach rolls hiding his navel in a lipless grin, the pants of a good suit misbuttoned and held up round the waist by a tie instead of a belt, and a pair of expensive sports shoes, worn without socks; a young Englishman in a worn greenish tweed suit with a neo-Edwardian cut to the waistcoat that labelled it a leftover from undergraduate days; a handsome white woman who, as the light fell upon her, was immediately recognizable to Jake Alexander.

He had never met her before but he knew the type well—had seen it over and over again at meetings of the Congress of Democrats, and other organizations where progressive whites met progressive blacks. These were the white women who, Jake knew, persisted in regarding themselves as your equal. That was even worse, he thought, than the parsons who persisted in regarding *you* as *their* equal. The parsons had had ten years at school and seven years at a university and theological school; you had carried sacks of vegetables from the market to white people's cars from the time you were eight years old until you were apprenticed to a printer, and your first woman, like your mother, had been a servant, whom you had visited in a backyard room, and your first gulp of whisky, like many of your other pleasures, had been stolen while a white man was not looking. Yet the good parson insisted that your picture of life was exactly the same as his own: *you* felt as *he* did. But these women—oh, Christ!— these women felt as *you* did. They were sure of it. They thought they understood the humiliation of the black man walking the streets only by the permission of a pass written out by a white person, and the guilt and swagger of the coloured man light-faced enough to slink, fugitive from his own skin, into the preserves—the cinemas, bars, libraries—marked 'EUROPEANS ONLY'. Yes, breathless with stout sensitivity, they insisted on walking the whole teeter-totter of the colour line. There was no escaping their understanding. They even insisted on feeling the resentment *you* must feel at their identifying themselves with your feelings . . .

Here was the black hair of a determined woman (last year they wore it pulled tightly back into an oddly perched knot; this year it was cropped and curly as a lap dog's), the round, bony brow unpowdered in order to show off the tan, the red mouth, the unrouged cheeks, the big, lively, handsome eyes, dramatically painted, that would look into yours with such intelligent, eager honesty—eager to mirror what Jake Alexander, a big, fat coloured man interested in women, money, brandy and boxing, was feeling. Who the hell wants a woman to look at you honestly, anyway? What has all this to do with a *woman*—with what men and women have for each other in their eyes? She was wearing a wide black skirt, a white cotton blouse baring a good deal of her breasts, and ear-rings that seemed to have been made by a blacksmith out of bits of scrap iron. On her feet she had sandals whose narrow thongs wound between her toes, and the nails of the toes were painted plum colour. By contrast, her hands were neglected-looking—sallow, unmanicured—and on one thin finger there swivelled a huge gold seal-ring. She was good-looking, he supposed with disgust.

He stood there, fat, greasy and grinning at the two visitors so lingeringly that his grin looked insolent. Finally he asked, 'What brings you this end of town, Mr Halford? Sight-seeing with the lady?'

The young Englishman gave Jake's arm a squeeze, where the short sleeve of the rayon shirt ended. 'Just thought I'd look you up, Jake,' he said, jolly.

'Come on in, come on in,' said Jake on a rising note, shambling ahead of them into the company of the back room. 'Here, what about a chair for the lady?' He swept a pile of handbills from the seat of a kitchen chair onto the dusty concrete floor, picked up the chair and planked it down again in the middle of the group of men who had risen awkwardly at the visitors' entrance. 'You know Maxie Ndube? And Temba?' Jake said, nodding at two of the men who surrounded him.

Alister Halford murmured with polite warmth his recognition of Maxie, a small, dainty-faced African in neat, businessman's dress, then said inquiringly and hesitantly to Temba, 'Have we? When?'

Temba was a coloured man—a mixture of the bloods of black slaves and white masters, blended long ago, in the days when the Cape of Good Hope was a port of refreshment for the Dutch East India Company. He was tall and pale, with a large Adam's apple, enormous black eyes, and the look of a musician in a jazz band; you could picture a trumpet lifted to the ceiling in those long yellow hands, that curved spine hunched forward to shield a low note. 'In Durban last year, Mr Halford, you remember?' he said eagerly. 'I'm sure we met—or perhaps I only saw you there.'

'Oh, at the Congress? Of course I remember you!' Halford apologized. 'You were in a delegation from the Cape?'

'Miss—?' Jake Alexander waved a hand between the young woman, Maxie, and Temba.

'Jennifer. Jennifer Tetzel,' she said again clearly, thrusting out her hand. There was a confused moment when both men reached for it at once and then hesitated, each giving way to the other. Finally the hand-shaking was accomplished, and the young woman seated herself confidently on the chair.

Jake continued, offhand, 'Oh, and of course Billy Boy—' Alister signalled briefly to a black man with sad, blood-shot eyes, who stood awkwardly, back a few steps, against some rolls of paper—'and Klaas and Albert.' Klaas and Albert had in their mixed blood some strain of the Bushman, which gave them a batrachian yellowness and toughness, like one of those toads that (prehistoric as the Bushman is) are mythically believed to have survived into modern times (hardly more fantastically than the Bushman himself has survived) by spending centuries shut up in an air bubble in a rock. Like Billy Boy, Klaas and Albert had backed away, and, as if abasement against the rolls of paper, the wall or the window were a greeting in itself, the two little coloured men and the big African only stared back at the masculine nods of Alister and the bright smile of the young woman.

'You up from the Cape for anything special now?' Alister said to Temba as he made a place for himself on a corner of a table that was littered with photographic blocks, bits of type, poster proofs, a bottle of souring milk, a bow-tie, a pair of red braces and a number of empty Coca-Cola bottles.

'I've been living in Durban for a year. Just got the chance of a lift to Jo'burg,' said the gangling Temba.

Jake had set himself up easily, leaning against the front of the stove and facing Miss Jennifer Tetzel on her chair. He jerked his head towards Temba and said, 'Real banana boy.' Young white men brought up in the strong Anglo-Saxon tradition of the province of Natal are often referred to, and refer to themselves, as 'banana boys', even though fewer and fewer of them have any connection with the dwindling number of vast banana estates that once made their owners rich. Jake's broad face, where the bright-pink cheeks of a Highland complexion—inherited, along with his name, from his Scottish father—showed oddly through his coarse, beige skin, creased up in appreciation of his own joke. And Temba threw back his head and laughed, his Adam's apple bobbing, at the idea of himself as a cricket-playing white public-school boy.

'There's nothing like Cape Town, is there?' said the young woman to him, her head charmingly on one side, as if this conviction were something she and he shared.

'Miss Tetzel's up here to look us over. She's from Cape Town,' Alister explained.

She turned to Temba with her beauty, her strong provocativeness, full on, as it were. 'So we're neighbours?'

Jake rolled one foot comfortably over the other and a spluttering laugh pursed out the pink inner membrane of his lips.

'Where did you live?' she went on, to Temba.

'Cape Flats,' he said. Cape Flats is a desolate coloured slum in the bush outside Cape Town.

'Me, too,' said the girl, casually.

Temba said politely, 'You're kidding,' and then looked down uncomfortably at his hands, as if they had been guilty of some clumsy movement. He had not meant to sound so familiar; the words were not the right ones.

'I've been there nearly ten months,' she said.

'Well, some people've got queer tastes,' Jake remarked, laughing, to no one in particular, as if she were not there.

'How's that?' Temba was asking her shyly, respectfully.

She mentioned the name of a social rehabilitation scheme that was in operation in the slum. 'I'm assistant director of the thing at the moment. It's connected with the sort of work I do at the university, you see, so they've given me fifteen months' leave from my usual job.'

Maxie noticed with amusement the way she used the word 'job', as if she were a plumber's mate; he and his educated African friends—journalists and schoolteachers—were careful to talk only of their 'professions'. 'Good works,' he said, smiling quietly.

She planted her feet comfortably before her, wriggling on the hard chair, and said to Temba with mannish frankness, 'It's a ghastly place. How in God's name did you survive living there? I don't think I can last out more than another few months, and I've always got my flat in Cape Town to escape to on Sundays, and so on.'

While Temba smiled, turning his protruding eyes aside slowly, Jake looked straight at her and said, 'Then why do you, lady, why *do* you?'

'Oh, I don't know. Because I don't see why anyone else—any one of the people who live there—should have to, I suppose.' She laughed before anyone else could at the feebleness, the philanthropic uselessness of what she was saying. 'Guilt, what-have-you . . .'

Maxie shrugged, as if at the mention of some expensive illness he had never been able to afford and whose symptoms he could not imagine.

There was a moment of silence; the two coloured men and the big black man standing back against the wall watched anxiously, as if some sort of signal might be expected, possibly from Jake Alexander, their boss, the man who, like themselves, was not white, yet who owned his own business and had a car and money and strange friends—sometimes even white people, such as these. The three of them were dressed in the ill-matched cast-off clothing that all humble workpeople who are not white wear in Johannesburg, and they had not lost the ability of rural people to stare, unembarrassed and unembarrassing.

Jake winked at Alister; it was one of his mannerisms—a bookie's wink, a stage comedian's wink. 'Well, how's it going, boy, how's it going?' he said. His turn of phrase was bar-room bonhomie; with luck, he *could* get into a bar, too. With a hat to cover his hair and his coat collar well up, and only a bit of greasy pink cheek showing, he had slipped into the bars of the shabbier Johannesburg hotels with Alister many times and got away with it. Alister, on the other hand, had got away with the same sort of thing narrowly several times, too, when he had accompanied Jake to a shebeen in a coloured location, where it was illegal for a white man to be, as well as illegal for anyone at all to have a drink; twice Alister had escaped a raid by jumping out of a window. Alister had been in South Africa only eighteen months, as correspondent for a newspaper in England, and because he was only two or three years away from under-graduate escapades such incidents seemed to give him a kind of nostalgic pleasure; he found them funny. Jake, for his part, had decided long ago (with the great help of the money he had made) that he would take the whole business of the colour bar as humorous. The combination of these two attitudes, stemming from such immeasurably different circumstances, had the effect of making their friendship less self-conscious than is usual between a white man and a coloured one.

'They tell me it's going to be a good thing on Saturday night?' said Alister, in the tone of questioning someone in the know. He was referring to a boxing match between two coloured heavyweights, one of whom was a protégé of Jake.

Jake grinned deprecatingly, like a fond mother. 'Well, Pikkie's a good boy,' he said. 'I tell you, it'll be something to see.' He danced about a little on his clumsy toes in pantomime of the way a boxer nimbles himself, and collapsed against the stove, his belly shaking with laughter at his breathlessness.

'Too much smoking, too many brandies, Jake,' said Alister.

'With me, it's too many women, boy.'

'We were just congratulating Jake,' said Maxie in his soft, precise voice, the indulgent, tongue-in-cheek tone of the protégé who is superior to his patron, for Maxie was one of Jake's boys, too—of a different kind. Though Jake had decided that for him being on the wrong side of a colour bar was ludicrous, he was as indulgent to those who took it seriously and politically, the way Maxie did, as he was to any up-and-coming youngster who, say, showed talent in the ring or wanted to go to America and become a singer. They could all make themselves free of Jake's pocket, and his printing shop, and his room in the lower end of the town, where the building had fallen below the standard of white people but was far superior to the kind of thing most coloureds and blacks were accustomed to.

'Congratulations on what?' the young white woman asked. She had a way of looking up around her, questioningly, from face to face, that came of long familiarity with being the centre of attention at parties.

'Yes, you can shake my hand, boy,' said Jake to Alister. 'I didn't see it, but these fellows tell me that my divorce went through. It's in the papers today.'

'Is that so? But from what I hear, you won't be a free man long,' Alister said teasingly.

Jake giggled, and pressed at one gold-filled tooth with a strong fingernail. 'You heard about the little parcel I'm expecting from Zululand?' he asked.

'Zululand?' said Alister. 'I thought your Lila came from Stellenbosch.' Maxie and Temba laughed.

'Lila? *What* Lila?' said Jake with exaggerated innocence.

'You're behind the times,' said Maxie to Alister.

'You know I like them—well, sort of round,' said Jake. 'Don't care for the thin kind, in the long run.'

'But Lila had red hair!' Alister goaded him. He remembered the incongruously dyed, straightened hair on a fine coloured girl whose nostrils dilated in the manner of certain fleshy water-plants seeking prey.

Jennifer Tetzel got up and turned the gas off on the stove, behind Jake. 'That bacon'll be like charred string,' she said.

Jake did not move—merely looked at her lazily. 'This is not the way to talk with a lady around.' He grinned, unapologetic.

She smiled at him and sat down, shaking her ear-rings. 'Oh, I'm divorced myself. Are we keeping you people from your supper? Do go ahead and eat. Don't bother about us.'

Jake turned around, gave the shrunken rashers a mild shake and put the pan aside. 'Hell, no,' he said. 'Any time. But—' turning to Alister— 'won't you have something to eat?' He looked about, helpless and unconcerned, as if to indicate an absence of plates and a general careless lack of equipment such as white women would be accustomed to use when they ate. Alister said quickly, no, he had promised to take Jennifer to Moorjee's.

Of course, Jake should have known; a woman like that would *want* to be taken to eat at an Indian place in Vrededorp, even though she was white, and free to eat at the best hotel in town. He felt suddenly, after all, the old gulf opening between himself and Alister: what did *they* see in such women—bristling, sharp, all-seeing, knowing women, who talked like men, who wanted to show all the time that, apart from sex, they were exactly the same as men? He looked at Jennifer and her clothes, and thought of the way a white woman could look: one of those big, soft, European women with curly yellow hair, with very high-heeled shoes that made them shake softly when they walked, with a strong scent, like hot flowers, coming up, it seemed, from their jutting breasts under the lace and pink and blue and all the other pretty things they wore—women with nothing resistant about them except, buried in white, boneless fingers, those red, pointed nails that scratched faintly at your palms.

'You should have been along with me at lunch today,' said Maxie to no one in particular. Or perhaps the soft voice, a vocal tiptoe, was aimed at Alister, who was familiar with Maxie's work as an organizer of African trade unions. The group in the room gave him their attention (Temba with the little encouraging grunt of one who has already heard the story), but Maxie paused a moment, smiling ruefully at what he was about to tell. Then he said, 'You know George Elson?' Alister nodded. The man was a white lawyer who had been arrested twice for his participation in anti-colour-bar movements.

'Oh, George? I've worked with George often in Cape Town,' put in Jennifer.

'Well,' continued Maxie, 'George Elson and I went out to one of the industrial towns on the East Rand. We were interviewing the bosses, you see, not the men, and at the beginning it was all right, though, once or twice the girls in the offices thought I was George's driver—"Your boy can wait outside."' He laughed, showing small, perfect teeth; everything about him was finely made—his straight-fingered dark hands, the curved African nostrils of his small nose, his little ears, which grew close to the sides of his delicate head. The others were silent, but the young woman laughed, too.

'We even got tea in one place,' Maxie went on. 'One of the girls came in with two cups and a tin mug. But old George took the mug.'

Jennifer Tetzel laughed again, knowingly.

'Then, just about lunch time, we came to this place I wanted to tell you about. Nice chap, the manager. Never blinked an eye at me, called me Mister. And after we'd talked, he said to George, "Why not come home with me for lunch?" So of course George said, "Thanks, but I'm with my friend here." "Oh, that's O.K.," said the chap. "Bring him along." Well, we go along to this house, and the chap disappears into the kitchen, and then he comes back and we sit in the lounge and have a beer, and then the servant comes along and says lunch is ready. Just as we're walking into the dining room, the chap takes me by the arm and says, "I've had *your* lunch laid on a table on the stoep. You'll find it's all perfectly clean and nice, just what we're having ourselves."'

'Fantastic,' murmured Alister.

Maxie smiled and shrugged, looking around at them all. 'It's true.'

'After he'd asked you, and he'd sat having a drink with you?' Jennifer said closely, biting in her lower lip, as if this were a problem to be solved psychologically.

'Of course,' said Maxie.

Jake was shaking with laughter, like some obscene Silenus. There was no sound out of him, but saliva gleamed on his lips, and his belly, at the level of Jennifer Tetzel's eyes, was convulsed.

Temba said soberly, in the tone of one whose goodwill makes it difficult for him to believe in the unease of his situation, 'I certainly find it worse here than at the Cape. I can't remember, y'know, about buses. I keep getting put off European buses.'

Maxie pointed to Jake's heaving belly. 'Oh, I'll tell you a better one than that,' he said. 'Something that happened in the office one day. Now, the trouble with me is, apparently, I don't talk like a native.' This time everyone laughed, except Maxie himself, who, with the instinct of a good raconteur, kept a polite, modest, straight face.

'You know that's true,' interrupted the young white woman. 'You have none of the usual softening of the vowels of most Africans. And you haven't got an Afrikaans accent, as some Africans have, even if they get rid of the African thing.'

'Anyway, I'd had to phone a certain firm several times,' Maxie went on, 'and I'd got to know the voice of the girl at the other end, and she'd got to know mine. As a matter of fact, she must have liked the sound of me, because she was getting very friendly. We fooled about a bit, exchanged first names, like a couple of kids—hers was Peggy—and she said, eventually, "Aren't you ever going to come to the office yourself?"' Maxie paused a moment, and his tongue flicked at the side of his mouth in a brief, nervous gesture. When he spoke again, his voice was flat, like the voice of a man who is telling a joke and suddenly thinks that perhaps it is not such a good one after all. 'So I told her I'd be in next day, about four. I walked in, sure enough, just as I said I would. She was a pretty girl, blonde, you know, with very tidy hair—I guessed she'd just combed it to be ready for me. She looked up and said "Yes?" holding out her hand for the messenger's book or parcel she thought I'd brought. I took her hand and shook it and said, "Well, here I am, on time—I'm Maxie—Maxie Ndube."'

'What'd she do?' asked Temba eagerly.

The interruption seemed to restore Maxie's confidence in his story. He shrugged gaily. 'She almost dropped my hand, and then she pumped it like a mad thing, and her neck and ears went so red I thought she'd burn up. Honestly, her ears were absolutely shining. She tried to pretend she'd known all along, but I could see she was terrified someone would come from the inner office and see her shaking hands with a native. So I took pity on her and went away. Didn't even stay for my appointment with her boss. When I went back to keep the postponed appointment the next week, we pretended we'd never met.'

Temba was slapping his knee. 'God, I'd have loved to see her face!' he said.

Jake wiped away a tear from his fat cheek—his eyes were light blue, and produced tears easily when he laughed—and said, 'That'll teach you not to talk swanky, man. Why can't you talk like the rest of us?'

'Oh, I'll watch out on the "Missus" and "Baas" stuff in future,' said Maxie.

Jennifer Tetzel cut into their laughter with her cool, practical voice. 'Poor little girl, she probably liked you awfully, Maxie, and was really disappointed. You mustn't be too harsh on her. It's hard to be punished for not being black.'

The moment was one of astonishment rather than irritation. Even Jake, who had been sure that there could be no possible situation between white and black he could not find amusing, only looked quickly from the young woman to Maxie, in a hiatus between anger, which he had given up long ago, and laughter, which suddenly failed him. On his face was admiration more than anything else—sheer, grudging admiration. This one was the best yet. This one was the coolest ever.

'Is it?' said Maxie to Jennifer, pulling in the corners of his mouth and regarding her from under slightly raised eyebrows. Jake watched. Oh, she'd have a hard time with Maxie. Maxie wouldn't give up his suffering-tempered blackness so easily. You hadn't much hope of knowing what Maxie was feeling at any given moment, because Maxie not only never let you know but made you guess wrong. But this one was the best yet.

She looked back at Maxie, opening her eyes very wide, twisting her sandalled foot on the swivel of its ankle, smiling. 'Really, I assure you it is.'

Maxie bowed to her politely, giving way with a falling gesture of his hand.

Alister had slid from his perch on the crowded table, and now, prodding Jake playfully in the paunch, he said, 'We have to get along.'

Jake scratched his ear and said again, 'Sure you won't have something to eat?'

Alister shook his head. 'We had hoped you'd offer us a drink, but—'

Jake wheezed with laughter, but this time was sincerely concerned. 'Well, to tell you the truth, when we heard the knocking, we just swallowed the last of the bottle off, in case it was someone it shouldn't be. I haven't a drop in the place till tomorrow. Sorry, chappie. Must apologize to you, lady, but we black men've got to drink in secret. If we'd've known it was you two . . .'

Maxie and Temba had risen. The two wizened coloured men, Klaas and Albert, and the sombre black Billy Boy shuffled helplessly, hanging about.

Alister said, 'Next time, Jake, next time. We'll give you fair warning and you can lay it on.'

Jennifer shook hands with Temba and Maxie, called 'Good-bye! Good-bye!' to the others, as if they were somehow out of earshot in that small room. From the door, she suddenly said to Maxie, 'I feel I must tell you. About that other story—your first one, about the lunch. I don't believe it. I'm sorry, but I honestly don't. It's too illogical to hold water.'

It was the final self-immolation by honest understanding. There was absolutely no limit to which that understanding would not go. Even if she could not believe Maxie, she must keep her determined good faith with him by confessing her disbelief. She would go to the length of calling him a liar to show by frankness how much she respected him—to insinuate, perhaps, that she was *with him*, even in the need to invent something about a white man that she, because she herself was white, could not believe. It was her last bid for Maxie.

The small, perfectly-made man crossed his arms and smiled, watching her go. Maxie had no price.

Jake saw his guests out of the shop, and switched off the light after he had closed the door behind them. As he walked back through the dark, where his presses smelled metallic and cool, he heard, for a few moments, the clear voice of the white woman and the low, noncommittal English murmur of Alister, his friend, as they went out through the archway into the street.

He blinked a little as he came back to the light and the faces that confronted him in the back room. Klaas had taken the dirty glasses from behind the curtain and was holding them one by one under the tap in the sink. Billy Boy and Albert had come closer out of the shadows and were leaning their elbows on a roll of paper. Temba was sitting on the table, swinging his foot. Maxie had not moved, and stood just as he had, with his arms folded. No one spoke.

Jake began to whistle softly through the spaces between his front teeth, and he picked up the pan of bacon, looked at the twisted curls of meat, jellied now in cold white fat, and put it down again absently. He stood a moment, heavily, regarding them all, but no one responded. His eye encountered the chair that he had cleared for Jennifer Tetzel to sit on. Suddenly he kicked it, hard, so that it went flying on to its side. Then, rubbing his big hands together and bursting into loud whistling to accompany an impromptu series of dance steps, he said 'Now, boys!' and as they stirred, he planked the pan down on the ring and turned the gas up till it roared beneath it.

The Day Mr Prescott Died

It was a bright day, a hot day, the day old Mr Prescott died. Mama and I sat on the side seat of the rickety green bus from the subway station to Devonshire Terrace and jogged and jogged. The sweat was trickling down my back, I could feel it, and my black linen was stuck solid against the seat. Every time I moved it would come loose with a tearing sound, and I gave Mama an angry 'so there' look, just like it was her fault, which it wasn't. But she only sat with her hands folded in her lap, jouncing up and down, and didn't say anything. Just looked resigned to fate is all.

'I say, Mama,' I'd told her after Mrs Mayfair called that morning, 'I can see going to the funeral even though I don't believe in funerals, only what do you mean we have to sit up and watch with them?'

'It is what you do when somebody close dies,' Mama said, very reasonable. 'You go over and sit with them. It is a bad time.'

'So it is a bad time,' I argued. 'So what can I do, not seeing Liz and Ben Prescott since I was a kid except once a year at Christmas time for giving presents at Mrs Mayfair's. I am supposed to sit around hold handkerchiefs, maybe?'

With that remark, Mama up and slapped me across the mouth, the way she hadn't done since I was a little kid and very fresh. 'You are coming with me,' she said in her dignified tone that means definitely no more fooling.

So that is how I happened to be sitting in this bus on the hottest day of the year. I wasn't sure how you dressed for waiting up with people, but I figured as long as it was black it was all right. So I had on this real smart black linen suit and a little veil hat, like I wear to the office when I go out to dinner nights, and I felt ready for anything.

Well, the bus chugged along and we went through the real bad parts of East Boston I hadn't seen since I was a kid. Ever since we moved to the country with Aunt Myra, I hadn't come back to my home town. The only thing I really missed after we moved was the ocean. Even today on this bus I caught myself waiting for that first stretch of blue.

'Look, Mama, there's the old beach,' I said, pointing.

Mama looked and smiled. 'Yes.' Then she turned around to me and her thin face got very serious. 'I want you to make me proud of you today. When you talk, talk. But talk nice. None of this fancy business about burning people up like roast pigs. It isn't decent.'

'Oh, Mama,' I said, very tired. I was always explaining. 'Don't you know I've got better sense. Just because old Mr Prescott had it coming. Just because nobody's sorry, don't think I won't be nice and proper.'

I knew that would get Mama. 'What do you mean nobody's sorry?' she hissed at me, first making sure people weren't near enough to listen. 'What do you mean, talking so nasty?'

'Now, Mama,' I said, 'you know Mr Prescott was twenty years older than Mrs Prescott and she was just waiting for him to die so she could have some fun. Just waiting. He was a grumpy old man even as far back as I remember. A cross word for everybody, and he kept getting that skin disease on his hands.'

'That was a pity the poor man couldn't help,' Mama said piously. 'He had a right to be crotchety over his hands itching all the time, rubbing them the way he did.'

'Remember the time he came to Christmas Eve supper last year?' I went on stubbornly. 'He sat at the table and kept rubbing his hands so loud you couldn't hear anything else, only the skin like sandpaper flaking off in little pieces. How would you like to live with *that* every day?'

I had her there. No doubt about it, Mr Prescott's going was no sorrow for anybody. It was the best thing that could have happened all around.

'Well,' Mama breathed, 'we can at least be glad he went so quick and easy. I only hope I go like that when my time comes.'

Then the streets were crowding up together all of a sudden, and there we were by old Devonshire Terrace and Mama was pulling the buzzer. The bus dived to a stop, and I grabbed hold of the chipped chromium pole behind the driver just before I would have shot out the front window. 'Thanks, mister,' I said in my best icy tone, and minced down from the bus.

'Remember,' Mama said as we walked down the sidewalk, going single file where there was a hydrant, it was so narrow, 'remember, we stay as long as they need us. And no complaining. Just wash dishes, or talk to Liz, or whatever.'

'But Mama,' I complained, 'how can I say I'm sorry about Mr Prescott when I'm really not sorry at all? When I really think it's a good thing?'

'You can say it is the mercy of the Lord he went so peaceful,' Mama said sternly. 'Then you will be telling the honest truth.'

I got nervous only when we turned up the little gravel drive by the old yellow house the Prescotts owned on Devonshire Terrace. I didn't feel even the least bit sad. The orange-and-green awning was out over the porch, just like I remembered, and after ten years it didn't look any different, only smaller. And the two poplar trees on each side of the door had shrunk, but that was all.

As I helped Mama up the stone steps onto the porch, I could hear a creaking and sure enough, there was Ben Prescott sitting and swinging on the porch hammock like it was any other day in the world but the one his Pop died. He just sat there, lanky and tall as life. What really surprised me was he had his favorite guitar in the hammock beside him. Like he'd just finished playing 'The Big Rock Candy Mountain', or something.

'Hello Ben,' Mama said mournfully. 'I'm so sorry.'

Ben looked embarrassed. 'Heck, that's all right,' he said. 'The folks are all in the living-room.'

I followed Mama in through the screen door, giving Ben a little smile. I didn't know whether it was all right to smile because Ben was a nice guy, or whether I shouldn't, out of respect for his Pop.

Inside the house, it was like I remembered too, very dark so you could hardly see, and the green window blinds didn't help. They were all pulled down. Because of the heat or the funeral, I couldn't tell. Mama felt her way to the living-room and drew back the portieres. 'Lydia?' she called.

'Agnes?' There was this little stir in the dark of the living-room and Mrs Prescott came out to meet us. I had never seen her looking so well, even though the powder on her face was all streaked from crying.

I only stood there while the two of them hugged and kissed and made sympathetic little noises to each other. Then Mrs Prescott turned to me and gave me her cheek to kiss. I tried to look sad again but it just wouldn't come, so I said, 'You don't know how surprised we were to hear about Mr Prescott.' Really, though, nobody was at all surprised, because the old man only needed one more heart attack and that would be that. But it was the right thing to say.

'Ah, yes,' Mrs Prescott sighed. 'I hadn't thought to see this day for many a long year yet.' And she led us into the living-room.

After I got used to the dim light, I could make out the people sitting around. There was Mrs Mayfair, who was Mrs Prescott's sister-in-law and the most enormous woman I've ever seen. She was in the corner by the piano. Then there was Liz, who barely said hello to me. She was in shorts and an old shirt, smoking one drag after the other. For a girl who had seen her father die that morning, she was real casual, only a little pale is all.

Well, when we were all settled, no one said anything for a minute, as if waiting for a cue, like before a show begins. Only Mrs Mayfair, sitting there in her layers of fat, was wiping away her eyes with a handkerchief, and I was reasonably sure it was sweat running down and not tears by a long shot.

'It's a shame,' Mama began then, very low, 'It's a shame, Lydia, that it had to happen like this. I was so quick in coming I didn't hear tell who found him even.'

Mama pronounced 'him' like it should have a capital H, but I guessed it was safe now that old Mr Prescott wouldn't be bothering anybody again, with that mean temper and those raspy hands. Anyhow, it was just the lead that Mrs Prescott was waiting for.

'Oh, Agnes,' she began, with a peculiar shining light to her face, 'I wasn't even here. It was Liz found him, poor child.'

'Poor child,' sniffed Mrs Mayfair into her handkerchief. Her huge red face wrinkled up like a cracked watermelon. 'He dropped dead right in her arms, he did.'

Liz didn't say anything, but just ground out one cigarette only half smoked and lit another. Her hands weren't even shaking. And believe me, I looked real carefully.

'I was at the rabbi's,' Mrs Prescott took up. She is a great one for these new religions. All the time it is some new minister or preacher having dinner at her house. So now it's a rabbi, yet. 'I was at the rabbi's, and Liz was home getting dinner when Pop came home from swimming. You know the way he always loved to swim, Agnes.'

Mama said yes, she knew the way Mr Prescott always loved to swim.

'Well,' Mrs Prescott went on, calm as this guy on the Dragnet program, 'it wasn't more than eleven-thirty. Pop always liked a morning dip, even when the water was like ice, and he came up and was in the yard drying off, talking to our next door neighbor over the hollyhock fence.'

'He just put up that very fence a year ago,' Mrs Mayfair interrupted, like it was an important clue.

'And Mr Gove, this nice man next door, thought Pop looked funny, blue, he said, and Pop all at once didn't answer him but just stood there staring with a silly smile on his face.'

Liz was looking out of the front window where there was still the sound of the hammock creaking on the front porch. She was blowing smoke rings. Not a word the whole time. Smoke rings only.

'So Mr Gove yells to Liz and she comes running out, and Pop falls like a tree right to the ground, and Mr Gove runs to get some brandy in the house while Liz holds Pop in her arms . . .'

'What happened then?' I couldn't help asking, just the way I used to when I was a kid and Mama was telling burglar stories.

'Then,' Mrs Prescott told us, 'Pop just . . . passed away, right there in Liz's arms. Before he could even finish the brandy.'

'Oh, Lydia,' Mama cried. 'What you have been through!'

Mrs Prescott didn't look as if she had been through much of anything. Mrs Mayfair began sobbing in her handkerchief and invoking the name of the Lord. She must have had it in for the old guy, because she kept praying, 'Oh, forgive us our sins,' like she had up and killed him herself.

'We will go on,' Mrs Prescott said, smiling bravely. 'Pop would have wanted us to go on.'

'That is all the best of us can do,' Mama sighed.

'I only hope I go as peacefully,' Mrs Prescott said.

'Forgive us our sins,' Mrs Mayfair sobbed to no one in particular.

At this point, the creaking of the hammock stopped outside and Ben Prescott stood in the doorway, blinking his eyes behind the thick glasses and trying to see where we all were in the dark. 'I'm hungry,' he said.

'I think we should all eat now,' Mrs Prescott smiled on us. 'The neighbors have brought over enough to last a week.'

'Turkey and ham, soup and salad,' Liz remarked in a bored tone, like she was a waitress reading off a menu. 'I just didn't know where to put it all.'

'Oh, Lydia,' Mama exclaimed, 'Let *us* get it ready. Let *us* help. I hope it isn't too much trouble. . . .'

'Trouble, no,' Mrs Prescott smiled her new radiant smile. 'We'll let the young folks get it.'

Mama turned to me with one of her purposeful nods and I jumped up like I had an electric shock. 'Show me where the things are, Liz,' I said, 'and we'll get this set up in no time.'

Ben tailed us out to the kitchen, where the black old gas stove was, and the sink, full of dirty dishes. First thing I did was pick up a big heavy glass soaking in the sink and run myself a long drink of water.

'My, I'm thirsty,' I said and gulped it down. Liz and Ben were staring at me like they were hypnotized. Then I noticed the water had a funny taste, as if I hadn't washed out the glass well enough and there were drops of some strong drink left in the bottom to mix with the water.

'That,' said Liz after a drag on her cigarette, 'is the last glass Pop drank out of. But never mind.'

'Oh Lordy, I'm sorry,' I said, putting it down fast. All at once I felt very much like being sick because I had a picture of old Mr Prescott, drinking his last from the glass and turning blue. 'I really am sorry.'

Ben grinned. 'Somebody's got to drink out of it someday.' I liked Ben. He was always a practical guy when he wanted to be.

Liz went upstairs to change then, after showing me what to get ready for supper.

'Mind if I bring in my guitar?' Ben asked, while I was starting to fix up the potato salad.

'Sure, it's okay by me,' I said. 'Only won't folks talk? Guitars being mostly for parties and all?'

'So let them talk. I've got a yen to strum.'

I made tracks around the kitchen and Ben didn't say much, only sat and played these hillbilly songs very soft, that made you want to laugh and sometimes cry.

'You know, Ben,' I said, cutting up a plate of cold turkey, 'I wonder, are you really sorry.'

Ben grinned, that way he has. 'Not really sorry, now, but I could have been nicer. Could have been nicer, that's all.'

I thought of Mama, and suddenly all the sad part I hadn't been able to find during the day came up in my throat. 'We'll go on better than before,' I said. And then I quoted Mama like I never thought I would: 'It's all the best of us can do.' And I went to take the hot pea soup off the stove.

'Queer, isn't it,' Ben said. 'How you think something is dead and you're free, and then you find it sitting in your own guts laughing at you. Like I don't feel Pop has really died. He's down there somewhere inside of me, looking at what's going on. And grinning away.'

'That can be the good part,' I said, suddenly knowing that it really could. 'The part you don't have to run from. You know you take it with you, and then when you go any place, it's not running away. It's just growing up.'

Ben smiled at me, and I went to call the folks in. Supper was kind of a quiet meal, with lots of good cold ham and turkey. We talked about my job at the insurance office, and I even made Mrs Mayfair laugh, telling about my boss Mr Murray and his trick cigars. Liz was almost engaged, Mrs Prescott said, and she wasn't half herself unless Barry was around. Not a mention of old Mr Prescott.

Mrs Mayfair gorged herself on three desserts and kept saying, 'Just a sliver, that's all. Just a sliver!' when the chocolate cake went round.

'Poor Henrietta,' Mrs Prescott said, watching her enormous sister-in-law spooning down ice cream. 'It's that psychosomatic hunger they're always talking about. Makes her eat so.'

After coffee which Liz made on the grinder, so you could smell how good it was, there was an awkward little silence. Mama kept picking up her cup and sipping from it, although I could tell she was really all through. Liz was smoking again, so there was a small cloud of haze around her. Ben was making an airplane glider out of his paper napkin.

'Well,' Mrs Prescott cleared her throat, 'I guess I'll go over to the parlor now with Henrietta. Understand, Agnes, I'm not old-fashioned about this. It said definitely no flowers and no one needs to come. It's only a few of Pop's business associates kind of expect it.'

'I'll come,' said Mama staunchly.

'The children aren't going,' Mrs Prescott said. 'They've had enough already.'

'Barry's coming over later,' Liz said. 'I have to wash up.'

'I will do the dishes,' I volunteered, not looking at Mama. 'Ben will help me.'

'Well, that takes care of everybody, I guess.' Mrs Prescott helped Mrs Mayfair to her feet, and Mama took her other arm. The last I saw of them, they were holding Mrs Mayfair while she backed down the front steps, huffing and puffing. It was the only way she could go down safe, without falling, she said.

DORIS LESSING

The Day Stalin Died

That day began badly for me with a letter from my aunt in Bournemouth. She reminded me that I had promised to take my cousin Jessie to be photographed at four that afternoon. So I had; and forgotten all about it. Having arranged to meet Bill at four, I had to telephone him to put it off. Bill was a film writer from the United States who, having had some trouble with an un-American Activities Committee, was blacklisted, could no longer earn his living, and was trying to get a permit to live in Britain. He was looking for someone to be a secretary to him. His wife had always been his secretary; but he was divorcing her after twenty years of marriage on the grounds that they had nothing in common. I planned to introduce him to Beatrice.

Beatrice was an old friend from South Africa whose passport had expired. Having been 'named' as a communist, she knew that once she went back she would not get out again, and wanted to stay another six months in Britain. But she had no money. She needed a job. I imagined that Bill and Beatrice might have a good deal in common; but later it turned out that they disapproved of each other. Beatrice said that Bill was corrupt, because he wrote sexy comedies for TV under another name and acted in bad films. She did not think his justification, namely, that a guy has to eat, had anything in its favour. Bill, for his part, had never been able to stand political women. But I was not to know about the incompatibility of my two dear friends; and I spent an hour following Bill through one switchboard after another, until at last I got him in some studio where he was rehearsing for a film about Lady Hamilton. He said it was quite all right, because he had forgotten about the appointment in any case. Beatrice was not on the telephone so I sent her a telegram.

That left the afternoon free for cousin Jessie. I was just settling down to work, when comrade Jean rang up to say she wanted to see me during lunch-hour. Jean was for many years my self-appointed guide or mentor towards a correct political viewpoint. Perhaps it would be more accurate to say she was one of several self-appointed guides. It was Jean who, the day after I had my first volume of short stories published, took the morning off work to come and see me, in order to explain that one of the stories, I forget which, gave an incorrect analysis of the class struggle. I remember thinking at the time that there was a good deal in what she said.

When she arrived that day at lunch-time, she had her sandwiches with her in a paper bag, but she accepted some coffee, and said she hoped I didn't mind her disturbing me, but she had been very upset by something she had been told I had said.

It appeared that a week before, at a meeting, I had remarked that there seemed to be evidence for supposing that a certain amount of dirty work must be going on in the Soviet Union. I would be the first to admit that this remark savoured of flippancy.

Jean was a small brisk woman with glasses, the daughter of a Bishop, whose devotion to the working class was proved by thirty years of work in the Party. Her manner towards me was always patient and kindly. 'Comrade,' she said, 'intellectuals like yourself are under greater pressure from the forces of capitalist corruption than any other type of party cadre. It is not your fault. But you must be on your guard.'

I said I thought I had been on my guard; but nevertheless I could not help feeling that there were times when the capitalist press, no doubt inadvertently, spoke the truth.

Jean tidily finished the sandwich she had begun, adjusted her spectacles, and gave me a short lecture about the necessity for unremitting vigilance on the part of the working class. She then said she must go; because she had to be at her office at two. She said that the only way an intellectual with my background could hope to attain to a correct working-class viewpoint was to work harder in the Party; to mix continually with the working class; and in this way my writing would gradually become a real weapon in the class-struggle. She said, further, that she would send me the verbatim record of the Trials in the thirties, and if I read this, I would find my at present vacillating attitude towards Soviet justice much improved. I said I had read the verbatim records a long time ago; and I always did think they sounded unconvincing. She said that I wasn't to worry; a really sound working-class attitude would develop with time.

With this she left me. I remember that, for one reason and another, I was rather depressed.

I was just settling down to work again when the telephone rang. It was cousin Jessie, to say she could not come to my flat as arranged, because she was buying a dress to be photographed in. Could I meet her outside the dress-shop in twenty minutes? I therefore abandoned work for the afternoon and took a taxi. On the way the taxi-man and I discussed the cost of living, the conduct of the government, and discovered that we had everything in common. Then he began telling me about his only daughter, aged eighteen, who wanted to marry his best friend, aged forty-five. He did not hold with this; had said so; and thereby lost daughter and friend at one blow. What made it worse was that he had just read an article on Psychology in the woman's magazine his wife took, from which he had suddenly gathered that his daughter was father-fixated. 'I felt real bad when I read that,' he said. 'It's a terrible thing to come on sudden-like, a thing like that.' He drew up smartly outside the dress-shop and I got out. 'I don't see why you should take it to heart,' I said. 'I wouldn't be at all surprised if we weren't all father-fixated.' 'That's not the way to talk,' he said, holding out his hand for the fare. He was a small bitter-looking man, with a head like a lemon or like a peanut, and his small blue eyes were brooding and bitter. 'My old woman's been saying to me for years that I favoured our Hazel too much. What gets me is she might have been in the right of it.' 'Well,' I said, 'look at it this way. It's better to love a child too much than too little.' 'Love?' he said. 'Love, is it? Precious little love or anything else these days if you ask me, and Hazel left home three months ago with my mate George and not so much as a post-card to say where or how.'

'Life's pretty difficult for everyone,' I said. 'What with one thing and another.'

'You can say that,' he said.

This conversation might have gone on for some time, but I saw my cousin Jessie standing on the pavement watching us. I said goodbye to the taxi-man and turned, with some apprehension, to face her.

'I saw you,' she said. 'I saw you arguing with him. It's the only thing to do. They're getting so damned insolent these days. My principle is, tip them sixpence regardless of the distance, and if they argue, let them have it. Only yesterday I had one shouting at my back all down the street because I gave him sixpence. But we've got to stand up to them.'

My cousin Jessie is a tall girl, broad-shouldered, aged about twenty-five. But she looks eighteen. She has light brown hair which she wears falling loose around her face, which is round and young and sharp-chinned. Her wide light-blue eyes are virginal and fierce. She is alto-gether like the daughter of a Viking, particularly when battling with bus conductors, taximen, and porters. She and my Aunt Emma carry on permanent guerilla warfare with the lower orders; an entertainment I begrudge neither of them, because their lives are dreary in the extreme. Besides, I believe their antagonists enjoy it. I remember once, after a set-to between cousin Jessie and a taxi-driver, when she had marched smartly off, shoulders swinging, he chuckled appreciatively and said: 'That's a real old-fashioned type, that one. They don't make them like that these days.'

'Have you bought your dress?' I asked.

'I've got it on,' she said.

Cousin Jessie always wears the same outfit: a well-cut suit, a round-necked jersey, and a string of pearls. She looks very nice in it.

'Then we might as well go and get it over,' I said.

'Mummy is coming too,' she said. She looked at me aggressively.

'Oh well,' I said.

'But I told her I would *not* have her with me while I was buying my things. I told her to come and pick me up here. I will *not* have her choosing my clothes for me.'

'Quite right,' I said.

My Aunt Emma was coming towards us from the tearoom at the corner, where she had been biding her time. She is a very large woman, and she wears navy-blue and pearls and white gloves like a policeman on traffic duty. She has a big, heavy-jowled, sorrowful face; and her bulldog eyes are nearly always fixed in disappointment on her daughter.

'There!' she said as she saw Jessie's suit. 'You might just as well have had me with you.'

'What do you mean?' said Jessie quickly.

'I went in to Renée's this morning; and told them you were coming, and I asked them to show you that suit. And you've bought it. You see, I do know your tastes as I know my own.'

Jessie lifted her sharp battling chin at her mother, who dropped her eyes in modest triumph, and began poking at the pavement with the point of her umbrella.

'I think we'd better get started,' I said.

Aunt Emma and Cousin Jessie, sending off currents of angry electricity into the air all around them, fell in beside me, and we proceeded up the street.

'We can get a bus at the top,' I said.

'Yes, I think that would be better,' said Aunt Emma. 'I don't think I could face the insolence of another taxi-driver today.'

'No,' said Jessie, 'I couldn't either.'

We went to the top of the bus, which was empty, and sat side by side along the two seats at the very front.

'I hope this man of yours is going to do Jessie justice,' said Aunt Emma.

'I hope so too,' I said. Aunt Emma believes that every writer lives in a whirl of photographers, press conferences, and publishers' parties. She thought I was the right person to choose a photographer. I wrote to say

I wasn't. She wrote back to say it was the least I could do. 'It doesn't matter in the slightest anyway,' said Jessie, who always speaks in short, breathless, battling sentences, as from an unassuageably painful inner integrity which she doesn't expect anyone else to understand.

It seems that at the boarding-house where Aunt Emma and Jessie live, there is an old inhabitant who has a brother who is a TV producer. Jessie had been acting in *Quiet Wedding* with the local Reps. Aunt Emma thought that if there was a nice photograph of Jessie, she could show it to the TV producer when he came to tea with his brother at the boarding-house, which he was expected to do any weekend now; and if Jessie proved to be photogenic, the TV producer would whisk her off to London to be a TV star.

What Jessie thought of this campaign I did not know. I never did know what she thought of her mother's plans for her future. She might conform or she might not; but it was always with the same fierce and breathless integrity of indifference.

'If you're going to take that attitude, dear,' said Aunt Emma, 'I really don't think it's fair to the photographer.'

'Oh, Mummy!' said Jessie.

'There's the conductor,' said Aunt Emma, smiling bitterly. 'I'm not paying a penny more than I did last time. The fare from Knightsbridge to Little Duchess Street is threepence.'

'The fares have gone up,' I said.

'Not a penny more,' said Aunt Emma.

But it was not the conductor. It was two middle-aged people, who steadied each other at the top of the stair, and then sat down, not side by side, but one in front of the other. I thought this was odd, particularly as the woman leaned forward over the man's shoulder and said in a loud parrot-voice: 'Yes, and if you turn my goldfish out of doors once more, I'll tell the landlady to turn *you* out. I've warned you before.'

The man, in appearance like a damp grey squashed felt hat, looked in front of him and nodded with the jogging of the bus.

She said: 'And there's fungus on my fish. You needn't think I don't know where it came from.'

Suddenly he remarked in a high insistent voice: 'There are all those little fishes in the depths of the sea, all those little fishes. We explode all these bombs at them, and we're not going to be forgiven for that, are we, we're not going to be forgiven for blowing up the poor little fishes.'

She said, in an amiable voice: 'I hadn't thought of that,' and she left her seat behind him and sat in the same seat with him.

I had known that the afternoon was bound to get out of control at some point; but this conversation upset me. I was relieved when Aunt Emma restored normality by saying: '*There*. There never used to be people like *that*. It's the Labour Government.'

'Oh Mummy,' said Jessie, 'I'm not in the mood for politics this afternoon.'

We had arrived at the place we wanted, and we got down off the bus. Aunt Emma gave the bus conductor ninepence for the three of us, which he took without comment. 'And they're inefficient as well,' she said.

It was drizzling and rather cold. We proceeded up the street, our heads together under Aunt Emma's umbrella.

Then I saw a news-board with the item: Stalin is Dying. I stopped and the umbrella went jerking up the pavement without me. The newspaper-man was an old acquaintance. I said to him, 'What's this, another of your sales-boosters?' He said: 'The old boy's had it if you ask me. Well the way he's lived, the way I look at it he's had it coming to him. Must have the constitution of a bulldozer.' He folded up a paper and gave it to me. 'The way I look at it is that it doesn't do anyone any good to live that sort of life. Sedentary. Reading reports and sitting at meetings. That's why I like this job, there's plenty of fresh air.' A dozen paces away Aunt Emma and Jessie were standing facing me, huddled together under the wet umbrella. 'What's the matter, dear?' shouted Aunt Emma. 'Can't you see, she's buying a newspaper,' said Jessie crossly.

The newspaperman said: 'It's going to make quite a change, with *him* gone. Not that I hold much with the goings-on out there. But they aren't used to democracy much, are they? What I mean is, if people aren't used to something, they don't miss it.'

I ran through the drizzle to the umbrella. 'Stalin's dying,' I said.

'How do you know?' said Aunt Emma suspiciously.

'It says so in the newspaper.'

'They said he was sick this morning but I expect it's just propaganda. I won't believe it till I see it.'

'Oh don't be silly, Mummy, how can you *see* it?' said Jessie.

We went on up the street. Aunt Emma said: 'What do you think, would it have been better if Jessie had bought a nice pretty afternoon dress?'

'Oh Mummy,' said Jessie, 'can't you see she's upset? It's the same for her as it would be for us if Churchill was dead.'

'Oh my *dear*!' said Aunt Emma, shocked, stopping dead. An umbrella spoke scraped across Jessie's scalp, and she squeaked. 'Do put that umbrella down now, can't you see it's stopped raining?' she said, irritably scratching at her parting.

Aunt Emma pushed and bundled at the umbrella until it collapsed, and Jessie took it and rolled it up. Aunt Emma, flushed and frowning, looked dubiously at me. 'Would you like a nice cup of tea?' she said.

'Jessie's going to be late,' I said. The photographer's door was just ahead.

'I do hope this man's going to get Jessie's expression,' said Aunt Emma. 'There's never been one yet that got her *look*.'

Jessie went crossly ahead of us up some rather plushy stairs, that had mauve-and-gold striped wall-paper. At the top there was a burst of Stravinsky as Jessie masterfully opened a door and strode in. We followed her into what seemed to be a drawing-room, all white and grey and gold. The *Rites of Spring* tinkled a baby chandelier overhead; and there was no point in speaking until our host, a charming young man in a black velvet jacket, switched off the machine, which he did with an apologetic smile.

'I do hope this is the right place,' said Aunt Emma. 'I have brought my daughter to be photographed.'

'Of course it's the right place,' said the young man. 'How delightful of you to come!' He took my Aunt Emma's white-gloved hands in his own, and seemed to press her down on to a large sofa; a pressure to which she responded with a confused blush. Then he looked at me. I sat down quickly on another divan, a long way from Aunt Emma. He looked professionally at Jessie, smiling. She was standing on the carpet, hands linked behind her back, like an admiral on the job, frowning at him.

'You don't look at all relaxed,' he said to her gently. 'It's really no use at all, you know, unless you are really relaxed all over.'

'I'm perfectly relaxed,' said Jessie. 'It's my cousin here who isn't relaxed.'

I said: 'I don't see that it matters whether I'm relaxed or not, because it's not me who is going to be photographed.' A book fell off the divan beside me on to the floor. It was *Prancing Nigger* by Ronald Firbank. Our host dived for it, anxiously.

'Do you read our Ron?' he asked.

'From time to time,' I said.

'Personally I never read anything else,' he said. 'As far as I am concerned he said the last word. When I've read him all through, I begin again at the beginning and read him through again. I don't see that there's any point in anyone ever writing another word after Firbank.'

This remark discouraged me, and I did not feel inclined to say anything.

'I think we could all do with a nice cup of tea,' he said. 'While I'm making it, would you like the gramophone on again?'

'I can't stand modern music,' said Jessie.

'We can't all have the same tastes,' he said. He was on his way to a door at the back, when it opened and another young man came in with a tea-tray. He was as light and lithe as the first; with the same friendly ease of manner. He was wearing black jeans and a purple sweater, and his hair looked like two irregular glossy black wings on his head.

'Ah, bless you, dear!' said our host to him. Then, to us: 'Let me introduce my friend and assistant, Jackie Smith. My name you know. Now if we all have a nice cup of tea, I feel that our vibrations might become just a *little* more harmonious.'

All this time Jessie was standing-at-ease on the carpet. He handed her a cup of tea. She nodded towards me saying: 'Give it to her.' He took it back and gave it to me. 'What's the matter, dear?' he asked. 'Aren't you feeling well?'

'I am perfectly well,' I said, reading the newspaper.

'Stalin is dying,' said Aunt Emma. 'Or so they would like us to believe.'

'Stalin?' said our host.

'That man in Russia,' said Aunt Emma.

'Oh you mean old Uncle Joe. Bless him.'

Aunt Emma started. Jessie looked gruffly incredulous.

Jackie Smith came and sat down beside me, and read the newspaper over my shoulder. 'Well, well,' he said. 'Well, well, well, well.' Then he giggled and said: 'Nine doctors. If there were fifty doctors I still wouldn't feel very safe, would you?'

'No, not really,' I said.

'Silly old nuisance,' said Jackie Smith. 'Should have bumped him off years ago. Obviously outlived his usefulness at the end of the war, wouldn't you think?'

'It seems rather hard to say,' I said.

Our host, a teacup in one hand, raised the other in a peremptory gesture. 'I don't like to hear that kind of thing,' he said. 'I really don't. God knows, if there's one thing I make a point of never knowing a thing about, it's politics, but during the war Uncle Joe and Roosevelt were absolutely my pin-up boys. But absolutely!'

Here Cousin Jessie, who had neither sat down, nor taken a cup of tea, took a stride forward and said angrily: 'Look, do you think we could get this *damned* business over with?' Her virginal pink cheeks shone with emotion, and her eyes were brightly unhappy.

'But, my *dear*!' said our host, putting down his cup. 'But of course. If you feel like that, of course.'

He looked at his assistant Jackie, who reluctantly laid down the newspaper, and pulled the cords of a curtain, revealing an alcove full of cameras and equipment. Then they both thoughtfully examined Jessie. 'Perhaps it would help,' said our host, 'if you could give me an idea what you want it for? Publicity? Dust-jackets? Or just for your lucky friends?'

'I don't know and I don't care,' said Cousin Jessie.

Aunt Emma stood up and said: 'I would like you to catch her expression. It's just a little *look* of hers. . . .'

Jessie clenched her fists at her.

'Aunt Emma,' I said, 'don't you think it would be a good idea if you and I went out for a little?'

'But my *dear*. . . .'

But our host had put his arm around her, and was easing her to the door. 'There's a duck,' he was saying. 'You do want me to make a good job of it, don't you? And I never could really do my best, even with the most sympathetic lookers-on.'

Again Aunt Emma went limp, blushing. I took his place at her side, and took her to the door. As we shut it, I heard Jackie Smith saying: 'Music, do you think?' And Jessie: 'I *loathe* music.' And Jackie again: 'We do rather find music helps, you know. . . .'

The door shut and Aunt Emma and I stood at the landing window, looking into the street.

'Has that young man done *you*?' she asked.

'He was recommended to me,' I said.

Music started up from the room behind us. Aunt Emma's foot tapped on the floor. 'Gilbert and Sullivan,' she said. 'Well, she can't say she loathes that. But I suppose she would, just to be difficult.'

I lit a cigarette. *The Pirates of Penzance* abruptly stopped.

'Tell me, dear,' said Aunt, suddenly roguish, 'about all the exciting things you are doing?'

Aunt Emma always says this; and always I try hard to think of portions of my life suitable for presentation to Aunt Emma. 'What have you been doing today, for instance?' I considered Bill; I considered Beatrice; I considered comrade Jean.

'I had lunch,' I said, 'with the daughter of a Bishop.'

'Did you, dear?' she said doubtfully.

Music again: Cole Porter. 'That doesn't sound right to me,' said Aunt Emma. 'It's modern, isn't it?' The music stopped. The door opened. Cousin Jessie stood there, shining with determination. 'It's no good,' she said. 'I'm sorry, Mummy, but I'm not in the mood.'

'But we won't be coming up to London again for another four months.'

Our host and his assistant appeared behind cousin Jessie. Both were smiling rather bravely. 'Perhaps we had better all forget about it,' said Jackie Smith.

Our host said: 'Yes, we'll try again later, when everyone is really themselves.'

Jessie turned to the two young men and thrust out her hand at them. 'I'm very sorry,' she said, with her fierce virgin sincerity. 'I am really terribly sorry.'

Aunt Emma went forward, pushed aside Jessie, and shook their hands. 'I must thank you both,' she said, 'for the tea.'

Jackie Smith waved my newspaper over the three heads. 'You've forgotten this,' he said.

'Never mind, you can keep it,' I said.

'Oh bless you, now I can read all the gory details.' The door shut on
their friendly smiles.

'Well,' said Aunt Emma, 'I've never been more ashamed.'

'I don't care,' said Jessie fiercely. 'I really couldn't care less.'

We descended into the street. We shook each other's hands. We kissed
each other's cheeks. We thanked each other. Aunt Emma and Cousin
Jessie waved at a taxi. I got on to a bus.

When I got home, the telephone was ringing. It was Beatrice. She said
she had got my telegram, but she wanted to see me in any case. 'Did you
know Stalin was dying?' I said.

'Yes of course. Look, it's absolutely essential to discuss this business
on the Copper Belt.'

'Why is it?'

'If we don't tell people the truth about it, who is going to?'

'Oh well, I suppose so,' I said.

She said she would be over in an hour. I set out my typewriter and
began to work. The telephone rang. It was comrade Jean. 'Have you
heard the news?' she said. She was crying.

Comrade Jean had left her husband when he became a member of the
Labour Party at the time of the Stalin-Hitler Pact, and ever since then
had been living in bed-sitting-rooms on bread, butter, and tea, with a
portrait of Stalin over her bed.

'Yes, I have,' I said.

'It's awful,' she said sobbing. 'Terrible. They've murdered him.'

'Who has? How do you know?' I said.

'He's been murdered by capitalist agents,' she said. 'It's perfectly
obvious.'

'He was 73,' I said.

'People don't die just like *that*,' she said.

'They do at 73,' I said.

'We will have to pledge ourselves to be worthy of him,' she said.

'Yes,' I said, 'I suppose we will.'

ELIZABETH TAYLOR

The Blush

They were the same age—Mrs Allen and the woman who came every day to do the housework. 'I shall never have children now,' Mrs Allen had begun to tell herself. Something had not come true; the essential part of her life. She had always imagined her children in fleeting scenes and intimations; that was how they had come to her, like snatches of a film. She had seen them plainly, their chins tilted up as she tied on their bibs at meal-times; their naked bodies had darted in and out of the water-sprinkler on the lawn; and she had listened to their voices in the garden and in the mornings from their beds. She had even cried a little dreaming of the day when the eldest boy would go off to boarding-school; she pictured the train going out of the station; she raised her hand and her throat contracted and her lips trembled as she smiled. The years passing by had slowly filched from her the reality of these scenes—the gay sounds; the grave peace she had longed for; even the pride of grief.

She listened—as they worked together in the kitchen—to Mrs Lacey's troubles with her family, her grumblings about her grown-up son who would not get up till dinner-time on Sundays and then expected his mother to have cleaned his shoes for him; about the girl of eighteen who was a hairdresser and too full of dainty ways which she picked up from the women's magazines, and the adolescent girl who moped and glowered and answered back.

My children wouldn't have turned out like that, Mrs Allen thought, as she made her murmured replies. 'The more you do for some, the more you may,' said Mrs Lacey. But from gossip in the village which Mrs Allen heard, she had done all too little. The children, one night after another, for years and years, had had to run out for parcels of fish and chips while their mother sat in The Horse & Jockey drinking brown ale. On summer evenings, when they were younger, they had hung about outside the pub: when they were bored they pressed their foreheads to the window and looked in at the dark little bar, hearing the jolly laughter, their mother's the loudest of all. Seeing their faces, she would swing at once from the violence of hilarity to that of extreme annoyance and, although ginger-beer and packets of potato crisps would be handed out through the window, her anger went out with them and threatened the children as they ate and drank.

'And she doesn't always care who she goes there *with*,' Mrs Allen's gardener told her.

'She works hard and deserves a little pleasure—she has her anxieties,' said Mrs Allen, who, alas, had none.

She had never been inside The Horse & Jockey, although it was nearer to her house than The Chequers at the other end of the village where she and her husband went sometimes for a glass of sherry on Sunday mornings. The Horse & Jockey attracted a different set of customers—for instance, people who sat down and drank, at tables all round the wall. At The Chequers no one ever sat down, but stood and sipped and chatted as at a cocktail-party, and luncheons and dinners were served, which made it so much more respectable: no children hung about outside, because they were all at home with their Nannies.

Sometimes in the evenings—so many of them—when her husband was kept late in London, Mrs Allen wished that she could go down to The Chequers and drink a glass of sherry and exchange a little conversation with someone; but she was too shy to open the door and go in alone: she imagined heads turning, a surprised welcome from her friends, who would all be safely in married pairs; and then, when she left, eyes meeting with unspoken messages and conjecture in the air.

Mrs Lacey left her at midday and then there was gardening to do and the dog to be taken for a walk. After six o'clock, she began to pace restlessly about the house, glancing at the clocks in one room after another, listening for her husband's car—the sound she knew so well because she had awaited it for such a large part of her married life. She would hear, at last, the tyres turning on the soft gravel, the door being slammed, then his footsteps hurrying towards the porch. She knew that it was a wasteful way of spending her years—and, looking back, she was unable to tell one of them from another—but she could not think what else she might do. Humphrey went on earning more and more money and there was no stopping him now. Her acquaintances, in wretched quandaries about where the next term's school-fees were to come from, would turn to her and say cruelly: 'Oh, *you're* all right, Ruth. You've no idea what you are spared.'

And Mrs Lacey would be glad when Maureen could leave school and 'get out earning'. 'I've got my geometry to do,' she says, when it's time to wash-up the tea-things. 'I'll geometry you, my girl,' I said. 'When I was your age, I was out earning.'

Mrs Allen was fascinated by the life going on in that house and the children seemed real to her, although she had never seen them. Only Mr Lacey remained blurred and unimaginable. No one knew him. He worked in the town in the valley, six miles away and he kept himself to himself; had never been known to show his face in The Horse & Jockey. 'I've got my own set,' Mrs Lacey said airily. 'After all, he's nearly twenty years older than me. I'll make sure neither of my girls follow my mistake. "I'd rather see you dead at my feet," I said to Vera.' Ron's young lady was lucky; having Ron, she added. Mrs Allen found this strange, for Ron had always been painted so black; was, she had been led to believe, oafish, ungrateful, greedy and slow to put his hands in his pockets if there was any paying out to do. There was also the matter of his shoe-cleaning, for no young woman would do what his mother did for him—or said she did. Always, Mrs Lacey would sigh and say: 'Goodness me, if only I was their age and knew what I know now.'

She was an envious woman: she envied Mrs Allen her pretty house and her clothes and she envied her own daughters their youth. 'If I had your figure,' she would say to Mrs Allen. Her own had gone: what else could be expected, she asked, when she had had three children? Mrs Allen thought, too, of all the brown ale she drank at The Horse & Jockey and of the reminiscences of meals past which came so much into her conversations. Whatever the cause was, her flesh, slackly corseted, shook as she trod heavily about the kitchen. In summer, with bare arms and legs she looked larger than ever. Although her skin was very white, the impression she gave was at once colourful—from her orange hair and bright lips and the floral patterns that she always wore. Her red-painted toe-nails poked through the straps of her fancy sandals; turquoise-blue beads were wound round her throat.

Humphrey Allen had never seen her; he had always left for the station before she arrived, and that was a good thing, his wife thought. When she spoke of Mrs Lacey, she wondered if he visualised a neat, homely woman in a clean white overall. She did not deliberately mislead him, but she took advantage of his indifference. Her relationship with Mrs Lacey and the intimacy of their conversations in the kitchen he would not have approved, and the sight of those calloused feet with their chipped nail-varnish and yellowing heels would have sickened him.

One Monday morning, Mrs Lacey was later than usual. She was never very punctual and had many excuses about flat bicycle-tyres or Maureen being poorly. Mrs Allen, waiting for her, sorted out all the washing. When she took another look at the clock, she decided that it was far too late for her to be expected at all. For some time lately Mrs Lacey had seemed ill and depressed; her eyelids, which were chronically rather inflamed, had been more angrily red than ever and, at the sink or ironing-board, she would fall into unusual silences, was absent-minded and full of sighs. She had always liked to talk about the 'change' and did so more than ever as if with a desperate hopefulness.

'I'm sorry, but I was ever so sick,' she told Mrs Allen, when she arrived the next morning. 'I still feel queerish. Such heartburn. I don't like the signs, I can tell you. All I crave is pickled walnuts, just the same as I did with Maureen. I don't like the signs one bit. I feel I'll throw myself into the river if I'm taken that way again.'

Mrs Allen felt stunned and antagonistic. 'Surely not at your age,' she said crossly.

'You can't be more astonished than me,' Mrs Lacey said, belching loudly. 'Oh, pardon. I'm afraid I can't help myself.'

Not being able to help herself, she continued to belch and hiccough as she turned on taps and shook soap-powder into the washing-up bowl. It was because of this that Mrs Allen decided to take the dog for a walk. Feeling consciously fastidious and aloof she made her way across the fields, trying to disengage her thoughts from Mrs Lacey and her troubles; but unable to. 'Poor woman,' she thought again and again with bitter animosity.

She turned back when she noticed how the sky had darkened with racing, sharp-edged clouds. Before she could reach home, the rain began. Her hair, soaking wet, shrank into tight curls against her head; her woollen suit smelt like a damp animal. 'Oh, I am drenched,' she called out, as she threw open the kitchen door.

She knew at once that Mrs Lacey had gone, that she must have put on her coat and left almost as soon as Mrs Allen had started out on her walk, for nothing was done; the washing-up was hardly started and the floor was unswept. Among the stacked-up crockery a note was propped; she had come over funny, felt dizzy and, leaving her apologies and respects, had gone.

Angrily, but methodically, Mrs Allen set about making good the wasted morning. By afternoon, the grim look was fixed upon her face. 'How dare she?' she found herself whispering, without allowing herself to wonder what it was the woman had dared.

She had her own little ways of cosseting herself through the lonely hours, comforts which were growing more important to her as she grew older, so that the time would come when not to have her cup of tea at four-thirty would seem a prelude to disaster. This afternoon, disorgan-ised as it already was, she fell out of her usual habit and instead of carrying the tray to the low table by the fire, she poured out her tea in the kitchen and drank it there, leaning tiredly against the dresser. Then she went upstairs to make herself tidy. She was trying to brush her frizzed hair smooth again when she heard the door-bell ringing.

When she opened the door, she saw quite plainly a look of astonishment take the place of anxiety on the man's face. Something about herself surprised him, was not what he had expected. 'Mrs Allen?' he asked uncertainly and the astonishment remained when she had answered him.

'Well, I'm calling about the wife,' he said. 'Mrs Lacey that works here.'

'I was worried about her,' said Mrs Allen.

She knew that she must face the embarrassment of hearing about Mrs Lacey's condition and invited the man into her husband's study, where she thought he might look less out-of-place than in her brocade-smothered drawing-room. He looked about him resentfully and glared down at the floor which his wife had polished. With this thought in his mind, he said abruptly: 'It's all taken its toll.'

He sat down on a leather couch with his cap and his bicycle-clips beside him.

'I came home to my tea and found her in bed, crying,' he said. This was true. Mrs Lacey had succumbed to despair and gone to lie down. Feeling better at four o'clock, she went downstairs to find some food to comfort herself with; but the slice of dough-cake was ill-chosen and brought on more heartburn and floods of bitter tears.

'If she carries on here for a while, it's all got to be very different,' Mr Lacey said threateningly. He was nervous at saying what he must and could only bring out the words with the impetus of anger. 'You may or may not know that she's expecting.'

'Yes,' said Mrs Allen humbly. 'This morning she told me that she thought. . . .'

'There's no "thought" about it. It's as plain as a pikestaff.' Yet in his eyes she could see disbelief and bafflement and he frowned and looked down again at the polished floor.

Twenty years older than his wife—or so his wife had said—he really, to Mrs Allen, looked quite ageless, a crooked, bow-legged little man who might have been a jockey once. The expression about his blue eyes was like a child's: he was both stubborn and pathetic.

Mrs Allen's fat spaniel came into the room and went straight to the stranger's chair and began to sniff at his corduroy trousers.

'It's too much for her,' Mr Lacey said. 'It's too much to expect.'

To Mrs Allen's horror she saw the blue eyes filling with tears. Hoping to hide his emotion, he bent down and fondled the dog, making playful thrusts at it with his fist closed.

He was a man utterly, bewilderedly at sea. His married life had been too much for him, with so much in it that he could not understand.

'Now I know, I will do what I can,' Mrs Allen told him. 'I will try to get someone else in to do the rough.'

'It's the late nights that are the trouble,' he said. 'She comes in dog-tired. Night after night. It's not good enough. "Let them stay at home and mind their own children once in a while," I told her. "We don't need the money."'

'I can't understand,' Mrs Allen began. She was at sea herself now, but felt perilously near a barbarous, unknown shore and was afraid to make any movement towards it.

'I earn good money. For her to come out at all was only for extras. She likes new clothes. In the daytimes I never had any objection. Then all these cocktail-parties begin. It beats me how people can drink like it night after night and pay out for someone else to mind their kids. Perhaps you're thinking that it's not my business, but I'm the one who has to sit at home alone till all hours and get my own supper and see next to nothing of my wife. I'm boiling over some nights. Once I nearly rushed out when I heard the car stop down the road. I wanted to tell your husband what I thought of you both.'

'My husband?' murmured Mrs Allen.

'What am I supposed to have, I would have asked him? Is she my wife or your sitter-in? Bringing her back at this time of night. And it's no use saying she could have refused. She never would.'

Mrs Allen's quietness at last defeated him and dispelled the anger he had tried to rouse in himself. The look of her, too, filled him with doubts, her grave, uncertain demeanour and the shock her age had been to him. He had imagined someone so much younger and—because of the cocktail-parties—flighty. Instead, he recognised something of himself in her, a yearning disappointment. He picked up his cap and his bicycle-clips and sat looking down at them, turning them round in his hands. 'I had to come,' he said.

'Yes,' said Mrs Allen.

'So you won't ask her again?' he pleaded. 'It isn't right for her. Not now.'

'No, I won't,' Mrs Allen promised and she stood up as he did and walked over to the door. He stooped and gave the spaniel a final pat. 'You'll excuse my coming, I hope.'

'Of course.'

'It was no use saying any more to her. Whatever she's asked, she won't refuse. It's her way.'

Mrs Allen shut the front door after him and stood in the hall, listening to him wheeling his bicycle across the gravel. Then she felt herself beginning to blush. She was glad that she was alone, for she could feel her face, her throat, even the tops of her arms burning, and she went over to a looking-glass and studied with great interest this strange phenomenon.

GRACE PALEY

An Interest in Life

My husband gave me a broom one Christmas. This wasn't right. No one can tell me it was meant kindly.

'I don't want you not to have anything for Christmas while I'm away in the Army,' he said. 'Virginia, please look at it. It comes with this fancy dustpan. It hangs off a stick. Look at it, will you? Are you blind or cross-eyed?'

'Thanks, chum,' I said. I had always wanted a dust-pan hooked up that way. It was a good one. My husband doesn't shop in bargain basements or January sales.

Still and all, in spite of the quality, it was a mean present to give a woman you planned on never seeing again, a person you had children with and got onto all the time, drunk or sober, even when everybody had to get up early in the morning.

I asked him if he could wait and join the Army in a half hour, as I had to get the groceries. I don't like to leave kids alone in a three-room apartment full of gas and electricity. Fire may break out from a nasty remark. Or the oldest decides to get even with the youngest.

'Just this once,' he said. 'But you better figure out how to get along without me.'

'You're a handicapped person mentally,' I said. 'You should've been institutionalized years ago.' I slammed the door. I didn't want to see him pack his underwear and ironed shirts.

I never got further than the front stoop, though, because there was Mrs Raftery, wringing her hands, tears in her eyes as though she had a monopoly on all the good news.

'Mrs Raftery!' I said, putting my arm around her. 'Don't cry.' She leaned on me because I am such a horsy build. 'Don't cry, Mrs Raftery, please!' I said.

'That's like you, Virginia. Always looking at the ugly side of things. "Take in the wash. It's rainin'!" That's you. You're the first one knows it when the dumb-waiter breaks.'

'Oh, come on now, that's not so. It just isn't so,' I said. 'I'm the exact opposite.'

'Did you see Mrs Cullen yet?' she asked, paying no attention.

'Where?'

'Virginia!' she said, shocked. 'She's passed away. The whole house knows it. They've got her in white like a bride and you never saw a beautiful creature like that. She must be eighty. Her husband's proud.'

'She was never more than an acquaintance; she didn't have any children,' I said.

'Well, I don't care about that. Now, Virginia, you do what I say now, you go downstairs and you say like this—listen to me—say, "I hear, Mr Cullen, your wife's passed away. I'm sorry." Then ask him how he is. Then you ought to go around the corner and see her. She's in Witson & Wayde. Then you ought to go over to the church when they carry her over.'

'It's not my church,' I said.

'That's no reason, Virginia. You go up like this,' she said, parting from me to do a prancy dance. 'Up the big front steps, into the church you go. It's beautiful in there. You can't help kneeling only for a minute. Then round to the right. Then up the other stairway. Then you come to a great oak door that's arched above you, then,' she said, seizing a deep, deep breath, for all the good it would do her, 'and then turn the knob slo-owly and open the door and see for yourself: Our Blessed Mother is in charge. Beautiful. Beautiful. Beautiful.'

I sighed in and I groaned out, so as to melt a certain pain around my heart. A steel ring like arthritis, at my age.

'You are a groaner,' Mrs Raftery said, gawking into my mouth.

'I am not,' I said. I got a whiff of her, a terrible cheap wine lush.

My husband threw a penny at the door from the inside to take my notice from Mrs Raftery. He rattled the glass door to make sure I looked at him. He had a fat duffel bag on each shoulder. Where did he acquire so much worldly possession? What was in them? My grandma's goose feathers from across the ocean? Or all the diaper-service diapers? To this day the truth is shrouded in mystery.

'What the hell are you doing, Virginia?' he said, dumping them at my feet. 'Standing out here on your hind legs telling everybody your business? The Army gives you a certain time, for God's sakes, they're not kidding.' Then he said, 'I beg your pardon,' to Mrs Raftery. He took hold of me with his two arms as though in love and pressed his body hard against mine so that I could feel him for the last time and suffer my loss. Then he kissed me in a mean way to nearly split my lip. Then he winked and said, 'That's all for now,' and skipped off into the future, duffel bags full of rags.

He left me in an embarrassing situation, nearly fainting, in front of that old widow, who can't even remember the half of it. 'He's a crock,' said Mrs Raftery. 'Is he leaving for good or just temporarily, Virginia?'

'Oh, he's probably deserting me,' I said, and sat down on the stoop, pulling my big knees up to my chin.

'If that's the case, tell the Welfare right away,' she said. 'He's a bum, leaving you just before Christmas. Tell the cops,' she said. 'They'll provide the toys for the little kids gladly. And don't forget to let the grocer in on it. He won't be so hard on you expecting payment.'

She saw that sadness was stretched world-wide across my face. Mrs Raftery isn't the worst person. She said, 'Look around for comfort, dear.' With a nervous finger she pointed to the truckers eating lunch on their haunches across the street, leaning on the loading platforms. She waved her hand to include in all the men marching up and down in search of a decent luncheonette. She didn't leave out the six longshoremen loafing under the fish-market marquee. 'If their lungs and stomachs ain't crushed by overwork, they disappear somewhere in the world. Don't be disappointed, Virginia. I don't know a man living'd last you a lifetime.'

Ten days later Girard asked, 'Where's Daddy?'

'Ask me no questions, I'll tell you no lies.' I didn't want the children to know the facts. Present or past, a child should have a father.

'Where *is* Daddy?' Girard asked the week after that.

'He joined the Army,' I said.

'He made my bunk bed,' said Phillip.

'The truth shall make ye free,' I said.

Then I sat down with pencil and pad to get in control of my resources. The facts, when I added and subtracted them, were that my husband had left me with fourteen dollars, and the rent unpaid, in an emergency state. He'd claimed he was sorry to do this, but my opinion is, out of sight, out of mind. 'The city won't let you starve,' he'd said. 'After all, you're half the population. You're keeping up the good work. Without you the race would die out. Who'd pay the taxes? Who'd keep the streets clean? There wouldn't be no Army. A man like me wouldn't have no place to go.'

I sent Girard right down to Mrs Raftery with a request about the whereabouts of Welfare. She responded RSVP with an extra comment in left-handed script: 'Poor Girard . . . he's never the boy my John was!'

Who asked her?

I called on Welfare right after the new year. In no time I discovered that they're rigged up to deal with liars, and if you're truthful it's disappointing to them. They may even refuse to handle your case if you're too truthful.

They asked sensible questions at first. They asked where my husband had enlisted. I didn't know. They put some letter writers and agents after him. 'He's not in the United States Army,' they said. 'Try the Brazilian Army,' I suggested.

They have no sense of kidding around. They're not the least bit lighthearted and they tried. 'Oh no,' they said. 'That was incorrect. He is not in the Brazilian Army.'

'No?' I said. 'How strange! He must be in the Mexican Navy.'

By law, they had to hound his brothers. They wrote to his brother who has a first-class card in the Teamsters and owns an apartment house in California. They asked his two brothers in Jersey to help me. They have large families. Rightfully they laughed. Then they wrote to Thomas, the oldest, the smart one (the one they all worked so hard for years to keep him in college until his brains could pay off). He was the one who sent ten dollars immediately, saying, 'What a bastard! I'll send something time to time, Ginny, but whatever you do, don't tell the authorities.' Of course I never did. Soon they began to guess they were better people than me, that I was in trouble because I deserved it, and then they liked me better.

But they never fixed my refrigerator. Every time I called I said patiently, 'The milk is sour . . .' I said, 'Corn beef went bad.' Sitting in that beer-stinking phone booth in Felan's for the sixth time (sixty cents) with the baby on my lap and Barbie tapping at the glass door with an American flag, I cried into the secretary's hardhearted ear, 'I bought real butter for the holiday, and it's rancid . . .' They said, 'You'll have to get a better bid on the repair job.'

While I waited indoors for a man to bid, Girard took to swinging back and forth on top of the bathroom door, just to soothe himself, giving me the laugh, dreamy, nibbling calcimine off the ceiling. On first sight Mrs Raftery said, 'Whack the monkey, he'd be better off on arsenic.'

But Girard is my son and I'm the judge. It means a terrible thing for the future, though I don't know what to call it.

It was from constantly thinking of my foreknowledge on this and other subjects, it was from observing when I put my lipstick on daily, how my face was just curling up to die, that John Raftery came from Jersey to rescue me.

On Thursdays, anyway, John Raftery took the tubes in to visit his mother. The whole house knew it. She was cheerful even before breakfast. She sang out loud in a girlish brogue that only came to tongue for grand occasions. Hanging out the wash, she blushed to recall what a remarkable boy her John had been. 'Ask the sisters around the corner,' she said to the open kitchen windows. 'They'll never forget John.'

That particular night after supper Mrs Raftery said to her son, 'John, how come you don't say hello to your old friend Virginia? She's had hard luck and she's gloomy.'

'Is that so, Mother?' he said, and immediately climbed two flights to knock at my door.

'Oh, John,' I said at the sight of him, hat in hand in a white shirt and blue-striped tie, spick-and-span, a Sunday-school man. 'Hello!'

'Welcome, John!' I said. 'Sit down. Come right in. How are you? You look awfully good. You do. Tell me, how've you been all this time, John?'

'How've I been?' he asked thoughtfully. To answer within reason, he described his life with Margaret, marriage, work, and children up to the present day.

I had nothing good to report. Now that he had put the subject around before my very eyes, every burnt-up day of my life smoked in shame, and I couldn't even get a clear view of the good half hours.

'Of course,' he said, 'you do have lovely children. Noticeable-looking, Virginia. Good looks is always something to be thankful for.'

'Thankful?' I said. 'I don't have to thank anything but my own foolishness for four children when I'm twenty-six years old, deserted, and poverty-struck, regardless of looks. A man can't help it, but I could have behaved better.'

'Don't be so cruel on yourself, Ginny,' he said. 'Children come from God.'

'You're still great on holy subjects, aren't you? You know damn well where children come from.'

He did know. His red face reddened further. John Raftery has had that color coming out on him boy and man from keeping his rages so inward.

Still he made more sense in his conversation after that, and I poured fresh tea to tell him how my husband used to like me because I was a passionate person. That was until he took a look around and saw how in the long run this life only meant more of the same thing. He tried to turn away from me once he came to this understanding, and make me hate him. His face changed. He gave up his brand of cigarettes, which we had in common. He threw out the two pairs of socks I knitted by hand. 'If there's anything I hate in this world, it's navy blue,' he said. Oh, I could have dyed them. I would have done anything for him, if he were only not too sorry to ask me.

'You were a nice kid in those days,' said John, referring to certain Saturday nights. 'A wild, nice kid.'

'Aaah,' I said, disgusted. Whatever I was then, was on the way to where I am now. 'I was fresh. If I had a kid like me, I'd slap her cross-eyed.'

The very next Thursday John gave me a beautiful radio with a record player. 'Enjoy yourself,' he said. That really made Welfare speechless. We didn't own any records, but the investigator saw my burden was lightened and he scribbled a dozen pages about it in his notebook.

On the third Thursday he brought a walking doll (twenty-four inches) for Linda and Barbie with a card inscribed, 'A baby doll for a couple of dolls.' He had also had a couple of drinks at his mother's, and this made him want to dance. 'La-la-la,' he sang, a ramrod swaying in my kitchen chair. 'La-la-la, let yourself go . . .'

'You gotta give a little,' he sang, 'live a little . . .' He said, 'Virginia, may I have this dance?'

'Sssh, we finally got them asleep. Please, turn the radio down. Quiet. Deathly silence, John Raftery.'

'Let me do your dishes, Virginia.'

'Don't be silly, you're a guest in my house,' I said. 'I still regard you as a guest.'

'I want to do something for you, Virginia.'

'Tell me I'm the most gorgeous thing,' I said, dipping my arm to the funny bone in dish soup.

He didn't answer. 'I'm having a lot of trouble at work,' was all he said. Then I heard him push the chair back. He came up behind me, put his arms around my waistline, and kissed my cheek. He whirled me around and took my hands. He said, 'An old friend is better than rubies.' He looked me in the eye. He held my attention by trying to be honest. And he kissed me a short sweet kiss on my mouth.

'Please sit down, Virginia,' he said. He kneeled before me and put his head in my lap. I was stirred by so much activity. Then he looked up at me and, as though proposing marriage for life, he offered—because he was drunk—to place his immortal soul in peril to comfort me.

First I said, 'Thank you.' Then I said, 'No.'

I was sorry for him, but he's devout, a leader of the Fathers' Club at his church, active in all the lay groups for charities, orphans, etc. I knew that if he stayed late to love with me, he would not do it lightly but would in the end pay terrible penance and ruin his long life. The responsibility would be on me.

So I said no.

And Barbie is such a light sleeper. All she has to do, I thought, is wake up and wander in and see her mother and her new friend John with his pants around his knees, wrestling on the kitchen table. A vision like that could affect a kid for life.

I said no.

Everyone in this building is so goddamn nosy. That evening I had to say no.

But John came to visit, anyway, on the fourth Thursday. This time he brought the discarded dresses of Margaret's daughters, organdy party dresses and glazed cotton for every day. He gently admired Barbara and Linda, his blue eyes rolling to back up a couple of dozen oohs and ahs.

Even Phillip, who thinks God gave him just a certain number of hellos and he better save them for the final judgment, Phillip leaned on John and said, 'Why don't you bring your boy to play with me? I don't have nobody who to play with.' (Phillip's a liar. There must be at least seventy-one children in this house, pale pink to medium brown, English-talking and gibbering in Spanish, rough-and-tough boys, the Lone Ranger's bloody pals, or the exact picture of Supermouse. If a boy wanted a friend, he could pick the very one out of his neighbors.)

Also, Girard is a cold fish. He was in a lonesome despair. Sometimes he looked in the mirror and said, 'How come I have such an ugly face? My nose is funny. Mostly people don't like me.' He was a liar too. Girard has a face like his father's. His eyes are the color of those little blue plums in August. He looks like an advertisement in a magazine. He could be a child model and make a lot of money. He is my first child, and if he thinks he is ugly, I think I am ugly.

John said, 'I can't stand to see a boy mope like that. . . . What do the sisters say in school?'

'He doesn't pay attention is all they say. You can't get much out of them.'

'My middle boy was like that,' said John. 'Couldn't take an interest. Aaah, I wish I didn't have all that headache on the job. I'd grab Girard by the collar and make him take notice of the world. I wish I could ask him out to Jersey to play in all that space.'

'Why not?' I said.

'Why, Virginia, I'm surprised you don't know why not. You know I can't take your children out to meet my children.'

I felt a lot of strong arthritis in my ribs.

'My mother's the funny one, Virginia.' He felt he had to continue with the subject matter. 'I don't know. I guess she likes the idea of bugging Margaret. She says, "You goin' up, John?" "Yes, Mother," I say. "Behave yourself, John," she says. "That husband might come home and hack-saw you into hell. You're a Catholic man, John," she says. But I figured it out. She likes to know I'm in the building. I swear, Virginia, she wishes me the best of luck.'

'I do too, John,' I said. We drank a last glass of beer to make sure of a peaceful sleep. 'Good night, Virginia,' he said, looping his muffler neatly under his chin. 'Don't worry. I'll be thinking of what to do about Girard.'

I got into the big bed that I share with the girls in the little room. For once I had no trouble falling asleep. I only had to worry about Linda and

Barbara and Phillip. It was a great relief to me that John had taken over
the thinking about Girard.

John was sincere. That's true. He paid a lot of attention to Girard,
smoking out all his sneaky sorrows. He registered him into a wild pack
of cub scouts that went up to the Bronx once a week to let off steam.
He gave him a Junior Erector Set. And sometimes when his family wasn't
listening he prayed at great length for him.

One Sunday, Sister Veronica said in her sweet voice from another life,
'He's not worse. He might even be a little better. How are *you*, Virginia?'
putting her hand on mine. Everybody around here acts like they know
everything.

'Just fine,' I said.

'We ought to start on Phillip,' John said, 'if it's true Girard's improving.'

'You should've been a social worker, John.'

'A lot of people have noticed that about me,' said John.

'Your mother was always acting so crazy about you, how come she
didn't knock herself out a little to see you in college? Like we did for
Thomas?'

'Now, Virginia, be fair. She's a poor old woman. My father was a weak
earner. She had to have my wages, and I'll tell you, Virginia, I'm not
sorry. Look at Thomas. He's still in school. Drop him in this jungle and
he'd be devoured. He hasn't had a touch of real life. And here I am with
a good chunk of a family, a home of my own, a name in the building
trades. One thing I have to tell you, the poor old woman is sorry. I said
one day (oh, in passing—years ago) that I might marry you. She stuck a
knife in herself. It's a fact. Not more than an eighth of an inch. You never
saw such a gory Sunday. One thing—you would have been a better
daughter-in-law to her than Margaret.'

'Marry me?' I said.

'Well, yes. . . . Aaah—I always liked you, then . . . Why do you think
I'd sit in the shade of this kitchen every Thursday night? For God's
sakes, the only warm thing around here is this teacup. Yes, sir, I did want
to marry you, Virginia.'

'No kidding, John? Really?' It was nice to know. Better late than never,
to learn you were desired in youth.

I didn't tell John, but the truth is, I would never have married him.
Once I met my husband with his winking looks, he was my only interest.
Wild as I had been with John and others, I turned all my wildness over
to him and then there was no question in my mind.

Still, face facts, if my husband didn't budge on in life, it was my fault.
On me, as they say, be it. I greeted the morn with a song. I had a hello
for everyone but the landlord. Ask the people on the block, come or go—

even the Spanish ones, with their sad dark faces—they have to smile when they see me.

But for his own comfort, he should have done better lifewise and moneywise. I was happy, but I am now in possession of knowledge that this is wrong. Happiness isn't so bad for a woman. She gets fatter, she gets older, she could lie down, nuzzling a regiment of men and little kids, she could just die of the pleasure. But men are different, they have to own money, or they have to be famous, or everybody on the block has to look up to them from the cellar stairs.

A woman counts her children and acts snotty, like she invented life, but men *must* do well in the world. I know that men are not fooled by being happy.

'A funny guy,' said John, guessing where my thoughts had gone. 'What stopped him up? He was nobody's fool. He had a funny thing about him, Virginia, if you don't mind my saying so. He wasn't much distance up, but he was all set and ready to be looking down on us all.'

'He was very smart, John. You don't realize that. His hobby was cross-word puzzles, and I said to him real often, as did others around here, that he ought to go out on the "$64 Question". Why not? But he laughed. You know what he said? He said, "That proves how dumb you are if you think I'm smart."'

'A funny guy,' said John. 'Get it all off your chest,' he said. 'Talk it out, Virginia; it's the only way to kill the pain.'

By and large, I was happy to oblige. Still I could not carry through about certain cruel remarks. It was like trying to move back into the dry mouth of a nightmare to remember that the last day I was happy was the middle of a week in March, when I told my husband I was going to have Linda. Barbara was five months old to the hour. The boys were three and four. I had to tell him. It was the last day with anything happy about it.

Later on he said, 'Oh, you make me so sick, you're so goddamn big and fat, you look like a goddamn brownstone, the way you're squared off in front.'

'Well, where are you going tonight?' I asked.

'How should I know?' he said. 'Your big ass takes up the whole goddamn bed,' he said. 'There's no room for me.' He bought a sleeping bag and slept on the floor.

I couldn't believe it. I would start every morning fresh. I couldn't believe that he would turn against me so, while I was still young and even his friends still liked me.

But he did, he turned absolutely against me and became no friend of mine. 'All you ever think about is making babies. This place stinks like the men's room in the BMT. It's a fucking *pissoir*.' He was strong on truth all through the year. 'That kid eats more than the five of us put together,' he said. 'Stop stuffing your face, you fat dumbbell,' he said to Phillip.

Then he worked on the neighbors. 'Get that nosy old bag out of here,' he said. 'If she comes on once more with "my son in the building trades" I'll squash her for the cat.'

Then he turned on Spielvogel, the checker, his oldest friend, who only visited on holidays and never spoke to me (shy, the way some bachelors are). 'That sonofabitch, don't hand me that friendship crap, all he's after is your ass. That's what I need—a little shitmaker of his using up the air in this flat.'

And then there was no one else to dispose of. We were left alone fair and square, facing each other.

'Now, Virginia,' he said, 'I come to the end of my rope. I see a black wall ahead of me. What the hell am I supposed to do? I only got one life. Should I lie down and die? I don't know what to do any more. I'll give it to you straight, Virginia, if I stick around, you can't help it, you'll hate me . . .'

'I hate you right now,' I said. 'So do whatever you like.'

'This place drives me nuts,' he mumbled. 'I don't know what to do around here. I want to get you a present. Something.'

'I told you, do whatever you like. Buy me a rattrap for rats.'

That's when he went down to the House Appliance Store, and he brought back a new broom and a classy dustpan.

'A new broom sweeps clean,' he said. 'I got to get out of here,' he said. 'I'm going nuts.' Then he began to stuff the duffel bags, and I went to the grocery store but was stopped by Mrs Raftery, who had to tell me what she considered so beautiful—death—then he kissed and went to join some army somewhere.

I didn't tell John any of this, because I think it makes a woman look too bad to tell on how another man has treated her. He begins to see her through the other man's eyes, a sitting duck, a skinful of flaws. After all, I had come to depend on John. All my husband's friends were strangers now, though I had always said to them, 'Feel welcome.'

And the family men in the building looked too cunning, as though they had all personally deserted me. If they met me on the stairs, they carried the heaviest groceries up and helped bring Linda's stroller down, but they never asked me a question worth answering at all.

Besides that, Girard and Phillip taught the girls the days of the week: Monday, Tuesday, Wednesday, Johnday, Friday. They waited for him once a week, under the hallway lamp, half asleep like bugs in the sun, sitting in their little chairs with their names on in gold, a birth present from my mother-in-law. At fifteen after eight he punctually came, to read a story, pass out some kisses, and tuck them into bed.

But one night, after a long Johnday of them squealing my eardrum split, after a rainy afternoon with brother constantly raising up his hand against brother, with the girls near ready to go to court over the proper ownership of Melinda Lee, the twenty-four-inch walking doll, the doorbell rang three times. Not any of those times did John's face greet me.

I was too ashamed to call down to Mrs Raftery, and she was too mean to knock on my door and explain.

He didn't come the following Thursday either. Girard said sadly, 'He must've run away, John.'

I had to give him up after two weeks' absence and no word. I didn't know how to tell the children: something about right and wrong, goodness and meanness, men and women. I had it all at my finger tips, ready to hand over. But I didn't think I ought to take mistakes and truth away from them. Who knows? They might make a truer friend in this world somewhere than I have ever made. So I just put them to bed and sat in the kitchen and cried.

In the middle of my third beer, searching in my mind for the next step, I found the decision to go on 'Strike It Rich.' I scrounged some paper and pencil from the toy box and I listed all my troubles, which must be done in order to qualify. The list when complete could have brought tears to the eye of God if He had a minute. At the sight of it my bitterness began to improve. All that is really necessary for survival of the fittest, it seems, is an interest in life, good, bad, or peculiar.

As always happens in these cases where you have begun to help yourself with plans, news comes from an opposite direction. The doorbell rang, two short and two long—meaning John.

My first thought was to wake the children and make them happy. 'No! No!' he said. 'Please don't put yourself to that trouble. Virginia, I'm dog-tired,' he said. 'Dog-tired. My job is a damn headache. It's too much. It's all day and it scuttles my mind at night, and in the end who does the credit go to?

'Virginia,' he said, 'I don't know if I can come any more. I've been wanting to tell you. I just don't know. What's it all about? Could you answer me if I asked you? I can't figure this whole thing out at all.'

I started the tea steeping because his fingers when I touched them were cold. I didn't speak. I tried looking at it from his man point of view, and I thought he had to take a bus, the tubes, and a subway to see me; and then the subway, the tubes, and a bus to go back home at 1 A.M. It wouldn't be any trouble at all for him to part with us forever. I thought about my life, and I gave strongest consideration to my children. If given the choice, I decided to choose not to live without him.

'What's that?' he asked, pointing to my careful list of troubles. 'Writing a letter?'

'Oh no,' I said, 'it's for "Strike It Rich." I hope to go on the program.'

'Virginia, for goodness' sakes,' he said, giving it a glance, 'you don't have a ghost. They'd laugh you out of the studio. Those people really suffer.'

'Are you sure, John?' I asked.

'No question in my mind at all,' said John. 'Have you ever seen that program? I mean, in addition to all of this—the little disturbances of man'—he waved a scornful hand at my list—'they *suffer*. They live in the forefront of tornadoes, their lives are washed off by floods—catastrophes of God. Oh, Virginia.'

'Are you sure, John?'

'For goodness' sake . . .'

Sadly I put my list away. Still, if things got worse, I could always make use of it.

Once that was settled, I acted on an earlier decision. I pushed his cup of scalding tea aside. I wedged myself onto his lap between his hard belt buckle and the table. I put my arms around his neck and said, 'How come you're so cold, John?' He has a kind face and he knew how to look astonished. He said, 'Why, Virginia, I'm getting warmer.' We laughed.

John became a lover to me that night.

Mrs Raftery is sometimes silly and sick from her private source of cheap wine. She expects John often. 'Honor your mother, what's the matter with you, John?' she complains. 'Honor. Honor.'

'Virginia dear,' she says. 'You never would've taken John away to Jersey like Margaret. I wish he'd've married you.'

'You didn't like me much in those days.'

'That's a lie,' she says. I know she's a hypocrite, but no more than the rest of the world.

What is remarkable to me is that it doesn't seem to conscience John as I thought it might. It is still hard to believe that a man who sends out the Ten Commandments every year for a Christmas card can be so easy buttoning and unbuttoning.

Of course we must be very careful not to wake the children or disturb the neighbors who will enjoy another person's excitement just so far, and then the pleasure enrages them. We must be very careful for ourselves too, for when my husband comes back, realizing the babies are in school and everything easier, he won't forgive me if I've started it all up again—noisy signs of life that are so much trouble to a man.

We haven't seen him in two and a half years. Although people have suggested it, I do not want the police or Intelligence or a private eye or anyone to go after him to bring him back. I know that if he expected to stay away forever he would have written and said so. As it is, I just don't know what evening, any time, he may appear. Sometimes, stumbling over a blockbuster of a dream at midnight, I wake up to vision his soft arrival.

He comes in the door with his old key. He gives me a strict look and says, 'Well, you look older, Virginia.' 'So do you,' I say, although he hasn't changed a bit.

He settles in the kitchen because the children are asleep all over the rest of the house. I unknot his tie and offer him a cold sandwich. He raps my backside, paying attention to the bounce. I walk around him as though he were a Maypole, kissing as I go.

'I didn't like the Army much,' he says. 'Next time I think I might go join the Merchant Marine.'

'What army?' I say.

'It's pretty much the same everywhere,' he says.

'I wouldn't be a bit surprised,' I say.

'I lost my cuff link, goddamnit,' he says, and drops to the floor to look for it. I go down too on my knees, but I know he never had a cuff link in his life. Still I would do a lot for him.

'Got you off your feet that time,' he says, laughing. 'Oh yes, I did.' And before I can even make myself half comfortable on that polka-dotted linoleum, he got onto me right where we were, and the truth is, we were so happy, we forgot the precautions.

1959

CHRISTINA STEAD

UNO 1945

❦

The Howards left before the conference ended and set out to drive to their new home in Beverly Hills. They had spent all this time and money on the UNO conference to write reports for the New York *Labor Daily* and the Washington *Liberator*, at a time when Emily's Hollywood agents were waiting for two scripts; and her New York agents for the manuscript of a new book in her moneymaking series, *Mr and Mrs Middletown*, humorous books of family life. The couple quarrelled before starting, about the opinions in Emily's article for the *Labor Daily*; but she posted it unchanged. As soon as the car started, the tiff began again.

'This is not for money, Stephen, and I'll say what I like; it's the truth.'

'Oh, damn the truth and damn not for money. You'll offend the left and you've wasted a week rewriting your article when your agents are screaming. But it's OK, your soul is white and the children won't eat next week.'

'Your goddamn article was a palimpsest by the time you'd finished achieving a wise, dry, prescient tone. You had to telephone it to Washington,' said Emily, but she began to laugh: 'In Europe contributors to radical sheets go about with the soles off their shoes and gnaw a dry crust in freezing attic rooms: and we live on the plunder of the land, best hotels, three-room suite, long-distance calls, swell car to run us home to our latest residence: that's American radicalism I suppose. They can't pay us so we pay them.'

'Well, it's worth it to see my name flown at the masthead,' said Stephen nastily.

'That's a petty selfish view. If we waste all this money, it's what we owe the country for our unnatural natural luck.'

They quarrelled again and the last part of the journey was passed in silence. When they got home, Emily went round the house fast, talking in a lively way with the servants, the children, the neighbours' children who were in. She looked through the children's clothing and the laundry, checked the contents of pantry, icebox, deepfreeze and bar, ordered dinner and took her large bundle of letters up to her room; a little room at the stairhead, and overlooking the side and back gardens. Manoel, the manservant, brought up a pot of black coffee; and she locked the door behind him. Her room was furnished mainly with steel files containing copies of her voluminous writings of all sorts, her diary, her correspondence, the material for many novels and stories, copies of all her lectures and articles, bundles of clippings, household bills and the children's school reports; as well as the exercise books in which she carefully went over their lessons with them. Besides this, there were wire baskets, a few reference books, a table, a chair and an excellent typewriter. She drank the coffee, took a pill from a little locked drawer in the table and began to read her letters, with shouts and great guffaws and sighs. She began typing replies at once.

Downstairs, in a large front room well furnished as study and library, in his own room, Stephen sat discontentedly going through the notes his research worker had sent him. He had a partners' desk, a pale blue-grey carpet. The panelled sliding door communicated with a charming living-room decorated with chintzes, French paintings and flowers arranged in Japanese style. Stephen found it hard to settle down to work, for Emily's agents, the studios and her publishers kept telephoning Emily; and every conversation in which, in her jolly, loving, languishing manner, full of good sense, outrageous hope and bonhomie, she promised and put off, threw him into a frenzy. Last year she had, without effort, made $80,000 in Hollywood. But she consumed hours, weeks in all, writing to friends and otherwise wasting time. A river of money was flowing through the telephone: she had only to direct it into their pockets. The thought poisoned him and stung him. Their expenses were large. The Portuguese couple who managed for them cost considerably over $400 a month; his own research worker had cost more than $5,000 in the course of five years.

Yet upstairs Emily flirted with the idea of writing a great novel. She sketched out one idea after another, and in each of them she wanted to tell some truth that would offend some section of the community. Some of the truths would offend everyone and get them on the black list. Also, she prepared lectures and courses for workers' and students' education. She wrote impassioned letters about her troubles to her friends, gave advice to young writers, worked harder on articles for 'those snoots' on the *Labor Daily* than on a script for Twentieth Century Fox.

Emily came downstairs, very cheery, bustling the children to wash their hands, fix their neckties, come in to dinner.

'What have you been doing?' he said sourly.

'Writing a letter to Phyl Robinson.'

'The house is full of unpaid bills and Hollywood and Bookman Bros

are telephoning and telegraphing every hour. You've got a market shrieking for your work. Why don't you do it?'

He said this before the children and Manoel the butler who was
serving. This was not unusual. They always talked with the greatest
freedom before intimates.

'My writing's crap,' she shouted, 'I don't want to do it. I'm not proud
they pay me gold for crap. That Mr and Mrs stuff is just custard pie I
throw in the face of the Mamma public, stupid, cruel and food crazy.
I find myself putting in recipes—ugh!—because I know they guzzle it.
They prefer a deepfreeze to a human being; it's cold, tailored and shiny.
I don't believe in a word I write. Do you know what that means, Stephen?
It's a terrible thing to say. You believe in what you write! Why should I
work my fingers stiff to pay off the mortgage on this goddamn shanty
with electric lights on the stair-treads so that the guests don't roll down
when they're full—let 'em roll—and with dried sweetpea on the airspray
in the linen closet—'

'That dried sweetpea makes me gag,' he sang out irately. 'All right!
Let's get out of the crappy place, though we've only just got in, and find
something cheap and nasty with no towel-rails. Let's go to one of my
family's modest little tax-saving apartments or a cabin in Arkansas. Let
my family see I'm a failure. Let's get rid of Manoel, who's my only friend
and get a char smelling of boiled rag and with hair in her nose. I'll do the
buttling. Why not get a job as a butler? I'd make a good sleek sneak
sipping the South African sherry in the outhouse. Let's wear our shirts
for a week and save on the laundry.'

'You're eating my heart with your aristocratic tastes,' she roared, beginning to cry, too. 'Moth and rust are nothing to what a refahned young
genteel gentleman from Princeton can do to an Arkansas peasant girl,
when a spot on the carpet to him is like pickles to a stomach-ulcer. Oh,
Jee-hosaphat, what was the matter with me, marrying a scion? You've
ruined my life, darn it. I want to be a writer. I don't want to write
cornmeal mush for fullbellied Bible belters. Did I leave my little Arkansas
share-cropper's shanty for that? I was going to be a great writer, Miss
America, the prairie flower. Now I'm writing Hh-umour and Pp-athos
for the commuters and hayseeds.'

She helped the children with their homework. Both parents went up to
sing to Giles in his cot, a song invented by Stephen,

> Oh G, oh I, oh L, oh E, oh S!
> Sle-ep, sle-ep, sle-ep, sleep!
> Oh, Gilesy, Gilesy, Gilesy, sleep!

Stephen ran a bath, while Emily went downstairs; and after writing out
the menu for the next day and saying, 'I will make the crêpes suzette,' she

went to the butler's pantry where she mixed herself a strong highball. Just as she was carrying it into the living-room, Stephen came down in fresh clothes. He scolded her for taking a drink and for the expense of some new handmade shirts which had just come in for the three boys; Lennie, aged twelve, Alun, eight, and Giles four. Emily defended herself: what was he just saying about a char with hair on her eyeballs? She was in a good humour. 'I've got an idea that will work for my script; it's so cheap I blushed for shame.'

Stephen picked up the evening paper and glanced over the headlines. They began once more to tear at the great wound which had opened in their love, mutual admiration and understanding and great need for each other. This was an equally fundamental thing, a disagreement about American exceptionalism; the belief widely held in the USA that what happened in Europe and the rest of the world belonged to other streams of history, never influencing that Mississippi which bears the USA. The flood of American energy could and perhaps would swallow those others: the watershed of European destiny was far back in time and drying up. To this belief, Stephen liked to adhere. Emily accused him of servility to a system which had made his grandparents and parents millionaires; and Stephen would not have been so tenacious, if the Government, and all the political parties right down to the extreme left, had not agreed that America's reason for invading Europe, joining the conflict, was to spread America's healthy and benevolent business democracy everywhere: the western answer to communism. Stephen had everyone at his back, but a few. Emily found this 'a pill too big for a horse to swallow', to quote Michael Gold; and she declared that this local doctrine, held even by the communists, was wrong.

'They know their theory better than you and me,' said Stephen querulously: 'at any rate better than me; and I don't know what to answer. I can only follow blindly; but I intend to follow. I went into Marxism for personal salvation, I know; a despicable reason; but I have to stick to it or where am I?'

'I'm not going to follow anyone into a quagmire. And I don't want to be saved.'

'You're an individualist: individualists become renegades.'

She sprang up from her chair, 'Don't you dare call me a renegade! I'll scratch your eyes out. I won't stand that.'

They quarrelled so bitterly and such unforgivable things were said that she packed a valise, got a seat on a plane going east the next morning and telephoned the studio that she'd post the scripts from New York. 'And I'll be able to work there,' she shouted, 'not worried to death by a limpet throttling me. Maybe I'll give up the whole crazy game, get myself a hall bedroom and really write.'

Before it was time to leave for the airport next day, Stephen took the car out. Emily telephoned for a taxi. But Stephen returned with a jewelcase, in the velvet lining of which lay a deep amethyst necklace from Russia. Emily loved stones in yellow, green and purple.

She was dressing and sat before her looking-glass in a linen slip with a square-cut neck embroidered in small scallops; and a bronze silk dressing gown, fallen round her hips: her hair was disordered, pushed back and in spikes. Arranged on her rosy solid bosom, set in the low bodice of white embroidery, the gems looked superb. Seeing her comical, robust fairness in the glass and Stephen beside her in pale blue, pliant, placating, absorbed, she began to laugh with tears in her eyes.

'Oh, Stephen, it's so beautiful and it's such a filthy insult, to think you can buy a writer's soul with money.'

Stephen said, 'Don't let Browder and such bagatelles separate us, Emily. What can I do without you? I know you can live without me.'

She sat thrown back in the dressing chair, looking at the necklace and her grotesque fair face. 'By golly, I look like a Polish peasant dressing as a countess,' she said laughing, her blue eyes bright and flushed, lucent, wet. 'I look like any kind of peasant, I'm so goddam earthy, no wonder I fell for a silk-stocking. I like to hear you talking to waiters in icy tones, "This *Graves* is not cool enough, wait-ah!"'

'I do not say waitah.'

'The prince and the pauper.' She began to take off the necklace, tugging impatiently at the catch. 'Help me with it, Stephen,' she continued in a hearty husky tone, 'it's lovely, I love it, but get thee behind me, Satan. I guess you don't know me after all. Hasn't any woman ever told you it's a damned insult to try to buy a woman's affections with Russian crown jewels and a fur coat? Is—our—whole—future,' she continued, breaking into sobs, 'to-be-built—on my selling out my belief in the future of the world for some gewgaws of Czarist Russia? It's a symbol, all right. I guess that's the kind of women you've known though.'

'Oh, Lord!'

'Of course, your mother and your sister are like that; they believe in Cincinnatus labouring the earth with a golden ploughshare. And what is the harvest? The corn is gold. The country's rich and right. Why dear Anna, your mother, would think it the hoith of foine morals intoirely to give up dirty radicalism and wear a clean fortune round your neck. I don't say sister Florence. Florence is not all lucre. She'd pawn it at once for a hundred cases of Bourbon—'

'I got this from Florence. I've got to pay her for it, somehow.'

'Take it back. It's for her sort,' said Emily decisively pushing it along the table. 'I like it; but after you saying you'd divorce me if I didn't believe in the American way of life—'

'I did not!' he shouted.

'American exceptionalism! What else is it? And you'd leave me for not believing in Hollywood, the art of the masses; do you think you can buy me back with a stick of candy? I don't think you could have done that to me, even as a child. The only thing you could buy me with then was affection. I loved people. They didn't love back.'

'I didn't mean to hurt your feelings; I don't seem to do anything right. So I've lost you!'

'Will you give up your belief that revolutionary Marxism is right; and consent to be led by the nose by the quiet man from nowhere, all for an amethyst necklace?' said Emily loudly and scornfully; and throwing the box with the thing in it on to the carpet, where she kicked it away. 'Pooh-ah! What triviality! Is that what you think of me, Emily White? You can buy me with a string of beads? When I whore, I'll whore for plenty, for the whole works. They'll have to come to me with the whole world wrapped up in their arms! And with the Bible too and the whole of revolutionary history, man's struggle, too, and say: Debs says you can, and you can prove it by the Haymarket Martyrs, the crimes of Cripple Creek; lynched labour organisers led to it and Sacco and Vanzetti died for it. Manoel! Is the car ready? Put my bags into it. Drive me to the airport. Stephen, I've left everything arranged; the children's diets, their dentists' appointments, when to change their clothes; everything; I've paid all the bills, I was up all night. Now, this is final. You can divorce me if you like.'

'Forgive me, Emily,' said Stephen.

'I don't forgive you. I'm goddam mad and I'm going to stay mad.'

But Stephen ordered Manoel out of the car, got in himself; and while he was driving Emily to the airport, he talked her round. In tears, quite overwhelmed with shame, Emily was brought back to the house. They spent the day together talking over many things quietly and sincerely; kisses and endearments were exchanged in the vegetable garden, down by the river, behind the trees that screened the barbecue, by the children's swing, in the dark of the garage and while they were spraying the vines with DDT against the Japanese beetle. Not far off, Manoel and Maria, in their rest hours, could be heard talking and laughing; once they screeched with laughter. Two or three times Emily ran to the children, who were being kept together by the English nurse named Thistleton. Emily hugged them all, kissed the eldest, their nephew Lennie, in the dark curls that fell over his pale narrow forehead. 'Oh, my darlings,' she said to them once, 'if you only knew what a mother you have! You'd do better with a snake, a gila monster, than an earthworm like me. Oh, Miss Thistledown, I'm a poor weak woman without character.' She hugged the nurse, 'Let me kiss you,' she said, pressing her wet round cheeks, rough and warm as fruit, to the middle-aged woman's thin face, 'you English are all so strong, you're just and strong. My God,' she said, turning away, and aloud, 'if my fighting forefathers heard that blather! I'm fat with the buttering and the licking afterwards.'

At dinner, Emily, a good chef, made the crêpes suzette as planned. She was wearing rings, a hair jewel and bracelets. She was flushed and her tongue wagged frenziedly. 'Oh, if only we were Jewish,' she cried; 'we'd stick together. What a beautiful family life the Jews have, so closewoven; and they make more of blood than we do. It's beautiful that tree of life with all its branches, under the mantle of all its leaves. Oh, how lucky you are, Lennie, to have had a Jewish father. If only I had Jewish blood I'd make you happy. I'd have the art of keeping the fire in the hearth forever. I used to go down to the Jewish quarter as a child and just stare in, glare in hungrily through their windows on Friday nights, when they had their candles in the windows! Oh, how tender it was, how touching and true! The family is the heart of man; how can you tear it open?'

Stephen listened, smiling, grinning: 'Lennie's father, my brother-in-law, was a nasty little man! Any family life is poison. I'm sure Miss Thistleton and Manoel think they're having a season in hell. Read what Plato said about the family!'

'Plato was a homosexual!' declared Emily. 'Stephen, listen to what I say! Family love is the only true selfless love; it's natural communism. That is the origin of our feeling for communism: to each according to his needs, from each according to his capacity; and everything is arranged naturally, without codes and without policing. Manoel, why don't you bring in the coffee? This coffee is not like we get at your sister Florence's. But of course, there's only one liquid that means anything to her—'

'Stop it!'

But she did not stop and held them at table while she discussed Stephen's family and their money habits, for a long time. Lennie's grand-uncle had dieted himself to death, being a miser: having apportioned his estate among his children to escape death duties and family hatred, he found them all sitting like buzzards around his semi-starved person to tear the pemmican from his bones. Stephen's mother, Stephen's sisters— the rich girl the family wanted Stephen to marry—

Miss Thistleton, embarrassed, half rose from her chair. 'Stay where you are!' roared Emily, 'I haven't finished speaking. You're the children's guardian. If I leave, you'll be their mother! You may as well know what's in them!' Last, with an imperial gesture she dismissed them, the children to their homework or beds; and when they had sung the Giles song, she said to Stephen, 'Let's go to the movies; I have a need to sit in the dark with you.'

They went downtown. At night, they went to bed but did not sleep. In the film, the word *fascist* was used and Stephen exulted, 'There you are! Hollywood is not all poison. Reaction is on the way out, when the radical writers in the studios can put over their ideas like that.'

'Oh, poohpooh,' said Emily; 'people don't even know what it means. It went by in a second! Who heard it but politicomaniacs like us?'

And with this one word, the bitter wound opened again.

'I shall be ill if you don't let me sleep,' said Stephen. 'Last night, too—'

'Sleep! When our futures and our souls, I mean that word, it's all we have that's worth fighting for—we've got to think this thing through. We can't sleep anyway.'

'I could if you'd let me. I've got you; my children are with me; I have no other wants. I don't want to have ideas. Ideas are civil war. Let us drown our ideas, Emmie: let's live in a friendly fug. I'm sick of it.'

'In the first place, what are we fighting about, Stephen? Let's get that clear. We're mixed up. We like New York, but you want us to stay here and make a fortune in the movies, so that dear Anna and Florence the Fuzzy and Uncle Shongo—'

'I have no Uncle Shongo!' he squealed.

'Uncle Mungo and Uncle Cha will see you are not a failure; you, too, can make money. I don't mind being a failure because my people remain in the mud of time; but you do. I'm from hoi-polloi and you're from hoity toity—'

'Stop it! Was there ever such a fool! I married a clown!'

'Anyway, for some reason, we've got to believe in MGM and the mistakes of the left.'

'Goddamn it, they are not mistakes. Who are you and I—'

'For myself, the writers like what I write when I like what I write; but the agents don't and you don't and even—but leave certain names out of this shameful story. If I write the way I like, it'll be poverty for us; not this monogrammed sheet, but mended shoes and tattered pants and not enough vitamins; and that's not fair to the kids.'

'We're not philanthropists. It's theory and practice for everyone in the world, except the unquestioning and thankless rich—lucky dogs! You don't want our kids to grow up like Clem Blake's, eating out of cans with many a fly twixt the can and the lip.'

'Golly!' she laughed: 'I guess they'll grow up, too.'

'If they don't die of botulism.'

'I thought that was from botflies.'

'What are botflies?'

'It shows I'm a farmer's daughter. Well, they'll grow up, too.' She sighed. 'Oh, well, what the hell! Maybe the oral hygiene and the hand-made shirts are just hanky-panky. Maybe that's no way to raise heroes of labour.'

'I don't want to live with heroes of labour,' he said pettishly. 'I've seen lots of them. Starvation and struggle are no good for the soul; nor the stomach. What are we fighting for? Not to make people like the workers are now. Good grief! I had "a love the worker" phase; but I wasn't sincere. I walked along working class streets and saw their stores and their baby-carriages and hated 'em. I wouldn't raise anyone to be like them. Why are the French so revolutionary? Because of their good cooking and good arts of life. And what the devil—you can make money, so make it! If we starved, it would be a whim, the whim of the rich. Why should we starve? You've only got to do two days' work and we'll be in $30,000. It's a whim and a selfish one to throw that kind of money back in the studio's face and talk about art and poverty and your soul. And if you're a red, you ought to show you're one just *because* you can come out on top; so they can't say it's grousing. You ought to be a shining-red-light. The rest is just moral filth, mental laziness and infantile behaviour. You want to be back in Arkansas, the schoolgirl who read through Shakespeare once every year, and dreamed about making a noise as a great writer. Fooey! You know I hated Princeton. Well, one of the reasons was, I spent my time trying to live up to the noble secular trees and noble secular presidents. I starved myself trying to live on what I thought a poor scholar would live on; and fancied my parents admired me for spending so little. Rich imbeciles like me think there's something mystic, some intellectual clarity and purification of the soul in sobriety, austerity and poverty. I got over that. Now anyone can keep me, my family, you—' he said bitterly, 'or Lennie or my son.'

'Lennie is your son,' she said: 'we'll get him.'

'My lazy vampirism feeds on my nearest and dearest: I gnaw their white breasts.'

'Oh, Stephen,' she wailed, 'oh, don't say that. I love you. Don't say those things. If I have a vulgar streak which enables me to make more money than you, aren't I, in those moments, like your moneymaking grandfathers that you despise? And I feel I'm tanned like a tanned rhino hide: I'm secretly afraid you'll leave me and get some decent woman who never sold out. Despise me; but don't despise yourself, Stephen. What else am I working and selling out for? You're my whole life, my rayzon d'ayter. If we haven't got each other, we've got nothing. Our life is so hideous. With each other, we can work it out, we can hope. Otherwise, what has it all been for? You gave up millions, I gave up my hopes, dreams and ideals; and our hearts are being squeezed dry.'

'You've made me better than I was,' said Stephen. 'First out of Princeton, I used to hang around with those wistful carping critics of the critics groups. I was young and stupid and I think I still am. I hated those arty people, Emily—all—with the bitterest hate of envy; and then I took up Marxism because I thought it gave me a key they didn't have; it raised me above them. I got out of the grovelling mass in the valley and felt the fresh air blowing on me; but it was all selfish—'

'It was NOT,' roared Emily, 'don't be crazy!'

'Yes, it was. They seemed to get women without even trying.'

'Jee-hosaphat! Did you want to get women?' She began to laugh, rolling about on the bed and looking at him with her red and yellow face, surrounded by loose fair hair. Her face was made for laughter—a pudgy comic face with deep lines only when she laughed, the deep lines of the comic mask. 'Oh, Stephen! And you so beautiful! Why on earth you picked a puttynose, a pieface like me—'

'A what?'

'I look as if some slapstick artist just threw a custard-pie in my puss—'

'Don't insult the woman I love!'

'And those freckles remind me of the oatmeal in a haggis—'

'You're the most beautiful woman I ever had in my life, that's all. It's the beauty of the mind—'

'Oh, if we could wear the mind inside out! I don't get it. You're fascinating, Stephen.'

'Well, the only women who go for me are those who wriggle down to the platform after meetings and ask me to explain. You know what that fellow in the bistro in Paris said to his son that day? "Don't fret son, study the cats. The females always go for the ragged, bleary-eyed, whiskery, dirty old tom with cobwebs on his eyebrows."'

'But is it true?'

'I envied them all,' said Stephen sourly, 'and you provide the final revenge against them. You're so wonderfully, truly, profoundly potent and you're nothing like them. They were so genteel; they wouldn't be caught in an enthusiasm: the sad little band of *nil admirari*. I had my intellectual revenge when I studied a few scraps of Marxism too. I learned they stood for nothing. They, if they learned a bit, they dropped out halfway. They married a bit of money, a schoolteacher with cheques appeal, took a house in a restricted suburb; no Jews, Irish or Italians, they're all too enthusiastic. They began to owe money and have plenty of nothing; they get sleek and terribly bright and wise—and so terribly empty. There's nothing to prevent them jumping off Brooklyn Bridge right now. Because only an idea and a belief can prevent you doing that.'

'Oh, well, who the hell cares for them? You got out.'

'Yes, but they've no doubts. I employed a poor scholar, a tailor's son, to teach me Marxism: the old noble getting out an insurance policy against the revolution! You're real. I knew right off you were a genuine person, a wise and rich woman, strong and meaningful.'

'How did you know that?'

'That awful dress you wore!'

'Stephen!' she cried, blushing; 'and you always said you loved it.'

'So I did and I do. I made you keep it forever. I love it. The vines and the grapes and the flowers—'

'Stephen! I did think it was lovely and warm,' she added thoughtfully. 'I loved it too. I still don't think it's awful. Of course, dear Florence wouldn't have—'

'Don't spoil it. And the story you told me of your growing up and the things that happened to you! The man in the house that fell down when you were in it: Jimmy—the man who rented out condemned buildings and introduced you to Donne—well, I never met such people. And then the rotten men—whom I understood, with all my failure, better than you. It all showed me the depth of life and love and passion and ability that could be. And lacking just one thing, the ability to be warped.'

Emily said nothing.

'I felt so cut off from the rest of mankind and you bridged that for me. I felt I was still up in that hospital in the snow slopes and pines, where I was cut off for three years. But I know I'm down on earth again when I'm with you. And I live for you,' he said obstinately, 'and only for you. Would I live for myself? You don't like me to say that; but I must. I want to call it out, to shout it out. I thirst for what you give me. My life drives me into sterility; I can't give and nothing bears for me. But you did.'

Emily turned about restlessly, 'You mustn't say that. I told you not to. It makes me feel ill. Suppose I died? Anyone can die.'

'Don't say that please.'

'All right. But you mustn't found your life on one person. It's dreadful. You throw yourself on another person's back and bear them down. They bow right down to earth with weeping and sobbing for you and them. You kill them. The feeling's unspeakable. I'll die.'

Stephen laughed, 'Well, that's me, though. Too bad. You must live for something. I think I'm lucky. A lot of those men I knew had nothing to live for and now they're slipping along a moral skid row. They're looking sideways furtively at the milestones. I guess the only thing that stops them putting their heads in the gas oven is that all they've got is an infrared grill. I know what I'm living for: for you. For anything you live for. I don't care what it is.'

'That's fabulous. I won't have it,' said Emily angrily.

'Perhaps I could be different in another society. I wonder. But I think a bad man, a real bastard but a strong villain, would be better for you than me. At least, he wouldn't pretend to be an intellectual or moral hero and take up your time and waste your affections.'

'Oh, I don't know what to do,' said Emily frantically. 'I'll give you a beating. It's more than I can stand. I'm going mad. You're killing me.' She threw herself from side to side as if avoiding bees. 'I'm burning. Don't, don't, don't!' She threw herself at him, 'Stop it, do you hear! It makes me feel desperate. I'll burst.'

She jumped out of bed, opened a small drawer in the dressing-table; and he at once snapped, 'What are you doing? Taking some of those damn pills?'

'I've got to calm down. How can I work tomorrow? And I've got a lecture in the evening.'

'What lecture?'

'Adult education.'

'That's it, that's it! Your whole life is filled with giving, doing. I'm nothing but a barnacle on the wheel of progress.'

She jumped back into bed and kissed him furiously, all over face, neck, hair, chest, arms. Then, she lay back and began to reason. 'This life doesn't suit you, Stevie. It's a gambling racecourse crazy life for touts and bums, not for you. You're a scholar and should live in peace. This double or nothing, boom or bust scares you and nauseates you. Your attitude towards money, so different from mine, is disturbed in this mad Hollywood carnival. You respect money. You shouldn't. Fancy respecting the filthy reeking stuff. I don't respect it. To me it's not part of a highly organised respectable society, the just reward of pioneering valour: nor a medal pinned on the virtuous starched bosom. To me there's just as much virtue in Skid Row, or as little. Moneymaking is gangdom, grab or someone else will. Of course, you're right too. It's the high established church of our great land. Lincoln said, "As a nation of freemen we must live through all time, or die by suicide." Suicide! Oh, God! A great nation cutting its throat! Could it really happen? As long as the razor is of gold and the noose of amethyst—'

'A country can't die,' said Stephen indignantly. 'We can, the poor lice on its hide, but thank God the country can't die. If I thought it could, I'd die of empty horror. Do you know the story that has haunted me since I was a boy? The man without a country.'

'But that's bamboozle.'

'I think I can even understand the cranks and crooks who are put out of Russia and write lies for bread. They want to be noticed; they're Russians too. It's the infant screaming for its mother.'

'Don't waste your sympathy,' she said drily.

'I suppose it's envy, too,' he conceded. 'They're bestsellers; though it's a nasty mean way to make a fortune, running down your country. I know you don't believe I am as good as that. I couldn't write a book that would sell, in any terms. So I ought to be out earning a living and giving you the chance you want.'

'I wish I could,' said Emily, thoughtfully and gently. Then she began to fire up, 'I'd like to write a book about the revolutionary movement, the way I see it and what's wrong with it. Here we have the greatest organisation for socialism in the western world. Look at the size of the labour union movement! A state within the state. When it says, Go, we go: when it says, Stop, we stop. Organised millions of conscious workers: what would the early socialists have said to that? The millenium! Though, it's not. But isn't it a great big poster saying, It can be done! Or is it already too late? Are there too many labour opportunists, too many finks and goons? Or are we what's wrong with it, the goddamn middle-class opportunists? I'd like to write this book. I'm dumb enough to think it would be good. But who would print it? We would all of us end up in the railroad wreck and not a single finger lifted to take the engine off our neck.'

'You could do it,' said Stephen without force; 'but you'd get nowhere. I ought to build fires under your ambition. It only shows the kind of punk I am. But I'm representative. You could have me for one of the characters; a clay lay figure covered with the fine patina of soft living, a radical arguing man, busy with top secrets and who's who in Washington, softshoeing in the antechambers of the lobbies of Congress, a radical dandy, dispensing the amenities of another caste, paying his way into the labour movement, following a boyish dream; take the underdog along with you to the White House; heel, sir, heel: misinterpreting everything to suit the silk-lined dream and with laughable ineffectiveness exhorting a stone-deaf working class out of the blind alley of porkchop opportunism to lead them down the blind alley of rigid righteousness. For what have we to offer them? Something we don't believe in ourselves; socialist austerity and puritanism for the better building of steel mills.'

'I wouldn't see it that way,' said Emily slowly. 'This would be a cruel book. I wouldn't spend much time on theoretical errors or an analysis of our peculiar applications of theory; but I'd try to put a finger on essential human weaknesses; the ignorance and self-indulgence that has led us into bohemia. On that score, there's plenty to say. Ought we all to live well, have our children in private schools, training them for the *gude braid claith*? I ought to say how everything becomes its opposite not only outside the besieged fortress but in: how we misinterpret the mission of America, the position in the unions, ourselves; and what our lives are, that are going so far astray. We would sneer at Utopian communities; but we are trying to live in Utopia.'

'It might be an epitaph of American socialism: I'd like to see it,' sang out Stephen.

'No, no! It would be for the real rebels, the real labour movement, against all vampires who take all that's best in the world, even the name of the most sacred causes and use them for promotion; shepherds killing and eating the lambs. That's it. Socialism can't die! Don't we believe that? But it can die—suffocated, here! By us! That's horrible.'

'It's horrible; especially when we're in it up to our necks,' said Stephen restlessly: 'if I had to be born in these days, why not a Russian, where it's all settled?'

'Why not a Jugoslav, a Frenchman, anyone but us? Yes. The world's going to be implacable towards us, Stephen. Let's face it. There's going to be a lot of stuff in between; but that time, the day before yesterday, was IT, *die Ende, Schluss, Fini.* I keep seeing the weirdest thing dancing before my eyes—like a dagger, like a cup of poison: choose fair maid, but both are death; ha-ha! Gromyko round the big table, eyes straight ahead, shoulders back, jaws grim, pad-pad, round and round, silent, but brain radiating what we all felt only too damn well: "If there's a war you can't win!" Oh, God! And we have to be on the WRONG side in the bad time coming! To be in America, to like America, to want to be an American and to be wrong, to be martyred by Americans—because, by golly, how the Americans love to make martyrs! They make them so wholesale, they never notice. Every few years some innocents have to be offered up on our altar, the giant footstool before the infinite altar of the brassfaced Philistine god. I know my people; I'm from deep America. What did Lincoln say in that address before the young men's Lyceum in Springfield, 1838: "—till dead men were seen literally dangling from the boughs of trees upon every roadside and in numbers almost sufficient to rival the native Spanish moss of the country as a drapery of the forest." I read that often as a child and I trembled. Later I thought, things have improved since then. But now I know they haven't. Can you see us as martyrs, Stephen? I'm not made for that. I don't believe in it.'

'Neither do I,' said Stephen, 'but it happens. Every day someone's name is called and he is conscripted into the army of blood.'

'I don't like to be a martyr, I won't be a martyr. I don't want to be on the wrong side. I wasn't born for that. How short life is! And what about the children? Oh, my, my! For them, one can't be on the wrong side: and yet we have to choose. What's the right side? I mean morally, and in terms of our natural lives? Oh, Lord! We can be torn to pieces. I won't give up the kids; and your mother and Florence will drag them from us like lightning. And they'd have every right if we became outcasts, outlaws with the community riding us on a rail and throwing stones through our windows. The court could be enquiring into our bank accounts and laundry baskets; and Grandma and Florence would be seen white as snow, for guzzling is not considered wrong in this country—'

'Oh, for pity's sake!'

'All right, Stephen,' she said, furious: 'you know you want to keep the children!'

'Yes, I need them: I love them and I need the boys' money.'

'You can't touch it,' she said.

'I could charge them for keep and education and foreign travel—we can travel maybe: and I can influence them, I hope. Imagine two little boys in my household are multimillionaires; and I'm a poor man. Life hoaxed me.'

'If they were settled, our hands would be free,' said Emily without joy. She sighed, 'It's the damnedest thing! But I won't let them go. And besides, with us they'll escape the tumbrils.'

'What tumbrils?' he said testily.

She sighed, 'Oh, well, if we weren't socialists, I suppose *agenbite of inwit* would make heroes of us anyway. We'd have to start out and join Daniel's little glorious band marching to extinction. Ugh! But that would finish us with your family. Now we can contend, with dear Anna and all our dear lucre-men, that communism was a youthful jag, "our Spanish Civil War phase", as the renegade hath it; and they can see it as an enthusiasm we're too decent to abandon. But, start in now and it would be crystal clear that we're middle-aged delinquents, not mad but bad. Yet we can't abandon and join those other bastards whose names are writ in shapes of crap.'

Stephen lay rigid and was silent. She became silent, too. They went to sleep.

Emily rose early, ordered the food for the day, and, taking a tray of black coffee up to her little room, she began on one of her scripts, a story with humour and pathos about a freckleface in the big city. She worked hard through the day, drove down to the village to buy some bottled French sauces and herbs from a specialist, visited a workman's coffee stall, the owner of which was a political friend, and hurried back to make over her UNO article into lecture notes for the evening.

In the evening she drove to downtown Los Angeles and in a small hall addressed forty to fifty people, among them Mexicans and Negroes, giving her impressions of the San Francisco Conference. Emily spoke in public as she spoke in private. On the platform, she was earnest and incisive and also rollicking and fatly funny. At the end she said, 'A man I knew in the Middle West had someone in City Hall tip him off about condemned houses; he rented them out privately as flophouses for whores and bums. He showed me a few of his houses and he used to recite John Donne to me. An ambulance-chaser I knew in my newspaper days used to sit outside the emergency waiting-room and read me William Blake. The first I ever heard of either poet! The way I collected my education, my high school having no use for same! Ha-ha. Very funny: I'm dying laughing. Imagine I have to go to work now on parsing and pluperfects, in my old age! Well, to the point, friends! I see you there and I am here and I see something ahead. The choice will come, the choice has come. Perhaps you don't see it clearly yet; but one day it will be as obvious as the cop's club and you will weep by teargas, because it is then too late to choose. Some of you will be in gaol, some will be silent with the silence that grows over a man like fungus; and some will be successes and able to appear anywhere in broad daylight. The choice is already taken out of our hands. Well, anyhow, this is the way William Blake puts it in one of his cloudy epics and I'm damned if I can remember anything else but this; and I'm damned remembering this, anyway, maybe. It goes,

> But Palambron called down a Great Solemn Assembly,
> That he who will not defend Truth, may be compelled to
> Defend a Lie, that he may be snared and caught and taken.'

After a pause, there was acclamation. She was forty minutes getting away from the meeting afterwards, for she talked with anyone who wanted to talk with her. Stephen was waiting for her in the car. She got in and they drove uptown. She remained silent.

'Did you wow them?' he asked.

'Were you in the hall?'

'No, I was sitting in the car.'

She grumbled, 'I recited to them a quote from William Blake.' She repeated it. 'They probably thought Palambron was an Indian chief,' she said, laughing. The laughing turned into uncontrollable sobbing.

The Rehabilitation of Ginevra Leake

❦

Ever since our State Department published that address of Khrushchev's to the Twentieth Congress of the Communist Party, in which he noted the 'posthumous rehabilitation' of a number of Russians who had been executed as enemies of the people, I've been nagged by the thought that I owe it to our bourgeois society to reveal what I know about the life of my friend Ginny Doll—or as she was known to her friends in the Party— Ginevra Leake. If you remember, Mr Khrushchev's speech was dotted with anecdotes that all wound to the same tender conclusion:

On February 4th Eihke was shot. It has been definitely established now that Eihke's case was fabricated; he has been posthumously rehabilitated . . . Sentence was passed on Rudzutak in twenty minutes and he was shot. (Indignation in the hall) . . . After careful examination of the case in 1955 it was established that the accusation against Rudzutak was false. He has been rehabilitated posthumously . . . Suffice it to say that from 1954 to the present time, the Military Collegium of the Supreme Court has rehabilitated 7,679 persons, many of whom were rehabilitated posthumously.

Being dead, Ginny Doll would certainly fall into the latter category if anyone chose to rehabilitate her, but since the manner of her death has elevated her, however erroneously, to martyrdom in the American branch of the Party, it's unlikely that any of her crowd will see the need of arousing indignation in the hall. The task therefore devolves on me, not only as a friend of her girlhood, but as her only non-Party friend—kept on because I represented the past, always so sacred to a Southerner, and therefore no more disposable than the rose-painted lamps, walnut commodes and feather-stitched samplers in the midst of which she pursued life on the New York barricades, right to the end. If to no one else, I owe to the rest of us Southrons the rehabilitation of Ginny Doll, even if, as is most likely, it's the last thing she'd want.

I first met Virginia Darley Leake, as she was christened, Ginny Doll as she was called by her mother and aunts, when she and I were about fifteen, both of us daughters of families who had recently emigrated from Virginia to New York, mine from Richmond, hers from Lynchburg, the town that, until I grew up, I assumed was spelled 'Lenchburg'. My father disliked professional Southerners, and would never answer invitations to join their ancestral societies. However, on one summer evening when he was feeling his age and there was absolutely no prospect of anyone dropping in to hear about it, he succumbed to momentary sentiment and went downtown to a meeting of the Sons and Daughters of the Confederacy. He came back snorting that they were nothing but old maids of both sexes, just as he'd expected; he'd been trapped into seeing home a Mrs Darley Lyon Leake who'd clung to him like a limpet when she'd found they both lived on Madison Avenue, and he warned my mother that he was afraid the woman would call—his actual phrase for Mrs Leake being 'one of those tiny, clinging ones you can't get off your hands—like peach fuzz'.

Mrs Leake—a tiny, coronet-braided woman with a dry, bodiless neatness—did call, but only, as she carefully explained to my mother, for the purpose of securing a Southern, presumably genteel playmate for her daughter. My mother was not Southern, but she shared her caller's opinion of the girls Ginny Doll and I brought home from school. The call was repaid once, by my mother with me in tow, after which it was understood that any *entente* was to be only between us girls; my parents and Mrs Leake never saw each other again.

On that first call I had been relieved to find how much the Leake household, scantily composed of only three females—Mrs Leake, Ginny Doll and Ida, the cook—still reminded me of our own crowded one, in its slow rhythm and antediluvian clutter. Three years spent trying to imitate the jumpy ways of my New York girl friends had made me ashamed of our peculiarities; it was comforting to be reminded that these were regional, and that at least there were two of us on Madison Avenue.

With the alchemic snobbery of her kind, Mrs Leake had decreed that the intimacy must be all one way; Ginny Doll could not come to us. So it was always I who went there, at first I didn't quite know why. For, like many of the children introduced to me by my parents, and as quickly shed, Ginny Doll was a lame duck. It would be unfair to suggest that she and her mother were types indigenous only to the South; nevertheless, anybody down there would have recognized them at once—the small woman whose specious femininity is really one of size and affectation, whose imperious ego always has a socially proper outlet (Mrs Leake wore her heart trouble on her sleeve), and whose single daughter is always a great lumpy girl with a clayey complexion. At fifteen, Ginny Doll was already extremely tall, stooped, and heavy in a waistless way; only her thin nose was pink, and her curves were neither joyous nor warm; her long hand lay in one's own like a length of suet just out of the icebox and her upper teeth preceded her smile. One glance at mother and daughter predicted their history; by producing a girl of such clearly unmarriageable aspect, the neatly turned Mrs Leake had assured herself of a well-serviced life until her own death—at a probable eighty. After that, Ginny Doll's fate would have been clearer in Lenchburg, for the South has never lost its gentle, feudal way of absorbing its maiden ladies in one family sinecure or another. But up here in the amorphous North, there was no foretelling what might happen, much less what did.

Ginny Doll also had manners whose archaic elegance I remembered from down home—it was these that my mother had hoped I would reacquire—but unfortunately hers were accompanied by a slippery voice, with a half-gushy catch to it, that gave her a final touch of the ridiculous. Still, I found myself unable to desert her. It appeared that I was her only friend (although her importunities were always so restrained that it took a keen ear to hear the tremor in them), and after I had gone there a few times I felt guilty at not liking her better, because I felt so sorry for her.

For it appeared also that my father had been accorded a signal honor in being allowed past their threshold. Mrs Leake was not a widow as we had assumed, but a deserted woman, and it was because of this that nothing more masculine than the old pug, which she sometimes boarded for a rich sister-in-law, was ever allowed past her door. According to Ginny Doll, her mother had done nothing to merit desertion, unless it was having committed the *faux pas* of marrying a Texan. Indeed, her position was so honorable that conscience money from the sister-in-law, the husband's sister, was the means by which she was quite adequately supported. Still, there was a stain upon them—it was the fact that Mr Leake still lived. Somehow this fact committed them to an infinite circumspection, and was responsible for the exhausted, yet virulent femininity of their ménage. It was also to blame for Mrs Leake's one perverted economy, for which Ginny Doll was never to forgive her—her refusal to get Ginny Doll's teeth straightened. When approached by the sister-in-law, Aunt Tot, on this matter, she would reply that she wouldn't use conscience money to tamper with the work of the Lord. When approached by Ginny Doll, her reply came nearer the truth: 'You didn't get them from me.' As I came to know the Leakes better, I concluded that the stain was increased by the fact that Mr Leake not only was, but was happy somewhere. Although Ginny Doll never spoke of him, I saw him clearly— a man still robust, with the slight coarseness of the too-far-south South, a man barreling along somewhere careless and carefree, a man who knew how to get peach fuzz off his hands.

By this time the household had won me, as it was to win so many—in later years I could well understand Ginny Doll's unique position in the

Party. How it must have salved Party spirits, after a hot day in the trenches of the *Daily Worker*, to enter an authentic version of that Southern parlor inside whose closed circle one sits so cozened and élite, pleating time's fan! Our famed hospitality consists really of a welcome whose stylized warmth is even more affecting than genuine interest, plus the kind of stately consideration for the trivial that makes everybody feel importantly human—Ginny Doll did both to perfection. In my case, it was summertime when I met the Leakes, and our people do have a genius for hot weather. Inside their living room the shades were drawn cool and gray, white dust covers were slippery under bare legs, and a music box was set purling. No one was ever there long before Ida, a frustrated artist with only two to feed, came in bearing an enormous, tinkling tea which she replenished at intervals, urging us to keep up our strength. When, during the first of my visits, Ginny Doll happened to remark, 'Your father is truly handsome; with that ahngree hair of his and that pahful nose, I declare he looks just like a sheik!' I took it for more of her Lenchburg manners. It was only later that I saw how the *idée fixe* 'Men!' was the pivot from which, in opposite ways, the two Leakes swung.

When I was sixteen, my parents gave me a coming-out dance. After a carefully primed phone call to Mrs Leake by my father, Ginny Doll was allowed to attend, on the stipulation that he bring her home at the stroke of twelve. At the dance I was too busy to pay her much mind, but later I heard my parents talking in their bedroom.

'She ought to take that girl back to Lenchburg,' said my father. 'Up here, they don't understand such takin' ways, 'less a pretty face goes with 'em. That girl'll get herself misunderstood—if she gets the chance.'

'Taking ways!' said my mother. 'Why she followed the boys around as if they were unicorns! As if she'd never seen one before!'

My father's shoes hit the floor. 'Reckon not,' he said.

The next day, Ginny Doll telephoned, eager for postmortems on the dance, but I'd already been through that with several of my own crowd, and I didn't get to see her until the end of the week. I found that she had spent the interval noting down the names of all the boys she had met at my house—out of a list of forty she had remembered twenty-nine names and some characteristic of each of the others, such as 'real short, and serious, kind of like the Little Minister'. Opening her leather diary, she revealed that ever since their arrival in New York, she had kept a list of every male she had met; my dance had been a strike of the first magnitude, bringing her total, with the inclusion of two doctors, the landlord and a grocery boy, almost to fifty. And in a special column opposite each name she had recorded the owner's type, much as an anthropologist might note 'brachycephalic', except that Ginny Doll's categories were all culled from their 'library', that collection of safely post-Augustan classics, bound *Harper's*, Thomas Nelson Page and E. P. Roe which used to be on half the musty bookshelves in the Valley of Virginia. There was a Charles Brandon, a Henry Esmond (one of the doctors), a Marlborough and a Bonnie Prince Charlie, as well as several other princes and chevaliers I'd never heard of before. A boy named Bobbie Locke, who'd brought a flask and made a general show of himself, was down as D'Artagnan, and my own beau, a nice quiet boy from St Mark's, was down as Gawain. My father was down as Rasselas, Prince of Abyssinia.

I remember being impressed at first; in Richmond we had been taught to admire 'great readers', even when female, and almost every family we knew had, or had had, at least one. But I also felt a faint, squirmy disquiet. Many of the girls I knew kept movie-star books, or had pashes on Gene Tunney or Admiral Byrd, but we never mixed up these legendary figures with the boys who took us to Huyler's. I was uncomfortably reminded of my father's cousin, old Miss Lavalette Buchanan, who still used more rouge than you could buy on Main Street, and wore gilt bows in her hair even to the Busy Bee.

From then on, my intimacy with Ginny Doll dwindled. Now and then I dropped by on a hot summer day when no one else was around and I simply had to talk about a new beau. For on this score she was the perfect confidante, of course, hanging breathless on every detail. After each time, I swore never to go back. It was embarrassing where there was no exchange. Besides, she drove me nuts with that list, bringing it out like an old set of dominoes, teasing me about my fickleness to 'Gawain'. I couldn't seem to get it through her head that this was New York, not Lenchburg, and that I hadn't seen any of those boys for years.

By the time I'd been away at college for a year, I was finished with her. Ginny Doll hadn't gone—Mrs Leake thought it made you hard. My mother occasionally met Ginny Doll on the avenue, and reported her as pursuing a round that was awesomely unchanged—errands for Mamma, dinners with the aunts, meetings of the Sons and Daughters—even the pug was the same. The Leakes, my father said once, had brought the art of the status quo to a hyaline perfection that was a rarity in New York, but one not much prized there. Who could have dreamed of the direction from which honor would one day be paid?

The last time I saw her was shortly after my engagement had been announced, when I received a formal note from the Leakes, requesting the pleasure of my and my fiancé's company on an afternoon. I remembered with a shock that long ago, 'down South', as we had learned to say now, within that circle of friends whom one did not shuffle but lost only to feud or death, a round of such visits was *de rigueur*. I went alone, unwilling to face the prospect of Ginny Doll studying my future husband for noble analogues, and found the two Leakes behind a loaded tea table.

Mrs Leake seemed the same, except for a rigidly 'at home' manner that she kept between us like a fire screen, as if my coming alliance with a man rendered me incendiary, and she was there to protect her own interests from flame. Ginny Doll's teeth had perhaps a more ivory polish from the constant, vain effort of her lips to close over them, and her dress had already taken a spinster step toward surplice necklines and battleship colors; it was hard to believe that she was, like myself, twenty-three. We were alone together only once, when I went to the bathroom and she followed me in, muttering something about hand towels, of which there were already a dozen or so lace-encrusted ones on the rod.

Once inside, she faced me eagerly, with the tight, held-in smile that always made her look as if she were holding a mashed daisy in her mouth. 'It's so exciting,' she said. 'Tell me all about it!'

'I have,' I said, referring to the stingy facts that had been extracted over the tea table—that we were both history instructors and were going to teach in Istanbul next year, that no, I had no picture with me, but he was 'medium' and dark, and from 'up here'.

'I mean—it's been so long,' she said. 'And Mamma made me dispose of my book.' It took me a minute to realize what she meant.

She looked down at the handkerchief she always carried, worrying the shred of cambric with the ball of her thumb, the way one worries a ticket to somewhere. 'I wondered,' she said. 'Is he one of the ones *we* knew?'

The Leakes sent us a Lenox vase for a wedding present, and my thank-you note was followed by one from Ginny Doll saying that I just must come by some afternoon and tell her about the wedding trip; Mamma napped every day at three and it would be just like old times. I never did, of course. I was afraid it would be.

Ten years passed, fifteen. We had long since returned from abroad and settled in East Hampton. My parents had died. The vase had been broken by the first of the children. I hadn't thought of Ginny Doll in years.

Then, one blinding August afternoon, I was walking along, of all places, Fourteenth Street, cursing the mood that had sent me into the city on such a day, to shop for things I didn't need and wouldn't find. I hadn't found them, but the rising masochism that whelms women at the height of an unsuccessful shopping tour had impelled me down here to check sewing-machine prices at a discount house someone had mentioned a year ago, on whose door I'd just found a sign saying 'Closed Month of August'. In another moment I would rouse and hail a cab, eager enough for the green routines I had fled that morning. Meanwhile I walked slowly west, the wrong way, still hunting for something, anything, peering into one after the other of the huge glass bays of the cheap shoe stores. Not long since, there had still been a chocolate shop down here, that had survived to serve teas in a cleanliness which was elegance for these parts, but I wouldn't find it either. New York lay flat, pooped, in air the color of sweat, but a slatternly nostalgia rose from it, as happens in the dead end of summer, for those who spent their youth there. This trip was a seasonal purge; it would be unwise to find anything.

'Why, Charlotte Mary! I do declare!'

I think I knew who it was before I turned. It was my youth speaking. Since my parents died, no one had addressed me in that double-barreled way in years.

'Why—why Ginny Doll!' Had she not spoken, I would have passed her; she was dressed in that black, short-sleeved convention which city women were just beginning to use and looked, at first glance, almost like anyone. But at the gaspy catch of that voice I remembered everything about her. Here was the one mortal who must have stayed as much the same as anyone could, preserved in the amber of her status quo.

'Why, believe it or not, I was just thinking of you!' I said. It wasn't strictly true; I had been thinking of Huyler's, of old, expunged summers to which she faintly belonged. But early breeding stays with one, returning at odd times like an accent. I can still tell a half-lie, for the sake of someone else's pleasure, as gracefully as anybody in Virginia.

While she extracted the number and names of my children, I revised my first impression of her. Age had improved her, as it does some unattractive girls—we were both thirty-seven. She still stooped heavily, as if the weight of her bust dragged at the high, thin shoulders, but she was better corseted, and had an arty look of heavy earrings and variegated bracelets, not Greenwich Village modern, but the chains of moonstones set in silver, links of carnelians and cameos that ladies used to bring back from Florence—I remembered Aunt Tot.

Something about her face had changed, however, and at first I thought it was merely the effect of her enormous hat (how had I missed it?)—the wide-brimmed 'picture' hat, with an overcomplicated crown, often affected by women who fancied a touch of Mata Hari, or by aging demimondaines. Later, I was to find that this hat was Ginny Doll's trademark, made for her in costume colors by the obscure family milliner to whom she still was loyal, whose fumbling, side-street touch saved the model from its own aspirations and kept it the hat of a lady. At the moment I thought only of how much it was just what Ginny Doll grown up would wear—one of those swooping discs under which romantic spinsters could visualize themselves leaning across a restaurant table at the not-impossible man, hats whose subfusc shadows came too heavy on the faces beneath them, and, well, too late. Here was her old aura of the ridiculous, brought to maturity.

'And how is your mother?' I asked, seeing Mrs Leake as she still must be—tiny, deathless companion fly.

'Mamma?' She smiled, an odd smile, wide and lifted, but closed, and then I saw the real difference in her face. Her teeth had been pulled in. She had had them straightened. 'Mamma's *dead*,' said Ginny Doll.

'Oh, I'm sorry; I hadn't heard—'

'Six years ago. It was her heart after all, think of it. And then I came into Aunt Tot's money.' She smiled on, like a pleased child; until the day of her death, as I was to find, she never tired of the wonder of smiling.

'But don't let's stand here in this awful heat,' she said. 'Come on up to the house, and Ida'll give us some iced tea. Oh, honey, there's so much to tell you!'

'Ida,' I said, enchanted. 'Still Ida? Oh I wish I could, but I'm afraid I haven't time to go all the way up there. I'll miss my train.'

'But I don't live uptown any more, darlin', I live right down here. Come on.' I gave in, and instinctively turned east. Toward Gramercy Park, it would surely be, or Irving Place.

'No, this way.' She turned me west. 'Right here on Fourteenth.'

I followed her, wondering, used as I was to the odd crannies that New Yorkers often seized upon with a gleefully inverted assumption of style. From Union Square just east of us, westward for several long blocks, this was an arid neighborhood even for tenements, an area of cranky shops being superseded by huge bargain chains, of lofts, piano factories, and the blind, shielded windows of textile agents. Nobody, really nobody lived here.

We turned in at the battered doorway of a loft building. Above us, I heard the chattering of machines. To the left, the grimy buff wall held a signboard with a row of company names in smudged gilt. Ginny Doll took out a key and opened a mailbox beneath. I was close enough to read the white calling card on it—*Ginevra Leake*.

At that moment she turned, holding a huge wad of mail. 'Honey, I guess I ought to tell you something about me, before you go upstairs,' she said. 'In case it might make a difference to you.'

In a flash I'd tied it all together—the hat, the neighborhood, the flossy new name, my mother's long-gone remark about unicorns. It wouldn't be need of money. She had simply gone one Freudian step past Miss Lavalette Buchanan. She'd become a tart. A tart with Ida in the background to serve iced tea, as a Darley Leake would.

'I—what did you say?' I said.

She looked down tenderly at her clutch of mail. 'I've joined the Party,' she said.

Familiar as the phrase had become to us all, for the moment I swear I thought she meant the Republican Party. 'What's that got—' I said, and then I stopped, understanding.

'Honey love,' she said. The moonstones rose, shining, on her breast. 'I mean the Communist Party.'

'Ginny Doll Leake! You haven't!'

'Cross my heart, I have!' she said, falling, as I had, into the overtones of our teens. 'Cross my heart hope to die or kiss a pig!' And taking my silence for consent, she tossed her head gaily and led me up, past the Miller Bodice Lining, past the Apex Art Trays, to the top floor.

Ida opened the door, still in her white uniform, and greeted me warmly, chortling 'Miss Charlotte! Miss Charlotte!' over and over before she released me.

I don't know what I expected to find behind her—divans perhaps, and the interchangeable furniture of Utopia built by R. H. Macy—certainly not what confronted me. For what I saw, gazing from the foyer where the abalone-shell lamp and the card tray reposed on the credenza as they had always done, was the old sitting room on Madison Avenue. Royal Doulton nymph vases, Chinese lamps, loveseats, 'ladies' chairs, and luster candelabras, it was all there, even to the Bruxelles curtains through which filtered the felt-tasting air of Fourteenth Street. Obviously the place had been a huge loft, reclaimed with much expense and the utmost fidelity, 'Lenchburg' Ascendant, wherever it might be. Even the positions of the furniture had been retained, with no mantel, but with the same feeling of orientation toward a nonexistent one. In the bathroom the rod held the same weight of ancestral embroidery. The only change I could discern was in the bedroom, where Ginny Doll's nursery chintz and painted rattan had been replaced by Mrs Leake's walnut wedding suite and her *point d'esprit* spread.

I returned to the parlor and sat down on the loveseat, where I had always sat, watching, bemused, while Ida bore in the tray as if she had been waiting all that time in the wings. 'The music box,' I asked. 'Do you still have it?' Of course they did, and while it purled, I listened to Ginny Doll's story.

After Mrs Leake's death, Aunt Tot had intended to take Ginny Doll on a world cruise, but had herself unfortunately died. For a whole year Ginny Doll had sat on in the old place, all Aunt Tot's money waiting in front of her like a Jack Horner pie whose strands she dared not pull. Above all she craved to belong to a 'crowd'; she spent hours weakly dreaming of suddenly being asked to join some 'set' less deliquescent than the First Families of Virginia, but the active world seemed closed against her, an impenetrable crystal ball. Finally the family doctor insisted on her getting away. She had grasped at the only place she could think of, an orderly mountain retreat run by a neo-spiritualistic group known as Unity, two of whose Town Hall lectures she had attended with an ardently converted Daughter. The old doctor, kindly insisting on taking charge of arrangements, had mistakenly booked her at a 'Camp Unity' in the Poconos. It had turned out to be a vacation camp, run, with a transparent disguise to which no one paid any attention, by the Communist Party.

'It was destiny,' said Ginny Doll, smiling absently at a wall on which hung, among other relics, a red-white-and-blue embroidered tribute to a distaff uncle who had been mayor of Memphis. 'Destiny'.

I had to agree with her. From her ingenuous account, and from my own knowledge of the social habits of certain 'progressives' at my husband's college, I could see her clearly, expanding like a *Magnolia grandiflora* in that bouncingly dedicated air. In a place where the really eminent were noncommittal and aliases were worn like medals, no one questioned her presence or affiliation; each group, absorbed in the general charivari, assumed her to be part of another. In the end she achieved the *réclame* that was to grow. She was a Southerner, and a moneyed woman. They had few of either, and she delighted them with her vigorous enmity toward the status quo. Meanwhile her heart recognized their romantic use of the bogus; she bloomed in this atmosphere so full of categories, and of men. In the end she had found, if briefly, a categorical man.

'Yes, it must have been destiny,' I said. Only kismet could have seen to it that Ginny Doll should meet, in the last, dialectic-dusted rays of a Pocono sunset, a man named Lee. 'Lighthorse Harry' or 'Robert E.', I wondered, but she never told me whether it was his first name or last, or gave any of the usual details, although in the years to come she often alluded to what he had said, with the tenacious memory of the woman who had once, perhaps only once, been preferred. It was not fantasy; I believed her. It had been one of those summer affairs of tents and flashlights, ending when 'Party work' reclaimed him, this kind of work apparently being as useful for such purpose as any other. But it had made her a woman of experience, misunderstood at last, able to participate in female talk with the rueful ease of the star-crossed—and to wear those hats.

'I'm not bitter,' she said. He had left her for the Party, and also to it. Her days had become as happily prescribed as a belle's, her mail as full. She had found her 'set'.

'And then—you know I went through analysis?' she said. She had chanced upon the Party during its great psychiatric era, when everybody was having his property-warped libido rearranged. Hers had resulted in the rearrangement of her teeth.

'The phases I went through!' She had gone through a period of wearing her hair in coronet braids; under her analyst's guidance she cut it. With his approval—he was a Party member—she had changed her name to Ginevra. He would have preferred her to keep the teeth as they were, as a symbol that she no longer hankered after the frivolities of class. But they were the one piece of inherited property for which she had no sentiment. Too impatient for orthodontia, she had had them extracted, and a bridge inserted. 'And do you know what I did with them?' she said. 'He said I could, if I had to, and I did.'

'With the teeth?'

She giggled. 'Honey, I put them in a bitty box, and I had the florist put a wreath around it. And I flew down to Lenchburg and put them on Mamma's grave.'

Something moved under my feet, and I gave a slight scream. It wasn't because of what she had just said. Down home, many a good family has its Poe touch of the weirdie, my own as well, and I quite understood. But something was looking out at me from under the sofa, with old, rheumy eyes. It was the pug.

'It's Junius! But it can't be!' I said.

'Basket, Junius! Go back to your basket!' she said. 'It's not the one you knew, of course. It's that one's child. Let's see, she married her own brother, so I guess this one's her cousin as well.' Her tone was rambling and genealogical, the same in which my old aunt still defined a cousinship as once, twice or thrice removed. And I saw that the tip of her nose could still blush. 'Old Junius was really a lady, you know,' she said.

When I rose to leave, Ida followed us to the hallway. 'You come back, Miss Charlotte,' she said. 'You come back, hear? And bring your family with you. I'll cook 'em a dinner. Be right nice to have you, 'stead all these tacky people Miss Ginny so took up with.'

'Now Ida,' said Ginny Doll. 'Charlotte,' she said, 'if there's one thing I've learned—' Her moonstones glittered again, in the mirror over the credenza. It was the single time she ever expounded theory. 'If there's one thing I've learned—it's that real people *are* tacky.'

I did go back of course, and now it was she who gave the social confidences, I who listened with fascination. Once or twice she had me to dinner with some of her 'set', not at all to convert me, but rather as a reigning hostess invites the quiet friend of other days to a brief glimpse of her larger orbit, the better to be able to talk about it later. For, as everyone now knows, she had become a great Party hostess. She gave little dinners, huge receptions, the *ton* of which was just as she would have kept it anywhere—excellent food, notable liqueurs and the Edwardian solicitude to which she had been born. As a Daughter and a DAR, she had a special exhibit value as well. Visiting dignitaries were brought to her as a matter of course; rising functionaries, when bidden there, knew how far they had risen. Her parlor was the scene of innumerable Young Communist weddings, and dozens of Marxian babies embarked on life with one of her silver spoons. The Party had had its Mother Bloor. Ginny Doll became its Aunt.

Meanwhile we kept each other on as extramural relaxation, the way people do keep the friend who knew them 'when'. Just because it was so unlikely for either of us (I was teaching again), we sometimes sewed together, took in a matinée. But I had enough glimpses of her other world to know what she ignored in it. No doubt she enjoyed the sense of conspiracy—her hats grew a trifle larger each year. And she did her share of other activities—if always on the entertainment committee. But her heart held no ruse other than the pretty guile of the Virginian, and I never heard her utter a dialectical word. Had she had the luck to achieve a similar success in 'Lenchburg' her response would have been the same— here, within a circle somewhat larger but still closed, the julep was minted for all. She lived for her friends, who happened to be carrying cards instead of leaving them.

She did *not*, however, die for her friends. Every newspaper reader, of course, knows how she died. She was blown up in that explosion in a union hall on Nineteenth Street, the one that also wrecked a delicatessen, a launderette and Mr Kravetz's tailoring shop next door. The union had had fierce anti-pro-Communist troubles for years, with beatings and dis-appearances for years, and when Ginny Doll's remains, not much but enough, were found, it was taken for granted that she had died in the Party. The Communist press did nothing to deny this. Some maintained that she had been wiped out by the other side; others awarded her a higher martyrdom, claiming that she had gone there equipped like a matronly Kamikaze, having made of herself a living bomb. Memorial services were held, the Ginevra Leake Camp Fund was set going, and she was awarded an Order of Stalin, second class. She is a part of their hagiolatry forever.

But I happen to know otherwise. I happen to know that she was on Nineteenth Street because it was her shopping neighborhood, and be-cause I had spoken to her on the telephone not an hour before. She was just going to drop a blouse by at Mr Kravetz's, she said, then she'd meet me at 2:30 at McCutcheon's, where we were going to pick out some gros-point she wanted to make for her Flint & Horner chairs.

I remember waiting for her for over an hour, thinking that she must be sweet-talking Mr Kravetz, who was an indifferent tailor but a real person. Then I phoned Ida, who knew nothing, and finally caught my train. We

left on vacation the next day, saw no papers, and I didn't hear of Ginny
Doll's death until my return.

When I went down to see Ida, she was already packing for Lynchburg.
She had been left all Ginny Doll's worldly goods and an annuity; the rest
of Aunt Tot's money must have gone you-know-where.

'Miss Charlotte, you pick yourself a momento,' said Ida. We were
standing in the bedroom, and I saw Ida's glance stray to the bureau,
where two objects reposed in *nature morte*. 'I just could'n leave 'em at the
morgue, Miss Charlotte,' she said. 'An' now I can't take 'em, I can't
throw 'em out.' It was Ginny Doll's hat, floated clear of the blast, and her
false teeth.

I knew Ida wanted me to take them. But I'm human. I chose the music
box. As I wrapped it, I felt Ida's eye on me. She knew what *noblesse oblige*
meant, better than her betters. So I compromised, and popped the teeth
in too.

When I got home, I hid them. I knew that the children, scavengers all,
would sooner or later come upon them, but it seemed too dreadful to
chuck them out. Finally, it came to me. I taped them in a bitty box,
masqued with a black chiffon rose, and took them to our local florist, who
sent them to a florist in Lynchburg, to be wreathed and set on Mrs
Leake's grave.

Nevertheless, whenever I heard the children playing the music box, I
felt guilty. I had somehow failed Ginny Doll, and the children too. Then,
when Mr Khrushchev's speech came along, I knew why. I saw that no
one but me could clear Ginny Doll's name, and give her the manifesto
she deserves.

Comrades! Fellow members of Bourgeois Society! Let there be indignation in the hall! It is my duty to tell you that Ginevra Leake, alias
Virginia Darley, alias Ginny Doll, was never an enemy of Our People at
all. She never deserted us, but died properly in the gracious world she
was born to, inside whose charmed circle everyone, even the Juniuses, are
cousins of one another! She was an arch-individualist, just as much as
Stalin. She was a Southern Lady.

And now I can look my children in the eye again. The Russians
needn't think themselves the only ones to rehabilitate people posthumously. We Southrons can take care of our own.

JEAN STAFFORD

The Tea Time of Stouthearted Ladies

❦

'As I tell Kitty, this summer job of hers is really more a vacation with pay
than work. What wouldn't *I* give to be up there in the mountains away
from the hurly-burly of this town! They have a lake right there below the
main lodge where the girls can cool off after they serve lunch. And quite
often they can have the horses to trot off here, there, and the other
place—go down to Brophy, for instance, and have a Coke. They can help
themselves to the books in the lounge, play the Victrola, sit in the sun and
get a good tan. They go to the square dances and dance with the dudes
as if they were dudes themselves, and if there's a home movie they're
invited to come and view. Mrs Bell and Miss Skeen are very democratic
along those lines and when they first hired Kitty, when she was just
fourteen, they told me they didn't look on their employees as servants but
as a part of the family.'

'Not my idea of work,' agreed Mrs Ewing, and made a hybrid sound,
half deprecating giggle, half longing sigh. 'Some different from *our*
summers, what with those scorching days in August and no let-up in the
way of a breeze. Oh, I'm by no means partial to summer on the plains.
And all those pesky grasshoppers spitting tobacco juice through the screens
onto your clean glass curtains, to say nothing of the fuss-budget old
school-marms—give me a dude any day of the week sooner than Miss
Prunes and Prisms from Glenwood Springs still plugging away at her
MA after fifteen years. Kitty's in luck all right.'

Lucky Kitty Winstanley, home from her last class for the day at Nevilles
College, stood in the middle of her small, shadowy bedroom, her arms
still full of books, and listened to the voices in the kitchen below her. She
visualized her mother and the turnip-shaped, bearded neighbor as they
lingered in the bright hollow of the dying May afternoon. Their ration of
icebox cookies eaten, their pale, scalding coffee drunk, they would be
sitting in the breakfast nook, facing each other through spotless, rimless
spectacles. Their tumid hands mutilated by work would be clasped loosely
on the tulip-patterned oilcloth and their swollen feet would be demurely
crossed as they glibly evaluated the silver lining of the cloud beneath

which they and their families lived, gasping for every breath. It was out
of habit, not curiosity, that Kitty listened; she knew all their themes by
heart and all of them embarrassed her. She listened with revulsion, with
boredom, pity, outrage, and she moved stealthily so that they would not
know she had come home.

Each afternoon, in one house or another along this broad, graveled
street, there was such an imitation tea party in such a fiercely clean
kitchen as Mrs Winstanley's when two women or more established
themselves in speckless cotton dresses in the breakfast nooks for a snack
and a confab. United in their profession, that of running boarding houses
for college students, and united more deeply but less admissibly in hardship and fatigue and in eternal worry over 'making ends meet', they
behaved, at this hour of day that lay tranquilly between the toasted
peanut-butter sandwiches of lunch and the Swedish meatballs of dinner,
like urban ladies of leisure gossiping after a matinee. Formal, fearful of
intimacy lest the full confrontation with reality shatter them to smither-
eens, they did not use each other's first names, asked no leading questions; it was surprising that they did not wear gloves and hats. They did
not refer, even by indirection, to personal matters, not to the monotonous
terror of debt that kept them wakeful at night despite the weariness that
was their incessant condition, or to the aching disappointment to which
they daily rose, or to their hopeless, helpless contempt for their unem-
ployed husbands who spent their days in the public park, clustering to
curse the national dilemma or scattering to brood alone upon their individual despair.

Valorously, the landladies kept their chins up, rationalized; they 'saw
the funny side of things', they never said die. One would not guess, to
listen to their light palaver, that they had been reduced to tears that same
morning by the dunning of the grocer and the coal man and had seen
themselves flung into debtors' prison for life. To hear their interchange of
news and commentary on their lodgers, one might have thought they
were the hostesses of prolonged, frolicsome houseparties. The cancer was
invisible, deep in their broken, bleeding hearts.

They sat at the social hour of four to five in the kitchens because their
parlors were either rented out or were used as a common room by the
lodgers, but even in this circumstance they contrived to find expansive
consolation. Often Mrs Winstanley, sitting at attention on the stark bench,
had said, 'I can relax so much better in a kitchen.' Did she think, her
daughter wondered, that the repetition of this humbug was one day going
to make it true? She sometimes went on from there to say, 'When I was
a girl back home in Missouri, we used to call our kitchen "the snuggery,"
and we used it more than any other room in the house.' As she complacently
glanced around, her manner invited her caller to believe that she saw a

Boston rocker and braided rugs, copper spiders hanging on whitewashed walls, a fireplace with a Dutch oven and cherry settles in the inglenooks, and a mantel crowded with pewter tankards and historic guns. In fact, the caller looked on a room all skin and bones: a coal-oil range with gaunt Queen Anne legs, a Hoosier cabinet ready to shudder into pieces, a linoleum rug worn down to gummy blackness save in the places that were inaccessible to feet and still showed forth its pattern of glossy bruises— a room, in short, in which there was nothing to recommend itself to the eye except the marmalade cat and the sunshine on the windowsill in which he slept.

But the neighbor conspiratorially played the game with her hostess, gladly breathed in these palliative fibs without which the ladies would have spent their days in tears. In one way or another, they had all 'come down in the world', but they had descended from a stratum so middling, so snobbish, and so uncertain of itself that it had looked on penury as a disgrace and to have joked about it would have been as alien to their upright natures as it would have been to say aloud the name of a venereal disease. They had come to Adams, this college town in the Rocky Mountains, from the South and the Midwest and New England, most of them driven there by tuberculosis in one member of the family, and now that the depression had slid to its nadir and there were no jobs for their husbands, they had taken up this hard, respectable work.

They bore their shame by refusing to acknowledge its existence: except in the bitter caverns of the night when they reproached their husbands in unflagging whispers, too soft for the boarders to hear but not too soft for their own sons and daughters. For years, Kitty had heard these static diatribes coming up through the hot-air register from her parents' bed-room off the kitchen; sometimes they lasted until the coyotes howled at sunup in the foothills. Rarely did her ruined father answer back; all the charges were true, brutally unfair as they were, and he had nothing to say for himself. He was a builder, but no one was building houses these days; he had only one lung and so he could not work in the mines. The oppressive facts of the depression and of his illness testified to his inno-cence, but his misery, so long drawn out and so unrelieved, had confused him until he was persuaded that he was jobless because he was no good at his work and he believed his wife when she, cruel out of fear, told him that if he had a little more gumption they would not have to live this way, hand to mouth, one jump ahead of the sheriff. Kitty hated her father's unmanliness (once she had seen him cry when a small roof-repairing job that he had counted on was given to someone else, and she had wanted to die for disgust) and she equally hated her mother for her injustice; and she hated herself for hating in them what they could not help.

In the daytime, the woe and bile were buried, and to her lodgers Mrs

Winstanley was a cheery, cherry-cheeked little red hen who was not too strict about quiet hours (their portable phonographs and radios drove Kitty nightly to the library) or about late dates.

With her friends, she liked to talk of her lodgers and of theirs: of their academic failures and successes ('I wasn't a bit surprised when Dolores got a con in psych,' Kitty once heard Mrs Ewing say, using the patois as self-confidently as if it were her own. 'She told me herself that she hadn't cracked a book all term,' and Mrs Winstanley, au courant and really interested, replied, 'But won't those A's in oral interp and business English bring her average up?'); they talked of the girls' love affairs, their plans for holidays, their clothes, their double dates. Gravely and with selfless affection, they told each other facts and sometimes mildly looked for overtones and meanings. Once, Kitty heard her mother say, 'Helen went to the Phi Delt tea dance on Thursday with the boy in Mrs McInerney's single front, but she didn't have a good time at all. She said afterward she was sorry that she had turned down an invitation to go to the show at the Tivoli, even though everyone said it was punk. Of course, I didn't ask any questions, but between you and me and the gatepost I think she was simply cutting off her nose to spite her face by going to the dance instead of keeping her regular date with her steady. Jerry Williams, that is, that big tall engineer with the Studebaker.'

They liked to speculate on the sort of homes their students came from; someone's mother's diabetes, someone's younger brother's practical jokes, someone else's widowed father's trip to Mexico were matters that mattered to them. They counted it an equal—and often thrilling—trade if one landlady, offering to her interlocutor the information that one of her girls or boys had been elected to Phi Beta Kappa, got in return the news that Helen or Joyce or Marie had been 'pinned' with his Chi Psi pin by a prominent member of the football team.

It was not often that they discussed their own sons and daughters who were working their way through college, but when they did their applause was warm. They were, said the landladies, a happy-go-lucky bunch of kids (though serious in their studies) despite the fact that they did not belong to fraternities and sororities (and were known, therefore, as Barbarians) and could not have exactly the clothes they wanted ('But they keep warm!' the ladies cried. 'And when you come right down to it, what else are clothes for?') and had to think twice about spending a nickel on a Coca-Cola. They mouthed their sweet clichés like caramels: 'Anything you work hard for means so much more than something just handed to you on a silver platter.' 'Our children's characters will be all the better for their having gone to the School of Hard Knocks.' 'For these youngsters of ours, Mrs Ewing, the depression is a blessing in disguise.'

With this honorable, aggressive, friendly mendacity, they armed themselves against the twilight return of their gray-faced husbands from the park and of their edgy children, exhausted from classes and study and part-time jobs and perpetually starved for status (they loathed the School of Hard Knocks, they hated being Barbarians) and clothes (a good deal of the time they were *not* warm) and fun. The husbands ate early, fed like dogs in the kitchen, and then, like dogs, they disappeared. Kitty's father spent his evenings in the furnace room where, under a weak light, he whittled napkin rings. But the landladies' sons and daughters, at the end of the day, became maids or footmen to the students whom they had earlier sat next to in Latin class or worked with on an experiment in chemistry. Kitty Winstanley, setting a plate of lamb stew in front of Miss Shirley Rogers, rejoiced that the girl had flubbed her translation in French and had got a scathing jeer from the instructor, but it was cold comfort because this did not detract at all from the professional set of Miss Rogers' fine blond hair or the chic of her flannel skirt and her English sweater on which, over her heart, was pinned the insignia of her current fiancé. Sometimes in the kitchen, as Kitty brought out dirty dishes or refilled the platter of meat, her mother whispered angrily, 'Don't look so down in the mouth! They'll go eat some place where they can find a cheerful smile and then what will we do?' Blackmailed, Kitty set her lips in a murderous grin.

A little work never hurt anyone, the landladies assured each other, and if it was not Mrs Winstanley yearning to trade places with Kitty in the debonair life she led as waitress and chambermaid at the Caribou Ranch, it was Mrs Ewing, similarly self-hypnotized, enumerating the advantages that accrued to her asthmatic son in nightly setting up pins in a bowling alley. What a lark she made of it! And what a solemn opportunity. It was a liberal education in itself, according to his mother, for Harry Ewing to mingle until one in the morning with coal miners and fraternity boys, a contrast of class and privilege she found profoundly instructive. A cricket match on the playing fields of Eton would not seem to offer more in the demonstration of sportsmanship than a bowling tournament between the Betas and the ATOs at the Pay Dirt Entertainment Hall. And, again, a stranger might have thought that Harry was only slumming when Mrs Ewing spoke, with a sociologist's objectivity, of the low mentality and lower morality of the men from the mines and the scandalous girls they brought with them on Ladies' Night. She never touched upon the sleep that Harry lost or on those occasions when a doctor had to be summoned on the double to give the pin boy an injection of adrenalin. 'I do believe Harry's outgrowing his asthma,' she said once, although that very morning Kitty had seen him across the hall in modern European history buffeted suddenly by an attack so debilitating that he had had to be led out by a monitor.

Kitty sat down at her study table and opened her Renaissance survey book to Donne, shutting her ears against the voices of the heroines below. But she was distracted and disconsolate, and the *Divine Poems* fled from her eyes before her mind could detain them. She turned to stare out of her narrow window at the sweet peas that her father's green thumb had coaxed to espalier the wall of the garage. Somewhere in the neighborhood, a music student was phrenetically practicing a polonaise, making villainous mistakes, and somewhere nearer a phonograph was playing 'I Wonder Who's Kissing Her Now', the singer's tribulation throbbing luxuriously in the light spring air. Beyond the garage, over the tops of the mongrel houses and through the feathery branches of mountain ash trees, Kitty could see the red rock terraces of the foothills and the mass of the range beyond where, in a high, wild, emerald and azure and bloodstone park, she would spend her summer.

She would not spend it exactly as her mother imagined. She thought of that lake Mrs Winstanley so much admired, sight unseen, where the girls could swim after lunch if they were not repelled by the mud puppies that abounded in the icy water; and then she thought of the lambent green pool in the main lodge for the exclusive use of the dudes. She thought of the one spooked and spavined old cow pony the kitchen help could ride if they wanted to go where he contrarily wanted to take them, up in the hot sage where the rattlers were or through thick copses of scratchy chokecherry or over sterile, stubbly fields pitted with gopher holes into which he maliciously stumbled when there was no need; and then she saw in her mind's eye the lively blooded bays and palominos that the dudes rode, never failing, as they mounted, to make some stale, soft-boiled joke about Western saddles. It was true, just as her mother said, that the help was asked to the square dances, only 'asked' was not the right word; they had to go to show the Easterners the steps, and there could not have been any dances at all if Wylie, the horse-wrangler, had not been there to call the turns. And it was hardly like going to Paris to go down to Brophy, all but a ghost town, where the only buildings that were not boarded up were a drugstore, a grocery, the post office, a filling station, and a barber-shop that was open on Tuesday and Saturday when an itinerant barber came to town. A handful of backward people, most of them named Brophy, lived in battered cabins in the shadows of the ore dumps of extinguished gold mines. In the wintertime, the story was, they often killed each other because they had nothing else to do.

The help at the Caribou blundered out of bed at five o'clock before the sun came up to begin a day that did not end until after nine at night, a day filled, besides work, with the fussy complaints about their cabins and their food from the older guests, pinches and propositions from the randy younger ones (who were not that young). There was ceaseless bickering among the staff who, xenophobic, despised the dudes and, misanthropic, despised each other. The kitchen was ruled by a fat red cook and a thin yellow pantry girl who did not speak to each other although they glared verbosely across the room, the cook from under the lowering hood of her enormous stove, the pantry girl over the counter of her bailiwick, where the smell of rancid butter was everlasting.

Every morning, as the girls and the wranglers drowsed through their breakfast of flapjacks and side meat, Miss Skeen appeared in the outer doorway of the kitchen, a homicidal German shepherd at her side (his name was Thor and he lived up to it; he had bitten many ankles and had abraded countless others), and boomed through the screen, 'Howdy, pardners!' Miss Skeen, a tall and manly woman, combined in her costume the cork helmet of the pukka sahib, the tweed jacket of the Cotswold squire, the close-fitting Levi's and the French-heeled boots of the wry American cowboy, and the silver and turquoise jewelry of the colorful Southwestern aborigine. Her hair was short, her face was made of crags, she spoke in a Long Island basso profundo.

While Miss Skeen gave the men their orders for the day, her partner, Mrs Bell, entered the kitchen to chirp admonitions to the female servants. Mrs Bell was stout, small-mouthed, doggishly dewlapped, and she wore the khaki uniform of a Red Cross ambulance driver; her contribution to the Great War still gave her great satisfaction, and her memories of France, which were extensive and fresh, were ever on the tip of her tongue. Quite often she lapsed from Western into Army lingo, called the dining room 'the mess hall', asked a guest how he liked his billet, spoke of the wranglers as 'noncoms'. Her awful greeting was, 'Cheerio, boys and girls! Everybody get out of the right side of bed this morning, I hope, I hope?'

The five waitress-chambermaids lived a mile from the main lodge down in a pine-darkened gulch in what had once been a chicken coop and what now Mrs Bell archly called 'the girls' dorm'. The door still latched on the outside and the ceilings were so low that no one taller than a child could stand up straight in any of the three small rooms. There was an outhouse, vile and distant; they were so plagued by trade rats that they had to keep everything they could in tin boxes if they did not want to find their money or their letters stolen and replaced by twigs or bluejay feathers. At that altitude it was freezing cold at night, and the laundry stove in which they burned pine knots could not be regulated, so that they had the choice of shivering or being roasted alive. They had a little time off in the afternoon, but, as often as not, Mrs Bell would dream up some task for them that she tried to make out was a game: they would have to go gather columbines for the tables in the dining room or look for puffballs to put in the pot roast. It was exhausting work; sometimes, after a thronged weekend or a holiday, Kitty's arms ached so much from carrying burdened trays that she could not sleep, and through the long night listened anxiously to the animals gliding and rustling like footpads through the trees.

But, all the same, each spring for the past four years Kitty had been wild with impatience to get to the Caribou, to get away from home, from the spectacle of her eaten father and from her mother's bright-eyed lies, from all the maniacal respectability with which the landladies straitjacketed the life of the town. The chicken coop was filthy and alarming, but it was not this genteel, hygienic house in which she was forced to live a double life. At the Caribou, she was a servant and she enjoyed a servant's prerogative of keeping her distance; for instance, to the rich and lascivious dude, Mr Kopf, a painter, she had been respectful but very firm in refusing to pose for him (he wanted to paint her as Hebe), had said, in a way that left no room for argument, 'I have to rest in my time off, sir.' But, at home, what could she do if a boarder, valuable to her mother for the rent she paid, asked for help with a translation or the loan of lecture notes? She could not put the girl, her contemporary and classmate, in her place by calling her 'ma'am', she could do nothing but supinely deliver the lecture notes together with the dumplings or lend a hand with *De Amicitia* after she had taken to the various rooms the underwear and blouses her mother had washed and ironed.

At the Caribou, there was no one she knew in any other context. Her fellow waitresses were local mountain girls, so chastely green that they were not really sure what a college was and certainly did not care. They never read, but it did not embarrass them that Kitty did. At Christmas she exchanged cards with them but they did not exist for her, or she for them, before the first of June or after Labor Day. And the dudes whose bathtubs she scoured and whose dietary idiosyncrasies she catered to came from a milieu so rich and foreign and Eastern that she could not even imagine it and therefore did not envy it.

Friendless, silent, long and exasperating, the summers, indeed, were no holiday. But she lived them in pride and without woe and with a physical intelligence that she did not exercise in the winter; there in the mountains, she observed the world acutely and with love—at dusk, the saddle horses grazing in the meadow were joined by deer seeking the salt lick; by day the firmament was cloudless and blinding and across the blue of it chicken hawks and eagles soared and banked in perpetual reconnaissance; by night the stars were near, and the mountains on the moon, when it was full, seemed to have actual altitude. On these wonders, Kitty mused, absorbed.

The voices downstairs invaded her trance. She began to calculate in pencil on the margin to the left of 'If poisonous minerals . . .' how many more hours there were to come before she got into the rattletrap mail coach that would take her, coughing spastically in its decrepitude, up the rivered canyons and over the quiet passes to her asylum. Her arithmetic did not deafen her. She heard:

'I grant you that the hours are long and the pay is low,' her mother said, 'but the Caribou attracts big spenders from the East and the tips more than make up for the poor wages. I don't mean your flashy tourists and I don't mean your snobby new rich but simply your settled, well-to-do people, mostly middle-aged and older. Mrs Bell and Miss Skeen are cultured—went to boarding school in Switzerland as I understand it—and they are ladies and, as a result, they are particular about their clientele—absolutely will not tolerate anything in the least out-of-the-way. For one thing, they don't allow drinking on the premises, and anyone who breaks the rule is given his walking papers without any further ado, I don't care if his name is Astor or John Doe. And with all the beer-drinking and what-not going on down here when those fast boys come flocking to town from heaven knows where in those covertible roadsters with the cut-outs open and those horns that play a tune, it's a comfort to me to know that my daughter is out of the way of loose living.'

'Oh, I agree,' said Mrs Ewing, and Kitty could imagine her nodding her head spiritedly and shaking loose the bone hairpins that held her gray braids in place. 'I happen to know that the drinking that goes on in this town is decidedly on the upgrade. In these bowling alleys and so on, they spike the three point two with grain alcohol. And that's the very least of it. There are many, many ether addicts in the frat houses. Oh, I'm telling you, there are plenty of statistics that would make your hair stand on end. DTs and so on among the young.'

For a few minutes then the ladies lowered their voices and Kitty could not hear what they said, but she knew the bypath they were joyfully ambling down; they were expounding the theory that beer-drinking led to dope and dope to free love and free love to hydrocephalic, albino, club-footed bastard babies or else to death by abortion.

The fact was that both Mrs Bell and Miss Skeen were lushes, and they fooled nobody with their high and mighty teetotal rule and their aura of Sen-Sen. The rule was at first a puzzle and a bore to the dudes, but then it became a source of surreptitious fun: outwitting the old girls became as much a part of the routine as fishing or hunting for arrowheads. For the last two years, Kitty Winstanley had acted as middleman between the guests and the bootlegger, Ratty Carmichael. There was local option in the state, but in Meade County where the Caribou lay there was nothing legal to drink but three point two. In an obscure, dry gully back of the cow pasture, Kitty kept her trysts with Ratty (his eyes were feral and his twitching nose was criminal) and gave him handfuls of money and orders for bottles of atrocious brown booze and demijohns of Dago Red. These he delivered at dinnertime when Miss Skeen and Mrs Bell were in their cabin, The Bonanza, oblivious to everything but their own elation, for which excellent Canadian whisky, bought honorably in Denver, was responsible. Kitty had no taste for this assignment of hers—she was not an adventurous girl—but she was generously tipped by the dudes for running their shady errands and for that reason she put up with the risks of it—being fired, being caught by the revenue officers and charged with collusion.

She smiled, finishing her multiplication. In 283 more hours, immediately after her last examination in final week, she would be putting her suitcase into the mail truck parked behind the post office. And a good many of those hours would be blessedly spent in sleep. Then she'd be gone from this charmless town on the singed plains where the cottonwoods were dusty and the lawns were straw. She'd be gone from the French dolls and baby pillows in the lodgers' rooms. And, in being gone, she would give her mother a golden opportunity to brag to the summer roomers: 'Kitty has the time of her life,' she could hear her mother say to some wispy, downtrodden schoolteacher waif, 'up there where the ozone is as good as a drink, as they say.'

Now the light was paling on the summit snows. Kitty heard her father's soft-footed, apologetic tread on the back porch and heard Mrs Ewing brightly say, 'Well, I must toddle along now and thanks a million for the treat. My turn next time.'

The music student was at work on *The Well-Tempered Clavichord* and the phonograph was playing 'The Object of My Affection' as fast as merry-go-round music. And down in the kitchen, as she clattered and banged her pots and pans, Mother Pollyana began to sing 'The Stein Song'.

MURIEL SPARK

The House of the Famous Poet

❧

In the summer of 1944, when it was nothing for trains from the provinces to be five or six hours late, I travelled to London on the night train from Edinburgh, which, at York, was already three hours late. There were ten people in the compartment, only two of whom I remember well, and for good reason.

I have the impression, looking back on it, of a row of people opposite me, dozing untidily with heads askew, and, as it often seems when we look at sleeping strangers, their features had assumed extra emphasis and individuality, sometimes disturbing to watch. It was as if they had rendered up their daytime talent for obliterating the outward traces of themselves in exchange for mental obliteration. In this way they resembled a twelfth-century fresco; there was a look of medieval unselfconsciousness about these people, all except one.

This was a private soldier who was awake to a greater degree than most people are when they are not sleeping. He was smoking cigarettes one after the other with long, calm puffs. I thought he looked excessively evil—an atavistic type. His forehead must have been less than two inches high above dark, thick eyebrows, which met. His jaw was not large, but it was apelike; so was his small nose and so were his deep, close-set eyes. I thought there must have been some consanguinity in the parents. He was quite a throw-back.

As it turned out, he was extremely gentle and kind. When I ran out of cigarettes, he fished about in his haversack and produced a packet for me and one for a girl sitting next to me. We both tried, with a flutter of small change, to pay him. Nothing would please him at all but that we should accept his cigarettes, whereupon he returned to his silent, reflective smoking.

I felt a sort of pity for him then, rather as we feel towards animals we know to be harmless, such as monkeys. But I realized that, like the pity we expend on monkeys merely because they are not human beings, this pity was not needed.

Receiving the cigarettes gave the girl and myself common ground, and we conversed quietly for the rest of the journey. She told me she had a job in London as a domestic helper and nursemaid. She looked as if she had come from a country district—her very blonde hair, red face and large bones gave the impression of power, as if she was used to carrying heavy things, perhaps great scuttles of coal, or two children at a time. But what made me curious about her was her voice, which was cultivated, melodious and restrained.

Towards the end of the journey, when the people were beginning to jerk themselves straight and the rushing to and fro in the corridor had started, this girl, Elise, asked me to come with her to the house where she worked. The master, who was something in a university, was away with his wife and family.

I agreed to this, because at that time I was in the way of thinking that the discovery of an educated servant girl was valuable and something to be gone deeper into. It had the element of experience—perhaps, even of truth—and I believed, in those days, that truth is stranger than fiction. Besides, I wanted to spend that Sunday in London. I was due back next day at my job in a branch of the civil service, which had been evacuated to the country and for a reason that is another story, I didn't want to return too soon. I had some telephoning to do, I wanted to wash and change. I wanted to know more about the girl. So I thanked Elise and accepted her invitation.

I regretted it as soon as we got out of the train at King's Cross, some minutes after ten. Standing up tall on the platform, Elise looked unbearably tired, as if not only the last night's journey but every fragment of her unknown life was suddenly heaping up on top of her. The power I had noticed in the train was no longer there. As she called, in her beautiful voice, for a porter, I saw that on the side of her head that had been away from me in the train, her hair was parted in a dark streak, which, by contrast with the yellow, looked navy blue. I had thought, when I first saw her, that possibly her hair was bleached, but now, seeing it so badly done, seeing this navy blue parting pointing like an arrow to the weighted weariness of her face, I, too, got the sensation of great tiredness. And it was not only the strain of the journey that I felt, but the foreknowledge of boredom that comes upon us unaccountably at the beginning of a quest, and that checks, perhaps mercifully, our curiosity.

And, as it happened, there really wasn't much to learn about Elise. The explanation of her that I had been prompted to seek, I got in the taxi between King's Cross and the house at Swiss Cottage. She came of a good family, who thought her a pity, and she them. Having no training for anything else, she had taken a domestic job on leaving home. She was engaged to an Australian soldier billeted also at Swiss Cottage.

Perhaps it was the anticipation of a day's boredom, maybe it was the effect of no sleep or the fact that the V-I sirens were sounding, but I felt some sourness when I saw the house. The garden was growing all over the place. Elise opened the front door, and we entered a darkish room almost wholly taken up with a long, plain wooden worktable. On this, were a half-empty marmalade jar, a pile of papers, and a dried-up ink bottle. There was a steel-canopied bed, known as a Morrison shelter, in one corner and some photographs on the mantelpiece, one of a schoolboy wearing glasses. Everything was tainted with Elise's weariness and my own distaste. But Elise didn't seem to be aware of the exhaustion so plainly revealed on her face. She did not even bother to take her coat off, and as it was too tight for her I wondered how she could move about so quickly with this restriction added to the weight of her tiredness. But, with her coat still buttoned tight Elise phoned her boy-friend and made breakfast, while I washed in a dim, blue, cracked bathroom upstairs.

When I found that she had opened my hold-all without asking me and had taken out my rations, I was a little pleased. It seemed a friendly action, with some measure of reality about it, and I felt better. But I was still irritated by the house. I felt there was no justification for the positive lack of consequence which was lying about here and there. I asked no questions about the owner who was something in a university, for fear of getting the answer I expected—that he was away visiting his grand-children, at some family gathering in the home counties. The owners of the house had no reality for me, and I looked upon the place as belonging to, and permeated with, Elise.

I went with her to a nearby public house, where she met her boy-friend and one or two other Australian soldiers. They had with them a thin Cockney girl with bad teeth. Elise was very happy, and insisted in her lovely voice that they should all come along to a party at the house that evening. In a fine aristocratic tone, she demanded that each should bring a bottle of beer.

During the afternoon Elise said she was going to have a bath, and she showed me a room where I could use the telephone and sleep if I wanted. This was a large, light room with several windows, much more orderly than the rest of the house, and lined with books. There was only one unusual thing about it: beside one of the windows was a bed, but this bed was only a fairly thick mattress made up neatly on the floor. It was obviously a bed on the floor with some purpose, and again I was angered to think of the futile crankiness of the elderly professor who had thought of it.

I did my telephoning, and decided to rest. But first I wanted to find something to read. The books puzzled me. None of them seemed to be automatically part of a scholar's library. An inscription in one book was signed by the author, a well-known novelist. I found another inscribed copy, and this had the name of the recipient. On a sudden idea, I went to the desk, where while I had been telephoning I had noticed a pile of unopened letters. For the first time, I looked at the name of the owner of the house.

I ran to the bathroom and shouted through the door to Elise, 'Is this the house of the famous poet?'

'Yes,' she called. 'I *told* you.'

She had told me nothing of the kind. I felt I had no right at all to be there, for it wasn't, now, the house of Elise acting by proxy for some unknown couple. It was the house of a famous modern poet. The thought that at any moment he and his family might walk in and find me there terrified me. I insisted that Elise should open the bathroom door and tell me to my face that there was no possible chance of their returning for many days to come.

Then I began to think about the house itself, which Elise was no longer accountable for. Its new definition, as the house of a poet whose work I knew well, many of whose poems I knew by heart, gave it altogether a new appearance.

To confirm this, I went outside and stood exactly where I had been when I first saw the garden from the door of the taxi. I wanted to get my first impression for a second time.

And this time I saw an absolute purpose in the overgrown garden, which, since then, I have come to believe existed in the eye of the beholder. But, at the time, the room we had first entered, and which had riled me, now began to give back a meaning, and whatever was, was right. The caked-up bottle of ink, which Elise had put on the mantelpiece, I replaced on the table to make sure. I saw a photograph I hadn't noticed before, and I recognized the famous poet.

It was the same with the upstairs room where Elise had put me, and I handled the books again, not so much with the sense that they belonged to the famous poet but with some curiosity about how they had been made. The sort of question that occurred to me was where the paper had come from and from what sort of vegetation was manufactured the black print, and these things have not troubled me since.

The Australians and the Cockney girl came around about seven. I had planned to catch an eight-thirty train to the country, but when I telephoned to confirm the time I found there were no Sunday trains running. Elise, in her friendly and exhausted way, begged me to stay without attempting to be too serious about it. The sirens were starting up again. I asked Elise once more to repeat that the poet and his family could by no means return that night. But I asked this question more abstractedly than before, as I was thinking of the sirens and of the exact proportions of the noise they made. I wondered, as well, what sinister genius of the Home Office could have invented so ominous a wail, and why. And I was thinking of the word 'siren'. The sound then became comical, for I imagined some maniac sea nymph from centuries past belching into the year 1944. Actually, the sirens frightened me.

Most of all, I wondered about Elise's party. Everyone roamed about the place as if it were nobody's house in particular, with Elise the best-behaved of the lot. The Cockney girl sat on the long table and gave of her best to the skies every time a bomb exploded. I had the feeling that the house had been requisitioned for an evening by the military. It was so hugely and everywhere occupied that it became not the house I had first entered, nor the house of the famous poet, but a third house—the one I had vaguely prefigured when I stood, bored, on the platform at King's Cross station. I saw a great amount of tiredness among these people, and heard, from the loud noise they made, that they were all lacking sleep. When the beer was finished and they were gone, some to their billets, some to pubs, and the Cockney girl to her Underground shelter where she had slept for weeks past, I asked Elise, 'Don't you feel tired?'

'No,' she said with agonizing weariness, 'I never feel tired.'

I fell asleep myself, as soon as I had got into the bed on the floor in the upstairs room, and overslept until Elise woke me at eight. I had wanted to get up early to catch a nine o'clock train, so I hadn't much time to speak to her. I did notice, though, that she had lost some of her tired look.

I was pushing my things into my hold-all while Elise went up the street to catch a taxi when I heard someone coming upstairs. I thought it was Elise come back, and I looked out of the open door. I saw a man in uniform carrying an enormous parcel in both hands. He looked down as he climbed, and had a cigarette in his mouth.

'Do you want Elise?' I called, thinking it was one of her friends.

He looked up, and I recognized the soldier, the throw-back, who had given us cigarettes in the train.

'Well, anyone will do,' he said. 'The thing is, I've got to get back to camp and I'm stuck for the fare—eight and six.'

I told him I could manage it, and was finding the money when he said, putting his parcel on the floor, 'I don't want to borrow it. I wouldn't think of borrowing it. I've got something for sale.'

'What's that?' I said.

'A funeral,' said the soldier. 'I've got it here.'

This alarmed me, and I went to the window. No hearse, no coffin stood below. I saw only the avenue of trees.

The soldier smiled. 'It's an abstract funeral,' he explained, opening the parcel.

He took it out and I examined it carefully, greatly comforted. It was very much the sort of thing I had wanted—rather more purple in parts than I would have liked, for I was not in favour of this colour of mourning. Still, I thought I could tone it down a bit.

Delighted with the bargain, I handed over the eight shillings and sixpence. There was a great deal of this abstract funeral. Hastily, I packed some of it into the holdall. Some I stuffed in my pockets, and there was still some left over. Elise had returned with a cab and I hadn't much time. So I ran for it, out of the door and out of the gate of the house of the famous poet, with the rest of my funeral trailing behind me.

You will complain that I am withholding evidence. Indeed, you may wonder if there is any evidence at all. 'An abstract funeral,' you will say, 'is neither here nor there. It is only a notion. You cannot pack a notion into your bag. You cannot see the colour of a notion.'

You will insinuate that what I have just told you is pure fiction.

Hear me to the end.

I caught the train. Imagine my surprise when I found, sitting opposite me, my friend the soldier, of whose existence you are so sceptical.

'As a matter of interest,' I said, 'how would you describe all this funeral you sold me?'

'Describe it?' he said. 'Nobody describes an abstract funeral. You just conceive it.'

'There is much in what you say,' I replied. 'Still, describe it I must, because it is not every day one comes by an abstract funeral.'

'I am glad you appreciate that,' said the soldier.

'And after the war,' I continued, 'when I am no longer a civil servant, I hope, in a few deftly turned phrases, to write of my experiences at the house of the famous poet, which has culminated like this. But of course,' I added, 'I will need to say what it looks like.'

The soldier did not reply.

'If it were an okapi or a sea-cow,' I said, 'I would have to say what it looked like. No one would believe me otherwise.'

'Do you want your money back?' asked the soldier. 'Because if so, you can't have it. I spent it on my ticket.'

'Don't misunderstand me,' I hastened to say. 'The funeral is a delightful abstraction. Only, I wish to put it down in writing.'

I felt a great pity for the soldier on seeing his worried look. The apelike head seemed the saddest thing in the world.

'I make them by hand,' he said, 'these abstract funerals.'

A siren sounded somewhere, far away.

'Elise bought one of them last month. She hadn't any complaints. I change at the next stop,' he said, getting down his kit from the rack. 'And what's more,' he said, 'your famous poet bought one.'

'Oh, did he?' I said.

'Yes,' he said. 'No complaints. It was just what he wanted—the idea of a funeral.'

The train pulled up. The soldier leaped down and waved. As the train started again, I unpacked my abstract funeral and looked at it for a few moments.

'To hell with the idea,' I said. 'It's a real funeral I want.'

'All in good time,' said a voice from the corridor.

'*You* again,' I said. It was the soldier.

'No,' he said. 'I got off at the last station. I'm only a notion of myself.'

'Look here,' I said, 'would you be offended if I throw all this away?'

'Of course not,' said the soldier. 'You can't offend a notion.'

'I want a real funeral,' I explained. 'One of my own.'

'That's right,' said the soldier.

'And then I'll be able to write about it and go into all the details,' I said.

'Your own funeral?' he said. 'You want to write it up?'

'Yes,' I said.

'But,' said he, 'you're only human. Nobody reports on their own funeral. It's got to be abstract.'

'You see my predicament?' I said.

'I see it,' he replied. 'I get off at this stop.'

This notion of a soldier alighted. Once more the train put on speed. Out of the window I chucked all my eight and sixpence worth of abstract funeral. I watched it fluttering over the fields and around the tops of camouflaged factories with the sun glittering richly upon it, until it was out of sight.

In the summer of 1944 a great many people were harshly and suddenly killed. The papers reported, in due course, those whose names were known to the public. One of these, the famous poet, had returned unexpectedly to his home at Swiss Cottage a few moments before it was hit direct by a flying bomb. Fortunately, he had left his wife and children in the country.

When I got to the place where my job was, I had some time to spare before going on duty. I decided to ring Elise and thank her properly, as I had left in such a hurry. But the lines were out of order, and the operator could not find words enough to express her annoyance with me. Behind this overworked, quarrelsome voice from the exchange I heard the high, long hoot which means that the telephone at the other end is not functioning, and the sound made me infinitely depressed and weary; it was more intolerable to me than the sirens, and I replaced the receiver; and, in fact, Elise had already perished under the house of the famous poet.

The blue cracked bathroom, the bed on the floor, the caked ink bottle, the neglected garden, and the neat rows of books—I try to gather them together in my mind whenever I am enraged by the thought that Elise and the poet were killed outright. The angels of the Resurrection will invoke the dead man and the dead woman, but who will care to restore the fallen house of the famous poet if not myself? Who else will tell its story?

When I reflect how Elise and the poet were taken in—how they calmly allowed a well-meaning soldier to sell them the notion of a funeral, I remind myself that one day I will accept, and so will you, an abstract funeral, and make no complaints.

FLANNERY O'CONNOR

Good Country People

❧

Besides the neutral expression that she wore when she was alone, Mrs Freeman had two others, forward and reverse, that she used for all her human dealings. Her forward expression was steady and driving like the advance of a heavy truck. Her eyes never swerved to left or right but turned as the story turned as if they followed a yellow line down the center of it. She seldom used the other expression because it was not often necessary for her to retract a statement, but when she did, her face came to a complete stop, there was an almost imperceptible movement of her black eyes, during which they seemed to be receding, and then the observer would see that Mrs Freeman, though she might stand there as real as several grain sacks thrown on top of each other, was no longer there in spirit. As for getting anything across to her when this was the case, Mrs Hopewell had given it up. She might talk her head off. Mrs Freeman could never be brought to admit herself wrong on any point. She would stand there and if she could be brought to say anything, it was something like, 'Well, I wouldn't of said it was and I wouldn't of said it wasn't,' or letting her gaze range over the top kitchen shelf where there was an assortment of dusty bottles, she might remark, 'I see you ain't ate many of them figs you put up last summer.'

They carried on their most important business in the kitchen at breakfast. Every morning Mrs Hopewell got up at seven o'clock and lit her gas heater and Joy's. Joy was her daughter, a large blonde girl who had an artificial leg. Mrs Hopewell thought of her as a child though she was thirty-two years old and highly educated. Joy would get up while her mother was eating and lumber into the bathroom and slam the door, and before long, Mrs Freeman would arrive at the back door. Joy would hear her mother call, 'Come on in,' and then they would talk for a while in low voices that were indistinguishable in the bathroom. By the time Joy came in, they had usually finished the weather report and were on one or the other of Mrs Freeman's daughters, Glynese or Carramae. Joy called them Glycerin and Caramel. Glynese, a redhead, was eighteen and had many admirers; Carramae, a blonde, was only fifteen but already married and pregnant. She could not keep anything on her stomach. Every morning Mrs Freeman told Mrs Hopewell how many times she had vomited since the last report.

Mrs Hopewell liked to tell people that Glynese and Carramae were two of the finest girls she knew and that Mrs Freeman was a *lady* and that she was never ashamed to take her anywhere or introduce her to anybody they might meet. Then she would tell how she had happened to hire the Freemans in the first place and how they were a godsend to her and how she had had them four years. The reason for her keeping them so long was that they were not trash. They were good country people. She had telephoned the man whose name they had given as a reference and he had told her that Mr Freeman was a good farmer but that his wife was the nosiest woman ever to walk the earth. 'She's got to be into everything,' the man said. 'If she don't get there before the dust settles, you can bet she's dead, that's all. She'll want to know all your business. I can stand him real good,' he had said, 'but me nor my wife neither could have stood that woman one more minute on this place.' That had put Mrs Hopewell off for a few days.

She had hired them in the end because there were no other applicants but she had made up her mind beforehand exactly how she would handle the woman. Since she was the type who had to be into everything, then, Mrs Hopewell had decided, she would not only let her be into everything, she would *see to it* that she was into everything—she would give her the responsibility of everything, she would put her in charge. Mrs Hopewell had no bad qualities of her own but she was able to use other people's in such a constructive way that she never felt the lack. She had hired the Freemans and she had kept them four years.

Nothing is perfect. This was one of Mrs Hopewell's favorite sayings. Another was: that is life! And still another, the most important, was: well, other people have their opinions too. She would make these statements, usually at the table, in a tone of gentle insistence as if no one held them but her, and the large hulking Joy, whose constant outrage had obliterated every expression from her face, would stare just a little to the side of her, her eyes icy blue, with the look of someone who has achieved blindness by an act of will and means to keep it.

When Mrs Hopewell said to Mrs Freeman that life was like that, Mrs Freeman would say, 'I always said so myself.' Nothing had been arrived at by anyone that had not first been arrived at by her. She was quicker than Mr Freeman. When Mrs Hopewell said to her after they had been on the place a while, 'You know, you're the wheel behind the wheel,' and winked, Mrs Freeman had said, 'I know it. I've always been quick. It's some that are quicker than others.'

'Everybody is different,' Mrs Hopewell said.

'Yes, most people is,' Mrs Freeman said.

'It takes all kinds to make the world.'

'I always said it did myself.'

The girl was used to this kind of dialogue for breakfast and more of it for dinner; sometimes they had it for supper too. When they had no guest they ate in the kitchen because that was easier. Mrs Freeman always managed to arrive at some point during the meal and to watch them finish it. She would stand in the doorway if it were summer but in the winter she would stand with one elbow on top of the refrigerator and look down on them, or she would stand by the gas heater, lifting the back of her skirt slightly. Occasionally she would stand against the wall and roll her head from side to side. At no time was she in any hurry to leave. All this was very trying on Mrs Hopewell but she was a woman of great patience. She realized that nothing is perfect and that in the Freemans she had good country people and that if, in this day and age, you get good country people, you had better hang onto them.

She had had plenty of experience with trash. Before the Freemans she had averaged one tenant family a year. The wives of these farmers were not the kind you would want to be around you for very long. Mrs Hopewell, who had divorced her husband long ago, needed someone to walk over the fields with her; and when Joy had to be impressed for these services, her remarks were usually so ugly and her face so glum that Mrs Hopewell would say, 'If you can't come pleasantly, I don't want you at all,' to which the girl, standing square and rigid-shouldered with her neck thrust slightly forward, would reply, 'If you want me, here I am—LIKE I AM.'

Mrs Hopewell excused this attitude because of the leg (which had been shot off in a hunting accident when Joy was ten). It was hard for Mrs Hopewell to realize that her child was thirty-two now and that for more than twenty years she had had only one leg. She thought of her still as a child because it tore her heart to think instead of the poor stout girl in her thirties who had never danced a step or had any *normal* good times. Her name was really Joy but as soon as she was twenty-one and away from home, she had had it legally changed. Mrs Hopewell was certain that she had thought and thought until she had hit upon the ugliest name in any language. Then she had gone and had the beautiful name, Joy, changed without telling her mother until after she had done it. Her legal name was Hulga.

When Mrs Hopewell thought the name, Hulga, she thought of the broad blank hull of a battleship. She would not use it. She continued to call her Joy to which the girl responded but in a purely mechanical way.

Hulga had learned to tolerate Mrs Freeman who saved her from taking

walks with her mother. Even Glynese and Carramae were useful when
they occupied attention that might otherwise have been directed at her.
At first she had thought she could not stand Mrs Freeman for she had
found that it was not possible to be rude to her. Mrs Freeman would take
on strange resentments and for days together she would be sullen but the
source of her displeasure was always obscure; a direct attack, a positive
leer, blatant ugliness to her face—these never touched her. And without
warning one day, she began calling her Hulga.

She did not call her that in front of Mrs Hopewell who would have
been incensed but when she and the girl happened to be out of the house
together, she would say something and add the name Hulga to the end of
it, and the big spectacled Joy-Hulga would scowl and redden as if her
privacy had been intruded upon. She considered the name her personal
affair. She had arrived at it first purely on the basis of its ugly sound and
then the full genius of its fitness had struck her. She had a vision of the
name working like the ugly sweating Vulcan who stayed in the furnace
and to whom, presumably, the goddess had to come when called. She saw
it as the name of her highest creative act. One of her major triumphs was
that her mother had not been able to turn her dust into Joy, but the
greater one was that she had been able to turn it herself into Hulga.
However, Mrs Freeman's relish for using the name only irritated her. It
was as if Mrs Freeman's beady steel-pointed eyes had penetrated far
enough behind her face to reach some secret fact. Something about her
seemed to fascinate Mrs Freeman and then one day Hulga realized that
it was the artificial leg. Mrs Freeman had a special fondness for the details
of secret infections, hidden deformities, assaults upon children. Of diseases,
she preferred the lingering or incurable. Hulga had heard Mrs Hopewell
give her the details of the hunting accident, how the leg had been literally
blasted off, how she had never lost consciousness. Mrs Freeman could
listen to it any time as if it had happened an hour ago.

When Hulga stumped into the kitchen in the morning (she could walk
without making the awful noise but she made it—Mrs Hopewell was
certain—because it was ugly-sounding), she glanced at them and did not
speak. Mrs Hopewell would be in her red kimono with her hair tied
around her head in rags. She would be sitting at the table, finishing her
breakfast and Mrs Freeman would be hanging by her elbow outward
from the refrigerator, looking down at the table. Hulga always put her
eggs on the stove to boil and then stood over them with her arms folded,
and Mrs Hopewell would look at her—a kind of indirect gaze divided
between her and Mrs Freeman—and would think that if she would only
keep herself up a little, she wouldn't be so bad looking. There was
nothing wrong with her face that a pleasant expression wouldn't help.

Mrs Hopewell said that people who looked on the bright side of things would be beautiful even if they were not.

Whenever she looked at Joy this way, she could not help but feel that it would have been better if the child had not taken the Ph.D. It had certainly not brought her out any and now that she had it, there was no more excuse for her to go to school again. Mrs Hopewell thought it was nice for girls to go to school to have a good time but Joy had 'gone through'. Anyhow, she would not have been strong enough to go again. The doctors had told Mrs Hopewell that with the best of care, Joy might see forty-five. She had a weak heart. Joy had made it plain that if it had not been for this condition, she would be far from these red hills and good country people. She would be in a university lecturing to people who knew what she was talking about. And Mrs Hopewell could very well picture her there, looking like a scarecrow and lecturing to more of the same. Here she went about all day in a six-year-old skirt and a yellow sweat shirt with a faded cowboy on a horse embossed on it. She thought this was funny; Mrs Hopewell thought it was idiotic and showed simply that she was still a child. She was brilliant but she didn't have a grain of sense. It seemed to Mrs Hopewell that every year she grew less like other people and more like herself—bloated, rude, and squint-eyed. And she said such strange things! To her own mother she had said—without warning, without excuse, standing up in the middle of a meal with her face purple and her mouth half full—'Woman! do you ever look inside? Do you ever look inside and see what you are *not*? God!' she had cried sinking down again and staring at her plate, 'Malebranche was right: we are not our own light. We are not our own light!' Mrs Hopewell had no idea to this day what brought that on. She had only made the remark, hoping Joy would take it in, that a smile never hurt anyone.

The girl had taken the Ph.D. in philosophy and this left Mrs Hopewell at a complete loss. You could say, 'My daughter is a nurse,' or 'My daughter is a school teacher,' or even, 'My daughter is a chemical engineer.' You could not say, 'My daughter is a philosopher.' That was something that had ended wth the Greeks and Romans. All day Joy sat on her neck in a deep chair, reading. Sometimes she went for walks but she didn't like dogs or cats or birds or flowers or nature or nice young men. She looked at nice young men as if she could smell their stupidity.

One day Mrs Hopewell had picked up one of the books the girl had just put down and opening it at random, she read, 'Science, on the other hand, has to assert its soberness and seriousness afresh and declare that it is concerned solely with what-is. Nothing—how can it be for science anything but a horror and a phantasm? If science is right, then one thing stands firm: science wishes to know nothing of nothing. Such is after all the strictly scientific approach to Nothing. We known it by wishing to know nothing of Nothing.' These words had been underlined with a blue pencil and they worked on Mrs Hopewell like some evil incantation in gibberish. She shut the book quickly and went out of the room as if she were having a chill.

This morning when the girl came in, Mrs Freeman was on Carramae. 'She thrown up four times after supper,' she said, 'and was up twice in the night after three o'clock. Yesterday she didn't do nothing but ramble in the bureau drawer. All she did. Stand up there and see what she could run up on.'

'She's got to eat,' Mrs Hopewell muttered, sipping her coffee, while she watched Joy's back at the stove. She was wondering what the child had said to the Bible salesman. She could not imagine what kind of a conversation she could possibly have had with him.

He was a tall gaunt hatless youth who had called yesterday to sell them a Bible. He had appeared at the door, carrying a large black suitcase that weighted him so heavily on one side that he had to brace himself against the door facing. He seemed on the point of collapse but he said in a cheerful voice, 'Good morning, Mrs Cedars!' and set the suitcase down on the mat. He was not a bad-looking young man though he had on a bright blue suit and yellow socks that were not pulled up far enough. He had prominent face bones and a streak of sticky-looking brown hair falling across his forehead.

'I'm Mrs Hopewell,' she said.

'Oh!' he said, pretending to look puzzled but with his eyes sparking, 'I saw it said "The Cedars," on the mailbox so I thought you was Mrs Cedars!' and he burst out in a pleasant laugh. He picked up the satchel and under cover of a pant, he fell forward into her hall. It was rather as if the suitcase had moved first, jerking him after it. 'Mrs Hopewell!' he said and grabbed her hand. 'I hope you are well!' and he laughed again and then all at once his face sobered completely. He paused and gave her a straight earnest look and said, 'Lady, I've come to speak of serious things.'

'Well, come in,' she muttered, none too pleased because her dinner was almost ready. He came into the parlor and sat down on the edge of a straight chair and put the suitcase between his feet and glanced around the room as if he were sizing her up by it. Her silver gleamed on the two sideboards; she decided he had never been in a room as elegant as this.

'Mrs Hopewell,' he began, using her name in a way that sounded almost intimate, 'I know you believe in Chrustian service.'

'Well yes,' she murmured.

'I know,' he said and paused, looking very wise with his head cocked on one side, 'that you're a good woman. Friends have told me.'

Mrs Hopewell never liked to be taken for a fool. 'What are you selling?' she asked.

'Bibles,' the young man said and his eye raced around the room before he added, 'I see you have no family Bible in your parlor, I see that is the one lack you got!'

Mrs Hopewell could not say, 'My daughter is an atheist and won't let me keep the Bible in the parlor.' She said, stiffening slightly, 'I keep my Bible by my bedside.' This was not the truth. It was in the attic somewhere.

'Lady,' he said, 'the word of God ought to be in the parlor.'

'Well, I think that's matter of taste,' she began. 'I think . . .'

'Lady,' he said, 'for a Chrustian, the word of God ought to be in every room in the house besides in his heart. I know you're a Chrustian because I can see it in every line of your face.'

She stood up and said, 'Well, young man, I don't want to buy a Bible and I smell my dinner burning.'

He didn't get up. He began to twist his hands and looking down at them, he said softly, 'Well lady, I'll tell you the truth—not many people want to buy one nowadays and besides, I know I'm real simple. I don't know how to say a thing but to say it. I'm just a country boy.' He glanced up into her unfriendly face. 'People like you don't like to fool with country people like me!'

'Why!' she cried, 'good country people are the salt of the earth! Besides, we all have different ways of doing, it takes all kinds to make the world go 'round. That's life!'

'You said a mouthful,' he said.

'Why, I think there aren't enough good country people in the world!' she said, stirred. 'I think that's what's wrong with it!'

His face had brightened. 'I didn't inraduce myself,' he said. 'I'm Manley Pointer from out in the country around Willohobie, not even from a place, just from near a place.'

'You wait a minute,' she said. 'I have to see about my dinner.' She went out to the kitchen and found Joy standing near the door where she had been listening.

'Get rid of the salt of the earth,' she said, 'and let's eat.'

Mrs Hopewell gave her a pained look and turned the heat down under the vegetables. '*I* can't be rude to anybody,' she murmured and went back into the parlor.

He had opened the suitcase and was sitting with a Bible on each knee.

'You might as well put those up,' she told him. 'I don't want one.'

'I appreciate your honesty,' he said. 'You don't see any more real honest people unless you go way out in the country.'

'I know,' she said, 'real genuine folks!' Through the crack in the door she heard a groan.

'I guess a lot of boys come telling you they're working their way through college,' he said, 'but I'm not going to tell you that. Somehow,' he said, 'I don't want to go to college. I want to devote my life to Chrustian service. See,' he said, lowering his voice, 'I got this heart condition. I may not live long. When you know it's something wrong with you and you may not live long, well then, lady . . .' He paused, with his mouth open, and stared at her.

He and Joy had the same condition! She knew that her eyes were filling with tears but she collected herself quickly and murmured, 'Won't you stay for dinner? We'd love to have you!' and was sorry the instant she heard herself say it.

'Yes mam,' he said in an abashed voice, 'I would sher love to do that!'

Joy had given him one look on being introduced to him and then throughout the meal had not glanced at him again. He had addressed several remarks to her, which she had pretended not to hear. Mrs Hopewell could not understand deliberate rudeness, although she lived with it, and she felt she had always to overflow with hospitality to make up for Joy's lack of courtesy. She urged him to talk about himself and he did. He said he was the seventh child of twelve and that his father had been crushed under a tree when he himself was eight year old. He had been crushed very badly, in fact, almost cut in two and was practically not recognizable. His mother had got along the best she could by hard working and she had always seen that her children went to Sunday School and that they read the Bible every evening. He was now nineteen year old and he had been selling Bibles for four months. In that time he had sold seventy-seven Bibles and had the promise of two more sales. He wanted to become a missionary because he thought that was the way you could do most for people. 'He who losest his life shall find it,' he said simply and he was so sincere, so genuine and earnest that Mrs Hopewell would not for the world have smiled. He prevented his peas from sliding onto the table by blocking them with a piece of bread which he later cleaned his plate with. She could see Joy observing sidewise how he handled his knife and fork and she saw too that every few minutes, the boy would dart a keen, appraising glance at the girl as if he were trying to attract her attention.

After dinner Joy cleared the dishes off the table and disappeared and Mrs Hopewell was left to talk with him. He told her again about his childhood and his father's accident and about various things that had happened to him. Every five minutes or so she would stifle a yawn. He sat for two hours until finally she told him she must go because she had an appointment in town. He packed his Bibles and thanked her and prepared to leave, but in the doorway he stopped and wrung her hand and said that not on any of his trips had he met a lady as nice as her and he asked if he could come again. She had said she would always be happy to see him.

Joy had been standing in the road, apparently looking at something in the distance, when he came down the steps toward her, bent to the side with his heavy valise. He stopped where she was standing and confronted her directly. Mrs Hopewell could not hear what he said but she trembled to think what Joy would say to him. She could see that after a minute Joy said something and that then the boy began to speak again, making an excited gesture with his free hand. After a minute Joy said something else at which the boy began to speak once more. Then to her amazement, Mrs Hopewell saw the two of them walk off together, toward the gate. Joy had walked all the way to the gate with him and Mrs Hopewell could not imagine what they had said to each other, and she had not yet dared to ask.

Mrs Freeman was insisting upon her attention. She had moved from the refrigerator to the heater so that Mrs Hopewell had to turn and face her in order to seem to be listening. 'Glynese gone out with Harvey Hill again last night,' she said. 'She had this sty.'

'Hill,' Mrs Hopewell said absently, 'is that the one who works in the garage?'

'Nome, he's the one that goes to chiropracter school,' Mrs Freeman said. 'She had this sty. Been had it two days. So she says when he brought her in the other night he says, "Lemme get rid of that sty for you," and she says, "How?" and he says, "You just lay yourself down acrost the seat of that car and I'll show you." So she done it and he popped her neck. Kept on a-popping it several times until she made him quit. This morning,' Mrs Freeman said, 'she ain't got no sty. She ain't got no traces of a sty.'

'I never heard of that before,' Mrs Hopewell said.

'He ast her to marry him before the Ordinary,' Mrs Freeman went on, 'and she told him she wasn't going to be married in no *office*.'

'Well, Glynese is a fine girl,' Mrs Hopewell said. 'Glynese and Carramae are both fine girls.'

'Carramae said when her and Lyman was married Lyman said it sure felt sacred to him. She said he said he wouldn't take five hundred dollars for being married by a preacher.'

'How much would he take?' the girl asked from the stove.

'He said he wouldn't take five hundred dollars,' Mrs Freeman repeated.

'Well we all have work to do,' Mrs Hopewell said.

'Lyman said it just felt more sacred to him,' Mrs Freeman said. 'The doctor wants Carramae to eat prunes. Says instead of medicine. Says them cramps is coming from pressure. You know where I think it is?'

'She'll be better in a few weeks,' Mrs Hopewell said.

'In the tube,' Mrs Freeman said. 'Else she wouldn't be as sick as she is.'

Hulga had cracked her two eggs into a saucer and was bringing them to the table along with a cup of coffee that she had filled too full. She sat down carefully and began to eat, meaning to keep Mrs Freeman there by questions if for any reason she showed an inclination to leave. She could perceive her mother's eye on her. The first roundabout question would be about the Bible salesman and she did not wish to bring it on. 'How did he pop her neck?' she asked.

Mrs Freeman went into a description of how he had popped her neck. She said he owned a '55 Mercury but that Glynese said she would rather marry a man with only a '36 Plymouth who would be married by a preacher. The girl asked what if he had a '32 Plymouth and Mrs Freeman said what Glynese had said was a '36 Plymouth.

Mrs Hopewell said there were not many girls with Glynese's common sense. She said what she admired in those girls was their common sense. She said that reminded her that they had had a nice visitor yesterday, a young man selling Bibles. 'Lord,' she said, 'he bored me to death but he was so sincere and genuine I couldn't be rude to him. He was just good country people, you know,' she said, —'just the salt of the earth.'

'I seen him walk up,' Mrs Freeman said, 'and then later—I seen him walk off,' and Hulga could feel the slight shift in her voice, the slight insinuation, that he had not walked off alone, had he? Her face remained expressionless but the color rose into her neck and she seemed to swallow it down with the next spoonful of egg. Mrs Freeman was looking at her as if they had a secret together.

'Well, it takes all kinds of people to make the world go 'round,' Mrs Hopewell said. 'It's very good we aren't all alike.'

'Some people are more alike than others,' Mrs Freeman said.

Hulga got up and stumped, with about twice the noise that was necessary, into her room and locked the door. She was to meet the Bible salesman at ten o'clock at the gate. She had thought about it half the night. She had started thinking of it as a great joke and then she had begun to see profound implications in it. She had lain in bed imagining dialogues for them that were insane on the surface but that reached below to depths that no Bible salesman would be aware of. Their conversation yesterday had been of this kind.

He had stopped in front of her and had simply stood there. His face was bony and sweaty and bright, with a little pointed nose in the center of it, and his look was different from what it had been at the dinner table. He was gazing at her with open curiosity, with fascination, like a child watching a new fantastic animal at the zoo, and he was breathing as if he had run a great distance to reach her. His gaze seemed somehow familiar but she could not think where she had been regarded with it before. For almost a minute he didn't say anything. Then on what seemed an insuck of breath, he whispered, 'You ever ate a chicken that was two days old?'

The girl looked at him stonily. He might have just put this question up for consideration at the meeting of a philosophical association. 'Yes,' she presently replied as if she had considered it from all angles.

'It must have been mighty small!' he said triumphantly and shook all over with little nervous giggles, getting very red in the face, and subsiding finally into his gaze of complete admiration, while the girl's expression remained exactly the same.

'How old are you?' he asked softly.

She waited some time before she answered. Then in a flat voice she said, 'Seventeen.'

His smiles came in succession like waves breaking on the surface of a little lake. 'I see you got a wooden leg,' he said. 'I think you're real brave. I think you're real sweet.'

The girl stood blank and solid and silent.

'Walk to the gate with me,' he said. 'You're a brave sweet little thing and I liked you the minute I seen you walk in the door.'

Hulga began to move forward.

'What's your name?' he asked, smiling down on the top of her head.

'Hulga,' she said.

'Hulga,' he murmured, 'Hulga. Hulga. I never heard of anybody name Hulga before. You're shy, aren't you, Hulga?' he asked.

She nodded, watching his large red hand on the handle of the giant valise.

'I like girls that wear glasses,' he said. 'I think a lot. I'm not like these people that a serious thought don't ever enter their heads. It's because I may die.'

'I may die too,' she said suddenly and looked up at him. His eyes were very small and brown, glittering feverishly.

'Listen,' he said, 'don't you think some people was meant to meet on account of what all they got in common and all? Like they both think serious thoughts and all?' He shifted the valise to his other hand so that the hand nearest her was free. He caught hold of her elbow and shook it a little. 'I don't work on Saturday,' he said. 'I like to walk in the woods and see what Mother Nature is wearing. O'er the hills and far away. Picnics and things. Couldn't we go on a picnic tomorrow? Say yes, Hulga,' he said and gave her a dying look as if he felt his insides about to drop out of him. He had even seemed to sway slightly toward her.

During the night she had imagined that she seduced him. She imagined that the two of them walked on the place until they came to the storage barn beyond the two back fields and there, she imagined, that things came to such a pass that she very easily seduced him and that then of course, she had to reckon with his remorse. True genius can get an idea across even to an inferior mind. She imagined that she took his remorse in hand and changed it into a deeper understanding of life. She took all his shame away and turned it into something useful.

She set off for the gate at exactly ten o'clock, escaping without drawing Mrs Hopewell's attention. She didn't take anything to eat, forgetting that food is usually taken on a picnic. She wore a pair of slacks and a dirty white shirt, and as an afterthought, she had put some Vapex on the collar of it since she did not own any perfume. When she reached the gate no one was there.

She looked up and down the empty highway and had the furious feeling that she had been tricked, that he had only meant to make her walk to the gate after the idea of him. Then suddenly he stood up, very tall, from behind a bush on the opposite embankment. Smiling, he lifted his hat which was new and wide-brimmed. He had not worn it yesterday and she wondered if he had bought it for the occasion. It was toast-colored with a red and white band around it and was slightly too large for him. He stepped from behind the bush still carrying the black valise. He had on the same suit and the same yellow socks sucked down in his shoes from walking. He crossed the highway and said, 'I knew you'd come!'

The girl wondered acidly how he had known this. She pointed to the valise and asked, 'Why did you bring your Bibles?'

He took her elbow, smiling down on her as if he could not stop. 'You can never tell when you'll need the word of God, Hulga,' he said. She had a moment in which she doubted that this was actually happening and then they began to climb the embankment. They went down into the pasture toward the woods. The boy walked lightly by her side, bouncing on his toes. The valise did not seem to be heavy today; he even swung it. They crossed half the pasture without saying anything and then, putting his hand easily on the small of her back, he asked softly, 'Where does your wooden leg join on?'

She turned an ugly red and glared at him and for an instant the boy looked abashed. 'I didn't mean you no harm,' he said. 'I only meant you're so brave and all. I guess God takes care of you.'

'No,' she said, looking forward and walking fast, 'I don't even believe in God.'

At this he stopped and whistled. 'No!' he exclaimed as if he were too astonished to say anything else.

She walked on and in a second he was bouncing at her side, fanning with his hat. 'That's very unusual for a girl,' he remarked, watching her out of the corner of his eye. When they reached the edge of the wood, he put his hand on her back again and drew her against him without a word and kissed her heavily.

The kiss, which had more pressure than feeling behind it, produced that extra surge of adrenalin in the girl that enables one to carry a packed trunk out of a burning house, but in her, the power went at once to the brain. Even before he released her, her mind, clear and detached and ironic anyway, was regarding him from a great distance, with amusement but with pity. She had never been kissed before and she was pleased to discover that it was an unexceptional experience and all a matter of the mind's control. Some people might enjoy drain water if they were told it was vodka. When the boy, looking expectant but uncertain, pushed her gently away, she turned and walked on, saying nothing as if such business, for her, were common enough.

He came along panting at her side, trying to help her when he saw a root that she might trip over. He caught and held back the long swaying blades of thorn vine until she had passed beyond them. She led the way and he came breathing heavily behind her. Then they came out on a sunlit hillside, sloping softly into another one a little smaller. Beyond, they could see the rusted top of the old barn where the extra hay was stored.

The hill was sprinkled with small pink weeds. 'Then you ain't saved?' he asked suddenly, stopping.

The girl smiled. It was the first time she had smiled at him at all. 'In my economy,' she said, 'I'm saved and you are damned but I told you I didn't believe in God.'

Nothing seemed to destroy the boy's look of admiration. He gazed at her now as if the fantastic animal at the zoo had put its paw through the bars and given him a loving poke. She thought he looked as if he wanted to kiss her again and she walked on before he had the chance.

'Ain't there somewheres we can sit down sometime?' he murmured, his voice softening toward the end of the sentence.

'In that barn,' she said.

They made for it rapidly as if it might slide away like a train. It was a large two-story barn, cool and dark inside. The boy pointed up the ladder that led into the loft and said, 'It's too bad we can't go up there.'

'Why can't we?' she asked.

'Yer leg,' he said reverently.

The girl gave him a contemptuous look and putting both hands on the ladder, she climbed it while he stood below, apparently awestruck. She pulled herself expertly through the opening and then looked down at him and said, 'Well, come on if you're coming,' and he began to climb the ladder, awkwardly bringing the suitcase with him.

'We won't need the Bible,' she observed.

'You never can tell,' he said, panting. After he had got into the loft, he was a few seconds catching his breath. She had sat down in a pile of straw. A wide sheath of sunlight, filled with dust particles, slanted over her. She lay back against a bale, her face turned away, looking out the front opening of the barn where hay was thrown from a wagon into the loft. The two pink-speckled hillsides lay back against a dark ridge of woods. The sky was cloudless and cold blue. The boy dropped down by her side and put one arm under her and the other over her and began methodically kissing her face, making little noises like a fish. He did not remove his hat but it was pushed far enough back not to interfere. When her glasses got in his way, he took them off of her and slipped them into his pocket.

The girl at first did not return any of the kisses but presently she began to and after she had put several on his cheek, she reached his lips and remained there, kissing him again and again as if she were trying to draw all the breath out of him. His breath was clear and sweet like a child's and the kisses were sticky like a child's. He mumbled about loving her and about knowing when he first seen her that he loved her, but the mumbling was like the sleepy fretting of a child being put to sleep by his mother. Her mind, throughout this, never stopped or lost itself for a second to her feelings. 'You ain't said you loved me none,' he whispered finally, pulling back from her. 'You got to say that.'

She looked away from him off into the hollow sky and then down at a black ridge and then down farther into what appeared to be two green swelling lakes. She didn't realize he had taken her glasses but this landscape could not seem exceptional to her for she seldom paid any close attention to her surroundings.

'You got to say it,' he repeated. 'You got to say you love me.'

She was always careful how she committed herself. 'In a sense,' she began, 'if you use the word loosely, you might say that. But it's not a word I use. I don't have illusions. I'm one of those people who see *through* to nothing.'

The boy was frowning. 'You got to say it. I said it and you got to say it,' he said.

The girl looked at him almost tenderly. 'You poor baby,' she murmured. 'It's just as well you don't understand,' and she pulled him by the neck, face-down, against her. 'We are all damned,' she said, 'but some of us have taken off our blindfolds and see that there's nothing to see. It's a kind of salvation.'

The boy's astonished eyes looked blankly through the ends of her hair. 'Okay,' he almost whined, 'but do you love me or don'tcher?'

'Yes,' she said and added, 'in a sense. But I must tell you something. There mustn't be anything dishonest between us.' She lifted his head and looked him in the eye. 'I am thirty years old,' she said. 'I have a number of degrees.'

The boy's look was irritated but dogged. 'I don't care,' he said. 'I don't care a thing about what all you done. I just want to know if you love me or don'tcher?' and he caught her to him and wildly planted her face with kisses until she said, 'Yes, yes.'

'Okay then,' he said, letting her go. 'Prove it.'

She smiled, looking dreamily out on the shifty landscape. She had seduced him without even making up her mind to try. 'How?' she asked, feeling that he should be delayed a little.

He leaned over and put his lips to her ear. 'Show me where your wooden leg joins on,' he whispered.

The girl uttered a sharp little cry and her face instantly drained of color. The obscenity of the suggestion was not what shocked her. As a child she had sometimes been subject to feelings of shame but education had removed the last traces of that as a good surgeon scrapes for cancer; she would no more have felt it over what he was asking than she would have believed in his Bible. But she was as sensitive about the artificial leg as a peacock about his tail. No one ever touched it but her. She took care of it as someone else would his soul, in private and almost with her own eyes turned away. 'No,' she said.

'I known it,' he muttered, sitting up. 'You're just playing me for a sucker.'

'Oh no no!' she cried. 'It joins on at the knee. Only at the knee. Why do you want to see it?'

The boy gave her a long penetrating look. 'Because,' he said, 'it's what makes you different. You ain't like anybody else.'

She sat staring at him. There was nothing about her face or her round freezing-blue eyes to indicate that this had moved her; but she felt as if her heart had stopped and left her mind to pump her blood. She decided that for the first time in her life she was face to face with real innocence. This boy, with an instinct that came from beyond wisdom, had touched the truth about her. When after a minute, she said in a hoarse high voice, 'All right,' it was like surrendering to him completely. It was like losing her own life and finding it again, miraculously, in his.

Very gently he began to roll the slack leg up. The artificial limb, in a white sock and brown flat shoe, was bound in a heavy material like canvas and ended in an ugly jointure where it was attached to the stump. The boy's face and his voice were entirely reverent as he uncovered it and said, 'Now show me how to take it off and on.'

She took it off for him and put it back on again and then he took it off himself, handling it as tenderly as if it were a real one. 'See!' he said with a delighted child's face. 'Now I can do it myself!'

'Put it back on,' she said. She was thinking that she would run away with him and that every night he would take the leg off and every morning put it back on again. 'Put it back on,' she said.

'Not yet,' he murmured, setting it on its foot out of her reach. 'Leave it off for a while. You got me instead.'

She gave a little cry of alarm but he pushed her down and began to kiss her again. Without the leg she felt entirely dependent on him. Her brain seemed to have stopped thinking altogether and to be about some other function that it was not very good at. Different expressions raced back and forth over her face. Every now and then the boy, his eyes like two steel spikes, would glance behind him where the leg stood. Finally she pushed him off and said, 'Put it back on me now.'

'Wait,' he said. He leaned the other way and pulled the valise toward him and opened it. It had a pale blue spotted lining and there were only two Bibles in it. He took one of these out and opened the cover of it. It was hollow and contained a pocket flask of whiskey, a pack of cards, and a small blue box with printing on it. He laid these out in front of her one at a time in an evenly-spaced row, like one presenting offerings at the shrine of a goddess. He put the blue box in her hand. THIS PRODUCT TO BE USED ONLY FOR THE PREVENTION OF DISEASE, she read, and dropped it. The boy was unscrewing the top of the flask. He stopped and pointed, with a smile, to the deck of cards. It was not an ordinary deck but one with an obscene picture on the back of each card. 'Take a swig,' he said, offering her the bottle first. He held it in front of her, but like one mesmerized, she did not move.

Her voice when she spoke had an almost pleading sound. 'Aren't you,' she murmured, 'aren't you just good country people?'

The boy cocked his head. He looked as if he were just beginning to understand that she might be trying to insult him. 'Yeah,' he said, curling his lip slightly, 'but it ain't held me back none. I'm as good as you any day in the week.'

'Give me my leg,' she said.

He pushed it farther away with his foot. 'Come on now, let's begin to have us a good time,' he said coaxingly. 'We ain't got to know one another good yet.'

'Give me my leg!' she screamed and tried to lunge for it but he pushed her down easily.

'What's the matter with you all of a sudden?' he asked, frowning as he screwed the top on the flask and put it quickly back inside the Bible. 'You just a while ago said you didn't believe in nothing. I thought you was some girl!'

Her face was almost purple. 'You're a Christian!' she hissed. 'You're a fine Christian! You're just like them all—say one thing and do another. You're a perfect Christian, you're . . .'

The boy's mouth was set angrily. 'I hope you don't think,' he said in a lofty indignant tone, 'that I believe in that crap! I may sell Bibles but I know which end is up and I wasn't born yesterday and I know where I'm going!'

'Give me my leg!' she screeched. He jumped up so quickly that she barely saw him sweep the cards and the blue box back into the Bible and throw the Bible into the valise. She saw him grab the leg and then she saw it for an instant slanted forlornly across the inside of the suitcase with a Bible at either side of its opposite ends. He slammed the lid shut and snatched up the valise and swung it down the hole and then stepped through himself.

When all of him had passed but his head, he turned and regarded her with a look that no longer had any admiration in it. 'I've gotten a lot of interesting things,' he said. 'One time I got a woman's glass eye this way. And you needn't to think you'll catch me because Pointer ain't really my name. I use a different name at every house I call at and don't stay nowhere long. And I'll tell you another thing, Hulga,' he said, using the name as if he didn't think much of it, 'you ain't so smart. I been believing in nothing ever since I was born!' and then the toast-colored hat disappeared down the hole and the girl was left, sitting on the straw in the dusty sunlight. When she turned her churning face toward the opening, she saw his blue figure struggling successfully over the green speckled lake.

Mrs Hopewell and Mrs Freeman, who were in the back pasture, digging up onions, saw him emerge a little later from the woods and head across the meadow toward the highway. 'Why, that looks like that nice dull young man that tried to sell me a Bible yesterday,' Mrs Hopewell said, squinting. 'He must have been selling them to the Negroes back in there. He was so simple,' she said, 'but I guess the world would be better off if we were all that simple.'

Mrs Freeman's gaze drove forward and just touched him before he disappeared under the hill. Then she returned her attention to the evil-smelling onion shoot she was lifting from the ground. 'Some can't be that simple,' she said. 'I know I never could.'

SYLVIA TOWNSEND WARNER

Heathy Landscape with Dormouse

❦

'Well, Leo, dear—here we are, all settled and comfortable!' Mrs Leslie, sitting on the ground, removed a couple of burrs from her stocking and looked round on a flattish expanse of heath. 'What heaven! Not a soul in sight.' As though reinforcing this statement, an owl hooted from a clump of alders.

People born into the tradition of English country life are accustomed to eccentric owls. Mrs Leslie and her daughter Belinda accepted the owl with vaguely acknowledging smiles. Her son-in-law, Leo Cooper, a Londoner whose contacts with nature had been made at the very expensive pleasure resorts patronized by his very rich parents, found midday hoots disconcerting, and almost said so. But did not, as he was just then in a temper and wholly engaged in not showing it.

He was in a temper for several reasons, all eminently adequate. For one thing, he had had a most unsatisfactory night with Belinda; for another, impelled by the nervous appetite of frustration he had eaten a traditional country breakfast and it was disagreeing with him; for yet another, he had been haled out on yet another of his mother-in-law's picnics; finally, there was the picnic basket. The picnic basket was a family piece, dating, as Mrs Leslie said on its every appearance, from an age of footmen. It was the size of a cabin trunk, built for eternity out of red wicker, equipped with massy cutlery and crockery; time had sharpened its red fangs, and however Leo took hold of it, they lacerated him. Also it caused him embarrassment to be seen carrying this rattling, creaking monstrosity, and today he had carried it farther than usual. The car was left where the track crossed a cattle bridge, and from there Mrs Leslie staggered unerringly over a featureless stretch of rough ground to the exact place where they always picnicked because it was there that Belinda as a little girl had found a dormouse.

'Yes, it was just here—by these particular whin bushes. Do you remember, darling? You were five.'

'I thought I was six.'

'No, five. Because Uncle Henry was with us that day, and next year he had that gun accident—God rest his soul!'

Having crossed herself with a sigh, and allowed time for the sigh's implications to sink in, Mrs Leslie pulled the picnic basket towards her and began fidgeting at the straps. 'Let me!' exclaimed Leo, unable to endure the intensified creakings, and at the same moment Belinda said, 'I will.'

She did—with the same negligent dexterity she showed in every activity but the act of love. Out came the plates and the cutlery and the mugs and the home-made ginger beer and the paste sandwiches and the lettuce sandwiches and the hard-boiled eggs; out came the cakes they had specially stopped to buy at Unwin the grocer's, because his old aunt made them and it was so nice and right of him to let her feel useful still. Out, too, a few minutes later, came the ants and the flies and those large predatory bluebottles that materialize from solitary places like depraved desert fathers.

'Brutes! Go away! How Delia used to swear at bluebottles! Poor Delia, I miss her to this day.'

'Leo will think we have a great many dead relations,' said Belinda. She glanced at him—a friendlier glance; as if she had temporarily forgotten who he was, thought Leo, and was ready to give him the kindness one extends to a stranger.

'We've got a whole new live one now,' said her mother. 'We've got Leo.'

The glance hardened to a stare. Replaced in his role of husband, he appealed no longer. 'There's that owl again,' he said. 'Is it usual for owls to hoot by day? Isn't it supposed to be a bad omen?'

'Frightfully.' Belinda's voice was so totally expressionless that it scalded him like an insult. He said with studied indifference, 'Never mind! I expect it's too late to do anything about it.'

She continued to stare at him and he stared back into her unreceiving eyes. Clear and round and wide-set, Belinda's eyes had the fatalistic melancholy of the eyes of hunting cats. Seeing her as a caged puma, silent, withdrawn in a stately sulk, turning her back on the public and on the bars of her cage, he had fallen in love with her at first sight. 'Belinda Leslie . . . Better look while you may; it's your only chance. She's in London for a week, being a bridesmaid, and then she'll go back to live with her widowed Mamma in a mouldering grange, and never get out again. She's one of those sacrificial daughters. . . . I believe the North of England's full of them.' A month later, she had snatched at his offer of marriage as though it were a still warm partridge; yes, exactly as though it were a still warm partridge—snatching the meat, ignoring the hand. So wild for liberty, he thought; later, she will love. But halfway through their honeymoon she insisted on pining for home, on pining for her mother even, so they travelled back to Snewdon and were welcomed as both her dear children by Mrs Leslie. Before I get away, he thought, and later on revised this to: if ever I get away, she will have sewn labels of 'Leo Leslie' on all my underclothes. Yet he felt a sneaking liking for her; she was always polite to him, and he was young.

Since then, three appalling weeks had passed. The weather was flawless; gooseberries appeared at every meal. There was no male society except for the deaf-and-dumb gardener and two rams who pastured on the former tennis court. They went nowhere except for picnics in the neighbourhood. Every picnicking place had associations. If he tried to escape the associations by suggestions of going farther afield in his swifter car, this merely provoked other picnics and more of the rattles and joltings of the family conveyance. And all the time things were as bad as ever between him and Belinda, and the only alleviation in their relationship was that he was now beginning to feel bored by it.

'I suppose that owl is an old admirer of yours. When does he produce the small guitar? After dark?' (For a little time, because of her melancholy, merciless eyes, he had called her Pussy.)

'I loathe Lear.'

'Darling!' To soften the rebuke in her voice, Mrs Leslie offered her daughter a hard-boiled egg, which was rejected. Turning to Leo, she said, 'Belinda and I do a lot of bird watching. We get such interesting migrants here—quite unexpected ones, sometimes.'

Belinda gave a brief, wounding laugh.

'Blown off their course, I suppose,' said Leo. 'I see I must learn about birds.'

'Oh, you should! It makes such a difference. There have been times when they were really my only support. Of course, I have always loved them. Quite the first book I remember is *The History of the Robins*. Flapsy, Pecksy—what were the others called? By Mrs Trimmer. Did you ever read it, Belinda?'

'No.'

Leo took out a slim note-book and wrote in it with a slender pencil. 'I'll make a note of the title. At last I may be able to give Belinda a book she hasn't read already.'

'How delicious lettuce sandwiches are!' Mrs Leslie said. 'So much the most comfortable way of managing lettuces, don't you think, Leo?'

'Infinitely. Do you know that lettuce is a mild sedative?'

'Is it? I never knew that. Belinda, do have another lettuce sandwich.'

'No, thank you.'

'But only very mild,' continued Leo.

Belinda sprang to her feet, took a cigarette from her bag, lit it, and walked away.

'She never really cares for Unwin's cakes,' explained her mother. 'But do try one. You might.'

'Thank you. I'd love one.'

Apparently he was doomed to failure in his loves, for the cake tasted of sweat and cough linctus. He laid it down where presently he would be able to trample on it, and stared after Belinda. Mrs Leslie noticed his stare.

'Belinda walks exactly like her father.'

'She walks beautifully.'

'Yes, doesn't she? I wonder where she's going.'

'She seems to be making for the car.'

'Perhaps she has left something in it. Or perhaps she wants to move it into the shade. She has always been so fond of it. She learned to drive it when she was twelve. Of course, yours is much newer. Is it an Austin, too?'

'A Bristol.'

'How nice!'

Belinda was certainly walking towards the car. Mrs Leslie's ringed hand, clasping a half eggshell, began to crumple it. Hearing her gasp, he realized that she had been holding her breath. Belinda walked on. They watched her cross the cattle bridge and get into the car. They saw her start the car, turn it and drive away.

'So now they know.' Belinda spoke in the tone of one who has achieved some stern moral purpose. 'Or they soon will.'

Belinda was one of those fortunate persons who fly into a rage as though into a refrigerator. Walking across the heath in the glaring post-meridian sun she had felt a film of ice encasing her, armouring her from head to foot in sleekness and invulnerability. She felt, too, the smile on her lips becoming increasingly rigid and corpselike. When she got into the car, though it was hot as an oven she seemed to be adjusting the hands of a marble effigy on the wheel. The car's smell, so familiar, so much part of her life, waylaid her with its ordinary sensuality, besought her to have a good cry. But righteousness sustained her. She turned the car and drove away, taking a studied pleasure in steering so skilfully among the ruts and ridges of the cart track. The track ran out into a lane, the car began to travel smoothly, she increased speed. The whole afternoon was before her; she could go where she pleased. The whole afternoon was also before Leo and her mother, and a wide range of reflections; for there on the heath, with not a soul in sight, they would have to remain till she drove back to collect them. When would that be? Not till she had forgiven them. And that would not be until she had forgotten them, forgotten their taunts and gibes and the silly smirks they had exchanged, making a party against her, looping their airy conversation over her silence—as though she were a child sulking in a corner. Well, they could practise airy conversation, sitting there on the heath with the picnic basket. Presently the conversation would falter, they would be forced to speculate, to admit, to learn their lesson. Slow scholars, they would be allowed plenty of time for the lesson to sink in.

With the whole afternoon before her, and in a landscape as familiar to her as the shrubberies of her birthplace, she drove with elegance through a network of lanes and lesser lanes, turning aside to skirt round villages or houses where someone in a gateway might recognize her. Once, she got out of the car and watched through a gap in a laurel hedge a charitable fête that was being held on the lawn beyond. There were the stalls, with their calico petticoats flapping; there were the little tables, and the en-listed schoolchildren bringing tea on trays, there were the ladies of the locality and their daughters. How dowdy they looked, and how cheerful! Six months ago, she had been quite as dowdy and quite often cheerful too; but now the secret was lost, never again would she wear a small floral pattern with a light heart. Dowdy, cheerful, dutiful and self-satisfied— that was the lot appointed for Belinda Leslie. And if she had had a living father, or a brother, a decent allowance, a taste for religion or blood sports, or had been sent to a secretarial college—any alternative to Mother's swaddle of affection, fidget and egotism—she might have accepted the lot appointed and been at this moment at one of the little tables, agreeing that raspberries were really nicer than strawberries: a reflection made by all when the strawberry season is over. But to get away from Mother she had married Leo, who was so much in love with her and whom she immediately didn't love; and then to get away from Leo, and with no-where else to run to, she had run home. Somehow it had not occurred to her that Leo would come too. For the first few days, he had stalked about being intolerably uncivil to his hostess. Then there had been that ghastly bedroom quarrel, the worst they had ever had. The next day, Mother, smelling the blood of his misery, had settled on him, assiduously sucking, assiduously soothing, showing him old snapshots and making him one of the family. And Leo, who had started up in her life as a sort of mother-slaying St George, lay down like a spaniel to be tickled, and like a spaniel snarled at her from under Mother's skirts. Well, the one-of-the-family process could be continued on the heath. There would be touchingly comic stories about little Belinda, a sweet child really, but perhaps a trifle spoilt, needing a firmer hand. . . . Mrs Whitadder and old Miss Groves at the table nearest the laurel hedge were startled to hear a car they hadn't known was there being so impetuously driven away.

In a landscape as familiar to her as the shrubberies of her birthplace

Belinda found she had managed to mislay the turning beyond Upton All
Saints and was temporarily lost. This, while it lasted, was quieting and
dreamlike. The high road banks, bulky with late-summer growth, with
scabious and toadflax and hemp agrimony, closed her in. Silvery, waning,
plumed grasses brushed against the car, swish-swish; smells of unseen
wheat, of turnips and once of a fox, puffed in at the open window. She
passed a pair of cottages, brick-built and of surpassing ugliness, called, as
one would expect, 'Rose' and 'Coronation'. A baker's van stood in front
of them, and the baker and Mrs Coronation were conversing across the
garden fence. It would be childish in the extreme to imagine herself into
that woman's shoes, with Mr Leo Coronation coming placidly home from
a day's work to eat a substantial meat tea in his shirtsleeves and then
go off to spend the evening at the pub—unless he did a little twilight
gardening. She managed not to imagine this, and drove on and soon after
approached the cottages, the baker's van and the conversation once more,
having driven in a circle. Quieting and dreamlike though this might be,
if she persevered in it the conversation would begin to feel itself being
hurried to a close. So this time she turned to the left, and, coming to a
road post, consulted it. Billerby & Frogwick. She was much farther east
than she supposed. Yet she could have known it, for in the very faint haze
spreading over the eastern sky one could read the sea. It was still a
beautiful, endless summer afternoon; the shadows of the whin bushes and
the clump of alders could be left to lengthen for a long time yet while
Mother and Leo got to know each other better and better. Having forgotten
them sufficiently to have to remember them she was nearer forgiving
them. They had looked so very silly, sitting on the hot heath and toying
with Unwin's uneatable cakes. By now they would be looking even sillier.
The longer she left them there, the better she would be to endure seeing
them again. Billerby & Frogwick. It was beyond Billerby that a track off
the road to Frogwick ran past a decoy wood and between fields of barley
and of rye to the barn that stood on the sea wall and had once been a
church. Years ago, exploring on her bicycle, she had found the barn, and
talked with the old man who was sheltering there from the rain; and even
then had known better than to report it. 'Time of the Danes,' he had said,
looking cautiously out across the saltings, as if the Danes might be coming
round the corner in their long-beaked ships. 'Or thereabouts.' But how
do you know it was a church?' 'Course it were a church. What prove it—
that there door ain't never been shut.' Not wanting to endanger her find,
she never went back to it.

Sure enough, the door was open. There were two farm workers in the
barn, tinkering at a reaper. She heard one say to the other, 'Tighten her
up a bit, and that will be all.' So she went and sat on the wall's farther

side, listening for the last clink of their spanners. They came out not long after, had a look at the car, called it a rum old Methusalem, and went away on motor bicycles. But she continued to sit on the slope of the wall, listening to the grasshoppers and watching the slow, ballet-postured mating of two blue butterflies. If you brush them apart, they die; yet from their fixed, quivering pattern they seem to be in anguish. Probably they don't feel much either way. It was then that she became aware of what for a stupid moment she thought to be a cuckoo, a disembodied, airy tolling of two notes, somewhere out to sea. But it was a bell buoy, rocking and ringing. It seemed as though a heart were beating—a serene, impersonal heart that rocked on a tide of salt water.

The breeze dropped, the music was silenced; but the breeze would resume, the heart begin to beat again. She sat among the grasshoppers, listening, so still that a grasshopper lit on her hand. All along the wall the yellow bedstraw was in bloom, its scent and colour stretching away on either side like a tidemark of the warm, cultivatable earth. If the silly Leslies had held on to their farmlands, it would be fun, uneconomic but fun, to take in another stretch of saltings: to embank and drain it, to sluice the salt out of it, to watch the inland weeds smothering glasswort and sea lavender, and bees adventuring, warm and furry, where little crabs had sidled along the creeks; then to plough, to sow, to reap the first, terrific harvest. But no one did that sort of thing nowadays. The sea continued to retreat, and the farmers to squat behind the wall and complain of the cost of its upkeep. There was that cuckoo again—no, that bell buoy. She addressed herself in a solemn voice: 'If you sit here much longer, you will fall asleep.' Exerting herself to sit erect, she heeled over and fell asleep.

Once, she stirred towards consciousness, and thought the Danes had arrived. Opening one eye, she caught sight of her yellow silk trousers, reasoned that the Danes could not possibly arrive when she was dressed like this and was asleep again. When next she woke, a different arrival had taken place. The sea mist had come inland, was walking in swathes over the saltings, had silenced the grasshoppers, extinguished the sun. Her blissful, Leo-less sleep was over. She was back in real life again, compelled to look at her wristwatch in order to see how long she had possessed her anonymity. It was past eight. Good God!—Mother and Leo on the heath!

She snatched up her bag and ran. Because she was in a hurry, the car wouldn't start. When it did, it baulked and hesitated. Just before the decoy, it stopped dead. It had run out of petrol.

It was useless to repine; she must leave the car on the marsh, as earlier in the day she had left Mother and Leo on the heath. Obviously, it was the kind of day when one leaves things. Billerby could not be more—at any rate, not much more—than four miles away; though it was a small village, it must be able to produce a gallon of petrol and a man to drive her out to the decoy. If not, she could ring up a garage. Walking briskly, she could reach Billerby in not much over an hour—once on the road, she might even get a lift. By half past nine at the latest . . . She stopped; a stone had got into her shoe, a thought had darted into her head. By half past nine those two would have finished their dinner, would be drinking coffee and wondering when foolish Belinda would come home, bringing her tail behind her. For of course, they had not remained on the heath. Mother would have sent Leo to look for a man. 'I think we ought to look for a man' was how she would have expressed it. And Leo, urban ignoramus though he was, would eventually have found one. Yes, they were all right. There was no call to waste pity on them. It was she who was cold and footsore and hungry and miles from home. Miles from home, and at least two miles from Billerby, and faint with hunger! Now that she had begun to think how hungry she was, she could think of nothing else. Two paste sandwiches, half a lettuce sandwich—Oh, why had she rejected that hard-boiled egg? Beasts! Gibing, guzzling beasts! By the time she walked into Billerby, Belinda was hating her husband and her mother as vehemently as when she walked away, leaving them on the heath.

But not with such righteous calm and elation. Her first sight of Billerby showed her that it would have been better to go to Frogwick. There was no inn. There was no filling station. There was a post office, but it was duly closed in accordance with government regulations. There were two small shops. One of them was vacant and for sale, the other appeared to sell only baby clothes. Nowhere held out the smallest promise of being able to produce a gallon of petrol. As for a man who would drive her, there was no man of any sort. At one moment there had been three. But they had mounted bicycles and ridden away, as though Billerby held no future for them. There was no sign of life in the one street and the two side streets of Billerby. Her footsteps disturbed various shut-up dogs, and in one house an aged person was coughing. That was the only house with a lighted window. Either the people of Billerby went to bed very early, or they all had television sets. There were, however, only a few aerials—as far as she could tell. The dusk and the gathering mist made it difficult to be sure.

However, there was the public call box, and when she shut herself into it the light went on like a public illumination. The light showed her that her purse held four pennies, one halfpenny and a five-pound note. Excellent! The pennies would pay the local call to some near-by garage; the note would look after the rest. Unfortunately, the call box had no Trades Directory book. She went and banged on the post office door. Nothing resulted except more barks and the wailing of an infant. She went back to the call box, and began to read through the ordinary directory, beginning with an Abacus Laundry. The public illumination did not seem so brilliant now, the print was small. She read from Abacus to Alsop, Mrs Yolande, and found no garage. Perseverance had never been Belinda's forte. Moreover, honour was satisfied, and when reduced by famine it is not disgraceful to yield. She took off the receiver. She dialled O. She gave the Snewdon number.

'Put ninepence in the box, please.'

'I can't. I've only got fourpence; the rest must be collect.'

'We don't usually . . .'

'I'm not usual. I'm desperate.'

The operator laughed and put her through.

'This is Snewdon Beeleigh two two-seven.'

'Mother.'

'This is Snewdon Beeleigh two two-seven.'

'Mother.'

'This is Snewdon Beeleigh two two-seven. Can't you hear me?'

'Mother!'

'This is Snewdon . . .'

'Press button A, caller,' said the operator.

Belinda pressed button A and said icily, 'Mother?'

'Belinda! Oh, thank heavens! Where are you, what happened to you? I've been in such a state—we both have. Leo! Leo! She's found!' The shriek seemed to be in the very call box.

'When did you get home?'

'When did we get home? I haven't the slightest idea. I was far too worried to notice when we got home. What I've been through! We waited and waited. At last I said to Leo, "I'll stay here in case she comes back, and you go and find a man to drive us." What I felt—every minute like an hour—and the flies! . . . By the way, I saw a nightjar.'

'A nightjar? Are you sure it wasn't a hawk?'

'My dear child, I wasn't so frantic about you that I didn't know the difference between a hawk and a nightjar. Well, then I began to think Leo was swallowed up, too. I'd told him exactly how to get to Gamble's farm, but for all that, he went wrong and wandered all over the place, till at last he saw a spire, and it turned out to be my dear old Archdeacon Brownlow, and he came at once and rescued us. And ever since then, we've been ringing up the police, and the hospital, and the AA and Leo has been driving everywhere we could think of to look for you, he's only just come in. Yes, Leo, she's perfectly all right, I'm talking to her. And I don't wish to judge you, Belinda, till I've heard what you've got to say for yourself, but this I must say—it was the most horrible picnic of my life and I never want to live through another. Now I suppose I shall have to ring up the police and say it was all a false alarm. How I hate grovelling to officials!'

'While you're about it, you might ring up the AA too—about the car.'

'The car? . . . Oh, my God!'

'And tell them to fetch it away tomorrow.'

'Fetch it? What's happened to it?'

'I ran out of petrol.'

'Well, why can't you have some put in, and bring it back? I can't do without it, I shall need it tomorrow, for I must take the Mothers' Union banner to Woffam to be invisibly darned and I want to take some goose-berries over to the Archdeacon, who was so very kind—and tactful. Not a single question, not one word of surprise. Just driving us home in such a soothing, understanding way. Leo thought him—'

Belinda slammed down the receiver. A minute later, the operator rang up Snewdon Beeleigh two two-seven to say there would be a collect charge of one and twopence on the call from Billerby. This time the telephone was answered by Leo.

The call-box door was not constructed to slam. Belinda closed it. The public illumination went out, and there was Billerby, unchanged. She had never lost her temper with so little satisfaction. She could not even enjoy her usual sensation of turning cold, for she was cold already. 'Well, at any rate, I've done my duty by them,' she said to herself. 'They know I'm alive and that the car isn't a wreck. And I've got five pounds and a halfpenny. With five pounds and a halfpenny I can at least buy one night to myself.'

But where was it to be bought, that idyllic night in a lumpy rural bed? For now it was ten o'clock, an hour at which people become disinclined to make up beds for strangers who arrive on foot and without luggage. Farther down the street, a light went on in an upper window—some carefree person going to bed as usual. She knocked on the door. The lighted window opened; an old man looked out.

'Who's there?'

'My car's broken down. Where can I find a bed for the night?'

'I don't know about that. It's a bit late to come asking for beds.' He looked up and down the street. 'Where's your car? I don't see no car.'

'On Frogwick Level. By the decoy.'

'That's a pity. If it had broken down nearer, you could have slept in it. Won't do it no good, either, standing out all night in the mermaid. These mermaids, they come from the sea, you see, so they're salt. That'll rust a car in no time.'

Like Mother, he thought of the car's welfare first. But he called the sea mist a mermaid: there must be some good in him.

'I don't want to stand out in it all night, either.'

'No, course you don't. So the best thing you can do, Missy, is to wait round about till the bus comes back.'

'The bus?'

'Bringing them back from the concert, you see. The concert at Shopdon, with the Comic. Everyone's gone to it. That's why there won't be no one here you could ask till they come back.'

'I see. Do you think . . .'

'They might and they mightn't. Of course, it will be a bit late by then.' He remained looking down, she remained looking up. Then he shook his head and closed the window. A moment later, the light went out. He must be undressing in the dark, as a safeguard.

Hunger and cold and discouragement narrowed her field of vision; she could see nothing to do but to walk up and down till the bus came back, and then plead with its passengers for a night's lodging. They would be full of merriment, flown with the Comic. . . . It wouldn't be very pleasant. She didn't look forward to it. Besides, they would be a crowd. It is vain to appeal to simple-hearted people when they are a crowd: embarrassment stiffens them, they shun the limelight of a good deed. She walked up and down and tried not to think of food—for this made her mouth water, which is disgraceful. She lit a cigarette. It made her feel sick. She threw it away.

It was a pity she couldn't throw herself away.

Opposite the shop that sold baby clothes was a Wesleyan chapel. It stood back from the road and produced an echo. Every time she passed by it she heard her footsteps sounding more dispirited. In front of the chapel was a railed yard, with some headstones and two table tombs. One can sit on a table tomb. She tried the gate. It was locked. Though she could have climbed the railings easily enough, she did not, but continued to walk up and down.

She might just as well throw herself away: she had always hated hoarding. Tomorrow it would all begin again—Mother's incessant shamming, rows and reconciliations with Leo. 'Darling, how could you behave like this?' 'Belinda, I despair of making you out.' 'It's not like you to be so callous.' 'Very well, very well! I am sorry I've been such a brute as to love you.' Or else they would combine to love her with all her faults. 'Darling, as you are back, I wonder if you could sometimes remember to turn off the hot tap properly.' But to throw oneself away—unless, like Uncle Henry, one is sensible and always goes about with a gun—one must do it off something or under something. The Wesleyan chapel was such a puny building that even if she were to scale it and throw herself off its pediment, she would be unlikely to do more than break her leg. And though there had once been a branch line to Frogwick, British Railways had closed it on the ground that it wasn't made use of. She could have made use of it. One would squirm through the wire fence, lie down on the track, hear the reliable iron approach, feel the rails tremble . . . 'and the light by which she had read the book filled with troubles, falsehoods, sorrow and evil . . .'

But she was in Billerby, not Moscow. On the outskirts of Billerby, and just about to turn round and walk back towards the Wesleyan chapel, the post office, the vacant shop that was for sale, the aged person coughing. An aged person coughing. That, too, lay ahead of her.

A light sprang up on the dark. A dazzle of headlights rushed towards her, creating vast shapes of roadside elms and overthrowing them, devouring night, perspective, space. She fluttered into its path like a moth. The Bristol swerved, braked, swung round on a skid, came to a stop across the road. Leo ran to where she stood motionless, with her mouth open.

'Damn you, Belinda, you fool!'

'Why are you here? Why can't I have a moment's peace? Go away!'

'I'd like to wring your neck.'

'Wring it then! Do something positive for a change.'

'Tripping out into the road like that. Do you realize I nearly killed you?'

'I wish you had! I wish you had!'

They clung together and shouted recriminations in each other's face. The driver of an approaching bus slowed down, and sounded his horn. As they ignored it, he stopped.

'Of course I did it deliberately. I drove away, and I stayed away, because I was tired of being talked at, and made a butt of—and bored, bored, bored! Do you think I've got no sensibilities?'

'Sensibilities? About as much as a rhinoceros.'

'Rhinoceros yourself!'

One by one, the party from the concert climbed out of the bus and walked cautiously towards this mysterious extra number.

'A pretty pair of fools you looked, sitting there with the picnic basket! And there you sat . . . and there you sat. . . .'

She broke into hysterical laughter. Leo cuffed her.

'Here! I say, young man. . . .'

They turned and saw the party from the concert gathering round them.

'Oh, damn these people!'

They ran to the car, leaped in, drove away. Several quick-witted voices exclaimed, 'Take the number! Take the number!' But the car went so fast, there wasn't time.

EDNA O'BRIEN

Irish Revel

❦

Mary hoped that the rotted, front tyre would not burst. As it was, the tube had a slow puncture, and twice she had to stop and use the pump, maddening, because the pump had no connection and had to be jammed on over the corner of a handkerchief. For as long as she could remember she had been pumping bicycles, carting turf, cleaning outhouses, doing a man's work. Her father and her two brothers worked for the forestry, so that she and her mother had to do all the odd jobs—there were three children to care for, and fowl and pigs and churning. Theirs was a mountainy farm in Ireland, and life was hard.

But this cold evening in early November she was free. She rode along the mountain road, between the bare thorn hedges, thinking pleasantly about the party. Although she was seventeen this was her first party. The invitation had come only that morning from Mrs Rodgers of the Commercial Hotel. The postman brought word that Mrs Rodgers wanted her down that evening, without fail. At first, her mother did not wish Mary to go, there was too much to be done, gruel to be made, and one of the twins had earache, and was likely to cry in the night. Mary slept with the year-old twins, and sometimes she was afraid that she might lie on them or smother them, the bed was so small. She begged to be let go.

'What use would it be?' her mother said. To her mother all outings were unsettling—they gave you a taste of something you couldn't have. But finally she weakened, mainly because Mrs Rodgers, as owner of the Commercial Hotel, was an important woman, and not to be insulted.

'You can go, so long as you're back in time for the milking in the morning; and mind you don't lose your head,' her mother warned. Mary was to stay overnight in the village with Mrs Rodgers. She plaited her hair, and later when she combed it it fell in dark crinkled waves over her shoulders. She was allowed to wear the black lace dress that had come from America years ago and belonged to no one in particular. Her mother had sprinkled her with Holy Water, conveyed her to the top of the lane and warned her never to touch alcohol.

Mary felt happy as she rode along slowly, avoiding the pot-holes that were thinly iced over. The frost had never lifted that day. The ground was hard. If it went on like that, the cattle would have to be brought into the shed and given hay.

The road turned and looped and rose; she turned and looped with it, climbing little hills and descending again towards the next hill. At the descent of the Big Hill she got off the bicycle—the brakes were unreliable—and looked back, out of habit, at her own house. It was the only house back there on the mountain, small, whitewashed, with a few trees around it, and a patch at the back which they called a kitchen-garden. There was a rhubarb bed, and shrubs over which they emptied tea-leaves and a stretch of grass where in the summer they had a chicken run, moving it from one patch to the next, every other day. She looked away. She was now free to think of John Roland. He came to their district two years before, riding a motor-cycle at a ferocious speed; raising dust on the milk-cloths spread on the hedge to dry. He stopped to ask the way. He was staying with Mrs Rodgers in the Commercial Hotel and had come up to see the lake, which was noted for its colours. It changed colour rapidly— it was blue and green and black, all within an hour. At sunset it was often a strange burgundy, not like a lake at all, but like wine.

'Down there,' she said to the stranger, pointing to the lake below, with the small island in the middle of it. He had taken a wrong turning.

Hills and tiny cornfields descended steeply towards the water. The misery of the hills was clear, from all the boulders. The cornfields were turning, it was midsummer; the ditches throbbing with the blood-red of fuchsia; the milk sour five hours after it had been put in the tanker. He said how exotic it was. She had no interest in views herself. She just looked up at the high sky and saw that a hawk had halted in the air above them. It was like a pause in her life, the hawk above them, perfectly still; and just then her mother came out to see who the stranger was. He took off his helmet and said 'Hello', very courteously. He introduced himself as John Roland, an English painter, who lived in Italy.

She did not remember exactly how it happened, but after a while he walked into their kitchen with them and sat down to tea.

Two long years since; but she had never given up hoping—perhaps this evening. The mail-car man said that someone special in the Commercial Hotel expected her. She felt such happiness. She spoke to her bicycle, and it seemed to her that her happiness somehow glowed in the pearliness of the cold sky, in the frosted fields going blue in the dusk, in the cottage windows she passed. Her father and mother were rich and cheerful; the twin had no earache, the kitchen fire did not smoke. Now and then, she smiled at the thought of how she would appear to him— taller and with breasts now, and a dress that could be worn anywhere. She forgot about the rotted tyre, got up and cycled.

The five street lights were on when she pedalled into the village. There had been a cattle fair that day, and the main street was covered with dung. The townspeople had their windows protected with wooden half-shutters and makeshift arrangements of planks and barrels. Some were out scrubbing their own piece of footpath with bucket and brush. There were cattle wandering around, mooing, the way cattle do when they are in a strange street, and drunken farmers with sticks were trying to identify their own cattle in dark corners.

Beyond the shop window of the Commercial Hotel, Mary heard loud conversation, and men singing. It was opaque glass so that she could not identify any of them, she could just see their heads moving about, inside. It was a shabby hotel, the yellow-washed walls needed a coat of paint as they hadn't been done since the time De Valera came to that village during the election campaign five years before. De Valera went upstairs that time, and sat in the parlour and wrote his name with a penny pen in an autograph book, and sympathized with Mrs Rodgers on the recent death of her husband.

Mary thought of resting her bicycle against the porter barrels under the shop window, and then of climbing the three stone steps that led to the hall door, but suddenly the latch of the shop door clicked and she ran in terror up the alley by the side of the shop, afraid it might be someone who knew her father and would say he saw her going in through the public bar. She wheeled her bicycle into a shed and approached the back door. It was open, but she did not enter without knocking.

Two townsgirls rushed to answer it. One was Doris O'Beirne, the daughter of the harness-maker. She was the only Doris in the whole village, and she was famous for that, as well as for the fact that one of her eyes was blue and the other a dark brown. She learnt shorthand and typing at the local technical school, and later she meant to be a secretary to some famous man or other in the Government, in Dublin.

'God, I thought it was someone important,' she said when she saw Mary standing there, blushing, pretty and with a bottle of cream in her hand. Another girl! Girls were two a penny in that neighbourhood. People said that it had something to do with the lime water that so many girls were born. Girls with pink skins, and matching eyes, and girls like Mary with long, wavy hair and good figures.

'Come in, or stay out,' said Eithne Duggan, the second girl, to Mary. It was supposed to be a joke but neither of them liked her. They hated shy mountainy people.

Mary came in carrying cream which her mother had sent to Mrs Rodgers, as a present. She put it on the dresser and took off her coat. The girls nudged each other when they saw her dress. In the kitchen was a smell of cow dung and fried onions.

'Where's Mrs Rodgers?' Mary asked.

'Serving,' Doris said in a saucy voice, as if any fool ought to know. Two old men sat at the table eating.

'I can't chew, I have no teeth,' said one of the men, to Doris. ' 'Tis like leather,' he said, holding the plate of burnt steak towards her. He had watery eyes and he blinked childishly. Was it so, Mary wondered, that eyes got paler with age, like bluebells in a jar?

'You're not going to charge me for that,' the old man was saying to Doris. Tea and steak cost five shillings at the Commercial.

' 'Tis good for you, chewing is,' Eithne Duggan said, teasing him.

'I can't chew with my gums,' he said again, and the two girls began to giggle. The old man looked pleased that he had made them laugh, and he closed his mouth and munched once or twice on a piece of fresh, shop bread. Eithne Duggan laughed so much that she had to put a dish-cloth between her teeth. Mary hung up her coat and went through to the shop.

Mrs Rodgers came from the counter for a moment to speak to her.

'Mary, I'm glad you came, that pair in there are no use at all, always giggling. Now first thing we have to do is to get the parlour upstairs straightened out. Everything has to come out of it except the piano. We're going to have dancing and everything.'

Quickly, Mary realized that she was being given work to do, and she blushed with shock and disappointment.

'Pitch everything into the back bedroom, the whole shootin' lot,' Mrs Rodgers was saying as Mary thought of her good lace dress, and of how her mother wouldn't even let her wear it to Mass on Sundays.

'And we have to stuff a goose too and get it on,' Mrs Rodgers said, and went on to explain that the party was in honour of the local Customs and Excise Officer who was retiring because his wife won some money in the Sweep. Two thousand pounds. His wife lived thirty miles away at the far side of Limerick and he lodged in the Commercial Hotel from Monday to Friday, going home for the weekends.

'There's someone here expecting me,' Mary said, trembling with the pleasure of being about to hear his name pronounced by someone else. She wondered which room was his, and if he was likely to be in at that moment. Already in imagination she had climbed the rickety stairs and knocked on the door, and heard him move around inside.

'Expecting you!' Mrs Rodgers said, and looked puzzled for a minute. 'Oh, that lad from the slate quarry was inquiring about you, he said he saw you at a dance once. He's as odd as two left shoes.'

'What lad?' Mary said, as she felt the joy leaking out of her heart.

'Oh, what's his name?' Mrs Rodgers said, and then to the men with empty glasses who were shouting for her. 'Oh all right, I'm coming.'

Upstairs Doris and Eithne helped Mary move the heavy pieces of furniture. They dragged the sideboard across the landing and one of the castors tore the linoleum. She was expiring, because she had the heaviest end, the other two being at the same side. She felt that it was on purpose: they ate sweets without offering her one, and she caught them making faces at her dress. The dress worried her too in case anything should happen to it. If one of the lace threads caught in a splinter of wood, or on a porter barrel, she would have no business going home in the morning. They carried out a varnished bamboo whatnot, a small table, knick-knacks and a chamber-pot with no handle which held some withered hydrangeas. They smelt awful.

'How much is the doggie in the window, the one with the waggledy tail?' Doris O'Beirne sang to a white china dog and swore that there wasn't ten pounds' worth of furniture in the whole shibeen.

'Are you leaving your curlers in, Dot, till it starts?' Eithne Duggan asked her friend.

'Oh def.,' Doris O'Beirne said. She wore an assortment of curlers—white pipe-cleaners, metal clips, and pink, plastic rollers. Eithne had just taken hers out and her hair, dyed blonde, stood out, all frizzed and alarming. She reminded Mary of a moulting hen about to attempt flight. She was, God bless her, an unfortunate girl with a squint, jumbled teeth and almost no lips; like something put together hurriedly. That was the luck of the draw.

'Take these,' Doris O'Beirne said, handing Mary bunches of yellowed bills crammed on skewers.

Do this! Do that! They ordered her around like a maid. She dusted the piano, top and sides, and the yellow and black keys; then the surround, and the wainscoting. The dust, thick on everything, had settled into a hard film because of the damp in that room. A party! She'd have been as well off at home, at least it was clean dirt attending to calves and pigs and the like.

Doris and Eithne amused themselves, hitting notes on the piano at random and wandering from one mirror to the next. There were two mirrors in the parlour and one side of the folding fire-screen was a blotchy mirror too. The other two sides were of water-lilies painted on black cloth, but like everything else in the room it was old.

'What's that?' Doris and Eithne asked each other, as they heard a hullabulloo downstairs. They rushed out to see what it was and Mary followed. Over the banisters they saw that a young bullock had got in the hall door and was slithering over the tiled floor, trying to find his way out again.

'Don't excite her, don't excite her I tell ye,' said the old, toothless man to the young boy who tried to drive the black bullock out. Two more boys were having a bet as to whether or not the bullock would do something on the floor when Mrs Rodgers came out and dropped a glass of porter. The beast backed out the way he'd come, shaking his head from side to side.

Eithne and Doris clasped each other in laughter and then Doris drew back so that none of the boys would see her in her curling pins and call her names. Mary had gone back to the room, downcast. Wearily she pushed the chairs back against the wall and swept the linoleumed floor where they were later to dance.

'She's bawling in there,' Eithne Duggan told her friend Doris. They had locked themselves into the bathroom with a bottle of cider.

'God, she's a right-looking eejit in the dress,' Doris said. 'And the length of it!'

'It's her mother's,' Eithne said. She had admired the dress before that, when Doris was out of the room, and had asked Mary where she bought it.

'What's she crying about?' Doris wondered, aloud.

'She thought some lad would be here. Do you remember that lad stayed here the summer before last and had a motor-cycle?'

'He was a Jew,' Doris said. 'You could tell by his nose. God, she'd shake him in that dress, he'd think she was a scarecrow.' She squeezed a blackhead on her chin, tightened a curling pin which had come loose and said, 'Her hair isn't natural either, you can see it's curled.'

'I hate that kind of black hair, it's like a gipsy's,' Eithne said, drinking the last of the cider. They hid the bottle under the scoured bath.

'Have a cachou, take the smell off your breath,' Doris said as she hawed on the bathroom mirror and wondered if she would get off with that fellow O'Toole, from the slate quarry, who was coming to the party.

In the front room Mary polished glasses. Tears ran down her cheeks so she did not put on the light. She foresaw how the party would be; they would all stand around and consume the goose, which was now simmering in the turf range. The men would be drunk, the girls giggling. Having eaten, they would dance, and sing, and tell ghost stories, and in the morning she would have to get up early and be home in time to milk. She moved towards the dark pane of window with a glass in her hand and looked out at the dirtied streets, remembering how once she had danced with John on the upper road to no music at all, just their hearts beating, and the sound of happiness.

He came into their house for tea that summer's day and on her father's suggestion he lodged with them for four days, helping with the hay and oiling all the farm machinery for her father. He understood machinery.

He put back doorknobs that had fallen off. Mary made his bed in the daytime and carried up a ewer of water from the rain-barrel every evening, so that he could wash. She washed the check shirt he wore, and that day, his bare back peeled in the sun. She put milk on it. It was his last day with them. After supper he proposed giving each of the grown-up children a ride on the motor-bicycle. Her turn came last, she felt that he had planned it that way, but it may have been that her brothers were more persistent about being first. She would never forget that ride. She warmed from head to foot in wonder and joy. He praised her as a good balancer and at odd moments he took one hand off the handlebar and gave her clasped hands a comforting pat. The sun went down, and the gorse flowers blazed yellow. They did not talk for miles; she had his stomach encased in the delicate and frantic grasp of a girl in love and no matter how far they rode they seemed always to be riding into a golden haze. He saw the lake at its most glorious. They got off at the bridge five miles away, and sat on the limestone wall, that was cushioned by moss and lichen. She took a tick out of his neck and touched the spot where the tick had drawn one pin-prick of blood; it was then they danced. A sound of larks and running water. The hay in the fields was lying green and ungathered, and the air was sweet with the smell of it. They danced.

'Sweet Mary,' he said, looking earnestly into her eyes. Her eyes were a greenish-brown. He confessed that he could not love her, because he already loved his wife and children, and anyhow he said, 'You are too young and too innocent.'

Next day, as he was leaving, he asked if he might send her something in the post, and it came eleven days later: a black-and-white drawing of her, very like her, except that the girl in the drawing was uglier.

'A fat lot of good, that is,' said her mother, who had been expecting a gold bracelet or a brooch. 'That wouldn't take you far.'

They hung it on a nail in the kitchen for a while and then one day it fell down and someone (probably her mother) used it to sweep dust on to, ever since it was used for that purpose. Mary had wanted to keep it, to put it away in a trunk, but she was ashamed to. They were hard people, and it was only when someone died that they could give in to sentiment or crying.

'Sweet Mary,' he had said. He never wrote. Two summers passed, devil's pokers flowered for two seasons, and thistle seed blew in the wind, the trees in the forestry were a foot higher. She had a feeling that he would come back, and a gnawing fear that he might not.

'Oh it ain't gonna rain no more, no more, it ain't gonna rain no more; How in the hell can the old folks say it ain't gonna rain no more.'

So sang Brogan, whose party it was, in the upstairs room of the Commercial Hotel. Unbuttoning his brown waistcoat, he sat back and said what a fine spread it was. They had carried the goose up on a platter and it lay in the centre of the mahogany table with potato stuffing spilling out of it. There were sausages also and polished glasses rim downwards, and plates and forks for everyone.

'A fork supper' was how Mrs Rodgers described it. She had read about it in the paper; it was all the rage now in posh houses in Dublin, this fork supper where you stood up for your food and ate with a fork only. Mary had brought knives in case anyone got into difficulties.

' 'Tis America at home,' Hickey said, putting turf on the smoking fire.

The pub door was bolted downstairs, the shutters across, as the eight guests upstairs watched Mrs Rodgers carve the goose and then tear the loose pieces away with her fingers. Every so often she wiped her fingers on a tea-towel.

'Here you are, Mary, give this to Mr Brogan, as he's the guest of honour.' Mr Brogan got a lot of breast and some crispy skin as well.

'Don't forget the sausages, Mary,' Mrs Rodgers said. Mary had to do everything, pass the food around, serve the stuffing, ask people whether they wanted paper plates or china ones. Mrs Rodgers had bought paper plates, thinking they were sophisticated.

'I could eat a young child,' Hickey said.

Mary was surprised that people in towns were so coarse and outspoken. When he squeezed her finger she did not smile at all. She wished that she were at home—she knew what they were doing at home; the boys at their lessons; her mother baking a cake of wholemeal bread, because there was never enough time during the day to bake; her father rolling cigarettes and talking to himself. John had taught him how to roll cigarettes, and every night since he rolled four and smoked four. He was a good man, her father, but dour. In another hour they'd be saying the Rosary in her house and going up to bed: the rhythm of their lives never changed, the fresh bread was always cool by morning.

'Ten o'clock,' Doris said, listening to the chimes of the landing clock.

The party began late; the men were late getting back from the dogs in Limerick. They killed a pig on the way in their anxiety to get back quickly. The pig had been wandering around the road and the car came round the corner; it got run over instantly.

'Never heard such a roarin' in all me born days,' Hickey said, reaching for a wing of goose, the choicest bit.

'We should have brought it with us,' O'Toole said. O'Toole worked in the slate quarry and knew nothing about pigs or farming; he was tall and thin and jagged. He had bright green eyes and a face like a greyhound; his hair was so gold that it looked dyed, but in fact it was bleached by the weather. No one had offered him any food.

'A nice way to treat a man,' he said.

'God bless us, Mary, didn't you give Mr O'Toole anything to eat yet?' Mrs Rodgers said as she thumped Mary on the back to hurry her up. Mary brought him a large helping on a paper plate and he thanked her and said that they would dance later. To him she looked far prettier than those good-for-nothing townsgirls—she was tall and thin like himself; she had long black hair that some people might think streelish, but not him, he liked long hair and simple-minded girls; maybe later on he'd get her to go into one of the other rooms where they could do it. She had funny eyes when you looked into them, brown and deep, like a bloody bog-hole.

'Have a wish,' he said to her as he held the wishbone up. She wished that she were going to America on an aeroplane and on second thoughts she wished that she would win a lot of money and could buy her mother and father a house down near the main road.

'Is that your brother the Bishop?' Eithne Duggan, who knew well that it was, asked Mrs Rodgers, concerning the flaccid-faced cleric over the fireplace. Unknown to herself Mary had traced the letter J on the dust of the picture mirror, earlier on, and now they all seemed to be looking at it, knowing how it came to be there.

'That's him, poor Charlie,' Mrs Rodgers said proudly, and was about to elaborate, but Brogan began to sing, unexpectedly.

'Let the man sing, can't you,' O'Toole said, hushing two of the girls who were having a joke about the armchair they shared; the springs were hanging down underneath and the girls said that at any minute the whole thing would collapse.

Mary shivered in her lace dress. The air was cold and damp even though Hickey had got up a good fire. There hadn't been a fire in that room since the day De Valera signed the autograph book. Steam issued from everything.

O'Toole asked if any of the ladies would care to sing. There were five ladies in all—Mrs Rodgers, Mary, Doris, Eithne, and Crystal the local hairdresser, who had a new red rinse in her hair and who insisted that the food was a little heavy for her. The goose was greasy and undercooked, she did not like its raw, pink colour. She liked dainty things, little bits of cold chicken breast with sweet pickles. Her real name was Carmel, but when she started up as a hairdresser she changed to Crystal and dyed her brown hair red.

'I bet you can sing,' O'Toole said to Mary.

'Where she comes from they can hardly talk,' Doris said.

Mary felt the blood rushing to her sallow cheeks. She would not tell them, but her father's name had been in the paper once, because he had seen a pine-marten in the forestry plantation; and they ate with a knife and fork at home and had oil cloth on the kitchen table, and kept a tin of coffee in case strangers called. She would not tell them anything. She just hung her head, making clear that she was not about to sing.

In honour of the Bishop O'Toole put 'Far away in Australia' on the horn gramophone. Mrs Rogers had asked for it. The sound issued forth with rasps and scratchings and Brogan said he could do better than that himself.

'Christ, lads, we forgot the soup!' Mrs Rodgers said suddenly, as she threw down the fork and went towards the door. There had been soup scheduled to begin with.

'I'll help you,' Doris O'Beirne said, stirring herself for the first time that night, and they both went down to get the pot of dark giblet soup which had been simmering all that day.

'Now we need two pounds from each of the gents,' said O'Toole, taking the opportunity while Mrs Rodgers was away to mention the delicate matter of money. The men had agreed to pay two pounds each, to cover the cost of the drink; the ladies did not have to pay anything, but were invited so as to lend a pleasant and decorative atmosphere to the party, and, of course, to help.

O'Toole went around with his cap held out, and Brogan said that as it was *his* party he ought to give a fiver.

'I ought to give a fiver, but I suppose ye wouldn't hear of that,' Brogan said, and handed up two pound notes. Hickey paid up, too, and O'Toole himself and Long John Salmon—who was silent up to then. O'Toole gave it to Mrs Rodgers when she returned and told her to clock it up against the damages.

'Sure that's too kind altogether,' she said, as she put it behind the stuffed owl on the mantelpiece, under the Bishop's watchful eye.

She served the soup in cups and Mary was asked to pass the cups around. The grease floated like drops of molten gold on the surface of each cup.

'See you later, alligator,' Hickey said, as she gave him his; then he asked her for a piece of bread because he wasn't used to soup without bread.

'Tell us, Brogan,' said Hickey to his rich friend, 'what'll you do, now that you're a rich man?'

'Oh go on, tell us,' said Doris O'Beirne.

'Well,' said Brogan, thinking for a minute, 'we're going to make some changes at home.' None of them had ever visited Brogan's home because it was situated in Adare, thirty miles away, at the far side of Limerick. None of them had ever seen his wife either, who it seems lived there and kept bees.

'What sort of changes?' someone said.

'We're going to do up the drawing-room, and we're going to have flower-beds,' Brogan told them.

'And what else?' Crystal asked, thinking of all the lovely clothes she could buy with that money, clothes and jewellery.

'Well,' said Brogan, thinking again, 'we might even go to Lourdes. I'm not sure yet, it all depends.'

'I'd give my two eyes to go to Lourdes,' Mrs Rodgers said.

'And you'd get 'em back when you arrived there,' Hickey said, but no one paid any attention to him.

O'Toole poured out four half-tumblers of whiskey and then stood back to examine the glasses to see that each one had the same amount. There was always great anxiety among the men, about being fair with drink. Then O'Toole stood bottles of stout in little groups of six and told each man which group was his. The ladies had gin and orange.

'Orange for me,' Mary said, but O'Toole told her not to be such a goody, and when her back was turned he put gin in her orange.

They drank a toast to Brogan.

'To Lourdes,' Mrs Rodgers said.

'To Brogan,' O'Toole said.

'To myself,' Hickey said.

'Mud in your eye,' said Doris O'Beirne, who was already unsteady from tippling cider.

'Well we're not sure about Lourdes,' Brogan said. 'But we'll get the drawing-room done up anyhow, and the flower-beds put in.'

'We've a drawing-room here,' Mrs Rodgers said, 'and no one ever sets foot in it.'

'Come into the drawing-room, Doris,' said O'Toole to Mary, who was serving the jelly from the big enamel basin. They'd had no china bowl to put it in. It was red jelly with whipped egg-white in it, but something went wrong because it hadn't set properly. She served it in saucers, and thought to herself what a rough-and-ready party it was. There wasn't a proper cloth on the table either, just a plastic one, and no napkins, and that big basin with the jelly in it. Maybe people washed in that basin, downstairs.

'Well someone tell us a bloomin' joke,' said Hickey, who was getting fed up with talk about drawing-rooms and flower-beds.

'I'll tell you a joke,' said Long John Salmon, erupting out of his silence.

'Good,' said Brogan, as he sipped from his whiskey glass and his stout glass alternately. It was the only way to drink enjoyably. That was why, in pubs, he'd be much happier if he could buy his own drink and not rely on anyone else's meanness.

'Is it a funny joke?' Hickey asked of Long John Salmon.

'It's about my brother,' said Long John Salmon, 'my brother Patrick.'

'Oh no, don't tell us that old rambling thing again,' said Hickey and O'Toole, together.

'Oh let him tell it,' said Mrs Rodgers who'd never heard the story anyhow.

Long John Salmon began, 'I had this brother Patrick and he died; the heart wasn't too good.'

'Holy Christ, not this again,' said Brogan, recollecting which story it was.

But Long John Salmon went on, undeterred by the abuse from the three men:

'One day I was standing in the shed, about a month after he was buried, and I saw him coming out of the wall, walking across the yard.'

'Oh what would you do if you saw a thing like that,' Doris said to Eithne.

'Let him tell it,' Mrs Rodgers said. 'Go on, Long John.'

'Well it was walking toward me, and I said to myself, "What do I do now?"; 'twas raining heavy, so I said to my brother Patrick, "Stand in out of the wet or you'll get drenched."'

'And then?' said one of the girls anxiously.

'He vanished,' said Long John Salmon.

'Ah God, let us have a bit of music,' said Hickey, who had heard that story nine or ten times. It had neither a beginning, a middle nor an end. They put a record on, and O'Toole asked Mary to dance. He did a lot of fancy steps and capering; and now and then he let out a mad 'Yippee'. Brogan and Mrs Rodgers were dancing too and Crystal said that she'd dance if anyone asked her.

'Come on, knees up Mother Brown,' O'Toole said to Mary, as he jumped around the room, kicking the legs of chairs as he moved. She felt funny: her head was swaying round and round, and in the pit of her stomach there was a nice, ticklish feeling that made her want to lie back and stretch her legs. A new feeling that frightened her.

'Come into the drawing-room, Doris,' he said, dancing her right out of the room and into the cold passage where he kissed her clumsily.

Inside Crystal O'Meara had begun to cry. That was how drink affected her; either she cried or talked in a foreign accent and said, 'Why am I talking in a foreign accent?' This time she cried.

'Hickey, there is no joy in life,' she said as she sat at the table with her head laid in her arms and her blouse slipping up out of her skirtband.

'What joy?' said Hickey, who had all the drink he needed, and a pound note which he slipped from behind the owl when no one was looking.

Doris and Eithne sat on either side of Long John Salmon, asking if they could go out next year when the sugar plums were ripe. Long John Salmon lived by himself, way up the country, and he had a big orchard. He was odd and silent in himself; he took a swim every day, winter and summer, in the river, at the back of his house.

'Two old married people,' Brogan said, as he put his arm round Mrs Rodgers and urged her to sit down because he was out of breath from dancing. He said he'd go away with happy memories of them all, and sitting down he drew her on to his lap. She was a heavy woman, with straggly brown hair that had once been a nut colour.

'There is no joy in life,' Crystal sobbed, as the gramophone made crackling noises and Mary ran in from the landing, away from O'Toole.

'I mean business,' O'Toole said, and winked.

O'Toole was the first to get quarrelsome.

'Now ladies, now gentlemen, a little laughing sketch, are we ready?' he asked.

'Fire ahead,' Hickey told him.

'Well, there was these three lads, Paddy th'Irishman, Paddy th'Englishman, and Paddy the Scotsman, and they were badly in need of a . . .'

'Now, no smut,' Mrs Rodgers snapped, before he had uttered a wrong word at all.

'What smut?' said O'Toole, getting offended. 'Smut!' And he asked her to explain an accusation like that.

'Think of the girls,' Mrs Rodgers said.

'Girls,' O'Toole sneered, as he picked up the bottle of cream—which they'd forgotten to use with the jelly—and poured it into the carcass of the ravaged goose.

'Christ's sake, man,' Hickey said, taking the bottle of cream out of O'Toole's hand.

Mrs Rodgers said that it was high time everyone went to bed, as the party seemed to be over.

The guests would spend the night in the Commercial. It was too late for them to go home anyhow, and also Mrs Rodgers did not want them to be observed staggering out of the house at that hour. The police watched her like hawks and she didn't want any trouble, until Christmas was over at least. The sleeping arrangements had been decided earlier on—there were three bedrooms vacant. One was Brogan's, the room he always slept in. The other three men were to pitch in together in the second big bedroom, and the girls were to share the back room with Mrs Rodgers herself.

'Come on, everyone, blanket street,' Mrs Rodgers said, as she put a guard in front of the dying fire and took the money from behind the owl.

'Sugar you,' O'Toole said, pouring stout now into the carcass of the goose, and Long John Salmon wished that he had never come. He thought of daylight and of his swim in the mountain river at the back of his grey, stone house.

'Ablution,' he said, aloud, taking pleasure in the word and in thought of the cold water touching him. He could do without people, people were waste. He remembered catkins on a tree outside his window, catkins in February as white as snow; who needed people?

'Crystal, stir yourself,' Hickey said, as he put on her shoes and patted the calves of her legs.

Brogan kissed the four girls and saw them across the landing to the bedroom. Mary was glad to escape without O'Toole noticing; he was very obstreperous and Hickey was trying to control him.

In the bedroom she sighed; she had forgotten all about the furniture being pitched in there. Wearily they began to unload the things. The room was so crammed that they could hardly move in it. Mary suddenly felt alert and frightened, because O'Toole could be heard yelling and singing out on the landing. There had been gin in her orangeade, she knew now, because she breathed closely on to the palm of her hand and smelt her own breath. She had broken her Confirmation pledge, broken her promise; it would bring her bad luck.

Mrs Rodgers came in and said that five of them would be too crushed in the bed, so that she herself would sleep on the sofa for one night.

'Two of you at the top and two at the bottom,' she said, as she warned them not to break any of the ornaments, and not to stay talking all night.

'Night and God bless,' she said, as she shut the door behind her.

'Nice thing,' said Doris O'Beirne, 'bunging us all in here; I wonder where she's off to?'

'Will you loan me curlers?' Crystal asked. To Crystal, hair was the most important thing on earth. She would never get married because you couldn't wear curlers in bed then. Eithne Duggan said she wouldn't put curlers in now if she got five million for doing it, she was that jaded. She threw herself down on the quilt and spread her arms out. She was a noisy, sweaty girl but Mary liked her better than the other two.

'Ah me old segotums,' O'Toole said, pushing their door in. The girls exclaimed and asked him to go out at once as they were preparing for bed.

'Come into the drawing-room, Doris,' he said to Mary, and curled his forefinger at her. He was drunk and couldn't focus her properly but he knew that she was standing there somewhere.

'Go to bed, you're drunk,' Doris O'Beirne said, and he stood very upright for an instant and asked her to speak for herself.

'Go to bed, Michael, you're tired,' Mary said to him. She tried to sound calm because he looked so wild.

'Come into the drawing-room, I tell you,' he said, as he caught her wrist and dragged her towards the door. She let out a cry, and Eithne Duggan said she'd brain him if he didn't leave the girl alone.

'Give me that flower-pot, Doris,' Eithne Duggan called, and then Mary began to cry in case there might be a scene. She hated scenes. Once she heard her father and a neighbour having a row about boundary rights and she'd never forgotten it; they had both been a bit drunk, after a fair.

'Are you cracked or are you mad?' O'Toole said, when he perceived that she was crying.

'I'll give you two seconds,' Eithne warned, as she held the flower-pot high, ready to throw it at O'Toole's stupefied face.

'You're a nice bunch of hard-faced aul crows, crows,' he said. 'Wouldn't give a man a squeeze,' and he went out cursing each one of them. They shut the door very quickly and dragged the sideboard in front of the door so that he could not break in when they were asleep.

They got into bed in their underwear; Mary and Eithne at one end with Crystal's feet between their faces.

'You have lovely hair,' Eithne whispered to Mary. It was the nicest thing she could think of to say. They each said their prayers, and shook hands under the covers and settled down to sleep.

'Hey,' Doris O'Beirne said a few seconds later, 'I never went to the lav.'

'You can't go now,' Eithne said, 'the sideboard's in front of the door.'

'I'll die if I don't go,' Doris O'Beirne said.

'And me, too, after all that orange we drank,' Crystal said. Mary was shocked that they could talk like that. At home you never spoke of such a thing, you just went out behind the hedge and that was that. Once a workman saw her squatting down and from that day she never talked to him, or acknowledged that she knew him.

'Maybe we could use that old pot,' Doris O'Beirne said, and Eithne Duggan sat up and said that if anyone used a pot in that room she wasn't going to sleep there.

'We have to use something,' Doris said. By now she had got up and had switched on the light. She held the pot up to the naked bulb and saw what looked to be a hole in it.

'Try it,' Crystal said, giggling.

They heard feet on the landing and then the sound of choking and coughing, and later O'Toole cursing and swearing and hitting the wall with his fist. Mary curled down under the clothes, thankful for the company of the girls. They stopped talking.

'I was at a party. Now I know what parties are like,' Mary said to herself, as she tried to force herself asleep. She heard a sound as of water running, but it did not seem to be raining outside. Later, she dozed, but at daybreak she heard the hall door bang, and she sat up in bed abruptly. She had to be home early to milk, so she got up, took her shoes and her lace dress, and let herself out by dragging the sideboard forward, and opening the door slightly.

There were newspapers spread on the landing floor and in the lavatory, and a heavy smell pervaded. Downstairs, porter had flowed out of the bar into the hall. It was probably O'Toole who had turned on the taps of the five porter barrels, and the stone-floored bar and sunken passage outside was swimming with black porter. Mrs Rodgers would kill somebody. Mary put on her high-heeled shoes and picked her steps carefully across the room to the door. She left without even making a cup of tea.

She wheeled her bicycle down the alley and into the street. The front tyre was dead flat. She pumped for a half-an-hour but it remained flat.

The frost lay like a spell upon the street, upon the sleeping windows, and the slate roofs of the narrow houses. It had magically made the dunged street white and clean. She did not feel tired, but relieved to be out, and stunned by lack of sleep she inhaled the beauty of the morning. She walked briskly, sometimes looking back to see the track which her bicycle and her feet made on the white road.

Mrs Rodgers wakened at eight and stumbled out in her big nightgown from Brogan's warm bed. She smelt disaster instantly and hurried downstairs to find the porter in the bar and the hall; then she ran to call the others.

'Porter all over the place; every drop of drink in the house is on the floor—Mary Mother of God help me in my tribulation! Get up, get up.' She rapped on their door and called the girls by name.

The girls rubbed their sleepy eyes, yawned, and sat up.

'She's gone,' Eithne said, looking at the place on the pillow where Mary's head had been.

'Oh, a sneaky country one,' Doris said, as she got into her taffeta dress and went down to see the flood. 'If I have to clean that, in my good clothes, I'll die,' she said. But Mrs Rodgers had already brought brushes and pails and got to work. They opened the bar door and began to bail the porter into the street. Dogs came to lap it up, and Hickey, who had by then come down, stood and said what a crying shame it was, to waste all that drink. Outside it washed away an area of frost and revealed the dung of yesterday's fair day. O'Toole the culprit had fled since the night; Long John Salmon was gone for his swim, and upstairs in bed Brogan snuggled down for a last-minute warm and deliberated on the joys that he would miss when he left the Commercial for good.

'And where's my lady with the lace dress?' Hickey asked, recalling very little of Mary's face, but distinctly remembering the sleeves of her black dress which dipped into the plates.

'Sneaked off, before we were up,' Doris said. They all agreed that Mary was no bloody use and should never have been asked.

'And 'twas she set O'Toole mad, egging him on and then disappointing him,' Doris said, and Mrs Rodgers swore that O'Toole, or Mary's father, or someone, would pay dear for the wasted drink.

'I suppose she's home by now,' Hickey said, as he rooted in his pocket for a butt. He had a new packet, but if he produced that they'd all be puffing away at his expense.

Mary was half-a-mile from home, sitting on a bank.

If only I had a sweetheart, something to hold on to, she thought, as she cracked some ice with her high heel and watched the crazy splintered pattern it made. The poor birds could get no food as the ground was frozen hard. Frost was general all over Ireland; frost like a weird blossom on the branches, on the river-bank from which Long John Salmon leaped in his great, hairy nakedness, on the ploughs left out all winter; frost on the stony fields, and on all the slime and ugliness of the world.

Walking again she wondered if and what she would tell her mother and her brothers about it, and if all parties were as bad. She was at the top of the hill now, and could see her own house, like a little white box at the end of the world, waiting to receive her.

The Butterfly and the Traffic Light

❦

... the moth for the star.

(Shelley)

Jerusalem, that phoenix city, is not known by its street-names. Neither is Baghdad, Copenhagen, Rio de Janeiro, Camelot, or Athens; nor Peking, Florence, Babylon, St Petersburg. These fabled capitals rise up ready-spired, story-domed and filigreed; they come to us at the end of a plain, behind hill or cloud, walled and moated by myths and antique rumors. They are built of copper, silver, and gold; they are founded on milkwhite stone; the bright thrones of ideal kings jewel them. Balconies, parks, little gates, columns and statuary, carriage-houses and stables, attics, kitchens, gables, tiles, yards, rubied steeples, brilliant roofs, peacocks, lapdogs, grand ladies, beggars, towers, bowers, harbors, barbers, wigs, judges, courts, and wines of all sorts fill them. Yet, though we see the shimmer of the smallest pebble beneath the humblest foot in all the great seats of legend, still not a single street is celebrated. The thoroughfares of beautiful cities are somehow obscure, unless, of course, we count Venice: but a canal is not really the same as a street. The ways, avenues, plazas, and squares of old cities are lost to us, we do not like to think of them, they move like wicked scratches upon the smooth enamel of our golden towns; we have forgotten most of them. There is no beauty in cross-section— we take our cities, like our wishes, whole.

It is different with places of small repute or where time has not yet deigned to be an inhabitant. It is different especially in America. They tell us that Boston is our Jerusalem; but, as anyone who has ever lived there knows, Boston owns only half a history. Honor, pomp, hallowed scenes, proud families, the Athenaeum and the Symphony are Boston's; but Boston has no tragic tradition. Boston has never wept. No Bostonian has ever sung, mourning for his city, 'If I do not remember thee, let my tongue cleave to the roof of my mouth'—for, to manage his accent, the Bostonian's tongue is already in that position. We hear of Beacon Hill and Back Bay, of Faneuil market and State Street: it is all cross-section, all map. And the State House with its gilt dome (it counts for nothing that

Paul Revere supplied the bottommost layer of gold leaf: he was business-man, not horseman, then) throws back furious sunsets garishly, boast-fully, as no power-rich Carthage, for shame, would dare. There is no fairy mist in Boston. True, its street-names are notable: Boylston, Washington, Commonwealth, Marlborough, Tremont, Beacon; and then the Squares, Kenmore, Copley, Louisburg, and Scollay—evidence enough that the whole, unlike Jerusalem, has not transcended its material parts. Boston has a history of neighborhoods. Jerusalem has a history of histories.

The other American towns are even less fortunate. It is not merely that they lack rudimentary legends, that their names are homely and unimag-inative, half ending in -burg and half in -ville, or that nothing has ever happened in them. Unlike the ancient capitals, they are not infixed in our vision, we are not born knowing them, as though, in some earlier migration, we had been dwellers there: for no one is a stranger to Jerusalem. And unlike even Boston, most cities in America have no landmarks, no age-enshrined graveyards (although death is famous everywhere), no green park to show a massacre, poet's murder, or high marriage. The American town, alas, has no identity hinting at immortality; we recognize it only by its ubiquitous street-names: sometimes Main Street, sometimes High Street, and frequently Central Avenue. Grandeur shuns such streets. It is all ambition and aspiration there, and nothing to look back at. Cicero said that men who know nothing of what has gone before them are like children. But Main, High, and Central have no past; rather, their past is now. It is not the fault of the inhabitants that nothing has gone before them. Nor are they to be condemned if they make their spinal streets conspicuous, and confer egregious luster and false acclaim on Central, High, or Main, and erect minarets and marquees indeed as though their city were already in dream and fable. But it is where one street in particular is regarded as the central life, the high spot, the main drag, that we know the city to be a prenatal trace only. The kiln of history bakes out these prides and these divisions. When the streets have been forgotten a thousand years, the divine city is born.

In the farm-village where the brewer Buldenquist had chosen to establish his Mighty College, the primitive commercial artery was called, not sur-prisingly, 'downtown', and then, more respectably, Main Street, and then, rather covetously looking to civic improvement, Buldenquist Road. But the Sacred Bull had dedicated himself to the foundation and per-petuation of scientific farming, and had a prejudice against putting money into pavements and other citifications. So the town fathers (for by that time the place *was* a town, swollen by the boarding houses and saloons frequented by crowds of young farm students)—the town fathers scratched their heads for historical allusions embedded in local folklore, but found nothing except two or three old family scandals, until one day a traveling salesman named Rogers sold the mayor an 'archive'—a wrinkled, torn, doused, singed, and otherwise quite ancient-looking holographic volume purporting to hold the records and diaries of one Colonel Elihu Bigghe. This rather obscure officer had by gratifying coincidence passed through the neighborhood during the war with a force of two hundred, the document claimed, encountering a skirmish with the enemy on the very spot of the present firehouse—the 'war' being, according to some, the Civil War, and in the positive authority of others, one of the lesser Indian Wars—in his private diary Bigghe was not, after all, expected to drop hints. At any rate, the skirmish was there in detail—one hundred or more of the enemy dead; not one of ours; ninety-seven of theirs wounded; our survivors all hale but three; the bravery of our side; the cowardice and brutality of the foe; and further pious and patriotic remarks on Country, Creator, and Christian Charity. A decade or so after this remarkable discovery the mayor heard of Rogers' arrest, somewhere in the East, for forgery, and in his secret heart began to wonder whether he might not have been taken in: but by then the Bigghe diaries were under glass in the antiseptic-smelling lobby of the town hall, school children were being herded regularly by their teachers to view it, boring Fourth of July speeches had been droned before the firehouse in annual commemoration, and most people had forgotten that Bigghe Road had ever been called after the grudging brewer. And who could blame the inhabitants if, after half a hundred years, they began to spell it Big Road? For by then the town had grown into a city, wide and clamorous.

For Fishbein it was an imitation of a city. He claimed (not altogether correctly) that he had seen all the capitals of Europe, and yet had never come upon anything to match Big Road in name or character. He liked to tell how the streets of Europe were 'employed', as he put it: he would people them with beggars and derelicts—'they keep their cash and their beds in the streets'; and with crowds assembled for riot or amusement or politics—'in Moscow they filled, the revolutionaries I mean, three troikas with White Russians and shot them, the White Russians I mean, and let them run wild in the street, the horses I mean, to spill all the corpses' (but he had never been to Moscow); and with travelers determined on objective and destination—'they use the streets there to go from one place to another, the original design of streets, *n'est-ce pas?*' Fishbein considered that, while a city exists for its own sake, a street is utilitarian. The uses of Big Road, on the contrary, were plainly secondary. In Fishbein's view Big Road had come into being only that the city might have a conscious center—much as the nucleus of a cell demonstrates the cell's character and maintains its well-being ('although', Fishbein argued, 'in the cell it is a moot question whether the nucleus exists for the sake of the cell or the cell for the sake of the nucleus: whereas it is clear that a formless city such as this requires a centrality from which to learn the idea of form'). But if the city were to have modeled itself after Big Road, it would have grown long, like a serpent, and unreliable in its sudden coilings. This had not happened. Big Road crept, toiled, and ran, but the city nibbled at this farmhouse and that, and spread and spread with no pattern other than exuberance and greed. And if Fishbein had to go to biology or botany or history for his analogies, the city was proud that it had Big Road to stimulate such comparisons.

Big Road was different by day and by night, weekday and weekend. Daylight, sunlight, and even rainlight gave everything its shadow, winter and summer, so that every person and every object had its Doppelgänger, persistent and hopeless. There was a kind of doubleness that clung to the street, as though one remembered having seen this and this and this before. The stores, hung with signs, had it, the lazy-walking old women had it (all of them uniformly rouged in the geometric centers of their cheeks like victims of some senile fever already dangerously epidemic), the traffic lights suspended from their wires had it, the air dense with the local accent had it.

This insistent sense of recognition was the subject of one of Fishbein's favorite lectures to his walking companion. 'It's America repeating itself! Imitating its own worst habits! Haven't I seen the same thing everywhere? It's a simultaneous urbanization all over, you can almost hear the cox-swain crow "Now all together, boys!"—This lamppost, I saw it years ago in Birmingham, that same scalloped bowl teetering on a wrought-iron stick. At least in Europe the lampposts look different in each place, they have individual characters. And this traffic light! There's no cross-street there, so what do they want it for in such a desert? I'll tell you: they put it up to pretend they're a real city—to tease the transients who might be naïve enough to stop for it. And that click and buzz, that flash and blink, why do they all do that in just the same way? Repeat and repeat, nothing meaningful by itself. . . .'

'I don't mind them, they're like abstract statues,' Isabel once replied to this. 'As though we were strangers from another part of the world and thought them some kind of religious icon with a red and a green eye. The ones on poles especially.'

He recognized his own fancifulness, coarsened, labored, and made literal. He had taught her to think like this. But she had a distressing disinclination to shake off logic; she did not know how to ride her intuition.

'No, no,' he objected, 'then you don't know what an icon is! A traffic light could never be anything but a traffic light.—What kind of religion would it be which had only one version of its deity—a whole row of identical icons in every city?'

She considered rapidly. 'An advanced religion. I mean a monotheistic one.'

'And what makes you certain that monotheism is "advanced"? On the contrary, little dear! It's as foolish to be fixed on one God as it is to be fixed on one idea, isn't that plain? The index of advancement is flexibility. Human temperaments are so variable, how could one God satisfy them all? The Greeks and Romans had a god for every personality, the way the Church has a saint for every mood. Savages, Hindus, and Roman Catholics understand all that. It's only the Jews and their imitators who insist on a rigid unitarian God—I can't think of anything more unfortunate for history: it's the narrow way, like God imposing his will on Job. The disgrace of the fable is that Job didn't turn to another god, one more germane to his illusions. It's what any sensible man would have done. And then wouldn't the boils have gone away of their own accord?—the Bible states clearly that they were simply a psychogenic nervous disorder— isn't that what's meant by "Satan"? There's no disaster that doesn't come of missing an imagination: I've told you that before, little dear. Now the Maccabean War for instance, for an altogether unintelligible occasion! All Antiochus the Fourth intended—he was Emperor of Syria at the time— was to set up a statue of Zeus on the altar of the Temple of Jerusalem, a harmless affair—who would be hurt by it? It wasn't that Antiochus cared anything for Zeus himself—he was nothing if not an agnostic: a philosopher, anyway—the whole movement was only to symbolize the Syrian hegemony. It wasn't worth a war to get rid of the thing! A little breadth of vision, you see, a little imagination, a little *flexibility*, I mean—there ought to be room for Zeus *and* God under one roof. . . . That's why traffic lights won't do for icons! They haven't been conceived in a pluralistic spirit, they're all exactly alike. Icons ought to differ from one another, don't you see? An icon's only a mask, that's the point, a representational mask which stands for an idea.'

'In that case,' Isabel tried it, 'if a traffic light were an icon it would stand for two ideas, stop and go—'

'Stop and go, virtue and vice, logic and law!—Why are you always on the verge of moralizing, little dear, when it's a fever, not morals, that keeps the world spinning! Are masks only for showing the truth? But no, they're for hiding, they're for misleading, too. . . . It's a maxim, you see: one mask reveals, another conceals.'

'Which kind is better?'

'Whichever you happen to be wearing at the moment,' he told her.

Often he spoke to her in this manner among night crowds on Big Road. Sometimes, too argumentative to be touched, she kept her hands in her pockets and, unexpectedly choosing a corner to turn, he would wind a rope of hair around his finger and draw her leashed after him. She always went easily; she scarcely needed to be led. Among all those night walkers the two of them seemed obscure, dimmed-out, and under a heat-screened autumn moon, one of those shimmering country-moons indigenous to midwestern America, he came to a kind of truce with the street. It was no reconcilement, nothing so friendly as that, not even a cessation of warfare, only of present aggression. To come to terms with Big Road would have been to come to terms with America. And since this was impossible, he dallied instead with masks, and icons, and Isabel's long brown hair.

After twilight on the advent of the weekend the clutter of banners, the parades, the caravans of curiously outfitted convertibles vanished, and the students came out to roam. They sought each other with antics and capers, brilliantly tantalizing in the beginning darkness. Voices hung in the air, shot upward all along the street, and celebrated the Friday madness. It was a grand posture of relief: the stores already closed but the display-windows still lit, and the mannequins leaning forward from their glass cages with leers of painted horror and malignant eyeballs; and then the pirate movie letting out (this is 1949, my hearties), and the clusters of students flowing in gleaming rows, like pearls on a string, past posters raging with crimson seas and tall-masted ships and black-haired beauties shrieking, out of the scented palace into drugstores and ice cream parlors. Sweet, sweet, it was all sweet there before the shops and among the crawling automobiles and under the repetitious street lamps and below the singular moon. On the sidewalks the girls sprouted like tapestry blossoms, their heads rising from slender necks like woven petals swaying on the stems. They wore thin dresses, and short capelike coats over them; they wore no stockings, and their round bare legs moved boldly through an eddy of rainbow skirts; the swift white bone of ankle cut into the breath of the wind. A kind of greed drove Fishbein among them. 'See that one,' he would say, consumed with yearning, turning back in the wake of the young lasses to observe their gait, and how the filaments of their dresses seemed to float below their arms caught in a gesture, and how the dry sparks of their eyes flickered with the sheen of spiders.

And he would halt until Isabel too had looked. 'Are you envious?' he asked, 'because you are not one of them? Then console yourself.' But he saw that she studied his greed and read his admiration. 'Take comfort,' he said again. 'They are not free to become themselves. They are different from you.' 'Yes,' Isabel answered, 'they are prettier.' 'They will grow corrupt. Time will overwhelm them. They have only their one moment, like the butterflies.' 'Looking at butterflies gives pleasure.' 'Yes, it is a kind of joy, little dear, but full of poison. It belongs to the knowledge of rapid death. The butterfly lures us not only because he is beautiful, but because he is transitory. The caterpillar is uglier, but in him we can regard the better joy of becoming. The caterpillar's fate is bloom. The butterfly's is waste.'

They stopped, and around them milled and murmured the girls in their wispy dresses and their little cut-off capes, and their yellow hair, whitish hair, tan hair, hair of brown-and-pink. The lithe, O the ladies young! It was all sweet there among the tousled bevies wormy with ribbon streamers and sashes, mock-tricked with make-believe gems, gems pinned over the breast, on the bar of a barrette, aflash even in the rims of their glasses. The alien gaiety took Fishbein in; he rocked in their strong sea-wave. From a record shop came a wild shiver of jazz, eyes unwound like coils of silk and groped for other eyes: the street churned with the laughter of girls. And Fishbein, arrested in the heart of the whirlpool, was all at once plunged again into war with the street and with America, where everything was illusion and all illusion led to disillusion. What use was it then for him to call O lyric ladies, what use to chant O languorous lovely November ladies, O lilting, lolling, lissome ladies—while corrosion sat waiting in their ears, he saw the maggots breeding in their dissolving jewels?

Meanwhile Isabel frowned with logic. 'But it's only that the caterpillar's future is longer and his fate farther off. In the end he will die too.' 'Never, never, never,' said Fishbein; 'it is only the butterfly who dies, and then he has long since ceased to be a caterpillar. The caterpillar never dies.—Neither to die nor to be immortal, it is the enviable state, little dear, to live always at the point of beautiful change! That is what it means to be extraordinary—when did I tell you that?—' He bethought himself. 'The first day, of course. It's always best to begin with the end—with the image of what is desired. If I had begun with the beginning I would have bored you, you would have gone away. . . . In my ideal kingdom, little dear, everyone, even the very old, will be passionately in the process of guessing at and preparing for his essential self. Boredom will be unnatural, like a curse, or unhealthy, like a plague. Everyone will be extraordinary.'

'But if the whole population were extraordinary,' Isabel objected, 'then nobody would be extraordinary.'

'Ssh, little dear, why must you insist on dialectics? Nothing true is ever found by that road. There are millions of caterpillars, and not one of them is intended to die, and they are all of them extraordinary. *Your* aim,' he admonished, as they came into the darkened neighborhood beyond Big Road, 'is to avoid growing into a butterfly. Come,' he said, and took her hand, 'let us live for that.'

JOYCE CAROL OATES

Scenes of Passion and Despair

❦

I

Walking quickly. The path become mud. She walked in the weeds at the edge of the path—then, her good luck, some planks had been put down in the mud, for cattle to walk on. She walked on the planks.

A hill leading down to the river, bumpy and desolate. Ragged weeds, bushes, piles of debris. NO DUMPING ALLOWED. The Hudson River: she stared at the wild gray water and its shapelessness. Familiar sight. She'd been seeing it from this path, hurrying along this path, for weeks. *Weeks?* It was only the end of June and it seemed to her the summer had lasted years already. *How to survive the summer?*

The planks wobbled in the mud. Her legs straining to go faster, faster. Down on the river bank were old bedsprings and mattresses, broken chairs, washing machines. . . . If one of these planks slipped she might tumble down there herself.

Her hands up to her face, warding off the stinging branches. Almost running. Sometimes she slipped off the cow plank and into the mud, her shoes splattered, damp; she felt with disgust her wet toes inside the gauze of her stockings. Heart thudding impatiently. The eerie light of this June morning, still half an hour before dawn: would it turn into an ordinary day later on? Could this gray still air turn into ordinary air, riddled with sunlight and the songs of June birds? Up at so early an hour, alone on the river bank, alone hurrying along the path, she felt her cunning and yet could not keep down a rising sense of panic—was this visit going to be a mistake? Did he want her? Why this particular June morning, before dawn? Why this particular dress of hers, a blue and white flowered dress, cotton, with a dipping white collar with machine-made lace, why this, why its looseness as if she'd lost weight, why the light splattering of mud and dew across her thighs? And why did she take the cowpath, why not dare the road?

Now she cut up from the path, up through a meager clump of trees. Legs aching from the climb. The house came into view suddenly: an old farmhouse, fixed up a little, the chimney restored. A car in the driveway, mud puddles stretching out long, narrow, glimmering around it, the water crystalline at this hour and at this distance, as if it meant something. Rehearsing her words: *I had to come—I had to see you*—Panting. Brushing strands of hair out of her face. Tried to imagine the exact appearance of her face—her face was very important—her face—her face and his face, confronting each other again—

She ran to the front door, up on the rickety porch. Uncut grass. *A real farmhouse in the country. Near the Hudson.* She did not knock, but opened the door, which was unlocked—*You don't even have to lock your doors*—went inside. Heart pounding desperately. She called his name, ran to his bedroom at the back of the house—in the air the smell of his tobacco, the smell of food from last night—the slight staleness of a body in these close, cluttered rooms—he was waking up, his hair matted from sleep—staring at her in amazement—

She ran to him. *I had to see you*—He interrupted her, they embraced, a feverish embrace. The blank startled love in his face: she saw it and could not speak. *Had to see you*—

Wonder. His voice, his surprise. Hips jammed together, bodies cool and yet slippery as if with the predawn dew, the start of the birds singing outside, ordinary singing for June, the rocky tumult of the run along the path, the planks, the mud puddles, the banks of the river, her mind flitting back to the house she had run from, running out in her blue and white cotton dress, no scarf on her head, shivering, reckless, calculating the amount of time she had before her husband—who had left for the airport at 5:30—might get to New York, might telephone her to check on her loneliness—

So long, you bastard.

II

Hips jammed together in languid violence. A need. A demand. Do the leaves glisten outside in the lead-gray air? Are they strong enough to last all summer? Only June, the flesh of her face is not firm enough to last. Her lover's hands, chest, stomach, his face, his soft kindly mouth, sucking at her mouth, the force of him jerking the bed out inches from the wall, the heaving of covers—she sees how grimy the khaki-colored blanket has become—her lover's parts are firm enough to last all summer, to last forever, even if she wears out.

How many times had they loved like this, exactly?

Lost count.

He is saying something: '. . . is he like now?'

'What is he like? . . .'

'With this, with us . . . doesn't he know, doesn't he sense it . . . what is he like now with you? Can't he guess?'

'I don't know. I don't think about it.'

'Does he drink a lot?'

'No more than before.'

'Can he sleep?'

'No more than before. He's always had insomnia. . . .'

'Do you sleep beside him, then, can you fall asleep while he's awake? . . .'

Wants to know if that other man, my husband, still makes love to me.

'I don't know. I don't know him at all.'

III

The cow planks sigh in the oozing mud, she runs holding her side, panting, her bowels feel like rocks this morning, poison, poisoned; she hates the man she is running from—eleven years invested in him—and she hates the man she is running toward, asleep in that room with the bedraggled wallpaper, and no telephone in his *authentic rented farmhouse on the Hudson River*, so he brags to his friends; she must run to him shivering, her face splotched from the slaps of branches, saliva gathering sourly in her mouth as if forcing her to spit—Can't stop running. Her heart pounds. Can't look down at the river because it is so brutal, a mass that would not support her weight if she suddenly slipped down the bank; imagine the shrieking, the lonely complexities of thought, the electric shocks of terror as she drowns, having a lot of time to reconsider her life—And then they would fish her body out of the river a hundred miles downstream. So long, my love.

The cow planks sigh and bounce. She runs up the hill to the farm he has rented, her flesh aches to be embraced, she scrambles up the hill in her muddy ruined shoes, panting, and she dreams suddenly of an ice pick—wide-awake, she dreams of an ice pick—remembers her mother with an ice pick twenty years ago, raising it to jam it down into a piece of ice—dreams of an ice pick raised in her two trembling hands and brought down hard into whose chest?—his chest?—but what about the wispy light-brown hairs of his chest, which she supposedly loves?

IV

Hips grinding, jammed together. You might imagine music in the background, the grinding is so fierce. An ancient bed: brass bedstead. It came with the house. *A semifurnished old farmhouse with a restored chimney!* The one time her lover ventured into her own home, her husband's handsome white Cape Cod, he clowned around and peeked into drawers nervously, joking about hidden tape recorders and other ingenious spying devices he'd just read about in a national newsmagazine, and then, serious with a sudden manly frown, he told her he had to leave, he couldn't make love to her *there*, in her husband's bed, that magical marriage bed with the satin bedspread.

Why not?

A manly code, a masculine code she couldn't appreciate, maybe?

Now she lies with him in his own rented bed, an old farmhouse bed with a brass headboard, and she sees at the back of his skull a shadowy area like a fatal shadow in an x-ray. Secret from her. Their toes tickle one another. Twenty toes together at the foot of the bed, under the khaki cover! Such loving toes! But the shadow inside his head isn't loving; she fears it growing bigger, darker; she shuts her eyes hard to keep it from oozing into her own skull, because she has always tried to be optimistic about life.

V

Ducks on the river. Mallards. Male and female in pairs and in loose busy groups, Canadian geese bouncing on the waves, going one way in a large confederation of birds, then turning unaccountably and going the other way, back and forth across the choppy waves, back and forth, their calls strident and dismal as she runs, her brow furrowed with some strange stray memory of her mother and an ice pick—

He, the husband, took the Volkswagen to the airport and left her the Buick. *I'll call you from New York*, he said. Darkness at the back of his skull. If his drinking got too bad and he really got sick, she would abandon her lover and nurse him. If he killed himself she would abandon her lover and wear black. Years of mourning. Guilt. Sin. If he found out about her lover and ran over and killed him, shot him right in that bed, she would wear black, she would not give evidence against him, she would come haggard to court, a faithful wife once again.

The husband will not get sick, will not kill himself, will not kill the lover or even find out about him; he will only grow old.

She will not need to wear black or to be faithful. She will grow old.

The lover will not even grow old: he will explode into molecules as into a mythology.

VI

I don't know him at all.

A stormy river, small cataclysms. Quakes, spouts, whirlpools a few yards deep. She doesn't dare to look at the water because her mind might suddenly go into a spin.

You take things too seriously before dawn.

Climbs up the path to his house, up the back way to his meager one-acre farm. Feet already wet from a lifetime of puddles that must be glimpsed far ahead of time in order to be avoided, and suddenly there is a blow against the back of her neck, she pitches forward, a man's feet stumble with her feet, she cries out at the sight of large muddy boots— The blow is so hard that her teeth seem shaken loose. She is thrown forward and would fall except he has caught hold of her.

Jerks her around to face him.

Small panicked screams. She hears someone screaming feebly—hears the sounds of toil, struggle—the man, whose face she can't see, trips her neatly with one ankle behind hers, she falls on her right side, on her hip and thigh and shoulder, already she is scrambling to get away—trying to slide sideways, backward in the mud—but the man has gripped her by the shoulders and lifts her and slams her back against the ground again, up, and then down again, as if trying to break her into pieces, and she sees a swirl of eyes, yellow-rimmed, the small hard dots of black at the center of each eye somehow familiar and eternal, even the dried mucus at the inside corner of each eye absolutely familiar, eternal—

A body jammed against hers. A bent knee, the strain of his thigh muscles communicated to her body, his wheezing, panting, his small cries overpowering hers, his grasping, nudging, glowering face, his leathery skin jammed against her skin; *I don't know him at all*, the bridge of his nose suddenly very important, lowered to her face again and again. Tufts of pale hair in his ears, swollen veins in his throat, his eager grunts, his groveling above her, the stale fury of his breath, his hands, his straining bent knees, the cold mud, the lead-gray patch of sky overhead; inch by inch she is being driven up the hill by his love for her, his thudding against her in a rapid series of blows that jar her entire body and seem to have loosened the teeth in her head—

VII

Once by chance but not really by chance she had met her lover in the general store in town, where he had a post-office box to insure his anonymity (exaggerating the world's interest in him, he imagined a crowd of curious friends sailing up the Hudson to claim him). That rushed exchange of hellos, that eager snatching of eyes, smiles. The anxiety: *Am I still loved?* Adultery makes people nervous. She saw that he hadn't shaved and was disappointed. They whispered between shelves of soup cans and cereal boxes and jars of instant coffee, the brand names and their heraldic colors and designs so familiar that she felt uneasy, as if spied upon by old friends. Her husband was at the lumberyard to buy a few things and would only be a few minutes, she had no time to waste; backing away, she put out her hands prettily as if to ward off her eager lover, and he, unshaven, dressed in a red-and-black checked wool jacket, took a step toward her, grinning, *Why are you so skittish?* Between the towering shelves of fading, souring food he lunged at her with his face, kissed her lips, more of a joke than a true kiss, and she felt a drop of his saliva on her lips and, involuntarily, she licked it off, and the drop was swept along by the powerful tiny muscles of her tongue, to the back of her throat, and down in a sudden pulsation of secret muscles to her insides, where it entered her bloodstream before she had even laughed nervously and backed away, paid for her jar of Maxwell House instant coffee and a leaky carton of milk, hurried outside without glancing back, walked over to the lumberyard where her husband was standing in a brightly lit little office made of concrete blocks talking with a fat man in a red-and-black checked wool jacket; by now the drop of saliva was soaring along her bloodstream, minute and bright and stable as a tiny balloon, rushing through the veins to the right ventricle—*I don't know you at all*—and faster and faster into the pulmonary artery, and into the secret left side of the heart, where it inflated itself suddenly, proudly, and caused her heart to pound—

Did you get the things you wanted? her husband asked.

VIII

Late winter. Freezing air. A car parked on the river bank, by the edge of the big park—barbecue fireplaces with tiny soiled drifts of snow on their grills, you have to imagine people at the picnic tables, you have to imagine a transistor radio squealing, and the smell of burning charcoal; but you can still see the remains of Sunday comics blown into the bushes.

She turns, twists herself eagerly in his arms. His mouth rubs against hers damply, the lips seem soft but they are also hard, or maybe it is the hardness of his youthful teeth behind them. Desperation. Struggle. The toiling of their breaths. On the radio is WKBT's 'Sunday Scene', a thumping tumult of voices and their echoes, yes, everything is wonderful—everything is desperate—he begins his frantic nudging, they are both eighteen, she discovers herself lying in the same position again, making the same writhing sharp twists with her body, as if fending him off and inviting him closer, she moves in time with the music, and then they are sitting up again and he is smoking a cigarette like someone in a movie. Small fixed uneasy smiles. They will marry, obviously.

IX

Early spring. Freezing air. The heater in his car won't work right. *State Police find lovers dead in an embrace.* They kiss each other wetly, hotly, eagerly on the lips, they slide their bodies out of their clothes, snakelike, eager and urgent, the man's breath is like a hiss, the woman's breath is shallow and seems to go no farther than the back of her throat, he lifts her legs up onto the front seat again, onto the scratchy plastic seat cover; such a difficult trick; after all, they are a lot older than eighteen.

X

A woman in a long blue dress. Her stockings white cotton; her shoes handmade. The man in a waistcoat, holding her hand, slipping down the incline to the river bank. They turn to each other eagerly and embrace. So friendly! So helpful! They kneel in the grass, whispering words that can't be heard by the children who are hiding in the bushes. The lovers undress each other. The woman is shy and efficient, the man keeps laughing in small nervous embarrassed delighted spurts, and the children in the bushes have to stand up to see more clearly what is happening—

XI

In his bed, before dawn, she notices the grimy blanket that she will think about with shame, hours later, and as he kneels above her she senses something fraudulent about him, no, yes, but it is too late; she grips his back and his legs though she is exhausted, and her constricted throat gives out small, gentle, fading, souring sounds of love, but she feels the toughness of his skin, like hide, and the leathery cracks of his skin, and down at his buttocks the cold little grainy pimples, like coarse sandpaper, and one hand darts in terror to his head as if she wanted to grip the hair and pull his head away from hers, and she feels his loosening hair—Ah, clumps of his thick brown hair come away in her hand! *I love you*, he is muttering, but she seems to recognize the pitch and rhythm of his voice, she has heard this before, in a movie perhaps, and now, as they kiss so urgently, she tries not to notice the way his facial structure sags, *dear God, the entire face can be moved from one side to the other, should she mention it?* And he didn't bother shaving again. He could have shaved before going to bed, guessing, hoping she might come this morning, before dawn. . . . The eyeballs can be pushed backward . . . and then they move slowly forward again, springing slowly forward, in slow motion, not the way you would expect eyeballs to spring forward. . . .

XII

God, her body aches. There is an itchiness too, probably an infection. That tiny bubble in the blood, exploding into splashes of excited colorless water, probably infected. His swarming germs, seed. The stain on her clothes.

At home, upstairs in the white Cape Cod, she cleans herself of him outside and inside.

No, she is not cleaning herself of him, but preparing herself for him: a shower the night before, the glimpse of her flushed face in the steamy mirror, the sorrow of those little pinched lines about her breasts, the urgent, slightly protruding bone of her forehead, wanting to push ahead to the next morning and through the impending sleepless night beside her husband. She has caught insomnia from him during the eleven years of their marriage.

No, she is not preparing herself for anyone. She is simply standing in the bathroom staring at herself. The bathtub with the bluebells on the shower curtain. Put the shower curtain on the *outside* of the tub when you take a bath, on the *inside* when you take a shower, her mother has explained for the hundredth time. Why are you always in a daze? What are you daydreaming about, may I ask? No, not daydreaming. She is just staring in the mirror at her small hard breasts, at the disappointing pallor of her chest, at her stomach where the faint brown hairs seem to grow in a circle, in a pale circle around her belly button. She is fourteen years old. She is just staring in the mirror, reluctant to leave the bathroom; she is not preparing herself for anyone, she is just standing on the fluffy blue rug from Woolworth's, she is not thinking about anything at all, she is reluctant to think.

XIII

Eight years old, the man finds himself again at a kitchen table, he glances up in surprise to see that it is the kitchen of his parents' house, and he is reduced in size—no more than eight years old! It's a rainy day and from the sound of the house (his father in the cellar) it must be a Saturday. He's fooling around with his clay kit. He has made four snakes by rolling clay between his hands; now he twists the snakes into circles, heads mashed against tails, and makes a pot, but it doesn't look right—too small. The clock is whirring above the stove: a yellow-backed General Electric clock. He is alone in the kitchen. His father is sawing something in the cellar and his mother is probably out shopping. He mashes all the clay together again and makes a column, about six inches high, and he molds the column into a body. With a pencil he pricks holes for the eyes and fashions a smiling mouth, pinches a little nose out, on the chest he pinches out two breasts, makes them very large and pointed, and between the legs he pokes a hole. Sits staring at this for a few minutes. He is aware of his father in the cellar, aware of the clock whirring, the rain outside, and suddenly a raw, sick sensation begins in him, in his bowels, and he is transfixed with dread. . . . He picks up a tiny piece of clay and makes a small wormlike thing and tries to press it against the figure, between her legs. It falls off. Perspiring, he presses it into place again and manages to make it stick. It is a small grub-sized thing but it makes sense. He stares at it and his panic subsides, slowly. He feels slightly sick the rest of the day.

XIV

He crouches above her, she notices his narrowed, squinting eyes, the hard dark iris, the tension of his mouth, and he buries his face against her shoulder and throat as if to hide himself from her, oh, she loves him, oh, she is dying for him, no one but him. Their stomachs rub and twist hotly together and she feels herself gathered up in his arms, is surprised at how small her body is, how good it is to be small, gathered in a man's strong arms, and she thinks that the two of them might be lying anywhere, making love anywhere, the walls of this farmhouse might fall away to show them on a river bank, in the sunshine, or in a car, at the edge of a large state park with Dixie cups blowing hollowly about them as they love, and small white plastic spoons in the grass. . . .

Suddenly exhausted, her hands stop their caressing of his back as if a thought had occurred to them, she instructs herself to caress him again but her fingers seem to have lost interest, grown stiff as if with arthritis, *what is wrong?* At the back of her throat she feels a ticklish sensation as if she is going to cough, but instead of coughing she whispers *I love you*, involuntarily, and they are toiling upstream on the cold river, ducks and geese around them sadly, morosely; the lead-gray sky and the lead-gray water are enough to convince them that this act is utterly useless, but who can stop? On the grass a few feet away is her wide-brimmed straw hat, a hat for Sunday in the country, and he has not had time to take off his waistcoat, and his whiskers scratch her soft skin; but when he whispers *Am I hurting you?* she answers at once *No, no, you never hurt me.* Someone calls out to them. A mocking scream. A shout. They freeze together, wondering if they heard correctly—what was that? Someone is shouting. It isn't in their imaginations, it isn't the cry of geese on the river, no, someone is really shouting at them—has her husband followed her here after all?—but no, it is a stranger who seems to know them. He stomps right over to them and they fall apart, dazed and embarrassed, they are so awkward together, being strangers themselves. The glaring lights make them squint. This stranger eyes them cynically. He squats, a more experienced lover, and arranges and rearranges arms, legs, the proper bending of the knee; with the palm of his practiced hand he urges the man's head down, down, just a few inches more, yes, hold it like that; he spreads the woman's hair in a fan around her head, a shimmering chestnut-brown fan, newly washed, and with his thumb he flecks something off her painted forehead—a drop of saliva, or a small leaf, or sweat from her lover's toiling face—yes, all right, hold this—now he backs away and the glare of the lights surrounds them again. Behind the lights is a crowd, in fact crowds of people, an audience, jostling one another and standing on tiptoe, elbowing one another aside, muttering and impatient. *Bring that camera in close! In close!* The itching raw reddened flesh between the woman's thighs, the moisture and the patch of hair, so forlorn with dampness, a monotonous detail; the camera itself slows with exhaustion and lingers too long upon this close-up, lacking the wit to draw back swiftly and dramatically. The woman with the hair fanned out around her head wonders if her make-up is smeared again, or if that slimy sensation is her skin coming loose. Someday, she knows, her skin must come loose and detach itself from her skull. So tired! She must not yawn. Must not. Must not even swallow her yawn because the tendons of her throat will move and her lover will notice and be hurt. Or angered. His whiskers rub against her face, her mouth and nose. She hates his whiskers. It is sickening how hair grows out of men's faces, constantly, pushing itself out. . . . There are tiny bits of hair on her lips. *Here is marriage. Permanent marriage*, she thinks. And he is whispering to her—*Am I hurting you?* and her pain fades as she realizes that she does love him and that though he hurts her, constantly and permanently, she must always whisper *no*, numb and smiling into his face, their bodies now comradely, soldierly in this grappling, their mouths hardened so that they are mainly teeth—the flesh seems to have rotted away—and she whispers *no, you're not hurting me, no, you have never hurt me.*

JANE GARDAM

Something to Tell the Girls

❦

Imagine a nonsense.

Imagine in *The Times* newspaper—perhaps the Personal Column—the following item:

'Miss Dee-Dee and Miss Gongers of Harrogate Hall, at present holidaying in the West Indies, today hired a motor car in the outskirts of Kingston, Jamaica, and set out on an expedition to the Blue Mountains.'

Imagine this. Suspend disbelief. Consider, as jaws revolve on toast, and bacon is eased from molars, as cornflakes crunch in several continents, this item being read. And imagine then a symphony of feminine shrieks, the scraping back of chairs, the rush of feet to telephones and the following conversation taking place, identical in several parts of the turning earth.

'They *can't* still be teaching!'

'They can't still be *alive*!'

'They certainly can't still be *driving*? Did they ever?'

'If they are it certainly won't be for long. I suppose it'll be Gongers?'

'Well it certainly won't be Dee-Dee.'

Shrieks and laughs.

And shrieks and laughs of not one generation only, for Miss Dee-Dee and Miss Gongers had been at Harrogate Hall (Junior French, Senior History) since before the flood. Since before the War anyway. Not one but half a dozen eras of girls had said, 'Since before the War', about Miss Dee-Dee and Miss Gongers, meaning quite different wars. They dressed —they had always dressed, the two of them—in a style suggesting even before the Boer War, though that of course, could certainly not be so. Could it?

Miss Dee-Dee and Miss Gongers were among the first batch of not very young young ladies to be allowed to go to Cambridge. They had met there, chaperoned by the mutual friend of an aunt. They had left Cambridge—chins held high under Leghorn straws—with the precious piece of paper—not of course a degree—to say that they had completed the course and satisfied the examiners. And they had left unencumbered by romance for they were stern days those and work was hard. Also it was important to try and pass out higher than the men. Miss Gongers was a shining example of this sternness and labour and spoke widely of the resultant glory to her sex of its full academic fruition now. Miss Dee-Dee of course agreed, though she was a pastel, gentle person and there had been a young man and a soft spring day in the Fellows' Garden . . . In the end however romance passed her by.

Nor did romance show itself much at Harrogate where the two young women proceeded, Miss Dee-Dee in a muslin dress and a brim of roses, Miss Gongers in more militant attire. It was Harrogate Hall for the Daughters of Gentlemen—believe it or believe it not—and they set about teaching with the same devotion and conviction that ever Florence Nightingale proclaimed at Scutari some time—well not all that long— before. They would have been quite at home with Miss Nightingale, both of them. Or anyway, Miss Gongers would.

They had taught grandmothers. Young grandmothers certainly, but grandmothers. More granddaughters wrote to grandmothers each year.

'Dear Granny,' they wrote,

Yes—Miss Dee-Dee and Miss Gongers *are* still here! Miss Dee-Dee's sweet. Wouldn't hurt a fly. She teaches the first years. She has a pink face and blue eyes and reads the new ones Beatrix Potters. We're far too old for Beatrix Potters but she still reads them. She's got terribly old editions—I expect *first* editions and our dormi head says if you're homesick you go and see Miss Dee-Dee and she'll give you Harrogate toffee and Mrs Tiggy Winkle. Actually she is absolutely exactly *like* Mrs Tiggy Winkle. She sends her love and says do you still get hay fever!!! Miss Gongers came up to me the first day and said, '*Elspeth's* granddaughter, I think. I hope you'll be better at dates.' She's *terrifying*. Like a sort of iron giraffe. I must say she's a bit of a prize, though. She wears long crêpe dresses—marvellous—and gold glasses, but someone said she does still go out sometimes and take hockey!!!! In knee socks!!!!! Oh, do come down and see them. And me. And thanks a million for the mun and records. Better not let D & G see those though. Buckets of love, Caroline. P.S. No, our letters don't get censored now.

And so on.

Miss Dee-Dee and Miss Gongers like the love of God stretched out from generation unto generation and such an item in *The Times* might have been read as widely and enthusiastically as anything else in it.

'But, Gongers,' said Miss Dee-Dee timidly as a great lorry whirled by in a cloud of dust.

Gongers did not speak. A bus called 'Sing to Jesus' squealed past on the crown of the road, its driver leaning out sideways pumping up and down a great black forearm.

'Gongers, I think—'

'Did you hear what he said?'

'No, but—'

A tremendous howling and screeching and two cars kindly opened before them passing on either side.

'Gongers, I believe it is the *left*-hand side.'

'Nonsense,' said Gongers. She proceeded on the right. They were on a quieter piece of road now, curving and climbing. 'They changed to the right when they threw us out. Naturally one respects their laws, however mistaken.'

Nevertheless, after a minute she changed to the left. The car laboured its way into the foothills of the forest.

'Do you know,' said Dee-Dee, 'do you know, Gongs, I had no idea that you could drive a motor.'

Miss Gongers's ancient Nefertiti neck strained forward as she kept her eyes upon the road. Her expression signified that she found this not extraordinary.

'I mean—the licence?'

'I have always possessed a licence.'

'But isn't there some—test one takes?'

'I never took a test.'

A disintegrating Rolls-Royce filled with two Jamaican families en vacances or en fête and also believing that since the fall of the Raj Jamaica drove on the right, shot past them with a terrible blast of wind.

'I never took a test,' said Miss Gongers. '(See, dear, where the river has taken away the verge.) I never took a test because my first licence was obtained before tests were invented. It was while you were in Schleswig I expect—that summer, just before the War. All through the War—the next War—oh!' (The car fell a foot on to an unexpected lower level.) 'All through the War I paid five shillings a year in order to preclude the necessity of taking a test at the end of it.'

'But you have never driven *since* then, dear, have you?'

'No—a bicycle is healthier in Harrogate. In the holidays there have been motor-coach tours. Well, you know there have.

'Anyway,' she added, narrowly missing a mongoose and swinging out towards the carpet of forest tree tops that bordered the outside edge of the hair-pin bend, 'I am not keen on driving in England now. It is unsafe . . . My word, Deeds,' she said in a minute and with a sudden spark, 'I'm glad we did it. We're climbing now all right. We'd never have got here without a car of our own. It's miles from a bus route.'

A man came out from the trees ahead of them and glared. Miss Gongers tooted at him. He spat.

'I hope we are wise,' Miss Dee-Dee said. 'I hope we don't meet trouble.'

'Wise?' said Gongers, 'you didn't want to spend the rest of the time on those wretched hot package beaches did you? Or in one of those private taxis going off to look at baskets in markets? And the organised tours are prohibitive.'

'Look out!' cried Dee-Dee. But it was only a group of children and their mothers, darting out at them from under the trees, their arms held out before them like sticks, holding pots of orchids.

'Orchids!' Miss Dee-Dee gasped.

'No good,' pronounced Gongers, taking a corner, on one wheel, 'we'd never get them home. Will you shut the windows?'

Dee-Dee wound up windows. One refused to wind. As she struggled with it she realised that she was experiencing an odd yet reminiscent sensation. 'Why, Gongers,' she said, 'it's getting quite cold.' She looked around her at the trees, they were not palm trees any more. They had damp trunks. They were ferny. They dripped with cold-looking water. Jamaica! 'And, goodness! It's getting foggy!'

'Aha,' said Gongers, speeding on.

In Newcastle they stopped and got out. 'Perhaps we ought to leave the engine running,' said Dee-Dee, but Miss Gongers put her mind to it and remembered the formula for switching off. 'Nonsense,' she said, 'they showed me the starter at the motor hire. Perfectly simple. I can't think why they seemed so nervous. It has all come back to me perfectly and, what is more, I *like* the four gears. They are stimulating. Come along, let's get out and walk about.'

On the wide terrace, the great parade ground of Newcastle where British soldiers had marched for so many years, the old ladies paced about. People began to gather in knots, the women with their arms folded and grinning under pink cotton head-gear. More children with orchids sidled up, automatically drifting towards Miss Dee-Dee, who as automatically spread out her arms.

'My dears,' she said, 'orchids. But you see we wouldn't be allowed to take them home. Back to England, you see.'

'You from England then, ma'am?'

'Yes, dear. From Harrogate, in England. Not far from another place called Newcastle.'

'You don't have no orchids there, ma'am?'

'Not like these, dear.'

'Harrogate has got *beautiful* flowers,' Miss Gongers broke in resonantly. 'And very beautiful Valley Gardens.'

'Oh, *look* at these orchids!' Dee-Dee begged, holding out small old hands.

'White face, white face,' a boy yelled, 'go home.' But his sister hit him.

'You like Jamaica, ma'am?' asked a lady in a nasturtium-coloured dress, standing with tilted hip.

'Oh, we *love* Jamaica.'

'The British,' announced Gongers, standing tall as the Duke of Wellington, 'have always loved Jamaica.' Pointing up at the high rock wall above her with the huge plaques of ancient regiments she said, 'My father was a member of that regiment and my grandfather before him.'

The Jamaicans were lost for a reply—then a little girl began to giggle, and a man standing at a little distance, propped against the iron railings, laughed. A breath of ill wind blew across the terrace.

'Hush,' said Miss Dee-Dee.

'You go home. Go home and call us Jamaican monkeys, hey?' a voice shouted.

'Hush! Good gracious!' Miss Dee-Dee exclaimed. She patted a woolly head and followed Miss Gongers back to the car. 'Back, I think,' she said, much flustered. 'Such nice people—Whatever did we do? How very horrible.'

'Back?' said Gongers, 'oh, come. We must go on.' With concentration she started the engine and moved forward with a rush, scattering the orchid bearers. 'Aha,' she said, and swept across the square, out of the high town and away off into the higher mountains.

The road was rough now and narrower, quite different from the way they had already travelled. It was more twisting and lonelier. The crags of the mountains were masked with pines—pines living in such a damp and sunless air that they had grown grey fur coats that hung in tattered rags, thick, ancient cobwebs that trailed the ground. There was not a flower beneath them, not a gleam of light.

'We're in the clouds,' said Dee-Dee.

'Proving that being in the clouds is not what it is thought to be,' said Gongers. 'It's something one might tell the girls.'

However, they swung soon out of the darkest part, over a splashing stream that crossed the road to where the air was clear. Pine woods rose rank on rank, almost black against a rainy sky to the very tops of the immense heights of the mountains. 'A mixture of the Tyrol,' said Miss Gongers, 'and Leatherhead.' They swooped upwards on a stony track and another swoop opened to the left. Miss Gongers put her pointed shoe down hard on the accelerator for this second swoop, swung magnificently round it and embedded the radiator and front bumper high up into a bank of giant blue lilies.

The engine stopped and silence fell over the mountains.

'Yes,' said Gongers, as if this was just what she had expected. 'Yes, yes, yes.' She switched off the engine, which in any case had stopped, and they both got out. The cloud, that had obligingly drifted away, now drifted back again, obscuring everything. Standing in the road in their cotton dresses the two old ladies shivered. 'Did you bring a cardigan, Deeds?' Miss Gongers was walking round the car and bending to look beneath it from various angles.

'No, dear. After all we've been so terribly hot—I never thought . . .'

'Ah well.' Miss Gongers straightened up. 'We came because they said it was cool in the mountains and cool we are.'

'Cool we are,' said Miss Dee-Dee unsurely. Shivering. 'You did put all the brakes on, dear? It does seem to be rather at a—tilt.'

'Of course,' said Gongers. The car in fact seemed to be almost vertical, belly to belly with the bank, desperate, like a climber surprised.

'There is something odd about the back wheel too, don't you think? The tyre seems to be flat. I think we'll have to walk, dear.'

'Down to Newcastle? Oh Gongers, it's miles.'

'We might go on a little upwards perhaps. There might be a village or a police post or something. After all we must be nearly at the top of the pass.'

'I don't see that that—' Miss Dee-Dee's voice had risen though, being Miss Dee-Dee's, it was not of course querulous.

'Why not?' Gongers asked sharply. 'There's always *something* at the top of a pass. Look at Switzerland.'

'But it's not Switzerland,' said Dee-Dee wishing profoundly that it were.

And her wish was answered for round the corner of the road the mists swam away again for a moment and a small Swiss chalet was astoundingly revealed, made of pine trunks, with pointed gables and check curtains at the windows. It stood on a little green alp all by itself surveying the clouds and the tree tops. It had a small stone terrace with an iron seat and round the door someone had planted beds of flowers. There was a child's teddy bear sitting on the terrace, very soggy. Otherwise there was no sign of life.

'Well, bless my soul. Dear Gongers, bless my soul!'

'There you are,' said Gongers triumphantly, 'now this is convenient,' and she marched over the lawn with Dee-Dee behind her and they knocked on the door.

Then they walked about and looked in the windows (rather untidy) and called a time or two, but nobody answered. There was a padlock properly fastened on the door and the windows were well barred.

'They can't be far though,' said Dee-Dee, thinking of the bear. 'There's washing-up to be done. Someone's been here very recently. If we wait about—'

'I thought I heard someone,' said Gongers and they stood quite still. But there was only the long clear pipe of the solitaires in the forest.

'Solitaires,' said Dee-Dee, 'oh, those must be the solitaires. Some people live in Jamaica all their lives and never hear the solitaires.'

Gongers, on steely tiptoe, made her way all round the chalet once again. 'There is no one,' she said, 'yet I'm sure I heard . . . It is a holiday house. Deeds, there may be nobody here for weeks.' The clouds swept slowly back, blotting out the view again and muffling the bird song. They stood looking at each other on the cold and now invisible lawn. 'I am afraid that we are quite alone,' said Miss Gongers in a voice that faced facts.

But back at the car she was proved wrong, for standing beside it quite silently were two men. Miss Gongers whose mind had been put to the test during the past minutes quickly shut her eyes and opened them again. 'Er—Deeds—Do you see?'

Dee-Dee joined her at the lily bank. 'Oh—*people*. Well! You were *right*. You *did* hear people! Oh what a blessing!'

'HellO!' Gongers called in hockey match tones and strode off to the road with Dee-Dee behind, 'How absolutely splendid. How *really* splendid. I cannot tell you how delighted we are to see you. We have really been very—How do you do?'

The two men had yellow whites to their eyes and were chewing something. They did not speak.

'Let me introduce—' said Gongers. 'I am Miss Gongham. This is my friend Miss Deeds. We are from England. This is our car.' She held out her hand and after a pause one of the men slowly took it, first moving his gun into his left hand. The other man turned away and gave the car wheel a kick.

'Yes,' said Gongers, 'yes, I know. I'm afraid it is a puncture on top of everything else. But if perhaps you could just get the car off the bank. Just a good heave. A *good* heave, perhaps—oh dear! Is that thunder?'

Neither of the men spoke but the one who had kicked the car kicked it again.

'Oh, I say,' said Gongers, 'I shouldn't do that. It will do no good whatsoever. Now just stay where you are and I will lean in and release the brake. Then both of you give a pull. Dee-Dee dear, just take the guns.'

Miss Gongers dived into the car and dealt with the hand-brake. Miss Dee-Dee smiled at the men and collected in the guns as though they had been exercise books. After an initial small shove by Miss Gongers the men quickly got out of the car's path and assisted it into a horizontal position.

'Now—the jack. Dee-Dee, put the guns in the car. They will get rusty.' It was raining hard now and thunder seemed very close at hand. 'Come along, Dee-Dee dear, you get in too. These kind friends will get the jack from the boot, I'm sure.'

Waiting until she saw them very slowly, and almost in a trance, begin to open up the boot, she herself got behind the wheel. Mutterings were heard without and the face of one of the men—his eyes were very strange and dead, his mouth not happy—appeared at the window. He said something in a hoarse voice. There was a strong, odd smell about him. He had gingerish crinkly hair, an orange skin and a chain round his neck. He seemed to be suggesting that they get out of the car again.

'We are making it too heavy,' said Dee-Dee and removed her tiny bird-like frame from the passenger seat. Gongers followed. 'Very well,' she said, 'do let's get a move on though, shall we?'

The second man, the kicker, swung the jack heavily about in his hands.

'Shall we?' Gongers gleamed over her arched nose. In the voice were forty-seven years of hockey, of supervision of the cross-country, of fixing in the mind the clauses of the Treaty of Amiens, of pressing home the iniquity of reading by torch beneath blankets, of . . .

The jack was placed and vigorously set to work and the back, left-hand corner of the car slowly rose into the air. The wheel however stayed upon the ground.

Even the two gunmen were surprised and the first one, the one who had shaken hands, met Miss Dee-Dee's eyes and gave a sudden huge crow of laughter. At almost the same moment there was a rending, blazing flash up behind them by the house and a crash of thunder like Armageddon. Gunmen and ladies leapt for the car with a composite leap and sat there rigid as the rain cracked down.

'Mind the guns,' said Miss Gongers, 'don't trample them on the floor. I am afraid of guns. I believe that they should be forbidden. I do not believe in shooting of any kind on any pretext whatsoever. I only hope,' she said glaring sternly at the wet men through the driving mirror, 'that you were not shooting solitaires.'

And half an hour later they still sat there stiffly.

The storm had turned the road into a stony brown river, thunder boomed and rattled above and the rain poured down. To assist things one of the men took off his jacket and fixed it over the window which did not wind up. He muttered to his friend now and then. They took out a bottle from a pocket and a strong smell of rum invaded the car.

'I suppose we ought to play a game or something,' said Miss Gongers.

'Or tell stories,' said Miss Dee-Dee.

The men had no views on this, but Miss Dee-Dee felt very tempted. '*The Tailor of Gloucester*?' she said. 'It is very adult.' But Miss Gongers thought not. Looking in the mirror again, she suggested a song. 'Shall we sing?' she asked, and as nothing resulted but rather heavier breathing struck up 'The Ash Grove'; and after a nervous false start Miss Dee-Dee joined in. The gunmen jumped out of the car and disappeared into the forest.

'Really,' said Miss Gongers, 'they are so very extraordinary. It makes me feel one will never understand them. Such good Christians too. Every denomination so well represented. I do like them all so much. Oh dear—we never even gave them a tip.'

A second nonsense:

The Times. April—197—
Personal.

A multiple puncture belonging to Miss Dee-Dee and Miss Gongers of Harrogate Hall was repaired late last evening by a policeman at a police box two miles down the mountain on which it occurred in the Jamaican rain forests. The ladies had rolled the two miles to the post on the car wheel's rim which Miss Gongers had cleverly and with Divine assistance freed from a faulty jack. As the clattering vehicle approached the police box, the officer was seen to buckle on his gun belt, but took it off again on examination of the passengers. He took them into his cement shed, made them tea on a Calor gas ring, tried the jack, flung it into the forest and loosed the wheel by the process of lifting the whole motor car up in his two hands. He then found the ladies blankets, coconut, and bread and accommodated them for the night—one in his bunk and the other on two chairs. He himself slept in the empty prison cell. In the morning he saw them off with the recommendation that they stop for nobody, adding that this was advice. Miss Gongers gave him her well-known handshake while Miss Dee-Dee took one of his hands in both her own and nearly kissed it.

'Trained by us of course,' said Gongers whirling down the mountain, 'the real old English policeman. A magnificent man. A very moving episode.'

'Yes,' said Miss Deeds. She was a little stiff this morning. 'It will be nice to have a bath and a proper rest though, and feel that it is over.'

'But it was a great experience,' said Gongers, 'and something to tell the girls.'

They had reached Kingston now and in the rush hour traffic Gongers was driving slowly in the slow lane. 'After all,' she said, 'this sort of experience is exactly what we came away from Europe for. A thrilling chapter. I'm almost sad that it is completed.'

And the car stopped.

They were crossing a bridge over some sort of underpass and the maniac traffic was hurtling by. It was the lunch-time rush hour, and the car baked and pulsated in the noon-day sun. Miss Gongers, after trying many things with fingers and toes, sat back and closed her eyes. 'I spoke too soon,' she said and let her hands drop into her lap. Her nose suddenly looked sharp and pale. 'What on earth can be the matter now?' she said and her voice had a most unfamiliar high and wavering quality.

'Now, don't worry,' said Dee-Dee at once, 'goodness we're nearly home. You've done wonderfully, Gongers. Now I'll just get out and tell someone. It'll be no time at all.' She was quickly back at the window. 'Dear,' she said, 'I've found someone. They'll come and get us at once. Now *don't worry*. A nice man in a van. Didn't you see him stop? I don't quite know where he's gone but . . . There. Now, we'll just sit a little. I wonder if it might be cooler out of the car. Shall we go and sit under the bridge down there? It might be in the shade.'

They got out and looked over the parapet. It did not look inviting. The underpass was not so much a road as—well, it might almost have been a great, dry drain (which it was) beating with heat and full of cracks. In one place someone had started a sort of allotment in the dust. There were some desperate looking tomatoes. Near them two black and white vultures were eating a dead dog. 'I don't think it looks cooler down there,' said Gongers.

'Perhaps under the bridge,' said Dee-Dee. They picked their way, tottering a little, down the steep ramp of the drain and sat upon a cement block inside the central pier, but it was, as Miss Gongers had thought, much hotter. It smelled quite dreadfully and beneath the bridge was unspeakable filth. 'This will not do,' said Gongers, 'we must go back.' But they sat on under the pitiless sun quite unable to move.

And presently the children began to appear all round them popping up from cracks and crannies, sliding out of the tin shacks that grew like sores along the banks of the drain. They were thin children—very thin about the legs and some of them were ugly and dressed in bits of rag. They stood round the old ladies in a circle and one or two began to call things out.

Soon they all began to call things out and when they found they were not answered they began to push forward and several started to do a sort of derisive dance. They came in closer. They clustered round.

'Children,' said Miss Gongers, 'not like the pretty ones up in the mountains.'

'Poor little dears,' was all Miss Dee-Dee could say.

The children began to laugh and shout and push, to come in close, to argue who should get nearest and feel brooches and bags and hats. A stone flew and someone began to cry. At the second stone Miss Gongers gave herself a great shake and stood up. Summoning all her powers she walked forward taking first one child by the hand and then a second. The others squealed and pressed forward but she still walked on, right into the middle of the drain and then stood still. 'Now,' she said.

'White face,' screamed a child.

'Dee-Dee, will you see to that one. He's so little. And take the other young ones will you? That's right.' Miss Dee-Dee with a sigh also stood up. Then clapped her hands.

'The little ones to Miss Deeds and the big ones to me,' called Miss Gongers. 'Two lines please. Now—who's to be leader? That's right. No fighting now. Straight lines, then off we go. Who knows "Oranges and Lemons?"'

'Sit now and be quiet,' said Miss Dee-Dee, 'quite, quite quiet—' Her voice died to a whisper and all the children's voices ceased, 'Once upon a time there was an old cat, called Mrs Tabitha Twitchit . . .'

'Oh very nice, very nice,' came Miss Gongers's voice as the lines took shape, 'and *lovely* singing. I wish my girls at home could see this dancing. My word. Now who can sing "Here we go gathering . . ."? That's the way. Now off you go.'

The rabble of children turned to dancers, skinny legs pranced, white teeth gleamed. A sort of song began to rise. First one line wavered forward, the the other to meet it, 'Here we come gathering . . .'

'You have the idea,' Miss Gongers cried.

It was Mrs Ingham who saw them. She was accompanying Miranda on the school run and a traffic jam on the bridge had caused Miranda to remark in passing or rather in sticking, that the bridge spanned a huge dry drain built against the hurricane floods but used in fact to grow tomatoes. Mrs Ingham nipped out of the car at once and jutted her chin over the parapet where she viewed the dead dog.

'Tomatoes,' she said, 'need *regular* fertiliser.'

Then, surveying a whirling group and a static group of children and two fragile scarecrows who appeared in some uncanny way to be in charge of them, she cried, 'Miranda! Come here. Quickly. It *can't* be!' and Miranda, heaving herself alongside said, 'Good Lord, it is!'

And so the two old things were rescued and lived to tell the tale.

In years to come anthropologists were to be interested and flummoxed by a legend of singing priestesses in a motor car in the mountains and by a localised calypso in the plain, about roly-poly puddings and rats, executions, and the churches of London, hawthorn, frost and citrus fruits and candles that light you to bed.

RUTH PRAWER JHABVALA

A Star and Two Girls

❦

No one knew who had brought the two English girls to the party. It was the usual kind of film star's party, with a lot of illicit liquor and heavy Indian food; and the usual kind of people were there, like directors and playback singers and actors and lots of hangers-on. It was the hangers-on who got drunk the quickest, and one of them had to be carried out quite early. There were also some well-known actresses, and they all wore plain white saris and no jewellery and sat very demurely with their eyes cast down so that it was evident at one glance that they were virtuous. The two English girls, on the other hand, were not a bit demure but looked around them with bright eyes and were ready to talk to anyone who talked to them. Their names were Gwen and Maggie.

Suraj, who gave the party in honour of his own birthday, had good reason to be satisfied with it. It went on till four o'clock in the morning, most people were drunk and some so drunk that they got sick; a lot of jokes were told which the actresses had to pretend not to understand. At the height of good spirits several men broke into a rough, spontaneous dance, while the others stood round in a circle and rhythmically clapped and cheered them on to dance more and more wildly till they collapsed in exhaustion on the floor, and then everyone laughed and helped them to their feet again. An excellent party in every way, and next day, lying in bed at noon, Suraj thought back on it with satisfaction. However, he found that what he thought most about was the two English girls, and here his satisfaction was not entirely unmixed. Although friendly, there had been something aloof about them, and Suraj even had a hazy memory—all memories of the party were hazy for he had drunk a good deal—of some kind of a rebuff. What had happened? What was it? He couldn't remember, he only had a vague idea that his advances—not even advances, his friendliness—were not met with the same eager gratitude that he was used to. And then quite suddenly, quite early too, the two girls had left. One minute they were there, and the next, just as he turned round to look for them again, they had gone. He frowned, then laughed. He was going to find them again; for nothing in particular, only for his own amusement. It was something to look forward to.

Gwen and Maggie were pleased to see him when he turned up at their hotel. Indeed, anyone would have been pleased to see Suraj: he was tremendously handsome and wore beautiful clothes and walked in the way people do who know everyone is looking at them. He had real star quality. Gwen and Maggie were not, however, absolutely bowled over by this; they kept their heads and this pleased Suraj and at the same time put him on his mettle. He wanted very much to have them like and admire him and found himself eager to do a great deal for them. He wanted to introduce them to the film world, to show them Bombay, to throw everything open for them. He escorted them to expensive restaurants and took them for long drives in his car. He invited them to his shooting sessions and showed them round the studios and introduced them to many famous stars. He was eager for them to pronounce an impossible wish so that he might be able to fulfil it. But all their wishes were quite possible and the most he could do was to fulfil them to the brim, doing everything on as large and grand a scale as possible. He took them to the races, and a polo match, and a wrestling bout, and a cricket match, and everywhere they had front seats and were made much of because they were with him. They accepted all this gladly and were always profuse in words of appreciation and gratitude. 'It was quite perfect,' they would say. 'Thank you so much for taking us.' 'Tremendous . . . fabulous . . . thanks most awfully . . . absolutely marvellous': but he sensed that it was only their words that were so profuse, and that actually they were not as overwhelmed as they pretended to be. On the contrary, he felt there was something detached and amused in their attitude, and indeed they took everything so much in their stride that he became quite frantic in trying to think up more and more, better and better treats for them. Sometimes he was annoyed at their level-headedness, and then annoyed at himself that he—he, Suraj!—should care to impress them.

He always thought of them together: Gwen and Maggie, as if they were one person. Yet they were very different. Maggie was large, pretty, ash-blonde, with a radiant smile and dimples in her healthy cheeks; Gwen, on the other hand, didn't look a bit healthy—in fact, she looked rather consumptive or at least as if she had a weak chest, very thin and with a deathly pale, transparent skin and light red hair. They had been at school together and had all sorts of jokes from that time which Suraj didn't understand; now they were on a world trip which their parents had given them as a present on their eighteenth birthdays. When they got back, Maggie hoped to start work on a fashion magazine, Gwen had been promised a job in an art gallery. Neither of them was in a hurry to return home, though, and start on this new life.

What they liked to do best was to lie for hours and hours on the beach.

Gwen would shelter herself under a parasol because her skin was so delicate, but Maggie would lie in full sunshine wearing a tight, bright yellow swimming-costume and smeared with suntan oil, lying now on her back and now on her stomach so that both sides should get done equally. Suraj would get restless and ask, 'What shall we do now?' but they wouldn't even answer him, they were so drowsy and content. Sometimes Maggie went off into the sea with him, and there she shrieked and kicked her arms and legs and fought with him among the waves, while Gwen watched them from under her parasol, looking composed and rather elegant in some sort of flowing, flowered shift. When they came back again, Suraj rubbed a towel vigorously to and fro across his back but Maggie simply flopped down on the sand and let the sun dry the drops of water from her skin.

'Aren't you hungry?' Suraj asked hopefully. He himself was starving—he always needed a lot of food at regular times and his swim in the sea combined with the idle morning had left him hungrier than ever. But those two, if they bothered to answer him at all, only shook their heads; it wasn't as if they didn't have hearty appetites—they did, whenever they settled down to a meal, he was amazed at the quantities they put away with unabashed relish—but only that they couldn't be bothered to move. 'It's restful here,' Gwen murmured, and Maggie, lying face down on the sand, said 'Hmm' in luxurious assent. Suraj was afraid they would drop off to sleep, and then he would patiently have to wait till they woke up before he could get anything to eat, so he began to talk rather desperately, using a loud, wide-awake voice to rouse them:

'Yesterday we saw my new rushes. Everyone said they are wonderful, this is going to be a big hit. Everyone said.'

'What fun.'

'They said it is my best role yet. I play a poor rickshaw-wallah and one day my sister is abducted by a rich man. The scene in which I realize what has happened is very emotional. There is no dialogue, only the expression on my face. It was a great strain playing this scene—ooph, afterwards I felt exhausted, terrible. You don't know what it is like for an actor: you see, we really *feel* what we are acting and it is, oh I can't explain, but a great burden here, here on the heart.' He clutched it.

'I know exactly what you mean,' Gwen said. 'I was in the school play once—you remember, Mag? It was only a small part but it was agony. Of course I muffed the whole thing and was never taken again in any other school play which was disappointing but also a tremendous relief because I honestly don't think I could ever have lived through such moments of fearful dread again.'

'Don't be an ass,' said Maggie and made amused sounds from out of the sand.

'I'm completely serious,' Gwen insisted, and then she looked at Suraj with wide, green eyes: 'She doesn't understand. But you do, don't you? You know what I mean.'

He felt uncomfortable. Was she laughing at him? But her eyes, as she looked at him unblinkingly, were clear and frank. He dared not answer but instead laughed to show that he understood the joke (if it was a joke). Then he shouted: 'But aren't you hungry yet? Aren't you starving?'

He enjoyed looking at them and beyond that he enjoyed the fact that they liked to be looked at. It was not so with pretty Indian girls—or if it was, they did their best to hide it, putting on a proud, injured air, giving little tosses of the head and twitching at their saris. But Gwen and Maggie bathed in admiration as if it were sunshine, they smiled and basked themselves like cats. When they were on the beach together, Suraj loved feasting his eyes on Maggie's naked thighs as they came bursting— so firm, golden and healthy, brushed with a down of blonde hair and grains of sand—from out of her tight yellow swimming-costume; and far from discouraging him, Maggie kept shifting them from here to there so that he could see them better, and sometimes she looked at them herself, likewise with admiration and approval, and tenderly brushed the sand off them. On the other hand, Suraj got very annoyed if anyone else looked at the two girls. Unfortunately most people did, not only because the two were young and pretty but also because they were foreign and different. Sometimes Suraj made scenes on this score—in restaurants, in cinema foyers, suddenly he would seize someone by the shirt-front and thrust his face forward and say rude, challenging things in Hindi. The two girls would try and calm him down and get him away as quickly as possible, almost hustling him off while he continued to throw furious glances at the offender and his big strong shoulders twitched inside the silk shirt, impatient for a fight.

But the worst scene was with one of his own friends. Suraj had many friends. They liked to be with him wherever he went, and he liked to have them there: they gave each other confidence, he to move in the middle of a crowd who applauded and, where possible, imitated his every word and action, they to be seen and known in the company of a celebrity. They sat in his house from early morning, eating his food and drinking his liquor and smoking his cigarettes, they accompanied him on the set and loudly applauded every shot of his, they thronged to his parties, they begged for passes to his premières, they accompanied him on his travels at his expense. When he wished them to go away—which was not very often, though more often than usual now that he had met Gwen and Maggie—he told them so quite without ceremony; and indeed they did not expect ceremony from him. He would not allow them to see much of the two English girls. He knew only too well what thoughts they would

have, what ribald comments they would pass about them to each other—
he had often enough made the same kind of comments himself. But now
the idea made him angry. The girls were his friends, they were under his
protection. His companions realized his feelings, so that when they did
meet the girls, which was sometimes unavoidable, they were on their
guard and were careful to throw nothing but covert glances in that direction and to pass their comments well out of their patron's earshot.

Once, however, one of them spoke too loudly. It was a very hot and
trying day, on the set of one of Suraj's films. An excellent scene, full of
dramatic and emotional content, had been planned for that day, and Suraj
had invited the two English girls to be present. However, everything
went wrong. The electricians could not fix the lights to the cameraman's
satisfaction and everyone had to sit around and wait, and then the leading
lady's make-up had to be done again. It was the sort of frustrating day
that happened often enough in Suraj's professional career; but today it
infuriated him because of his two guests whom he had specially invited to
witness one of his great scenes. He sat and smoked cigarette after cigarette,
frowning and not speaking much, and feeling very hot in his costume
which consisted of silk leggings, a cloth of gold coat, and a huge silk
turban with a jewel and a feather in it. Everyone was in a bad mood. The
director and the cameraman shouted at each other, and the assistant
director had an argument with the sound recordist, and the leading lady
got angry with the tailor who kneeled on the floor sewing spangles on to
her Moghul princess dress. Suraj's friends yawned and were restless and
called for many bottles of Coca Cola. Only Gwen and Maggie were not
bored. They sat on the two chairs allotted to them, one in a raspberry
pink dress and the other in a lemon yellow one, sucking cold drinks
through a straw and looking very happy to be there and grateful that they
had been invited.

The heat, the boredom, the fact that Suraj seemed to be preoccupied
made his friends more careless than usual. They began to point out
certain characteristics of the two English girls to each other—for instance,
that they happened to be showing a great deal of long leg—and they
tittered together and one of them volunteered a remark which was certainly
funny but was unfortunately overheard by Suraj. Quick as a flash he
jumped up (his chair fell over) and the next thing that was heard was a
resounding slap. Those that had been quarrelling or arguing stopped
doing so and it was suddenly very quiet in that noisy place so that the
next slap sounded even louder than the first. The leading lady let out a
little cry of terror. After the second slap, Suraj's victim hid his head in his
arms; otherwise he made no attempt to defend himself, nor did he offer
to run away but stood as if awaiting any further chastisement his patron

might wish to inflict. Suraj began to belabour him with his fists, the feather in his turban shook and trembled furiously as he rained blows on the young man's head and shoulders; since no resistance was offered, he continued to do so until others begged him to desist and hung on to his arms. The leading lady cried 'Oh, oh' as she watched, and from time to time she flung her hands before her face as if she could not bear to see any more. Gwen and Maggie averted their eyes from the scene of violence, and when it was over, they sat very quiet, no longer bright and interested and happy to be there but, on the contrary, as if they were uncomfortable and wished to be away.

When next he saw them, Suraj had forgotten about this incident and was surprised when they brought it up. 'It's all right,' he said, waving his hand to wave it all away. 'He apologized to me.'

'*He* apologized to *you*!'

'Yes,' Suraj said and stared at them and they stared back at him. There was a brief silence. Then Suraj said, 'Hurry up, aren't you ready yet?' He had come to the hotel to fetch them and take them out to witness a gala beauty contest.

Gwen said, 'You know, I think I don't feel like it.'

'Me neither,' Maggie said. They both took off their shoes and lay down on their twin beds.

'Are you ill?'

'Not ill exactly,' Gwen said.

'Our table is booked! Everyone is expecting us!'

'You go, Suraj. Who cares if we're there or not. You're the big attraction.'

He paced the room in agitation. He ran his hand through his hair. 'What is this? Good heavens. First you say yes, we are coming, and now—'

'I know. We're awful.'

He stood by the window. The room, on the third floor of the hotel, overlooked the sea and the curtains were drawn right back, giving a clear view out. Dusk had fallen and the sea looked silver and so did the sky and the ships that lay out on the water. Suraj looked out, and it was so peaceful that his agitation subsided, leaving him instead sad, melancholy. He said, 'Something is wrong.' He turned back into the room and looked at them.

'It's what you did yesterday,' Gwen said at once, and Maggie too came in with 'It made us feel dreadful.' Both seemed relieved to be able to talk about it to him, and they went on in a rush: 'It was so unfair, Suraj. That poor boy, after all, what had he done? Nothing.'

'Wait,' Suraj said.

To humiliate him like that in front of everyone—how could you? It was so shaming. Unbearable. Oh God, Suraj.' And they blushed, their faces red with someone else's shame.

'Wait,' Suraj said again. But strangely enough, he was grateful to them for being so frank with him. He remembered the differences he had had with Indian women of his acquaintance—not only with girl friends but with relatives too, with his own mother or sisters. If for some reason they were offended with him, they would be haughty, toss their head, shrug one shoulder, push out their underlip, be eloquent in injured silence; and it was not until he had done a hundred little acts of propitiation that they would at last consent to tell him what he had done to offend them. Gwen and Maggie's directness surprised and pleased him. His feelings towards them grew very warm, and while of course he wanted to acquit himself, he was also at the same time eager to meet their frankness with an even greater one of his own, to explain and to describe his life, his whole world, and make them understand him utterly.

He told them about his own earlier years when he had run away from home and come to Bombay to become a film star. He had been very poor and dependent on other people's goodwill even for food and shelter. Fortunately, he had acquired a patron, a successful film star who had allowed him to join his retinue and follow him around wherever he went. How grateful Suraj had been for this privilege! It had enabled him to penetrate straightaway into that world which he had come to conquer, to pass freely in and out of studios, be present at story conferences, see the newest rushes, go to film-world parties, drink the whisky and smoke the cigarettes which he would never have been able to afford on his own. In return, all that his patron required was perfect obedience and perfect allegiance, to be there when he was feeling bored or lonely, to laugh at his jokes, to praise him and run down his rival. All this Suraj and the star's other friends did gladly, vying with each other as to who could do it the best; and not only because the star was who he was, no, but because they genuinely loved and admired and looked up to him. 'He was like a god to me!' Suraj exclaimed, and his whole face shone with this past adoration.

Gwen and Maggie, still lying on their beds, smiled at his fervour. They appreciated it very much. Maggie said, 'I wish I could feel like that about someone.'

Gwen said, 'Did you know that in the fourth I was mad about Miss Kemp? Except I couldn't stand the way she spat when she spoke.'

'Even today,' Suraj said, 'well—he is not so great any more, I will tell you, he doesn't get half the amount, not one quarter, for a film that I get, and everyone knows he drinks too much and other vices also. Well, he is old now. But even today, when I meet him—he can say, Suraj, run out and get me a packet of cigarettes, and I would run if he ordered me like that, yes today! Once, years ago, he humiliated me in front of everyone because he was angry with me. I felt bad, of course, I went away and cried and wanted to be dead; but not for one moment did I feel angry with him—only with myself because I had offended him. Next day I went back and touched his feet and begged his pardon and he forgave me. How I loved him at that moment, how grateful I was to him. He was my father, my guide, my guru. I owed everything to him.'

'I'm starving,' Maggie suddenly said.

Suraj jumped up and said, 'Let's go out! Let me take you to—' He racked his brains for somewhere glorious and wonderful enough where he could spend a lot of money and make them happy.

But they preferred to stay in the hotel. They rang the bell and a lot of food was ordered and brought up. They all three ate heartily and sent for several more dishes so that the room became cluttered with used plates and silver dishcovers. Afterwards they leaned out of the window and looked at the sea and the strings of light on the shore and those on the ships far out on the water, and they threw out bread crumbs for the seagulls though these were all asleep. They competed as to who could throw them the furthest, and Suraj won hands down and that made him happier than ever—he loved winning games; and he thought, leaning out of the window between them both, that never in all his life had he enjoyed such a grand friendship, such jolly times as he had with these two English girls.

Yet there were occasions when he was annoyed with them. Suddenly he would suspect that they didn't take him seriously enough; that they didn't realize quite who he was. Then he felt compelled to tell them. Last year he had been voted Actor of the Year by the All India Critics Association; he had more than five hundred fan letters every day; all over the country there were Suraj Fan Clubs who wore badges and celebrated his birthday and organized teas at which to meet each other and talk about him. Gwen and Maggie listened to him politely and made their usual appreciative remarks of 'How fascinating' or 'How lovely' or 'What fun'. It wasn't enough: he couldn't quite say what more it was he wanted from them but only that he wanted more, much more, he wanted them to get excited and look at him the way other girls did. And because they didn't do that, they didn't lose their heads, he went and lost his: he became very boastful and told them not only of the grand things he had done and was doing but the even grander ones that lay waiting for him in the future. They continued to listen politely though they no longer commented, and their silence made him talk louder and bigger, his claims became exaggerated and ridiculous, and the worst of it was that he himself was aware of this and was ashamed of it: but instead of keeping quiet, he felt compelled to talk more and more, even thrusting out his chest and beating the flat of his hand against it, at the same time hating himself, and hating them for bringing him to this pass.

On the next day he lay in bed and thought resentful thoughts about them. They were really nothing more than two very ordinary English girls of whom he himself had seen plenty; there was absolutely no reason why they should have so high an opinion of themselves. He decided that he hated people who had a high opinion of themselves. He also decided that he would not see them any more. He stayed in bed and had his breakfast and then his friends came and sat round the bed and they all played cards and had a lot of jokes. It was good fun. Later in the day he sent them away and got dressed very nicely and went to visit an actress friend. He was pleased with the reception he got there. She fussed over him and so did her mother and they pampered him with a rich tea of fritters and sweetmeats. He sat with them in their drawing-room which was rather dark but had lots of furniture and ornaments and red velvet curtains. There was teasing and tittering and the actress sat with her hands demurely in her lap and her eyelids lowered except sometimes when she raised them a tiny bit to dart a look of fire at him. A crumb of sweetmeat had got enticingly stuck to her lip and, when her mother left the room for a moment, he darted forward to kiss it away while she tried to ward him off with her soft, weak arms. Then some photographers came to take her publicity pictures, and although Suraj wanted her to send them away, she wouldn't but posed for them in various attitudes in her drawing-room. Now she looked reflective by a vase of flowers and holding one flower in her hand, now she stuck her finger through the bars of her parrot's cage and tenderly puckered her mouth at him, now she was gay and threw back her head and laughed with spontaneous laughter into the cameras. All the time she was very sweet with the photographers, dazzling them with charm, while Suraj watched and got more and more cross. When they had gone, he began to pick a quarrel with her to which she was not slow to respond, and soon they were taunting each other with their shortcomings in both their personal and professional lives. The mother, after attempting to soothe them down, joined in on the daughter's side, but before the quarrel could reach its climax, Suraj got up in disgust and left them. Surprised and disappointed, they called after him, 'What's the matter? Why are you going?' but he didn't bother to answer. When he got home, there was a telephone message from the actress, and she kept trying to ring him the whole evening till in the end he took the receiver off the hook.

He felt terrible. His whole life seemed to him empty and futile. He sat all alone in his large, modern drawing-room which had been done up by an interior decorator and contained several modern paintings which Suraj secretly disliked; indeed, the whole room was only pleasant to him when it was full of his friends or had a big party going. He drank one whisky after the other. He perspired, he wept a little, his mind became soaked and soft. He heard the doorbell ring but he didn't take any notice and it rang again and he still didn't take any notice. Then Gwen and Maggie came in and said they'd been trying to phone and phone, and where had he been all the time and what was the matter? All his misery disappeared like a flash and he tried to rise to his feet but he was very unsteady and they said he had better sit down again. They sat down with him, one on each side. He tried to tell them a lot of things but his tongue was too big and furry. Finally he only waved his hand at them to express everything he wanted to but couldn't say and he cried a bit more but now it was with contentment. They suggested he should go to bed and he let them help him into his pyjamas, and when they had settled him and made him comfortable, he fell asleep at once with a smile of satisfaction on his face.

This incident drew them, if anything, closer together. The girls did not speak about it much but neither did they try to avoid the subject, and whenever they referred to it, it was in a light, amused way. Suraj even became quite proud of it and felt it was a manly thing to get drunk and have to be put to bed. And now that they had seen him in this state, he felt there was nothing he need hide from them; he trusted them completely and wanted them to know everything about him, not only the things of which he was very proud but others also. He told them more and more about his early days, his childhood in a town in the North, his family who expected him to go to college and from whom in the end he had had to run away because they could never sympathize with his higher ambitions. He also told them a lot about his early days of hardship in Bombay, before he met his patron and began to do well: how he had attached himself to groups of people on the outskirts of the film industry and had followed them around and sat with them in cheap restaurants, hoping that someone would buy him a meal and yet so shy to accept it that often he had walked away the moment the menu was brought. He had lived with anyone who was ready to put him up, and there were always people who didn't mind if he unrolled his bedding on their veranda or, during the monsoon, in whatever space he could find inside; on hot nights he often slept out on the beach. His greatest fear was always that his family would find him before he had achieved what he wanted and had become rich and famous (he never had any doubts that he would). He missed them and wanted to be with them, but he dared not even write to them. Sometimes he did write to them but he never sent the letters, he crumpled them up and threw them away. He also wrote some poetry. He was often alone at that time and went for long walks and had many strange thoughts and feelings. Sometimes these thoughts were very happy and then he wouldn't walk but run on the empty beach and even cry out and jump into the air; but sometimes they were sad, and then he would lie down on the sand and bury his head in his arms and fall asleep like one falling into a heavy, unpleasant stupor. He spent his eighteenth birthday like that, alone and asleep.

Gwen and Maggie were eager to tell him about their lives too. Only they did not have very much to tell. Their present world tour was their first big adventure; before that they had simply been at boarding school and the holidays they had spent at home with their families or gone to stay on the Continent with family friends. They looked forward, however, to a lot of things happening to them in the future.

'What things?' Suraj asked them.

They smiled and looked thoughtful. They were on a deserted beach several miles out of town. Suraj had brought them here in his car, and he had also carried lunch along in a big picnic basket. There were chickens and fried pancakes stuffed with potatoes, and he had gone to a lot of trouble and managed to procure a bottle of champagne which he twirled lovingly in its ice bucket. He had wanted to bring a servant along to serve the food and make everything comfortable for them, but they said they preferred to manage on their own. Indeed, it was surprising how well they did manage. Whereas Suraj was inclined rather roughly to pull things out of the basket, throw away the paper and begin to eat, they first spread a scarf (he had forgotten, or rather, never thought of a tablecloth) and set everything out very nicely, and Gwen even took a few steps away to see what it looked like and then came back and touched up the arrangement with her long, pale hands.

They told him about what they hoped to do in London. They were both trying to persuade their families to let them take a flat together instead of living at home. They even described how they would furnish the flat with a Victorian chest-of-drawers and commercial posters on the walls. Gwen would keep a Siamese cat and Maggie a bull-terrier. They would probably go out a lot—they both liked dancing and good food in good restaurants—but they also expected to be at home quite often for Maggie wanted to learn Spanish and Gwen to do a lot of reading. They loved cooking and looked forward to making all sorts of delicious, unusual little dishes and entertaining their friends.

'What friends?' Suraj said with a knowing smile.

They shrugged and smiled back: 'Just friends.'

'Boy friends?'

'Those too, I expect,' Maggie said with cheerful pleasure.

'Ah-ha!' said Suraj and winked; and when they didn't take him up on it, he said, 'I think in England all the girls have a lot of boy friends and they have a very good time together. Isn't it? Tell me. The truth now.' He became quite roguish and even shook a finger at them, so that they both burst out laughing and said, 'Get along with you,' in nasal cockney accents.

'Please don't try to put me off the scent,' he said. 'I know all about it. The parties where you switch the lights off and petting in cars and all that pre-marital sex. I think it's a very good thing. I believe in a free society, and I think it is a sign of backwardness when society is not free in this respect.'

Maggie rolled around in the sand, from her stomach to her back, covering herself with tiny golden grains in the process. She said, 'Gwen didn't sleep with anyone till last year, but I was only fifteen. I developed early.'

The expression on Suraj's face changed suddenly, utterly. Perhaps Maggie noticed, perhaps she didn't, but in any case she went on: 'My first time wasn't terribly successful. It was at the end of the hols and I was feeling awful and wondering would school never stop, would nothing ever happen, and then I met this man in Kensington Gardens. You know how at that age one is absolutely panting for new experiences. But it didn't come up to expectations really. In fact, it was such a disappointment that it put me off sex for more than a year.'

'Who is coming for a swim!' Suraj shouted with unnatural brightness and jumped up and dashed towards the sea. He was glad when they did not follow. He swam strongly, taking pleasure in battling against the waves. When he was tired, he lay on his back and floated, letting himself be carried out a little further than was quite wise. His mind and feelings were in turmoil. He found he could not bear the idea of the two girls with other men. Not because he was personally jealous but because it was outrageous to think of them that way: Maggie so wholesome, untouched, firm-fleshed, and Gwen who was frail and pale and grown too tall like a girl who's been ill and lying in bed for a long time. They were not women, they were friends, his friends. He felt it was his duty to protect them, and it made him furious to think of them going back to England where he would no longer be able to do so and they would be prey to anyone who came along, to all those people who believed in pre-marital sex and other loose practices.

One day he decided to take them to his mother's house. They were surprised—they hadn't realized his mother was in Bombay, they thought she was still far away in the place from which he had run away. Now they

learned that, after his father's death a few years ago, he had brought her
and the rest of the family to Bombay and had bought a house for them
and kept them there. He seemed shy to speak of all this and was indeed
quite irritable, as if he resented having broken his silence on the subject.
The two girls dressed up carefully in silk frocks and stockings and high-
heeled shoes, so that they looked as if they were going to church. Suraj
was rather silent and even a little surly all the way he drove them there,
and his mood did not improve when they reached their destination. The
house was large and full of women. There was not only his mother but
also various unmarried sisters and a lot of old aunts and other dependants.
They crowded round and touched and patted Suraj and said he was
looking weak. A lot of food was brought, and the girls were urged to eat
which they did—even the strangest and most outrageous pickles—with
their usual grateful enthusiasm. Everyone looked at them from top to toe
and smiled at them to show goodwill, and the girls smiled back; only
Suraj was frowning.

'Are you married?' one of the sisters asked the girls in English. 'Any
children?'

'I'm afraid not,' Gwen said. She stretched her hand out for another
fritter and murmured, 'Delicious,' as she popped it, piping hot, into her
mouth.

'Look at that one,' said an aunt in Hindi. 'Thin as a fish-bone, but how
she eats.'

They all laughed, and the girls too laughed though they hadn't understood what was said. Suraj suddenly shouted, 'Be quiet!' and hit his fist
on the table. The girls looked at him in surprise, but the relatives composed their faces and were quiet at once.

'Rest, son,' said his mother. 'Don't upset yourself.' She stroked his
hair and his cheeks soothingly; an aunt kneeled on the floor and began to
press his ankles but he drew them away ungraciously. 'Listen,' said his
mother; she put her hand secretively to the side of her mouth and began
to whisper in his ear. He did not seem to like what he heard. Other
relatives came and whispered in his other ear. Suddenly he stood up; he
told the girls, 'Come on, we are going.'

They held a glass of sherbet in one hand, a coloured sweetmeat in the
other. 'What, already?'

'Come on.'

He did not look like a person with whom one could argue. They took
a last gulp of their sherbet and hastily ate up the remains of their sweetmeats. They got up, still chewing, and dusting crumbs from their hands.

'But you have eaten nothing!' cried the relatives. They snatched up the
platters of food and followed the departing guests with them. 'One little

piece of barfi,' they pleaded. 'Only to taste.' Gwen and Maggie lingered and looked willing enough, but Suraj hustled them out of the house and into the car and slammed the car-door after them decisively. He did not speak to them much on the way home and left them at their hotel with a curt, half-angry good-bye.

Next day he said to them aggressively, 'You don't know anything about our Indian way of life.'

'You didn't give us much time to find out,' Gwen said.

They were in the girls' hotel room, and Gwen was lying on the bed with a book and Maggie sat in an armchair with one foot drawn up and painting her toenails silver.

'I could see you were very bored there,' he said after a while.

'Bored!'

'Yes.' Then he said again: 'You don't know anything about the way we live.'

'We were having a simply marvellous time. Everyone was so kind, and those fabulous sweets! Only you were cross and disagreeable.'

Suddenly he roared: 'Because I was bored! Yes, it was I! I was bored! Very bored!' He turned from the window and glared at his two friends as if he hated them. Embarrassed by so much strong feeling, Maggie blushed and bent her head closer over her toenails. Gwen too avoided looking at Suraj.

'Our Indian families are like that,' he said. 'What do you know of it. Yes, I love them but—they want so much! They eat me up! You know nothing.'

He wandered to their dressing-table and absentmindedly sprayed himself from one of the bottles. A dewy English flower-smell enveloped him and he liked it and sprayed himself some more. This seemed to calm him.

'How did you like the house?' he said. 'I bought it for them for six lakhs of rupees. And the furniture? Do you think it is in good taste?'

'It looked awfully comfortable.'

'They want a silver tea-set.' He laughed. 'And another car. They say they need two. Supposing someone wants to go shopping and another person wants to go to the temple, then what? They quarrel a lot about the car. Do your families also have many quarrels?'

The two girls looked at each other and began to laugh. Gwen said, 'They have differences of opinion. It's very subtle.'

'First thing when I go there I have to hear about all the quarrels. Next thing I have to hear is the girls they have found for me to marry. Ooph! It's always the same: after half an hour I want to run away and then they begin to cry and then I stay. What sort of people we are! I think you must be having a good laugh at us.'

He sprayed himself again from the atomizer, he worked the lever up and down vigorously so that a lot of scent came out and enveloped him in a cool, fragrant mist. Maggie, whose bottle it was, cried 'Hey!'

'I like it.' He took out some more and shut his eyes with pleasure. 'Yesterday they again had a girl for me. Very good family, very pretty, sixteen years old. I wanted to say: But I'm going to marry these two! Only to see the fun. And why not?' he said suddenly. 'Why shouldn't I marry you two? I can do what I like. We can all stay together in my apartment, there are many rooms I never use. Or I will build a new house for us— yes, I'll do that, a brand-new house to most modern design!' He became enthusiastic. He imagined himself always enveloped in an atmosphere of English floral scent. He would buy English clothes for them. They would have a cook who knew how to prepare all English dishes. 'Will you like it?' he asked them. 'Do you think it will be nice?' But although they said it would be wonderful, he frowned and said, 'No, you wouldn't like it. You don't want to stay here. You think our poor India is very backward.'

He was often dissatisfied nowadays. He had always enjoyed being surrounded by his friends and talking and laughing with them and having them run little errands for him. Now he tired of them quickly, and in the middle of a friendly session—drinking, joking, having fun—he would tell them to go away. They were surprised, and he was surprised himself; and when they had gone, he wandered round the big, empty apartment by himself and wished for them back again. He had become used to having many people laugh when he made a joke and hearing from them what a big actor he was and how much better than all his rivals. He wanted to hear that, he needed it. Yet, all the same, when they said it now, he became irritated with them. Their jokes too no longer amused him, and the whole tenor of their conversation—which he had lived on and thrived on, which had been *his*—now often filled him with boredom and even disgust. It was the same not only with his friends but with his mistresses too. Everything that had once excited him about them now had the opposite effect. Their intensely feminine being—their soft, fat bodies, their long oiled hair, the heavy, heady Indian perfumes they used, the transparent sari drawn coyly over the enticing cleft that emerged from their low-cut blouses, the little jingle that rang out from bracelets and anklets and golden chains as they moved, their demure, clinging, giggling ways, their little sulks and tantrums—all this, which had once spelled everything feminine and desirable to him, now affected him unpleasantly. As a result, he was tough with his girls, sometimes brutal, and deliber- ately picked quarrels with them.

But he also quarrelled with Gwen and Maggie. He felt obscurely that they were the cause of his dissatisfaction with what had up till now been a satisfying or, at any rate, an enviable life. Although they never uttered a critical word, he thought of them as critical, as setting themselves up as superior, and it angered him. He defended things against them that they had never attacked and had no thoughts of attacking. These ranged from his family to the Bombay film industry to the whole of India which he admitted was not very advanced in the material sense but which amply made up for this shortcoming by the richness of its spiritual heritage. The two girls did not deny it, in fact they even agreed with him—politely rather than enthusiastically: they had not come here on any higher quest but were ready to concede that such a quest was possible, indeed they knew that many people came on it. Yet their agreement far from soothing only exasperated him further for it made him feel as if they were humouring him. Then he would turn right round and say that no, India *was* poor and backward, he felt ashamed when he thought of how far behind it lagged other countries like England and America and also when he thought of the starving people in the streets and the fact that after so many years of Independence no further progress had been made: but of course, he said, they wouldn't understand that, they were only foreigners and could have no conception of the deep feelings that an Indian had for his country. The girls took these changes of mood very well although sometimes, if he carried on for too long a time or at too high a pitch, they said, 'Oh do shut up, Suraj,' but so calmly, even patiently, that there was no offence in it. Indeed, when they said that, he at once stopped talking that way and became instead extremely attentive and proposed all sorts of outings and other amusements for them and did everything he could to make amends and show them how much he cared for them. But one thing he could not bear and that was when they talked of going away. He had already made them cancel a visit to Isphahan they had planned on their way back, and now he kept persuading them to postpone going home to England, even though their parents and their jobs were waiting for them there and anxious letters were already beginning to arrive.

He wanted them with him everywhere nowadays. Even when they would have much preferred to stay doing nothing on the beach, he made them come and watch him shooting or took them along to some film-world function that he had to attend. But he did not like to see them enjoying themselves too much there. If he noticed them talking too long to any one person, he would come and take them away to meet someone else; and afterwards he would ask them, 'What were you talking so much to him?' and while they were trying to recollect what had been said (which was rarely interesting enough to remember), he went on to suggest, 'It is best not to know such people very well.'

'But, Suraj, he was charming!'

'Yes, yes, for you he must have put on a very nice face.'

'Oh dear. What's he done then? What's the matter with him?'

But Suraj would not tell them. He became indeed rather prim and said it was not necessary for them to know such things, and all their entreaties could not unseal his lips any further. Then they became exasperated, furious with him, but he enjoyed that and laughed with pleasure at the names they called him.

A producer gave a party in the banquet-room of a big hotel. Everyone was there. Long buffet tables had been laid out with huge platters of pilau, lobster and prawn curries, mountains of kebabs heaped with sliced raw onions. The less important guests jostled and pushed each other in piling up their plates as if they had never eaten before and would perhaps never eat again. Streamers and paper lanterns festooned the ceiling, and everything was done just as it should be for the management of the hotel had plenty of practice in putting on these kind of parties. In deference to the prohibition laws, drinks were served—with a secrecy which had become ostentatious and pleasurable—in a little side-room to which many people took many trips and always came back with a wink and a joke ('They are serving very good Coca Colas in there'). The producer was in an excellent mood to see his party going so well. He rallied everyone to momentous feats of eating and drinking, joked and slapped backs, clapped his hands with enjoyment, was simultaneously paternal and slyly jovial with all the actresses in white saris. He made a big fuss of Gwen and Maggie who were not really enjoying themselves much—they had been to too many parties like this one by now—but pretended they were. Later there was music, and a playback singer rendered a love-song with so much feeling that it made people shake their heads at the beauty of life and filled them with sadness and longing. The host turned to Gwen and Maggie and asked, 'Did you like it?' They saw that his eyes were swimming in tears.

'Jolly nice,' they replied, embarrassed for him and tactfully looking the other way.

He was not ashamed but proud of his tears: 'What songs we have,' he said, 'what feeling,' and since further words failed him, he shut his eyes and pressed his heart where it hurt him. But then he became cheerful again and, putting an arm round the waist of each girl, said: 'Now we would like to hear an English song.'

Gwen and Maggie looked at each other over the top of his head. They gave the tiniest shrug, their eyebrows were ever so slightly raised.

People clapped and shouted 'Yes yes! Let us have a Beatle song!'

But what Gwen and Maggie chose to give was not a Beatle song. An imperceptible sign passed between them, and then they stood side by side very correctly, and began to sing:

> Go, stranger! track the deep,
> Free, free, the white sails spread!
> Wave may not foam, nor wild wind sweep,
> Where rest not England's dead.

They sang the way they had been taught at school, with spirit and expression. They lifted their heads and their voices high and every time the refrain came round they made a conductor's gesture with their hands as if encouraging their audience to join in. Each rhythmically tapped a foot on the floor. It was rousing and stirring and brave. When they had finished, there was tremendous applause. Many people were laughing; some of the actresses had taken out little lace handkerchiefs and tittered into them. The producer was enchanted, he stretched up and kissed their cheeks and he squeezed their hips ('But how *thin* you are,' he whispered, deeply concerned, when he had done this to Gwen). The girls accepted the applause with a graceful mixture of pride and modesty. They knew their performance could not be judged by the highest standards, but they were happy to have given pleasure. They avoided looking at Suraj.

All the way home in his car he upbraided, scolded them. 'Why did you do it?' he said several times. 'Because we were asked,' they replied, but when he kept repeating his question, they were silent and looked out of the car window at the lights stretching like jewels all round the sea-front.

'Everyone was laughing at you,' he said.

'So what.'

He groaned; he seemed in real pain. 'And not only laughing . . . Gwen, Maggie, you don't know what these people are. What thoughts they have.' When they didn't answer but went on looking out of the window, he said desperately, 'Especially about English girls.'

'I nearly got stuck in that Egypt's burning plain bit,' Maggie said to Gwen.

'I know you did.'

'But it went rather well on the whole, don't you think?'

'Frightfully well. I'm proud of us.'

'They think all English girls are loose in their morals,' Suraj said. 'When they look at you, they laugh because of the thoughts they have about you. Such dirty thoughts.'

'Oh do shut up, Suraj.'

'Yes, when truth is to be heard then you say shut up.'

But he did not speak again. He sat between the two of them with his arms folded and staring grimly ahead of him at the back of his chauffeur's neck. He did not move even when they reached the hotel and the girls got out, nor did he answer to their cheerful good-nights. He was angry with them.

But next day he turned up in great excitement at the hotel. A famous

American saxophone-player was passing through Bombay, and Suraj had got three tickets. 'You try and get tickets on your own,' he said triumphantly. 'Only try. Even if you pay Rs.500 on the black market you won't be able to get.'

'You are clever.' Then they asked: 'When is it?'

'On the fifteenth.'

They smiled sadly and told him that they had booked their return tickets for the twelfth. Suraj was thunderstruck. He looked from one to the other. He said, 'It is because I was angry with you in the car.'

'Of course not,' they said, laughing a little uneasily and avoiding his eyes.

He insisted it was. He accused himself for his bad temper and then accused them for taking such spiteful revenge on him. He wouldn't listen when they tried to tell him that it was time they went home, they couldn't stay here for ever, and that their decision had nothing to do with what had happened the night before. He knew that wasn't true and wanted to draw them out to admit it. But they just kept on saying no, they had to go, and no, it wasn't because of anything he had said or done. Then he tried to persuade them at least to postpone their departure by two weeks, one week—all right, not a week, just a few days, just till the concert—but here too they would not budge from their position.

Finally he changed. He became resigned and deeply melancholy and recognized that the pain of parting had to be endured. This attitude remained with him in the days that were left. He sighed often, and quoted Urdu couplets about the tears of friends whose paths lie in separate directions. This led him further, and he became even more philosophical and quoted verses about the transience of all worldly pleasures and how nothing ever stayed—not the song of the nightingale nor the bloom of the rose nor the throne of kings—but everything dissolved and disappeared as if it had never been. The girls too became depressed; they said, 'It's going to be awful without you.' When they said that, he became more cheerful and made plans for the future: how they would come back again, or he would go and visit them in England, and meanwhile, of course, there would be letters, many many letters, between them.

The girls did write very often. He loved getting their letters which were very lively and were just the way they spoke. He marvelled at the way they could write like that. When he himself sat down to write, the words came out stiff like words that are written not like words that are spoken. And when he had put down that he was well and hoped that they were also and that the weather was not good and that he was going up to Simla to shoot some scenes in snow, then he didn't know what else to say. Their letters were filled with so many things that happened to them—

how they had discovered a marvellous little new restaurant, and that skirts were so short now that they had had to take up all their hems—but he could not think of anything to write. Nothing new ever happened to him: it was just shooting, and sitting with his friends, and premières, always the same. It was not worth writing in a letter all the way to England. He would start writing—slowly and laboriously, with his lips moving—and then he would stop and not know what to say next. When he came back to it a few days later and read it over again, he was dissatisfied because it did not sound very well, nor was he sure of his spelling, and then he tore the letter up and told himself he would start again tomorrow. In the end he didn't write at all, and after a time their letters stopped too.

Sometimes his friends talked about the two English girls. At first they did so hesitantly, looking at him out of the corner of their eyes, but when he said nothing they became bolder and soon they were laughing and everyone had something humorous to contribute. Suraj smiled good-naturedly and allowed himself to be teased. He did not contradict when they made references to events that had never happened, or assumed that there had been more than there actually had been. Sometimes he wondered to himself that there had not been more. At the time he had been proud of this fact, of the purity of their friendship; now he felt slightly ashamed of it, and would not have liked his friends to know. It was like a shortcoming, or like having been cheated. He did not understand how he could have allowed it to happen, and a hint of resentment entered into his memory of the English girls. Indeed, he did not like to think of them much any more, and whenever he could not help doing so, he would go out and visit one of his actress friends.

JEAN RHYS

Overture and Beginners Please

❦

We were sitting by the fire in the small dining-room when Camilla said 'I hate my parents, don't you?' Hail was rattling against the curtained windows. I had been told all about snow long before I left the West Indies, hail was a surprise and exciting in its way. I thought I'd be laughed at if I asked what it was.

Another dark yellow curtain hung over the door which led into a passage and beyond that were the empty classrooms, for this was the week after Christmas and the day girls and other seven boarders had gone home for their holidays.

'And what's more,' said Camilla, 'they hate me. They like my younger sister. A lot of that sort of thing goes on in families but it's hushed up of course.'

It was almost dark, I was almost warm, so I said, 'I don't hate mine. They gave a farewell dance for me before I left. We had a band. It's funny, I can remember exactly the face of the man with the shak-shak.'

'How comic,' said Camilla who seemed annoyed.

'They play well. Different music of course.'

'Why did they send you to the old Perse if they were so fond of you?'

'Because my English aunt said it was a good school.'

'That's the one who won't have you with her for Christmas, isn't it?'

'Well she is sick—ill, I mean.'

'*She says!* How do you like it now you are here?'

'I like it all right, but the chilblains on my hands hurt.'

Then she said I would have lots of time to find out if I did like it as she was leaving the next day to stay with friends at Thaxted. 'Miss Born has all of Charlotte M. Yonge's novels lined up for you to read in the evenings.'

'Oh Lord, she hasn't!'

'Just you wait,' said Camilla.

The maid came in to light up and soon it would be time to go upstairs and change for dinner. I thought this woman one of the most fascinating I had ever seen. She had a long thin face, dead white, or powdered dead white. Her hair was black and lively under her cap, her eyes so small that the first time I saw her I thought she was blind. But wide open, they were the most astonishing blue, cornflower blue, no, more like sparks of blue fire. Then she would drop her eyelids and her face would go dead and lifeless again. I never tired of watching this transformation.

After dinner there I was, reading aloud *The Dove in the Eagle's Nest*. Camilla didn't listen, nor did Miss Rode, our headmistress, who was a middle-aged very imposing woman with quantities of black-grey hair arranged like a coronet. She dressed in various shades of brown, purple, puce or mustard and her face was serene and kind.

Miss Born however never took her eyes off me. Miss Born was old, she wore black, she never taught. She represented breeding and culture and was a great asset to the school. 'Drop your voice,' she would say, 'drop it. An octave at least'; or 'That will do, don't go on, I really cannot bear any more tonight.'

We sat around the fire till the clock struck nine. 'Good night Miss Rode.' 'Good night, dear child' said Miss Rode, who was wearing her purple, always a good sign. 'Good night Miss Born.' Miss Born inclined her head very slightly and as I went out remarked, 'Why did you insist on that girl playing Autolycus? Tony Lumpkin in person.'

'Not in person, surely,' said Miss Rode mildly.

'In manner then, in manner,' said Miss Born.

Camilla shut the door and I heard no more.

The staircase was slippery and smelt of floor polish. All the way up to the bedroom floor I thought about Miss Born's black clothes, her small active body. A mouse with a parrot's head. I hadn't even wanted to be in the old *Winter's Tale* and I told them so. However, I said nothing of all this to Camilla for I had been five months in England and was slowly learning to be cautious. Besides the bedrooms were unheated and I had already begun to shiver and shake.

'Don't you think it's frightfully cold, Camilla?'

'No, not particularly. Hop into bed and you'll soon get warm.' She went off to her own room four doors away.

I knew of course that I would not sleep or get warm for on top of everything else an icy wind was blowing through the window, which for some mysterious reason must be left open six inches at the top.

Do not shut your window. This window must not be closed.

I was still awake and shivering, clutching my ankles with my hands, when the maid, who was called Jarvis, knocked. 'I've brought you up a hot water bottle miss.'

'Oh thank you. How awfully kind of you.'

'It is my own hot water bottle,' she said. She asked why I didn't shut my window.

'Well, I thought we weren't supposed to.'

She pushed the sash up without answering. I stretched my legs out and put the bottle where my back hurt and thanked her again. I hoped she'd go away but she lingered.

'I wanted to tell you miss, that I enjoyed the school play this term very much. You were good in that boy's part.'

'Autolycus.'

'Well, I don't remember the name but you quite cheered me up.'

'I'm very glad,' I said. 'Good night Jarvis, don't catch cold in this icy little room.'

'I had a great success once in an amateur theatrical performance,' she went on dreamily. 'I played the part of a blind girl.'

'You played a blind girl? How strange, because when I saw you first I thought . . .' I stopped. 'I thought you might be able to act because you don't look at all wooden.'

'The flowers I had sent me,' she said. 'Roses and that. Of course, it was long ago, when I was a girl, but I still remember my part, every word of it.'

'How very nice' was all I could think of to say. She snapped the light out and shut the door, rather loudly.

She played a blind girl. I thought she was blind. But this sort of thing had happened to me before. I'd stopped trying to make sense of clues that led nowhere.

When, next day after breakfast, Camilla left I got through the morning thinking no bicycle ride anyhow. Patey isn't here.

Miss Patey had been trying to teach me to bicycle. She always skimmed gracefully ahead as though she had nothing to do with me and I followed her, wobbling dangerously from side to side. Once when I'd fallen into a ditch on the way to Newnham, she turned back and asked in a detached way if I'd hurt myself. 'Oh no, Miss Patey, not at all.' I climbed out of the ditch and picked up the bicycle. 'I see your stocking is torn and that is quite a bruise on your knee.' She did not speak again until we got to the Trumpington Road. 'You had better get down and wheel your bicycle here.' 'Yes, Miss Patey.'

Limping along the Trumpington Road . . . past Mrs G's house, a distant relative of my father's. I was allowed to have tea with her every Saturday afternoon . . . She was called Jeanette and was a very lovely, stately old lady with thick white hair, huge black eyes and a classic profile. She didn't wear spectacles except for reading and her hands were slender and transparent looking. She talked about Cambridge when she was young and the famous men she'd known. 'Poor Darwin. He threaded the labyrinths of creation and lost his Creator.' Or 'Of course Fitzgerald's translation from the Persian was not really accurate . . .'; and the Song of Solomon was an allegory of Christ and His Church.

Another day she told me that she had nearly eloped (tired of her absent-minded old husband, I suppose). She was packed and ready to leave but when she was pinning on her hat she saw in the looking-glass the devil grinning over her shoulder. She was so frightened that she changed her mind.

'And what did the devil look like?' I asked, very curious. But she never told me that.

Like so many beautiful old ladies then she had a devoted maid whom I was rather afraid of, she looked at me so sternly, so unsmilingly when she opened the door. Now I come to think of it, Jarvis didn't smile either.

None of the girls could believe that I'd never owned a bicycle before or that there were very few in the island. 'How do you get about then, if there are no trains, buses, cars or bicycles?' they would say. 'Horses, mules, carriages, buggies, traps.' Winks, smiles. 'Is it "honey don't try so hard" or "honey don't cry so hard"?' 'How should I know?' 'Well, it's a coon song, you ought to know.' But when I discovered that though they never believed the truth, they swallowed the most fantastic lies, I amused myself a good deal.

That first afternoon when I had walked along the gravel path which circled the muddy green hockey field, I crossed a flower bed and looked into one of the dim classrooms. It was a grey-yellow day. Not so bad as the white glaring days or the icy wind days. Still, bad enough. The sky was the colour of no hope, but they don't notice it, they are used to it, they expect me to grow used to it.

It was while I was staring at the empty ghostly-looking desks that I felt a lump in my throat. Tears—my heart a heavy jagged weight. Of course premonitions, presentiments had brushed me before, cold and clammy as a bat's wing, but nothing like this. Despair, grey-yellow like their sky. I stayed by the window in the cold thinking 'What is going to become of me? Why am I here at all?'

One hot silent July afternoon I was told that I was to go to England with my Aunt Clare, who had been staying with us for the last six months. I was to go to a school called The Perse in Cambridge.

'It is very good of her to take charge of you.' I noticed that my father was looking at me in a critical, disapproving way. 'I am sure,' he said, 'that it will do you a great deal of good.'

'I sincerely hope so,' said Aunt Clare dubiously.

This interview chilled me and I was silent all that evening. (So, I noticed, was my mother.) I went up to my bedroom early and took out the exercise book that I called 'Secret Poems.'

> I am going to England
> What shall I find there?
>
> 'No matter what
> Not what I sought' said Byron.
>
> Not what I sought,
> Not what I seek.

I wrote no more poems for a very long time.

Unfortunately it was a grey lowering August in London, not cold but never bright or fresh. My Aunt Clare, a tireless walker, dragged me round to see all the sights and after a week I went to sleep in the most unlikely places; St Paul's, Westminster Abbey, Madame Tussaud's, the Wallace Collection, the zoo, even a shop or two. She was a swift but absentminded walker and I could easily lag behind and find a chair or bench to droop on.

'She can't help it,' I heard her explain once. 'It's the change of climate, but it can really be very annoying.'

Mistake after mistake.

But I knew the exact day when I lost belief in myself and cold caution took control. It was when she bought me the ugly dress instead of the pretty wine-coloured one.

'It's a perfect fit,' said the saleswoman, 'and the young lady is so pale, she needs colour.'

My aunt looked at the price ticket. 'No, not at all suitable,' she said and chose a drab dress which I disliked. I didn't argue for the big shop and the saleswoman whom I thought very beautiful bewildered me. But I was heart-broken. I'd have to appear before a lot of strange girls in this hideous garment. 'They're bound to dislike me.'

Outside in the hostile street we got into the hateful bus (always squashed up against perfect strangers—millions of perfect strangers in this horrible place). The bus wheels said 'And *when* we say we've *always* won, and *when* they ask us *how* it's done.' (You wouldn't dare say how you do it, not straight out you wouldn't, it's too damned mean the way you do it.)

At Cambridge I refused to say anything except 'Oh yes, that's very nice indeed. This bridge, that building. King's College Chapel. Oh yes. Very nice.'

'Is that all you can say about King's College Chapel?' said Miss Born disdainfully.

Privately I thought that a Protestant service was all wrong in King's College Chapel, that it missed the smell of incense, splendid vestments,

Latin prayers. 'You've forgotten that you stole it from the Catholics but it hasn't forgotten,' I thought. Fortunately I didn't say this.

'They sang very nicely indeed.'

Well, I walked up and down the hockey field till I'd stopped crying then went back to the small dining-room where there was always a blazing fire, I will say. But I could not eat anything and Miss Rode sent me to bed.

'I hear,' she said, 'that you feel the cold, so you'll find extra blankets and Jarvis will bring you up a hot water bottle and hot milk.'

Lying in bed, warm and comfortable, I tried to argue my fears away. After all, it's only for another eighteen months at the worst and though I don't particularly want to go back, there it is, solid and safe, the street, the sandbox tree, the stone steps, the long gallery with the round table at the top. But I was astonished to discover how patchy, vague and uncertain my memory had become. I had forgotten so much so soon.

I remembered the stars, but not the moon. It was a different moon, but different in what way? I didn't know. I remembered the shadows of trees more clearly than the trees, the sound of rain but not the sound of my mother's voice. Not really. I remembered the smell of dust and heat, the coolness of ferns but not the scent of any of the flowers. As for the mountains, the hills and the sea, they were not only thousands of miles away, they were years away.

About three days before the holidays ended, Miss Rode handed me a letter from Switzerland. 'But I don't know anyone in Switzerland.'

'Open it and find out,' she said.

I put the letter under my pillow for a time, thinking it would be something to look forward to the next morning, but I was too curious to wait. I opened it—it was signed Myrtle. I was disappointed. What on earth had Myrtle, a girl I hardly knew, to write to me about? This was the letter which was to change my life.

Dear West Indies,

I have been thinking about you a lot since I came to Switzerland, perhaps because my mother is getting divorced. I see now what a silly lot of fools we were about everything that matters and I don't think you are. It was all those words in *The Winter's Tale* that Miss Born wanted to blue pencil, you rolled them out as though you knew what they meant. My mother said you made the other girls look like waxworks and when you dropped your cap you picked it up so naturally, like a born actress. She says that you ought to go on the stage and why don't you? I like Switzerland all right. There are a lot of English here and my mother says what a pity! She can be very sarcastic. Let me hear from you soon. I felt I simply had to write this.

Yours ever,
MYRTLE

I read this letter over and over again, then rolled about from side to side making up an answer. 'Dear Myrtle, Thanks for letter. I did not know what the words meant, I just liked the sound of them. I thought your mother very pretty, but yes, a bit sarky.'

Then I stopped writing the imaginary letter to Myrtle for suddenly, like an illumination, I knew exactly what I wanted to do. Next day I wrote to my father. I told him that I longed to be an actress and that I wanted to go to the Academy of Dramatic Art in Gower Street.

'I am *quite* sure. Please think very seriously about it. I don't mind this place and some of the mistresses are quite all right but it's really a waste of money my being here . . .'

When the answer arrived it was yes and I was happier than I'd ever been in my life. Nothing could touch me, not praise, nor blame. Nor incredulous smiles. A new term had started but Myrtle hadn't come back and Camilla was still away in Thaxted.

'There is an entrance examination,' they'd say. 'You won't pass it.'

'Yes I will,' but really I was extremely nervous about this examination and surprised when I did pass. The judges had seemed so very bored. The place was not Royal then and was known colloquially as 'Tree's school'. It wasn't so choosy then perhaps.

My aunt installed me in an Upper Bedford Place boarding-house and left me to it; she strongly disapproved of the whole business. However she soon came back to London and took a small flat near Baker Street to see for herself how I was getting on.

'When you're stabbed in the back you fall like this, and when you're stabbed in front you fall like this, but if you stab yourself you fall differently. Like this.'

'Is that all you've learnt?'

'No.' I told her about fencing classes, ballet, elocution, gesture. And so on. 'No plays?' she wanted to know. 'Yes of course. I was Celia in *As You Like It* and we did Paolo and Francesca once.' And I was Francesca in the little dark sitting-room.

> 'Now I am free and gay,
> Light as a dancer when the strings begin
> All ties that held me I cast off . . .'

'You'll find that very expensive,' my aunt said.

I spent the vacation with relatives in Yorkshire and one morning early my uncle woke me with a cablegram of the news of my father's sudden death. I was quite calm and he seemed surprised, but the truth was that I hadn't taken it in, I didn't believe him.

Harrogate was full of music that late summer. Concertinas, harpists, barrel organs, singers. One afternoon in an unfamiliar street, listening to a man singing 'It may be for years and it may be for ever', I burst into tears and once started I couldn't stop.

Soon I was packed off to responsible Aunt Clare in Wales. 'You cry without reticence,' she told me the day after I arrived. 'And you watch me without reticence,' I thought.

There was a calm slow-moving river called the Afon that flowed at the bottom of my aunt's garden. Walking up and down looking at the water she said that she could understand my grief. My father's death meant that it was impossible to keep me in London at a theatrical school. 'Quite out of the question.' She had heard from my mother who wished me to return home at once. I said that I didn't want to go, 'not yet.' 'But you'll have to.' 'I won't . . .'

Aunt Clare changed the subject. 'What a lovely day. Straight from the lap of the gods' (she talked like that). As her voice went on I was repeating to myself 'Straight from the lap of the gods'.

At last we went up to London to do some shopping for hot weather clothes and one afternoon when she was visiting friends I went to Blackmore's agency in the Strand and after some palaver was engaged as one of the chorus of a touring musical comedy. I was astonished when Aunt Clare told me that I'd behaved deceitfully, outrageously. A heated argument followed.

She said that my contract had no legal value at my age and threatened to stop me. I said that if she stopped me I'd marry a young man at the Academy whom I knew she detested. He'd been to tea at the Marylebone flat. 'He may be a horrid boy but he's got a lot of money.' 'How do you know that?' said my aunt in a different voice, a sharp voice.

'He showed me the letter from his trustees. He's twenty-one. Besides at the Academy everyone knows who has money and who hasn't. That's one thing they do know.'

'If this young man is well-off you ought to think very carefully before you answer him.'

'I have answered him. I said no. But if you interfere with my contract I'll marry him and be miserable. And it will be your fault.'

This went on for a long time. Then Aunt Clare said that it was unfair to expect her to deal with me, that she'd write to my mother. 'Perhaps we'll be rehearsing before she answers,' I said hopefully. But when my mother's letter arrived it was very vague. She didn't approve, neither did she altogether disapprove. It seemed as if what with her grief for my father and her worry about money she was relieved that I'd be earning my own living in England. 'Not much of a living,' said my aunt.

'Some people manage. Why shouldn't I?'

The company was playing a musical comedy called *Our Miss Gibbs*. We rehearsed at the National Sporting Club somewhere in the Leicester Square/Covent Garden area. A large room with a stage up one end. Sometimes boxers would pass through looking rather shy on their way to other rooms, I supposed. It was foggy. First a black fog then a yellow one. I didn't feel well but I never missed a rehearsal. Once my aunt came with me and the girls approved of her so enthusiastically that I saw her in a new light. 'Is that your auntie? Oh, isn't she nice.'

She was a nice woman, I see that now. It was kind of her to take charge of me to please her favourite brother. But she wasn't exactly demonstrative. Even pecks on the cheek were very rare. And I craved for affection and reassurance. By far my nicest Cambridge memory was of the day an undergraduate on a bicycle knocked me flat as I was crossing the road. I wasn't hurt but he picked me up so carefully and apologized so profusely that I thought about him for a long time.

Talking to the other girls I realized that several of them dreaded the tour up North in the winter. We were going to Oldham, Bury, Leeds, Halifax, Huddersfield and so on. As for the boys, one of them showed me a sketch he'd done of a street in a northern town. He'd called it 'Why we drink'. But none of this prevented me from being excited and happy.

The man who engaged me at the agent's was at one rehearsal. He came up to me and said in a low voice: 'Don't tell the other girls that you were at Tree's school. They mightn't like it.' I hadn't any idea what he meant. But 'No, I won't tell anybody,' I promised.

MARGARET ATWOOD

Hair Jewellery

There must be some approach to this, a method, a technique, that's the word I want, it kills germs. Some technique then, a way of thinking about it that would be bloodless and therefore painless; devotion recollected in tranquillity. I try to conjure up an image of myself at that time, also one of you, but it's like conjuring the dead. How do I know I'm not inventing both of us, and if I'm not inventing then it really is like conjuring the dead, a dangerous game. Why should I disturb those sleepers, sleep-walkers, as they make their automaton rounds through the streets where we once lived, fading from year to year, their voices thinning to the sound of a thumb drawn across a wet window: an insect squeak, transparent as glass, no words. You can never tell with the dead whether it is they who wish to return or the living who want them to. The usual explanation is that they have something to tell us. I'm not sure I believe it; in this case it's more likely that I have something to tell them.

Be careful, I want to write, *there is a future*, God's hand on the temple wall, clear and unavoidable in the new snow, just in front of them where they are walking—I see it as December—along the brick sidewalk in Boston, city of rotting dignities, she in her wavering high heels, getting her feet wet from sheer vanity. Boots were ugly then, heavy shapeless rubber like rhinoceros paws, flight boots they called them, or furred at the tops like old ladies' or bedroom slippers, with stringy bows; or there were those plastic wedge-shaped rain boots, they would yellow quickly and become encrusted with dirt on the inside, they looked like buried teeth.

That's my technique, I resurrect myself through clothes. In fact it's impossible for me to remember what I did, what happened to me, unless I can remember what I was wearing, and every time I discard a sweater or a dress I am discarding a part of my life. I shed identities like a snake, leaving them pale and shrivelled behind me, a trail of them, and if I want any memories at all I have to collect, one by one, those cotton and wool fragments, piece them together, achieving at last a patchwork self, no defence anyway against the cold. I concentrate, and this particular lost soul rises miasmic from the Crippled Civilians Clothing Donation Box in the Loblaws parking lot in downtown Toronto, where I finally ditched that coat.

The coat was long and black. It was good quality—good quality mattered then, and the women's magazines had articles about basic wardrobes and correct pressing and how to get spots out of camel's hair—but it was far too big for me, the sleeves came to my knuckles, the hem to the tops of my plastic rain boots, which did not fit either. When I bought it I meant to alter it, but I never did. Most of my clothes were the same, they were all too big, perhaps I believed that if my clothes were large and shapeless, if they formed a sort of tent around me, I would be less visible. But the reverse was true; I must have been more noticeable than most as I billowed along the streets in my black wool shroud, my head swathed in, was it a plaid angora scarf, also good quality; at any rate, my head swathed.

I bought these clothes, when I bought clothes at all—for you must remember that, like you, I was poor, which accounts for at least some of our desperation—in Filene's Basement, where good quality clothes that failed to sell at the more genteel levels were disposed of at slashed prices. You often had to try them on in the aisles, as there were few dressing rooms, and the cellar, for it was a cellar, low-ceilinged, dimly lit, dank with the smell of anxious armpits and harassed feet, was filled on bargain days with struggling women in slips and bras, stuffing themselves into torn and soiled designer originals to the sound of heavy breathing and a hundred sticking zippers. It is customary to laugh at bargain-hunting women, at their voraciousness, their hysteria, but Filene's Basement was, in its own way, tragic. No one went there who did not aspire to a shape-change, a transformation, a new life, but the things never did quite fit.

Under the black coat I wear a heavy tweed skirt, grey in colour, and a brown sweater with only one not very noticeable hole, valued by me because it was your cigarette that burned it. Under the sweater I have a slip (too long), a brassiere (too small), some panties with little pink roses on them, also from Filene's Basement, only twenty-five cents, five for a dollar, and a pair of nylon stockings held up by a garter belt which, being too large, is travelling around my waist, causing the seams at the backs of my legs to spiral like barbers' poles. I am lugging a suitcase which is far too heavy—no one carried packsacks then except at summer camp—as it contains another set of my weighty, oversized clothes as well as six nineteenth-century Gothic novels and a sheaf of clean paper. On the other side, counterbalancing the suitcase, are my portable typewriter and my Filene's Basement handbag, gargantuan, bottomless as the tomb. It is February, the wind whips the black coat out behind me, my plastic rain boots skid on the ice of the sidewalk, in a passing store window I see a woman thick and red and bundled. I am hopelessly in love and I am going to the train station to escape.

If I had been richer it would have been the airport. I would have gone to California, Algiers, somewhere oily and alien and above all warm. As it was, I had just enough money for a return ticket and three days in Salem, the only other place both accessible and notable being Walden Pond, which was not much good in winter. I had already justified the trip to myself: it would be more educational to go to Salem than to Algiers, for I was supposed to be 'doing work' on Nathaniel Hawthorne. 'Doing work,' they called it; they still call it that. I would be able to soak up atmosphere; perhaps from this experience, to which I did not look forward, the academic paper required for my survival as a scholar would emerge, like a stunted dandelion from a crack in the sidewalk. Those dismal streets, that Puritanical melancholy combined with the sodden February sea winds would be like a plunge into cold water, shocking into action my critical faculties, my talent for word-chopping and the construction of plausible footnotes which had assured so far the trickle of scholarship money on which I subsisted. For the past two months these abilities had been paralysed by unrequited love. I thought that several days away from you would give me time to think things over. In my subsequent experience, this does no good at all.

Unrequited love was, at that period of my life, the only kind I seemed to be capable of feeling. This caused me much pain, but in retrospect I see it had advantages. It provided all the emotional jolts of the other kind without any of the risks, it did not interfere with my life, which, although meagre, was mine and predictable, and it involved no decisions. In the world of stark physical reality it might call for the removal of my ill-fitting garments (in the dark or the bathroom, if possible: no woman wants a man to see her safety pins), but it left undisturbed their metaphysical counterparts. At that time I believed in metaphysics. My Platonic version of myself resembled an Egyptian mummy, a mysteriously wrapped object that might or might not fall into dust if uncovered. But unrequited love demanded no stripteases.

If, as had happened several times, my love was requited, if it became a question of the future, of making a decision that would lead inevitably to the sound of one's beloved shaving with an electric razor while one scraped congealed egg from his breakfast plate, I was filled with panic. My academic researches had made me familiar with the moment at which one's closest friend and most trusted companion grows fangs or turns into a bat; this moment was expected, and held few terrors for me. Far more disconcerting was that other moment, when the scales would fall from my eyes and my current lover would be revealed not as a demigod or a monster, impersonal and irresistible, but as a human being. What Psyche saw with the candle was not a god with wings but a pigeon-chested youth with pimples, and that's why it took her so long to win her way back to true love. It is easier to love a daemon than a man, though less heroic.

You were, of course, the perfect object. No banal shadow of lawn mowers and bungalows lurked in your melancholy eyes, opaque as black marble, recondite as urns, you coughed like Roderick Usher, you were, in your own eyes and therefore in mine, doomed and restless as Dracula. Why is it that dolefulness and a sense of futility are so irresistible to young women? I watch this syndrome among my students: those febrile young men who sprawl on the carpets which this institution of higher learning has so thoughtfully provided for them, grubby and slack as hookworm victims, each with some girl in tow who buys cigarettes and coffee for him and who receives in turn his outpourings of spleen, his condemnations of the world and his mockery of her in particular, of the way she dresses, of the recreation room and two television sets owned by her parents, who may be in fact identical to his, of her friends, of what she reads, of how she thinks. Why do they put up with it? Perhaps it makes them feel, by contrast, healthful and life-giving; or perhaps these men are their mirrors, reflecting the misery and chaos they contain but are afraid to acknowledge.

Our case was different only in externals; the desperation, I'm sure, was identical. I had ended up in academia because I did not want to be a secretary, or, to put it another way, because I did not want always to have to buy my good-quality clothes in Filene's Basement; you, because you did not want to be drafted, and at that time the university dodge still worked. We were both from small, unimportant cities, whose Rotary Club denizens, unaware of our actual condition, believed that their minute bursaries were helping us to pursue arcane but glamorous careers which would in some vague way reflect credit on the community. But neither of us wanted to be a professional scholar, and the real ones, some of whom had brush-cuts and efficient briefcases and looked like junior executives of shoe companies, filled us with dismay. Instead of 'doing work' we would spend our time drinking draft beer in the cheapest of the local German restaurants, ridiculing the pomposity of our seminars and the intellectual mannerisms of our fellow students. Or we would wander through the stacks of the library, searching for recondite titles no one could possibly have heard of so we could drop them into the next literary debate in that reverential tone soon mastered by every future departmental chairman, and watch the ripples of dismay spread through the eyes of our fellow inmates. Sometimes we would sneak into the Music Department, co-opt a vacant piano and sing maudlin Victorian favourites or bouncy choruses from Gilbert and Sullivan, or a plaintive balled by Edward Lear from which we had been compelled, earlier in the year, to extract the Freudian symbols. I associate it with a certain brown corduroy skirt which I had made myself, the hem of which was stapled in several places because I had not had the moral energy to sew it.

> On the coast of Coromandel,
> Where the early pumpkins blow
> In the middle of the woods
> Lived the Yonghy-Bonghy-Bo . . .
>
> Two old chairs, and half a candle
> One old jug without a handle,
> These were all his worldly goods
> In the middle of the woods . . .

The mutilated candle and the broken jug had caused much snide merriment at the seminar, but for us they held a compelling pathos. The state of affairs in Coromandel, its squalor and hopelessness, seemed too apt a comment on our own.

Our problem, I thought, was that neither the world around us nor the future stretching before us contained any image of what we might conceivably become. We were stranded in the present as in a stalled, otherwise empty subway train, and in this isolation we clutched morosely at each other's shadows. That at any rate was my analysis as I lugged my suitcase through the icy twilight towards the only hotel in Salem that was open, or so the conductor had told me. I have trouble seeing this, but I think the railroad station was condensed and dark, lit by a muddy orange light like the subway stations in Boston, and it too had the smell of weak disinfectant unsuccessfully applied to a layer of dried urine so old as to be almost respectable. It did not remind me of Puritans or witches or even of overstuffed shipbuilders, but of undernourished mill-workers with lung trouble, a later generation.

The hotel, too, smelt of decay and better days. It was being repainted, and the painters' canvas cloths and stepladders almost blocked the corridors. The hotel was open only because of the renovations; otherwise, said the desk clerk, who seemed also to be the bellboy, the manager and possibly the owner, he would have shut it down and gone to Florida. 'People only come here in the summer,' he said, 'to see the House of the Seven Gables and that.' He resented my being there at all, and more especially for refusing to give a satisfactory explanation. I told him I had come to look at the tombstones but he did not believe this. As he hauled my suitcase and my typewriter towards the windswept cupboard in which he was about to deposit me, he kept looking back over my shoulder as though there ought to have been a man behind me. Illicit sex, he knew, was the only conceivable reason for Salem in February. He was right, of course.

The bed was narrow and hard as a mortuary slab, and I soon discovered that although there was a brisk sea breeze blowing through the closed window, the management was aware of it and had compensated; each fresh onslaught of central heating was announced by the sound of hammers and leaden gongs from the radiator.

Between my fits of sleep I thought about you, rehearsing our future, which I knew would be brief. Of course we would sleep together, though this topic had not yet been discussed. In those days, as you recall, it had to be discussed first, and so far we had not progressed beyond a few furtive outdoor gropings and one moment when, under a full moon on one of those deserted brick streets, you had put your hand on my throat and announced that you were the Boston Strangler; a joke which, for one with my literary predilections, amounted to a seduction. But though sex was a necessary and even a desirable ritual, I dwelt less on it than on our parting, which I visualized as sad, tender, inevitable and final. I rehearsed it in every conceivable location: doorways, ferry-boat docks, train, plane and subway stations, park benches. We would not say much, we would look at each other, we would *know* (though precisely what we would know I wasn't sure); then you would turn a corner and be lost forever. I would be wearing a trench coat, not yet purchased, though I had seen the kind of thing I wanted in Filene's Basement the previous autumn. The park bench scene—I set it in spring, to provide a contrast to the mood—was so affecting that I cried, though since I had a horror of being overheard, even in an empty hotel, I timed it to coincide with the radiator. Futility is so attractive to the young, and I had not yet exhausted its possibilities.

By the next morning I was tired of brooding and snivelling. I decided to seek out the main derelict graveyard, which might provide me with a quaint seventeenth-century tombstone epitaph suitable for my Hawthorne paper. In the hall the workmen were hammering and painting; as I walked down the corridor they stared after me like frogs in a pond. The desk clerk grudgingly relinquished a Chamber of Commerce tourist brochure, which had a map and a short list of the points of interest.

There was no one in the streets outside, and very few cars. The houses, filmed with soot, their paint peeled by the salty air, seemed deserted, though in several of the front windows behind the greying lace curtains I could see the shadowy outline of a face. The sky was grey and furrowed, like the inside of a mattress, and there was a high wind blowing. I skidded over the sidewalks in my slippery boots, the wind pushing my black coat like a sail, making good progress until I turned a corner and the wind was no longer behind me. Soon after that I gave up the graveyard idea.

Instead I turned into a small restaurant; I had not yet had breakfast—the hotel had been surly about it—and I wanted to eat and to consider what to do next. I ordered an egg sandwich and a glass of milk and studied the brochure. The waitress and the proprietor, who were the only other people in the room, retreated to the far end and stood with folded arms, watching me suspiciously while I ate as though expecting me to leap up and perform some act of necromancy with the butter knife. Meanwhile, the House of the Seven Gables was closed for the winter. It had nothing to do with Hawthorne anyway; it was just an old house that had avoided being torn down, and which people now paid money to see because it had been given the name of a novel. No genuine author's sweat on the banisters. I think this was the moment at which I started to become cynical about literature.

The only other point of interest, according to the Chamber of Commerce, was the library. Unlike everything else it was open in February, and was apparently world-famous for its collection of genealogies. The last thing I wanted was a visit to the library, but returning to the hotel with its noise and chemical smells was pointless, and I couldn't stay in the restaurant all day.

The library was empty, except for a middle-aged man in a felt hat who was looking doggedly at the rows of genealogies, palpably killing time. An official woman with a bun and a scowl was sitting behind a blunt desk doing crossword puzzles. The library served also as a museum of·sorts. There were several ship's figureheads, maidens with rigid eyes, wooden men, ornate fish and lions, their gilt worn thin; and, displayed in glass cases, a collection of Victorian hair jewellery; brooches and rings, each with a crystal front protecting a design of woven hair; flowers, initials, wreaths or weeping willows. The more elaborate ones had hair of different colours. Though originally they must have shone, the strands by now had aged to the texture of something you find under a chair cushion. It struck me that Donne had been wrong about the circlet of bright hair about the bone. A hand-lettered card explained that many of these pieces were memorial jewellery, intended for distribution to the mourners at funerals.

'The funeral ones,' I said to the woman at the desk. 'I mean, how did they . . . did they cut the hair off before or after?'

She looked up from her puzzle. She did not understand at all what I was talking about.

'Before or after the person died,' I said. If it was before, it seemed to me a callous thing to do. If after, how did they have time to weave all those willow trees before the funeral? And why would they want to? I

could not imagine wearing at my throat one of those heavy brooches, like
a metal pillow, stuffed with the gradually dimming tresses of one I loved.
It would be like a dried hand. It would be like a noose.

'I'm sure I don't know,' she said with distaste. 'This is a travelling
exhibition.'

The man in the felt hat was lying in wait for me outside the door. He
asked me to join him for a drink. He must have been staying at the hotel.

'No, thank you,' I said, adding, 'I'm with someone.' I said this to
mollify him—women always feel compelled to mollify men by whom
they are declining to be picked up—but as I said it I realized I had come
here not to get away from you, as I had thought, but to be with you, more
completely than your actual presence would allow. In the flesh your irony
was impenetrable, but alone I could wallow uninterrupted in romantic
doom. I've never understood why people consider youth a time of freedom and joy. It's probably because they have forgotten their own. Surrounded now by the doleful young, I can only feel grateful for having
escaped, hopefully forever (for I no longer believe in reincarnation), from
the intolerable bondage of being twenty-one.

I had told you I was going away for three days, but undiluted fantasy
was too much for me. Salem was a vacuum and you were expanding to fill
it. I knew whose hair that was in the massive black and gold *memento mori*
in the second row of brooches, I knew who I had heard in the vacant hotel
room to the left of mine, breathing almost inaudibly between the spasms
of the radiator. Luckily there was an afternoon train; I took it, and fled
back to the present.

I called you from the Boston train station. You accepted my early
return with your usual fatalism, expressing neither glee nor surprise. You
were supposed to be doing work on ambiguity in Tennyson's 'Locksley
Hall', which, you informed me, was clearly out of the question. Ambiguity
was big in those days. We went for a walk instead. It was milder and the
snow was turning to mush; we ended up at the Charles River, where we
rolled snowballs and pitched them into the water. After that we constructed
a damp statue of Queen Victoria, complete with jutting bosom, monumental
bustle and hooked nose, then demolished it with snowballs and chunks of
ice, sniggering at intervals with what I then thought was liberated abandon
but now recognize as hysteria.

And then, and then. What did I have on? My coat, of course, and a
different skirt, a sickly greenish plaid; the same sweater with the burnt
hole in it. We slithered together through the partially frozen slush beside
the river, holding each other's chilly hands. It was evening and getting
colder. From time to time we stopped, to jump up and down and kiss
each other, in order to keep warm. On the oily surface of the Charles

were reflected, like bright mirages, the towers and belfries from which the spring examination hopeless ones would later hurl themselves, as they did every year; in its sludgy depths floated the literary suicides, Faulkner's among them, encrusted with crystalline words and glittering like eyes; but we were reckless, we sang in mockery of them, a ragged duet:

> Two old chairs, and half a candle,
> One old jug without a handle, . . .

For once you were laughing. I renounced my carefully constructed script, the ending I had planned for us. The future opened like a wide-screen vista, promising and dangerous, any direction was possible. I felt as if I was walking along the edge of a high bridge. It seemed to us—at least it seemed to me—that we were actually happy.

When the cold was finally too much for us and you had begun to sneeze, we went to one of the cheap restaurants where, it was rumoured, you could live for nothing by eating the free packets of ketchup, relish and sugar and drinking the cream out of the cream-jugs when no one was looking. There we debated the advisability of sleeping together, the pros and cons and, quite soon after that, the ways and means. It was not done lightly, especially by female graduate students, who were supposed to be like nuns, dedicated and unfleshly. Not that in those monastic surroundings they had much chance to be anything else, as the male ones mostly went to the opera together in little groups and had sherry parties to which they invited only each other. We both lived in residence; we both had cell-mates who were always in the room, biting their nails and composing bibliographies. Neither of us had a car, and we were sure the local hotels would reject us. It would have to be somewhere else. We settled on New York at Easter Break.

The day before the trip I went to Filene's Basement and bought, after some deliberation, a red nylon baby-doll nightgown, only one size too big and with a shoulder strap that could easily be sewed back on. I lingered over a mauve one with Carmen-like flounces, but I could wear only one at a time and the money would be needed for other things. On Good Friday I took the bus down to New York. You had left several days earlier, but I had stayed to finish an overdue essay on Mrs Radcliffe's *The Italian*. You yourself had three overdue papers by that time, but you no longer seemed to care. You had been spending a lot of time taking showers, which had annoyed your roommate; you had also been suffering from extended nightmares, which featured, as I recall, elephants, alligators and other large animals rolling down hills in wheelchairs, and people being nailed to crosses and incinerated. I viewed these as evidence of your sensitivity.

The plan was that you would stay at the apartment of an old friend from your hometown, while I was to get a single hotel room. This would defeat suspicion, we hoped; also it would be less expensive.

At that time I had never been to New York and I was not prepared for it. At first it made me dizzy. I stood in the Port Authority in my long black coat, with my heavy suitcase and my bottomless purse, looking for a phone booth. The crowd was like a political demonstration, though at that time I had never seen a real one. Women jostled each other and spat insults as if they were slogans, hauling grumpy children in their wake; there was a lineup of seedy old men on the benches, and the floor was dotted with gum, candy wrappers and cigarette stubs. I'm not sure but I think there were pinball machines; can that be possible? I wished now that I had asked you to meet the bus, but such dependencies were not part of our understanding.

As I headed for what I guessed was the exit, a black man grabbed hold of my suitcase and began to pull. He had a fresh cut on his forehead from which the blood was running, and his eyes were filled with such desperation that I almost let go. He was not trying to steal my suitcase, I realized after a minute; he just wanted to carry it to a taxi for me.

'No thank you,' I said. 'No money.'

He glanced with scorn at my coat—it was, after all, good quality—and did not let go. I pulled harder and he gave up. He shouted something after me that I didn't understand; those words had not yet become common currency.

I knew the address of the hotel, but I didn't know how to get there. I began to walk. The sun was out and I was sweating, from fright as well as heat. I found a telephone booth: the phone had been eviscerated and was a tangle of wires. The next one was intact, but when I called you there was no answer. This was strange, as I'd told you what time I was arriving.

I leaned against the side of the phone booth, making an effort not to panic. New York had been designed like a barred window, so by looking at the street signs and counting, I should be able to deduce the location of the hotel. I did not want to ask anyone: the expressions of blank despair or active malice made me nervous, and I had passed several people who were talking out loud to themselves. New York, like Salem, appeared to be falling to pieces. A rich person might have seen it as potential urban renewal, but the buildings with chunks missing, the holes in the sidewalks, did not reassure me.

I set out to drag my suitcase to the hotel, stopping at every phone booth to dial your number. In one of these I left your copy of *The Education of Henry Adams*, by mistake. It was just as well, as it was the only thing of yours I had; it would have been unlucky to have kept it.

The hotel clerk was nearly as suspicious of me as the one in Salem had been. I had ascribed the distrust of me there to small-town xenophobia, but it occurred to me now for the first time that it might be the way I was dressed. With my cuffs down to my knuckles, I did not look like someone with a credit card.

I sat in my room, which was really very much like the one in Salem, wondering what had happened to you, where you were. I phoned every half hour. There was not much I could do while waiting. I unpacked the red nightgown with the broken strap, only to find I'd forgotten the needle and thread with which I'd intended to repair it; I didn't even have a safety pin. I wanted to take a bath, but the handle of my door kept turning, and although I had fastened the chain I did not want to take the chance. I even kept my coat on. I began to think that you had given me the wrong number, or, worse, that you were something I had invented.

Finally at about seven o'clock someone answered the phone at your end. It was a woman. When I asked for you she laughed, not pleasantly.

'Hey, Voice of Doom,' I heard her say. 'Some chick wants you.' When you came on your voice was even more remote than usual.

'Where are you?' I said, trying not to sound like a nagging wife. 'I've been trying to get hold of you since two-thirty.'

'It's my friend,' you said. 'She swallowed a bottle of sleeping pills this morning. I had to walk her around a lot.'

'Oh,' I said. I'd had the impression that the friend was male. 'Couldn't you have taken her to a hospital or something?'

'You don't take people to hospitals here unless you really have to.'

'Why did she do it?' I asked.

'Who knows?' you said, in the voice of someone annoyed at being involved, however peripherally. 'To pass the time, I guess.' In the background the woman said something that sounded like 'You shit.'

The soles of my feet turned cold, my legs went numb. I had realized suddenly that she was not just an old friend, as you had told me. She had been a lover, she was still a lover, she was serious, she had taken the pills because she found out I was arriving that day and she was trying to stop you; yet all this time you were calmly writing down the room number, the phone number, that I was just as calmly giving you. We arranged to meet the next day. I spent the night lying on the bed with my coat on.

Of course you failed to arrive, and by that time I had thought twice about phoning. You did not even return to Boston. In May I got a cryptic note from you on a postcard with a picture of the Atlantic City boardwalk on the front:

I ran off to join the Navy but they wouldn't have me, they didn't think Ancient Greek was a good enough qualification. I got a job in a hash joint by lying about

my literacy. It's better than jumping off the bell tower. Give my regards to
Coromandel. Ever yours, Bo.

As usual, I couldn't decide whether or not you were sneering.

Of course I mourned; not so much for your departure, as that had
been, I now saw, a foregone conclusion, but for its suddenness. I had
been deprived of that last necessary scene, the park bench, the light
spring wind, the trench coat (which I was destined never to buy), your
vanishing figure. Even after I realized that our future would have contained neither the dreaded bungalow and electric razor nor those vague,
happy possibilities I had once imagined, but, inevitable as a rhymed
couplet, an emptied bottle of sleeping pills whose effects you might not
have helped me walk off, I continued to mourn.

Because you had not left in the proper way it seemed as though you
had never left at all. You hung around, like a miasma or the smell of mice,
waiting to deflate my attempts at optimism—for out of sheer fright I soon
began to make them—with your own jaundiced view of my behaviour. As
if you were my darker twin or an adept in sinister telepathy I could sense
on every occasion what your opinion would be. When I became engaged
(seven months later, to an architect who designed, and continues to
design, apartment buildings), you let me know you had expected other
things of me. The actual wedding, and yes, I had all the trimmings
including a white gown, filled you with scorn. I could see you in your
dingy room, surrounded by empty sardine tins and lint-covered socks,
living on nothing but your derision and your refusal to sell out, as I was
so palpably doing. (To what? To whom? Unlike later generations, we
were never able to pinpoint the enemy.)

My two children did not impress you, nor did the academic position
which I subsequently achieved. I have become, in a minor way, an authority
on women domestic novelists of the nineteenth century. I discovered
after my marriage that I really had more in common with them than I did
with Gothic romances; I suppose this insight into my true character
signifies maturity, a word you despise. The most prominent of my subjects is Mrs Gaskell, but you may have heard of Mrs J. H. Riddell as
well; she wrote also under the pen name of F. G. Trafford. I gave quite
a creditable paper on her *George Geith of Fen Court*, which was later
published in a reputable journal. Needless to say I have tenure, as my
department, averse to women for many years, has recently been under
some pressure to justify its hiring policies. I am a token, as you never tire
of pointing out. I dress well, too, as befits a token. The drab, defiantly
woollen wardrobe you may remember vanished little by little into the
bins of the Salvation Army as I grew richer, and was replaced by a

moderately chic collection of pantsuits and brisk dresses. My male colleagues think of me as efficient and rather cold. I no longer have casual affairs, as I hate mementoes that cannot be thrown away. My coats no longer flap, and when I attend academic conferences nobody stares.

It was at one of these, the big one, the central flesh market and hiring fair, that I saw you last. Curiously enough, it was held in New York that year. I was giving a paper on Amelia Edwards and other female journalists of the period. When I saw your name on the agenda I thought it must be someone else. But it was you, all right, and you spent the entire session discussing whether or not John Keats had had syphilis. You had done a considerable amount of research on the medical uses of mercury in the early part of the century, and your last paragraph was a masterpiece of inconclusion. You had gained weight, in fact you looked healthy, you looked as if you played golf. Though I watched in vain for a sardonic smile: your delivery was deadpan.

Afterwards I went up to congratulate you. You were surprised to see me; you had never thought of me, you said, ending up quite like this, and your possibly dismayed gaze took in my salon haircut, my trim-fitting red jump suit, my jaunty boots. You yourself were married, with three children, and you hastily showed me wallet snapshots, holding them out like protective talismans. I matched them with my own. Neither of us suggested having a drink. We wished each other well; we were both disappointed. You had wanted me, I saw now, to die young of consumption or some equally operatic disease. Underneath it all you too were a romantic.

That should have been that, and I can't understand why it isn't. It is absolutely true that I love my husband and children. In addition to attending faculty meetings, where I crochet afghan squares during discussions of increments and curricula, I cook them nourishing meals, arrange birthday parties and make my own bread and pickles, most of the time. My husband admires my achievements and is supportive, as they say, during my depressions, which become rarer. I have a rich and rewarding sex life, and I can already hear you ridiculing the adjectives, but it is rich and rewarding in spite of you. And you have done no better than I have.

But when I returned from the conference to the house where I live, which is not a bungalow but a two-storey colonial and in which, ever since I moved in, you have occupied the cellar, you were not gone. I expected you to have been dispelled, exorcised: you had become real, you had a wife and three snapshots, and banality is after all the magic antidote for unrequited love. But it was not enough. There you were, in your accustomed place, over by the shelf to the right of the cellar stairs where I keep the preserves, standing dusty and stuffed like Jeremy Bentham in his glass case, looking at me not with your former scorn, it's true, but with reproach, as if I had let it happen, as if it was my fault. Surely you don't want it back, that misery, those decaying buildings, that seductive despair and emptiness, that fear? Surely you don't want to be stuck on that slushy Boston street forever. You should have been more careful. I try to tell you it would have ended badly, that it was not the way you remember, you are deceiving yourself, but you refuse to be consoled. *Goodbye*, I tell you, waiting for your glance, pensive, regretful. You are supposed to turn and walk away, past the steamer trunks, around the corner into the laundry room, and vanish behind the twinset washer-dryer; but you do not move.

ANGELA CARTER

Puss-in-Boots

❦

Figaro here; Figaro, there, I tell you! Figaro upstairs, Figaro downstairs and—oh, my goodness me, this little Figaro can slip into my lady's chamber smart as you like at any time whatsoever that he takes the fancy for, don't you know, he's a cat of the world, cosmopolitan, sophisticated; he can tell when a furry friend is the Missus' best company. For what lady in all the world could say 'no' to the passionate yet toujours discret advances of a fine marmalade cat? (Unless it be her eyes incontinently overflow at the slightest whiff of fur, which happened once, as you shall hear.)

A tom, sirs, a ginger tom and proud of it. Proud of his fine, white shirtfront that dazzles harmoniously against his orange and tangerine tessellations (oh! what a fiery suit of lights have I); proud of his bird-entrancing eye and more than military whiskers; proud, to a fault, some say, of his fine, musical voice. All the windows in the square fly open when I break into impromptu song at the spectacle of the moon above Bergamo. If the poor players in the square, the sullen rout of ragged trash that haunts the provinces, are rewarded with a hail of pennies when they set up their makeshift stage and start their raucous choruses, then how much more liberally do the citizens deluge me with pails of the freshest water, vegetables hardly spoiled and, occasionally, slippers, shoes and boots.

Do you see these fine, high, shining leather boots of mine? A young cavalry officer made me the tribute of, first, one; then, after I celebrate his generosity with a fresh obbligato, the moon no fuller than my heart—whoops! I nimbly spring aside—down comes the other. Their high heels will click like castanets when Puss takes his promenade upon the tiles, for my song recalls flamenco, all cats have a Spanish tinge although Puss himself elegantly lubricates his virile, muscular, native Bergamasque with French, since that is the only language in which you can purr.

'Merrrrrrrrrrrci!'

Instanter I draw my new boots on over the natty white stockings that terminate my hinder legs. That young man, observing with curiosity by moonlight the use to which I put his footwear, calls out: 'Hey, Puss! Puss, there!'

'At your service, sir!'

'Up to my balcony, young Puss!'

He leans out, in his nightshirt, offering encouragement as I swing succinctly up the façade, forepaws on a curly cherub's pate, hindpaws on a stucco wreath, bring them up to meet your forepaws while, first paw forward, hup! on to the stone nymph's tit; left paw down a bit, the satyr's bum should do the trick. Nothing to it, once you know how, rococo's no problem. Acrobatics? Born to them; Puss can perform a back somersault whilst holding aloft a glass of vino in his right paw and *never spill a drop*.

But, to my shame, the famous death-defying triple somersault en plein air, that is, in middle air, that is, unsupported and without a safety net, I, Puss, have never yet attempted though often I have dashingly brought off the double tour, to the applause of all.

'You strike me as a cat of parts,' says this young man when I'm arrived at his window-sill. I made him a handsome genuflection, rump out, tail up, head down, to facilitate his friendly chuck under my chin; and, as involuntary free gift, my natural, my habitual smile.

For all cats have this particularity, each and every one, from the meanest alley sneaker to the proudest, whitest she that ever graced a pontiff's pillow—we have our smiles, as it were, painted on. Those small, cool, quiet Mona Lisa smiles that smile we must, no matter whether it's been fun or it's been not. So all cats have a politician's air; we smile and smile and so they think we're villains. But, I note, this young man is something of a smiler hisself.

'A sandwich,' he offers. 'And, perhaps, a snifter of brandy.'

His lodgings are poor, though he's handsome enough and even en déshabillé, nightcap and all, there's a neat, smart, dandified air about him. Here is one who knows what's what, thinks I; a man who keeps up appearances in the bedchamber can never embarrass you out of it. And excellent beef sandwiches; I relish a lean slice of roast beef and early learned a taste for spirits, since I started life as a wine-shop cat, hunting cellar rats for my keep, before the world sharpened my wits enough to let me live by them.

And the upshot of this midnight interview? I'm engaged, on the spot, as Sir's valet: valet de chambre and, from time to time, his body servant, for, when funds are running low, as they must do for every gallant officer when the pickings fall off, he pawns the quilt, doesn't he. Then faithful Puss curls up on his chest to keep him warm at nights. And if he don't like me to knead his nipples, which, out of the purest affection and the desire—ouch! he says—to test the retractability of my claws, I do in moments of absence of mind, then what other valet could slip into a young girl's sacred privacy and deliver her a billet-doux at the very moment when she's reading her prayerbook with her sainted mother? A task I once or twice perform for him, to his infinite gratitude.

And, as you will hear, brought him at last to the best of fortunes for us all.

So Puss got his post at the same time as his boots and I dare say the Master and I have much in common for he's proud as the devil, touchy as tin-tacks, lecherous as liquorice and, though I say it as loves him, as quick-witted a rascal as ever put on clean linen.

When times were hard, I'd pilfer the market for breakfast—a herring, an orange, a loaf; we never went hungry. Puss served him well in the gaming salons, too, for a cat may move from lap to lap with impunity and cast his eye over any hand of cards. A cat can jump on the dice—he can't resist to see it roll! poor thing, mistook it for a bird; and, after I've been, limp-spined, stiff-legged, playing the silly buggers, scooped up to be chastised, who can remember how the dice fell in the first place?

And we had, besides, less . . . gentlemanly means of maintenance when they closed the tables to us, as, churlishly, they sometimes did. I'd perform my little Spanish dance while he went round with his hat: *olé*! But he only put my loyalty and affection to the test of this humiliation when the cupboard was as bare as his backside; after, in fact, he'd sunk so low as to pawn his drawers.

So all went right as ninepence and you never saw such boon companions as Puss and his master; until the man must needs go fall in love.

'Head over heels, Puss.'

I went about my ablutions, tonguing my arsehole with the impeccable hygienic integrity of cats, one leg stuck in the air like a ham bone; I choose to remain silent. Love? What has my rakish master, for whom I've jumped through the window of every brothel in the city, besides haunting the virginal back garden of the convent and god knows what other goatish errands, to do with the tender passion?

'And she. A princess in a tower. Remote and shining as Aldebaran. Chained to a dolt and dragon-guarded.'

I withdrew my head from my privates and fixed him with my most satiric smile; I dare him warble on in *that* strain.

'All cats are cynics,' he opines, quailing beneath my yellow glare.

It is the hazard of it draws him, see.

There is a lady sits in a window for one hour and one hour only, at the tenderest time of dusk. You can scarcely see her features, the curtains almost hide her; shrouded like a holy image, she looks out at the piazza as the shops shut up, the stalls go down, the night comes on. And that is all the world she ever sees. Never a girl in all Bergamo so secluded except, on Sundays, they let her go to Mass, bundled up in black, with a veil on. And then she is in the company of an aged hag, her keeper, who grumps along grim as a prison dinner.

How did he see that secret face? Who else but Puss revealed it?

Back we come from the tables so late, so very late at night we found, to our emergent surprise, that all at once it was early in the morning. His pockets were heavy with silver and both our guts sweetly a-gurgle with champagne; Lady Luck had sat with us, what fine spirits were we in! Winter and cold weather. The pious trot to church already with little lanterns through the chill fog as we go ungodly rolling home.

See, a black barque, like a state funeral; and Puss takes it into his bubbly-addled brain to board her. Tacking obliquely to her side, I rub my marmalade pate against her shin; how could any duenna, be she never so stern, take offence at such attentions to her chargeling from a little cat? (As it turns out, this one: *attishooo!* does.) A white hand fragrant as Arabia descends from the black cloak and reciprocally rubs behind his ears at just the ecstatic spot. Puss lets rip a roaring purr, rears briefly on his high-heeled boots; jig with joy and pirouette with glee—she laughs to see and draws her veil aside. Puss glimpses high above, as it were, an alabaster lamp lit behind by dawn's first flush: her face.

And she smiling.

For a moment, just that moment, you would have thought it was May morning.

'Come along! Come! Don't dawdle over the nasty beast!' snaps the old hag, with the one tooth in her mouth, and warts; she sneezes.

The veil comes down; so cold it is, and dark, again.

It was not I alone who saw her; with that smile he swears she stole his heart.

Love.

I've sat inscrutably by and washed my face and sparkling dicky with my clever paw while he made the beast with two backs with every harlot in the city, besides a number of good wives, dutiful daughters, rosy country girls come to sell celery and endive on the corner, and the chambermaid who strips the bed, what's more. The Mayor's wife, even, shed her diamond earrings for him and the wife of the notary unshuffled her petticoats and, if I could, I would blush to remember how her daughter shook out her flaxen plaits and jumped in bed between them and she not sixteen years old. But never the word, 'love', has fallen from his lips, nor in nor out of any of these transports, until my master saw the wife of Signor Panteleone as she went walking out to Mass, and she lifted up her veil though not for him.

And now he is half sick with it and will go to the tables no more for lack of heart and never even pats the bustling rump of the chambermaid in his new-found, maudlin celibacy, so we get our slops left festering for days and the sheets filthy and the wench goes banging about bad-temperedly with her broom enough to fetch the plaster off the walls.

I'll swear he lives for Sunday morning, though never before was he a religious man. Saturday nights, he bathes himself punctiliously, even, I'm glad to see, washes behind his ears, perfumes himself, presses his uniform so you'd think he had a right to wear it. So much in love he very rarely panders to the pleasures, even of Onan, as he lies tossing on his couch, for he cannot sleep for fear he miss the summoning bell. Then out into the cold morning, harking after that black, vague shape, hapless fisherman for this sealed oyster with such a pearl in it. He creeps behind her across the square; how can so amorous bear to be so inconspicuous? And yet, he must; though, sometimes, the old hag sneezes and says she swears there is a cat about.

He will insinuate himself into the pew behind milady and sometimes contrive to touch the hem of her garment, when they all kneel, and never a thought to his orisons; she is the divinity he's come to worship. Then sits silent, in a dream, till bed-time; what pleasure is his company for me?

He won't eat, either. I brought him a fine pigeon from the inn kitchen, fresh off the spit, parfumé avec tarragon, but he wouldn't touch it so I crunched it up, bones and all. Performing, as ever after meals, my meditative toilette, I pondered, thus: one, he is in a fair way to ruining us both by neglecting his business; two, love is desire sustained by unfulfilment. If I lead him to her bedchamber and there he takes his fill of her lily-white, he'll be right as rain in two shakes and next day tricks as usual.

Then Master and his Puss will soon be solvent once again.

Which, at the moment, very much not, sir.

This Signor Panteleone employs, his only servant but the hag, a kitchen cat, a sleek, spry tabby whom I accost. Grasping the slack of her neck firmly between my teeth, I gave her the customary tribute of a few firm thrusts of my striped loins and, when she got her breath back, she assured me in the friendliest fashion the old man was a fool and a miser who kept herself on short commons for the sake of the mousing and the young lady a soft-hearted creature who smuggled breast of chicken and sometimes, when the hag-dragon-governess napped at midday, snatched this pretty kitty out of the hearth and into her bedroom to play with reels of silk and run after trailed handkerchiefs, when she and she had as much fun together as two Cinderellas at an all-girls' ball.

Poor, lonely lady, married so young to an old dodderer with his bald pate and his goggle eyes and his limp, his avarice, his gore belly, his rheumaticks, and his flag hangs all the time at half-mast indeed; and jealous as he is impotent, tabby declares—he'd put a stop to all the rutting in the world, if he had his way, just to certify his young wife don't get from another what she can't get from him.

'Then shall we hatch a plot to antler him, my precious?'

Nothing loath, she tells me the best time for this accomplishment should be the one day in all the week he forsakes his wife and his counting-house to ride off into the country to extort most grasping rents from starveling tenant farmers. And she's left all alone, then, behind so many bolts and bars you wouldn't believe; all alone—but for the hag!

Aha! This hag turns out to be the biggest snag; an iron-plated, copper-bottomed, sworn man-hater of some sixty bitter winters who—as ill luck would have it—shatters, clatters, erupts into paroxysms of the _sneeze_ at the very glimpse of a cat's whisker. No chance of Puss worming his winsome way into _that_ one's affections, nor for my tabby, neither! But, oh my dear, I say; see how my ingenuity rises to this challenge. . . . So we resume the sweetest part of our conversation in the dusty convenience of the coalhole and she promises me, least she can do, to see the fair, hitherto-inaccessible one gets a letter safe if I slip it to her and slip it to her forthwith I do, though somewhat discommoded by my boots.

He spent three hours over his letter, did my master, as long as it takes me to lick the coaldust off my dicky. He tears up half a quire of paper, splays five pen-nibs with the force of his adoration: 'Look not for any peace, my heart; having become a slave to this beauty's tyranny, dazzled am I by this sun's rays and my torments cannot be assuaged.' _That's_ not the high road to the rumpling of the bedcovers; she's got _one_ ninny between them already!

'Speak from the heart,' I finally exhort. 'And all good women have a missionary streak, sir; convince her her orifice will be your salvation and she's yours.'

'When I want your advice, Puss, I'll ask for it,' he says, all at once hoity-toity. But at least he manages to pen ten pages; a rake, a profligate, a card-sharper, a cashiered officer well on the way to rack and ruin when first he saw, as if it were a glimpse of grace, her face . . . his angel, his good angel, who will lead him from perdition.

Oh, what a masterpiece he penned!

'Such tears she wept at his addresses!' says my tabby friend. 'Oh, Tabs, she sobs—for she calls me "Tabs"—I never meant to wreak such havoc with a pure heart when I smiled to see a booted cat! And put his paper next to her heart and swore, it was a good soul that sent her his vows and she was too much in love with virtue to withstand him. If, she adds, for she's a sensible girl, he's neither old as the hills nor ugly as sin, that is.'

An admirable little note the lady's sent him in return, per Figaro here and there; she adopts a responsive yet uncompromising tone. For, says she, how can she usefully discuss his passion further without a glimpse of his person?

He kisses her letter once, twice, a thousand times; she must and will see me! I shall serenade her this very evening!

So, when dusk falls, off we trot to the piazza, he with an old guitar he pawned his sword to buy and most, if I may say so, outlandishly rigged out in some kind of vagabond mountebank's outfit he bartered his gold-braided waistcoat with poor Pierrot braying in the square for, moonstruck zany, lovelorn loon he was himself and even plastered his face with flour to make it white, poor fool, and so ram home his heartsick state.

There she is, the evening star with the clouds around her; but such a creaking of carts in the square, such a clatter and crash as they dismantle the stalls, such an ululation of ballad-singers and oration of nostrum-peddlers and perturbation of errand boys that though he wails out his heart to her: 'Oh, my beloved!', why she, all in a dream, sits with her gaze in the middle distance, where there's a crescent moon stuck on the sky behind the cathedral pretty as a painted stage, and so is she.

Does she hear him?

Not a grace-note.

Does she see him?

Never a glance.

'Up you go, Puss; tell her to look my way!'

If rococo's a piece of cake, that chaste, tasteful, early Palladian stumped many a better cat than I in its time. Agility's not in it, when it comes to Palladian; daring alone will carry the day and, though the first storey's graced with a hefty caryatid whose bulbous loincloth and tremendous pects facilitate the first ascent, the Doric column on her head proves a horse of a different colour, I can tell you. Had I not seen my precious Tabby crouched in the gutter above me keening encouragement, I, even I, might never have braved that flying, upward leap that brought me, as if Harlequin himself on wires, in one bound to her window-sill.

'Dear god!' the lady says, and jumps. I see she, too, ah, sentimental thing! clutches a well-thumbed letter. 'Puss in boots!'

I bow her with a courtly flourish. What luck to hear no sniff or sneeze; where's hag? A sudden flux sped her to the privy—not a moment to lose.

'Cast your eye below,' I hiss. 'Him you know of lurks below, in white with the big hat, ready to sing you an evening ditty.'

The bedroom door creaks open, then, and: whee! through the air Puss goes, discretion is the better part. And, for both their sweet sakes I did it, the sight of both their bright eyes inspired me to the never-before-attempted, by me or any other cat, in boots or out of them—the death-defying triple somersault!

And a three-storey drop to ground, what's more; a grand descent.

Only the merest trifle winded, I'm proud to say, I neatly land on all my fours and Tabs goes wild, huzzah! But has my master witnessed my triumph? Has he, my arse. He's tuning up that old mandolin and breaks, as down I come, again into his song.

I would never have said, in the normal course of things, his voice would charm the birds out of the trees, like mine; and yet the bustle died for him, the homeward-turning costers paused in their tracks to hearken, the preening street girls forgot their hard-edged smiles as they turned to him and some of the old ones wept, they did.

Tabs, up on the roof there, prick up your ears! For by its power I know my heart is in his voice.

And now the lady lowers her eyes to him and smiles, as once she smiled at me.

Then, bang! a stern hand pulls the shutters to. And it was as if all the violets in all the baskets of all the flower-sellers drooped and faded at once; and spring stopped dead in its tracks and might, this time, not come at all; and the bustle and the business of the square, that had so magically quieted for his song, now rose up again with the harsh clamour of the loss of love.

And we trudge drearily off to dirty sheets and a mean supper of bread and cheese, all I can steal him, but at least the poor soul manifests a hearty appetite now she knows he's in the world and not the ugliest of mortals; for the first time since that fateful morning, sleeps sound. But sleep comes hard to Puss tonight. He takes a midnight stroll across the square, soon comfortably discusses a choice morsel of salt cod his tabby friend found among the ashes on the hearth before our converse turns to other matters.

'Rats!' she says. 'And take your boots off, you uncouth bugger; those three-inch heels wreak havoc with the soft flesh of my underbelly!'

When we'd recovered ourselves a little, I ask her what she means by those 'rats' of hers and she proposes her scheme to me. How my master must pose as a *rat-catcher* and I, his ambulant marmalade rat-trap. How we will then go kill the rats that ravage milady's bedchamber, the day the old fool goes to fetch his rents, and she can have her will of the lad at leisure for, if there is one thing the hag fears more than a cat, it is a rat and she'll cower in a cupboard till the last rat is off the premises before she comes out. Oh, this tabby one, sharp as a tack is she! I congratulate her ingenuity with a few affectionate cuffs round the head and home again, for breakfast, ubiquitous Puss, here, there and everywhere, who's your Figaro?

Master applauds the rat ploy; but, as to the rats themselves, how are they to arrive in the house in the first place? he queries.

'Nothing easier, sir; my accomplice, a witty soubrette who lives among the cinders, dedicated as she is to the young lady's happiness, will personally strew a large number of dead and dying rats she has herself collected about the bedroom of the said ingénue's duenna, and, most particularly, that of the said ingénue herself. This to be done tomorrow morning, as soon as Sir Pantaloon rides out to fetch his rents. By good fortune, down in the square, plying for hire, a rat-catcher! Since our hag cannot abide either a rat or a cat, it falls to milady to escort the rat-catcher, none other than yourself, sir, and his intrepid hunter, myself, to the site of the infestation.

'Once you're in her bedroom, sir, if *you* don't know what to do, then I can't help you.'

'Keep your foul thoughts to yourself, Puss.'

Some things, I see, are sacrosanct from humour.

Sure enough, prompt at five in the bleak next morning, I observe with my own eyes the lovely lady's lubberly husband hump off on his horse like a sack of potatoes to rake in his dues. We're ready with our sign: SIGNOR FURIOSO, THE LIVING DEATH OF RATS; and in the leathers he's borrowed from the porter, I hardly recognize him myself, not with the false moustache. He coaxes the chambermaid with a few kisses—poor, deceived girl! love knows no shame—and so we install ourselves under a certain shuttered window with the great pile of traps she's lent us, the sign of our profession, Puss perched atop them bearing the humble yet determined look of a sworn enemy of vermin.

We've not waited more than fifteen minutes—and just as well, so many rat-plagued Bergamots approach us already and are not easily dissuaded from employing us—when the front door flies open on a lusty scream. The hag, aghast, flings her arms round flinching Furioso; how fortuitous to find him! But, at the whiff of me, she's sneezing so valiantly, her eyes awash, the vertical gutters of her nostrils aswill with snot, she barely can depict the scenes inside, rattus domesticus dead in her bed and all; and worse! in the Missus' room.

So Signor Furioso and his questing Puss are ushered into the very sanctuary of the goddess, our presence announced by a fanfare from her keeper on the noseharp. *Attishhoooo!!!*

Sweet and pleasant in a morning gown of loose linen, our ingénue jumps at the tattoo of my boot heels but recovers instantly and the wheezing, hawking hag is in no state to sniffle more than: 'Ain't I seen that cat before?'

'Not a chance,' says my master. 'Why, he's come but yesterday with me from Milano.'

So she has to make do with that.

My Tabs has lined the very stairs with rats; she's made a morgue of the hag's room but something more lively of the lady's. For some of her prey she's very cleverly not killed but crippled; a big black beastie weaves its way towards us over the turkey carpet, Puss, pounce! Between screaming and sneezing, the hag's in a fine state, I can tell you, though milady exhibits a most praiseworthy and collected presence of mind, being, I guess, a young woman of no small grasp so, perhaps, she has a sniff of the plot, already.

My master goes down hands and knees under the bed.

'My god!' he cries. 'There's the biggest hole, here in the wainscoting, I ever saw in all my professional career! And there's an army of black rats gathering behind it, ready to storm through! To arms!'

But, for all her terror, the hag's loath to leave the Master and me alone to deal with the rats; she casts her eye on a silver-backed hairbrush, a coral rosary, twitters, hovers, screeches, mutters until milady assures her, amidst scenes of rising pandemonium:

'I shall stay here myself and see that Signor Furioso doesn't make off with my trinkets. You go and recover yourself with an infusion of friar's balsam and don't come back until I call.'

The hag departs; quick as a flash, la belle turns the key in the door on her and softly laughs, the naughty one.

Dusting the slut-fluff from his knees, Signor Furioso now stands slowly upright; swiftly, he removes his false moustache, for no element of the farcical must mar this first, delirious encounter of these lovers, must it. (Poor soul, how his hands tremble!)

Accustomed as I am to the splendid, feline nakedness of my kind, that offers no concealment of that soul made manifest in the flesh of lovers, I am always a little moved by the poignant reticence with which humanity shyly hesitates to divest itself of its clutter of concealing rags in the presence of desire. So, first, these two smile, a little, as if to say: 'How strange to meet you here!', uncertain of a loving welcome, still. And do I deceive myself, or do I see a tear a-twinkle in the corner of his eye? But who is it steps towards the other first? Why, she; women, I think, are, of the two sexes, the more keenly tuned to the sweet music of their bodies. (A penny for my foul thoughts, indeed! Does she, that wise, grave personage in the négligé, think you've staged this grand charade merely in order to kiss her hand?) But, then—oh, what a pretty blush! steps back; now it's his turn to take two steps forward in the saraband of Eros.

I could wish, though, they'd dance a little faster; the hag will soon recover from her spasms and shall she find them in flagrante?

His hand, then, trembling, upon her bosom; hers, initially more hesitant, sequentially more purposeful, upon his breeches. Then their strange trance breaks; that sentimental havering done, I never saw two fall to it with such appetite. As if the whirlwind got into their fingers, they strip each other bare in a twinkling and she falls back on the bed, shows him the target, he displays the dart, scores an instant bullseye. Bravo! Never can that old bed have shook with such a storm before. And their sweet, choked mutterings, poor things: 'I never . . .' 'My darling . . .' 'More . . .' And etc. etc. Enough to melt the thorniest heart.

He rises up on his elbows once and gasps at me: 'Mimic the murder of the rats, Puss! Mask the music of Venus with the clamour of Diana!'

A-hunting we shall go! Loyal to the last, I play catch as catch can with Tab's dead rats, giving the dying the coup de grâce and baying with resonant vigour to drown the extravagant screeches that break forth from that (who would have suspected?) more passionate young woman as she comes off in fine style. (Full marks, Master.)

At that, the old hag comes battering at the door. What's going on? Whyfor the racket? And the door rattles on its hinges.

'Peace!' cries Signor Furioso. 'Haven't I just now blocked the great hole?'

But milady's in no hurry to don her smock again, she takes her lovely time about it; so full of pleasure gratified her languorous limbs you'd think her very navel smiled. She pecks my master prettily thank-you on the cheek, wets the gum on his false moustache with the tip of her strawberry tongue and sticks it back on his upper lip for him, then lets her wardress into the scene of the faux carnage with the most modest and irreproachable air in the world.

'See! Puss has slaughtered all the rats.'

I rush, purring proud, to greet the hag; instantly, her eyes o'erflow.

'Why the bedclothes so disordered?' she squeaks, not quite blinded, yet, by phlegm and chosen for her post from all the other applicants on account of her suspicious mind, even (oh, dutiful) when in grande peur des rats.

'Puss had a mighty battle with the biggest beast you ever saw upon this very bed; can't you see the bloodstains on the sheets? And now, what do we owe you, Signor Furioso, for this singular service?'

'A hundred ducats,' says I, quick as a flash, for I know my master, left to himself, would, like an honourable fool, take nothing.

'That's the entire household expenses for a month!' wails avarice's well-chosen accomplice.

'And worth every penny! For those rats would have eaten us out of house and home.' I see the glimmerings of sturdy backbone in this little lady. 'Go, pay them from your private savings that I know of, that you've skimmed off the housekeeping.'

Muttering and moaning but nothing for it except do as she is bid; and the furious Sir and I take off a laundry basket full of dead rats as souvenir—we drop it, plop! in the nearest sewer. And sit down to one dinner honestly paid for, for a wonder.

But the young fool is off his feed, again. Pushes his plate aside, laughs, weeps, buries his head in his hands and, time and time again, goes to the window to stare at the shutters behind which his sweetheart scrubs the blood away and my dear Tabs rests from her supreme exertions. He sits, for a while, and scribbles; rips the page in four, hurls it aside. I spear a falling fragment with a claw. Dear God, he's took to writing poetry.

'I must and will have her for ever,' he exclaims.

I see my plan has come to nothing. Satisfaction has not satisfied him; that soul they both saw in one another's bodies has such insatiable hunger no single meal could ever appease it. I fall to the toilette of my hinder parts, my favourite stance when contemplating the ways of the world.

'How can I live without her?'

You did so for twenty-seven years, sir, and never missed her for a moment.

'I'm burning with the fever of love!'

Then we're spared the expense of fires.

'I shall steal her away from her husband to live with me.'

'What do you propose to live on, sir?'

'Kisses,' he said distractedly. 'Embraces.'

'Well, you won't grow fat on that, sir; though *she* will. And then, more mouths to feed.'

'I'm sick and tired of your foul-mouthed barbs, Puss,' he snaps. And yet my heart is moved, for now he speaks the plain, clear, foolish rhetoric of love and who is there cunning enough to help him to happiness but I? Scheme, loyal Puss, scheme!

My wash completed, I step out across the square to visit that charming she who's wormed her way directly into my own hitherto-untrammelled heart with her sharp wits and her pretty ways. She exhibits warm emotion to see me; and, oh! what news she has to tell me! News of a rapt and personal nature, that turns my mind to thoughts of the future, and, yes, domestic plans of most familial nature. She's saved me a pig's trotter, a whole, entire pig's trotter the Missus smuggled to her with a wink. A feast! Masticating, I muse.

'Recapitulate,' I suggest, 'the daily motions of Sir Pantaloon when he's at home.'

They set the cathedral clock by him, so rigid and so regular his habits. Up at the crack, he meagrely breakfasts off yesterday's crusts and a cup of cold water, to spare the expense of heating it up. Down to his counting-house, counting out his money, until a bowl of well-watered gruel at midday. The afternoon he devotes to usury, bankrupting, here, a small tradesman, there, a weeping widow, for fun and profit. Dinner's luxurious, at four; soup, with a bit of rancid beef or a tough bird in it—he's an arrangement with the butcher, takes unsold stock off his hands in return for a shut mouth about a pie that had a finger in it. From four-thirty until five-thirty, he unlocks the shutters and lets his wife look out, oh, don't I know! while hag sits beside her to make sure she doesn't smile. (Oh, that blessed flux, those precious loose minutes that set the game in motion!)

And while she breathes the air of evening, why, he checks up on his chest of gems, his bales of silk, all those treasures he loves too much to share with daylight and if he wastes a candle when he so indulges himself, why, any man is entitled to one little extravagance. Another draught of Adam's ale healthfully concludes the day; up he tucks besides Missus and, since she is his prize possession, consents to finger her a little. He palpitates her hide and slaps her flanks: 'What a good bargain!' Alack, can do no more, not wishing to profligate his natural essence. And so drifts off to sinless slumber amid the prospects of tomorrow's gold.

'How rich is he?'

'Croesus.'

'Enough to keep two loving couples?'

'Sumptuous.'

Early in the uncandled morning, groping to the privy bleared with sleep, were the old man to place his foot upon the subfusc yet volatile fur of a shadow-camouflaged young tabby cat—

'You read my thoughts, my love.'

I say to my master: 'Now, you get yourself a doctor's gown, impedimenta all complete or I'm done with you.'

'What's this, Puss?'

'Do as I say and never mind the reason! The less you know of why, the better.'

So he expends a few of the hag's ducats on a black gown with a white collar and his skull cap and his black bag and, under my direction, makes himself another sign that announces, with all due pomposity, how he is Il Famed Dottore: *Aches cured, pains prevented, bones set, graduate of Bologna, physician extraordinary.* He demands to know, is she to play the invalid to give him further access to her bedroom?

'I'll clasp her in my arms and jump out of the window; we too shall both perform the triple somersault of love.'

'You just mind your own business, sir, and let me mind it for you after my own fashion.'

Another raw and misty morning! Here in the hills, will the weather ever change? So bleak it is, and dreary; but there he stands, grave as a sermon in his black gown and half the market people come with coughs and boils and broken heads and I dispense the plasters and the vials of coloured water I'd forethoughtfully stowed in his bag, he too agitato to sell for himself. (And, who knows, might we not have stumbled on a profitable profession for future pursuit, if my present plans miscarry?)

Until dawn shoots his little yet how flaming arrow past the cathedral on which the clock strikes six. At the last stroke, that famous door flies open once again and—*eeeeeeeeeeeech!* the hag lets rip.

'Oh, Doctor, oh, Doctor, come quick as you can; our good man's taken a sorry tumble!'

And weeping fit to float a smack, she is, so doesn't see the doctor's apprentice is most colourfully and completely furred and whiskered.

The old booby's flat out at the foot of the stair, his head at an acute angle that might turn chronic and a big bunch of keys, still, gripped in his right hand as if they were the keys to heaven marked: *Wanted on voyage.* And Missus, in her wrap, bends over him with a pretty air of concern.

'A fall—' she begins when she sees the doctor but stops short when she sees your servant, Puss, looking as suitably down-in-the-mouth as his chronic smile will let him, humping his master's stock-in-trade and hawing like a sawbones. 'You, again,' she says, and can't forbear to giggle. But the dragon's too blubbered to hear.

My master puts his ear to the old man's chest and shakes his head dolefully; then takes the mirror from his pocket and puts it to the old man's mouth. Not a breath clouds it. Oh, sad! Oh, sorrowful!

'Dead, is he?' sobs the hag. 'Broke his neck, has he?'

And she slyly makes a little grab for the keys, in spite of her well-orchestrated distress; but Missus slaps her hand and she gives over.

'Let's get him to a softer bed,' says Master.

He ups the corpse, carries it aloft to the room we know full well, bumps Pantaloon down, twitches an eyelid, taps a kneecap, feels a pulse.

'Dead as a doornail,' he pronounces. 'It's not a doctor you want, it's an undertaker.'

Missus has a handkerchief very dutifully and correctly to her eyes.

'You just run along and get one,' she says to hag. 'And then I'll read the will. Because don't think he's forgotten you, thou faithful servant. Oh, my goodness, no.'

So off goes hag; you never saw a woman of her accumulated Christ-mases sprint so fast. As soon as they are left alone, no trifling, this time;

they're at it, hammer and tongs, down on the carpet since the bed is occupé. Up and down, up and down his arse; in and out, in and out her legs. Then she heaves him up and throws him on his back, her turn at the grind, now, and you'd think she'll never stop.

Toujours discret, Puss occupies himself in unfastening the shutters and throwing the windows open to the beautiful beginnings of morning in whose lively yet fragrant air his sensitive nostrils catch the first and vernal hint of spring. In a few moments, my dear friend joins me. I notice already—or is it only my fond imagination?—a charming new *portliness* in her gait, hitherto so elastic, so spring-heeled. And there we sit upon the window-sill, like the two genii and protectors of the house; ah, Puss, your rambling days are over. I shall become a hearthrug cat, a fat and cosy cushion cat, sing to the moon no more, settle at last amid the sedentary joys of a domesticity we two, she and I, have so richly earned.

Their cries of rapture rouse me from this pleasant revery.

The hag chooses, naturellement, this tender if outrageous moment to return with the undertaker in his chiffoned topper, plus a brace of mutes black as beetles, glum as bailiffs, bearing the elm box between them to take the corpse away in. But they cheer up something wonderful at the unexpected spectacle before them and he and she conclude their amorous interlude amidst roars of approbation and torrents of applause.

But what a racket the hag makes! Police, murder, thieves! Until the Master chucks her purseful of gold back again, for a gratuity. (Meanwhile, I note that sensible young woman, mother-naked as she is, has yet the presence of mind to catch hold of her husband's keyring and sharply tug it from his sere, cold grip. Once she's got the keys secure, she's in charge of all.)

'Now, no more of your nonsense!' she snaps to hag. 'If I hereby give you the sack, you'll get a handsome gift to go along with you for now'— flourishing the keys—'I am a rich widow and here'—indicating to all my bare yet blissful master—'is the young man who'll be my second husband.'

When the governess found Signor Panteleone had indeed remembered her in his will, left her a keepsake of the cup he drank his morning water from, she made not a squeak more, pocketed a fair sum with thanks and, sneezing, took herself off with no more cries of 'murder', neither. The old buffoon briskly bundled in his coffin and buried; Master comes into a great fortune and Missus rounding out already and they as happy as pigs in plunk.

But my Tabs beat her to it, since cats don't take much time about engendering; three fine, new-minted ginger kittens, all complete with snowy socks and shirtfronts, tumble in the cream and tangle Missus's knitting and put a smile on every face, not just their mother's and proud father's for Tabs and I smile all day long and, these days, we put our hearts in it.

So may all your wives, if you need them, be rich and pretty; and all your husbands, if you want them, be young and virile; and all your cats as wily, perspicacious and resourceful as:

PUSS-IN-BOOTS.

PATRICIA HIGHSMITH

The Terrors of Basket Weaving

Diane's terror began in an innocent and fortuitous way. She and her husband Reg lived in Manhattan, but had a cottage on the Massachusetts coast near Truro where they spent most weekends. Diane was a press relations officer in an agency called Retting. Reg was a lawyer. They were both thirty-eight, childless by choice, and both earned good salaries.

They enjoyed walks along the beach, and usually they took walks alone, not with each other. Diane liked to look for pretty stones, interesting shells, bottles of various sizes and colours, bits of wood rubbed smooth by sand and wind. These items she took back to the unpainted gray cottage they called 'the shack', lived with them for a few weeks or months, then Diane threw nearly all of them out, because she didn't want the shack to become a magpie's nest. One Sunday morning she found a wicker basket bleached nearly white and with its bottom stoved in, but its frame and sides quite sturdy. This looked like an old-fashioned crib basket for a baby, because one end of it rose higher than the other, the foot part tapered, and it was just the size for a new-born or for a baby up to a few months. It was the kind called a Moses basket, Diane thought.

Was the basket even American? It was amusing to think that it might have fallen overboard or been thrown away, old and broken, from a passing Italian tanker, or some foreign boat that might have had a woman and child on board. Anyway, Diane decided to take it home, and she put it for the nonce on a bench on the side porch of the shack, where coloured stones and pebbles and sea glass already lay. She might try to repair it, for fun, because in its present condition it was useless. Reg was then shifting sand with a snow shovel from one side of the wooden front steps, and was going to plant more beach grass from the dunes, like a second line of troops, between them and the sea to keep the sand in place. His industry, which Diane knew would go on another hour or so until lunch time—and cold lobster and potato salad was already in the fridge—inspired her to try her hand at the basket now.

She had realized a few minutes before that the kind of slender twigs she needed stood already in a brass cylinder beside their small fireplace.

Withes or withies—the words sounded nice in her head—might be more appropriate, but on the other hand the twigs would give more strength to the bottom of a basket which she might use to hold small potted plants, for instance. One would be able to move several pots into the sun all at once in a basket—if she could mend the basket.

Diane took the secateurs, and cut five lengths of reddish brown twigs—results of a neighbour's apple-tree pruning, she recalled—and then snipped nine shorter lengths for the crosspieces. She estimated she would need nine. A ball of twine sat handy on a shelf, and Diane at once got to work. She plucked out what was left of the broken pieces in the basket, and picked up one of her long twigs. The slightly pointed ends, an angle made by the secateurs, slipped easily between the sturdy withes that formed the bottom rim. She took up a second and a third. Diane then, before she attempted to tie the long pieces, wove the shorter lengths under and over the longer, at right angles. The twigs were just flexible enough to be manageable, and stiff enough to be strong. No piece projected too far. She had cut them just the right length, measuring only with her eye or thumb before snipping. Then the twine.

Over and under, around the twig ends at the rim and through the withes already decoratively twisted there, then a good solid knot. She was able to continue with the cord to the next twig in a couple of places, so she did not have to tie a knot at each crosspiece. Suddenly to her amazement the basket was repaired, and it looked splendid.

In her first glow of pride, Diane looked at her watch. Hardly fifteen minutes had passed since she had come into the house! How had she done it? She held the top end of the basket up, and pressed the palm of her right hand against the floor of the basket. It gave out firm-sounding squeaks. It had spring in it. And strength. She stared at the neatly twisted cord, at the correct over-and-under lengths, all about the diameter of pencils, and she wondered again how she had done it.

That was when the terror began to creep up on her, at first like a faint suspicion or surmise or question. Had she some relative or ancestor not so far in the past, who had been an excellent basket-weaver? Not that she knew of, and the idea made her smile with amusement. Grandmothers and great-grandmothers who could quilt and crochet didn't count. This was more primitive.

Yes, people had been weaving baskets thousands of years before Christ, and maybe even a million years ago, hadn't they? Baskets might have come before clay pots.

The answer to her question, how had she done it, might be that the ancient craft of basket-weaving had been carried on for so long by the human race that it had surfaced in her this Sunday morning in the late twentieth century. Diane found this thought rather frightening.

As she set the table for lunch, she upset a wine glass, but the glass was empty and it didn't break. Reg was still shoveling, but slowing up, nearly finished. It was still early for lunch, but Diane had wanted the table set, the salad dressing made in the wooden bowl, before she took a swat at the work she had brought with her. Finally she sat with a yellow pad and pencil, and opened the plastic-covered folder marked RETTING, plus her own name Diane Clarke in smaller letters at the bottom. She had to write three hundred words about a kitchen gadget that extracted air from plastic bags of apples, oranges, potatoes or whatever. After the air was extracted, the bags could be stored in the bottom of the fridge as usual, but the product kept much longer and took up less space because of the absence of air in the bag. She had seen the gadget work in the office, and she had a photograph of it now. It was a sixteen-inch-long tube which one fastened to the cold water tap in the kitchen. The water from the tap drained away, but its force moved a turbine in the tube, which created a vacuum after a hollow needle was stuck into the sealed bag. Diane understood the principle quite well, but she began to feel odd and disoriented.

It was odd to be sitting in a cottage built in a simple style more than a hundred years ago, to have just repaired a basket in the manner that people would have made or repaired a basket thousands of years ago, and to be trying to compose a sentence about a gadget whose existence depended upon modern plumbing, sealed packaging, transport by machinery of fruit and vegetables grown hundreds of miles (possibly thousands) from the places where they would be consumed. If this weren't so, people could simply carry fruit and vegetables home in a sack from the fields, or in baskets such as the one she had just mended.

Diane put down the pencil, picked up a ballpoint pen, lit a cigarette, and wrote the first words. 'Need more space in your fridge? Tired of having to buy more lemons at the supermarket than you can use in the next month? Here is an inexpensive gadget that might interest you.' It wasn't particularly inexpensive, but no matter. Lots of people were going to pay thousands of dollars for this gadget. She would be paid a sizeable amount also, meaning a certain fraction of her salary for writing about it. As she worked on, she kept seeing a vision of her crib-shaped basket and thinking that the basket—*per se*, as a thing to be used—was far more important than the kitchen gadget. However, it was perfectly normal to consider a basket more important or useful, she supposed, for the simple reason that a basket was.

'Nice walk this morning?' Reg asked, relaxing with a pre-lunch glass of cold white wine. He was standing in the low-ceilinged living-room, in shorts, an unbuttoned shirt, sandals. His face had browned further, and the skin was pinkish over his cheekbones.

'Yes. Found a basket. Rather nice. Want to see it?'

'Sure.'

She led the way to the side porch, and indicated the basket on the wooden table. 'The bottom was all broken—so I fixed it.'

'*You* fixed it?' Reg was leaning over it with admiration. 'Yeah, I can see. Nice job, Di.'

She felt a tremor, a little like shame. Or was it fear? She felt uncomfortable as Reg picked up the basket and looked at its underside. 'Might be nice to hold kindling—or magazines, maybe,' she said. 'We can always throw it away when we get bored with it.'

'Throw it away, no! It's sort of amusing—shaped like a baby's cradle or something.'

'That's what I thought—that it must have been made for a baby.' She drifted back into the living-room, wishing now that Reg would stop examining the basket.

'Didn't know you had such talents, Di. Girl Scout lore?'

Diane gave a laugh. Reg knew she'd never joined the Girl Scouts. 'Don't forget the Gartners are coming at seven-thirty.'

'Um-m. Yes, thanks. I didn't forget.—What's for dinner? We've got everything we need?'

Diane said they had. The Gartners were bringing raspberries from their garden plus cream. Reg had meant he was willing to drive to town in case they had to buy anything else.

The Gartners arrived just before eight, and Reg made daquiris. There was scotch for any who preferred it, and Olivia Gartner did. She was a serious drinker and held it well. An investment counsellor, she was, and her husband Pete was a professor in the maths department at Columbia.

Diane, after a swim around four o'clock, had collected some dry reeds from the dunes and among these had put a few long-stemmed blossoming weeds and wild flowers, blue and pink and orangy-yellow. She had laid all these in the crib-shaped basket which she had set on the floor near the fireplace.

'Isn't this pretty!' said Olivia during her second scotch, as if the drink had opened her eyes. She meant the floral arrangement, but Reg at once said:

'And look at the basket, Olivia! Diane found it on the beach today and *repaired* it.' Reg lifted the basket as high as his head, so Olivia and Pete could admire its underside.

Olivia chuckled. 'That's fantastic, Diane! Beautiful! How long did it take you?—It's a sweet basket.'

'That's the funny thing,' Diane began, eager to express herself. 'It took me about twelve minutes!'

'Look how proud she is of it!' said Reg, smiling.

Pete was running his thumb over the apple twigs at the bottom, nodding his approval.

'Yes, it was almost terrifying,' Diane went on.

'Terrifying?' Pete lifted his eyebrows.

'I'm not explaining myself very well.' Diane had a polite smile on her face, though she was serious. 'I felt as if I'd struck some hidden talent or knowledge—just suddenly. Everything I did, I felt sure of. I was amazed.'

'Looks strong too,' Pete said, and set the basket back where it had been.

Then they talked about something else. The cost of heating, if they used their cottages at all in the coming winter. Diane had hoped the basket conversation would continue a little longer. Another round of drinks, while Diane put their cold supper on the table. Bowls of jellied consommé with a slice of lemon to start with. They sat down. Diane felt unsatisfied. Or was it a sense of disturbance? Disturbance because of what? Just because they hadn't pursued the subject of the basket? Why should they have? It was merely a basket to them, mended the way anyone could have mended it. Or could just anyone have mended it that well? Diane happened to be sitting at the end of the table, so the basket was hardly four feet from her, behind her and to her right. She felt bothered somehow even by the basket's nearness. That was very odd. She must get to the bottom of it—that was funny, in view of the basket repair—but now wasn't the time, with three other people talking, and half her mind on seeing that her guests had a good meal.

While they were drinking coffee, Diane lit three candles and the oil lamp, and they listened to a record of Mozart *divertimenti*. They didn't listen, but it served as background music for their conversation. Diane listened to the music. It sounded skilful, even modern, and extremely civilized. Diane enjoyed her brandy. The brandy too seemed the epitome of human skill, care, knowledge. Not like a basket any child could put together. Perhaps a child in years couldn't, but a child as to progress in the evolution of the human race could weave a basket.

Was she possibly feeling her drinks? Diane pulled her long cotton skirt farther down over her knees. The subject was lobbies now, the impotence of any president, even Congress against them.

Monday morning early Diane and Reg flew back to New York by helicopter. Neither had to be at work before eleven. Diane had supposed that New York and work would put the disquieting thoughts *re* the basket out of her head, but that was not so. New York seemed to emphasize what she had felt up at the shack, even though the origin of her feelings had stayed at the shack. What were her feelings, anyway? Diane disliked vagueness, and was used to labelling her emotions jealousy, resentment, suspicion or whatever, even if the emotion was not always to her credit. But this?

What she felt was most certainly not guilt, though it was similarly troubling and unpleasant. Not envy either, not in the sense of desiring to master basketry so she could make a truly great basket, whatever that was. She'd always thought basket-weaving an occupation for the simple-minded, and it had become in fact a symbol of what psychiatrists advised disturbed people to take up. That was not it at all.

Diane felt that she had lost herself. Since repairing that basket, she wasn't any longer Diane Clarke, not completely, anyway. Neither was she anybody else, of course. It wasn't that she felt she had assumed the identity, even partially, of some remote ancestor. How remote, anyway? No. She felt rather that she was living with a great many people from the past, that they were in her brain or mind (Diane did not believe in a soul, and found the idea of a collective unconscious too vague to be of importance), and that people from human antecedents were bound up with her, influencing her, controlling her every bit as much as, up to now, she had been controlling herself. This thought was by no means comforting, but it was at least a partial explanation, maybe, for the disquietude that she was experiencing. It was not even an explanation, she realized, but rather a description of her feelings.

She wanted to say something to Reg about it and didn't, thinking that anything she tried to say along these lines would sound either silly or fuzzy. By now five days had passed since she had repaired the basket up at Truro, and they were going up to the shack again this weekend. The five working days at the office had passed as had a lot of other weeks for Diane. She had had a set-to with Jan Heyningen, the art director, on Wednesday, and had come near telling him what she thought of his stubbornness and bad taste, but she hadn't. She had merely smouldered. It had happened before. She and Reg had gone out to dinner at the apartment of some friends on Thursday. All as usual, outwardly.

The unusual was the schizoid atmosphere in her head. Was that it? Two personalities? Diane toyed with this possibility all Friday afternoon at the office while she read through new promotion-ready material. Was she simply imagining that several hundred prehistoric ancestors were somehow dwelling within her? No, frankly, she wasn't. That idea was even less credible than Jung's collective unconscious. And suddenly she rejected the simple schizo idea or explanation also. Schizophrenia was a catch-all, she had heard, for a lot of derangements that couldn't otherwise be diagnosed. She didn't feel schizoid, anyway, didn't feel like two people, or three, or more. She felt simply scared, mysteriously terrified. But only one thing in the least awkward happened that week: she had let one side of the lettuce-swinger slip out of her hand on the terrace, and lettuce flew everywhere, hung from the potted bamboo trees, was caught on rose thorns, lay fresh and clean on the red tile paving, and on the seat of the glider. Diane had laughed, even though there was no more lettuce in the house. She was tense, perhaps, therefore clumsy. A little accident like that could happen any time.

During the flight to the Cape, Diane had a happy thought: she'd use the basket not just for floral arrangements but for collecting more *objets trouvés* from the beach, or better yet for potatoes and onions in the kitchen. She'd treat it like any old basket. That would take the mystique out of it, the terror. To have felt terror was absurd.

So Saturday morning while Reg worked on the non-electric typewriter which they kept at the shack, Diane went for a walk on the beach with the basket. She had put a piece of newspaper in the basket, and she collected a greater number than usual of coloured pebbles, a few larger smooth rocks—one orange in colour, making it almost a *trompe l'oeil* for a mango —plus an interesting piece of sea-worn wood that looked like a boomerang. Wouldn't that be odd, she thought, if it really were an ancient boomerang worn shorter, thinner, until only the curve remained unchanged? As she walked back to the shack, the basket emitted faint squeaks in unison with her tread. The basket was so heavy, she had to carry it in two hands, letting its side rest against her hip, but she was not at all afraid that the twigs of the bottom would give. *Her work.*

Stop it, she told herself.

When she began to empty the basket on the porch's wooden table, she realized she had gathered too many stones, so she dropped more than half of them, quickly choosing the less interesting, over the porch rail onto the sand. Finally she shook the newspaper of its sand, and started to put it back in the basket. Sunlight fell on the glossy reddish-brown apple twigs. Over and under, not every one secured by twine, because for some twigs it hadn't been necessary. New work, and yet—Diane felt the irrational fear creeping over her again, and she pressed the newspaper quickly into the basket, pressed it at the crib-shaped edges, so that all her work was hidden. Then she tossed it carelessly on the floor, could have transferred some potatoes from a brown paper bag into it but she wanted to get away from the basket now.

An hour or so later, when she and Reg were finishing lunch, Reg laughing and about to light a cigarette, Diane felt an inner jolt as if— What? She deliberately relaxed, and gave her attention, more of it, to what Reg was saying. But it was as if the sound had been switched off a TV set. She saw him, but she wasn't listening or hearing. She blinked and forced herself to listen. Reg was talking about renting a tractor to clear some of their sand away, about terracing, and maintaining their property with growing things. They'd drawn a simple plan weeks ago, Diane remembered. But again she was feeling not like herself, as if she had lost herself in millions of people as an individual might get lost in a huge crowd. No, that was too simple, she felt. She was still trying to find solace in words. Or was she even dodging something? If so, what?

'What?' Reg asked, leaning back in his chair now, relaxed.

'Nothing. Why?'

'You were lost in thought.'

Diane might have replied that she had just had a better idea for a current project at Retting, might have replied several things, but she said suddenly, 'I'm thinking of asking for a leave of absence. Maybe just a month. I think Retting would do it, and it'd do me good.'

Reg looked puzzled. 'You're feeling tired, you mean? Just lately?'

'No. I feel somehow upset. Turned around, I don't know. I thought maybe a month of just being away from the office . . .' But work was supposed to be good in such a situation as hers. Work kept people from dwelling on their problems. But she hadn't a problem, rather a state of mind.

'Oh . . . well,' Reg said. 'Heyningen getting on your nerves maybe.'

Diane shifted. It would have been easy to say yes, that was it. She took a cigarette, and Reg lit it. 'Thanks. You're going to laugh, Reg. But that basket bothers me.' She looked at him, feeling ashamed, and curiously defensive.

'The one you found last weekend? You're worried a child might've drowned in it, lost at sea?' Reg smiled as if at a mild joke he'd just made.

'No, not at all. Nothing like that. I told you last weekend. It simply bothers me that I repaired it so easily. There. That's it. And you can say I'm cracked—I don't care.'

'I do not—quite—understand what you mean.'

'It made me feel somehow—prehistoric. And funny. Still does.'

Reg shook his head. 'I can sort of understand. Honestly. But—another way of looking at it, Di, is to realize that it's a very simple activity after all, mending or even making a basket. Not that I don't admire the neat job you did, but it's not like—sitting down and playing Beethoven's Emperor Concerto, for instance, if you've never had a piano lesson in your life.'

'No.' She'd never had a basket-making lesson in her life, she might have said. She was silent, wondering if she should put in her leave of absence request on Monday, as a gesture, a kind of appeasement to the uneasiness she felt? Emotions demanded gestures, she had read some-where, in order to be exorcized. Did she really believe that?

'Really, Di, the leave of absence is one thing, but that basket—It's an interesting basket, sure, because it's not machine-made and you don't see that shape any more. I've seen you get excited about stones you find. I understand. They're beautiful. But to let yourself get upset about—'

'Stones are different,' she interrupted. 'I can admire them. I'm not upset about them. I told you I feel I'm not exactly myself—me—any longer. I feel lost in a strange way—*Identity*, I mean,' she broke in again, when Reg started to speak.

'Oh, Di!' He got up. 'What do you mean you told me that? You didn't.'

'Well, I have now. I feel—as if a lot of other people were inside me besides myself. And I feel lost because of that. Do you understand?'

Reg hesitated. 'I understand the words. But the feeling—no.'

Even that was something. Diane felt grateful, and relieved that she had said this much to him.

'Go ahead with the leave of absence idea, darling. I didn't mean to be so abrupt.'

Diane put her cigarette out. 'I'll think about it.' She got up to make coffee.

That afternoon, after tidying the kitchen, Diane put another newspaper in the basket, and unloaded the sack of potatoes into it, plus three or four onions—familiar and contemporary objects. Perishable too. She made herself not think about the basket or even about the leave of absence for the rest of the day. Around 7.30, she and Reg drove off to Truro, where there was a street party organized by an ecology group. Wine and beer and soft drinks, hotdogs and juke-box music. They encountered the Gartners and a few other neighbours. The wine was undrinkable, the atmosphere marvellous. Diane danced with a couple of merry strangers and was for a few hours happy.

A month's leave of absence, she thought as she stood under the shower that night, was absurd and unnecessary. Temporary aberration to have considered it. If the basket—a really simple object as Reg had said—annoyed her so much, the thing to do was to get rid of it, burn it.

Sunday morning Reg took the car and went to deliver his Black and Decker or some appliance of it to the Gartners who lived eight miles away. As soon as he had left, Diane went to the side porch, replaced the potatoes and onions in the brown paper bag which she had saved as she saved most bags that arrived at the shack, and taking the basket with its newspaper and a book of matches, she walked out onto the sand in the direction of the ocean. She struck a match and lit the newspaper, and laid the basket over it. After a moment's hesitation, as if from shock, the basket gave a crack and began to burn. The drier sides burned more

quickly than the newer apple twigs, of course. With a stick, Diane poked
every last pale withe into the flames, until nothing remained except black
ash and some yellow-glowing embers, and finally these went out in the
bright sunshine and began to darken. Diane pushed sand with her feet
over the ashes, until nothing was visible. She breathed deeply as she
walked back to the shack, and realized that she had been holding her
breath, or almost, the entire time of the burning.

She was not going to say anything to Reg about getting rid of the
basket, and he was not apt to notice its absence, Diane knew.

Diane did mention, on Tuesday in New York, that she had changed
her mind about asking for a leave of absence. The implication was that
she felt better, but she didn't say that.

The basket was gone, she would never see it again, unless she deliberately
tried to conjure it up in memory, and that she didn't want to do. She felt
better with the thing out of the shack, destroyed. She knew that the
burning had been an action on her part to get rid of a feeling within her,
a primitive action, if she thought about it, because though the basket had
been tangible, her thoughts were not tangible. And they proved damned
hard to destroy.

Three weeks after the burning of the basket, her crazy idea of being a
'walking human race' or some such lingered. She would continue to listen
to Mozart and Bartók, they'd go to the shack most weekends, and she
would continue to pretend that her life counted for something, that she
was part of the stream or evolution of the human race, though she felt
now that she had spurned that position or small function by burning the
basket. For a week, she realized, she had grasped something, and then she
had deliberately thrown it away. In fact, she was no happier now than
during that week when the well-mended basket had been in her possession. But she was determined not to say anything more about it to Reg.
He had been on the verge of impatience that Saturday before the Sunday
when she had burned it. And in fact could she even put any more into
words? No. So she had to stop thinking about it. Yes.

ELIZABETH JOLLEY

The Play Reading

'Whatever shall I get for Mr Hodgetts and Aunty Shovell for their teas?'
Mother sat down at the kitchen table. She was so tired coming straight
from South Heights the luxury apartments where she cleans every day.

'How about a nice mutton and sardine yoghurt?' my brother said. 'It
might make them change their minds about coming here for tea every
night.' Mother looked at him as if she was seeing him very tall suddenly
there by the door.

All this winter Mother's been going to night classes. She says she can
feel her brain expanding out of her head.

'I know!' Mother brightened up, 'We'll have a play reading.' She took
her night-school book out of her bag. 'It's a play by a man called Ibsen.
He had this idea that it's only when the body dies that people really come
to life.'

'What's it called?' I asked.

'*When We Dead Awake.*'

'Is there any sex interest in it?' I asked.

'Nice girls don't ask questions like that.'

'It seems they've had it,' my brother turned the pages quickly. 'Here
you are,' he said, 'page 226, *He* says, "It reminds me of the night we
spent in the train on our way up here." And *she* says back to him, "Why
you sat in the compartment and slept the whole way." And *he* says—'

'That'll do,' Mother said. 'It's all highly symbolic. The writer sees the
human body all laid out over the Bush and the fences and the paddicks.'

'How?' I asked.

'The human contours and emotions are expressed in the landscape,'
Mother said, her voice all posh.

'Here you are,' my brother said. 'Page 252. It's *her* talking again, here
she goes. "Right down there in the foothills, where the forest's thickest.
Places where ordinary people could never penetrate—"' Mother took the
book off him pretty sharply.

'You'll understand when you're older,' she said to me. 'The play's like
a quartet,' she said getting posh again, her nose turning red the way it
does when she's excited about something.

'What's a quartet?' I asked.

Mother cut an apple into four.

'I'll explain,' she said spreading out the bits of apple. 'These are the four characters,' she said. 'Here's Professor Rubek and his young wife, Maia, sitting beside the teapot—'

'Why ever would they sit by a teapot!' my brother said.

'It represents the hotel,' Mother said patiently. 'Professor Rubek and his wife are sitting drinking champagne after their breakfasts and these other two', she arranged the other pieces of apple further away on the tablecloth, 'are Irene and the bear hunter. And this banana here can be the hotel manager, just a minor part in the play. Oh! You've eaten Professor Rubek!' Mother accused my brother.

'Irene and the bear hunter have gone too,' I said.

'Why you son of a Bitch!' Mother jumped up and my brother ran round and round the kitchen table with Mother after him. Suddenly my brother turned and Mother crashed into him. He sat backwards into the wood box.

'Halp! I'm choking!' My brother put on his idiot's face, 'Halp!'

I thought we should all die laughing. The Professor's wife looked lonely there on the table cloth so I ate her.

'Whatever shall I get for Shovell's tea!' Mother sat down to get her breath back.

The door opened and Aunty Shovell and Mr Hodgetts came in with all their shopping.

'Talk of Angels!' Mother said, very white.

'Nothing I wouldn't say about myself I hope,' Aunty Shovell made herself comfortable in the best chair. 'Tea ready?'

'You're just in time for the play reading,' my brother said. 'The Professor and his wife are just getting stuck into the booze after their cornflakes.'

'Oh?' said Aunt Shovell.

'Oh yes,' Mother said quickly. 'Mr Hodgetts you can be Professor Rubek.' Mr Hodgetts smiled at himself in the mirror over the sink, he smoothed his hair and examined his tongue. 'Delighted Dear Lady,' he said, 'delighted.'

'Put this lace curtain round you,' Mother said. 'Professor Rubek wears a shawl over his clothes to show the audience he's getting old—it's a writer's symbol,' she explained.

'Mr Hodgetts isn't getting old,' Aunt Shovell said. 'Mr Hodgetts is in the Prime of Life. You've only got to look at his neck to see he's in his Prime.'

'I'll be Ireene,' Mother said ignoring Aunt Shovell. 'Ireene's the Professor's nood model. They haven't seen each other for quite a while. He wants her to come with him up the mountain—'

'That's enough!' Aunt Shovell began gathering up her shopping bags.

'Oh Cheryl lovey it's only a play!' Mr Hodgetts smiled from inside his lace curtain.

'Let Aunty Shovell be Irene then.' My brother consulted the book, 'It says here she's supposed to be mad with knitting pins stuck in her hair and a knife hidden between her—'

'Just you watch your language!' Mother said. 'Shovell,' she said, 'you can be the Nun, that's a lovely part, when they all get swallowed up in an avalanche at the end of the play, the Nun's the only one left.'

'How can I be a Nun when Mr Hodgetts and me have an understanding!' Aunty Shovell's nose was as red as Mother's. They both asked my brother if their noses were red as if he cared.

'Come along Herbert, we'll get the half-past-five bus.' Aunty Shovell went out and Mr Hodgetts followed her. The door banged shut.

'He's got the lace curtains on,' I said.

'Never mind!' Mother said. I didn't know whether she was laughing or crying but she said she'd be all right directly. To keep himself going while Mother went down the road for three steakburgers my brother ate the hotel manager.

FAY WELDON

In the Great War

❧

Enid's mother Patty didn't stand a chance. That was in the Great War, in the fifties, when women were at war with women. Victory meant a soft bed and an easy life: defeat meant loneliness and the humiliation of the spinster. These days, of course, women have declared themselves allies, and united in a new war, a cold war, against the common enemy, man. But then, in the Great War, things were very different. And Patty didn't stand a chance against Helene. She was, for one thing, badly equipped for battle. Her legs were thick and practical, her breasts floppy, and her features, though pleasant enough, lacked erotic impact. Her blue eyes were watery and her hair frizzy and cut brusquely for easy washing and combing. 'I can't stand all this dolling up,' she'd say. 'What's the point?'

Patty cooked with margarine because it was cheaper than butter and her white sauces were always lumpy. She wouldn't keep pot plants, or souvenirs, or even a cat. What was the point?
She didn't like sex and, though she never refused her husband Arthur, she washed so carefully before and after, she made him feel he must have been really rather dirty.

Patty, in other words, was what she was, and saw no point in pretending to be anything else. Or in cooking with mushrooms or holidaying abroad or buying a new pair of shoes for Enid, her only child, when she had a perfectly good pair already, or going with her husband to the pub. And, indeed, there very often was no point in these things, except surely life must be more than something just to be practically and sensibly *got through*?

Enid thought so. Enid thought she'd do better than her mother in the Great War. Enid buffed her pre-pubertal nails and arranged wild flowers in jam jars and put them on the kitchen table. Perhaps she could see what was coming!

For all Patty's good qualities—cleanliness, honesty, thrift, reliability, kindness, sobriety, and so on—did her no good whatsoever when Helene came along. Or so Enid observed. Patty was asleep on duty, and there all of a sudden was Helene, the enemy at the gate, with her slim legs and her bedroom eyes, enticing Arthur away. 'But what does she *see* in Arthur?' asked Patty, dumbfounded. What you don't! the ten-year-old Enid thought, but did not say.

In fact, the Second World Male War, from 1939 to 1945, which men had waged among themselves in the name of Democracy, Freedom, Racial Supremacy and so forth, to the great detriment of women and children everywhere, had sharpened the savagery of the Female War. There just weren't enough men to go around. In ordinary times Helene would have gone into battle for some unmarried professional man—accountant or executive—but having lost country, home, family and friends in the ruins of Berlin now laid claim to Arthur, Patty's husband, a railway engineer in the north of England, who painted portraits as a hobby. The battle she fought for him was short and sharp. She shaved her shapely legs and flashed her liquid eyes.

'She's no better than a whore,' said Patty. 'Shaving her legs!' If God put hairs on your legs, thought Patty, then a woman's duty, and her husband's, too, is to put up with them.

Helene thought otherwise. And in her eyes Arthur saw the promise of secret bliss, the complicity of abandon, and all the charm of sin: the pink of her rosy nipples suffused the new world she offered him. And so, without much difficulty Helene persuaded Arthur to leave Patty and Enid, give up his job, paint pictures for a living and think the world well lost for love.

By some wonderful fluke—wonderful, that is, for Arthur and Helene, if infuriating for Patty—Arthur's paintings were an outstanding commercial success. They became the worst bestselling paintings of the sixties, and Arthur, safely divorced from Patty, lived happily ever after with Helene, painting the occasional painting of wide-eyed deer, and sipping champagne by the side of swimming pools. 'Nasty acidy stuff, champagne,' said Patty.

Enid—Patty and Arthur's daughter—never really forgave her mother for losing the war. As if poor Patty didn't have enough to put up with already, without being blamed by her daughter for something she could hardly help! But that's the way these things go—life is the opposite of fair. It stuns you one moment and trips your feet from under you the next, and then jumps up and down on you, pound, pound, pound for good measure.

You should have seen Enid, when she was twelve, twisting the knife in her mother's wounds, poking about among the lumps of the cauliflower cheese, saying: 'Do we *have* to eat this? No wonder Dad left home!' 'Eat it up, it's good for you,' her mother would reply. 'If you want something fancy go and live with your stepmother.'

And, indeed, Enid had been asked, but Enid never went. Enid would twist a knife but not deliver a mortal wound, not to her mother. Instead she took up the armoury her mother never wore, breathed on it, burnished it, sharpened its cutting edges, prepared for war herself. Long after the war was over, Enid was still fighting. She was like some mad Aussie soldier hiding out in the Malayan jungle, still looking for a foe that had years since thrown away its grenades and taken to TV assembly instead.

At sixteen Enid scanned the fashion pages and read hints on make-up and how to be an interesting person; she went weekly to the theatre and art galleries and classical music concerts and exercised every day, and not until she was eighteen did she feel properly prepared to step into the battlefield. She was intelligent, and thought it sensible enough to go to university, although she chose English literature as the subject least likely to put men off.

'Nothing puts a man off like a clever woman,' said Helene when Enid visited. Now warriors in the Great War thought nothing of swapping secrets. Intelligence services of warring countries, hand in glove, glove in hand! It's always been so. Just as there's always been trade with enemy nations, unofficially if not officially. Helene lisped out quite a few secrets to Enid: her accent tinged with all the poise and decadence of a vanished Europe. 'My foreign wife!' Arthur would say, proudly in his honest, northern, jovial, middle-aged voice. Arthur was the J. B. Priestley of the art world—good in spite of himself.

Oh, Patty had lost a lovely prize, Enid knew it! Her beloved father! What a victory Patty's could have been—and yet she chose defeat. She'd chosen a bra to flatten an already flat chest. 'What's the point?' she asked, when Enid said she was going off to university. Couldn't she even see that?

Little Enid, so bright and knowledgeable and determined! So young, so ruthless—a warrior! And fortune favours the brave, the strong, the ruthless. That was the point. Enid's professor, Walter Walther, looked at Enid in a lingering way, and Enid looked straight back. Take me! Well, not quite take me. Love me now, take me eventually.

Walter Walther was forty-eight. Enid was nineteen. Enid was studying Chaucer. Enid said in an essay that Chaucer's Parfait Gentle Knight was no hero but a crude mercenary, and Chaucer, in his adulation, was being ironic; Walter Walther hadn't thought of that before, and at forty-eight it is delightful to meet someone who says something you haven't thought of before. And she was so young, and dewy, almost downy, so that if she was out in the rain the drops lay like silver balls upon her skin; and she was surprisingly knowledgeable for one so young, and knew all about music and painting, which Walter didn't, much, and she had an interesting, rich father, if a rather dowdy, vague, distant little mother. And Enid was warm.

Oh, Enid was warm! Enid was warm against his body on stolen nights. Walter's wife Rosanne, four years older than he, was over fifty. Rain fell off her like water off a duck's back—her skin being oily, not downy. Enid had met Rosanne once or twice baby-sitting; or rather adolescent-sitting, for Walter and Rosanne's two children, Barbara and Bernadette.

Rosanne didn't stand a chance against Enid. Enid still fought the old, old war, and Rosanne had put away her weapons long ago.

'He's so unhappy with his wife,' said Enid to Margot. 'She's such a cold unfeeling bitch. She's only interested in her career, not in him at all, or the children.' Margot was Enid's friend. Margot had owl eyes and a limpid handshake and not a hope of seducing, let alone winning, a married professor. But Margot understood Enid, and was a good friend to her, and had most of the qualities Enid's mother Patty had, and one more important one besides—self-doubt.

'Men never leave their wives for their mistresses,' warned Margot. It was a myth much put about, no doubt by wives, in the days of the Great War, to frighten the enemy. Enid knew better: she could tell a savage war mask from the frightened face of a foe in retreat. Enid knew Rosanne was frightened by the way she would follow Enid into the kitchen if Walter Walther was there alone, getting ice for drinks or scraping mud from the children's shoes.

Enid was pleased. A frightened foe seldom wins. The attacker is usually victorious, even if the advantage of surprise is gone, especially if the victim is old: Rosanne was old. She'd had the children late. It wasn't as if Walter Walther had really wanted children. He knew what kind of mother she'd make—cold.

Enid was warm. She knew how to silhouette her head against the sunlight so that her hair made a halo round her head, and then turn her face slowly so that the pure line of youth, the one that runs from ear to chin, showed to advantage. Rosanne had trouble with her back. Trouble with her back! Rosanne was a hag with one foot in the grave and with the iron bonds of matrimony would drag Walter Walther down there with her, if Walter didn't somehow break the bonds.

And Enid knew how to behave in bed, too: always keeping something in reserve, never taking the initiative, always the pupil, never the teacher. Enid had seen the *Art of Love* in Rosanne's bookshelves, and guessed her to be sexually experimental and innovatory. And she was later proved right, when Walter managed to voice one of his few actual complaints about his wife: there was, he felt, something indecent about Rosanne's sexual prowess: something disagreeably insatiable in her desires; it made Walter, from time to humiliating time, impotent.

Otherwise, it wasn't so much lack of love for Rosanne that Walter suffered from, as surfeit of love for Enid.

Enid exulted. And Rosanne was using worn-out old weapons: that particular stage in the war had ended long ago. The battle these days went to the innocent, not to the experienced. Modern man, Enid knew by instinct, especially those with a tendency to impotence, requires docility in bed and admiration and exultation—not excitement and exercise.

'He'll never leave the children,' said Margot. 'Men don't.' But Enid had been left. Enid knew very well that men did. And Barbara and Bernadette were not the most lovable of children—how could they be? With such a mother as Rosanne—a working mother who never even remembered her children's birthdays, never baked a cake, never ironed or darned, never cleaned the oven? Rosanne was a translator with the International Cocoa Board—a genius at languages, but not at motherhood. She was cold, stringy and sour—all the things soft, warm, rounded Enid was not. Walter said so, in bed, and increasingly out of it.

'What are you playing at?' asked Helene, crossly. Her own attitude to the world was moderating. She was an old retired warrior, sitting in a castle she'd won by force of arms, shaking her head at the shockingness of war.

Patty now lived alone in a little council flat in Birmingham. As Enid had left home Arthur no longer paid Patty maintenance. Why should he?

'You want Walter because Walter's Rosanne's,' observed Patty to Enid one day in a rare rush of insight to the head. Patty's doctor had started giving her oestrogen for her hot flushes, and side-effects were beginning to show. There was a geranium in a pot on Patty's windowsill, when Enid went to break the news to her mother that Walter was finally leaving Rosanne. A geranium! Patty, who never could see the point in pot plants!

All the same, something, if only oestrogen, was now putting a sparkle in Patty's eye, and she turned up at Walter and Enid's wedding in a kind of velvet safari jacket which made her look almost sexy, and when Arthur crossed the room to speak to his ex-wife, she did not turn away, but actually saw the point of shaking his hand, and even laying her cheek against his, in affection and forgiveness.

Enid, in her white velvet trouser suit, saw: and a pang of almost physical pain roared through her, and for a second, just a second, looking at Walter, she saw not her great love but an elderly, paunchy, lecherous stranger. Even though he'd slimmed down quite remarkably during the divorce. It wasn't surprising! Rosanne had behaved like a bitch, and it had told on them both. Nevertheless, people remarked at the wedding that they'd never seen Walter looking so well—or Enid so elegant. He'd somehow scaled down to forty, and she up to thirty. Hardly a difference at all!

Barbara and Bernadette were bridesmaids. Rosanne had been against the idea, out of envy and malice mixed. She hadn't even been prepared to make their dresses, which Enid thought particularly spiteful. 'I'd never have made a bridesmaid's dress for you,' said Patty. 'Not to wear at your father's wedding.' 'That's altogether different,' said Enid, hurt and confused by the way Patty was seeing the war, almost as if she, Patty, were Rosanne's ally; more Helene's enemy than Enid's mother.

And then Helene upset her. 'I hope you're not thinking of having children,' she said, during the reception. 'Of course I am,' said Enid. 'Some men can't stand it,' said Helene. 'Your father, for one. Why do you think

I never had any?' 'Well, I'm sure he could stand me,' said Enid, with a
self-confidence she did not feel. For perhaps he just plain couldn't?
Perhaps some of the blame for his departure was Enid's, not Patty's.
Perhaps if she'd been nicer her father would never have left? And
perhaps, indeed, he wouldn't!

Well, if we can't be nice, we can at least try to be perfect. Enid set out on
her journey through life with perfection in mind. Doing better! Oh, how
neat the corners of the beds she tucked, how fresh the butter, how crisp
the tablecloth! Her curtains were always fully lined, her armpits smooth
and washed, never merely sprayed. Enid never let her weapons get rusty.
She would do better, thank you, than Patty, or Helene, or Rosanne.

Walter Walther clearly adored his Enid and let the world know it. His
colleagues half envied, half pitied him. Walter would ring Enid from the
department twice a day and talk baby-talk at her. Until recently he'd
talked to his daughter Barbara in just such a manner. His colleagues came
to the conclusion, over many a coffee table, that now the daughter had
reached puberty the father, in marrying a girl of roughly the same age,
was acting out incest fantasies too terrible to acknowledge. No one mentioned the word love: for this was the new language of the post-war age.
If there was to be no hate, how could there be love?

In the meantime, for Walter and Enid, there was perpetual trouble with
Rosanne. She insisted at first on staying in the matrimonial home, and it
took a lawsuit and some fairly sharp accountants to drive her out: presently she lived with the girls in a little council flat. Oddly enough, it was
rather like Patty's. Practical, but somehow depressing. 'You see,' said
Enid. 'No gift for living! Poor Walter! What a terrible life she gave him.'
In the Great War men gave women money, and women gave men life.

Barbara and Bernadette came to stay at weekends. They had their old
rooms. Enid prettified them, and lined the curtains. She was a better
mother to Barbara and Bernadette than Rosanne had ever been. Walter
said so. Enid remembered their birthdays, and saw to their verrucas and
had their hair styled. They looked at her with sullen gratitude, like slaves
saved from slaughter.

Rosanne lost her job. Rosanne said—of course, it was because the responsibility of being a one-parent family and earning a living was too much for
her, but Enid and Walter knew the loss of her job was just a simple
matter of redundancy combined with lack of charm. Bernadette's asthma

got worse. 'Of course the poor child's ill,' said Enid. 'With such a mother!' Enid didn't believe in truces. She ignored white flags and went in for the kill.

Enid had a pond built in the garden and entertained Walter's friends on Campari and readings of Shakespeare's sonnets. They were literary people, after all, or claimed to be. 'Couldn't we do without the sonnets?' said Walter.

But Enid insisted on the sonnets, and the friends drifted away. 'It's Rosanne's doing,' said Enid. 'She's turned them against us.' And she twined her white, soft, serpent's arms round his grizzly, stranger body and he believed her. His students, he noticed, seemed less respectful of him than they had been: not as if he had grown younger but they had grown older. Air came through the lecture-room windows, on a hot summer's day, like a sigh. Well, at least he was married, playing honestly and fair, unlike his colleagues, who were for the most part hit-and-run seducers. As for Rosanne, he knew she knew how to look after herself. She always had. A man, in the Great War, usually preferred a woman who couldn't.

'Let's have a baby of our own soon,' said Enid. A baby! He hadn't thought of that. She was his baby. Or was he hers?

'We're so happy,' said Enid. 'You and I. It doesn't matter what the world thinks or says. We were just both a little out of step, that's all, time-wise. God meant us for each other. Don't you feel that?'

He queried her use of the word God, but otherwise agreed with what she said. Her words came as definite instruction from some powerful, knowledgeable source. They flowed, unsullied by doubt. He, being older, had to grope for meanings. He was too wise, and this could only diffuse his certainty, since wisdom is the acknowledgment of ignorance.

'Of course you should have a baby, Enid,' said Patty. 'Why not?' But she wasn't really thinking. She was having an affair with a mini-cab driver, and had forgotten about Enid. 'Your behaviour is obscene and disgusting,' Enid shouted at her mother. '*He's young*.'

'What's the point in your making all this fuss?' asked Patty. 'I deserve a little happiness in my life, and I'm sure you brought me precious little!'

Enid got pregnant, straight away. Walter went out and got drunk when he heard, with old friends of himself and Rosanne. Enid was so upset by this double disloyalty she went and stayed with her friend Margot for at least three days.

Margot was married and pregnant, too, and by one of Walter Walther's students, who had spots and bad breath. They lived on their grants, and beans and cider. Nevertheless, her husband went with her to the antenatal clinic and they pored over baby books together. Walter Walther took the view, common in the Great War, that the begetting of children was something to do with the one-upmanship of woman against woman, and very little to do with the man.

'Look, Enid,' said Walter, a new Walter, briskly and unkindly, 'you just get on with it by yourself.' Arthur had left Patty to get on with it by herself, too. Her very name, Enid, had been a last-minute choice by Patty with the registrar hovering over her hospital bed, because Arthur just left it to her.

'You can't have everything,' was what Helene said, when Enid murmured a complaint or two. 'You can't have status, money, adoration and what Margot has as well.'
'Why not?' demanded Enid. 'I want *everything*!'

Enid saw herself on a mountain top, a million women bowing down before her, acknowledging her victory. Her foot would be heavy on the necks of those she humbled. That was how it ought to be. She pulled herself together. She knew that, in the Great War, being pregnant could make you or break you. Great prizes were to be won—the best mother, the prettiest child, the whitest white—but much was risked. The enemy could swoop down, slender-waisted and laughing and lively, and deliver any number of mortal wounds. So Enid wore her prettiest clothes, and sighed a little but never grunted when the baby lay on some pelvic nerve or other, and never let Walter suffer a moment because of what he had done to her. (In those pre-pill days men made women pregnant: women didn't just get pregnant.)

His boiled egg and toast soldiers and freshly milled coffee and the single flower in the silver vase were always there on the breakfast table at half past eight sharp and they'd eat together, companionably. Rosanne had slopped Sugar Puffs into bowls for the family breakfast, and they'd eaten among the uncleared children's homework and students' essays. Slut!

Walter was protective. 'We have to take extra special care of you,' he'd say, helping her across roads. But he seemed a little embarrassed. Something grated: she didn't know what. They ate in rather more often than before.

Then Rosanne, who ought by rights to have been lying punch-drunk in some obscure corner of the battlefield, rose up and delivered a nasty body-blow. Barbara and Bernadette were to come to live with Enid and Walter. Rosanne couldn't cope, in such crowded surroundings. She had a new job, and couldn't always be rushing home for Bernadette's asthma. Could she?

'A new boyfriend, more like,' said Walter, bitterly. Enid restrained from pointing out that Rosanne was an old, old woman with a bad back and hardly in the field for admirers.

Now six perfectly cooked boiled eggs on the table each morning—Bernadette and Barbara demanded two each—is twelve times as difficult to achieve as two. By the time the last one's in, the first one's cooked, but which one is it?

Walter looked at his bowl of Sugar Puffs one morning and said, 'Just like old times,' and the girls looked knowingly and giggled. They looked at Enid and her swelling tum with contempt and pity. They borrowed her clothes and her make-up. They refused to be taken to art galleries, or theatres; they refused even to play Monopoly, let alone Happy Families. They referred to their father as the Old Goat.

Sometimes she hated them. But Walter would not let her. 'Look,' said Walter, 'you did come along and disrupt their lives. You owe them something, at least.' As if it was all nothing to do with him. Which in a way it wasn't. It was between Rosanne and Enid.

Enid locked herself out of the house one day and, though she knew the girls were inside, when she knocked they wouldn't let her in. It was raining. Afterwards they just said they hadn't heard. And she'd fallen and hurt her knee trying to climb in the window, and might have lost the baby. Bernadette threw a bad asthma attack and got all the attention.

Walter spent more and more time in the department. She and he hardly made love at all any more. It didn't seem right.

Enid went into labour at eight o'clock one evening. She rang Walter
Walther at the English Department where he said he was, but he wasn't.
She rang Margot and wept, and Margot said, 'I don't think I've ever
known you cry, Enid,' and Margot's spotty husband said, 'You'll probably find him round at Rosanne's. I wouldn't tell you, if it wasn't an
emergency.'

'Yes,' said Barbara and Bernadette. 'He goes round to see Mum quite a
lot. We didn't like to tell you because we didn't want to upset you.

'Really,' they said, 'the whole thing was a plot to get rid of us. The thing
is, neither of them can stand us.' (Barbara and Bernadette went to one of
the large new comprehensive schools, where there were pupil–counsellors,
who could explain everything and anything, and were never lost for
words.)

Enid screamed and wept all through her labour, not just from pain.
They'd never known a noisier mother, they said: and she'd been so quiet
and elegant and self-controlled throughout her pregnancy.

Enid gave birth to a little girl. Now in the Great War, the birth of a
girl was, understandably, and unlike now, cause for commiseration rather
than rejoicing. Nevertheless, Enid rejoiced. And in so doing, abandoned
a battle which was really none of her making; she laid down her arms: she
kissed her mother and Helene when they came to visit her, clasped her
baby and admitted weakness and distress to Barbara and Bernadette, who
actually then seemed quite to like her.

Walter Walther did not come home. He stayed with Rosanne. Enid,
Barbara and Bernadette lived in the same house, shared suspender belts,
shampoo and boyfriends, and looked after baby Belinda. Walter and
Rosanne visited, sheepishly, from time to time, and sent money. Enid
went back to college and took a degree in psychology, and was later to
earn a good living as a research scientist.

Later still she was to become something of a propagandist in the new cold
war against men; she wore jeans and a donkey jacket and walked round
linked arm-in-arm with women. But that was, perhaps, hardly surprising,
so treacherous had the old male allies turned out to be. All the same,
yesterday's enemy, tomorrow's friend! Who is to say what will happen
next?

ELLEN GILCHRIST

Victory Over Japan

❦

When I was in the third grade I knew a boy who had to have fourteen shots in the stomach as the result of a squirrel bite. Every day at two o'clock they would come to get him. A hush would fall on the room. We would all look down at our desks while he left the room between Mr Harmon and his mother. Mr Harmon was the principal. That's how important Billy Monday's tragedy was.

Mr Harmon came along in case Billy threw a fit. Every day we waited to see if he would throw a fit but he never did. He just put his books away and left the room with his head hanging down on his chest and Mr Harmon and his mother guiding him along between them like a boat.

'Would you go with them like that?' I asked Letitia at recess. Letitia was my best friend. Usually we played girls chase the boys at recess or pushed each other on the swings or hung upside down on the monkey bars so Joe Franke and Bobby Saxacorn could see our underpants but Billy's shots had even taken the fun out of recess. Now we sat around on the fire escape and talked about rabies instead.

'Why don't they put him to sleep first?' Letitia said. 'I'd make them put me to sleep.'

'They can't,' I said. 'They can't put you to sleep unless they operate.'

'My father could,' she said. 'He owns the hospital. He could put me to sleep.' She was always saying things like that but I let her be my best friend anyway.

'They couldn't give them to me,' I said. 'I'd run away to Florida and be a beachcomber.'

'Then you'd get rabies,' Letitia said. 'You'd be foaming at the mouth.'

'I'd take a chance. You don't always get it.' We moved closer together, caught up in the horror of it. I was thinking about the Livingstons' bulldog. I'd had some close calls with it lately.

'It was a pet,' Letitia said. 'His brother was keeping it for a pet.'

It was noon recess. Billy Monday was sitting on a bench by the swings. Just sitting there. Not talking to anybody. Waiting for two o'clock, a small washed-out-looking boy that nobody paid any attention to until he got bit. He never talked to anybody. He could hardly even read. When Mrs Jansma asked him to read his head would fall all the way over to the side of his neck. Then he would read a few sentences with her having to tell him half the words. No one would ever have picked him out to be the center of a rabies tragedy. He was more the type to fall in a well or get sucked down the drain at the swimming pool.

Fourteen days. Fourteen shots. It was spring when it happened and the schoolroom windows were open all day long and every afternoon after Billy left we had milk from little waxy cartons and Mrs Jansma would read us chapters from a wonderful book about some children in England that had a bed that took them places at night. There we were, eating graham crackers and listening to stories while Billy was strapped to the table in Doctor Finley's office waiting for his shot.

'I can't stand to think about it,' Letitia said. 'It makes me so sick I could puke.'

'I'm going over there and talk to him right now,' I said. 'I'm going to interview him for the paper.' I had been the only one in the third grade to get anything in the Horace Mann paper. I got in with a story about how Mr Harmon was shell-shocked in the First World War. I was on the lookout for another story that good.

I got up, smoothed down my skirt, walked over to the bench where Billy was sitting and held out a vial of cinnamon toothpicks. 'You want one,' I said. 'Go ahead. She won't care.' It was against the rules to bring cinnamon toothpicks to Horace Mann. They were afraid someone would swallow one.

'I don't think so,' he said. 'I don't need any.'

'Go on,' I said. 'They're really good. They've been soaking all week.'

'I don't want any,' he said.

'You want me to push you on the swings?'

'I don't know,' he said. 'I don't think so.'

'If it was my brother's squirrel, I'd kill it,' I said. 'I'd cut its head off.'

'It got away,' he said. 'It's gone.'

'What's it like when they give them to you?' I said. 'Does it hurt very much?'

'I don't know,' he said. 'I don't look.' His head was starting to slip down onto his chest. He was rolling up like a ball.

'I know how to hypnotize people,' I said. 'You want me to hypnotize you so you can't feel it?'

'I don't know,' he said. He had pulled his legs up on the bench. Now his chin was so far down into his chest I could barely hear him talk. Part of me wanted to give him a shove and see if he would roll. I touched him on the shoulder instead. I could feel his little bones beneath his shirt. I could smell his washed-out rusty smell. His head went all the way down under his knees. Over his shoulder I saw Mrs Jansma headed our way.

'Rhoda,' she called out. 'I need you to clean off the blackboards before we go back in. Will you be a sweet girl and do that for me?'

'I wasn't doing anything but talking to him,' I said. She was beside us now and had gathered him into her wide sleeves. He was starting to cry, making little strangled noises like a goat.

'Well, my goodness, that was nice of you to try to cheer Billy up. Now go see about those blackboards for me, will you?'

I went on in and cleaned off the blackboards and beat the erasers together out the window, watching the chalk dust settle into the bricks. Down below I could see Mrs Jansma still holding on to Billy. He was hanging on to her like a spider but it looked like he had quit crying.

That afternoon a lady from the PTA came to talk to us about the paper drive. 'One more time,' she was saying. 'We've licked the Krauts. Now all we have left is the Japs. Who's going to help?' she shouted.

'I am,' I shouted back. I was the first one on my feet.

'Who do you want for a partner?' she said.

'Billy Monday,' I said, pointing at him. He looked up at me as though I had asked him to swim the English Channel, then his head slid down on the desk.

'All right,' Mrs Jansma said. 'Rhoda Manning and Billy Monday. Team number one. To cover Washington and Sycamore from Calvin Boulevard to Conner Street. Who else?'

'Bobby and me,' Joe Franke called out. He was wearing his coonskin cap, even though it was as hot as summer. How I loved him! 'We want downtown,' he shouted. 'We want Dirkson Street to the river.'

'Done,' Mrs Jansma said. JoEllen Scaggs was writing it all down on the blackboard. By the time Billy's mother and Mr Harmon came to get him the paper drive was all arranged.

'See you tomorrow,' I called out as Billy left the room. 'Don't forget. Don't be late.'

When I got home that afternoon I told my mother I had volunteered to let Billy be my partner. She was so proud of me she made me some cookies even though I was supposed to be on a diet. I took the cookies and a pillow and climbed up into my treehouse to read a book. I was getting to be more like my mother every day. My mother was a saint. She fed hoboes and played the organ at early communion even if she was sick and gave away her ration stamps to anyone that needed them. She had only had one pair of new shoes the whole war.

I was getting more like her every day. I was the only one in the third grade that would have picked Billy Monday to help with a paper drive. He probably couldn't even pick up a stack of papers. He probably couldn't even help pull the wagon.

I bet this is the happiest day of her life, I was thinking. I was lying in my treehouse watching her. She was sitting on the back steps putting liquid hose on her legs. She was waiting for the Episcopal minister to come by for a drink. He'd been coming by a lot since my daddy was overseas. That was just like my mother. To be best friends with a minister.

'She picked out a boy that's been sick to help her on the paper drive,' I heard her tell him later. 'I think it helped a lot to get her to lose weight. It was smart of you to see that was the problem.'

'There isn't anything I wouldn't do for you, Ariane,' he said. 'You say the word and I'll be here to do it.'

I got a few more cookies and went back up into the treehouse to finish my book. I could read all kinds of books. I could read Book-of-the-Month Club books. The one I was reading now was called *Cakes and Ale*. It wasn't coming along too well.

I settled down with my back against the tree, turning the pages, looking for the good parts. Inside the house my mother was bragging on me. Above my head a golden sun beat down out of a blue sky. All around the silver maple leaves moved in the breeze. I went back to my book. 'She put her arms around my neck and pressed her lips against mine. I forgot my wrath. I only thought of her beauty and her enveloping kindness.

'"You must take me as I am, you know," she whispered.'

'"All right," I said.'

Saturday was not going to be a good day for a paper drive. The sky was gray and overcast. By the time we lined up on the Horace Mann playground with our wagons a light rain was falling.

'Our boys are fighting in rain and snow and whatever the heavens send,' Mr Harmon was saying. He was standing on the bleachers wearing an old baseball shirt and a cap. I had never seen him in anything but his gray suit. He looked more shell-shocked than ever in his cap.

'They're working over there. We're working over here. The Germans are defeated. Only the Japs left to go. There're canvas tarps from Gentilly's Hardware, so take one to cover your papers. All right now. One grade at a time. And remember, Mrs Winchester's third grade is still ahead by seventy-eight pounds. So you're going to have to go some to beat that.

Get to your stations now. Get ready, get set, go. Everybody working together . . .'

Billy and I started off. I was pulling the wagon, he was walking along beside me. I had meant to wait awhile before I started interviewing him but I started right in.

'Are you going to have to leave to go get it?' I said.

'Go get what?'

'You know. Your shot.'

'I got it this morning. I already had it.'

'Where do they put it in?'

'I don't know,' he said. 'I don't look.'

'Well, you can feel it, can't you?' I said. 'Like, do they stick it in your navel or what?'

'It's higher than that.'

'How long does it take? To get it.'

'I don't know,' he said. 'Till they get through.'

'Well, at least you aren't going to get rabies. At least you won't be foaming at the mouth. I guess you're glad about that.' I had stopped in front of a house and was looking up the path to the door. We had come to the end of Sycamore, where our territory began.

'Are you going to be the one to ask them?' he said.

'Sure,' I said. 'You want to come to the door with me?'

'I'll wait,' he said. 'I'll just wait.'

We filled the wagon by the second block. We took that load back to the school and started out again. On the second trip we hit an attic with bundles of the *Kansas City Star* tied up with string. It took us all afternoon to haul that. Mrs Jansma said she'd never seen anyone as lucky on a paper drive as Billy and I. Our whole class was having a good day. It looked like we might beat everybody, even the sixth grade.

'Let's go out one more time,' Mrs Jansma said. 'One more trip before dark. Be sure and hit all the houses you missed.'

Billy and I started back down Sycamore. It was growing dark. I untied my Brownie Scout sweater from around my waist and put it on and pulled the sleeves down over my wrists. 'Let's try that brick house on the corner,' I said. 'They might be home by now.' It was an old house set back on a high lawn. It looked like a house where old people lived. I had noticed old people were the ones who saved things. 'Come on,' I said. 'You go to the door with me. I'm tired of doing it by myself.'

He came along behind me and we walked up to the door and rang the bell. No one answered for a long time although I could hear footsteps and saw someone pass by a window. I rang the bell again.

A man came to the door. A thin man about my father's age.

'We're collecting papers for Horace Mann School,' I said. 'For the war effort.'

'You got any papers we can have?' Billy said. It was the first time he had spoken to anyone but me all day. 'For the war,' he added.

'There're some things in the basement if you want to go down there and get them,' the man said. He turned a light on in the hall and we followed him into a high-ceilinged foyer with a set of winding stairs going up to another floor. It smelled musty, like my grandmother's house in Clarksville. Billy was right beside me, sticking as close as a burr. We followed the man through the kitchen and down a flight of stairs to the basement.

'You can have whatever you find down here,' he said. 'There're papers and magazines in that corner. Take whatever you can carry.'

There was a large stack of magazines. Magazines were the best thing you could find. They weighed three times as much as newspapers.

'Come on,' I said to Billy. 'Let's fill the wagon. This will put us over the top for sure.' I picked up a bundle and started up the stairs. I went in and out several times carrying as many as I could at a time. On the third trip Billy met me at the foot of the stairs. 'Rhoda,' he said. 'Come here. Come look at this.'

He took me to an old table in a corner of the basement. It was a walnut table with grapes carved on the side and feet like lion's feet. He laid one of the magazines down on the table and opened it. It was a photograph of a naked little girl, a girl smaller than I was. He turned the page. Two naked boys were standing together with their legs twined. He kept turning the pages. It was all the same. Naked children on every page. I had never seen a naked boy. Much less a photograph of one. Billy looked up at me. He turned another page. Five naked little girls were grouped together around a fountain.

'Let's get out of here,' I said. 'Come on. I'm getting out of here.' I headed for the stairs with him right behind me. We didn't even close the basement door. We didn't even stop to say thank you.

The magazines we had collected were in bundles. About a block from the house we stopped on a corner, breathless from running. 'Let's see if there're any more,' I said. We tore open a bundle. The first magazine had pictures of naked grown people on every page.

'What are we going to do?' he said.

'We're going to throw them away,' I answered, and started throwing them into the nandina bushes by the Hancock's vacant lot. We threw them into the nandina bushes and into the ditch that runs into Mills Creek. We threw the last ones into a culvert and then we took our wagon and got on out of there. At the corner of Sycamore and Wesley we went our separate ways.

'Well, at least you'll have something to think about tomorrow when you get your shot,' I said.

'I guess so,' he replied.

'Look here, Billy. I don't want you to tell anyone about those magazines. You understand?'

'I won't.' His head was going down again.

'I mean it, Billy.'

He raised his head and looked at me as if he had just remembered something he was thinking about. 'I won't,' he said. 'Are you really going to write about me in the paper?'

'Of course I am. I said I was, didn't I? I'm going to do it tonight.'

I walked on home. Past the corner where the Scout hikes met. Down the alley where I found the card shuffler and the Japanese fan. Past the yard where the violets grew. I was thinking about the boys with their legs twined. They looked like earthworms, all naked like that. They looked like something might fly down and eat them. It made me sick to think about it and I stopped by Mrs Alford's and picked a few iris to take home to my mother.

Billy finished getting his shots. And I wrote the article and of course they put it on page one. BE ON THE LOOKOUT FOR MAD SQUIRREL, the headline read. By Rhoda Katherine Manning. Grade 3.

We didn't even know it was mean, the person it bit said. That person is in the third grade at our school. His name is William Monday. On April 23 he had his last shot. Mrs Jansma's class had a cake and gave him a pencil set. Billy Monday is all right now and things are back to normal.

I think it should be against the law to keep dangerous pets or dogs where they can get out and get people. If you see a dog or squirrel acting funny go in the house and stay there.

I never did get around to telling my mother about those magazines. I kept meaning to but there never seemed to be anywhere to start. One day in August I tried to tell her. I had been to the swimming pool and I thought I saw the man from the brick house drive by in a car. I was pretty sure it was him. As he turned the corner he looked at me. *He looked right at my face.* I stood very still, my heart pounding inside my chest, my hands as cold and wet as a frog, the smell of swimming pool chlorine rising from my skin. What if he found out where I lived? What if he followed me home and killed me to keep me from telling on him? I was

terrified. At any moment the car might return. He might grab me and put
me in the car and take me off and kill me. I threw my bathing suit and
towel down on the sidewalk and started running. I ran down Linden
Street and turned into the alley behind Calvin Boulevard, running as fast
as I could. I ran down the alley and into my yard and up my steps and
into my house looking for my mother to tell her about it.

She was in the living room, with Father Kenniman and Mr and Mrs
DuVal. They lived across the street and had a gold star in their window.
Warrene, our cook, was there. And Connie Barksdale, our cousin who
was visiting from the Delta. Her husband had been killed on Corregidor
and she would come up and stay with my mother whenever she couldn't
take it anymore. They were all in the living room gathered around the
radio.

'Momma,' I said. 'I saw this man that gave me some magazines . . .'

'Be quiet, Rhoda,' she said. 'We're listening to the news. Something's
happened. We think maybe we've won the war.' There were tears in her
eyes. She gave me a little hug, then turned back to the radio. It was a
wonderful radio with a magic eye that glowed in the dark. At night when
we had blackouts Dudley and I would get into bed with my mother
and we would listen to it together, the magic eye glowing in the dark like
an emerald.

Now the radio was bringing important news to Seymour, Indiana.
Strange, confused, hush-hush news that said we had a bomb bigger than
any bomb ever made and we had already dropped it on Japan and half of
Japan was sinking into the sea. Now the Japs had to surrender. Now they
couldn't come to Indiana and stick bamboo up our fingernails. Now it
woud all be over and my father would come home.

The grown people kept on listening to the radio, getting up every now
and then to get drinks or fix each other sandwiches. Dudley was sitting
beside my mother in a white shirt acting like he was twenty years old. He
always did that when company came. No one was paying any attention to
me.

Finally I went upstairs and lay down on the bed to think things over.
My father was coming home. I didn't know how to feel about that. He
was always yelling at someone when he was home. He was always yelling
at my mother to make me mind.

'What do you mean, you can't catch her,' I could hear him yelling. 'Hit
her with a broom. Hit her with a table. Hit her with a chair. But, for
God's sake, Ariane, don't let her talk to you that way.'

Well, maybe it would take a while for him to get home. First they had
to finish off Japan. First they had to sink the other half into the sea. I
curled up in my soft old eiderdown comforter. I was feeling great. We

had dropped the biggest bomb in the world on Japan and there were plenty more where that one came from.

I fell asleep in the hot sweaty silkiness of the comforter. I was dreaming I was at the wheel of an airplane carrying the bomb to Japan. Hit 'em, I was yelling. Hit 'em with a mountain. Hit 'em with a table. Hit 'em with a chair. Off we go into the wild blue yonder, climbing high into the sky. I dropped one on the brick house where the bad man lived, then took off for Japan. Down we dive, spouting a flame from under. Off with one hell of a roar. We live in flame. Buckle down in flame. For nothing can stop the Army Air Corps. Hit 'em with a table, I was yelling. Hit 'em with a broom. Hit 'em with a bomb. Hit 'em with a chair.

A. S. BYATT

On the Day that E. M. Forster Died

❦

This is a story about writing. It is a story about a writer who believed, among other things, that time for writing about writing was past. 'Our art', said T. S. Eliot, 'is a substitute for religion and so is our religion.' The writer in question, who, on the summer day in 1970 when this story takes place, was a middle-aged married woman with three small children, had been brought up on art about art which saw art also as salvation. *Portrait of the Artist as a Young Man, Death in Venice, À la Recherche du Temps Perdu.* Or, more English and moral, more didactic, D. H. Lawrence. 'The novel is the highest form of human expression yet attained.' 'The novel is the one bright book of life.' Mrs Smith was afraid of these books, and was also naturally sceptical. She did not believe that life aspired to the condition of art, or that art could save the world from most of the things that threatened it, endemically or at moments of crisis. She had written three brief and elegant black comedies about folly and misunder-standing in sexual relationships, she had sparred with and loved her husband, who was deeply interested in international politics and the world economy, and only intermittently interested in novels. She had three children, who were interested in the television, small animals, model armies, other small children, the sky, death and occasional narratives and paintings. She had a cleaning lady, who was interested in wife-battery and diabetes and had that morning opened a button-through dress to display to Mrs Smith a purple and chocolate and gold series of lumps and swellings across her breasts and belly. Mrs Smith's own life made no sense to her without art, but she was disinclined to believe in it as a cure, or a duty, or a general necessity. Nor did she see the achievement of the work of art as a paradigm for the struggle for life, or virtue. She had somehow been inoculated with it, in the form of the novel, before she as a moral being had had anything to say to it. It was an addiction. The bright books of life were the shots in the arm, the warm tots of whisky which kept her alive and conscious and lively. Life itself was related in complicated ways to this addiction. She often asked herself, without receiving any satisfactory answer, why she needed it, and why this form of it? Her answers would have appeared to Joyce, or Mann, or Proust to be frivolous. It was because she had become sensuously excited in early childhood by Beatrix Potter's sentence structure, or Kipling's adjectives. It was because she was a voyeur and liked looking in through other people's windows on warmer, brighter worlds. It was because she was secretly deprived of power, and liked to construct other worlds in which things would be as she chose, lovely or horrid. When she took her art most seriously it was because it focused her curiosity about things that were not art; society, education, science, death. She did a lot of research for her little books, most of which never got written into them, but it satisfied her somehow. It gave a temporary coherence to her perception of things.

So this story, which takes place on the day when she decided to commit herself to a long and complicated novel, would not have pleased her. She never wrote about writers. Indeed, she wrote witty and indignant reviews of novels which took writing for a paradigm of life. She wrote about the metaphysical claustrophobia of the Shredded Wheat Box on the Shredded Wheat Box getting smaller ad infinitum. She liked things to happen. Stories, plots. History, facts. If I do not entirely share her views, I am much in sympathy with them. Nevertheless, it seems worth telling this story about writing, which is a story, and does have a plot, is indeed essentially plot, overloaded with plot, a paradigmatic plot which, I believe, takes it beyond the narcissistic consideration of the formation of the writer, or the aesthetic closure of the mirrored mirror.

On a summer day in 1970, then, Mrs Smith, as was her habit when her children were at school, was writing in the London Library. (She preferred to divide art and life. She liked to write surrounded by books, in a closed space where books were what mattered most. In her kitchen she thought about cooking and cleanliness, in her living room about the children's education and different temperaments, in bed about her husband, mostly.) She had various isolated ideas for things she might write about. There was a story which dealt with the private lives of various people at the time of the public events of the Suez landings and the Russian invasion of Hungary. There was a tragi-comedy about a maverick realist painter in a Fine Art department dedicated to hard-edge abstract work. There was a tale based, at a proper moral distance, on her husband's accounts, from his experience in his government department, of the distorting effects on love, marriage and the family, of the current complicated British immigration policy. There was a kind of parody of *The Lord of the Rings* which was designed to show why that epic meant so much to many and to wind its speech into incompatible 'real' modern events. None of these enterprises attracted her quite enough. She sat on her not comfortable hard chair at the library table with its peeling leather top and looked from shelved dictionaries to crimson carpet to elegantly sleeping elderly gentlemen in leather armchairs to the long windows onto St James's Square. One of these framed a clean, large Union Jack, unfurled from a flagpole on a neighbouring building. The others were filled by the green tossing branches of the trees in the Square and the clear blue of the sky. (Her metabolism was different in summer. Her mind raced clearly. Oxygen made its way to her brain.)

It was suddenly clear to her that all her beginnings were considerably more interesting if they were part of the same work than if they were seen separately. The painter's aesthetic problem was more complicated in the same story as the civil servant's political problem, the Tolkien parody gained from being juxtaposed or interwoven with a cast of Hungarian refugees, intellectuals and Old Guard, National Servicemen at Suez and Angry Young Men. They *were* all part of the same thing. They were part of what she knew. She was a middle-aged woman who had led a certain, not very varied but perceptive, life, who had lived through enough time to write a narrative of it. She sat mute and motionless looking at the trees and the white paper, and a fantastically convoluted, improbably possible plot reared up before her like a snake out of a magic basket, like ticker-tape, or football results out of the television teleprinter.

It would have to be a very long book. Proust came to mind, his cork-lined room stuffed with the transformation of life into words, everything he knew, feathers on hats, Zeppelins, musical form, painting, vice, reading, snobbery, sudden death, slow death, food, love, indifference, the telephone, the table-napkin, the paving-stone, a lifetime.

Such moments are—if one allows oneself to know that they have happened—as terrible as falling in love at first sight, as the shock of a major physical injury, as gaining or losing huge sums of money. Mrs Smith was a woman who was capable, she believed, of not allowing herself to know that they had happened. She was a woman who could, and on occasion did, successfully ignore love at first sight, out of ambition before her marriage, out of moral terror after it. She sat there in the sunny library and watched the snake sway and the tape tick, and the snake-dance grew more, not less, delightful and powerful and complicated. She remembered Kékulé seeing the answer to a problem of solid state physics in a metaphysical vision of a snake eating its tail in the fire. Why does condensation of thought have such authority? Like warning, or imperative, dreams. Mrs Smith could have said at any time that of course all her ideas were part of a whole, they were all hers, limited by her history, sex, language, class, education, body and energy. But to experience this so sharply, and to experience it as intense pleasure, to know limitation as release and power, was outside Mrs Smith's pattern. She had probably been solicited by such aesthetic longings before. And rejected them. Why else be so afraid of the bright books?

She put pen to paper then, and noted the connections she saw between the disparate plots, the developments that seemed so naturally to come to all of them, branching and flowering like speeded film, seed to shoot to spring to summer from this new form. She wrote very hard, without looking up, for maybe an hour, doing more work in that time than in times of lethargy or distraction she did in a week. A week? A month. A year even, though work is of many kinds and she had the sense that this form was indeed a growth, a form of life, her life, its own life.

Then, having come full circle, having thought her way through the planning, from link to link back to the original perception of linking that had started it all, she got up, and went out of the Library, and walked. She was overexcited, there was too much adrenalin, she could not be still.

She went up and down Jermyn Street, through the dark doorway, the windowed umber quiet of St James's Piccadilly, out into the bright church-yard with its lettered stones smoothed and erased by the passage of feet. Along Piccadilly, past Fortnum and Mason's, more windows full of dec-orous conspicuous consumption, down an arcade bright with windowed riches like Aladdin's cave, out into Jermyn Street again. Everything was transformed. Everything was hers, by which phrase she meant, thinking fast in orderly language, that at that time she felt no doubt about being able to translate everything she saw into words, her own words, English words, English words in 1970, with their limited and meaningful and endlessly rich histories, theirs as hers was hers. This was not the same as Adam in Eden naming things, making nouns. It was not that she said nakedly as though for the first time, tree, stone, grass, sky, nor even, more particularly, omnibus, gas-lamp, culottes. It was mostly adjectives. Ele-phantine bark, eau-de-nil paint on Fortnum's walls, Nile-water green, a colour fashionable from Nelson's victories at the time when this street was formed, a colour for old drawing-rooms or, she noted in the chem-ist's window, for a new eyeshadow, Jeepers Peepers, Occidental Jade, what nonsense, what vitality, how lovely to know. Naming with nouns, she thought absurdly, is the language of poetry, There is a Tree, of many One. The Rainbow comes and goes. And Lovely is the Rose. Adjectives go with the particularity of long novels. They limit nouns. And at the same time give them energy. Dickens is full of them. And Balzac. And Proust.

Nothing now, she knew, whatever in the moral abstract she thought about the relative importance of writing and life, would matter to her more than writing. This illumination was a function of middle age. Novels—as opposed to lyrics, or mathematics—are essentially a middle-aged form. The long novel she meant to write acknowledged both the length and shortness of her time. It would not be History, nor even a history, nor certainly, perish the thought, her history. Autobiographies tell more lies than all but the most self-indulgent fiction. But it would be written in the knowledge that she had lived through and noticed a certain amount of history. A war, a welfare state, the rise (and fall) of the meritocracy, European unity, little England, equality of opportunity, comprehensive schooling, women's liberation, the death of the individual, the poverty of liberalism. How lovely to trace the particular human events that might chart the glories and inadequacies, the terrors and absurdities, the hopes and fears of those words. And biological history too. She had lived now through birth, puberty, illness, sex, love, marriage, other births, other kinds of love, family and kinship and local manifestations of these universals, Drs Spock, Bowlby, Winnicott, Flower Power, gentrification, the transformation of the adjective gay into a politicized noun. How extraordinary and interesting it all was, how adequate language turned out to be, if you thought in terms of long flows of writing, looping tightly and loosely round things, joining and knitting and dividing, or, to change the metaphor, a Pandora's box, an Aladdin's cave, a bottomless dark bag into which everything could be put and drawn out again, the same and not the same. She quoted to herself, in another language, 'Nel mezzo del cammin di nostra vita.' Another beginning in a middle. Mrs Smith momentarily Dante, in the middle of Jermyn Street.

Where is the plotting and over-plotting I wrote of? It is coming, it is proceeding up Lower Regent Street, it is stalking Mrs Smith, a terror by noonday. It is not, aesthetic pride compels me to add, a straying terrorist's bullet, or anything contrived by the IRA. Too many stories are curtailed by these things, in life and in literature.

In the interim, Mrs Smith read the newspaper placards. 'Famous Novelist Dies.' She bought an early paper and it turned out that it was E. M. Forster who was dead. He was, or had been, ninety-one. A long history. Which, since 1924, he had not recorded in fiction. 'Only connect,' he had said, 'the prose and the passion.' He had been defeated apparently by the attenuation of the world he knew, the deep countryside, life in families in homes, a certain social order. Forster, much more than Lawrence, corresponded to Mrs Smith's ideal of the English novel. He wrote civilized comedy about the value of the individual and his responsibilities: he was aware of the forces that threatened the individual, unreason, belief in causes, political fervour. He believed in tolerance, in the order of art, in recognizing the complicated energies of the world in which art didn't matter. In Cambridge, Mrs Smith had had a friend whose window had overlooked Forster's writing desk. She had watched him pass mildly to and fro, rearranging heaps of papers. Never writing. She honoured him.

She was surprised therefore to feel a kind of quick, delighted, automatic survivor's pleasure at the sight of the placards. 'Now,' she thought wordlessly, only later, because of the unusual speed and accuracy with which she was thinking, putting it into words, 'Now I have room to move, now I can do as I please, now he can't overlook or reject me.' Which was absurd, since he did not know she was there, would not have wished to overlook or reject her.

What she meant, she decided, pacing Jermyn Street, was that he was removed, in some important sense, by his death, as a measure. Some obligation she had felt, which tugged both ways, to try to do as well as he did, and yet to do differently from him, had been allayed. Because his work was now truly closed into the past it was now in some sense her own, more accessible to learn from, and formally finished off. She passed the church again, thinking of him, agnostic and scrupulous. She envied him his certainties. She enjoyed her own difference. She thought, 'On the day that E. M. Forster died I decided to write a long novel.' And heard in the churchyard a Biblical echo. 'In the year that King Uzziah died I saw also the Lord . . .'

He had written, 'The people I respect most behave as if they were immortal and society was eternal. Both assumptions are false: both of them must be accepted as true if we are to keep on eating and working and loving and are to keep open a few breathing holes for the spirit.'

Mrs Smith was still exalted. A consuming passion streamlines everything, like stripes in a rolled ribbon, one weaving: newsprint, smudged black lines on the placard, Wren church, Famine Relief posters, the order of male living in Jermyn Street shop windows, shoes mirror-bright, embroidered velvet slippers, brightly coloured shirts, the cheese shop with its lively smell of decay, Floris the perfumer with the ghost of pot-pourri. And for the ear the organ, heard faintly, playing baroque music. A pocket of civilization or a consumers' display-area. She came to Grima the jeweller, a recent extravaganza, expensively primitive, huge, matt, random slabs of flint-like stone, bolted apparently randomly to the shop-frame, like a modern theatre-set for an ancient drama, black and heavy, *Oedipus, Lear, Macbeth*. And in the interstices of these louring slabs the bright tiny boxes of windows—lined with scarlet kid, crimson silk, vermilion velvet.

The jewels were artfully random, not precision polished, but fretted, gold and silver, as stone or bone might be by the incessant action of the sea. And the stones—huge, glowing lumpen uneven pearls, a pear-shaped fiery opal, a fall of moonstones like water on gold mail—were both opulent and primitive, set in circlets or torques that might have come from the Sutton Hoo ship, a Pharaoh's tomb, the Museum of Modern Art. Windows, frames, Mrs Smith thought, making metaphors of everything, out of the library window I saw the national flag and summer trees, in here is the fairy cavern and all the sixties myths, and in the tailor was Forster's Edwardian world of handmade shirts and slippers. The windows order it. But it is not disorderly. Even the *names*—Turnbull and Asser, Floris, Grima—can work in a Tolkien-tale, a realist novel, or a modern fantasy. It is all *there*. There is time.

And then the man, who had turned the corner into Jermyn Street, plucked her by her sleeve, called her by her name, said how delighted he was to see her. She took time to recognize him: he had aged considerably since they last met. He was not a man she considered herself to know well, though at their rare meetings he behaved, as now, as if they were old and intimate friends. His history, which I shall now tell, was in most ways the opposite of Mrs Smith's, given that most histories of the university-educated English would appear very similar to a creature from another planet or even from Japan, Brazil or Turkey. Mrs Smith and Conrad had been to the same university, attended the same parties, had the same acquaintances and one or two friends in common in the worlds of education and the arts in London in 1970. Conrad had studied psychology whereas Mrs Smith had studied English literature. He had made passes at Mrs Smith, but he made passes at most people, and Mrs Smith did not see that as a token of intimacy. He had been, and remained, a friend of friends.

In Jermyn Street, as always before, he radiated boundless enthusiasm, as though there was no one he would rather have met at that moment, as though chance, or Providence, or God had answered his need, and hers almost certainly too, by bringing them haphazardly together. He leaped about on the pavement, a heavy man with a new, pear-shaped belly propped on his jeans like a very large egg on an inadequate egg-cup. He had a jean jacket over a cotton polo-neck through which rusty specks and wires of hair pierced here and there. He leaped with a boyish eagerness, although he was a middle-aged man with a bald brow and crown, and long, kinked, greasy fringes of hair over his collar. She particularly noticed the hair in the first moments. As an undergraduate he had had a leonine bush of it which gave him presence.

'Come and have a cup of coffee,' he said, 'I have so much to tell you. You are the ideal person.'

In the past she would, out of fear, or distaste for being cornered and having her knee pressed or stroked, have refused this invitation. In the past, she had refused more of his invitations than she had accepted. There were resilient moods in which the writer in her was prepared to fend off the patting, stroking and breathing for the sake of information Conrad purveyed about things she knew too little about. Psychology, for instance. It was Conrad who had told her about the effects of experiments in total sensory deprivation, men suspended in lightless baths of warm liquid so that sight, and the sense of the body and then the sense of time and the self were annihilated. It was Conrad who had said that there were unrevealed numbers of volunteer students, whose personalities had disintegrated forever in this bodiless floating. Mrs Smith was curious about what held the personality together, what constituted the self. Conrad, whose life experience was varied, told her also, when she could bear to be told, about forms of bullying and torture, and about experiments on the readiness of ordinary men to inflict pain under orders. Mrs Smith was extensively curious but lacked the journalist's readiness to ask questions. Conrad's talkativeness was, in its way, a godsend.

But on that June day, she went to have coffee because of the music. She felt particularly warm to Conrad because of the music.

The story of the music was, is, a plot almost needing no character. All that need initially be known about Conrad to tell the story of the music is that he was a man of extraordinary nervous, physical and mental energy. He was not still, he did not stop, he was perpetually mobile. He bedded women with an extravagant greed and need which Mrs Smith found sensuously unattractive but interesting to be told about. He had married a rich and beautiful wife, very young, but all other women interested him. He liked activity: he had taken his academic psychological skills into the army, into the prison service, into commerce. He had an interest in advising television advertisers. As I said, he was to Mrs Smith a friend of friends, and in her early days of childbearing she had heard from friends tales of Conrad's restless activity. He had set out and joined in the Hungarian uprising. He had spent his honeymoon in the Ritz, three weeks without getting out of bed, he had been heard of as accompanying a filming expedition to Central New Guinea, to study cannibals, he had several children by actresses, au pair girls, students. He had been very busy. He had had a routine medical examination for a job with another film company working abroad and had been discovered to have tuberculosis. He had been sent to a sanatorium, and the friends had not seen him for several years. His wife had left him. All this filtered through friends to Mrs Smith, quietly running her house, feeding her children, reading George Eliot and Henry James.

In the sanatorium, Conrad had, in his enforced stillness, had a vision. He had seen that his life was finite, that it came only once, that a man must decide what was the most important thing to him and pursue that, and that only, with all his power. The most important thing in life to Conrad was, he decided, music. In the sanatorium that seemed clear to him. When he came out, gaunt and quiet, he had resigned all his lucrative work and had enrolled as a music student, a student of composition. He had married a second quiet wife. Meeting him at that time, a man submitted to a new discipline in middle age for the sake of an ideal vision, Mrs Smith had felt a mixture of envy and cautious scepticism. He was shining with certainty. The routine pass was couched almost as an invitation to a religious laying-on of hands. Mrs Smith rejected it, and went home to a flooded washing-machine, a threatening letter from a released anarchist drug-pusher to her husband, and the reflection that in the past much great art had been produced by the peculiar vitality and vision afforded by TB, which could now of course be cured, to our human gain and aesthetic loss.

She had seen Conrad once again between then and now, when he had knocked on her door and said she *must* come to lunch. The lunch had been expensive—mussels, turbot, zabaglione, wine. Mrs Smith had scrutinized Conrad, who ate and drank with passion. He ate all her new potatoes and all his, glistening with hollandaise sauce, and left an empty sauceboat. He wiped his lips with a damask napkin: his face also glistened with exertion and butter: his second wife, he said, had left him, taking the children. He was paying a lot of alimony. He had had a motet played at a Contemporary Music Festival in Leamington Spa. He was working for a cigarette company, devising ways of suggesting that cigarettes produced sexual pleasure, without this being apparent. The decline of lipstick-wearing amongst women made this harder. Once you could use a glamorous scarlet lip, wet-looking. Now it had to be clean and healthy. He wasn't happy about this; he had seen too much in the lung ward in the sanatorium. But there was the alimony. Did she know any good modern love poems he could set to music? He wanted to write for single voices, very plain. He had met an extraordinary Israeli singer. With an extraordinary range. Did women write love poems? Did she know women ate mussels because they reminded them of sex? Was it the marine smell, or the hint of the embryonic? Would she care for a brandy? An armagnac? A ticket for

Stockhausen at the Festival Hall? The nature of our concept of musical sound, musical form, was being radically changed, as never before. He was engaged, too, in research about how to interest women in fortified wines. Of course, physiologically speaking, they couldn't take much. Up-market port and lemon. Class drink preferences were not wholly determined by money. Would she like a cigar? He rubbed her knee with his. Big and hot. She dodged efficiently.

All the same, there was the music. He had been *in extremis*, and had put music first.

They sat in front of cappucinos in an unassuming coffee bar. Now she was near him, she saw that he looked ill. There was thick beard stubble, his face was patterned by broken capillary tubes, his eyes were veined, his neck tendons stood out. His shoulders were sprinkled with dandruff and traced by fallen hairs.

'How's the music?' asked Mrs Smith.

'Marvellous. Wonderful. New. Never better. You look radiant. You look so *lovely*. It's *marvellous* to see you, looking so lovely. Not a day older—not a *day*—than when we walked along the Backs together and sat side by side in the University Library.'

Mrs Smith did not recall that they had done either of these things. Perhaps her memory—which she must now trust to be so sharp—was at fault.

'I've just been thinking how pleasant it is to be middle-aged.'

'You aren't middle-aged. You're as old as you feel. That's true, not just something to say. I'm young, you're young, we can do anything. I've never in my whole life felt so young, so healthy.'

There were panels of sweat down his nose, in the crease of his chin, on his clammy brow. The ends of his fingers were dead white and his fingernails had dirt under them. He smelled. Across the new coffee smell he smelled of new sweat and old sweat under it, mortality.

'Tell me how the music is.'

'I told you, it's fantastic. Every day, new discoveries. Revolutionary techniques. New machines. A new range of possibilities. I can't get over how *fresh* you look.'

Mrs Smith knew that she had grey hairs, a marked fan of lines in her eye-corners, a neck better covered, a body loosened by childbearing. She did not attract wolf whistles. She was not generally considered to expect or hope that advances would be made.

'Don't say that, I'm thinking how happy I am to be irretrievably middle-aged. Because of time, because I'm *in time*. Listen—I've decided to write a long book—about my time, the time I've lived and won't have again.'

It was the first time, possibly, she had volunteered a serious confidence in their acquaintance. It was because of the music.

'By the time we're middle-aged I can tell you they'll have discovered how to arrest the ageing process forever. They're working on it. It'll be quite possible soon to stop death, to stop death in most cases. I assure you, I've gone into it. You deprive the body of the signals—hormone decrease, loss of calcium, those things—that trigger off ageing. There's a political problem, they don't want everyone to know, naturally, they haven't solved the world population problem. But I have my sources of information. You trick your genes into working to perpetuate themselves in the body you've got, not a new one. It can be done. I had a vasectomy. No more kids, no more alimony, no more splurging my genes on other beings. Conserve. Perpetuate. Live. Don't talk about middle age.'

'But I *like* it.' She wanted him, for once, to hear. 'I've just discovered I practise a middle-aged art. Spread over time. Time's of the essence.'

'There's no such thing as time. Time's an illusion. The new music knows that. It's all in the present. Now. It isn't interested in the past, or in harmony, or in keeping time, in tempo, any of all that. We've broken the idea of time and sequence. We play with the random, the chaotic. Einstein destroyed the illusion of linear time.'

'Not biological time,' said Mrs Smith, bravely, having heard these arguments before, though not from Conrad.

'Instantaneous and disposable sounds,' said Conrad, excited. 'Always different, always now. Biological time's an illusion too. Only the more complicated organisms die. Simple cells are immortal. We can reverse that. We must make a better world to live in. That's what matters. We must survive. Can I trust you?'

Mrs Smith lowered her eyelids and said nothing. She expected a sexual confidence.

'I know I can trust you, that's why I met you. These things are not fortuitous. I was followed here. I'm in danger.'

Mrs Smith did not know what to do with this introduction of espionage plotting. She continued to look non-committally intelligent, and to say nothing.

'There's a dark man across there, across the street, with an evil umbrella. Don't look now.'

Paranoia, said Mrs Smith's mind. 'Why?' said Mrs Smith, more neutrally.

'I am carrying', said Conrad, leaning forward across the formica table top, breathing stale smoke and sour fear in her face, 'this folder of secret plans. It's a matter of life and death. I've got to get them to the Israeli embassy.'

He laid a rubbed and filthy package before her, tied with various kinds of string, sprouting faded edges of xerox paper.

'This may prevent nuclear war. They have a Bomb, you know, they may be driven to let it off. Everyone's against them, fighting for survival, history conspiring . . .'

'I don't think . . .'

'You don't know. I worked for British Intelligence, you know. On some very hush-hush research. All those trips to eastern university conferences weren't what they seemed. I know my way around. In Israel everyone's in Intelligence. They have to be. I recognized it in Miriam immediately. I can't get her to trust me. I want the Israelis to accept this. In token of good faith. British good faith.'

Mrs Smith was driven to ask, in a small voice, what 'this' was, though not, she hoped, as though she really wanted to know. Across the road the man in a dark overcoat lit a cigarette, shifted his umbrella, looked through the café window, looked back at the gentlemen's shirts in their bold colours, scarlet stripes, roseate flowers, black and gold paisley. He did not look the sort of man to wear such shirts.

'The music department in this university has made an instrument— constructed a machine—that disintegrates solid bodies with sound waves. By shaking them. Sound broadcast by this instrument at certain frequencies disorientates people completely. Drives them round the bend. Arabs are peculiarly susceptible to sound. They hear a greater frequency range. I'm taking these plans to the Israeli embassy.'

'How terrible,' said Mrs Smith.

'Of course it's terrible. Life is terrible. Destroy or be destroyed. What I want you to do is keep the duplicate plans safe—just sit here and keep them safe—and if I'm not back in one hour take them to one of these people in the BBC Music Department. The BBC's full of spies. I know them. I have the list.'

'Terrible I meant,' said Mrs Smith, 'to use the music. The *music* . . .'

He brushed this aside. 'I'll give you £100. £500. Just for *half an hour*. As an insurance?'

'I don't want anything to do with it.' Mrs Smith stood up. 'I don't like it. I'm going.'

'Oh no,' said Conrad. 'Oh no, you don't. You may be part of the plot, after all. You will stay here where I can see you.'

He clasped Mrs Smith's wrist. The man on the opposite pavement looked at them again, pulled his hat over his eyes, became absorbed in the contemplation of a pair of black velvet slippers, embroidered with a pair of gold stags' heads. Mrs Smith thought of *The Thirty-Nine Steps*. Her desire to get out of this story, international incident, paranoid fantasy, became overmastering. She tried to pull away.

'I'm going, I'm afraid. I have work to do.'

'You can't go out there. Those people have poison-darts in their umbrella-tips. Fatal. No known antidote.'

'No, they don't,' said Mrs Smith.

Mrs Smith pulled. 'You have got to help.' She raised her handbag and banged it against Conrad's bald head and red ear. He, breathing loudly, grabbed her crisp white shirt by the collar. Both pulled. The shirt came apart, leaving most of one sleeve and the left front portion in Conrad's hand. The restaurant proprietor, assuming rape, approached from behind the bar. Conrad's parcel fell under the table. As he bent towards it, Mrs Smith, her face scratched, one lace-covered breast exposed, ran out into Jermyn Street, attracting the brief, unsmiling attention of the window-watcher. When she was at the corner of Jermyn Street she heard Conrad's voice, plaintive and wild, 'Come back, help me, help me.'

Mrs Smith ran on, down Duke of York Street, along St James's Square, into the solid Victorian mahogany sanctuary of the London Library, which, at its inception, at the behest of Thomas Carlyle, historian and founder member, stocked the fiction of only one writer, George Eliot, who he believed had so deep an insight into the thought and nature of the times that her work was classified, by him, as philosophy.

In the mahogany ladies' room, with water from a Victorian brass tap, Mrs Smith mopped her face and wept for the music. She would have to borrow a cardigan to go home respectably. She had lost some virtue. (In the old sense of that word, from the Latin, *virtus*, manliness, worth, power; and in newer ones too.) She was shaken. She was a determined and practical woman and would go back to work, however her elation had been broken.

Conrad was mad. She would not inhabit his plot of deathly music-machines and lethal umbrellas.

How precarious it was, the sense of self in the dark bath of uncertainty, the moment of knowing, the certainty that music is the one thing needful.

'Death destroys a man,' said Forster, the liberal humanist, the realist, who died on that day. 'The idea of death saves him.' It would take more than Conrad's local madness to deflect or deter Mrs Smith.

I have to record, however, that only two weeks later she went to see a surgeon in the Marylebone Road. She had a pain in her side, not much, not a bad pain, a small lump, a hernia.

She had a sort of growth, said the surgeon, a thickening of old scar tissue. He thought it would be better if he took it out.

'Not just now,' said Mrs Smith. 'I am busy, I have a lot of work to do, I work best in the summer, it's the school holidays. In the autumn.'

'Next week,' said the surgeon, and added in answer to her unspoken question; 'it is certainly benign.'

This is not what he said to Mr Smith, and indeed, how could he have said with such certainty, before the event, what it was, malignant or benign?

Mrs Smith, during the three weeks that in fact supervened before she entered the hospital, went as usual to the London Library. She stared a lot out of the window and tried to think of short tales, of compressed, rapid forms of writing, in case there was not much time.

BHARATI MUKHERJEE

A Wife's Story

❦

Imre says forget it, but I'm going to write David Mamet. So Patels are hard to sell real estate to. You buy them a beer, whisper Glengarry Glen Ross, and they smell swamp instead of sun and surf. They work hard, eat cheap, live ten to a room, stash their savings under futons in Queens, and before you know it they own half of Hoboken. You say, where's the sweet gullibility that made this nation great?

Polish jokes, Patel jokes: that's not why I want to write Mamet.

Seen their women?

Everybody laughs. Imre laughs. The dozing fat man with the Barnes & Noble sack between his legs, the woman next to him, the usher, everybody. The theater isn't so dark that they can't see me. In my red silk sari I'm conspicuous. Plump, gold paisleys sparkle on my chest.

The actor is just warming up. *Seen their women?* He plays a salesman, he's had a bad day and now he's in a Chinese restaurant trying to loosen up. His face is pink. His wool-blend slacks are creased at the crotch. We bought our tickets at half-price, we're sitting in the front row, but at the edge, and we see things we shouldn't be seeing. At least I do, or think I do. Spittle, actors goosing each other, little winks, streaks of makeup.

Maybe they're improvising dialogue too. Maybe Mamet's provided them with insult kits, Thursdays for Chinese, Wednesdays for Hispanics, today for Indians. Maybe they get together before curtain time, see an Indian woman settling in the front row off to the side, and say to each other: 'Hey, forget Friday. Let's get *her* today. See if she cries. See if she walks out.' Maybe, like the salesmen they play, they have a little bet on.

Maybe I shouldn't feel betrayed.

Their women, he goes again. *They look like they've just been fucked by a dead cat.*

The fat man hoots so hard he nudges my elbow off our shared armrest.

'Imre. I'm going home.' But Imre's hunched so far forward he doesn't hear. English isn't his best language. A refugee from Budapest, he has to listen hard. 'I didn't pay eighteen dollars to be insulted.'

I don't hate Mamet. It's the tyranny of the American dream that scares me. First, you don't exist. Then you're invisible. Then you're funny. Then you're disgusting. Insult, my American friends will tell me, is a kind of acceptance. No instant dignity here. A play like this, back home, would cause riots. Communal, racist, and antisocial. The actors wouldn't make it off stage. This play, and all these awful feelings, would be safely locked up.

I long, at times, for clear-cut answers. Offer me instant dignity, today, and I'll take it.

'What?' Imre moves toward me without taking his eyes off the actor. 'Come again?'

Tears come. I want to stand, scream, make an awful scene. I long for ugly, nasty rage.

The actor is ranting, flinging spittle. *Give me a chance. I'm not finished, I can get back on the board. I tell that asshole, give me a real lead. And what does that asshole give me? Patels. Nothing but Patels.*

This time Imre works an arm around my shoulders. 'Panna, what is Patel? Why are you taking it all so personally?'

I shrink from his touch, but I don't walk out. Expensive girls' schools in Lausanne and Bombay have trained me to behave well. My manners are exquisite, my feelings are delicate, my gestures refined, my moods undetectable. They have seen me through riots, uprootings, separation, my son's death.

'I'm not taking it personally.'

The fat man looks at us. The woman looks too, and shushes.

I stare back at the two of them. Then I stare, mean and cool, at the man's elbow. Under the bright blue polyester Hawaiian shirt sleeve, the elbow looks soft and runny. 'Excuse me,' I say. My voice has the effortless meanness of well-bred displaced Third World women, though my rhetoric had been learned elsewhere. 'You're exploiting my space.'

Startled, the man snatches his arm away from me. He cradles it against his breast. By the time he's ready with come-backs, I've turned my back on him. I've probably ruined the first act for him. I know I've ruined it for Imre.

It's not my fault; it's the *situation*. Old colonies wear down. Patels—the new pioneers—have to be suspicious. Idi Amin's lesson is permanent. AT&T wires move good advice from continent to continent. Keep all assets liquid. Get into 7–11s, get out of condos and motels. I know how both sides feel, that's the trouble. The Patel sniffing out scams, the sad salesmen on the stage: postcolonialism has made me their referee. It's hate I long for; simple, brutish, partisan hate.

After the show Imre and I make our way toward Broadway. Sometimes he holds my hand; it doesn't mean anything more than that crazies and drunks are crouched in doorways. Imre's been here over two years, but he's stayed very old-world, very courtly, openly protective of women. I met him in a seminar on special ed. last semester. His wife is a nurse somewhere in the Hungarian countryside. There are two sons, and miles of petitions for their emigration. My husband manages a mill two hundred miles north of Bombay. There are no children.

'You make things tough on yourself,' Imre says. He assumed Patel was a Jewish name or maybe Hispanic; everything makes equal sense to him. He found the play tasteless, he worried about the effect of vulgar language on my sensitive ears. 'You have to let go a bit.' And as though to show me how to let go, he breaks away from me, bounds ahead with his head ducked tight, then dances on amazingly jerky legs. He's a Magyar, he often tells me, and deep down, he's an Asian too. I catch glimpses of it, knife-blade Attila cheekbones, despite the blondish hair. In his faded jeans and leather jacket, he's a rock video star. I watch MTV for hours in the apartment when Charity's working the evening shift at Macy's. I listen to WPLJ on Charity's earphones. Why should I be ashamed? Television in India is so uplifting.

Imre stops as suddenly as he'd started. People walk around us. The summer sidewalk is full of theatergoers in seersucker suits; Imre's year-round jacket is out of place. European. Cops in twos and threes huddle, lightly tap their thighs with night sticks and smile at me with benevolence. I want to wink at them, get us all in trouble, tell them the crazy dancing man is from the Warsaw Pact. I'm too shy to break into dance on Broadway. So I hug Imre instead.

The hug takes him by surprise. He wants me to let go, but he doesn't really expect me to let go. He staggers, though I weigh no more than 104 pounds, and with him, I pitch forward slightly. Then he catches me, and we walk arm in arm to the bus stop. My husband would never dance or hug a woman on Broadway. Nor would my brothers. They aren't stuffy people, but they went to Anglican boarding schools and they have a well-developed sense of what's silly.

'Imre.' I squeeze his big, rough hand. 'I'm sorry I ruined the evening for you.'

'You did nothing of the kind.' He sounds tired. 'Let's not wait for the bus. Let's splurge and take a cab instead.'

Imre always has unexpected funds. The Network, he calls it, Class of '56.

In the back of the cab, without even trying, I feel light, almost free. Memories of Indian destitutes mix with the hordes of New York street people, and they float free, like astronauts, inside my head. I've made it. I'm making something of my life. I've left home, my husband, to get a

Ph.D. in special ed. I have a multiple-entry visa and a small scholarship for two years. After that, we'll see. My mother was beaten by her mother-in-law, my grandmother, when she'd registered for French lessons at the Alliance Française. My grandmother, the eldest daughter of a rich zamindar, was illiterate.

Imre and the cabdriver talk away in Russian. I keep my eyes closed. That way I can feel the floaters better. I'll write Mamet tonight. I feel strong, reckless. Maybe I'll write Steven Spielberg too; tell him that Indians don't eat monkey brains.

We've made it. Patels must have made it. Mamet, Spielberg: they're not condescending to us. Maybe they're a little bit afraid.

Charity Chin, my roommate, is sitting on the floor drinking Chablis out of a plastic wineglass. She is five foot six, three inches taller than me, but weighs a kilo and a half less than I do. She is a 'hands' model. Orientals are supposed to have a monopoly in the hands-modelling business, she says. She had her eyes fixed eight or nine months ago and out of gratitude sleeps with her plastic surgeon every third Wednesday.

'Oh, good,' Charity says. 'I'm glad you're back early. I need to talk.'

She's been writing checks. MCI, Con Ed, Bonwit Teller. Envelopes, already stamped and sealed, form a pyramid between her shapely, knee-socked legs. The checkbook's cover is brown plastic, grained to look like cowhide. Each time Charity flips back the cover, white geese fly over sky-colored checks. She makes good money, but she's extravagant. The difference adds up to this shared, rent-controlled Chelsea one-bedroom.

'All right. Talk.'

When I first moved in, she was seeing an analyst. Now she sees a nutritionist.

'Eric called. From Oregon.'

'What did he want?'

'He wants me to pay half the rent on his loft for last spring. He asked me to move back, remember? He *begged* me.'

Eric is Charity's estranged husband.

'What does your nutritionist say?' Eric now wears a red jumpsuit and tills the soil in Rajneeshpuram.

'You think Phil's a creep too, don't you? What else can he be when creeps are all I attract?'

Phil is a flutist with thinning hair. He's very touchy on the subject of *flautists* versus *flutists*. He's touchy on every subject, from music to books to foods to clothes. He teaches at a small college upstate, and Charity bought a used blue Datsun ('Nissan', Phil insists) last month so she could spend weekends with him. She returns every Sunday night, exhausted and exasperated. Phil and I don't have much to say to each other—he's the only musician I know; the men in my family are lawyers, engineers, or in business—but I like him. Around me, he loosens up. When he visits, he bakes us loaves of pumpernickel bread. He waxes our kitchen floor. Like many men in this country, he seems to me a displaced child, or even a woman, looking for something that passed him by, or for something that he can never have. If he thinks I'm not looking, he sneaks his hands under Charity's sweater, but there isn't too much there. Here, she's a model with high ambitions. In India, she'd be a flat-chested old maid.

I'm shy in front of the lovers. A darkness comes over me when I see them horsing around.

'It isn't the money,' Charity says. Oh? I think. 'He says he still loves me. Then he turns around and asks me for five hundred.'

What's so strange about that, I want to ask. She still loves Eric, and Eric, red jump suit and all, is smart enough to know it. Love is a commodity, hoarded like any other. Mamet knows. But I say, 'I'm not the person to ask about love.' Charity knows that mine was a traditional Hindu marriage. My parents, with the help of a marriage broker, who was my mother's cousin, picked out a groom. All I had to do was get to know his taste in food.

It'll be a long evening, I'm afraid. Charity likes to confess. I unpleat my silk sari—it no longer looks too showy—wrap it in muslin cloth and put it away in a dresser drawer. Saris are hard to have laundered in Manhattan, though there's a good man in Jackson Heights. My next step will be to brew us a pot of chrysanthemum tea. It's a very special tea from the mainland. Charity's uncle gave it to us. I like him. He's a humpbacked, awkward, terrified man. He runs a gift store on Mott Street, and though he doesn't speak much English, he seems to have done well. Once upon a time he worked for the railways in Chengdu, Szechwan Province, and during the Wuchang Uprising, he was shot at. When I'm down, when I'm lonely for my husband, when I think of our son, or when I need to be held, I think of Charity's uncle. If I hadn't left home, I'd never have heard of the Wuchang Uprising. I've broadened my horizons.

Very late that night my husband calls me from Ahmadabad, a town of textile mills north of Bombay. My husband is a vice president at Lakshmi Cotton Mills. Lakshmi is the goddess of wealth, but LCM (Priv.), Ltd., is doing poorly. Lockouts, strikes, rock-throwings. My husband lives on digitalis, which he calls the food for our *yuga* of discontent.

'We had a bad mishap at the mill today.' Then he says nothing for seconds.

The operator comes on. 'Do you have the right party, sir? We're trying to reach Mrs Butt.'

'Bhatt,' I insist. '*B* for Bombay, *H* for Haryana, *A* for Ahmadabad, double *T* for Tamil Nadu.' It's a litany. 'This is she.'

'One of our lorries was firebombed today. Resulting in three deaths. The driver, old Karamchand, and his two children.'

I know how my husband's eyes look this minute, how the eye rims sag and the yellow corneas shine and bulge with pain. He is not an emotional man—the Ahmadabad Institute of Management has trained him to cut losses, to look on the bright side of economic catastrophes—but tonight he's feeling low. I try to remember a driver named Karamchand, but can't. That part of my life is over, the way *trucks* have replaced *lorries* in my vocabulary, the way Charity Chin and her lurid love life have replaced inherited notions of marital duty. Tomorrow he'll come out of it. Soon he'll be eating again. He'll sleep like a baby. He's been trained to believe in turnovers. Every morning he rubs his scalp with cantharidine oil so his hair will grow back again.

'It could be your car next.' Affection, love. Who can tell the difference in a traditional marriage in which a wife still doesn't call her husband by his first name?

'No. They know I'm a flunky, just like them. Well paid, maybe. No need for undue anxiety, please.'

Then his voice breaks. He says he needs me, he misses me, he wants me to come to him damp from my evening shower, smelling of sandal-wood soap, my braid decorated with jasmines.

'I need you too.'

'Not to worry, please,' he says. 'I am coming in a fortnight's time. I have already made arrangements.'

Outside my window, fire trucks whine, up Eighth Avenue. I wonder if he can hear them, what he thinks of a life like mine, led amid disorder.

'I am thinking it'll be like a honeymoon. More or less.'

When I was in college, waiting to be married, I imagined honeymoons were only for the more fashionable girls, the girls who came from slightly racy families, smoked Sobranies in the dorm lavatories and put up posters of Kabir Bedi, who was supposed to have made it as a big star in the West. My husband wants us to go to Niagara. I'm not to worry about foreign exchange. He's arranged for extra dollars through the Gujarati Network, with a cousin in San Jose. And he's bought four hundred more on the black market. 'Tell me you need me. Panna, please tell me again.'

I change out of the cotton pants and shirt I've been wearing all day and put on a sari to meet my husband at JFK. I don't forget the jewelry; the

marriage necklace of *mangalsutra*, gold drop earrings, heavy gold bangles.
I don't wear them every day. In this borough of vice and greed, who
knows when, or whom, desire will overwhelm.

My husband spots me in the crowd and waves. He has lost weight, and
changed his glasses. The arm, uplifted in a cheery wave, is bony, frail,
almost opalescent.

In the Carey Coach, we hold hands. He strokes my fingers one by one.
'How come you aren't wearing my mother's ring?'

'Because muggers know about Indian women,' I say. They know with
us it's 24-karat. His mother's ring is showy, in ghastly taste anywhere but
India: a blood-red Burma ruby set in a gold frame of floral sprays. My
mother-in-law got her guru to bless the ring before I left for the States.

He looks disconcerted. He's used to a different role. He's the knowing,
suspicious one in the family. He seems to be sulking, and finally he comes
out with it. 'You've said nothing about my new glasses.' I compliment
him on the glasses, how chic and Western-executive they make him look.
But I can't help the other things, necessities until he learns the ropes.
I handle the money, buy the tickets. I don't know if this makes me
unhappy.

Charity drives her Nissan upstate, so for two weeks we are to have the
apartment to ourselves. This is more privacy than we ever had in India.
No parents, no servants, to keep us modest. We play at housekeeping.
Imre has lent us a hibachi, and I grill saffron chicken breasts. My husband marvels at the size of the Perdue hens. 'They're big like peacocks,
no? These Americans, they're really something!' He tries out pizzas,
burgers, McNuggets. He chews. He explores. He judges. He loves it all,
fears nothing, feels at home in the summer odors, the clutter of Manhattan
streets. Since he thinks that the American palate is bland, he carries a
bottle of red peppers in his pocket. I wheel a shopping cart down the
aisles of the neighborhood Grand Union, and he follows, swiftly, greed-
ily. He picks up hair rinses and high-protein diet powders. There's so
much I already take for granted.

One night, Imre stops by. He wants us to go with him to a movie. In
his work shirt and red leather tie, he looks arty or strung out. It's only
been a week, but I feel as though I am really seeing him for the first time.
The yellow hair worn very short at the sides, the wide, narrow lips. He's
a good-looking man, but self-conscious, almost arrogant. He's picked the
movie we should see. He always tells me what to see, what to read. He
buys the *Voice*. He's a natural avant-gardist. For tonight he's chosen
Numéro Deux.

'Is it a musical?' my husband asks. The Radio City Music Hall is on his list of sights to see. He's read up on the history of the Rockettes. He doesn't catch Imre's sympathetic wink.

Guilt, shame, loyalty. I long to be ungracious, not ingratiate myself with both men.

That night my husband calculates in rupees the money we've wasted on Godard. 'That refugee fellow, Nagy, must have a screw loose in his head. I paid very steep price for dollars on the black market.'

Some afternoons we go shopping. Back home we hated shopping, but now it is a lovers' project. My husband's shopping list startles me. I feel I am just getting to know him. Maybe, like Imre, freed from the dignities of old-world culture, he too could get drunk and squirt Cheez Whiz on a guest. I watch him dart into stores in his gleaming leather shoes. Jockey shorts on sale in outdoor bins on Broadway entrance him. White tube socks with different bands of color delight him. He looks for microcassettes, for anything small and electronic and smuggleable. He needs a garment bag. He calls it a 'wardrobe', and I have to translate.

'All of New York is having sales, no?'

My heart speeds watching him this happy. It's the third week in August, almost the end of summer, and the city smells ripe, it cannot bear more heat, more money, more energy.

'This is so smashing! The prices are so excellent!' Recklessly, my prudent husband signs away traveller's checks. How he intends to smuggle it all back I don't dare ask. With a microwave, he calculates, we could get rid of our cook.

This has to be love, I think. Charity, Eric, Phil: they may be experts on sex. My husband doesn't chase me around the sofa, but he pushes me down on Charity's battered cushions, and the man who has never entered the kitchen of our Ahmadabad house now comes toward me with a dish tub of steamy water to massage away the pavement heat.

Ten days into his vacation my husband checks out brochures for sight-seeing tours. Shortline, Grayline, Crossroads: his new vinyl briefcase is full of schedules and pamphlets. While I make pancakes out of a mix, he comparison-shops. Tour number one costs $10.95 and will give us the World Trade Center, Chinatown, and the United Nations. Tour number three would take us both uptown *and* downtown for $14.95, but my husband is absolutely sure he doesn't want to see Harlem. We settle for tour number four: Downtown and the Dame. It's offered by a new tour company with a small, dirty office at Eighth and Forty-eighth.

The sidewalk outside the office is colorful with tourists. My husband sends me in to buy the tickets because he has come to feel Americans don't understand his accent.

The dark man, Lebanese probably, behind the counter comes on too friendly. 'Come on, doll, make my day!' He won't say which tour is his. 'Number four? Honey, no! Look, you've wrecked me! Say you'll change your mind.' He takes two twenties and gives back change. He holds the tickets, forcing me to pull. He leans closer. 'I'm off after lunch.'

My husband must have been watching me from the sidewalk. 'What was the chap saying?' he demands. 'I told you not to wear pants. He thinks you are Puerto Rican. He thinks he can treat you with disrespect.'

The bus is crowded and we have to sit across the aisle from each other. The tour guide begins his patter on Forty-sixth. He looks like an actor, his hair bleached and blow-dried. Up close he must look middle-aged, but from where I sit his skin is smooth and his cheeks faintly red.

'Welcome to the Big Apple, folks.' The guide uses a microphone. 'Big Apple. That's what we native Manhattan degenerates call our city. Today we have guests from fifteen foreign countries and six states from this US of A. That makes the Tourist Bureau real happy. And let me assure you that while we may be the richest city in the richest country in the world, it's okay to tip your charming and talented attendant.' He laughs. Then he swings his hip out into the aisle and sings a song.

'And it's mighty fancy on old Delancey Street, you know. . . .'

My husband looks irritable. The guide is, as expected, a good singer. 'The bloody man should be giving us histories of buildings we are passing, no?' I pat his hand, the mood passes. He cranes his neck. Our window seats have both gone to Japanese. It's the tour of his life. Next to this, the quick business trips to Manchester and Glasgow pale.

'And tell me what street compares to Mott Street, in July. . . .'

The guide wants applause. He manages a derisive laugh from the Americans up front. He's working the aisles now. 'I coulda been somebody, right? I coulda been a star!' Two or three of us smile, those of us who recognize the parody. He catches my smile. The sun is on his harsh, bleached hair. 'Right, your highness? Look, we gotta maharani with us! Couldn't I have been a star?'

'Right!' I say, my voice coming out a squeal. I've been trained to adapt; what else can I say?

We drive through traffic past landmark office buildings and churches. The guide flips his hands. 'Art deco,' he keeps saying. I hear him confide to one of the Americans: 'Beats me. I went to a cheap guide's school.' My husband wants to know more about this Art Deco, but the guide sings another song.

'We made a foolish choice,' my husband grumbles. 'We are sitting in the bus only. We're not going into famous buildings.' He scrutinizes the pamphlets in his jacket pocket. I think, at least it's air-conditioned in here. I could sit here in the cool shadows of the city forever.

Only five of us appear to have opted for the 'Downtown and the Dame' tour. The others will ride back uptown past the United Nations after we've been dropped off at the pier for the ferry to the Statue of Liberty.

An elderly European pulls a camera out of his wife's designer tote bag. He takes pictures of the boats in the harbor, the Japanese in kimonos eating popcorn, scavenging pigeons, me. Then, pushing his wife ahead of him, he climbs back on the bus and waves to us. For a second I feel terribly lost. I wish we were on the bus going back to the apartment. I know I'll not be able to describe any of this to Charity, or to Imre. I'm too proud to admit I went on a guided tour.

The view of the city from the Circle Line ferry is seductive, unreal. The skyline wavers out of reach, but never quite vanishes. The summer sun pushes through fluffy clouds and dapples the glass of office towers. My husband looks thrilled, even more than he had on the shopping trips down Broadway. Tourists and dreamers, we have spent our life's savings to see this skyline, this statue.

'Quick, take a picture of me!' my husband yells as he moves toward a gap of railings. A Japanese matron has given up her position in order to change film. 'Before the Twin Towers disappear!'

I focus, I wait for a large Oriental family to walk out of my range. My husband holds his pose tight against the railing. He wants to look relaxed, an international businessman at home in all the financial markets.

A bearded man slides across the bench toward me. 'Like this,' he says and helps me get my husband in focus. 'You want me to take the photo for you?' His name, he says, is Goran. He is Goran from Yugoslavia, as though that were enough for tracking him down. Imre from Hungary. Panna from India. He pulls the old Leica out of my hand, signaling the Orientals to beat it, and clicks away. 'I'm a photographer,' he says. He could have been a camera thief. That's what my husband would have assumed. Somehow, I trusted. 'Get you a beer?' he asks.

'I don't. Drink, I mean. Thank you very much.' I say those last words very loud, for everyone's benefit. The odd bottles of Soave with Imre don't count.

'Too bad.' Goran gives back the camera.

'Take one more!' my husband shouts from the railing. 'Just to be sure!'

The island itself disappoints. The Lady has brutal scaffolding holding her in. The museum is closed. The snack bar is dirty and expensive. My husband reads out the prices to me. He orders two french fries and two Cokes. We sit at picnic tables and wait for the ferry to take us back.

'What was that hippie chap saying?'

As if I could say. A day-care center has brought its kids, at least forty of them, to the island for the day. The kids, all wearing name tags, run around us. I can't help noticing how many are Indian. Even a Patel, probably a Bhatt if I looked hard enough. They toss hamburger bits at pigeons. They kick styrofoam cups. The pigeons are slow, greedy, persistent. I have to shoo one off the table top. I don't think my husband thinks about our son.

'What hippie?'

'The one on the boat. With the beard and the hair.'

My husband doesn't look at me. He shakes out his paper napkin and tries to protect his french fries from pigeon feathers.

'Oh, him. He said he was from Dubrovnik.' It isn't true, but I don't want trouble.

'What did he say about Dubrovnik?'

I know enough about Dubrovnik to get by. Imre's told me about it. And about Mostar and Zagreb. In Mostar white Muslims sing the call to prayer. I would like to see that before I die: white Muslims. Whole peoples have moved before me; they've adapted. The night Imre told me about Mostar was also the night I saw my first snow in Manhattan. We'd walked down to Chelsea from Columbia. We'd walked and talked and I hadn't felt tired at all.

'You're too innocent,' my husband says. He reaches for my hand. 'Panna,' he cries with pain in his voice, and I am brought back from perfect, floating memories of snow, 'I've come to take you back. I have seen how men watch you.'

'What?'

'Come back, now. I have tickets. We have all the things we will ever need. I can't live without you.'

A little girl with wiry braids kicks a bottle cap at his shoes. The pigeons wheel and scuttle around us. My husband covers his fries with spread-out fingers. 'No kicking,' he tells the girl. Her name, Beulah, is printed in green ink on a heart-shaped name tag. He forces a smile, and Beulah smiles back. Then she starts to flap her arms. She flaps, she hops. The pigeons go crazy for fries and scraps.

'Special ed. course is two years,' I remind him. 'I can't go back.'

My husband picks up our trays and throws them into the garbage before I can stop him. He's carried disposability a little too far. 'We've been taken,' he says, moving toward the dock, though the ferry will not arrive for another twenty minutes. 'The ferry costs only two dollars

round-trip per person. We should have chosen tour number one for
$10.95 instead of tour number four for $14.95.'

With my Lebanese friend, I think. 'But this way we don't have to
worry about cabs. The bus will pick us up at the pier and take us back to
midtown. Then we can walk home.'

'New York is full of cheats and whatnot. Just like Bombay.' He is not
accusing me of infidelity. I feel dread all the same.

That night, after we've gone to bed, the phone rings. My husband listens,
then hands the phone to me. 'What is this woman saying?' He turns on
the pink Macy's lamp by the bed. 'I am not understanding these Negro
people's accents.'

The operator repeats the message. It's a cable from one of the directors
of Lakshmi Cotton Mills. 'Massive violent labor confrontation anticipated. Stop. Return posthaste. Stop. Cable flight details. Signed Kantilal
Shah.'

'It's not your factory,' I say. 'You're supposed to be on vacation.'

'So, you are worrying about me? Yes? You reject my heartfelt wishes
but you worry about me?' He pulls me close, slips the straps of my
nightdress off my shoulder. 'Wait a minute.'

I wait, unclothed, for my husband to come back to me. The water is
running in the bathroom. In the ten days he has been here he has learned
American rites: deodorants, fragrances. Tomorrow morning he'll call Air
India; tomorrow evening he'll be on his way back to Bombay. Tonight I
should make up to him for my years away, the gutted trucks, the degree
I'll never use in India. I want to pretend with him that nothing has
changed.

In the mirror that hangs on the bathroom door, I watch my naked body
turn, the breasts, the thighs glow. The body's beauty amazes. I stand here
shameless, in ways he has never seen me. I am free, afloat, watching
somebody else.

AMY TAN

A Pair of Tickets

❧

The minute our train leaves the Hong Kong border and enters Shenzhen, China, I feel different. I can feel the skin on my forehead tingling, my blood rushing through a new course, my bones aching with a familiar old pain. And I think, My mother was right. I am becoming Chinese.

'Cannot be helped,' my mother said when I was fifteen and had vigorously denied that I had any Chinese whatsoever below my skin. I was a sophomore at Galileo High in San Francisco, and all my Caucasian friends agreed: I was about as Chinese as they were. But my mother had studied at a famous nursing school in Shanghai, and she said she knew all about genetics. So there was no doubt in her mind, whether I agreed or not: Once you are born Chinese, you cannot help but feel and think Chinese.

'Someday you will see,' said my mother. 'It is in your blood, waiting to be let go.'

And when she said this, I saw myself transforming like a werewolf, a mutant tag of DNA suddenly triggered, replicating itself insidiously into a *syndrome*, a cluster of telltale Chinese behaviors, all those things my mother did to embarrass me—haggling with store owners, pecking her mouth with a toothpick in public, being color-blind to the fact that lemon yellow and pale pink are not good combinations for winter clothes.

But today I realize I've never really known what it means to be Chinese. I am thirty-six years old. My mother is dead and I am on a train, carrying with me her dreams of coming home. I am going to China.

We are first going to Guangzhou, my seventy-two-year-old father, Canning Woo, and I, where we will visit his aunt, whom he has not seen since he was ten years old. And I don't know whether it's the prospect of seeing his aunt or if it's because he's back in China, but now he looks like he's a young boy, so innocent and happy I want to button his sweater and pat his head. We are sitting across from each other, separated by a little table with two cold cups of tea. For the first time I can ever remember, my father has tears in his eyes, and all he is seeing out the train window is a sectioned field of yellow, green, and brown, a narrow canal flanking the tracks, low rising hills, and three people in blue jackets riding an ox-driven cart on this early October morning. And I can't help myself. I also have misty eyes, as if I had seen this a long, long time ago, and had almost forgotten.

In less than three hours, we will be in Guangzhou, which my guide-book tells me is how one properly refers to Canton these days. It seems all the cities I have heard of, except Shanghai, have changed their spellings. I think they are saying China has changed in other ways as well. Chung-king is Chongqing. And Kweilin is Guilin. I have looked these names up, because after we see my father's aunt in Guangzhou, we will catch a plane to Shanghai, where I will meet my two half-sisters for the first time.

They are my mother's twin daughters from her first marriage, little babies she was forced to abandon on a road as she was fleeing Kweilin for Chungking in 1944. That was all my mother had told me about these daughters, so they had remained babies in my mind, all these years, sitting on the side of a road, listening to bombs whistling in the distance while sucking their patient red thumbs.

And it was only this year that someone found them and wrote with this joyful news. A letter came from Shanghai, addressed to my mother. When I first heard about this, that they were alive, I imagined my iden-tical sisters transforming from little babies into six-year-old girls. In my mind, they were seated next to each other at a table, taking turns with the fountain pen. One would write a neat row of characters: *Dearest Mama. We are alive.* She would brush back her wispy bangs and hand the other sister the pen, and she would write: *Come get us. Please hurry.*

Of course they could not know that my mother had died three months before, suddenly, when a blood vessel in her brain burst. One minute she was talking to my father, complaining about the tenants upstairs, schem-ing how to evict them under the pretense that relatives from China were moving in. The next minute she was holding her head, her eyes squeezed shut, groping for the sofa, and then crumpling softly to the floor with fluttering hands.

So my father had been the first one to open the letter, a long letter it turned out. And they did call her Mama. They said they always revered her as their true mother. They kept a framed picture of her. They told her about their life, from the time my mother last saw them on the road leaving Kweilin to when they were finally found.

And the letter had broken my father's heart so much—these daughters calling my mother from another life he never knew—that he gave the letter to my mother's old friend Auntie Lindo and asked her to write back and tell my sisters, in the gentlest way possible, that my mother was dead.

But instead Auntie Lindo took the letter to the Joy Luck Club and discussed with Auntie Ying and Auntie An-mei what should be done, because they had known for many years about my mother's search for her twin daughters, her endless hope. Auntie Lindo and the others cried over this double tragedy, of losing my mother three months before, and now again. And so they couldn't help but think of some miracle, some possible way of reviving her from the dead, so my mother could fulfill her dream.

So this is what they wrote to my sisters in Shanghai:

Dearest Daughters, I too have never forgotten you in my memory or in my heart. I never gave up hope that we would see each other again in a joyous reunion. I am only sorry it has been too long. I want to tell you everything about my life since I last saw you. I want to tell you this when our family comes to see you in China. . . .

They signed it with my mother's name.

It wasn't until all this had been done that they first told me about my sisters, the letter they received, the one they wrote back.

'They'll think she's coming, then,' I murmured. And I had imagined my sisters now being ten or eleven, jumping up and down, holding hands, their pigtails bouncing, excited that their mother—*their* mother— was coming, whereas my mother was dead.

'How can you say she is not coming in a letter?' said Auntie Lindo. 'She is their mother. She is your mother. You must be the one to tell them. All these years, they have been dreaming of her.' And I thought she was right.

But then I started dreaming, too, of my mother and my sisters and how it would be if I arrived in Shanghai. All these years, while they waited to be found, I had lived with my mother and then had lost her. I imagined seeing my sisters at the airport. They would be standing on their tiptoes, looking anxiously, scanning from one dark head to another as we got off the plane. And I would recognize them instantly, their faces with the identical worried look.

'*Jyejye, Jyejye*. Sister, Sister. We are here,' I saw myself saying in my poor version of Chinese.

'Where is Mama?' they would say, and look around, still smiling, two flushed and eager faces. 'Is she hiding?' And this would have been like my mother, to stand behind just a bit, to tease a little and make people's patience pull a little on their hearts. I would shake my head and tell my sisters she was not hiding.

'Oh, that must be Mama, no?' one of my sisters would whisper excitedly, pointing to another small woman completely engulfed in a tower of presents. And that, too, would have been like my mother, to bring mountains of gifts, food, and toys for children—all bought on sale—shunning thanks, saying the gifts were nothing, and later turning the labels over to show my sisters, 'Calvin Klein, 100% wool'.

I imagined myself starting to say, 'Sisters, I am sorry, I have come alone . . .' and before I could tell them—they could see it in my face—they were wailing, pulling their hair, their lips twisted in pain, as they ran away from me. And then I saw myself getting back on the plane and coming home.

After I had dreamed this scene many times—watching their despair turn from horror into anger—I begged Auntie Lindo to write another letter. And at first she refused.

'How can I say she is dead? I cannot write this,' said Auntie Lindo with a stubborn look.

'But it's cruel to have them believe she's coming on the plane,' I said. 'When they see it's just me, they'll hate me.'

'Hate you? Cannot be.' She was scowling. 'You are their own sister, their only family.'

'You don't understand,' I protested.

'What I don't understand?' she said.

And I whispered, 'They'll think I'm responsible, that she died because I didn't appreciate her.'

And Auntie Lindo looked satisfied and sad at the same time, as if this were true and I had finally realized it. She sat down for an hour, and when she stood up she handed me a two-page letter. She had tears in her eyes. I realized that the very thing I had feared, she had done. So even if she had written the news of my mother's death in English, I wouldn't have had the heart to read it.

'Thank you,' I whispered.

The landscape has become gray, filled with low flat cement buildings, old factories, and then tracks and more tracks filled with trains like ours passing by in the opposite direction. I see platforms crowded with people wearing drab Western clothes, with spots of bright colors: little children wearing pink and yellow, red and peach. And there are soldiers in olive green and red, and old ladies in gray tops and pants that stop mid-calf. We are in Guangzhou.

Before the train even comes to a stop, people are bringing down their belongings from above their seats. For a moment there is a dangerous shower of heavy suitcases laden with gifts to relatives, half-broken boxes wrapped in miles of string to keep the contents from spilling out, plastic bags filled with yarn and vegetables and packages of dried mushrooms, and camera cases. And then we are caught in a stream of people rushing, shoving, pushing us along, until we find ourselves in one of a dozen lines waiting to go through customs. I feel as if I were getting on the number 30 Stockton bus in San Francisco. I am in China, I remind myself. And somehow the crowds don't bother me. It feels right. I start pushing too.

I take out the declaration forms and my passport. 'Woo', it says at the top, and below that, 'June May', who was born in 'California, USA', in 1951. I wonder if the customs people will question whether I'm the same person as in the passport photo. In this picture, my chin-length hair is swept back and artfully styled. I am wearing false eyelashes, eye shadow, and lip liner. My cheeks are hollowed out by bronze blusher. But I had not expected the heat in October. And now my hair hangs limp with the humidity. I wear no makeup; in Hong Kong my mascara had melted into dark circles and everything else had felt like layers of grease. So today my face is plain, unadorned except for a thin mist of shiny sweat on my forehead and nose.

Even without makeup, I could never pass for true Chinese. I stand five-foot-six, and my head pokes above the crowd so that I am eye level only with other tourists. My mother once told me my height came from my grandfather, who was a northerner, and may have even had some Mongol blood. 'This is what your grandmother once told me,' explained my mother. 'But now it is too late to ask her. They are all dead, your grandparents, your uncles, and their wives and children, all killed in the war, when a bomb fell on our house. So many generations in one instant.'

She had said this so matter-of-factly that I thought she had long since gotten over any grief she had. And then I wondered how she knew they were all dead.

'Maybe they left the house before the bomb fell,' I suggested.

'No,' said my mother. 'Our whole family is gone. It is just you and I.'

'But how do you know? Some of them could have escaped.'

'Cannot be,' said my mother, this time almost angrily. And then her frown was washed over by a puzzled blank look, and she began to talk as if she were trying to remember where she had misplaced something. 'I went back to that house. I kept looking up to where the house used to be. And it wasn't a house, just the sky. And below, underneath my feet, were four stories of burnt bricks and wood, all the life of our house. Then off to the side I saw things blown into the yard, nothing valuable. There was a bed someone used to sleep in, really just a metal frame twisted up at one corner. And a book, I don't know what kind, because every page had turned black. And I saw a teacup which was unbroken but filled with ashes. And then I found my doll, with her hands and legs broken, her hair burned off. . . . When I was a little girl, I had cried for that doll, seeing it all alone in the store window, and my mother had bought it for me. It was an American doll with yellow hair. It could turn its legs and arms.

The eyes moved up and down. And when I married and left my family home, I gave the doll to my youngest niece, because she was like me. She cried if that doll was not with her always. Do you see? If she was in the house with that doll, her parents were there, and so everybody was there, waiting together, because that's how our family was.'

The woman in the customs booth stares at my documents, then glances at me briefly, and with two quick movements stamps everything and sternly nods me along. And soon my father and I find ourselves in a large area filled with thousands of people and suitcases. I feel lost and my father looks helpless.

'Excuse me,' I say to a man who looks like an American. 'Can you tell me where I can get a taxi?' He mumbles something that sounds Swedish or Dutch.

'Syau Yen! Syau Yen!' I hear a piercing voice shout from behind me. An old woman in a yellow knit beret is holding up a pink plastic bag filled with wrapped trinkets. I guess she is trying to sell us something. But my father is staring down at this tiny sparrow of a woman, squinting into her eyes. And then his eyes widen, his face opens up and he smiles like a pleased little boy.

'*Aiyi! Aiyi!*'—Auntie Auntie!—he says softly.

'Syau Yen!' coos my great-aunt. I think it's funny she has just called my father 'Little Wild Goose'. It must be his baby milk name, the name used to discourage ghosts from stealing children.

They clasp each other's hands—they do not hug—and hold on like this, taking turns saying, 'Look at you! You are so old. Look how old you've become!' They are both crying openly, laughing at the same time, and I bite my lip, trying not to cry. I'm afraid to feel their joy. Because I am thinking how different our arrival in Shanghai will be tomorrow, how awkward it will feel.

Now Aiyi beams and points to a Polaroid picture of my father. My father had wisely sent pictures when he wrote and said we were coming. See how smart she was, she seems to intone as she compares the picture to my father. In the letter, my father had said we would call her from the hotel once we arrived, so this is a surprise, that they've come to meet us. I wonder if my sisters will be at the airport.

It is only then that I remember the camera. I had meant to take a picture of my father and his aunt the moment they met. It's not too late.

'Here, stand together over here,' I say, holding up the Polaroid. The camera flashes and I hand them the snapshot. Aiyi and my father still stand close together, each of them holding a corner of the picture, watching as their images begin to form. They are almost reverentially quiet.

Aiyi is only five years older than my father, which makes her around seventy-seven. But she looks ancient, shrunken, a mummified relic. Her thin hair is pure white, her teeth are brown with decay. So much for stories of Chinese women looking young forever, I think to myself.

Now Aiyi is crooning to me: '*Jandale*'. So big already. She looks up at me, at my full height, and then peers into her pink plastic bag—her gifts to us, I have figured out—as if she is wondering what she will give to me, now that I am so old and big. And then she grabs my elbow with her sharp pincerlike grasp and turns me around. A man and woman in their fifties are shaking hands with my father, everybody smiling and saying, 'Ah! Ah!' They are Aiyi's oldest son and his wife, and standing next to them are four other people, around my age, and a little girl who's around ten. The introductions go by so fast, all I know is that one of them is Aiyi's grandson, with his wife, and the other is her granddaughter, with her husband. And the little girl is Lili, Aiyi's great-granddaughter.

Aiyi and my father speak the Mandarin dialect from their childhood, but the rest of the family speaks only the Cantonese of their village. I understand only Mandarin but can't speak it that well. So Aiyi and my father gossip unrestrained in Mandarin, exchanging news about people from their old village. And they stop only occasionally to talk to the rest of us, sometimes in Cantonese, sometimes in English.

'Oh, it is as I suspected,' says my father, turning to me. 'He died last summer.' And I already understood this. I just don't know who this person, Li Gong, is. I feel as if I were in the United Nations and the translators had run amok.

'Hello,' I say to the little girl. 'My name is Jing-mei.' But the little girl squirms to look away, causing her parents to laugh with embarrassment. I try to think of Cantonese words I can say to her, stuff I learned from friends in Chinatown, but all I can think of are swear words, terms for bodily functions, and short phrases like 'tastes good', 'tastes like garbage', and 'she's really ugly'. And then I have another plan: I hold up the Polaroid camera, beckoning Lili with my finger. She immediately jumps forward, places one hand on her hip in the manner of a fashion model, juts out her chest, and flashes me a toothy smile. As soon as I take the picture she is standing next to me, jumping and giggling every few seconds as she watches herself appear on the greenish film.

By the time we hail taxis for the ride to the hotel, Lili is holding tight onto my hand, pulling me along.

In the taxi, Aiyi talks nonstop, so I have no chance to ask her about the different sights we are passing by.

'You wrote and said you would come only for one day,' says Aiyi to my father in an agitated tone. 'One day! How can you see your family in one day! Toishan is many hours' drive from Guangzhou. And this idea to call us when you arrive. This is nonsense. We have no telephone.'

My heart races a little. I wonder if Auntie Lindo told my sisters we would call from the hotel in Shanghai?

Aiyi continues to scold my father. 'I was so beside myself, ask my son, almost turned heaven and earth upside down trying to think of a way! So we decided the best was for us to take the bus from Toishan and come into Guangzhou—meet you right from the start.'

And now I am holding my breath as the taxi driver dodges between trucks and buses, honking his horn constantly. We seem to be on some sort of long freeway overpass, like a bridge above the city. I can see row after row of apartments, each floor cluttered with laundry hanging out to dry on the balcony. We pass a public bus, with people jammed in so tight their faces are nearly wedged against the window. Then I see the skyline of what must be downtown Guangzhou. From a distance, it looks like a major American city, with highrises and construction going on everywhere. As we slow down in the more congested part of the city, I see scores of little shops, dark inside, lined with counters and shelves. And then there is a building, its front laced with scaffolding made of bamboo poles held together with plastic strips. Men and women are standing on narrow platforms, scraping the sides, working without safety straps or helmets. Oh, would OSHA have a field day here, I think.

Aiyi's shrill voice rises up again: 'So it is a shame you can't see our village, our house. My sons have been quite successful, selling our vegetables in the free market. We had enough these last few years to build a big house, three stories, all of new brick, big enough for our whole family and then some. And every year, the money is even better. You Americans aren't the only ones who know how to get rich!'

The taxi stops and I assume we've arrived, but then I peer out at what looks like a grander version of the Hyatt Regency. 'This is communist China?' I wonder out loud. And then I shake my head toward my father. 'This must be the wrong hotel.' I quickly pull out our itinerary, travel tickets, and reservations. I had explicitly instructed my travel agent to choose something inexpensive, in the thirty-to-forty-dollar range. I'm sure of this. And there it says on our itinerary: Garden Hotel, Huanshi Dong Lu. Well, our travel agent had better be prepared to eat the extra, that's all I have to say.

The hotel is magnificent. A bellboy complete with uniform and sharp-creased cap jumps forward and begins to carry our bags into the lobby. Inside, the hotel looks like an orgy of shopping arcades and restaurants all encased in granite and glass. And rather than be impressed, I am worried about the expense, as well as the appearance it must give Aiyi, that we rich Americans cannot be without our luxuries even for one night.

But when I step up to the reservation desk, ready to haggle over this booking mistake, it is confirmed. Our rooms are prepaid, thirty-four dollars each. I feel sheepish, and Aiyi and the others seem delighted by our temporary surroundings. Lili is looking wide-eyed at an arcade filled with video games.

Our whole family crowds into one elevator, and the bellboy waves, saying he will meet us on the eighteenth floor. As soon as the elevator door shuts, everybody becomes very quiet, and when the door finally opens again, everybody talks at once in what sounds like relieved voices. I have the feeling Aiyi and the others have never been on such a long elevator ride.

Our rooms are next to each other and are identical. The rugs, drapes, bedspreads are all in shades of taupe. There's a color television with remote-control panels built into the lamp table between the two twin beds. The bathroom has marble walls and floors. I find a built-in wet bar with a small refrigerator stocked with Heineken beer, Coke Classic, and Seven-Up, mini-bottles of Johnnie Walker Red, Bacardi rum, and Smirnoff vodka, and packets of M & M's, honey-roasted cashews, and Cadbury chocolate bars. And again I say out loud, 'This is communist China?'

My father comes into my room. 'They decided we should just stay here and visit,' he says, shrugging his shoulders. 'They say, Less trouble that way. More time to talk.'

'What about dinner?' I ask. I have been envisioning my first real Chinese feast for many days already, a big banquet with one of those soups steaming out of a carved winter melon, chicken wrapped in clay, Peking duck, the works.

My father walks over and picks up a room service book next to a *Travel & Leisure* magazine. He flips through the pages quickly and then points to the menu. 'This is what they want,' says my father.

So it's decided. We are going to dine tonight in our rooms, with our family, sharing hamburgers, french fries, and apple pie à la mode.

Aiyi and her family are browsing the shops while we clean up. After a hot ride on the train, I'm eager for a shower and cooler clothes.

The hotel has provided little packets of shampoo which, upon opening, I discover is the consistency and color of hoisin sauce. This is more like it, I think. This is China. And I rub some in my damp hair.

Standing in the shower, I realize this is the first time I've been by myself in what seems like days. But instead of feeling relieved, I feel forlorn. I think about what my mother said, about activating my genes and becoming Chinese. And I wonder what she meant.

Right after my mother died, I asked myself a lot of things, things that couldn't be answered, to force myself to grieve more. It seemed as if I wanted to sustain my grief, to assure myself that I had cared deeply enough.

But now I ask the questions mostly because I want to know the answers. What was that pork stuff she used to make that had the texture of sawdust? What were the names of the uncles who died in Shanghai? What had she dreamt all these years about her other daughters? All the times when she got mad at me, was she really thinking about them? Did she wish I were they? Did she regret that I wasn't?

At one o'clock in the morning, I awake to tapping sounds on the window. I must have dozed off and now I feel my body uncramping itself. I'm sitting on the floor, leaning against one of the twin beds. Lili is lying next to me. The others are asleep, too, sprawled out on the beds and floor. Aiyi is seated at a little table, looking very sleepy. And my father is staring out the window, tapping his fingers on the glass. The last time I listened my father was telling Aiyi about his life since he last saw her. How he had gone to Yenching University, later got a post with a newspaper in Chungking, met my mother there, a young widow. How they later fled together to Shanghai to try to find my mother's family house, but there was nothing there. And then they traveled eventually to Canton and then to Hong Kong, then Haiphong and finally to San Francisco. . . .

'Suyuan didn't tell me she was trying all these years to find her daughters,' he is now saying in a quiet voice. 'Naturally, I did not discuss her daughters with her. I thought she was ashamed she had left them behind.'

'Where did she leave them?' asks Aiyi. 'How were they found?'

I am wide awake now. Although I have heard parts of this story from my mother's friends.

'It happened when the Japanese took over Kweilin,' says my father.

'Japanese in Kweilin?' says Aiyi. 'That was never the case. Couldn't be. The Japanese never came to Kweilin.'

'Yes, that is what the newspapers reported. I know this because I was working for the news bureau at the time. The Kuomintang often told us what we could say and could not say. But we knew the Japanese had come into Kwangsi Province. We had sources who told us how they had captured the Wuchang-Canton railway. How they were coming overland, making very fast progress, marching toward the provincial capital.'

Aiyi looks astonished. 'If people did not know this, how could Suyuan know the Japanese were coming?'

'An officer of the Kuomintang secretly warned her,' explains my father. 'Suyuan's husband also was an officer and everybody knew that officers and their families would be the first to be killed. So she gathered a few possessions and, in the middle of the night, she picked up her daughters and fled on foot. The babies were not even one year old.'

'How could she give up those babies!' sighs Aiyi. 'Twin girls. We have never had such luck in our family.' And then she yawns again.

'What were they named?' she asks. I listen carefully. I had been planning on using just the familiar 'Sister' to address them both. But now I want to know how to pronounce their names.

'They have their father's surname, Wang,' says my father. 'And their given names are Chwun Yu and Chwun Hwa.'

'What do the names mean?' I ask.

'Ah.' My father draws imaginary characters on the window. 'One means "Spring Rain", the other "Spring Flower",' he explains in English, 'because they born in the spring, and of course rain come before flower, same order these girls are born. Your mother like a poet, don't you think?'

I nod my head. I see Aiyi nod her head forward, too. But it falls forward and stays there. She is breathing deeply, noisily. She is asleep.

'And what does Ma's name mean?' I whisper.

'"Suyuan",' he says, writing more invisible characters on the glass. 'The way she write it in Chinese, it mean "Long-Cherished Wish". Quite a fancy name, not so ordinary like flower name. See this first character, it mean something like "Forever Never Forgotten". But there is another way to write "Suyuan". Sound exactly the same, but the meaning is opposite.' His finger creates the brushstrokes of another character. 'The first part look the same: "Never Forgotten". But the last part add to first part make the whole word mean "Long-Held Grudge". Your mother get angry with me, I tell her her name should be Grudge.'

My father is looking at me, moist-eyed. 'See, I pretty clever, too, hah?'

I nod, wishing I could find some way to comfort him. 'And what about my name,' I ask, 'what does "Jing-mei" mean?'

'Your name also special,' he says. I wonder if any name in Chinese is not something special. ' "Jing" like excellent *jing*. Not just good, it's something pure, essential, the best quality. *Jing* is good leftover stuff when you take impurities out of something like gold, or rice, or salt. So what is left—just pure essence. And "Mei", this is common *mei*, as in *meimei*, "younger sister".'

I think about this. My mother's long-cherished wish. Me, the younger sister who was supposed to be the essence of the others. I feed myself with the old grief, wondering how disappointed my mother must have been. Tiny Aiyi stirs suddenly, her head rolls and then falls back, her mouth opens as if to answer my question. She grunts in her sleep, tucking her body more closely into the chair.

'So why did she abandon those babies on the road?' I need to know, because now I feel abandoned too.

'Long time I wondered this myself,' says my father. 'But then I read that letter from her daughters in Shanghai now, and I talk to Auntie Lindo, all the others. And then I knew. No shame in what she done. None.'

'What happened?'

'Your mother running away—' begins my father.

'No, tell me in Chinese,' I interrupt. 'Really, I can understand.'

He begins to talk, still standing at the window, looking into the night.

After fleeing Kweilin, your mother walked for several days trying to find a main road. Her thought was to catch a ride on a truck or wagon, to catch enough rides until she reached Chungking, where her husband was stationed.

She had sewn money and jewelry into the lining of her dress, enough, she thought, to barter rides all the way. If I am lucky, she thought, I will not have to trade the heavy gold bracelet and jade ring. These were things from her mother, your grandmother.

By the third day, she had traded nothing. The roads were filled with people, everybody running and begging for rides from passing trucks. The trucks rushed by, afraid to stop. So your mother found no rides, only the start of dysentery pains in her stomach.

Her shoulders ached from the two babies swinging from scarf slings. Blisters grew on her palms from holding two leather suitcases. And then the blisters burst and began to bleed. After a while, she left the suitcases behind, keeping only the food and a few clothes. And later she also dropped the bags of wheat flour and rice and kept walking like this for many miles, singing songs to her little girls, until she was delirious with pain and fever.

Finally, there was not one more step left in her body. She didn't have the strength to carry those babies any farther. She slumped to the ground. She knew she would die of her sickness, or perhaps from thirst, from starvation, or from the Japanese, who she was sure were marching right behind her.

She took the babies out of the slings and sat them on the side of the road, then lay down next to them. You babies are so good, she said, so quiet. They smiled back, reaching their chubby hands for her, wanting to be picked up again. And then she knew she could not bear to watch her babies die with her.

She saw a family with three young children in a cart going by. 'Take my babies, I beg you,' she cried to them. But they stared back with empty eyes and never stopped.

She saw another person pass and called out again. This time a man turned around, and he had such a terrible expression—your mother said it looked like death itself—she shivered and looked away.

When the road grew quiet, she tore open the lining of her dress, and stuffed jewelry under the shirt of one baby and money under the other. She reached into her pocket and drew out the photos of her family, the picture of her father and mother, the picture of herself and her husband on their wedding day. And she wrote on the back of each the names of the babies and this same message: 'Please care for these babies with the money and valuables provided. When it is safe to come, if you bring them to Shanghai, 9 Weichang Lu, the Li family will be glad to give you a generous reward. Li Suyuan and Wang Fuchi.'

And then she touched each baby's cheek and told her not to cry. She would go down the road to find them some food and would be back. And without looking back, she walked down the road, stumbling and crying, thinking only of this one last hope, that her daughters would be found by a kindhearted person who would care for them. She would not allow herself to imagine anything else.

She did not remember how far she walked, which direction she went, when she fainted, or how she was found. When she awoke, she was in the back of a bouncing truck with several other sick people, all moaning. And she began to scream, thinking she was now on a journey to Buddhist hell. But the face of an American missionary lady bent over her and smiled, talking to her in a soothing language she did not understand. And yet she could somehow understand. She had been saved for no good reason, and it was now too late to go back and save her babies.

When she arrived in Chungking, she learned her husband had died two weeks before. She told me later she laughed when the officers told her this news, she was so delirious with madness and disease. To come so far, to lose so much and to find nothing.

I met her in a hospital. She was lying on a cot, hardly able to move, her dysentery had drained her so thin. I had come in for my foot, my missing toe, which was cut off by a piece of falling rubble. She was talking to herself, mumbling.

'Look at these clothes,' she said, and I saw she had on a rather unusual dress for wartime. It was silk satin, quite dirty, but there was no doubt it was a beautiful dress.

'Look at this face,' she said, and I saw her dusty face and hollow cheeks, her eyes shining back. 'Do you see my foolish hope?'

'I thought I had lost everything, except these two things,' she murmured. 'And I wondered which I would lose next. Clothes or hope? Hope or clothes?'

'But now, see here, look what is happening,' she said, laughing, as if all her prayers had been answered. And she was pulling hair out of her head as easily as one lifts new wheat from wet soil.

*

It was an old peasant woman who found them. 'How could I resist?' the peasant woman later told your sisters when they were older. They were still sitting obediently near where your mother had left them, looking like little fairy queens waiting for their sedan to arrive.

The woman, Mei Ching, and her husband, Mei Han, lived in a stone cave. There were thousands of hidden caves like that in and around Kweilin so secret that the people remained hidden even after the war ended. The Meis would come out of their cave every few days and forage for food supplies left on the road, and sometimes they would see something that they both agreed was a tragedy to leave behind. So one day they took back to their cave a delicately painted set of rice bowls, another day a little footstool with a velvet cushion and two new wedding blankets. And once, it was your sisters.

They were pious people, Muslims, who believed the twin babies were a sign of double luck, and they were sure of this when, later in the evening, they discovered how valuable the babies were. She and her husband had never seen rings and bracelets like those. And while they admired the pictures, knowing the babies came from a good family, neither of them could read or write. It was not until many months later that Mei Ching found someone who could read the writing on the back. By then, she loved these baby girls like her own.

In 1952 Mei Han, the husband, died. The twins were already eight years old, and Mei Ching now decided it was time to find your sisters' true family.

She showed the girls the picture of their mother and told them they had been born into a great family and she would take them back to see their true mother and grandparents. Mei Chang told them about the reward, but she swore she would refuse it. She loved these girls so much, she only wanted them to have what they were entitled to—a better life, a fine house, educated ways. Maybe the family would let her stay on as the girls' amah. Yes, she was certain they would insist.

Of course, when she found the place at 9 Weichang Lu, in the old French Concession, it was something completely different. It was the site of a factory building, recently constructed, and none of the workers knew what had become of the family whose house had burned down on that spot.

Mei Ching could not have known, of course, that your mother and I, her new husband, had already returned to that same place in 1945 in hopes of finding both her family and her daughters.

Your mother and I stayed in China until 1947. We went to many different cities—back to Kweilin, to Changsha, as far south as Kunming. She was always looking out of one corner of her eye for twin babies, then little girls. Later we went to Hong Kong, and when we finally left in 1949 for the United States, I think she was even looking for them on the boat. But when we arrived, she no longer talked about them. I thought, At last, they have died in her heart.

When letters could be openly exchanged between China and the United States, she wrote immediately to old friends in Shanghai and Kweilin. I did not know she did this. Auntie Lindo told me. But of course, by then, all the street names had changed. Some people had died, others had moved away. So it took many years to find a contact. And when she did find an old schoolmate's address and wrote asking her to look for her daughters, her friend wrote back and said this was impossible, like looking for a needle on the bottom of the ocean. How did she know her daughters were in Shanghai and not somewhere else in China? The friend, of course, did not ask, How do you know your daughters are still alive?

So her schoolmate did not look. Finding babies lost during the war was a matter of foolish imagination, and she had no time for that.

But every year, your mother wrote to different people. And this last year, I think she got a big idea in her head, to go to China and find them herself. I remember she told me, 'Canning, we should go, before it is too late, before we are too old.' And I told her we were already too old, it was already too late.

I just thought she wanted to be a tourist! I didn't know she wanted to go and look for her daughters. So when I said it was too late, that must have put a terrible thought in her head that her daughters might be dead. And I think this possibility grew bigger and bigger in her head, until it killed her.

Maybe it was your mother's dead spirit who guided her Shanghai schoolmate to find her daughters. Because after your mother died, the schoolmate saw your sisters, by chance, while shopping for shoes at the Number One Department Store on Nanjing Dong Road. She said it was like a dream, seeing these two women who looked so much alike, moving down the stairs together. There was something about their facial expressions that reminded the schoolmate of your mother.

She quickly walked over to them and called their names, which of course, they did not recognize at first, because Mei Ching had changed their names. But your mother's friend was so sure, she persisted. 'Are you not Wang Chwun Yu and Wang Chwun Hwa?' she asked them. And then these double-image women became very excited, because they remembered the names written on the back of an old photo, a photo of a young man and woman they still honored, as their much-loved first parents, who had died and become spirit ghosts still roaming the earth looking for them.

At the airport, I am exhausted. I could not sleep last night. Aiyi had followed me into my room at three in the morning, and she instantly fell asleep on one of the twin beds, snoring with the might of a lumberjack. I lay awake thinking about my mother's story, realizing how much I have never known about her, grieving that my sisters and I had both lost her.

And now at the airport, after shaking hands with everybody, waving good-bye, I think about all the different ways we leave people in this world. Cheerily waving good-bye to some at airports, knowing we'll never see each other again. Leaving others on the side of the road, hoping that we will. Finding my mother in my father's story and saying good-bye before I have a chance to know her better.

Aiyi smiles at me as we wait for our gate to be called. She is so old. I put one arm around her and one arm around Lili. They are the same size, it seems. And then it's time. As we wave good-bye one more time and enter the waiting area, I get the sense I am going from one funeral to another. In my hand I'm clutching a pair of tickets to Shanghai. In two hours we'll be there.

The plane takes off. I close my eyes. How can I describe to them in my broken Chinese about our mother's life? Where should I begin?

'Wake up, we're here,' says my father. And I awake with my heart pounding in my throat. I look out the window and we're already on the runway. It's gray outside.

And now I'm walking down the steps of the plane, onto the tarmac and toward the building. If only, I think, if only my mother had lived long enough to be the one walking toward them. I am so nervous I cannot even feel my feet. I am just moving somehow.

Somebody shouts, 'She's arrived!' And then I see her. Her short hair. Her small body. And that same look on her face. She has the back of her hand pressed hard against her mouth. She is crying as though she had gone through a terrible ordeal and were happy it is over.

And I know it's not my mother, yet it is the same look she had when

I was five and had disappeared all afternoon, for such a long time, that she was convinced I was dead. And when I miraculously appeared, sleepy-eyed, crawling from underneath my bed, she wept and laughed, biting the back of her hand to make sure it was true.

And now I see her again, two of her, waving, and in one hand there is a photo, the Polaroid I sent them. As soon as I get beyond the gate, we run toward each other, all three of us embracing, all hesitations and expectations forgotten.

'Mama, Mama,' we all murmur, as if she is among us.

My sisters look at me, proudly. '*Meimei jandale*,' says one sister proudly to the other. 'Little Sister has grown up.' I look at their faces again and I see no trace of my mother in them. Yet they still look familiar. And now I also see what part of me is Chinese. It is so obvious. It is my family. It is in our blood. After all these years, it can finally be let go.

My sisters and I stand, arms around each other, laughing and wiping the tears from each other's eyes. The flash of the Polaroid goes off and my father hands me the snapshot. My sisters and I watch quietly together, eager to see what develops.

The gray-green surface changes to the bright colors of our three images, sharpening and deepening all at once. And although we don't speak, I know we all see it: Together we look like our mother. Her same eyes, her same mouth, open in surprise to see, at last, her long-cherished wish.

ALICE MUNRO

Meneseteung

❧

I

Columbine, bloodroot,
And wild bergamot,
Gathering armfuls,
Giddily we go.

Offerings the book is called. Gold lettering on a dull-blue cover. The author's full name underneath: Almeda Joynt Roth. The local paper, the *Vidette*, referred to her as 'our poetess'. There seems to be a mixture of respect and contempt, both for her calling and for her sex—or for their predictable conjuncture. In the front of the book is a photograph, with the photographer's name in one corner, and the date: 1865. The book was published later, in 1873.

The poetess has a long face; a rather long nose; full, sombre dark eyes, which seem ready to roll down her cheeks like giant tears; a lot of dark hair gathered around her face in droopy rolls and curtains. A streak of gray hair plain to see, although she is, in this picture, only twenty-five. Not a pretty girl but the sort of woman who may age well, who probably won't get fat. She wears a tucked and braid-trimmed dark dress or jacket, with a lacy, floppy arrangement of white material—frills or a bow—filling the deep V at the neck. She also wears a hat, which might be made of velvet, in a dark color to match the dress. It's the untrimmed, shapeless hat, something like a soft beret, that makes me see artistic intentions, or at least a shy and stubborn eccentricity, in this young woman, whose long neck and forward-inclining head indicate as well that she is tall and slender and somewhat awkward. From the waist up, she looks like a young nobleman of another century. But perhaps it was the fashion.

'In 1854,' she writes in the preface to her book, 'my father brought us—my mother, my sister Catherine, my brother William, and me—to the wilds of Canada West (as it then was). My father was a harness-maker by trade, but a cultivated man who could quote by heart from the Bible, Shakespeare, and the writings of Edmund Burke. He prospered in this newly opened land and was able to set up a harness and leather-goods store, and after a year to build the comfortable house in which I live (alone) today. I was fourteen years old, the eldest of the children, when we came into this country from Kingston, a town whose handsome streets I have not seen again but often remember. My sister was eleven and my brother nine. The third summer that we lived here, my brother and sister were taken ill of a prevalent fever and died within a few days of each other. My dear mother did not regain her spirits after this blow to our family. Her health declined, and after another three years she died. I then became housekeeper to my father and was happy to make his home for twelve years, until he died suddenly one morning at his shop.

'From my earliest years I have delighted in verse and I have occupied myself—and sometimes allayed my griefs, which have been no more, I know, than any sojourner on earth must encounter—with many floundering efforts at its composition. My fingers, indeed, were always too clumsy for crochetwork, and those dazzling productions of embroidery which one sees often today—the overflowing fruit and flower baskets, the little Dutch boys, the bonneted maidens with their watering cans—have likewise proved to be beyond my skill. So I offer instead, as the product of my leisure hours, these rude posies, these ballads, couplets, reflections.'

Titles of some of the poems: 'Children at Their Games', 'The Gypsy Fair', 'A Visit to my Family', 'Angels in the Snow', 'Champlain at the Mouth of the Meneseteung', 'The Passing of the Old Forest', and 'A Garden Medley'. There are other, shorter poems, about birds and wildflowers and snowstorms. There is some comically intentioned dog-gerel about what people are thinking about as they listen to the sermon in church.

'Children at Their Games': The writer, a child, is playing with her brother and sister—one of those games in which children on different sides try to entice and catch each other. She plays on in the deepening twilight, until she realizes that she is alone, and much older. Still she hears the (ghostly) voices of her brother and sister calling. *Come over, come over, let Meda come over.* (Perhaps Almeda was called Meda in the family, or perhaps she shortened her name to fit the poem.)

'The Gypsy Fair': The Gypsies have an encampment near the town, a 'fair', where they sell cloth and trinkets, and the writer as a child is afraid that she may be stolen by them, taken away from her family. Instead, her family has been taken away from her, stolen by Gypsies she can't locate or bargain with.

'A Visit to My Family': A visit to the cemetery, a one-sided conversation.

'Angels in the Snow': The writer once taught her brother and sister to make 'angels' by lying down in the snow and moving their arms to create wing shapes. Her brother always jumped up carelessly, leaving an angel with a crippled wing. Will this be made perfect in Heaven, or will he be flying with his own makeshift, in circles?

'Champlain at the Mouth of the Meneseteung': This poem celebrates the popular, untrue belief that the explorer sailed down the eastern shore of Lake Huron and landed at the mouth of the major river.

'The Passing of the Old Forest': A list of all the trees—their names, appearance, and uses—that were cut down in the original forest, with a general description of the bears, wolves, eagles, deer, waterfowl.

'A Garden Medley': Perhaps planned as a companion to the forest poem. Catalogue of plants brought from European countries, with bits of history and legend attached, and final Canadianness resulting from this mixture.

The poems are written in quatrains or couplets. There are a couple of attempts at sonnets, but mostly the rhyme scheme is simple—*a b a b* or *a b c b*. The rhyme used is what was once called 'masculine' ('shore'/ 'before'), though once in a while it is 'feminine' ('quiver'/'river'). Are those terms familiar anymore? No poem is unrhymed.

II

> White roses cold as snow
> Bloom where those 'angels' lie.
> Do they but rest below
> Or, in God's wonder, fly?

In 1879, Almeda Roth was still living in the house at the corner of Pearl and Dufferin streets, the house her father had built for his family. The house is there today; the manager of the liquor store lives in it. It's covered with aluminum siding; a closed-in porch has replaced the veranda. The woodshed, the fence, the gates, the privy, the barn—all these are gone. A photograph taken in the eighteen-eighties shows them all in place. The house and fence look a little shabby, in need of paint, but perhaps that is just because of the bleached-out look of the brownish photograph. The lace-curtained windows look like white eyes. No big shade tree is in sight, and, in fact, the tall elms that overshadowed the town until the nineteen-fifties, as well as the maples that shade it now, are skinny young trees with rough fences around them to protect them from the cows. Without the shelter of those trees, there is a great exposure— back yards, clotheslines, woodpiles, patchy sheds and barns and privies— all bare, exposed, provisional-looking. Few houses would have anything like a lawn, just a patch of plantains and anthills and raked dirt. Perhaps petunias growing on top of a stump, in a round box. Only the main street is gravelled; the other streets are dirt roads, muddy or dusty according to season. Yards must be fenced to keep animals out. Cows are tethered in vacant lots or pastured in back yards, but sometimes they get loose. Pigs get loose, too, and dogs roam free or nap in a lordly way on the boardwalks. The town has taken root, it's not going to vanish, yet it still has some of the look of an encampment. And, like an encampment, it's busy all the time—full of people, who, within the town, usually walk wherever they're going; full of animals, which leave horse buns, cow pats, dog turds that ladies have to hitch up their skirts for; full of the noise of building and of drivers shouting at their horses and of the trains that come in several times a day.

I read about that life in the *Vidette*.

The population is younger than it is now, than it will ever be again. People past fifty usually don't come to a raw, new place. There are quite a few people in the cemetery already, but most of them died young, in accidents or childbirth or epidemics. It's youth that's in evidence in town. Children—boys—rove through the streets in gangs. School is compulsory for only four months a year, and there are lots of occasional jobs that even a child of eight or nine can do—pulling flax, holding horses, delivering groceries, sweeping the boardwalk in front of stores. A good deal of time they spend looking for adventures. One day they follow an old woman, a drunk nicknamed Queen Aggie. They get her into a wheelbarrow and trundle her all over town, then dump her into a ditch to sober her up. They also spend a lot of time around the railway station. They jump on shunting cars and dart between them and dare each other to take chances, which once in a while result in their getting maimed or killed. And they keep an eye out for any strangers coming into town. They follow them, offer to carry their bags, and direct them (for a five-cent piece) to a hotel. Strangers who don't look so prosperous are taunted and tormented. Speculation surrounds all of them—it's like a cloud of flies. Are they coming to town to start up a new business, to persuade people to invest in some scheme, to sell cures or gimmicks, to preach on the street corners? All these things are possible any day of the week. Be on your guard, the *Vidette* tells people. These are times of opportunity and danger. Tramps, confidence men, hucksters, shysters, plain thieves are travelling the roads, and particularly the railroads. Thefts are announced: money invested and never seen again, a pair of trousers taken from the clothesline, wood from the woodpile, eggs from the henhouse. Such incidents increase in the hot weather.

Hot weather brings accidents, too. More horses run wild then, upsetting buggies. Hands caught in the wringer while doing the washing, a man lopped in two at the sawmill, a leaping boy killed in a fall of lumber at the lumberyard. Nobody sleeps well. Babies wither with summer complaint, and fat people can't catch their breath. Bodies must be buried in a hurry. One day a man goes through the streets ringing a cowbell and calling, 'Repent! Repent!' It's not a stranger this time, it's a young man who works at the butcher shop. Take him home, wrap him in cold wet cloths, give him some nerve medicine, keep him in bed, pray for his wits. If he doesn't recover, he must go to the asylum.

Almeda Roth's house faces on Dufferin Street, which is a street of considerable respectability. On this street, merchants, a mill owner, an operator of salt wells have their houses. But Pearl Street, which her back windows overlook and her back gate opens onto, is another story. Work-men's houses are adjacent to hers. Small but decent row houses—that is all right. Things deteriorate toward the end of the block, and the next, last one becomes dismal. Nobody but the poorest people, the unrespectable and undeserving poor, would live there at the edge of a boghole (drained since then), called the Pearl Street Swamp. Bushy and luxuriant weeds grow there, makeshift shacks have been put up, there are piles of refuse and debris and crowds of runty children, slops are flung from doorways. The town tries to compel these people to build privies, but they would just as soon go in the bushes. If a gang of boys goes down there in search of adventure, it's likely they'll get more than they bargained for. It is said that even the town constable won't go down Pearl Street on a Saturday night. Almeda Roth has never walked past the row housing. In one of those houses lives the young girl Annie, who helps her with her housecleaning. That young girl herself, being a decent girl, has never walked down to the last block or the swamp. No decent woman ever would.

But that same swamp, lying to the east of Almeda Roth's house, presents a fine sight at dawn. Almeda sleeps at the back of the house. She keeps to the same bedroom she once shared with her sister Catherine—she would not think of moving to the large front bedroom, where her mother used to lie in bed all day, and which was later the solitary domain of her father. From her window she can see the sun rising, the swamp mist filling with light, the bulky, nearest trees floating against that mist and the trees behind turning transparent. Swamp oaks, soft maples, tamarack, bitternut.

III

Here where the river meets the
   inland sea,
Spreading her blue skirts from the
   solemn wood,

> I think of birds and beasts and
>   vanished men,
> Whose pointed dwellings on these
>   pale sands stood.

One of the strangers who arrived at the railway station a few years ago
was Jarvis Poulter, who now occupies the next house to Almeda Roth's—
separated from hers by a vacant lot, which he has bought, on Dufferin
Street. The house is plainer than the Roth house and has no fruit trees or
flowers planted around it. It is understood that this is a natural result of
Jarvis Poulter's being a widower and living alone. A man may keep his
house decent, but he will never—if he is a proper man—do much to
decorate it. Marriage forces him to live with more ornament as well as
sentiment, and it protects him, also, from the extremities of his own
nature—from a frigid parsimony or a luxuriant sloth, from squalor, and
from excessive sleeping or reading, drinking, smoking, or freethinking.

In the interests of economy, it is believed, a certain estimable gentleman of our
town persists in fetching water from the public tap and supplementing his fuel
supply by picking up the loose coal along the railway track. Does he think to
repay the town or the railway company with a supply of free salt?

This is the *Vidette*, full of shy jokes, innuendo, plain accusation that no
newspaper would get away with today. It's Jarvis Poulter they're talking
about—though in other passages he is spoken of with great respect, as
a civil magistrate, an employer, a churchman. He is close, that's all. An
eccentric, to a degree. All of which may be a result of his single condition,
his widower's life. Even carrying his water from the town tap and filling
his coal pail along the railway track. This is a decent citizen, prosperous:
a tall—slightly paunchy?—man in a dark suit with polished boots. A
beard? Black hair streaked with gray. A severe and self-possessed air,
and a large pale wart among the bushy hairs of one eyebrow? People
talk about a young, pretty, beloved wife, dead in childbirth or some
horrible accident, like a house fire or a railway disaster. There is no
ground for this, but it adds interest. All he has told them is that his wife
is dead.

He came to this part of the country looking for oil. The first oil well in
the world was sunk in Lambton County, south of here, in the eighteen-
fifties. Drilling for oil, Jarvis Poulter discovered salt. He set to work to
make the most of that. When he walks home from church with Almeda
Roth, he tells her about his salt wells. They are twelve hundred feet deep.
Heated water is pumped down into them, and that dissolves the salt.
Then the brine is pumped to the surface. It is poured into great evapor-
ator pans over slow, steady fires, so that the water is steamed off and the

pure, excellent salt remains. A commodity for which the demand will never fail.

'The salt of the earth,' Almeda says.

'Yes,' he says, frowning. He may think this disrespectful. She did not intend it so. He speaks of competitors in other towns who are following his lead and trying to hog the market. Fortunately, their wells are not drilled so deep, or their evaporating is not done so efficiently. There is salt everywhere under this land, but it is not so easy to come by as some people think.

Does this not mean, Almeda says, that there was once a great sea?

Very likely, Jarvis Poulter says. Very likely. He goes on to tell her about other enterprises of his—a brickyard, a limekiln. And he explains to her how this operates, and where the good clay is found. He also owns two farms, whose woodlots supply the fuel for his operations.

Among the couples strolling home from church on a recent, sunny Sabbath morning we noted a certain salty gentleman and literary lady, not perhaps in their first youth but by no means blighted by the frosts of age. May we surmise?

This kind of thing pops up in the *Vidette* all the time.

May they surmise, and is this courting? Almeda Roth has a bit of money, which her father left her, and she has her house. She is not too old to have a couple of children. She is a good enough housekeeper, with the tendency toward fancy iced cakes and decorated tarts that is seen fairly often in old maids. (Honorable mention at the Fall Fair.) There is nothing wrong with her looks, and naturally she is in better shape than most married women of her age, not having been loaded down with work and children. But why was she passed over in her earlier, more marriageable years, in a place that needs women to be partnered and fruitful? She was a rather gloomy girl—that may have been the trouble. The deaths of her brother and sister, and then of her mother, who lost her reason, in fact, a year before she died, and lay in her bed talking nonsense—those weighed on her, so she was not lively company. And all that reading and poetry—it seemed more of a drawback, a barrier, an obsession, in the young girl than in the middle-aged woman, who needed something, after all, to fill her time. Anyway, it's five years since her book was published, so perhaps she has got over that. Perhaps it was the proud, bookish father encouraging her?

Everyone takes it for granted that Almeda Roth is thinking of Jarvis Poulter as a husband and would say yes if he asked her. And she is thinking of him. She doesn't want to get her hopes up too much, she doesn't want to make a fool of herself. She would like a signal. If he attended church on Sunday evenings, there would be a chance, during some months of the year, to walk home after dark. He would carry a lantern. (There is as yet no street lighting in town.) He would swing the lantern to light the way in front of the lady's feet and observe their narrow and delicate shape. He might catch her arm as they step off the boardwalk. But he does not go to church at night.

Nor does he call for her, and walk with her *to* church on Sunday mornings. That would be a declaration. He walks her home, past his gate as far as hers; he lifts his hat then and leaves her. She does not invite him to come in—a woman living alone could never do such a thing. As soon as a man and woman of almost any age are alone together within four walls, it is assumed that anything may happen. Spontaneous combustion, instant fornication, an attack of passion. Brute instinct, triumph of the senses. What possibilities men and women must see in each other to infer such dangers. Or, believing in the dangers, how often they must think about the possibilities.

When they walk side by side, she can smell his shaving soap, the barber's oil, his pipe tobacco, the wool and linen and leather smell of his manly clothes. The correct, orderly, heavy clothes are like those she used to brush and starch and iron for her father. She misses that job—her father's appreciation, his dark, kind authority. Jarvis Poulter's garments, his smell, his movements all cause the skin on the side of her body next to him to tingle hopefully, and a meek shiver raises the hairs on her arms. Is this to be taken as a sign of love? She thinks of him coming into her— *their*—bedroom in his long underwear and his hat. She knows this outfit is ridiculous, but in her mind he does not look so; he has the solemn effrontery of a figure in a dream. He comes into the room and lies down on the bed beside her, preparing to take her in his arms. Surely he removes his hat? She doesn't know, for at this point a fit of welcome and submission overtakes her, a buried gasp. He would be her husband.

One thing she has noticed about married women, and that is how many of them have to go about creating their husbands. They have to start ascribing preferences, opinions, dictatorial ways. Oh, yes, they say, my husband is very particular. He won't touch turnips. He won't eat fried meat. (Or he will only eat fried meat.) He likes me to wear blue (brown) all the time. He can't stand organ music. He hates to see a woman go out bareheaded. He would kill me if I took one puff of tobacco. This way, bewildered, sidelong-looking men are made over, made into husbands, heads of households. Almeda Roth cannot imagine herself doing that. She wants a man who doesn't have to be made, who is firm already and determined and mysterious to her. She does not look for companionship. Men—except for her father—seem to her deprived in some way, incurious. No doubt that is necessary, so that they will do what they have to do. Would she herself, knowing that there was salt in the earth, discover how to get it out and sell it? Not likely. She would be thinking about the ancient sea. That kind of speculation is what Jarvis Poulter has, quite properly, no time for.

Instead of calling for her and walking her to church, Jarvis Poulter might make another, more venturesome declaration. He could hire a horse and take her for a drive out to the country. If he did this, she would be both glad and sorry. Glad to be beside him, driven by him, receiving this attention from him in front of the world. And sorry to have the countryside removed for her—filmed over, in a way, by his talk and preoccupations. The countryside that she has written about in her poems actually takes diligence and determination to see. Some things must be disregarded. Manure piles, of course, and boggy fields full of high, charred stumps, and great heaps of brush waiting for a good day for burning. The meandering creeks have been straightened, turned into ditches with high, muddy banks. Some of the crop fields and pasture fields are fenced with big, clumsy uprooted stumps; others are held in a crude stitchery of rail fences. The trees have all been cleared back to the woodlots. And the woodlots are all second growth. No trees along the roads or lanes or around the farmhouses, except a few that are newly planted, young and weedy-looking. Clusters of log barns—the grand barns that are to dominate the countryside for the next hundred years are just beginning to be built—and mean-looking log houses, and every four or five miles a ragged little settlement with a church and school and store and a blacksmith shop. A raw countryside just wrenched from the forest, but swarming with people. Every hundred acres is a farm, every farm has a family, most families have ten or twelve children. (This is the country that will send out wave after wave of settlers—it's already starting to send them—to northern Ontario and the West.) It's true that you can gather wildflowers in spring in the woodlots, but you'd have to walk through herds of horned cows to get to them.

IV

> The Gypsies have departed.
> Their camping-ground is bare.
> Oh, boldly would I bargain now
> At the Gypsy Fair.

Almeda suffers a good deal from sleeplessness, and the doctor has given her bromides and nerve medicine. She takes the bromides, but the drops gave her dreams that were too vivid and disturbing, so she has put the bottle by for an emergency. She told the doctor her eyeballs felt dry, like hot glass, and her joints ached. Don't read so much, he said, don't study; get yourself good and tired out with housework, take exercise. He believes that her troubles would clear up if she got married. He believes this in spite of the fact that most of his nerve medicine is prescribed for married women.

So Almeda cleans house and helps clean the church, she lends a hand to friends who are wallpapering or getting ready for a wedding, she bakes one of her famous cakes for the Sunday-school picnic. On a hot Saturday in August, she decides to make some grape jelly. Little jars of grape jelly will make fine Christmas presents, or offerings to the sick. But she started late in the day and the jelly is not made by nightfall. In fact, the hot pulp has just been dumped into the cheesecloth bag to strain out the juice. Almeda drinks some tea and eats a slice of cake with butter (a childish indulgence of hers), and that's all she wants for supper. She washes her hair at the sink and sponges off her body to be clean for Sunday. She doesn't light a lamp. She lies down on the bed with the window wide open and a sheet just up to her waist, and she does feel wonderfully tired. She can even feel a little breeze.

When she wakes up, the night seems fiery hot and full of threats. She lies sweating on her bed, and she has the impression that the noises she hears are knives and saws and axes—all angry implements chopping and jabbing and boring within her head. But it isn't true. As she comes further awake, she recognizes the sounds that she has heard sometimes before—the fracas of a summer Saturday night on Pearl Street. Usually the noise centers on a fight. People are drunk, there is a lot of protest and encouragement concerning the fight, somebody will scream, 'Murder!' Once, there was a murder. But it didn't happen in a fight. An old man was stabbed to death in his shack, perhaps for a few dollars he kept in the mattress.

She gets out of bed and goes to the window. The night sky is clear, with no moon and with bright stars. Pegasus hangs straight ahead, over the swamp. Her father taught her that constellation—automatically, she counts its stars. Now she can make out distinct voices, individual contributions to the row. Some people, like herself, have evidently been wakened from sleep. 'Shut up!' they are yelling. 'Shut up that caterwauling or I'm going to come down and tan the arse off yez!'

But nobody shuts up. It's as if there were a ball of fire rolling up Pearl Street, shooting off sparks—only the fire is noise; it's yells and laughter and shrieks and curses, and the sparks are voices that shoot off alone. Two voices gradually distinguish themselves—a rising and falling howling cry and a steady throbbing, low-pitched stream of abuse that contains all those words which Almeda associates with danger and depravity

and foul smells and disgusting sights. Someone—the person crying out,
'Kill me! Kill me now!'—is being beaten. A woman is being beaten. She
keeps crying, 'Kill me! Kill me!' and sometimes her mouth seems choked
with blood. Yet there is something taunting and triumphant about her
cry. There is something theatrical about it. And the people around are
calling out, 'Stop it! Stop that!' or 'Kill her! Kill her!' in a frenzy, as if at
the theatre or a sporting match or a prizefight. Yes, thinks Almeda, she
has noticed that before—it is always partly a charade with these people;
there is a clumsy sort of parody, an exaggeration, a missed connection. As
if anything they did—even a murder—might be something they didn't
quite believe but were powerless to stop.

Now there is the sound of something thrown—a chair, a plank?—and
of a woodpile or part of a fence giving way. A lot of newly surprised cries,
the sound of running, people getting out of the way, and the commotion
has come much closer. Almeda can see a figure in a light dress, bent over
and running. That will be the woman. She has got hold of something like
a stick of wood or a shingle, and she turns and flings it at the darker figure
running after her.

'Ah, go get her!' the voices cry. 'Go baste her one!'

Many fall back now; just the two figures come on and grapple, and
break loose again, and finally fall down against Almeda's fence. The sound
they make becomes very confused—gagging, vomiting, grunting, pounding. Then a long, vibrating, choking sound of pain and self-abasement,
self-abandonment, which could come from either or both of them.

Almeda has backed away from the window and sat down on the bed.
Is that the sound of murder she has heard? What is to be done, what is
she to do? She must light a lantern, she must go downstairs and light a
lantern—she must go out into the yard, she must go downstairs. Into the
yard. The lantern. She falls over on her bed and pulls the pillow to her
face. In a minute. The stairs, the lantern. She sees herself already down
there, in the back hall, drawing the bolt of the back door. She falls asleep.

She wakes, startled, in the early light. She thinks there is a big crow
sitting on her windowsill, talking in a disapproving but unsurprised way
about the events of the night before. 'Wake up and move the wheelbarrow!' it says to her, scolding, and she understands that it means
something else by 'wheelbarrow'—something foul and sorrowful. Then
she is awake and sees that there is no such bird. She gets up at once and
looks out the window.

Down against her fence there is a pale lump pressed—a body.

Wheelbarrow.

She puts a wrapper over her nightdress and goes downstairs. The front
rooms are still shadowy, the blinds down in the kitchen. Something goes

plop, plup, in a leisurely, censorious way, reminding her of the conversation of the crow. It's just the grape juice, straining overnight. She pulls the bolt and goes out the back door. Spiders have draped their webs over the doorway in the night, and the hollyhocks are drooping, heavy with dew. By the fence, she parts the sticky hollyhocks and looks down and she can see.

A woman's body heaped up there, turned on her side with her face squashed down into the earth. Almeda can't see her face. But there is a bare breast let loose, brown nipple pulled long like a cow's teat, and a bare haunch and leg, the haunch showing a bruise as big as a sunflower. The unbruised skin is grayish, like a plucked, raw drumstick. Some kind of nightgown or all-purpose dress she has on. Smelling of vomit. Urine, drink, vomit.

Barefoot, in her nightgown and flimsy wrapper, Almeda runs away. She runs around the side of her house between the apple trees and the veranda; she opens the front gate and flees down Dufferin Street to Jarvis Poulter's house, which is the nearest to hers. She slaps the flat of her hand many times against the door.

'There is the body of a woman,' she says when Jarvis Poulter appears at last. He is in his dark trousers, held up with braces, and his shirt is half unbuttoned, his face unshaven, his hair standing up on his head. 'Mr Poulter, excuse me. A body of a woman. At my back gate.'

He looks at her fiercely. 'Is she dead?'

His breath is dank, his face creased, his eyes bloodshot.

'Yes. I think murdered,' says Almeda. She can see a little of his cheerless front hall. His hat on a chair. 'In the night I woke up. I heard a racket down on Pearl Street,' she says, struggling to keep her voice low and sensible. 'I could hear this—pair. I could hear a man and a woman fighting.'

He picks up his hat and puts it on his head. He closes and locks the front door, and puts the key in his pocket. They walk along the boardwalk and she sees that she is in her bare feet. She holds back what she feels a need to say next—that she is responsible, she could have run out with a lantern, she could have screamed (but who needed more screams?), she could have beat the man off. She could have run for help then, not now.

They turn down Pearl Street, instead of entering the Roth yard. Of course the body is still there. Hunched up, half bare, the same as before.

Jarvis Poulter doesn't hurry or halt. He walks straight over to the body and looks down at it, nudges the leg with the toe of his boot, just as you'd nudge a dog or a sow.

'You,' he says, not too loudly but firmly, and nudges again.

Almeda tastes bile at the back of her throat.

'Alive,' says Jarvis Poulter, and the woman confirms this. She stirs, she grunts weakly.

Almeda says, 'I will get the doctor.' If she had touched the woman, if she had forced herself to touch her, she would not have made such a mistake.

'Wait,' says Jarvis Poulter. 'Wait. Let's see if she can get up.'

'Get up, now,' he says to the woman. 'Come on. Up, now. Up.'

Now a startling thing happens. The body heaves itself onto all fours, the head is lifted—the hair all matted with blood and vomit—and the woman begins to bang this head, hard and rhythmically, against Almeda Roth's picket fence. As she bangs her head, she finds her voice and lets out an openmouthed yowl, full of strength and what sounds like an anguished pleasure.

'Far from dead,' says Jarvis Poulter. 'And I wouldn't bother the doctor.'

'There's blood,' says Almeda as the woman turns her smeared face.

'From her nose,' he says. 'Not fresh.' He bends down and catches the horrid hair close to the scalp to stop the head-banging.

'You stop that, now,' he says. 'Stop it. Gwan home, now. Gwan home, where you belong.' The sound coming out of the woman's mouth has stopped. He shakes her head slightly, warning her, before he lets go of her hair. 'Gwan home!'

Released, the woman lunges forward, pulls herself to her feet. She can walk. She weaves and stumbles down the street, making intermittent, cautious noises of protest. Jarvis Poulter watches her for a moment to make sure that she's on her way. Then he finds a large burdock leaf, on which he wipes his hand. He says, 'There goes your dead body!'

The back gate being locked, they walk around to the front. The front gate stands open. Almeda still feels sick. Her abdomen is bloated; she is hot and dizzy.

'The front door is locked,' she says faintly. 'I came out by the kitchen.' If only he would leave her, she could go straight to the privy. But he follows. He follows her as far as the back door and into the back hall. He speaks to her in a tone of harsh joviality that she has never before heard from him. 'No need for alarm,' he says. 'It's only the consequences of drink. A lady oughtn't to be living alone so close to a bad neighborhood.' He takes hold of her arm just above the elbow. She can't open her mouth to speak to him, to say thank you. If she opened her mouth, she would retch.

What Jarvis Poulter feels for Almeda Roth at this moment is just what he has not felt during all those circumspect walks and all his own solitary calculations of her probable worth, undoubted respectability, adequate comeliness. He has not been able to imagine her as a wife. Now that is possible. He is sufficiently stirred by her loosened hair—prematurely gray but thick and soft—her flushed face, her light clothing, which nobody but a husband should see. And by her indiscretion, her agitation, her foolishness, her need?

'I will call on you later,' he says to her. 'I will walk with you to church.'

At the corner of Pearl and Dufferin streets last Sunday morning there was discovered, by a lady resident there, the body of a certain woman of Pearl Street, thought to be dead but only, as it turned out, dead drunk. She was roused from her heavenly—or otherwise—stupor by the firm persuasion of Mr Poulter, a neighbour and a Civil Magistrate, who had been summoned by the lady resident. Incidents of this sort, unseemly, troublesome, and disgraceful to our town, have of late become all too common.

V

> I sit at the bottom of sleep,
> As on the floor of the sea.
> And fanciful Citizens of the Deep
> Are graciously greeting me.

As soon as Jarvis Poulter has gone and she has heard her front gate close, Almeda rushes to the privy. Her relief is not complete, however, and she realizes that the pain and fullness in her lower body come from an accumulation of menstrual blood that has not yet started to flow. She closes and locks the back door. Then, remembering Jarvis Poulter's words about church, she writes on a piece of paper, 'I am not well, and wish to rest today.' She sticks this firmly into the outside frame of the little window in the front door. She locks that door, too. She is trembling, as if from a great shock or danger. But she builds a fire, so that she can make tea. She boils water, measures the tea leaves, makes a large pot of tea, whose steam and smell sicken her further. She pours out a cup while the tea is still quite weak and adds to it several dark drops of nerve medicine. She sits to drink it without raising the kitchen blind. There, in the middle of the floor, is the cheesecloth bag hanging on its broom handle between the two chairbacks. The grape pulp and juice has stained the swollen cloth a dark purple. *Plop, plup*, into the basin beneath. She can't sit and look at such a thing. She takes her cup, the teapot, and the bottle of medicine into the dining room.

She is still sitting there when the horses start to go by on the way to church, stirring up clouds of dust. The roads will be getting hot as ashes. She is there when the gate is opened and a man's confident steps sound on her veranda. Her hearing is so sharp she seems to hear the paper taken out of the frame and unfolded—she can almost hear him reading it, hear the words in his mind. Then the footsteps go the other way, down the steps. The gate closes. An image comes to her of tombstones—it makes her laugh. Tombstones are marching down the street on their little booted feet, their long bodies inclined forward, their expressions preoccupied and severe. The church bells are ringing.

Then the clock in the hall strikes twelve and an hour has passed.

The house is getting hot. She drinks more tea and adds more medicine. She knows that the medicine is affecting her. It is responsible for her extraordinary languor, her perfect immobility, her unresisting surrender to her surroundings. That is all right. It seems necessary.

Her surroundings—some of her surroundings—in the dining room are these: walls covered with dark-green garlanded wallpaper, lace curtains and mulberry velvet curtains on the windows, a table with a crocheted cloth and a bowl of wax fruit, a pinkish-gray carpet with nosegays of blue and pink roses, a sideboard spread with embroidered runners and holding various patterned plates and jugs and the silver tea things. A lot of things to watch. For every one of these patterns, decoration seems charged with life, ready to move and flow and alter. Or possibly to explode. Almeda Roth's occupation throughout the day is to keep an eye on them. Not to prevent their alteration so much as to catch them at it—to understand it, to be a part of it. So much is going on in this room that there is no need to leave it. There is not even the thought of leaving it.

Of course, Almeda in her observations cannot escape words. She may think she can, but she can't. Soon this glowing and swelling begins to suggest words—not specific words but a flow of words somewhere, just about ready to make themselves known to her. Poems, even. Yes, again, poems. Or one poem. Isn't that the idea—one very great poem that will contain everything and, oh, that will make all the other poems, the poems she has written, inconsequential, mere trial and error, mere rags? Stars and flowers and birds and trees and angels in the snow and dead children at twilight—that is not the half of it. You have to get in the obscene racket on Pearl Street and the polished toe of Jarvis Poulter's boot and the plucked-chicken haunch with its blue-black flower. Almeda is a long way now from human sympathies or fears or cozy household considerations. She doesn't think about what could be done for that woman or about keeping Jarvis Poulter's dinner warm and hanging his long underwear on the line. The basin of grape juice has overflowed and is running over her kitchen floor, staining the boards of the floor, and the stain will never come out.

She has to think of so many things at once—Champlain and the naked Indians and the salt deep in the earth, but as well as the salt the money, the money-making intent brewing forever in heads like Jarvis Poulter's. Also the brutal storms of winter and the clumsy and benighted deeds on Pearl Street. The changes of climate are often violent, and if you think about it there is no peace even in the stars. All this can be borne only if it is channelled into a poem, and the word 'channelled' is appropriate, because the name of the poem will be—it *is*—'The Meneseteung'. The name of the poem is the name of the river. No, in fact it is the river, the Meneseteung, that is the poem—with its deep holes and rapids and blissful pools under the summer trees and its grinding blocks of ice thrown up at the end of winter and its desolating spring floods. Almeda looks deep, deep into the river of her mind and into the tablecloth, and she sees the crocheted roses floating. They look bunchy and foolish, her mother's crocheted roses—they don't look much like real flowers. But their effort, their floating independence, their pleasure in their silly selves do seem to her so admirable. A hopeful sign. *Meneseteung*.

She doesn't leave the room until dusk, when she goes out to the privy again and discovers that she is bleeding, her flow has started. She will have to get a towel, strap it on, bandage herself up. Never before, in health, has she passed a whole day in her nightdress. She doesn't feel any particular anxiety about this. On her way through the kitchen, she walks through the pool of grape juice. She knows that she will have to mop it up, but not yet, and she walks upstairs leaving purple footprints and smelling her escaping blood and the sweat of her body that has sat all day in the closed hot room.

No need for alarm.

For she hasn't thought that crocheted roses could float away or that tombstones could hurry down the street. She doesn't mistake that for reality, and neither does she mistake anything else for reality, and that is how she knows that she is sane.

VI

> I dream of you by night,
> I visit you by day.
> Father, Mother,
> Sister, Brother,
> Have you no word to say?

April 22, 1903. At her residence, on Tuesday last, between three and four o'clock in the afternoon, there passed away a lady of talent and refinement whose pen, in days gone by, enriched our local literature with a volume of sensitive, eloquent verse. It is a sad misfortune that in later years the mind of this fine person had become somewhat clouded and her behaviour, in consequence, somewhat rash and unusual. Her attention to decorum and to the care and adornment of her person had suffered, to the degree that she had become, in the eyes of those unmindful of her former pride and daintiness, a familiar eccentric, or even, sadly, a figure of fun. But now all such lapses pass from memory and what is recalled is her excellent published verse, her labours in former days in the Sunday school, her dutiful care of her parents, her noble womanly nature, charitable concerns, and unfailing religious faith. Her last illness was of mercifully short duration. She caught cold, after having become thoroughly wet from a ramble in the Pearl Street bog. (It has been said that some urchins chased her into the water, and such is the boldness and cruelty of some of our youth, and their observed persecution of this lady, that the tale cannot be entirely discounted.) The cold developed into pneumonia, and she died, attended at the last by a former neighbour, Mrs Bert (Annie) Friels, who witnessed her calm and faithful end.

January, 1904. One of the founders of our community, an early maker and shaker of this town, was abruptly removed from our midst on Monday morning last, whilst attending to his correspondence in the office of his company. Mr Jarvis Poulter possessed a keen and lively commercial spirit, which was instrumental in the creation of not one but several local enterprises, bringing the benefits of industry, productivity, and employment to our town.

So the *Vidette* runs on, copious and assured. Hardly a death goes undescribed, or a life unevaluated.

I looked for Almeda Roth in the graveyard. I found the family stone. There was just one name on it—Roth. Then I noticed two flat stones in the ground, a distance of a few feet—six feet?—from the upright stone. One of these said 'Papa', the other 'Mama'. Farther out from these I found two other flat stones, with the names William and Catherine on them. I had to clear away some overgrowing grass and dirt to see the full name of Catherine. No birth or death dates for anybody, nothing about being dearly beloved. It was a private sort of memorializing, not for the world. There were no roses, either—no sign of a rose-bush. But perhaps it was taken out. The grounds keeper doesn't like such things; they are a nuisance to the lawnmower and if there is nobody left to object he will pull them out.

I thought that Almeda must have been buried somewhere else. When this plot was bought—at the time of the two children's deaths—she would still have been expected to marry, and to lie finally beside her husband. They might not have left room for her here. Then I saw that the stones in the ground fanned out from the upright stone. First the two for the parents, then the two for the children, but these were placed in such a way that there was room for a third, to complete the fan. I paced out from 'Catherine' the same number of steps that it took to get from

'Catherine' to 'William', and at this spot I began pulling grass and scrabbling in the dirt with my bare hands. Soon I felt the stone and knew that I was right. I worked away and got the whole stone clear and I read the name 'Meda'. There it was with the others, staring at the sky.

I made sure I had got to the edge of the stone. That was all the name there was—Meda. So it was true that she was called by that name in the family. Not just in the poem. Or perhaps she chose her name from the poem, to be written on her stone.

I thought that there wasn't anybody alive in the world but me who would know this, who would make the connection. And I would be the last person to do so. But perhaps this isn't so. People are curious. A few people are. They will be driven to find things out, even trivial things. They will put things together. You see them going around with notebooks, scraping the dirt off gravestones, reading microfilm, just in the hope of seeing this trickle in time, making a connection, rescuing one thing from the rubbish.

And they may get it wrong, after all. I may have got it wrong. I don't know if she ever took laudanum. Many ladies did. I don't know if she ever made grape jelly.

ANJANA APPACHANA

The Prophecy

❦

In the end we decided to visit the astrologer before going to the gynaecologist. After an hour's wait in the relentless afternoon sun, a scooter
finally stopped for us. When we told the scooterwalla where we wanted to
go, he snorted and spat out a copious stream of paan.

'I don't go such short distances,' he said contemptuously. We turned
away wearily. 'It will be ten rupees!' he shouted.

'Go to hell,' said Amrita. 'You scooterwallas are all the same.'

I dragged her back. 'Forget your principles today. We'll both collapse
in this heat.'

We sat inside the scooter. To the scooterwalla's left was a picture of
Goddess Lakshmi with a tinsel garland around it, to his right, one of a
film actress, bare-bosomed and smiling. Surveying us through the rear
view mirror, the scooterwalla grinned. He lit a beedi with a flourish and
started the scooter. Loudly and at breakneck speed, the scooter weaved
its way through the traffic. We clung to the sides and helplessly tried to
hold our sarees down.

'Maybe I'll be lucky and have a miscarriage now,' gasped Amrita.

'Slow down,' I shouted above the noise of the scooter. He accelerated.
'Slow down will you!'

He turned to me, grinning. 'What did you say?'

I screamed, 'Look at the road, don't look at me! Slow down!'

He missed a car by an inch, swerved violently, threw back his head
and laughed. 'Which college are you from?' We did not answer. He
accelerated.

'Slow down! Do you want us to die!'

'Memsahib,' he said, 'death is neither in your hands or in mine. If we
have to die, we will die. It is all written down.'

'You die if you want to. At the rate you're going you'll kill us too.'

He bounded up and down in his seat gleefully. 'Who cares,' he sang,
'Who cares if I die, who cares if you die, what difference does it make!'

'Stop talking to him,' Amrita told me, 'he's enjoying it.'

The scooterwalla accelerated again and looked at me hopefully in the rear view mirror. I looked out at the road. We had passed our destination. *'Stop, stop!'*

He turned to me again and winked. 'What is there to be so scared about? People die all the time.'

'Will you please stop, we've passed the place!'

He braked immediately and we almost fell over him. He leered at our bosoms and said, 'Madam, you should have warned me. This is how accidents happen.'

I thrust a ten rupee note into his outstretched hand. He took it, caressing my hands as he did, smiled slowly and drove off. Shakily we began walking to Chachaji's house. Chachaji, as the astrologer was called, was very popular with the girls in our college. His prophecies came true and he was cheaper than the rest. He could read your minds. One look at you and he knew everything—your past, your present, your future.

His wife opened the door to us and led us to the living room. I could hear the pressure cooker in the kitchen and the house was redolent with the smell of chicken curry. Somewhere inside a baby cried. The smell of incense wafted in and Chachaji entered. Spotless white pyjama-kurta, soft white beard, frail frame, startling eyes . . . mystic . . . ethereal. We stared at him, dumbstruck.

He sat opposite us and gazed into our faces. He smiled. 'Yes, my children?'

I looked at Amrita. It had been her idea to come here. When she didn't say anything, I spoke. 'We wanted to consult you.'

'Yes, yes, they all want to consult me.' How soft his voice was.

I looked again at Amrita. Her eyes were deep with tears. I knew how she felt. I could have confessed anything to him.

He turned to Amrita. Almost imperceptibly, he shook his head. 'Beti, you are in a forest, lost, wandering. You do not know where to go.' Dumbly, Amrita nodded. He sighed and closed his eyes. 'I see a boy.' We started. 'I see trouble. It all began with this boy. What is the date, time and place of your birth?' She told him. On a piece of paper he did some rapid calculations. He shook his head. 'The stars are not good. The shadow of Shani is falling on you. It is a very unlucky year for you.'

Amrita whispered. 'Chachaji, what will happen?'

'Happen? Has it not already happened?'

She flinched and lowered her eyes. Her fingers gathered and ungathered her pleats. 'What will I do, Chachaji, what will I do?'

He closed his eyes once again. I was sweating profusely and there were beads of perspiration above Amrita's mouth.

His wife entered with two glasses of water for us. We drank thirstily. She smiled at us. 'You are both so pretty.' We smiled gratefully. 'But you don't know how to wear sarees,' she said, clicking her tongue. 'Stand up for a moment.' We stood up obediently. She bent and pulled our sarees down. 'Always wear your sandals before wearing sarees. Or else it'll ride high,' she adjusted our pleats, then stood up and surveyed her work with satisfaction.

'Champa's mother,' sighed Chachaji, 'they have not come here to talk of sarees.'

'Oh you,' she dismissed him with a gesture. 'Don't frighten these children with all your talk.' She picked up the glasses, gave us another sunny smile and walked out of the room, her payals tinkling softly.

Apologetically, we looked at Chachaji. He smiled indulgently. 'Yes, children, what else do you want to know?'

'What should I do?' asked Amrita.

'I will do a puja for you. It will negate the bad influence of Shani. After six months I will perform a second puja. Your stars will change. The shadow of Shani will no longer envelop you.' Worshipfully, we nodded. 'For the puja,' he continued, his eyes fixed at the wall behind us, 'you will have to give a donation.'

'How much?' Amrita asked, fumbling in her purse.

'Whatever you wish, beti, whatever you wish. With the blessings of God all will be well. I will do a special puja for you.'

Amrita gave him twenty rupees. He took it and fingered the notes meditatively. 'My child, this will suffice only for a small puja. For you I will have to perform a big puja. Or else the trouble may become worse.'

'Chachaji, I have very little money.'

He shrugged his shoulders. 'If that is your wish, then. This may not suffice to negate the evil influence of Shani.' I took out ten rupees from my bag and gave it to him. 'Chachaji, this is all we have.'

He smiled, took the money with one hand, and patted my cheek with the other. 'You are a true friend, beti. You are a loyal friend. Your stars are good. You will do an MA. It is possible that you will work. You will marry a handsome man and have one son, one daughter.'

'When will I get married, Chachaji?'

'How old are you?'

'Seventeen.'

'In six, seven years, beti.'

'Will it be arranged?'

'It will be love. You will have a love marriage.'

'Will I go abroad, Chachaji?'

'Many times, many, many times.'

'Thank you, Chachaji,' I said, quietly ecstatic.

He turned to Amrita. 'After I perform the puja, your stars will change.

You will marry a handsome, fair, rich, influential man. You will have two sons who will rise to powerful positions in the government. They will bring you power, fame, respect. And you will also travel abroad, many, many times.'

He rose. We folded our hands.

The heat hit us as we stepped out of the house. We walked towards the bus stop.

'Oh no, Patram!' I gasped and pulled Amrita back from the road. In silence, breathing heavily, we stood where we were. A khaki-clad man walked past us. He was not Patram. Feeling foolish, we continued walking.

Patram was the omnipresent, omniscient peon-cum-bodyguard-cum-regulator-of-rules, employed by our college, who watched the boarders like a hawk and reported all our goings-on to the superintendent. He knew who sneaked out of the gates before the rules permitted, who returned after 8 pm, who smoked, who had a boyfriend. Just last month two girls had been expelled from the hostel after Patram smelt cigarette smoke in the corridor outside their room and informed the superintendent. The case went up to the principal. The girls pleaded with her but she would not budge. She said that she would not have girls of such loose character in her college. They had to leave. If someone decided to sneak out of the college gates and see a 1.30 film show, Patram was sure to know. He was everywhere—in the markets, cinema, theatres, Connaught Place. We lived in dread of the famous khaki dress and cap and the permanent grin on his face. That morning we had walked out of the college before official going-out time, and there had been no sign of Patram. Dressed in sarees for the first time in an effort to look older, we had walked out of the gates, awkwardly and with trepidation. Still no Patram.

And now, weak with relief at the false alarm, we waited for the bus that would take us to the gynaecologist. It arrived almost immediately, and for once, it was not crowded. 'Forty rupees,' Amrita said as the bus began to move. 'We've spent forty rupees today.'

I said nothing. We had just a hundred between us. We had no idea how much the gynaecologist would take. The previous day, in a desperate bid to make some money, we had gone around the hostel collecting old newspapers, empty jars and bottles. We had fitted these into six polythene bags and trudged to the nearby market, trying to appear oblivious to the noise they made as we walked, praying that the polythene bags would not fall apart. In the market we had squatted before the kabadiwalla and bargained at length. He had said he would give us twenty rupees for the whole lot. We had asked for thirty. He had refused. We walked away and he had called us back. Twenty-five, he had said. So we struck the bargain. On the way back, overcome by the sight of pastries in the bakery, we had spent most of it on black forests, lemon tarts, chocolate eclairs and chicken patties. And now we had barely enough for the gynaecologist, let alone the abortion. Maybe, I thought, she isn't pregnant after all.

The clinic was plush, beautiful and smelt rich. Our hearts sank. We sat at the reception and waited Amrita's turn. There was just one other person there, in a bright pink chiffon saree. She stared at us. We thumbed unseeingly through the magazines. She continued staring.

'She's going to ask questions,' Amrita murmured.

'Lie.'

'What?'

'So,' said the woman, 'you have come to visit Dr Kumar?'

We nodded distantly and went back to our magazines.

'How old are you both?'

'Twenty,' I lied. Beneath my saree my legs began to tremble.

'Acha? You look younger.'

Amrita smiled. 'That's good.'

She continued surveying us and her face grew grim. She drew her palla over her shoulders. 'Are you married?'

'Yes,' I said.

'No,' said Amrita.

'Acha?' She turned a shocked face towards Amrita. 'Then what are you doing here?'

'Period problems,' said Amrita and went back to her magazine.

'What problems?'

'Irregular,' I said.

'Too frequent,' said Amrita.

She smiled knowingly. 'There seems to be some confusion about the problem, yes?' We did not reply. She turned her gaze on me. 'So are you the married one?'

'Yes.'

'You don't look married. How old are you?'

'Twenty.'

'So what is *your* problem?'

'I'm accompanying my friend.'

'Acha! So the married friend is accompanying the unmarried friend to the gynaecologist!' She knew, she knew. She fingered her mangalsutra. 'It seems to me that neither of you is married.' She waited. 'And if that is so, God knows what you are doing here.'

The nurse called, 'Mrs Mehta, your turn please.'

She rose, exuding a strong whiff of Intimate as she did, and walked in.

'Bitch,' said Amrita.

Ten minutes later, Mrs Mehta emerged, gave us a meaningful look and left.

We went in, sat opposite Dr Kumar and began to cry.

She was wonderful. She spoke to us in low, comforting tones, gave us tissues, got us cold water and had the nurse serve us tea. Finally, red-nosed and swollen-eyed, we were quiet.

She turned to Amrita. 'You're pregnant?'

'I think so.'

'Let me check you.'

I sat in the room while she and Amrita went into the adjoining room. When they emerged, I knew it was confirmed. Amrita sat next to me. She was trembling. I put my hand on her knee.

Dr Kumar's eyes, brown and gentle, looked troubled. She reminded me of my mother. But I could not tell my mother if I were pregnant.

'How much will an abortion cost?' asked Amrita.

Dr Kumar rested her face against her hand. 'Does the boy know?'

'No. There's no need for him to know.'

'So, you don't intend marrying him?'

'No. How much will it cost?'

Dr Kumar was silent. Finally she said, 'It's a thousand rupees in this clinic.' Amrita and I looked at each other in despair. We didn't even have a hundred. Dr Kumar, her eyes full of compassion, suggested that there were government hospitals where it could be done for about a hundred rupees. She would give us the addresses. Sensing my apprehension, she assured me that they were perfectly safe. As for the abortion—people were having it all the time. She paused, then said, 'Amrita, would you like to take your parents into your confidence?' Seeing Amrita's face, she gently continued, 'Sometimes, beti, we tend to misjudge our parents. Often they're the best people to turn to at such times.'

'Last year,' Amrita whispered, 'our neighbour's daughter got pregnant. She threw herself in front of a passing train. Her parents refused to claim her body. And my father said, that is how it should be.'

'Your mother?'

'What could she say? She cried for days. And Ma can't keep anything to herself. She'll tell my father.'

Dr Kumar seemed lost in thought. After some time she sighed and said, 'Are you both in the hostel?' We nodded. 'So, your parents are not in Delhi?' We shook our heads. 'I see.' She wrote down a few addresses and gave them to us. We rose to leave. 'Wait,' she said, and proceeded to give us a fifteen-minute talk on contraception. Wide-eyed and quivering with embarrassment, I listened. I could barely look Dr Kumar in the eye as she systematically went through it all. How did people ever buy these things? How did they look chemists in the eye? How did they ever get down to it? Amrita looked tired but unembarrassed, nodding from time to time. After Dr Kumar finished, she said, 'Don't be so foolish next time.' We got up. She said, 'Amrita, you're already two months gone. Don't wait much longer.' Amrita nodded.

Dr Kumar refused to take any money.

It was five when we reached the hostel. We changed out of our sarees and looked at each other.

'Marry him, Amrita,' I said tentatively.

'Please,' Amrita replied, 'you'll never understand.'

I didn't. I didn't understand at all. I liked Rakesh; he was handsome, bright, fun to be with. He smelt wonderfully of aftershave and had given us our first motorcycle rides. He's so *nice* I had often told Amrita, so *nice*. But she said he had no aesthetic sense. She didn't *want* nice. She didn't *want* to get married after college. She didn't *want* to end up like her parents. She wanted adventure. I, half in love with Rakesh, his aftershave and his motorcycle, was sure he would provide adventure. She scoffed at the very idea.

Often I wondered why Amrita had gone into this strange, loveless relationship. Normally so communicative with me, she was unusually reticent about her affair with Rakesh. Was it just the sex? My mind recoiled at the thought. Nevertheless, I wondered. It's nothing so great, she told me once, and I tried to school my expression at this unexpected revelation. She had done it! How often? She looked the same. On our occasional outings together, I watched them covertly. They laughed, talked, ate, drank. I could see no hidden fire in Rakesh's eyes, no answering flame in Amrita's. In my own fantasies, I was beautiful but enigmatic, virginal, but willing to surrender it all to the man I married. If it happened before marriage he would not respect me. I would tame the beast in him. Did Rakesh respect Amrita? Did she drive him crazy with desire. I waited to hear more, but she said nothing. I continued feeding my fantasies of handsome men on motorcycles, smelling of aftershave, with deep voices and British accents. I would happily have settled for one after college, happily married one. He would never tire of me, nor I of him. Marriage would be that wondrous path of rapid heartbeats and unending, intimate discoveries.

Amrita spent the weekends with Rakesh in his hostel. 'This bloody college and those frustrated spinsters make me sick,' she would tell me every Sunday evening, referring to the superintendent and the principal. 'I'll be glad to get out of this hole.' Rakesh never seemed to figure in her plans for the future. She wanted to be a journalist and I had no doubt that she would succeed. Not only did she write expressively, but had strong feelings and a strange kind of courage, an indifference to what people thought of her. While I seemed to spend my life looking over my shoulder to see who was watching, starting, for fear someone was listening, always fearful that 'they' would know. Amrita, as long as I had known her, had done exactly what she wanted. Now, on Amrita's behalf, it was I who was guilty, scared of discovery, certain that retribution was imminent.

We could not use the hostel phone to fix up the appointment as it was out of order. We began walking towards the gate again since the taxi-stand outside the college had a public phone. But Nemesis in the form of Patram was just behind us. Grinning, he led us to the superintendent's office. He had seen us outside the college gates that morning, he said. The superintendent, sullen, but with a predatory gleam in her eyes, lectured us on our dishonesty, the wickedness of our actions and on our parents' inability to inculcate in us the virtues of restraint and politeness. As she took a deep breath to renew her attack, Amrita told her that she was an ignorant, power-hungry, narrow-minded, perverse woman and stormed out of the room. Weak with shock and fear, I gave the super-intendent an ingratiating smile and followed Amrita.

Back in our room, Amrita raged. She damned the college and the authorities. 'One day,' she fumed, 'I'm going to expose this place for what it is. I'll write about it and publish it. No one will want to attend this wretched place.' I replied, 'It'll have exactly the opposite effect—your article will reassure every middle-class parent like yours and mine.'

We were gated for two weeks. But the next week we sneaked out and waited for a scooter or bus that would take us to one of the clinics Dr Kumar had suggested. Patram's voice called us from across the road, precipitating another return. Once again he escorted us to the super-intendent's office. Our gating was extended to four weeks. Two weeks passed, then three weeks. One day someone casually mentioned that her sister had had a miscarriage after eating pickles. That evening I made Amrita eat half a bottle of mango pickle. The room smelled of it for days and she was violently sick, but nothing happened. She said, 'If I starve myself maybe it'll die,' and didn't eat for three days. She almost collapsed, but nothing happened. I said, 'Eat, you'll need your strength for the abortion.' 'When,' she whispered, 'when?' As the days passed I felt Amrita's rising fear. The more fearful she was, the quieter she became. Daily I murmured reassurances while unobtrusively examining her stomach. It seemed to grow no bigger. Would an abortion at this stage kill her? I imagined Amrita's prolonged, bloody death at the clinic, with me left behind to break the news to her parents, to the superintendent, to the principal, to my parents. The horror. Would they hold me responsible? And then I was ridden with guilt for thinking such thoughts, for feeling not sorrow, but terror for the seemingly endless repercussions of such a death. My fantasies turned to nightmares.

As our gating entered the fourth week, Amrita fell ill. She refused to let me call a doctor for fear he would find out that she was pregnant. At midnight her temperature rose to 104 degrees. The superintendent did not take kindly to my knock at her door at that hour, urging her to call a doctor. This was no time to come knocking at her door, she snapped, handing me two aspirins and banging the door on my face. I stood outside her door for a long time. Then I went back to ours.

Amrita's temperature remained the same the next day. The superintendent called a doctor. The diagnosis—measles.

'Oh my God, oh my God,' said the superintendent wringing her hands. 'Now everyone in the hostel will get it. She had better leave the hostel.'

'She has nowhere to go,' I said.

She gave me a look of pure hatred and left the room hurriedly. Half an hour later I was summoned to her office where the principal had joined her. 'What is this I hear?' the principal asked me.

'All what?'

The principal looked at me in amazement and then spoke to me for ten minutes on the subject of respect for elders. Subsequently she expressed her outrage that Amrita had no local guardians in Delhi who could take her away, and her deeper outrage that I couldn't ask my local guardians to look after her. She ordered the superintendent to send a telegram to Amrita's parents in Bangalore. In the meantime Amrita and I were to have our meals in our room. On no account were we to enter the dining-hall. To attend classes, we were to use the back door of the hostel. It would be opened especially for us.

The superintendent placed a call to Amrita's parents but could not get through. She sent a telegram but there was no response. For a week Amrita stayed confined to our room. I continued attending classes, leaving through the back door of the hostel. For some unaccountable reason, it did not matter to them if I infected the others in class, but the dining-room was taboo. Amrita wept silently throughout, and when she was asleep, I did. Often I would wake up at night to find Amrita awake, gazing at the ceiling, her face now full of spots, her large eyes swollen and red. We hardly spoke. Finally the superintendent got through to Amrita's parents. They said they would fly to Delhi the next day. Turning to the wall, Amrita said, 'This is the end. My father will have nothing to do with me. Where will I go? Where will I go?' I could offer no comfort, no sanctuary. I kept saying, 'He won't do that, he won't do that.' Then I said, 'Rakesh is there, he'll see you through, he'll have to.' She was silent and then said, 'Call him, tell him.'

The hostel phone was out of order again. I asked the superintendent if I could use hers. She refused. In the end I walked out of the college gates, my pocket full of fifty paisa coins, while Patram followed me, calling, 'Hemlathaji, come back, come back, I'll report you to the superintendent, I'll tell the principal, you will see what I will do, you will see what happens.' He followed me to the gate and watched me walk to the taxi-stand. The taxiwallas stared at me while I dialled Rakesh's number at his engineering college. I got a wrong number the first time. The second time the call got disconnected. The third time I got through. Rakesh was out, I was told, but would be back in ten minutes. I waited, while the taxiwallas eyed me. One lay down on the charpoi next to me. 'It is so hot,' he groaned. He removed his banyan, lowered his pyjamas and looked at me. I looked away.

It was growing dark and every emerging shadow seemed khaki-clad and wore a wide grin. I walked down the road slowly. Five minutes. A cyclist swerved towards me and I stepped back. He groaned and cycled away rapidly. I walked back and tried the number again. I got through. Rakesh was back. I told him what I could and he said he would be there immediately. I walked a slight distance away from the taxi-stand and waited. 'Madam,' said a voice behind me. I shuddered and looked back. It was the same taxiwalla. He looked me over and scratched his groin. 'Can I help you in any way?' 'No,' I said and turned away. He remained where he was. 'Do you need any fifty paisa coins?' 'No,' I said, 'No.' I walked further away. He followed me. I crossed the road. He stood opposite, staring at me. Ten minutes later Rakesh's motorcycle came to a halt beside me. The taxiwalla walked back.

Rakesh was in a state of shock and incomprehension. He would sell his motorcycle and pay for the abortion, he declared hoarsely. He would protect her from her parents. He would leave college. As I tried to calm him down, a familiar khaki-clad apparition emerged silently from the shadows and stood before us, grinning.

For the third time Patram escorted me back to the superintendent's office. The principal was there too. It was girls like me who ruined the reputation of the college—breaking rules, making boyfriends, smoking, she said. I didn't smoke, I replied. The principal snorted. Next I would say I didn't have a boyfriend. She pulled the telephone towards her. She was going to phone my local guardians to take me away. I could start packing my things.

I wish I could say at this point that I had let her phone them. I wish I could say that I had walked out of the room with an appropriate remark.

I wish I could say that I had told them what I thought of them. Even today I relive that scene and say all that I did not at that time. I wish I didn't have to say that I began to cry hysterically while they watched me with satisfaction. That I begged them to give me another chance. That I told them my parents would never understand. That I kept repeating, please, please don't expel me, I'll never repeat my mistakes. That the superintendent said she wanted all this in writing. That I gave her a written apology, still sobbing, still begging. They both smiled and shook their heads. And the principal asked the superintendent, 'So you think she has realised?' And the superintendent replied, 'Who knows with these girls, they are such good actresses.' And I said, (oh God), I said, 'I will do anything you want me to do, but please don't expel me, please forgive me, please forgive me.' And they said, 'We cannot give you an answer now, we shall have to think about it. We will watch your behaviour and then we will decide.' And I thanked them.

The next morning, from our first floor window, I saw Rakesh's figure next to his motorcycle, waiting outside the gate. I sent him a note through my next-door neighbour, explaining the situation, but he continued waiting in the afternoon sun while I helped Amrita pack her belongings. Her parents arrived in the evening. Her father waited in the superintendent's office while her mother came up to our room and sat next to her daughter, stroking her hair. 'My poor baby,' she said, 'my poor, poor child.' And she smiled at me and said, 'Hemu, beti, thank you for looking after her all this time. My daughter is lucky to have such a friend.' She continued stroking Amrita's hair. 'Ma,' Amrita said, 'Ma, I'm pregnant.' Her mother's hands stopped. 'Ma,' Amrita said, grasping her thigh, 'I'm three months pregnant Ma. Ma, where will I go? Where will I go?' Her mother was still, so still. She closed her eyes and whispered, 'Bhagwan, hai Bhagwan.'

In the distance a clock struck six. From my position at the window I could see Rakesh outside the gate, waiting.

'*Ma!*'

We started. Amrita's voice sounded strange.

'Ma, I think I'm bleeding.'

She was. Slowly, the white sheets were staining. Amrita began to cry, loud, harsh sounds. Fascinated, I watched the white sheets turning red while the room filled with the horrible sound, till I thought it would have to burst open to let out what it could not possibly contain. And then there was a knock on the door and the superintendent entered. I threw a bedcover over Amrita and her sounds stopped abruptly. The superintendent's eyes bulged. 'What is the matter?'

Amrita's mother began stroking her hair again. 'My daughter is tired.

It has been a strain. Please call a taxi. We must leave now.' The superintendent eyed us suspiciously. She came closer to Amrita and whipped the bedcover away. Amrita's mother gasped. The superintendent gave a strangled scream. Amrita closed her eyes and the superintendent said, 'I should have known.'

'Please call a taxi,' her mother said.

'Taxi—nothing doing, I'm calling the principal.' She rushed out of the room and we heard her heavy footsteps echoing down the corridor.

'Beti,' her mother's face was distorted, 'Please call a taxi.'

'I can't, I can't, I'll be expelled. You call one from outside the gate, I'll stay with her.'

'Ma, don't leave me,' Amrita moaned.

I held her hands tightly. 'I'm here.'

Small, incoherent sounds escaped her mother's throat. She looked at us and then went out rapidly.

I was with Amrita for fifteen minutes while she continued bleeding. I used up all the sheets we had to use below and between her. The blood soaked through them all, right down to the mattress, and the room was heavy with its smell. Amrita moaned and twisted and turned and held on to my hand until I felt I could no longer bear the pain of it all. Then the superintendent entered the room with the principal. The principal took the scene in and hit her forehead with her hand.

'Tell her parents to take her away,' she told me. 'Tell them she cannot come back to this college. Where are they?'

'Her mother's gone to get a taxi.' I was shivering violently.

I heard footsteps in the corridor and her mother entered the room, panting. She ignored the superintendent and the principal. 'Beti,' she told me, 'help me carry her down.'

'And don't bring her back,' the principal said, tight-lipped. 'We don't want such girls here.'

'Madam, madam,' the superintendent said hysterically, 'it isn't my fault—she broke the rules and got into this mess.'

They called Patram to carry her suitcases down, while her mother and I carried Amrita downstairs to the waiting taxi, past the superintendent's room, past her amazed father, followed by the principal and the superintendent. We laid Amrita down on the back seat of the taxi and her mother said to me, 'Come with me, beti, please come with me.'

'Nothing doing,' the principal said, holding my arm. 'This girl is going nowhere. We have had enough trouble. Now Amrita is your responsibility.' I stood between them, helpless.

'Will someone tell me what is happening?' her father asked.

'Yes, I will tell you,' the principal said. 'Your daughter is pregnant and at this moment she is aborting. You do what you want with her and don't bring her back to this college.'

Her father's face seemed to shrink. He shook his head uncomprehendingly. Her mother took his arm gently and opened the door of the taxi. 'Get inside,' she said, 'we have to go to the hospital.' She sat at the back with Amrita. Slowly, the taxi drove away.

'So, Hemlathaji,' said the superintendent, but I walked away, away from her, away from the hostel, away from it all, towards the college building. I climbed up the stairs to the first floor and sat there, against the wall.

Much later I looked at my watch. It was 9.45 pm. They would lock the hostel door at 10.00. I walked back slowly and went upstairs to our room. The stench of blood greeted me, and on the bed, an accumulation of sheets, all red and white. I bolted the door and walked to the window. He was still there. I drew the curtains.

The rest, I heard from my mother's sister in Bangalore, who is a good friend of Amrita's mother. She stayed with us for a week and, in the strictest of confidence, gave us a blow-by-blow account of everything. Amrita was in hospital for a day and then flew back with her parents to Bangalore. The following month she was married off. 'That is *luck*,' my aunt said. '*Such* a nice boy, you cannot imagine. *So* fair, *so* handsome and on top of that, the *only* son. And the wedding . . . what a wedding! She wore a lahenga studded with *real* pearls.' I asked, 'Isn't she going to complete her BA?' My aunt replied, 'What will she do with a BA now? And anyway, her father forbade it. He was a broken man. Do you know, his hair turned grey overnight? Poor man,' she sighed. My mother turned to me. She said, 'I cannot believe you were friendly with a girl like that. You act as though she did nothing wrong. I hope she hasn't influenced you. You'll never understand what a mother goes through till you become a mother. It is my only prayer to God these days, that you make the correct decisions, that you know right from wrong, that you do not go astray.'

Rakesh came to visit me the following term. I told him about Amrita. At the end he said, 'I see.' That is all.

The rules in the hostel became stricter. Patram kept a strict eye on me. Like the Cheshire cat his grin followed me everywhere.

The year I graduated, Amrita wrote. She had no time for letter-writing, she said, at least not for the kind she wished to write to me. There had been too much to cope with that first year—the abortion, her marriage, her first child. And the second year, her second child. So much for Dr Kumar's advice on contraception! she said. Her father began speaking to her after her son was born. Her mother never referred to what happened. But she stood by her.

Of course, her husband knew nothing. He's nice, she said, and also tall and fair and by that definition, they say, handsome. He's all set to groom our sons to be good IAS officers like him, extending his dreary dreams of all that is proper, permanent and powerful. Work was taking her husband abroad the following year. She would probably accompany him. She asked if I could come and stay with her for a while, for more than a while, whenever possible. She longed to talk to me, letters were so difficult. And all the interruptions, babies crying, meals to be cooked . . . you know how it can be, she said. Oh, Hemu, no, you cannot know. Not yet, not yet. She asked, remember Chachaji? He got it all right, didn't he? He will always get it right, won't he? For this is how it will always be, yes, this is how it will always be. Oh, Hemu, Hemu, my stars have changed, haven't they?'

And mine, Amrita, and mine.

BIOGRAPHICAL NOTES

ANJANA APPACHANA. Born in India. Moved to the United States in 1984 where she graduated from the Pennsylvania State University. Author of some highly acclaimed and distinctive short stories. *Incantations and Other Stories*—her first collection—was published in 1991.

MARGARET ATWOOD (1939–). Born in Ottawa, Ontario. Among the leading contemporary Canadian writers; poet, novelist, and outstanding short-story writer, whose collections include *Dancing Girls* (1977) and *Bluebeard's Egg* (1983).

ELIZABETH BOWEN (1899–1973). Born in Dublin. Anglo-Irish novelist, and one of the most highly regarded short-story writers of the century. Author of seven collections of stories, of which *Look at All Those Roses* (1941) and *The Demon Lover* (1945) are probably the most striking.

A. S. BYATT (1936–). Born in Sheffield. Distinguished novelist and critic, and author of *Sugar and Other Stories* (1987).

HORTENSE CALISHER (1911–). Born in New York. Novelist and short-story writer of exceptional quality, with both subject-matter and location ranging widely. Described in 1963 by Brigid Brophy as 'an American of European sympathies, taut artistry and stupendous talent'.

ANGELA CARTER (1940–92). Born in London. Exuberant and inventive novelist, critic, and short-story writer. *The Bloody Chamber*—retellings of traditional tales—was published in 1979.

WILLA CATHER (1873–1947). Born in Virginia. Acclaimed American novelist and short-story writer, best known for *O Pioneers!* (1913) and *My Antonia* (1918).

JANE GARDAM (1928–). Born in Coatham, Yorkshire. Began as a children's writer (*A Long Way from Verona* was published in 1971) before going on to produce some striking and original novels and short stories. The collection *Black Faces, White Faces* came out in 1975.

ELLEN GILCHRIST (1935–). Born in Vicksburg, Mississippi. Satirical and engaging novelist and short-story writer. Work is set mostly in New Orleans, and her subject is 'discordances in contemporary society' (as one critic put it). Extends the image of the traditional 'Southern' writer. *Victory Over Japan* was published in 1984.

NADINE GORDIMER (1923–). Born in South Africa. Regarded as one of the finest living writers in English. Author of many distinguished novels and short stories (including the remarkable *Burger's Daughter*, 1979). A strongly political writer.

CAROLINE GORDON (1895–1981). Born in Todd County, Kentucky. Distinguished novelist and short-story writer; associated with the Old South. Married Allen Tate in 1924. First novel *Penhally* published in 1931; *Old Red and Other Stories* in 1963.

PATRICIA HIGHSMITH (1921–95). Born in Fort Worth, Texas; grew up in New York. Has lived in Europe since 1963. Came to prominence with *Strangers on a Train* (1950); a suspense writer who has transcended the boundaries of genre fiction.

RUTH PRAWER JHABVALA (1927–). Born in Germany to Polish parents; came to England at the age of 12. Married to an Indian and has lived in India where most of her novels and stories are set. Author of four collections of stories. Her novel *Heat and Dust* won the Booker Prize in 1975.

ELIZABETH JOLLEY (1923–). Born in the Midlands of England; moved to Western Australia in 1959 with her husband and family. Has perfected a completely original literary manner, compounded of apparent dottiness and actual razor-sharp perception. *Woman in a Lampshade* (short stories) was published in 1983.

DORIS LESSING (1919–). Born in Persia, but grew up in Southern Rhodesia. Has lived in London since 1949. Distinguished novelist and short-story writer, whose novel *The Golden Notebook* (1962) was acclaimed both as an innovative work of fiction and as a textbook for feminism.

MARY McCARTHY (1912–89). Born in Seattle. Novelist, critic, and woman of letters. Achieved fame with *The Group* in 1963; also wrote two autobiographies.

OLIVIA MANNING (1908–80). Born in Portsmouth, but grew up mostly in Ireland. Married British Council lecturer R. D. Smith just before the Second World War and went with him to Bucharest. One result of this was her acclaimed *Balkan Trilogy* (1960–5), followed by the *Levant Trilogy* of 1977–80; these six novels capture the essence of wartime exigencies, and the whole unsettled expatriate existence. Olivia Manning's stories are collected in two volumes, *Growing Up* (1948) and *A Romantic Hero* (1967).

KATHERINE MANSFIELD (1888–1923). Born in Wellington, New Zealand. First collection of stories *In a German Pension*, published in 1911, by which time she was living in London and associated with A. R. Orage's magazine *New Age*. Died in France at the age of 34 having written eighty-eight masterly stories (some uncompleted).

F. M. MAYOR (1872–1932). English novelist, and author of one collection of stories, *The Room Opposite* (published posthumously in 1935).

BHARATI MUKHERJEE (1940–). Born in Calcutta. Left India for University of Iowa in 1961; has lived in Montreal and New York and is currently a professor at Berkeley. Novelist and short-story writer of great diversity and imaginative power. Her collection *The Middleman* was published in 1988.

ALICE MUNRO (1931–). Born in Wingham, Ontario. One of the most outstanding and accomplished of contemporary short-story writers. Collections include *Lives of Girls and Women* (1971) and *Friend of My Youth* (1990).

JOYCE CAROL OATES (1938–). Born in Lockport, New York. One of the most prolific and distinctive of recent writers; author of many novels and short stories, including *A Bloodsmoor Romance* (1982), *American Appetites* (1986), and the short-story collection *Marriages and Infidelities* (1972). Since 1978 she has been on the faculty of Princeton University.

EDNA O'BRIEN (1932–). Born in Co. Clare, Ireland. Achieved instant celebrity with *The Country Girls* (1960) and has written a handful of stories which equal the charm and lucidity of her earliest novels, 'Irish Revel' among them.

FLANNERY O'CONNOR (1925–64). Born in Savannah, Georgia. Among the most powerful and original of American short-story writers; takes provincial Southern life as her theme and presents it in a variety of modes: comic, grotesque, disabused, idiosyncratic. Died young of an inherited disease.

CYNTHIA OZICK (1928–). Born in New York. A dazzling and original short-story writer, essayist, and novelist. Best known for her story 'The Shawl', an uncompromising Holocaust episode; but has also produced much striking work in a lighter vein.

GRACE PALEY (1922–). Born in New York, to Jewish immigrant parents. Short-story collections include *The Little Disturbances of Man* (1959) and *Enormous Changes at the Last Minute* (1974). Has a completely individual voice; gives a comic slant to domestic trials and upsets.

SYLVIA PLATH (1932–63). Born Massachusetts. Author of four collections of poetry, a novel, *The Bell Jar* (1963), and a few short stories. Committed suicide in London in 1963.

KATHERINE ANNE PORTER (1890–1980). Born in Indian Creek, Texas. Regarded as a superb stylist right from the publication of her earliest work; her *Collected Stories* won the Pulitzer Prize in 1965.

JEAN RHYS (1890–1979). Born in Dominica in the West Indies. Came to England in 1907; worked briefly as a touring actress. Began to write in the 1920s, encouraged by Ford Maddox Ford. Celebrated for her bittersweet, candid, disabused approach, and for the insight her novels and stories provide into the lives of insecure women between the wars.

STEVIE SMITH (1902–71). Born in Hull, but brought up in Palmers Green, London. Famous as a poet, with a wonderfully idiosyncratic voice; also wrote three novels, starting with *Novel on Yellow Paper* in 1936, and a number of sketches and stories.

MURIEL SPARK (1918–). Born in Edinburgh, came to prominence in post-war London, first winning an *Observer* short-story competition (1951), and going on to write an accomplished and original first novel, *The Comforters* (1957). One of the most outstanding stylists in English fiction and a writer of great depth and ingenuity.

JEAN STAFFORD (1915–79). Born in Covina, California; brought up in the Rocky Mountains of Colorado. Novelist and short-story writer of considerable verve and edginess. Married the poet Robert Lowell in 1940. First novel *Boston Adventure* published to great acclaim in 1944. Her *Collected Stories* (1969) won the Pulitzer Prize.

CHRISTINA STEAD (1902–83). Born in Sydney, Australia, but spent most of her life in Europe and America before returning to Australia in 1968. Author of some extraordinarily dense, intricate, and rewarding novels, of which the best-known is probably *The Man Who Loved Children* (1940).

AMY TAN (1952–). Born in Oakland, California, to Chinese immigrant parents. *The Joy Luck Club* (1989) is a collection of related episodes dealing with the experience of growing up as a Chinese-American, and—like her novel of 1991, *The Kitchen God's Wife*, is a work of great charm and astuteness.

ELIZABETH TAYLOR (1912–75). Born in Reading. Novelist and short-story writer; first novel *At Mrs Lippincote's* published in 1946, followed by the best-selling *A Wreath of Roses* in 1950. A meticulous craftswoman with an individualistic slant; goes in for a kind of comic sedateness and English decorum, always tempered by sharpness.

SYLVIA TOWNSEND WARNER (1893–1978). Born in Harrow, daughter of a schoolmaster. Author of poems, essays, a biography, seven idiosyncratic novels, and eight volumes of stories, all displaying her singular imaginative power and narrative gifts.

FAY WELDON (1933–). Born in New Zealand, but has spent most of her life in England. Novelist, short-story writer, stage and screen writer. Her custom is to subject the lives of women to sardonic scrutiny. The didactic element in her writing is tempered by wit and audacity. *Polaris and Other Stories* was published in 1985.

EUDORA WELTY (1909–). Born in Jackson, Mississippi. Among the most remarkable and distinguished of twentieth-century American writers. Author of five novels, beginning with *The Robber Bridegroom* of 1942, and four volumes of entrancing stories.

EDITH WHARTON (1862–1937). Born in New York. Author of more than fifty volumes of work, including fiction and non-fiction, and one of the most prominent and successful American writers of her day. Awarded the Pulitzer Prize for her novel *The Age of Innocence* (1920). Also wrote many short stories, of which those dealing with the supernatural are especially impressive.

VIRGINIA WOOLF (1882–1941). Born in London, daughter of Sir Leslie Stephen of the *Dictionary of National Biography*. Married Leonard Woolf in 1912. One of the luminaries of the modern movement, with novels such as *To the Lighthouse* (1927) and *The Waves* (1931) establishing her reputation permanently in the field of English literature. Subject to bouts of insanity, and eventually committed suicide by drowning. *A Haunted House and Other Stories* published posthumously in 1944.

ACKNOWLEDGEMENTS

The editor and publishers are grateful for permission to include the following copyright material:

Anjana Appachana, from *Incantations and Other Stories*, © Anjana Appachana. Published by Virago Press 1991 and Rutgers University Press, New Jersey.

Margaret Atwood, from *Dancing Girls and Other Stories* (Cape, 1982).

Elizabeth Bowen, from *Collected Stories*, © 1981 by Curtis Brown Ltd., Literary Executors of the Estate of Elizabeth Bowen. Reprinted by permission of Alfred A. Knopf Inc., and Curtis Brown Ltd.

A. S. Byatt, from *Sugar and Other Stories* (Chatto & Windus, 1987). Reprinted by permission of the publisher.

Hortense Calisher, from *Collected Stories* (Arbor House Pub. Co., 1975), © 1975 Hortense Calisher.

Angela Carter, from *The Bloody Chamber and Other Stories*. Reprinted by permission of Victor Gollancz Ltd.

Willa Cather, from *The Troll Garden* (1905).

Jane Gardam, from *Black Faces, White Faces* (Hamish Hamilton, 1975), © Jane Gardam, 1975. Reprinted by permission of Hamish Hamilton Ltd. and David Higham Associates Ltd.

Ellen Gilchrist, from *Victory Over Japan*. Reprinted by permission of Faber & Faber Ltd., and Sheil Land Associates Ltd.

Nadine Gordimer, from *Selected Stories* (Gollancz, 1956), © Nadine Gordimer 1956, 1978.

Caroline Gordon, from *The Collected Stories of Caroline Gordon* (Farrar, Straus & Giroux, 1981).

Patricia Highsmith, from *The Black House*, © Patricia Highsmith 1981. Reprinted by permission of William Heinemann Ltd., and Diogenes Verlag AG for the author.

Ruth Prawer Jhabvala, from *How I Became a Holy Mother and Other Stories*, © Ruth Prawer Jhabvala 1976. Reprinted by permission of John Murray (Publishers) Ltd., and Harriet Wasserman Literary Agency.

Elizabeth Jolley, from *Woman In a Lampshade*, © 1983 Elizabeth Jolley. Published by Penguin Books Australia.

Doris Lessing, from *The Habit of Loving*, © 1957 Doris Lessing. Reprinted by permission of Jonathan Clowes Ltd., London, on behalf of Doris Lessing. Published in the US by HarperCollins Publishers Inc.

Mary McCarthy, first published in *The New Yorker*, 1949, © 1949 Mary McCarthy.

Olivia Manning, from *A Romantic Hero* (1967). Reprinted by permission of William Heinemann Ltd.

Katherine Mansfield, from *The Short Stories of Katherine Mansfield*, copyright 1920 by Alfred A. Knopf Inc., and renewed 1948 by John Middleton Murry. Reprinted by permission of the publisher.

Bharati Mukherjee, from *The Middleman and Other Stories*, © 1988 Bharati

522   *Acknowledgements*

Mukherjee. Published by Virago Press 1990, and Penguin Books of Canada Ltd. Used with permission.

Alice Munro, from *Friend of My Youth* (Chatto & Windus, 1990). Reprinted by permission of the publisher.

Joyce Carol Oates, from *Marriages and Infidelities* (Gollancz, 1974), © 1974 Joyce Carol Oates. Reprinted by permission of Murray Pollinger Literary Agent and John Hawkins & Associates, New York.

Edna O'Brien, from *The Love Object* (Jonathan Cape, 1968). Reprinted by permission of A. M. Heath & Company Ltd.

Flannery O'Connor, from *A Good Man is Hard to Find* (The Women's Press, 1980) & *The Complete Stories* (Faber). Reprinted by permission of Peters Fraser & Dunlop Group. Published in the US by Harcourt Brace & Company.

Cynthia Ozick, from *The Pagan Rabbi and Other Stories*. Reprinted by permission of Campbell Thomson & McLaughlin Ltd., Authors' Agents. Published in the US by Alfred A. Knopf Inc. © 1972 Cynthia Ozick.

Grace Paley, from *The Little Disturbances of Man* (Viking Press, 1959), © Grace Paley 1959.

Sylvia Plath, from *Johnny Panic and the Bible of Dreams*. Reprinted by permission of Faber & Faber Ltd. Published in the US by HarperCollins Publishers Inc.

Katherine Anne Porter, from *Collected Stories* (Cape, 1964). Reprinted by permission of the publisher.

Jean Rhys, from *Sleep It Off Lady* (Penguin Books, 1979, first published by Andre Deutsch), © Jean Rhys, 1976. Reprinted by permission of Penguin Books Ltd. Published in the US by HarperCollins Publishers Inc.

Stevie Smith, from *The Uncollected Writings of Stevie Smith*, © James Macgibbon. Published by Virago Press 1981. Used with permission.

Muriel Spark, from *Collected Stories* (Penguin). Reprinted by permission of David Higham Associates.

Jean Stafford, from *The Collected Stories of Jean Stafford*. Reprinted by permission of A. M. Heath & Co. Ltd.

Christina Stead, from *Ocean Story: The Uncollected Stories of Christina Stead*, © Christina Stead, 1985. Published by Penguin Books Australia Ltd.

Amy Tan, from *The Joy Luck Club*, © 1989 by Amy Tan. Reprinted by permission of The Putnam Publishing Group and Sandra Dijkstra Literary Agency.

Elizabeth Taylor, from *The Blush and Other Stories*, © Elizabeth Taylor, 1958. Reprinted by permission of A. M. Heath & Co.

Sylvia Townsend Warner, from *A Stranger With a Bag and Other Stories* (Chatto & Windus, 1966).

Fay Weldon, from *Polaris and Other Stories*. Reprinted by permission of Hodder & Stoughton Ltd. and Sheil Land Associates Ltd.

Eudora Welty, from *The Wide Net*. Reprinted by permission of A. M. Heath & Co. Ltd.

Virginia Woolf, from *A Haunted House and Other Short Stories*, copyright 1944 and renewed 1972 by Harcourt Brace & Company. Reprinted by permission of Harcourt Brace Jovanovich and Hogarth Press Ltd.

Any errors or omissions in the above list are entirely unintentional. If notified the publisher will be pleased to make any necessary corrections at the earliest opportunity.

OXFORD POPULAR FICTION
THE ORIGINAL MILLION SELLERS!

This series boasts some of the most talked-about works of British and US fiction of the last 150 years—books that helped define the literary styles and genres of crime, historical fiction, romance, adventure, and social comedy, which modern readers enjoy.

Riders of the Purple Sage	Zane Grey
The Four Just Men	Edgar Wallace
Trilby	George Du Maurier
Trent's Last Case	E C Bentley
The Riddle of the Sands	Erskine Childers
Under Two Flags	Ouida
The Lost World	Arthur Conan Doyle
The Woman Who Did	Grant Allen

Forthcoming in October:

Olive	Dinah Craik
The Diary of a Nobody	George and Weedon Grossmith
The Lodger	Belloc Lowndes
The Wrong Box	Robert Louis Stevenson

PAST MASTERS

General Editor: Keith Thomas

SHAKESPEARE

Germaine Greer

'At the core of a coherent social structure as he viewed it lay marriage, which for Shakespeare is no mere comic convention but a crucial and complex ideal. He rejected the stereotype of the passive, sexless, unresponsive female and its inevitable concommitant, the misogynist conviction that all women were whores at heart. Instead he created a series of female characters who were both passionate and pure, who gave their hearts spontaneously into the keeping of the men they loved and remained true to the bargain in the face of tremendous odds.'

Germaine Greer's short book on Shakespeare brings a completely new eye to a subject about whom more has been written than on any other English figure. She is especially concerned with discovering why Shakespeare 'was and is a popular artist', who remains a central figure in English cultural life four centuries after his death.

'eminently trenchant and sensible . . . a genuine exploration in its own right' John Bayley, *Listener*

'the clearest and simplest explanation of Shakespeare's thought I have yet read' Auberon Waugh, *Daily Mail*

OXFORD POETS

FLEUR ADCOCK

Time Zones

In this lively new collection, Fleur Adcock's subjects range from domestic matters—recalling the birth of her son some years back; remembering her father, the news of whose death in New Zealand reaches her, the expatriate, in England; working in her own London garden—to matters of contemporary concern, such as the Romanian bid for freedom in 1989, and support for Green causes, including the anti-nuclear stand.

'She is an eminently readable poet, whose quiet accuracy sometimes makes me laugh out loud.'
Wendy Cope, *Guardian*

ILLUSTRATED HISTORIES IN
OXFORD PAPERBACKS

THE OXFORD ILLUSTRATED HISTORY
OF ENGLISH LITERATURE

Edited by Pat Rogers

Britain possesses a literary heritage which is almost
unrivalled in the Western world. In this volume, the
richness, diversity, and continuity of that tradition
are explored by a group of Britain's foremost literary scholars.

Chapter by chapter the authors trace the history
of English literature, from its first stirrings in Anglo-
Saxon poetry to the present day. At its heart towers
the figure of Shakespeare, who is accorded a special
chapter to himself. Other major figures such as
Chaucer, Milton, Donne, Wordsworth, Dickens,
Eliot, and Auden are treated in depth, and the story
is brought up to date with discussion of living
authors such as Seamus Heaney and Edward Bond.

'[a] lovely volume . . . put in your thumb and pull
out plums' Michael Foot

'scholarly and enthusiastic people have written in-
spiring essays that induce an eagerness in their readers to return to the writers they admire' *Economist*

OXFORD REFERENCE

THE CONCISE OXFORD COMPANION TO ENGLISH LITERATURE

Edited by Margaret Drabble and Jenny Stringer

Based on the immensely popular fifth edition of the *Oxford Companion to English Literature* this is an indispensable, compact guide to the central matter of English literature.

There are more than 5,000 entries on the lives and works of authors, poets, playwrights, essayists, philosophers, and historians; plot summaries of novels and plays; literary movements; fictional characters; legends; theatres; periodicals; and much more.

The book's sharpened focus on the English literature of the British Isles makes it especially convenient to use, but there is still generous coverage of the literature of other countries and of other disciplines which have influenced or been influenced by English literature.

From reviews of *The Oxford Companion to English Literature*:

'a book which one turns to with constant pleasure . . . a book with much style and little prejudice' Iain Gilchrist, *TLS*

'it is quite difficult to imagine, in this genre, a more useful publication' Frank Kermode, *London Review of Books*

'incarnates a living sense of tradition . . . sensitive not to fashion merely but to the spirit of the age' Christopher Ricks, *Sunday Times*